The top of the keep, sharp as a dragon's fang and towering high over the island, afforded a sweeping view. The dense belt of enemy vessels massed on the horizon had begun to move. It arced and crept toward them, and, though some ships were faster than others, nowhere was there a break in their formation. The countless throng of humans devoured sea and sky, and the winged legions of the Castle of All the Ancients reached almost to the very sun. The thane saw Rakoth slant swift through the azure in his fiery cloak. His detachments still held their position.

The Generation's forces were near enough now for the observers to make out the details of the ships' rigging. The vessels resembled those that had mounted the unsuccessful attack on Hedinseigh some days previously—tall they were, steep-sided and many-masted, with rosy sails. Filling the gaps between them moved long yellow galleys towed by huge sea-beasts, whale-like but with webbed flippers, enormous tusks protruding from their mouths, and sharp, high, bony fins. Through the air floated astonishing constructions with immense rhythmically beating canvas wings, some harnessed to giant eagles. Even higher soared small dragons, winged wolves and other beings assembled in haste by their overlords to die in a bloody battle whose purpose was unknown to the vast majority of the warriors that marched under the banners of the Castle of All the Ancients.

Fear, an icy serpent, slithered into Hagen's heart. Never before had he faced such a force. How many could Rakoth have brought? And could his servants stand against the combined might of an untold multitude of worlds?

GODSDOOM

THE BOOK OF HAGEN

BY

NICK PERUMOV

ZUMAYA OTHERWORLDS   AUSTIN TX

2007

This book is a work of fiction. Names, characters, places and incidents are products of the author's imagination or are used fictitiously. Any resemblance to actual persons or events is purely coincidental.

GODSDOOM
© 2007 by Nick Perumov

ISBN 13: 978-1-934135-38-9
ISBN 10: 1-934135-38-0

Cover art used by permission
Cover design by Martine Jardin

Look for us online at http://www.zumayapublications.com

Library of Congress Cataloging-in-Publication Data

Perumov, Nikolai.
  [Gibel' bogov. English]
  Godsdoom : the book of Hagen / by Nick Perumov.
    p. cm.
  ISBN-13: 978-1-934135-38-9
  ISBN-10: 1-934135-38-0
  I. Title.
  PG3485.E642G5313 2007
  891.73'5--dc22
                          2007009959

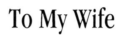
To My Wife

PART THE FIRST

CHAPTER I

"ILL TIDINGS FROM GNIPAHELLIR, MY THANE."

The horses ambled along the surfline, where the waves lazily licked at the verge of a gentle rocky slope. Away from the shore, gray carcasses of cliffs reached skyward, their faces fissured with cracks where stunted pines clung. Keen-edged fangs of rock, the ocean's best weapon, pierced the water, now wave-covered, now laid bare again. The air stank of rotting seaweed, and seagulls wheeled overhead.

Six riders in thick gray cloaks of coarse cloth traveled two abreast along the coast—four with longswords strapped on the left, the fifth with a blade slung over his back, the hilt jutting up over his right shoulder, and the sixth content to wield a gnarled and hefty cudgel. Their heads were covered with identical felt caps, much like those blacksmiths wear to keep from singeing their hair.

Looking at their faces, no one could have distinguished them by rank or calling. They were all men in the prime of life. By their ease with their weapons they might have been members of the royal guard of Vidrir; the cut of their clothes and their way with each other bore the mark of free peasants from the neighborhood of the Iron Wood, but their mounts were saddled and harnessed like those of the Rogheim horseherds.

"Ill tidings from Gnipahellir, my thane." The man spoke low, leaning toward the rider with the sword hilt rising above his shoulder, who nodded as if to bid him continue.

"The dwarves of Roedulsfoel have set Ialini's Wood afire again—the sky in the north is all smoke, and the darkness is so deep that birds are flying into the cliffs. But worse, Garm has smelled the burning. The Hound is awake."

The baleful words carried on the wind. The one addressed as "thane" heard the news in silence, his head bent at the slightest angle.

"What more?" he asked curtly.

"The mood in Himinvagar," the other replied. "Milord Hjorleif has declared war on Vidrir."

"On Vidrir?" The leader's eyebrows arched. "I was not expecting Hjorleif to be so hasty."

The other lowered his voice. "There is a rumor, uncertain and obscure, spread about by the Darkling Riders, that Hjorleif has received a secret envoy from the Isle of Brandeigh."

"The Island of the Black Mages, terror of Earth," the thane murmured. "What scent have those carrion-eaters picked up there? But continue. Is the battle over?"

"When we left Ervasund, Vidrir had only begun to muster his regiments, and Hjorleif had crossed the River Hator on the northern boundary of the Sheltered Kingdom."

"I see," the thane said tersely, and lapsed into a frowning, pondering silence. His companions waited.

"Lodin, Knut, Isung! Skirt that cliff and take the path to the Forest of Valla, then proceed by the highroad to Stave Ness. The gnomes there are to furnish you with weapons. Pay them nothing—it has all been settled in advance. The dragonships will arrive at the ness three days later. Load the weapons then make for Hedinseigh.

"Frodi, Gudmund! You shall accompany me as far as the Living Crags then turn off to Roedulsfoel. Seek out the Keepers of Ialini's Veil and alert them that Garm has awoken. Then strike westward to the Gulf of Unavagar. At the settlement there, buy a boat—spare no expense, mind—and set sail. You must reach Hedinseigh before the storm breaks. Wait for me there until the next moon. If I do not return, take Ilving and...find a new land for yourselves and for my men. Heed my Teacher.

"And remember that you have all sworn by the Eight Iron Nails of the Gates of Niflhel that you will serve my son!"

"We remember, Thane Hagen," one of the riders said in a hollow voice. It was Frodi, the one with a mighty cudgel laid across his saddle. "We will keep our vow, or Hel shall have our despicable hides. But, my thane, although we never question your commands, I must know why you're going to certain death at the Living Crags. That is a place from which no one returns."

"You have your orders, Frodi, as do you all!" the thane replied harshly, stopping the conversation short. He flicked his horse's reins and rode on. His companions straggled behind him, visibly out of humor.

Dawn had barely tinged the sky to the east, while everywhere else—in ravines, gullies and clefts—the night still lay. A short-statured, shapely figure passed through the trees, descending to a purling brook, feet in soft leather half-boots stepping noiselessly over the rotted pine needles. Once by the brook, the figure halted, stooped and plunged two slim, girlish hands into the water.

Ceaselessly and almost inaudibly, lips shaped words, the words settled into phrases; and with each new set of rhythmic, tumbling couplets it was as if the darkness returned to the bottom of the deep ravine with its lush growth of young trees. The outlines of roots, trunks and branches trembled into shapelessness, as if swathed in mist; the brook's voice grew muffled as it seemed to slide into sleep.

The slender hands moved in studied gestures over an earthenware chalice filled to the brim with fresh-drawn water.

A hero of bygone days who had gone to battle under the command of the Ancient Gods against the new masters of this world on Borgild Field would have known what to do, had he seen that girl in the ravine. The Black Mages of Brandeigh Isle would, for their part, have made her their ward.

A man in gray, his face covered with a soft mask, stood silent and motionless, watching. In his hand, he held four steel-rayed stars with sword-sharp edges, a weapon he had learned to trust above magic. He was sure of himself and therefore unafraid. Besides, the Preceptor had ordered him to watch the ritual to the end.

The water in the chalice took on a light sheen of ice and hissed, serpentlike. The girl's hands flew apart, and her shapeless cap fell off, disheveling her thick, dark-blond, carelessly sheared hair. Each couplet fell like a hammer blow. The ice began to crimson, and real blood flowed across it.

The man in gray had to take his will hard in hand so as not to yield to a sudden surge of fear. As if water had been splashed into his eyes, all around him smeared and blurred. It was as the Preceptor had said it would be.

With a short, sharp, sighing cry, the girl smashed her fist into the chalice. The ice cracked, and crimson drops flew. The slender body arched in pain, the head fell back.

And the warrior in gray, with a quick movement of his hand, sent the steel star flying straight for the exposed throat.

But the girl's slim, delicate hands were faster still. Scooping fiery liquid from the chalice, she flung it against the death-dealing weapon. The metal flared up like the flimsiest paper and vanished into invisible ash. Macabre laughter rang out such as no human could ever have uttered, no matter how

3

loutish or malign.

The warrior in gray stood as stone, unable to reach for the hilt of his short curved sword. A stream of liquid flame burst from the chalice, enveloping him from head to foot. He fell without a word, and the fire, obedient to an imperious gesture, returned to the chalice and disappeared.

The girl leaned over the prostrate form. She turned the heavy body this way and that with unwomanly strength but found no insignia, no crest, no amulets. She took up the curved sword. Scarcely touching the steel, she ran her tender fingers lightly along the blade—once, twice, thrice.

Her lips trembled. Submitting to the Words of Strength, the liquid fire boiled and seethed in the chalice. The blade, she discovered, had been thrust into flame but had not melted or liquefied there, as any other human weapon would. Instead, it had been flooded with a sudden, dense blackness, the dark obstinacy of one strong of spirit turning haughtily away from his inquisitors.

That sufficed. Her eyes blazed with irrepressible hatred; her nails dug into her palms.

She knew.

A movement of the hand, and the chalice was thickly coated with a crust that resembled coagulated human blood. The vessel of fire was nestled in a scrip, and she was gone, the bushes closing with a slight rustle behind her. The Darkling Rider had picked up the trail.

"Brunevagar!"

It rang like a curse.

FRODI AND GUDMUND RODE THEIR HORSES HARD, PUSHING NORTHEAST. THERE, BEHIND A low ridge of hills long eroded by wind and water, lay Roedulsfoel, the lush garden of Ialini, Great Lady of the Green World and one of the seven Young Gods.

That once cheerless and barren land had been made a token of the Goddess's might. Over many ages of unrelenting toil, she had strewn it with trees, bushes and grasses that grew there and nowhere else.

Many leagues before they reached those forbidden realms, though, they saw the sky shot through with smoke. Low clouds, nourished by thousands upon thousands of ascending gray-black pillars, hung like a baleful canopy. The wind tore at their margins, but new eddies pressed ever upward from below and the gaps quickly filled.

Exchanging glances, Frodi and Gudmund spurred their mounts.

The road made a sharp turn, the riders detoured around an alder thicket…and came upon the strangest of bands, perched on a fallen tree that blocked the road.

Swinging legs shod in red leather boots, and deep in lively conversation sat five squat wood-gnomes, each with a bow across its knees. Muttering something and rolling owl-yellow eyes, a marsh troll crouched in a shaggy pile. A kobold sat in silence, workworn hands with flat, callused palms limp on its lap. And at the very end of the log was an elf—still, tense and straight, wearing wondrous azure armor and holding atilt a long, narrow blade that danced with every color of the rainbow. At its back was an alv, dressed in a suit embroidered with hundreds of fletched steel quills, a loaded crossbow lying by its side.

Something extraordinary must have happened to bring all these beings together. Frodi and Gudmund drew rein.

"Permit us to pass, O Honored Ones!" Frodi spoke in the common tongue used between men and nomen, which was a compilation of the languages of the most diverse races. Of course, he felt he owed no honor to the bloodsucking marsh troll—or to the mischief-making wood-gnomes, for that matter, so unlike were they to their kinsmen in the far mountains, who were great adepts and master craftsmen.

"Who are—" the elf began then suddenly fell silent in mid-phrase. Magpies raised a rattlebrained commotion among the trees, and a second later another gnome hurtled through the bushes.

"She's here! Coming right this way! She's here!" it squealed, struggling for breath.

"The two of you may pass."

The elf's eyes held a frigid gleam. Most of the motley detachment had already scattered into hiding, but the alv tarried, holding its crossbow at the ready and watching the elf expectantly.

"We do not flee from danger," Gudmund replied, unsheathing his sword.

"Fool!" the elf said, its patience spent and its voice rising. "We are keeping watch for a Darkling Rider in hot pursuit. You are a hindrance here, not a help! You must—"

As if woven of layers of air, a shapely figure swaddled in a green cloak with the hood thrown back appeared soundlessly on the road, and Hagen's warriors could not believe what they saw. How could this be a Darkling Rider, this sweet, gentle-looking, rosy-cheeked young thing with short dark-blond curls, holding an earthenware chalice?

A tightly double-woven net fell from above, but before it could cover the

Darkling Rider—or, simply put, the wiccan—she raised the chalice, which disgorged a stream of fire. The cords flared, becoming ashes in the blink of an eye. Drops of liquid fire, scooped out by her narrow hand, flew in every direction, and where they fell ruddy tongues of flame shot up. Only then did Frodi realize he was witnessing the unthinkable.

All Darkling Riders were afraid of the Burning, a primordial and pristine divine principle. But this one—how in the name of Iambren the Merciful had she mastered Fire?

To Gudmund it seemed that, during those instants, he was thinking those very thoughts; but in truth, the astonishment came much later. No sooner had he and Frodi flung themselves face-first on the ground than everything around them was ablaze. Lucky it was for them that none of the spurting drops of flame fell on their clothing or armor.

So dense was the smoke that Hagen's warriors did not see what happened next. A roar, a howl, a scream rose from many throats, setting bowstrings twanging; then all was unexpectedly still. A dumbfounded Frodi raised his head. The fire had died as if doused by a heavy downpour, and seemingly in response to an unspoken command. The embers had turned blue and hissed maliciously. And the entire volunteer detachment was still there.

The troll lay dead in a charred heap, muzzle down and paws spread. Nearby were the gnomes, all burned like hideous pieces of kindling. The kobold had slipped into a ditch, apparently to hide, and there had breathed its last. And right in front of the smoking tree-trunk that blocked the road, the elf and the alv lay side-by-side, to all appearances whole, unscathed and sleeping. The alv still held its loaded crossbow.

Frodi leaned over the elf. He could not see a single wound on the First-Begotten's body but still it was dying. Perplexed, not knowing how to help, the humans stood motionless.

The elf slowly lifted its eyelids. Its eyes were as penetrating and severe as before, but with every moment life was draining from them. Gudmund brought his ear close to the scarce-moving lips of the dying creature.

"Someone…make to the Vale of Brunevagar. To the convocation. Warn…the Preceptor…"

The elf gave an almost inaudible sigh and was no more.

The Darkling Rider had disappeared.

It being a mortal sin for any true warrior to leave unburied the corpse of one who had fought bravely, Frodi and Gudmund delayed their departure. The blackened bodies of the gnomes were taken up by their weeping kin, who also helped drag the troll to its final resting place—a deep, marshy pit out in the fens. The kobold was given a home in the cliffs, in a tiny cave whose entrance was then walled up tight.

Finally, Hagen's warriors placed the elf and the alv on a hastily constructed raft and sent them floating down a quiet forest rill.

For such is the law: no matter where death finds one of the First-Begotten, it must be laid in a boat or even on a simple pontoon, and that mournful cargo must be consigned to even the most minuscule stream. The water will bear its burden through all its windings, past every snag, to the seashore from whence, it is said, the souls of elves follow their bodies unseen to the sunset and there, in wondrous, uncharted lands, are reborn.

"Where is Brunevagar?" a gloomy Frodi asked his companion.

"Seven or eight days' journey to the east," Gudmund replied. "I've heard tell of that place. The convocation is really a monastery. It has stood on that spot since the Second Incursion of Rakoth."

"So, indeed, it has. Well, what now?"

"With a wiccan in hot pursuit, and armed with that fiery chalice of hers? There's no telling what harm she can do. We have to warn them."

"But we're under orders. Have the Keepers slipped your mind?"

"Nothing's slipped my mind. Very well, then, we'll part ways. I'll go to Brunevagar and make my own reckoning with the thane later. Farewell!"

Frodi only grunted, knowing it was pointless to argue. Gudmund turned his horse to face the east.

HEDIN

I LEANED ON AN ORNATE SILVER RAILING OF THE CASTLE OF ALL THE ANCIENTS, WHICH stands on the very summit of the Pillar of the Titans, silently gazing down on the indistinct outlines of many worlds swathed in a cloudy haze. Far below, in the world named Hjorvard, which lies within the confines of the Mortal Lands—a world fresh in my memory and far from these filigreed parapets— in a pauper's pitiful hovel, my apprentice was being born.

Behind me, and barely audible even to me, delicate crystal bells chimed. The lot had been cast, and a human destiny had fallen from the circle of fortune that circumscribed the rest of mortalkind. My apprentice! I had waited ten long centuries while the others shared the power amongst themselves, but the Law of Lots is inexorable. A Mage must have apprentices as tools to know a world and to act upon it. The Council of the Generation cannot interdict him forever. And I had already served a most rigorous sentence.

I believe that Makran and Esteri would have gladly dispensed with me altogether, had not the Behest of the Ancients forbidden the murder of one Mage by another. But my term of exile was over; and I had returned now, far stronger than they could ever have expected. Passing along the tracks of snakes and the burrows of mice, the aerial paths of dragonflies and the invisible highways of spirits, biding a while at sunrise and sunset, conferring with alvs and dwarves, gnomes and elfs, humans and goblins, trolls and harrids, kheddees and kobolds, and even venturing into the forbidden realms of the Shades, I had returned—and returned with knowledge.

In marshes that breathed a deathly miasma, gray beings with never a bone in them had revealed to me the enigmas of their origins. Over long nights, in ravines strewn with skeletons, moonwolves—distant descendents of the Moonbeast—had imparted to me the secrets of their changes. And in the bottomless pits of Moraia hissing black creatures much like giant worms had told me tales of the pathways to Hel and the Laws of the Black Highway.

I had spoken with the dead—the Unquiet Ones. With mortal wizards and shamans to whom the Ancients had disclosed not a little of all they had discovered. Since my own kin had closed off my path to the mystery, I had perforce sought out other ways. I knew much. I was not the same. Had the others understood that?

A wind was born in the meanders of the sky and blew over the Castle towers, toying with the fanciful pennants. Even after the air calmed, the bells still spoke together. Clouds floated below me.

Someone was silently at my back. I stiffened at once but made no hurry to turn around. It was she—again it was she! What now, more games?

"Greetings, Hedin." Her voice was soft and enveloping, yet so candid it seemed incapable of lies. Was she glad for me? After she had exerted such effort to bury without trace all my earlier undertakings?

"Had someone other than I done that, the thirst for vengeance would have stolen your sanity," she remarked quietly, not hiding that she had read my thoughts—forgetting herself, I thought openly, like any human. "I had hoped you would not seek to revenge yourself on me—or, at least, not immediately. I had hoped that, your anger cooled, you would understand the Council, myself among them, was denied all alternatives by your own foolhardiness."

"Sigrlinn." I allow her name came hard to me. But she would never read anything in me again. "Enough of the past. What's done is done. It is gone and cannot be changed. But I never did repent. Remember that."

"Would I have wasted my time on you, had you disavowed yourself? You are as you are. As I…remember you." It was obvious she had wanted to end with other words.

Sigrlinn the Sorceress. One of the most powerful of our Generation, one of the fourteen members of the Council of the Generation, and…my foremost adversary, who had cast my long-wrought Empire of Night into the dust and on the ruins of my offspring built her own dear Sheltered Kingdom.

Once, at the very dawn of our Generation, Sigrlinn had been my beloved.

"Very well." I could not contain myself. "What shall we speak of, enemy mine? Shall we remember how we raised the Cerulean City and knew no discord? Or shall I tell you of the recent past? I could instruct you on how to survive amid the eternal ice once deprived, by the will of your most evenhanded Council, of the power over fire. You'd best listen. One day you may have need—"

She stopped me with a gesture—not angry, not contemptuous, but seemingly full of sympathy.

"Why do you speak so, Hedin?" She tilted her head reproachfully. "Rather tell me what is in store for your new apprentice. I'll warrant you've contrived something uncommon for him."

By the Law of the Ancients, no Mage can interfere in the dealings between another Mage and his apprentice. Not even the Council had that right. I failed to understand what benefit she could be deriving from this conversation.

"No silence," she implored of a sudden. "You have closed yourself off. I don't know what you are thinking now, but all your talk of the Code of the Generation—I could cite the same myself. Oh, away with these laws and regulations! I'm interested, that's all. We kn—I mean, you know," she corrected herself, "that I never betrayed you, never did aught behind your back. I issued my challenge to you by all the canons of the Ancients, twenty-one days before the outright declaration of war. And before that—"

"Before that? What does it matter now?" Probably the bitterness inside me was only too evident, and at that moment I saw in Sigrlinn's eyes something resembling surprise. She had found the chink in my armor. Did that gladden her?

My blood asimmer, I forged ahead with visor raised.

"I shall have an apprentice," I said slowly, meeting her gaze. "An apprentice who will far outstrip all the rest. I will give him that which I have given no other. I will teach him to thirst for knowledge and to slake that thirst, and he will raise a kingdom such as mortal history has never seen. He will be a warrior among warriors!"

Sigrlinn's face was a picture of disappointment, and I instantly stopped short, as I had in bygone years at the slightest sign of her displeasure—all to avoid a quarrel.

"And that is all?" She drew the question out. "I was expecting more, Hedin. Can you think only of war, and nothing else?"

I knew very well what she meant by that "else."

"What else but war is a fitting occupation for a man?" I was teasing her, doing my very best to make every word sound like a covert thought long brooded over and finally allowed to surface. "War is the pinnacle of the human spirit and the human destiny. And this time I shall try to ensure that nothing will prevent my apprentice from reaching the acme of his fame. What good that will do me…I beg your pardon, but for now that's a secret. Although you did send me that challenge, you will understand."

"That is your strength," she said, oddly calm. "No one can tell if you're speaking in earnest or in jest. But can the past have taught you nothing? You created fighters, mighty and strong, and they were victorious, indeed; but it all ended in terrible routs, and your followers shed rivers of blood."

She was wrong to take that tone. I can't bear being preached at.

"That's for me to decide," I growled. "Why do women in general—and sorceresses in particular—so love to stick their noses in other people's business? I'll be damned if I don't make sure my apprentice knows to keep his distance from you girls."

"Could you plan to make the one assigned to you a monk only because you yourself have never been a resounding success with us 'girls?'"

That was a low blow.

"I don't meddle in what and how you teach your pupils," I flared. I could feel the muscles along my jawline working, and was unable to stop them. "So leave me be!"

"I will, Hedin," she replied, sadness in her voice. "But others won't."

"I'll settle my scores with the others myself!" I snapped.

"And be exiled as before? Take care. Merlin may not content himself with that."

Had she ever let slip before that the last word in the argument would not be hers?

Sigrlinn disappeared—she had either dissolved into the air, as she so loved to do when returning to Earth, or had chosen another way unknown to me. I never did know where she went, but in any event she was no longer in attendance at the Council.

Gradually, I regained my composure. Sigrlinn. What was she to me now? An erstwhile enemy, giving me to know she was not averse to ending our hostilities? An old friend trying to prevent me from making a fateful mistake?

But then the Great Bell of the Keep pealed, and all extraneous thoughts flew out of my head.

That bell returning now to life had been cast in ages so distant the events of those days had seemed mythical even to the Ancients. How many years had it been since I last heard those proud, imperious notes flowing out into the infinity of the Middle Sky? I had completely forgotten what they could do to such as I—my head was caught in a vice of dull, crushing pain, for the Council had not yet fully absolved me of guilt. Had I approached the Castle during my exile, the sound of the Bell would have driven me stark mad.

The bloody murk that filmed my eyes retreated slowly, reluctantly. I was bent in three, my face drenched with sweat. A Mage cannot dispense with a physical shell, but, Great Spirit, what inconveniences it can cause at times. On the other hand, what pleasures it can afford.

"Hedin, Sage of Darkness!" The cold voice came from everywhere and nowhere, and for the first time in a thousand years I heard my name spoken together with my title.

Merlin the Great, Leader of the Council of the Generation.

It was precisely thus, without a hint of feeling, that he had pronounced judgment in the evil days of my devastation. Wish it as I might, I could not contend with his strength here. Not yet, anyway.

The stone slabs parted, and I saw the Hall of the Council, familiar to the last detail and changed not a whit—an enormous black wooden table in the center; on the walls, tapestries with the crests of the Council members worked in gold and silver; the crystal Sphere of Lots on a marble pedestal at the back of the room.

And thirteen pairs of eyes, all fixed on me. Only thirteen, because the fourteenth—Sigrlinn—was absent.

I gritted my teeth. The confrontation had begun, and I had not yet crossed the threshold.

Not one of them trusted me, yet they could not change a decision that had been set with the Seal of Eternity, which was the only reason I was standing there instead of hanging in chains in one of the Lowerlands. Still, I knew the next time they would not even stop at that, but would send an Astral Messenger to the chambers of the Lords Everlasting for permission to act further. That was how they had dealt with Rakoth.

But I was not going to be the first to breach this peace, poor one though it was. Obedient to the strictures of etiquette, I bowed, my right hand on my heart. Beneath my feet, a silvery path blazed from the threshold all the way to the Sphere of Lots.

I took the first few steps. For some reason, they were very difficult—my head swam, and blood pounded in my temples. I forced myself with every iota of my strength to stand erect; deep inside, a wild, frenetic joy roiled, gradually pushing up into my higher mind. It was as if I had emerged from a musty, mirage-ridden bog and stepped out onto the solid rocks of the real world.

Apprentice!

To me, that word had the rolling resonance of a myriad organs, and burned bright with all the flames of the universe and the Light of the Hallowed Land. I had returned to life. I lived!

Thirteen pairs of very calm, dispassionate eyes followed my every movement. I felt the powerful, probing pressure of mind-gazes, and I had to close myself off, although I knew this would only fuel suspicion. Besides, if Merlin were to take it upon himself to...

Of course, I could protect myself against him, even here, but then he would know the secret of my new defense—it was advisable not to underestimate the power of the Archmage. So, although I sensed his heedfulness, sensed his sharp gaze penetrating deeper and deeper into me, I limited myself to a piece of our ordinary defensive magic, which is as much good against Merlin as the lock on the door of a long-abandoned house is against real thieves.

"Sage of Darkness, the term of your allotted punishment is over." He did not rise from his seat to speak. He stared directly into my eyes, and it was all I could do not to look away. "We can no longer deprive you of the right to teach. I entertain no great hope of your reformation, and I say this openly, for all to hear.

"I must warn you that if you return to your old ways you will not be facing Sigrlinn alone. I, too, will be there, and will spare no effort in dispatching an Astral Messenger for permission to mete out the punishment due, if you rebel once more. I would not advise you to follow Rakoth's path. And now..."

In violation of all custom and tradition, Merlin did not stand in order to join me in removing the Grain of Fate from the Sphere of Lots but instead demonstratively settled more comfortably in his seat.

"Approach, and take what is yours by the Law of the Ancients. I swear by the Moonbeast that were there no such Law, you would not be standing here."

Merlin was not one to stoop to deceit, ambush or sneak attacks. I was not surprised by the malice in his words, although they sounded barbarous at this time and in this place. Punishments, some quite severe, had been inflicted before, but when the time had been served everyone—and Merlin foremost among them—had tried to treat the miscreant as cordially and warmly as they might, harking back to the past with neither word nor glance.

Yet, I say again, this was no cause for wonder. Merlin had amply earned his title of the Great. He knew something none of the others seated at the Council table would grasp for a long time to come—that I would not rest until I had taken his place or was cast out of this world.

I had set myself too great a task, had conceived the unheard-of; and as the first small step along that way, leadership of the Council would serve me well. Had Merlin not spoken those words, it would not have been easy for me to take up arms against him. Now the opposite was true—war had been declared. The thirteen who sat in the Council hall today had given me clearly to know they would not permit me to stray one single step from that which was customary for any Mage.

Excellent, then. Just try and stop me this time.

Yet this was naught but bravado, for I was all the while aware that, for the time being, two or three Council members would be able to scotch anything I had planned, although certainly not at a stroke. And if Merlin should ever quit his Avalon, I would have trouble enough.

Strange it was—all these thoughts flared up ready-formed, as if I had been pondering this matter long and hard, whereas I had stepped onto the flagstones of the Ethereal Wharf of the Castle of All the Ancients with the certainty there need be no feud with the Council, except perhaps with Makran and Esteri. But the last thing I could do was lie to myself.

You've always known that, even on your return from exile, you would never be forgiven, I told myself. You knew it, but would not admit it. So, then...better late than never.

Then I had to halt those thoughts, because Merlin's unceremonious invasion of my mind had already almost completely made away with my last defenses. Yet my long wanderings among mortal men had not been time wasted. As if to compensate for the brevity of their sojourn on Earth, humans are, on occasion, endowed with strange talents, among which is the art of inner silence and a lightning-fast shift of thought. That is what I did then, keeping the precious secret of my new defense for a rainy day; and if Merlin the Great read anything in my mind at that moment it was only that I was irritated by his overly intrusive attention.

I halted before the Sphere of Lots. The Grain of Fate of the apprentice assigned to me by the Eternal Ones gleamed crimson, snuggled comfortably in its crystal nest and pulsing with the beat of a heart not yet emerged from its mother's womb. I stared at it; never before had its color so resembled that of blood. This would, I realized, be a warrior, a great warrior. The Masters of Fate never hid aught. But, by the Almighty Ancients, how much cruelty was in him, even from birth!

That was good. It meant he would accept my lessons on the instant, inasmuch as they would answer to his own inner needs. It would have been difficult to wish for a better apprentice, given the deed I had planned.

The bells finally fell silent. The choice had been made, and all that remained was to take up the Grain. I slowly stretched out my hand toward it, focussing my thoughts on how it had been the last time. Then, Merlin had assisted me, as he should, while this time the Leader of the Council was a mere observer, cold and detached.

My mind cleared. They wanted me to be my apprentice's undoing now, at the very moment of his birth; then all would proceed according to the Law. A Mage unable to take up the Grain must wait out the time until he was entitled to try for another—though that time would, of course, seem like nothing compared with the length of my exile. What is a hundred years alongside a thousand?

So, I accepted the challenge. There was nothing else for me to do. Slowly, very slowly, I touched the Grain—and a beggarwoman in a tumbledown hut went into labor.

I reached out with all my mind's strength and saw a dismal, rickety scrap-wood table littered with cracked and dented utensils, a bed piled high with unimaginably filthy rags and the woman who lay on those rags, groaning. She was alone.

I had no time either to be vexed with the Lot or to curse Merlin. When a Mage's apprentice is born, the pangs are invariably harder and many times more dangerous than with an ordinary birth. The mother often dies, and the child with her.

I bent all my strength to quenching the Grain's sinister glitter, its inner fire. And quench it I did, although the sensation was that of grasping red-hot metal with bare hands. The woman's agony eased, for the moment.

But that only won me a brief respite The challenge remained unmet, and I could see no simple way of meeting it. There was only one thing I could do, and that was forbidden—not only to me but to all of us, even Merlin. It had been attempted only a handful of times, and always the entire Council, convened in the Castle of the Ancients, had had to help so the whole world would not be upended as a result.

For all his powers and knowledge, a Mage cannot act directly to protect anyone against physical destruction from there—from the Castle of the Ancients. He has to rely upon intermediaries appearing in the right place at the right time.

I screwed up my eyes. As clearly as would a bird on the wing, I saw the hut, the fields that surrounded it, the meadows and vegetable gardens, the fences, barns, other houses and roads. Gathering my will hard in hand, searing it in the cold fire of the Castle hearth like a blazing, celestial fireball, I crashed down into the world.

A fiery blade ripping apart the layers of the Real and making the River of

Time seethe and bubble, I displaced the layers of Being with an imperious hand, drawing lavish quantities of strength from an arsenal stocked by All the Ancients. I fell out of ordinary space, seeing nothing before me and feeling only the floor trembling under my feet. A cyclone of fire began to rage around the Castle, a supple wave that pounded those seemingly invulnerable battlements.

I was struck dumb, second by second absorbing new torrents of improbable visions. I searched for the one who could save my apprentice, and before the spectral Dragons of Time I had freed from their home in the boundless waves of Time could thrust into the Worldframe fangs that naught could check, I finally found the one I had been seeking. Cleaving and slashing everything in my way, I rushed headlong to him.

The merchant felt a slight vertigo and, being careful of his health, decided, even though the light-headedness passed an instant later, to rest a while for safety's sake. The caravan turned from the high road, and there both the merchant and his stewards saw a lopsided little hut, whose occupant was groaning in pain. The groans were most certainly those of a woman.

"Go and see what is there," the merchant ordered an underling, who squeamishly stuck his head through a chink in the door.

"A wench in childbed, your worship," he called back. "And suffering much, 'tis clear to see."

"Help her, Anselm," commanded the merchant, who was at heart by no means a bad man, nor callous.

One of his companions, wearing a physician's cloak and cap, made a hurried bow and disappeared inside the hut.

The Castle walls were shaken by such a storm as had never been. The unseen billows of Forces run mad rolled over it, threatening at any moment to sweep it away, to loosen the nail that secured all the layers of the Real. The entire Council, Merlin foremost among them, leapt to their feet, forming a great circle—if they did not immediately still the earthquake I had called forth the Castle of All the Ancients would crumble to dust. It would be hard to prevent, but not impossible.

Not allowing myself even a moment's respite, I carefully removed the Grain of Fate from its delicate crystal repository. The storm raging in the Real and the Mid-Real was of little concern to me once the Grain's spark was pulsating in my hands. Carefully, trying to make no uneven or unsteady movements and not even daring to breathe, I drew it toward me.

Merlin stood over the blazing hearth, raising a great clamor. Entirely engrossed as I was in capturing the Grain, I could not but be startled by the titanic might he was pouring into that spell. The forces he had set in motion would easily have matched strength with an average-sized Dark Army.

But as he intoned that powerful charm, I finally had my prize. The Grain of Fate lay on my palm.

Anselm the physician, meanwhile, was cradling a red and wrinkled little bundle that promptly let out a fretful cry.

When Merlin had completed his spell, the storm began to abate; and the trembling in the floor and walls faded slowly away. I felt the powerful blows dealt as one by the combined forces of the Council of Mages; the Layers of All Creation I had shifted gradually returned to their places. I hid the Grain of Fate in an amulet next to my skin and immediately felt its warmth.

My next thought, which came in the heat of the moment, was that I had no further business in the Castle. I had no interest in visiting my apartments there and saw no sense in bidding anyone farewell. Without so much as a glance at any of them, I departed. All the way to the parapet, I felt the cold gaze of Merlin the Great on my back.

LEAVING A LITTLE MONEY AND FOOD FOR THE WOMAN, WHO WAS ALREADY SOMEWHAT ALERT after that hard birth, the kindly merchant bade his company continue their journey. Doctor Anselm, saddling his placid horse, seemed greatly disturbed, almost fearful.

"It seems you're not yourself, my good Anselm," the merchant observed, now wholly forgetful of his earlier desire to rest a while. "What has surprised you so?"

"Surprised me, my liege?" The doctor glanced around, bent close to the other's ear and whispered feverishly, "Horrified me, rather! I have attended any number of births, but never before have I seen an infant with such timeworn eyes."

"You say so?" The merchant, a man of ample common sense, had his doubts.

"I've never been more certain, my liege," Anselm nodded. "Those were the eyes of an evil old man who had lived long and seen much. And then—I felt I would run mad—those terrible eyes suddenly shrank, changed, grew vacant, became those of any newborn. Ugh! Fair Iamerth preserve us from the false visions of the Gloom!"

Anselm made a gesture of protection, which the merchant repeated but with no particular piety. Clearly, the young doctor's tale had made no particular impression on him.

The caravan slowly disappeared around a bend in the road. I followed them with my gaze, wrapping my pauper's cloak more tightly around me. It was not a bad place after all—clean, and with a spring nearby, a village a half-mile distant, a forest and a river not far away.

Now, then, where would be the best location? Probably here, behind this hillock, to be shielded somewhat from the damp.

I untied my knapsack and took out a keen-edged carpenter's ax. An hour later I had an entirely serviceable shelter that would serve until I could acquire more seemly lodgings. In general, though, I would have to put palaces, featherbeds and pillows from my mind for a while. I scattered my modest belongings around and set off to the hut across the way.

"May I come in?" Carefully, I tapped my staff against the doorpost. My question was a pure formality, since the cracked, chipped door already stood ajar.

"And who, by the Darkness, are you?" The reply came in a hoarse, weak voice that only faintly resembled a woman's.

"I heard you had given birth today and came to ask if you need anything," I explained, remaining outside the door. "Water or firewood? I'll be your new neighbor."

"Well, I never!" There was a malicious chuckle in the squalid darkness. *And where does she find the strength?* I wondered. "All my life nothing but blows and kicks, never a kind word from anybody, and today it's been just one soft heart after another. Well and good. Come in and let's see who my benefactor is this time."

The child gave a sharp, petulant cry.

THE VILLAGE CLOSEST TO OUR HOVELS WAS NAMED JOL. A NEWCOMER WISHING TO SETTLE there had to pay a levy, and anyone who could not was not permitted to set up within half a mile of the village outskirts. Svava, my apprentice's mother, and I were soon getting along famously. As I understood it, she had never really been a beggarwoman. She spoke of the past unwillingly, and I did not press her or discover the truth by my own devices. What did I care who she had been?

Yet before long she could not do without me. Her baby boy cried in her arms even after being fed, while when I held him he was instantly silent and fell into a peaceful sleep. I also made common cause with an alderman in Jol, paying for the use of both man and beast when need arose.

Then I began predicting the weather, putting the village experts to shame;

and by the spring of the following year, Svava and I could have lived in the village, had we wished. But she would have none of it; she could not forget the insults. That fell in well with my own plans—the fewer witnesses, the better.

I must admit Svava was no mother. She had become so accustomed to my help that a few months after my arrival she was requesting—no, demanding—money for drink. I gave it to her so I could spend more time with Hagen, named thus in honor of another apprentice, who had perished in front of my eyes. Hagen of Tronje was confidante to the kings of Vorms, his terrible end hymned now in song and saga.

Presently, the boy was entirely in my care.

A year passed, rich and bountiful, followed by another. Hagen grew and was soon calling me "Grandfather," asking endlessly "Why?" Then, on what was for me a truly fine day, when he had just turned six, he announced to me he wanted to learn to fight.

Mentally, I wiped the honest sweat from my brow and began to teach him.

Six months later, Hagen was feared by all the village boys, up to and including the fourteen-year-olds. When he was eight he took his first life—that of a full-grown wolf—armed with nothing more than a child's knife.

Three years after that, the village was burned down for falling into arrears on its levies. A drunken constable ran Svava through in passing to loosen her hold on a sack of flour but then measured his own length on the ground when Hagen leapt onto his back from a ceiling beam and, without the slightest hesitation, plunged his knife in below the ear. All the while I lay apparently insensate, pretending to have been knocked unconscious by the constable when he burst into the hut, watching Hagen in silence.

He did not let me down.

Then he was shaking me by the shoulders, calling my name at the top of his voice. His distress lasted only seconds—he took the physic he needed from my bag and I "came to."

"You're alive? You're not hurt?" He stood over me with the blood of his victim fresh on his hands and petulant tears in his eyes.

"Just a little hurt, Hagen, but it's nothing, it will pass. And you did well."

"We'd have shown them, if you hadn't fallen!"

"No matter, Hagen. We'll show them yet. We'll pay them back for everything, and for your mother, too. But that will take study."

"I'll study, I will! But...will you teach me?"

"Of course, Hagen."

19

CHAPTER II

Having parted with Frodi and Gudmund, Hagen traveled south. While his warriors, on their way to Roedulsfoel, might still encounter human habitations, he came upon no villages nor another living soul. Only disfigured and sickly pines clung to the rocky slopes of the deep ravine through which he passed. His jet-black stallion, though obedient to its rider, would snort in fear and balk at times, at which Hagen would have to dismount and calm the frightened beast.

Though the sun beat mercilessly down, the thane did not remove his armor, for hour after hour a hostile and inhuman gaze had been pursuing him. Hagen felt it but did not turn around, knowing the noman would either attack of a sudden or not at all. There were no harrids or kheddees near the Living Crags, although mormaths—those solitary eaters of human flesh, half-octopus, half-bird, Rakoth's nightmare handiwork from the heyday of his power—might wander to those parts to sleep the black sleep in the Hollow of Fire.

The one other creature dwelling there was the aim of Hagen's present journey. It would, of course, have been best to confer on Garm with his Teacher, but Hedin was away on one of his mysterious journeys, and it wanted two more months—he never came late—before his return.

The Hound, fed on corpseflesh in Hel, had to be brought to heel with all speed, for otherwise...

A sorcerer had once said that, otherwise, the Gods would descend from the Heavens out of season, and that would signal the end of even the best-laid plans. Before the news reached the Lordly Thrones, he—Hagen of Jol, the Thane of Hedinseigh—must defeat the monster alone.

But who, in pity's name, was staring so hard at his back? Everyone knew there were no casual visits made to the Living Crags—the fright that reigned there would repulse all except such as Hagen, who possessed the knowledge of Command and Subjugation. But why peer at the back of an adept of such skills, and so brazenly and doggedly to boot? What tailing was this? Or had he simply happened on something young and foolish with a fondness for manflesh?

The thane made a demonstration once again of checking that his sword moved freely from its sheath. The blue steel would certainly serve as a warning to his pursuer. It was known to all, even the most stupid harrids and brainless kheddees, not to mention the Darkling Riders.

But that alien gaze remained fixed on his back. All Hagen could do was shrug. *If its pleasure is looking, then let it look...but nothing more.* To capture the noman dogging his steps might not be difficult, but why go to the trouble? Surely, no one would dare to square off against Old Hropt, the one whom Hagen was going to see.

Everyone knew about Hropt, but few would ever venture into his domains. Loose tongues said he had certain dealings with Orlangur and Demogorgon, whom everything living—except, of course, the Wise Ones—feared more than death and disgrace, over which the two were said to rule. So, Hropt dealt with many, with all, with whomever he wished, but almost no one took the risk of returning the favor.

Hagen strongly suspected, and his Teacher had hinted, that the powers of the Living Crags bowed to none other than Hropt. By dint of long effort, he had managed to create for himself a small corner where he was almost impervious to harm.

The ravine became a narrow rocky cleft, damp and cold. There was a sudden rumble beneath the horse's hooves, and several stones rolled off the precipice. It was the last warning to whatever brainsick fool had dared penetrate to the very Gates. Now came the time to stop and await the appearance of the Stone Sentinels. How would whatever was following him treat with them?

Hagen took a spare cloak from his saddlebag and wrapped it around his horse's head. He removed the sword from his baldric and laid aside his bow and quiver. Weapons, even such as these, were powerless against the Stone Sentinels. Only bare hands would avail. And a strong will, of course.

A great chunk of rock rolled down, colliding noisily with another in a shower of sparks. The Sentinels were close by, and the follower was still there, too—and, to all appearances, in no hurry to be away. That individual was

,py Hagen no less than his upcoming meeting with Hropt.

ne thane's right-hand side burst like an over-ripe fruit, with a

)ar. Shards spattered all around, but not before Hagen had spoken a _ ction Charm to shield both him and his mount. Then, from the tumbled wreckage of rock, there rose a being the very sight of which would have sent anyone, even the most foolhardy valiant, into a dead faint.

Its huge head swung from side to side on a slim, snakelike neck; the powerful trunk stood on four columnar legs. It came in a rush, stretching out long, menacing clawed paws twined about with thick corded muscles. Or, rather, they looked for all the world like muscles, whereas in fact the Stone Sentinel's entire body was made up of small and mid-sized boulders.

Hagen briefly tensed and relaxed his own muscles. Only mortals who had never passed through the Consecrations will meet fire with fire. Sword deflects sword, word turns aside word—though only for a time, to be sure—and, faced with this stone monster, they would no doubt have picked up a cobblestone.

But the Wise Ones taught differently. Though in nature a spruce grows from a spruce, a wolf brings forth a wolf cub, and all that lives gives birth to its own likeness, Magic works by the rule of opposites. A skimming stone will not split a cliff, but a human hand divested of its steel sheath can. That was why Hagen dared go against a Stone Sentinel with his fists cocked, as if wading into a lusty brawl.

But the Stone Sentinel paid the young thane not the slightest attention. It raced by him, roaring like a hundred hungry lions hard on their prey. Hagen was thunderstruck. He had never seen the like, had never heard the like, had never even *imagined* the like. The Stone Sentinel, monstrous being born of the Living Crags, was making not for him, a creature of flesh and blood, but for his unseen pursuer.

On the ground! Before Hagen's mind had grasped the order screamed at him, his body obeyed it, and not a moment too soon. Whoever had been on his trail evidently knew well enough what a Stone Sentinel was and what it could do when angered, so was trying to bring down the quarry while there was still time. A gleaming steel disc sheared off a lock of hair on the back of Hagen's head and dove shrilly into a nearby rock. Giving off a sickening grating noise, it trembled in the crevice, surrounded by tiny clouds of rock dust.

Hagen went cold. The legendary weapon being used against him was so deadly that even his Teacher could only remember two who, being its target, had lived to tell of it.

The Disc of Iamerth!

His Teacher had spoken of the great Temple of the Sun in the capital of the Sheltered Kingdom where, on high terraces open to the daystar's rays, five such disks were kept in crystal cubes, like a holy of holies. The priests of Iamerth were masters of powerful forces; they had bewitched and now commanded legions of magical beings. But why had the Temple of the Sun suddenly decided to make an end of *him*, of Thane Hagen?

The Stone Sentinel had reached the bushes where the envoy of Light, wielder of the Disc, was hiding. Hagen heard the monster's deep-chested bellow and then the throaty kind of cry, full of hate and rage, with which warriors dispatch their foes. It was a woman's voice. In reply, the Sentinel gave a deafening roar, and the fight was on.

But Hagen could not follow its progress. His eyes were locked on the Disc. There was no way escaping it—once thrown, it invariably found its target. In the vanishingly rare instances when the hunted contrived to dodge it, and it drilled a rock, a tree or the ground, or plunged into a river, the Disc of Iamerth would free itself and again make for its mark. The Disc cared nothing for armor; it sliced through iron like fine linen. Only when cooled in its victim's blood would it peacefully return to its owner's hand.

Quivering, humming gently, the Disc was extracting itself by degrees from the deep crevice in the rock. Hagen knew there would be no second chance. Soon…soon…any moment now…

He slashed his knife across his left wrist, and warm, heavy streams of scarlet blood ran down into his cupped palms. *Quickly, quickly—another inch and the Disc will be free.* Not waiting for the makeshift receptacle to fill, Hagen hastily bent over the wondrous weapon and poured the blood over it.

In that same instant, the deadly, glistening circle wrenched itself from the rock…and hung motionless, confused by the blood of the one whom it had been sent to destroy.

Hagen sprinkled it with another hasty handful. With a light, ringing sound, the Disc rolled over the stones, back to the bushes whence it had come.

It had believed.

Panting, Hagen fell back onto the rocks, too winded even to feel the pain.

He had deceived it.

Hagen was, though, a true Mage's apprentice. A moment later, he had roughly bandaged his slashed wrist and was bounding after the Disc, drawing his sword as he ran. There was very little time left—mere instants—until it returned to its master's hand.

He ran as he had been taught; only an inhumanly sharp eye could have made out his shadow flickering headlong across the patches of light between the boulders. Such a run is very difficult. Words of Strength are needed, but they must also be pronounced in such a way they will work as they should.

The Stone Sentinel and Hagen's unseen pursuer were still locked in bitter battle. Something was slicing through the air with a thin whistle. It was not steel but a short whip, its sibilant sound ever and again drowned out by a furious roar from the Sentinel. What opponent had the strength to withstand that all but invincible foe? The thane himself, as he prepared for battle, had not been counting on victory. The Stone Sentinel would have to have seen him as one of its own.

Yet the offspring of the Living Crags would never have attacked him so hatefully, and if whatever was following Hagen was so strong, then how was he to match strength with it?

The Stone Sentinel gave a wild, unanticipated howl. It bellowed once, in the throes of death, and was silent, crashing lifeless to the ground. Hardly had the din of its fall faded away than Hagen's ear caught a short dying groan, low and piteous, full of astonished, almost childlike, umbrage.

Just above the Stone Sentinel's head, now disintegrated into pebbles, among the broken, trampled bushes, the thane saw a slim girlish figure. The glassy eyes stared upward, the Darkling Rider's gray cloak was spattered with blood, and her right arm was bent at an unnatural angle.

Had Frodi and Gudmund been there, they would have thought the deceased to be the sister of the wiccan whom they had encountered and who had made such short work of the ambush laid across her path. They would have been close to the truth.

Hagen surveyed the body closely. At first glance, she looked nothing like the common run of Darkling Riders, except for the vertical, raptor-like pupils they all had. The lessons had not been wasted—he was looking at her as he would at any object that needed to be studied, no more. Without hesitation, he searched the corpse.

The Disc of Iamerth lay meekly alongside, but Hagen did not even reach out a hand to it. His Teacher could have picked it up, but he, Hagen, still had much to learn. Soon the glittering circle would receive the order to return to the temple and would set off on its long journey—and woe to him who dared to seize it!

The Darkling Rider had no other weapon; Hagen found only an intricate key of gnomish workmanship, and pocketed it to investigate it later. He was far more intrigued by the yet-unextinguished shadow of the young sorceress's mind. Too much that was unusual for a Darkling Rider revealed itself to him as he stood there, his eyes closed and his hand extended over her head. Monotone in humans and unambiguously gray in an ordinary wiccan, here the mind-shadow was multicolored, gray and black alternating with blue and green, and at its very edge was the almost indistinguishable, fading gleam of a thin golden thread. His Teacher had told him of this—it was the sign of communication with magical forces.

What would Hagen have said had he known that in the shadow of his own mind there was an identical thread, as there is in every mortal who has become a Mage's apprentice?

The thane hurried now, driving on his mount as it stepped uncertainly across the sharp stones. It was but a few leagues' more to Old Hropt's home; but night was coming on, and with it the time when all the forces of the Living Crags would turn upon him, scorching and dehydrating his brain; he would crumple to the ground with empty, leaking eye-sockets. The Stone Sentinel had perished before Hagen could obtain from him the Charm of Passage, so to the Living Crags he was still no more than a hated, ambulant, warm-blooded thing. When the sun set and the pale, ravaging moon rose, the Crags would gain their true strength. It would not go well with him if he had not reached Hropt's home by then.

And here's another puzzle, Hagen thought. *Someone very powerful is seriously intent on doing away with me. But who and why?*

He began trying to reckon up those who might wish him dead and had not yet been dispatched to Hel but quickly lost the thread. Which of them was so highly placed as to be able to convince the very priests of Iamerth to rise up against him? Yet perhaps—the thought was brief but disturbing—this betokened, rather, some enmity toward his Teacher?

It made no sense to rack his brains, though, so Hagen abandoned the fruitless guesswork. His Teacher had taught him to concentrate on the achievable. At that point, the achievable was to settle in under Hropt's roof. *So let's think on that.*

He was in good time. The sunset's fires still lingered on the mountains' gray bulk when a round hollow opened up to him. Against the slope opposite the outlet from the ravine along which he had been traveling rested the home of Old Hropt, built of unimaginably ancient logs, each at least three spans in girth. Two long walls jutting out from the mountainside were joined by a rather narrow facade with one window and one doorway, low and broad. Slightly to one side stood a barn with a hitching post.

Hagen hooked his horse's reins to the post, gave him some oats and knocked loudly with his sword hilt on the bronze-clad door.

"Step in, whoever you be!" a very deep voice almost growled in reply. "Come along. It's not locked."

Hagen pushed the door and entered, bowing low under the lintel.

It was twilight in the spacious vestibule, which was filled with the savory aroma of the bunches of herbs that wreathed the walls. *But where does Hropt gather them? There is desolation all around.* The host opened the second door to greet his guest.

Old Hropt was both tall and broad in the shoulders, his back unbent under the weight of years. He had a truly regal bearing, and his deeply lined face, with its aquiline nose and wide, smooth brow-arch, was the face of a warrior who had seen much, had suffered all, but had yet to be subdued by anyone. He could have been taken for a very distinguished jarl or a king of the Southern Shores, yet such a fire burned in his eyes that only very few could bear to meet that gaze. Mage Hedin, Hagen's Teacher, was such a one.

Hropt was dressed simply in a costume of coarse gray cloth, though a short broadsword hung from his wide ornate belt in a transparent sheath that could have been fashioned from crystal. The blade seemed forged of pure gold, and the sword gleamed with the slightly muted, dense hue of maple leaves in fall.

"Ah, Hagen!" Hropt burst out laughing, clapping his guest on the shoulder. "'Tis long enough since you last showed yourself in these parts. You completely forgot this old man! Well, then, come in, come in. I need to lock the door, now the evening's drawing on."

He laughed again, and Hagen smiled at the joke. Who did not know that neither mortals nor immortals, neither begotten nor created would dare approach that dwelling with malice aforethought?

"Come in, my ale is just ready to tap," Hropt continued, leading his guest through a long room with two hearths, one by the door and the other at the back, near a great wide bed strewn with furs. "Sit down, take tankard in hand, and tell me—to what do I owe the pleasure? How fares the estimable Hedin?"

Hard on the young thane's first few words, Hropt stopped playing the clown. The fiery gaze bored into Hagen, as if bent on burning two holes in his skin; the angular, powerful fingers grasped the table's edge.

"'Tis long enough since I heard worse," he muttered when Hagen fell silent, raising to his lips a stoup brimming with dark, foamy ale. "And it's not only Garm, either. He can be dealt with. He's a hound and no more, big as he is. The dame who was following you disturbs me far more. Would we could talk with Hedin..." His voice trailed away; he rubbed his forehead and plunged into deep thought, his brows knit over the bridge of his nose.

Hropt thought hard for a few minutes then slapped a decisive hand on the sturdy table.

"Well and good! Whatever you and I think up here—sithee, it'll all go athwart. So sleep now, and tomorrow I'll tell you how to treat with Garm. The Rider shall be mine...after I've had a word with your Teacher. Sleep! And whatever you hear or see this night do not be surprised, do not be afraid and do not stir. For now, it's no business of yours—although you're growing fast."

Hagen knew that in this place there must be obedience, with no ifs, ands or buts, and he obeyed. That he could do—one unable to submit could never command, so said his Teacher.

"If I hear you aright, Garm is no threat."

Hropt shook his head. "I said not so. Alone—no, he's no threat. His hour is distant yet. Only on the appointed day, at the battle of Ragnarok, will he acquire the power to devour the Gods, tear them to shreds. But on one thing you're correct—his awakening may bring us uninvited guests..." He ground his teeth, narrowing his eyes malevolently. He clearly had lengthy accounts to settle with those who might descend from the High Thrones to pacify the Hound. "Of course, were Garm to break free now, he would do much harm to mortal men, whom the Gods love. Then they would have to intervene. And if the heralds of Iamerth were to appear...no, that were better avoided. Sleep, then! While morning may not be wiser than evening, thinking is best done with a clear head."

"But what about the Stone Sentinel?"

"What of it?" a disgruntled Hropt muttered. "I'll just make another one, a stronger one."

"What killed it?"

"Someone's will was greater than mine." It was, at best, a grudging response. "That Darkling Rider had somehow laid her hands on a White Blade, and she could only have gotten it from a Mage. Well and good!" He rose. The conversation was over. "I haven't the time to be chin-wagging with you." He flung a thick black cloak, its huge hood hanging waist-low, over his shoulders, settled the sword at his side and took a hefty stave in his right hand. "Stay here. There's bread on the table, ale in the jug and a hock hanging yonder. But shilly-shally—you've no reason at all to see what I'm doing."

"As you wish, mine host." Hagen inclined his head. There was no sense in playing fast and loose with the Lord of the Living Crags by trying to spy or eavesdrop. Without the advantage of superior strength, one must be true to one's word.

It was almost morning when Hropt re-entered the room, weary and somber. The walls had been shaking all night long, with pale glimmerings running across the ceiling. In the darkness behind the wall cold voices called one to another, but Hagen was at a loss to tell what forces had gathered at Hropt's bidding.

A thirsty Hropt drained a tankard the size of a half-bucket, had a bite to eat and turned to Hagen, his eyes baleful and resolute and burning with a doleful fire.

"Have you eaten? Then listen close and remember well. You can forget for now about the wiccan who was on your trail. First, you must meet with Hedin. But, forget her though you may, you must go very carefully. When you settle for the night, don't be shiftless—conjure a Charmline around yourself.

"You must journey all the way to Utnordri, to the Field of Gnipahellir." Hropt looked Hagen sharply in the eye—did he falter? But no, the thane was calm. "That, as you should well know, is the beginning of the Black Highway to Near Niflhel. There is Garm's underground den. The Servants of the Lowerworld feed it constantly with dead bodies—the corpses of traitors, of perjurers who set the Heavens at naught. Still sleeping, the Hound eats it all.

"Once there, you must add this poppy juice to its feed." He handed Hagen a small flask. "And don't you be thinking that it's not enough. One drop of that potion will kill a man, though it will barely suffice to send the Hound back to sleep. Hedin bade you hurry. There are other pressing matters, but this he deems a simple commission for you. You will, he said, deal smartly with the first outpost manned by the Sentinels of the Dark Way, it being simpler for you as the one on the offensive. And because you must make your way to Utnordri unnoticed and as fast as you can, I'll give you a guide.

"Three days from here, midway between sunrise and midnight, in the Wilds of Bastier, lives Brann Shrunkenhand. He will lead you all the way to Gnipahellir. If you went as ordinary men do it would take four weeks, or even six, but Brann knows the entrance into the Forestway."

"The Forestway?" Hagen shook himself alert. His Teacher had spoken of this. The Forest there was not merely a jumble of pines and spruces sprouting from the soil; it was a huge yet single being, with its own language, unimaginably complex and all but incomprehensible, and a mind of enormous power. One of its wonders was the Forestway. A human, gnome, or elf—in short, any that the Forest acknowledged as its own—could petition for help, and then use special spells to open up a path along secret tracks so as to be able in a day to cover a distance that would have taken one traveling along the best roads a month. That was the Forestway, the Way Through.

"The Forestway, yes," Hropt nodded. "It has its dangers, mind. There are still mormaths, for instance, and woodland kheddes. But it is fast, and the Darkling Riders won't come after you. To make sure Brann knows who sends you and why, give him this."

The Master of the Living Crags handed Hagen a small scrap of parchment bearing a few elaborate runes. Hagen knew the meaning of each one, but combined they looked to him like arrant nonsense. To the note Hropt added a whimsically shaped folding knife that was clearly the work of lowland craftsmen.

"Tell him it's a gift from me. Brann likes a good knife. And for yourself, know that if you want to please Shrunkenhand, present him with a dagger."

"But who is he, this Brann?" Hagen asked.

"A man." Hropt replied. "Just as you are. A mortal with Knowledge, although, unlike you, no one ever taught it to him, except the Forest and the Speaking Land."

"He has the skill to hear the Speaking Land?" The thane raised his brows.

"No. He doesn't squeeze magical secrets out of her, as you would for certain, Hedin's apprentice. You're right in thinking that takes a special ability. He hears her as an ordinary man would catch the music of the wind or the sea or the merest rustle of a pinewood at night. What Brann can do, he does unawares. Like as not, he simply fell asleep once on a tract of Speaking Land. Any ordinary traveler would have paid for that with his reason, but Shrunkenhand has lived his whole life in the Forest, and belike it helped him that first time. In short, watch him close. Be honest with him and, sithee, he'll be of use to you yet."

"But I'd like to know—" Hagen began.

"How I could speak with Hedin, what he told me, where he is, and when you'll see him again?" Hropt had run ahead. "Then I'll tell you. I spoke with help from the Band of Erith that he gave me long, long ago. It is a kind of key to the Astral Plane, you know. Alas, men cannot use it. Or, rather, Hedin has not yet found the way. What he told me—well, those things are as yet in many respects beyond your reach. Beyond your reach because were you to know of them, you would be many times more vulnerable than you are.

"If any Mage now conceives the notion of doing away with you, he…or she…must perforce set someone on your trail and resort to the services of such vulgarities—to their minds, anyway—as steel or poison.

"But if you knew anything of my discussion with Hedin today, your enemies would need only to make certain motions and you would die in pain beyond understanding, with no way of protecting yourself. You slipped away from the Disc of Iamerth, but what the Mages could hurl against you is a hundred times more deadly.

"As to when you shall see Hedin, that will be as soon as you're done with the Hound. You will convene here, with Shrunkenhand as escort. Your Teacher has been forced to cut his travels short. We're in a sorry state."

"And what of the Sheltered Kingdom?"

"Vidrir has gone against Hjorlief, leading the first regiments of the city guard of the seaboard and his own militias. The forces will meet in four days. Like as not, Vidrir will carry it off, but it will cost him dear."

Hagen bade farewell to Hropt and journeyed on, the time he had fixed for his men—to the next moon—forcing him to hurry. He spared his horse but not himself. Remembering the words of the Master of the Living Crags, he traveled carefully, and was glad he did—twice he caught sight of mormaths but was able to take cover, so that the gray brutes did not even know he was there.

Toward the evening of the first day, he emerged from the mountains and spent the night in a tidy little spruce grove. He listened long and strained his eyes for anything crawling, creeping, flying, but he noticed nothing suspicious.

The next day, though, the forest suddenly grew dense, reared up in impenetrable thickets, blocked the way with deep gullies and countless marshy-banked streams, and bristled with trees fallen at an impassable angle. Even so, here and there, the thane's practiced eye glimpsed a scarcely distinguishable old ax-scar on a trunk or lopped spruce boughs or the broken stem of a recently gathered mushroom. There were humans in the forest and they were close, but just try to seek them out. Look around all you wanted, even from the top of the highest tree, everywhere it would be the same—a green carpet without end or boundary, and not a clearing in sight.

Such a forest is death to a southerner pampered by sunshine and open spaces, not knowing how to move amid endless mossy marshes overgrown with crooked little pines, or how to find food and shelter. A northern forest is uninhabited only at first glance, though, for in truth it is seething with life. Mischievous wood sprites lay their unremarkable trails; sullen trolls, shunned by all—even by the Father of Night who created them—fashion their lairs in the very heart of remote fens; and wood gnomes sell their logs and planks to their canny neighbors, the merchant-dwarves, and to mountain gnomes. Miners and smiths, they, who arrive with convoys of carts to purchase pit-props and clean birch charcoal for their forges.

Ghourees wander in search of prey. Gloomy kheddees hide from the searing arrows of humans, once in a while gathering in magical assemblies that are terrible to eye and ear. And that only describes the ones that may be encountered in physical form, by those who know how. No less a number Fate has cheated of a bodily shell and left fleshless. There are many masters in the Forest, called so by time-honored custom, although they cede governance of this wooded kingdom to humans, elves and gnomes. Every marsh, every spruce grove has its Master, hiding under snag or root, or in an entanglement of branches. They are not easy to spy, and few are they who may speak with them.

All these sprites are subjects and servants of Ialini, Everlasting Mistress of the Green World. The life of all growing things comes under their unsleeping watch, and if some stupid peasant were to lumber in, brandishing an ax with no good reason, not a week would pass before wolves would be ripping his cow apart or his garden plot would be rank with goose-foot or a ferret would find a cranny in his henhouse. The Forest Masters know all. Never a pinecone falls, never a blade of grass withers without their being privy to it. It seems they rule the Forest.

Yet at the same time it rules them, and there is no way of knowing who truly commands whom in such a place.

In the deep cleft of an old burned stump, Hagen noticed—thanks be to his Teacher—barely visible sparks of pale-green eyes. He dismounted, extinguished all other thoughts and rhythmically recited a charm of his own, a source of pride for him, not particularly strong but unfailing in cases such as this. The snippet of a woodland sprite had no escape.

"I know you," it announced, emerging unwillingly from its hiding place. "You are Hagen, apprentice of Mage Hedin known as the Sage of Darkness. You have spoken Words of Strength. So ask, then, and I will answer."

Hagen set his jaw—that was a bad sign. The denizens of the forest can be vengeful so should never know their questioner's name. They could have him trailed, or do him several hundred other kinds of harm. Yet they do love a good talk; a charm works less by restraining them than by enabling the listener to understand them.

But if a sprite says "Ask and I will answer," that means it is noways inclined to conversation and is only submitting to superior strength.

"How do I reach Roedulsfoel?" That was not at all what Hagen had originally wanted to ask.

"That's all? For this you disturb me?" the sprite griped. Then it pulled itself up, the charm forcing it to answer—and truthfully, too. "Make your way towards midnight. On the evening of the second day, you will pass by the house of Brann Shrunkenhand. Then..." And it launched into a rather lengthy description of the way to Roedulsfoel, which Hagen already knew very well.

When it was done, he asked it point-blank, "Why don't you want to talk with me of your own free will?"

Sprites are fortunate: they never blush and cannot be embarrassed.

"You are the enemy," the translucent little creature replied guilelessly. "You and your Teacher."

"Whose enemies are we?" Hagen barked, forgetting he was not speaking to a human being.

But the sprite did not answer; Hagen had passed beyond the bounds of his own charm.

Realizing there was nothing more for him here, and greatly vexed, he lashed his horse on. Now he had to cover his tracks to confuse the forest denizens and reach the home of Shrunkenhand in secret, for Ialini, sweet as she herself was, had powerful servants. Even Hropt could not help Brann here.

The task was hard. Phantoms of his own creation—his exact spectral doubles—galloped off in various directions while he, hidden as under a shield of invisibility by all the charms he knew, traveled on to Shrunkenhand's homestead. He should not, of course, have gone there in his own person, for who knew if all possible stalkers had been shaken from his trail? But no other choice remained to him.

Could the Green Mages have joined forces against him and his Teacher? That Darkling Rider had some connection with them—she had received the White Blade and a Disc of Iamerth from one of them. The forest sprites were Ialini's servants, and Ialini was Mistress of the Forests, the younger and much-loved sister of Iamerth, Lord of the Sun's Light...

But had the bearers of the Supreme Powers really got wind of all this, they would surely have taken up arms not against him, Hagen the mortal man, but against Mage Hedin, his Teacher. The apprentice would be of secondary importance, at best.

A familiar surge of sharp malice sent the rapid blood pounding in his veins. *Only wait, you eaters of dead things, wait until I'm done with Garm! Were you gods thrice over…*

It was a heady emotion, but the thane held it in check, malice being but a poor helpmeet to one uttering Words of Strength. Only for an instant had he let the magic shield that hid him weaken, and had distinctly sensed that even the little forest creatures he had left behind were aware of it. Besides, just as an animal is drawn by the scent of fresh blood, so powerful a draw is another's hatred. He must think no more on those who had set this hunt in train. He would engage them later, in his own good time, but for now he had to find his way to Shrunkenhand.

Doubt suddenly seized him. Brann was flesh of the Forest's flesh, and must perforce be subject to, or at least pay honor to, Ialini. Then had he been given his orders, too?

Hagen thought long and hard as he circled back and forth through the thickets. That Hropt had told him to travel with Brann meant nothing at all. If a Mage-war in the Real was imminent, the situation would be changing faster than in the fiercest affray. As Thane of Hedinseigh he had taken many a town by storm before his twenty-first year and could break out of any trap…except a snare set by wizardry. He shuddered. If his Teacher was under assault, he— Hagen, apprentice of an unruly Mage—would be squeezed for the last drop of information. Hedin had told him enough about the ways and customs of the Mages, and had good cause for having parted company with them.

Still, he found no alternative—only Brann could lead him to Gnipahellir through the Forestway. So, even were he three times an enemy, he must made to serve. Shrunkenhand understood the language of the Speaking Land, but that only made him a more worthy adversary, assuming he were able to call into play everything he had heard from it.

Again Hagen cleared his mind, displacing all thoughts with a resounding gray emptiness, and reached out to his intended guide. He had used this expedient several times in the past to determine if he were going to friend or enemy. This time, he sensed no response. Where he was going, there was plain indifference to such things.

Even better, he thought, abandoning his fruitless efforts. *Neither yes nor no is an answer, too. We'll take that as impartiality. We'll try to make an ally of Shrunkenhand…on our journey at least, and then we'll see.*

The thane touched his heels lightly to his horse's flanks, urging it forward. He had done all he could with distracting, deceitful phantoms and new-made canopies of mist that concealed both him and his horse. His brow and cheeks were slick with sweat, but here at last the forest parted and he was riding along a slatted fence built to keep livestock from wandering far. In the middle of a circlet of fields, under three mighty elms, he saw a small, neat log house, a thriving farmstead surrounded by a high palisade. A well-sweep pointed skyward, and there were barns roofed with gray planking. Dogs began barking at the stranger's approach, although he was downwind of them.

He dismounted and knocked on a gate with a massive iron ring. The gate, of course, opened only outward, so that storming it would involve breaking the locks and hinges; and any attacker would have to shiver stout oaken planks into splinters. Brann was a thoughtful builder.

There was another flurry of barks behind the high fence, then the sound of a bolt being drawn. The thane pulled the gate toward him, and two fluffy, sharp-eared dogs with tails curled like clover-leaf rolls promptly shot through the narrow opening to hem the newcomer in on both sides. Right behind the shaggy guards came their master.

He was easily old enough to be Hagen's father. His hair was abundantly gray, his forehead deeply wrinkled and his face windworn and sunburned. But his eyes were calm, and there was no guile in them. He was but a few inches shorter than the thane, who considered himself very tall. In his right hand, he held an almost finished hunting arrow, and his left hand was, indeed, shrunken and twisted. Brann held it close to his side, the wrist against his chest.

The dagger in his broad belt was a surprise—the weapon seemed placed not so that he could use the hand on the healthy right arm, with its mounds of powerful muscles, to reach it but so that it would be accessible to the maimed left hand.

"Peace be unto this house, master!" Hagen bowed his head courteously. "I come to you from Hropt, with business in mind and gift in hand." He proffered the knife given to him by the Lord of the Living Crags.

At the sight of the costly blade, warmth crept into Brann's eyes.

"Greetings to you, and thanks to the esteemed Hropt for the honor. Enter." He stood aside. "Enter, and be welcome. What's your name? Whose son are you? And what business have you with me?"

Hagen gave his name. Brann did not bat an eye and showed no particular deference to one who called himself thane.

"Let's go up," he said. "'Tis not decent to be talking in the doorway."

HEDIN

Hagen and I left the ruins of Jol—charred bones now, picked bare by hungry flames—in the pouring rain, following the trail of the large mounted contingent that had obeyed the Jarl Sviurr's cruel orders to the letter. My apprentice was holding up quite well; one would never have thought him to be only ten and a half years old.

He had a difficult task ahead of him—difficult not because it meant slitting the throats of three dozen seasoned warriors by night but because he had never before had to walk through blood and kill unarmed men. I had no doubt he would pass through their ranks unheeded, but would the rest of it be too much for him?

I had withstood that test, but not he, not yet. Had my teaching been all it could have been? Before taking up the magic arts, he would first have to grasp the human skills, one of which was the ability to carry one's intentions through without a qualm. Frustrated intentions are a plaguey thing, and sap the strength. Follow your desires and you will always be in the right.

Ahead of us, we could already see the outbuildings of the village where the contingent had halted for the night. Just then, from the slanting, spinning curtains of rain, there emerged a slim cloaked figure I instantly recognized.

"Well met, Sigrlinn," I said, politely and even gaily, while inwardly clenching and preparing for battle. "What brings you here? What are you doing out in such a storm?"

"Stay your steps, Sage of Darkness." She had not taken up my tone. Now she bore a very strong and unpleasant resemblance to the one who had dictated the terms of my surrender. Hagen, fine lad that he was, was also immediately aware of the threat.

"What's she want? Why's she in our way?" he said in the whiny voice of an

35

offended child, while deftly turning away from the sorceress and thrusting his hand surreptitiously under his cloak to reach for his strong knife with its curved blade.

I laid a calming hand on his shoulder.

"Sage of Darkness, this will be your first and last warning from the Council. If you disobey, you will meet the fate of Rakoth, or worse. You are planning a war, and for it you are training this boy—"

"Boy yourself!" Hagen snapped. "I'll teach you to call me that, I will. Boy, indeed. I am a warrior!"

"Merlin's not letting you out of his sight, Hedin." Sigrlinn words came fast and feverish, while with a familiar gesture she conjured a Deflecting Circle around herself. "He's certain you're aiming for his position. The Council is obliged by law to warn you and has sent me for that purpose. Stop now, or bear the consequences. If you have no pity on yourself, then at least pity him." She pointed at Hagen. "Or…or me!"

She spoke from the heart, and that had me completely perplexed. What could she mean by her "at least pity me?" It had been a long—an immemorially long—time since I had heard her say anything of the sort; the memories that rose up, unbidden, were ones from which I had shielded myself for many years. Sigrlinn and I, creating together, day and night— young, inseparable, happy…

"Very well. You came to give me the Council's warning." I spoke with difficulty, driving the uninvited thoughts away by sheer willpower. "And that you have done. What else? What do you want? Would you have me believe you are on my side and prepared to tell me all the plans Merlin has for me? Would you have me forget our battles?"

"You never change, Hedin." She gave a hard laugh. "You can't help looking for traps, can't help suspecting me of perfidy. You probably won't believe me when I tell you that I hold dear the memory of what we had together, and that I was drawn here by pity, both for you, you poor madman, and for your apprentice, this child."

Once again, Hagen intruded into our conversation by unceremoniously flinging a lump of wet road clay at her.

"Go away! Be off with you! What do you want with us?"

I took a step back. His eyes were blazing. The knife glinted in his right hand, a perfect pairing with the bristling, battle-ready young wolfcub he had become.

The corner of Sigrlinn's perfectly drawn mouth trembled and twitched. I readied myself to parry a stream of flame that would have unfailingly incinerated my young saucebox on the spot. Instead, she stretched out her right hand to Hagen in an unexpectedly gentle, open gesture.

"You'd give your life for him, would you?" she said to my apprentice, without a shadow of a smile. "He's everything to you now."

Hagen was taken aback. So, I must admit, was I. I had no idea what was happening. There was the fleeting thought that if we ever disentangled ourselves from this fix I would have a lot to teach the boy. He was bewildered right now, and that was bad. One must know how to hate one's enemies regardless of what comes out of their mouths.

"Then this is what I would say to you," Sigrlinn continued in the same gentle, confiding voice. "Your Teacher is in great danger. Those who live above, in the sky…" She pointed upward with an elegant finger. "…are greatly vexed with him. He wants to kill them, to seize their thrones, and you are only a tool he is creating for that purpose. If the two of you don't stop, they will sweep you away. That was the warning I wanted to give, but it seems to have been a wasted effort."

Lightning shot from her eyes. She was barely holding herself in check.

"If you'll excuse us, we'll be on our way," I said, touching Hagen's head. "I believe we are as soaked as we care to be."

"Then I'm done with you, you miserable fool!" Sigrlinn stamped her foot in fury. Two silver lightning bolts darted from her fingers into a roadside puddle. The water instantly boiled and seethed, giving off clouds of steam. "I wash my hands of you for good and all. I'll not shield you any longer. Get clear of it as best you can."

She was at once terrifying and stupendous and bewitching. Since our days in the Cerulean City, I had never seen her so ravishing—anger always made her more beautiful. Transparent tongues of pale iridescent flame danced around her; a cascade of blue sparks streamed from the ends of her rain-soaked hair, and a scarlet glow rose from the hem of her cloak.

"I thank you for the warning," I said. "Don't be so cross, and let's not squabble. But I'll still be going my own way. If I were to turn aside I would no longer be myself. Wasn't it you who said you would have nothing more to do with me if I repented before the Council?"

"Hedin." She raised her hands as if holding an unseen but heavy burden. "They'll kill you."

"What did you say?" It sounded so absurd I was sure I had misheard.

"Merlin has found a way to outflank the Law of the Ancients," Sigrlinn let fall wearily, obviously not striving for effect. "He has dispatched a Star Messenger."

"Merlin found it? Or Merlin was told it?" It was a thick-headed question, but at the time nothing better came to mind.

"Merlin has been given the right to punish with Unbeing anyone who upsets the World Balance," Sigrlinn said crisply. "Sentence is passed by a majority vote in the Council."

"How did it come about that Merlin first vouchsafed himself the honor of sending a Messenger and then was granted such unprecedented power? I felt nothing."

"Merlin didn't go into the reasons for his decision. He created the Messenger himself, and no one knows what was in the message laid at the feet of the thrones of the Hallowed Land. We can only guess. Could it have had something to do with Rakoth?"

"With Rakoth?" I exclaimed. "What could it have to do with him? He's fettered and confined."

Sigrlinn shrugged. "But now perhaps you'll think on this?" she asked by way of answer, with an almost timid note of hope in her voice. Or, rather, I heard that hope but then I brusquely told myself not to be ridiculous. Sigrlinn would not have spoken so even if racked by a deathbed delirium.

"The Council would never go so far," I replied with a hard-won smile. "Even Makran and Esteri, no matter how much they hate me, understand perfectly well that if I am first there will be others after me. And precisely what is so harmful about an upset of the Balance? A Mage's entire life is one upset after another."

"Enough, I can't stand it!" Sigrlinn suddenly groaned, dropping her hands. And she was instantly gone, leaving only that smoking puddle, heated to extinction by her lightning bolts.

"Hold your questions, Hagen," I checked my apprentice, who was already trembling with impatience. "First we have work to do."

We covered the remainder of the way in silence. Sigrlinn had deluged me with news, but I made myself forget that for the moment. The important thing now was Hagen.

I helped him scramble onto the roof of a coaching inn, and that was the full extent of my participation in his revenge. He managed marvelously all alone. He did, I own, emerge pale and shaken, but that soon passed. He had learned his lessons well—not one superfluous move, not a creak, not a groan. Sharp as a razor, the knife cut noiselessly and unerringly.

"Was it frightening?" I asked him, but Hagen simply jerked his shoulders and peppered me with all the questions he had been longing to ask.

I answered them throughout the following day, as we sat in a gloomy ravine waiting out the turmoil that had been going on in the village since morning. When the owner of the inn found the bodies of Sviurr's warriors, you'd have thought the trump of doom had sounded. Snatching up pitchforks and axes, the peasants began roaming around the outskirts, less to catch the unknown murderers, of whom they themselves were mortally afraid, than to earn the jarl's forgiveness. He was a flinty man, and could well have ordered the village razed to the ground, as he had with Jol.

While the hapless hue and cry went on in the distance, I opened up some secrets to Hagen. I had to tell him everything I knew about the history of the Order of the Mages so he could understand who Sigrlinn and Merlin were.

"She's beautiful, though, Teacher," he suddenly announced in a completely grown-up way, in the very midst of my tale. "But bad. She doesn't want you to teach me."

I was silent. Who knows—perhaps it would have been better for Hagen if the Grain of his Fate had never fallen into my hands.

I had spoken of the Gods and the other Great Powers, both Ancient and Distant, only in passing. Hagen also needed to hear no more of Merlin for the time being, having immediately grasped that Merlin was at present the prime enemy. That said, it was no small effort to keep the conversation away from Rakoth. I did not want to lie to my own apprentice, but neither, for now, could I tell him the truth.

Finally, he was worn out and fell asleep, his nose nuzzled into the crook of my elbow. I covered him with a cloak, and only then could I catch my breath and think about what Sigrlinn had told me.

The right to punish with Unbeing. How could that be? What an abyss of knowledge must have opened up before Merlin—or been opened to him by the Lords Everlasting—to give the Archmage access to the heretofore unthinkable. Everything I knew told me the Law of the Ancients was inviolate, meaning that Merlin must have reached a completely new level of knowledge.

A Mage's life is not directly tied to the body. The body can be wounded, hacked to pieces, burned to a crisp, but none of that will kill a Mage. The weapon the Powers of the World had placed into Merlin's hands was one of colossal might. Were they so naive as to be certain he would not turn it against them in good time?

But assume that it is all true, and Merlin really can destroy me. Then the question is, can he truly do it only after the Council has passed sentence or can he do it on his own volition, informing the others only after the event? And how is it done?

I was, I admit, extremely uneasy at the thought I could disappear at that very moment, without so much as a by-your-leave, and melt into the shoreless ocean. In fact, I was dripping with cold sweat.

Wait, though, I said to myself. Be calm. If Merlin had really wanted to make off with you and has the means to do so, it would already be done. Something is holding him back. I need to ferret out everything I can, as quickly as I can, about that weapon of his, and find out what Sigrlinn meant when she spoke of Rakoth.

And then my thoughts surprised me by going their own way. Suddenly, instead of pondering the Leader of the Council of the Generation's new and incredible ability to dispose of undesirables with greater dispatch than was afforded by exile and confinement, I found myself assailed by that dread name: Rakoth.

I was only now becoming aware of the ominous import of what my once-beloved had said. Had she meant to say it, or had it escaped her accidentally? In either event, it was just too close to one of the components of my carefully guarded plan.

Rakoth. Rakoth the Rebel, the Lord of Gloom, who with his Dark Armies had thrice stormed the Castle of the Ancients, and had in his time even laid siege to the Hallowed Land. Rakoth, brought low and confined, and—my friend. My only friend down the long ages.

We had begun together, which was why mine was also a title that invoked the Dark Powers; but then he had unwisely developed a thirst for absolute power. Having acquired enormous amounts of knowledge that was his and his alone, he frittered his whole self away on the creation of countless Black Legions and Twilight Kingdoms. He declared war on the Lords Everlasting, hoping to see them away with his ordinary, everyday armamentarium.

I had tried to stop him, but he would have none of my advice, and we quarreled. I did not go to his aid when his armies began perishing one after another under the furious onslaught of the Young Gods and their resplendent troops; and my treachery, be it intentional or accidental, was a searing pain to me. I could find only one way of escaping from myself.

The victors ground Rakoth's strongholds into the dust and took him prisoner. There was a trial. I did not help my friend, but neither did I ally myself with the Gods, as did every other Mage of my Generation. In punishment for that, they made me read Rakoth his sentence—a humiliation I had not forgotten and would not forget to the end of my days. The fettered and partially disembodied Rakoth sank into oblivion, while I...

I began to create my Empire of Night.

A great many sundry events ensued; time passed and the day grew near when I would be able to repay my debt to each and all, including to Rakoth. It was a slippery path, though, and all too easy to lose one's balance on it. Now came Sigrlinn with her veiled hints...

I caught myself thinking how long it had been since I had been able to predict any action of hers. Had she been sent to me, or had she come of her own accord? Was it all mere invention? Where could I go for advice?

I remembered Hropt.

I had not seen him for more than a decade—since my return from exile, all my days had been Hagen's. Now, evidently, the time had come to meet again. Besides, I was dutybound to present my apprentice to him.

And so our journey began.

By an old trade route out of Jarlsland, past the barons' domains and through the free plowlands to the edges of the Rogheim wolds, then southward on the only road that offered us any safety. Through the Land of Oak Groves, giving a wide berth to the fearsome Iron Wood—Hagen was still a little too young for that excursion—we made our way to the Living Crags.

Old Hropt. He had been old already when I was but a lad. Being indelibly marked by the Seal of the Wrath of the Lords Everlasting, he was shunned by all. The dictate of the gods was honored as sacred writ, and I chanced to be the first of my Generation to violate their order, partly out of curiosity, and partly out of contrariness. I had always been drawn to that mighty, magical being who had come into our world from who knows where, was neither one of the ruling Gods nor one of the Ancient Ones and was, to boot, utterly alone. He had no apprentices, no followers; he was, to all appearances, an outcast.

That was probably why he had been so tremendously surprised that a young Mage of a Generation that had only just found its feet had dared defy the divine precepts and turn up on his doorstep. He seemed glad of my visit, although he made every effort to hide it; in fact, he almost turned me out. But then, relenting and realizing I was no spy—I was dismayed he could even think that of me—he grew open to me, and I learned from him that which turned my back to the Light and plunged me into so assiduous a study of Darkness.

Hropt and I never became friends. Nor can I say he was my Teacher, although he gave me much. Something other, and far stronger, than the attachments and duties of apprenticeship brought us together. We felt we could not do without each other for the fulfillment of our innermost desires. I was Hropt's only hope, and he was my only source of truly invaluable knowledge. You might say he was the one who upended all my notions of the Real, the Mid-Real, the gods, demons and other magical beings, of the Light and the Dark within the compass of the world.

Before I met Hropt, existence, although full of unsettling secrets and incredible adventures, was to me a flower-strewn meadow between two menacing fortresses, one white and the other black. I was certain of myself and of the side I was on. Hropt opened my eyes to the great diversity of Powers, Ancient and Distant; and I will never forget the day when I finally understood who he was and why the Lords had placed him under their ban.

I had always wondered why that mighty spirit, that proud heart, that profound mind had accepted his place as a piteous castaway who spent weeks and months in listless gloom, cooped up in his silent shack and indulging rather too heartily in the roughest, strongest ale known to anyone. Age upon age would yet sink into nothingness before the cry "All hail to fallen grandeur!" would go up, but as the Moonbeast is my witness, it fit Hropt to a nicety.

I quite soon understood he was not of the Ancients who had proceeded and been supplanted by the Mage Generation, but who he truly was, and whence he came, long remained an enigma to me. Once, when his mood was especially cloudy and the bottom of the ale jug was showing through, he touched fleetingly on Bifrost and Midgard and other things that meant nothing to me. I steeled myself to ask.

"Whence come I?" Hropt narrowed his eyes. "You haven't guessed? Time was when I sat on a golden throne surrounded by faithful friends. Time was when I commanded and passed judgment, and all bowed before me. Who am I? Come."

He dragged me off into the stables. There, dejected and drooping, stood a wondrous stallion, the like of which I had never seen. It was not his points, strength and beauty that surprised me, though, but his eight slim yet well-muscled legs.

Only one such steed existed in the Real.

And only one rider would he ever bear.

"To the hour of Ragnarok there remained measureless abysses of time," Hropt said, staring unseeing at the wall. "But They came beforetime, unheralded and no one knows from whence. We fought and...failed. Then,

42

they say, the rest fell, too. The slayer of Beli, the son of Fjorgyn, the brother of Byleist—all, and all our wives. They perished, every one. I was alone, and the world had new masters. So I am here, since fire sated itself on my chambers' high walls. My strength was spent in battle, and now my abilities are but a remnant of what they once were."

The hazy legends and hints bandied about among the gnomes, that most ancient and wisest race of mortals, which I had been gathering so long and so eagerly, were all at once fleshed out. A multitude of scattered details fell into place. The world had been ruled by others before the coming of the Young Gods, and the old suzerains had fallen before the interlopers' onslaught.

"And you..." I hesitated, but Hropt waved it away.

"No need for titles—they're as empty as the skull of a corpse rolling in the surf. I know what you want to ask. No, I cared to try no more, because I no longer know how to fight. But I will do everything I can to learn it again. Stay with me, if you wish, but I warn you that if you ever take it into your head to betray me..."

His brows drew together, his eyes blazed, and before me stood the Father of Hosts, terrible as he ever had been when galloping at the head of a mighty force into a great battle.

That was when I did become Hropt's apprentice, and a strange apprenticeship it was, like none before it. I realized very quickly that almost everything at his command was open to me, while he lacked the strength to imitate my skills. He liberally shared with me a different kind of knowledge—not charms and the martial crafts of magic but the true history of the world and the minutiae of the various Powers that were active in it, my tally of them having ere then fallen far short.

There came the day when my apprenticeship imperceptibly gave way to an alliance; and then, as my own powers grew, Old Hropt began paying me more heed, following my advice and eventually doing what I asked him to do. He had acknowledged my superior strength. Understanding that the old stock-in-trade would not suffice in future times, he became an eager student, although the New Magic came hard to him. Still, he was in no hurry.

The victors, having banished him and slaughtered all his comrades-in-arms, had for some reason spared his life—I assumed the renowned soft-heartedness of Ialini, who hated bloodshed, had been instrumental in that—but had placed him under constant watch. I had immediately sensed the presence of the Unslumbering Eye, even though it was concerned only with Hropt, not with anything around him.

The Father of Hosts made no secret of his goals. He wanted everything to be as before, and if it could not, then he wanted revenge. He was not insisting I fight shoulder-to-shoulder with him—in those days, after all, I did not even know my own desires. I did help him, though, because I was already aware that the Young Gods and I were ripe for a parting of the ways. Sigrlinn and the Cerulean City were in the past, Rakoth was keeping his distance as he prepared his First Rebellion, and I was at loose ends, not really knowing what I wanted.

Then the vortex of wars that shook all the Real sucked me into its gigantic funnel. I made my own plan and began to pursue it, and finally was hugely astonished to see, at the window of my citadel apartments in the capital of the Empire of Night, the huge black Castle Raven, harbinger of war. The Raven from the Castle of All the Ancients, bringing me Sigrlinn's summons.

In the hateful ages of my exile, Hropt had been my only friend, the imprisoned Rakoth having, as I thought, fallen forever from this world. Hropt really did spare no effort in helping me. He even on occasion left his lonely refuge by the Living Crags to go with me on long and risky journeys, such as to the dead cathedral cities of the South, where the wind wails over the dilapidated altars of decayed gods—a place I would never have left had it not been for Hropt.

So, Hagen and I were on our way to the Living Crags. In a few years, my apprentice would be a full-fledged warrior. First, he would become a thane, and later...

THE STONE SENTINEL WAS ALL SET TO CRIPPLE HAGEN, WHO HAD RUSHED, WITHOUT FEAR but also without much common sense, to head it off. But the youngster darted aside and needed no help from me, although he was soundly shaken. I had not said a word to him about what awaited him amidst the Crags.

Hropt was enduringly pleased with my apprentice. We lived there a full four years, which were probably the best four years of my life. Then the fifteen-year-old Hagen, no longer a boy but a man, and I left our safe haven and traveled southwest toward inhabited lands. The time had come to cast away stones, as one of Merlin's luckless followers was later to say.

My apprentice's weapon was forged by gnomes, for despite everything, Hropt still commanded vast respect among them, and they were glad to do as he asked. To be equal to the tasks that lay ahead, Hagen would, of course, need something made at least by the Ancient Mages, or better yet by the Ancient Gods; but a gnomish blade would first be required to reach their secret stores. I loosened my pursestrings, and the craftsmen of Hauberk Mount took the gold, although the thought of riches could not have been further from their minds.

Gnomes belong to a strange race that creates and destroys with equal passion, though none of their formidable *hirds*, those indestructible battle arrays, had been seen afoot for many a long year. They lived at peace with humans, entirely engrossed in their work, yet their hearts were perpetually aflame with a gloomy fire, the Creating and Devouring Ardor; and that was why they were so willing to forge swords or any other military gear. As he took our order, Droni, an old gnome whose unpronounceable title translated in human parlance into something like "he-who-makes-glittering-killing-cleaving-spikes-to-wound," said in a low tone, eyeing my apprentice closely, "'Tis a pleasure to work for such as he. He will put the sword to good use. Steel should drink its fill of blood." And his eyes gleamed with such unlooked-for ferocity it almost knocked me back on my heels.

No one knows how many times the steel of the sword-to-be was forged and reforged, how many millions of layers were fused together in that underground furnace. The old rumors of the miraculous strength of a weapon crafted by moonlight were to me no more than rumors. Yet I had more faith in the gnomes' craftsmanship than in Sigrlinn's elusive hints, since she had never had any serious dealings with simple metal playthings; my duel with her had been conducted by other means.

Hagen clasped the glittering blade to his chest, his eyes burning. He bowed low to the old craftsman, and Droni gave a satisfied grin.

"Don't forget to let it out for air often," he said. "A sword, you know, is not fond of dozing idly in its sheath. It can lose its strength."

Hagen straightened, and his hand abruptly sliced through the air. With a slight hiss, the blade inscribed a pearly half-circle, felling a young pine as broad as a strong man's arm at the root. The gnomes knew what they were about.

Droni also made a helmet, hauberk, shield and other essential accouterments for my apprentice. Now we could strike south. There, beyond the Oak Groves, lay the mountains of Alvland, where no one ventured on a whim. To the west, the young and voracious kingdom of Himinvagar stretched greedy hands composed of numerous well-armed regiments to snatch up any undefended land. And to the southwest of Himinvagar, the defensive ramparts of the Sheltered Kingdom ran league after league, although everyone knew it was protected with a might far greater than any human sword or lance.

Yet farther southward, from the frontiers of Vidrir's dominion to the very gulf that separated Eastern Hjorvard from the southern continent, lay the lands of the free peasants, each region living by its own rules. Some decided everything down to the pettiest detail by fistfights in their assembly rooms; others invited princes in to lead their militias and dispense impartial justice. There was never peace among those communities for long.

The lands to the east of the free peasants' settlements belonged to the barons, small independent rulers of diminutive states who spent their days in knightly merriment, feasts giving way to tournaments and tournaments to feasts. The barons were at odds with the jarls, who were always after new lands to pay them tribute, while the barons persisted in pursuit of their cherished dream of having an outlet to the sea.

The jarls themselves were snugly ensconced far down on the eastern coast, where the sea-swell met the raw and ancient bones of Earth, the hills of Ossor. The sea drove deep into the land with long, lapping inlets and sinuous fjords that were perfect places to hide the elongated, narrow war vessels known as dragon-ships. By one such fjord lay Jol of happy memory, which had probably been rebuilt by now, with ant-like obstinacy.

Midway between the domains of the jarls and the lands of the free peasants sprawled Haithabu, the capital of the independent Mercantile Republic and the crossroads of Eastern and Southern, Northern and Western Hjorvard. People and goods streamed there from all quarters, the most insane and reckless schemes were contrived there; and there, too, was refuge and employment for any who no longer had a home in the old lands. There, all held stubbornly to the law of primogeniture, whereby each homestead passed to the oldest son, leaving the younger to hire himself out to his own brother or throw it all up and seek his fortune elsewhere.

Both the jarls and the grasping leaders of the free peasant communities had long had their eyes on the riches of Haithabu, but the Mercantile Republic could afford to enlist the best men-at-arms. For the most well-to-do merchants of the town, three hundred gold belts was a small price to pay.

I wanted to show the city to Hagen, lead him through all the illusory enticements of tasty food and lovely things, of seductive and easy women, so that later he would know exactly what he was rejecting. Besides, he needed to gather an entourage of followers and comrades-in-arms. We were about to challenge the might of the Sheltered Kingdom, and he would have to win that first war on his own, with no more of my help than the advice I would give him.

Approximately a day's passage, with a following wind, from the entrance to

Vidvagar Cove, on whose banks lay the Sovereign City, capital of Vidrir's kingdom, the sea disgorged the rugged hulks of the sea-cliffs of Hedinseigh Island.

My island.

Once, long, long ago, I had founded there the capital of my Empire of Night, before the hurricane of war swept all the fruits of my labors into nothingness. The island had fallen into Sigrlinn's hands, and she had given it to her apprentices, who then created the Sheltered Kingdom under the sovereignty of the Young Gods in what had once been my domain. The island had remained uninhabited from that time, although inside the ring of precipices that protected it on all sides were meadows, fields and streams aplenty. That was what had first drawn me to it; it was a land that could feed many.

For the sake of order, Vidrir, the present ruler of the Sheltered Kingdom, maintained a small garrison there.

Between the boundaries of the Kingdom and the lands of the free peasants stretched a narrow strip of land belonging to the self-ruling thanes, vassals of Vidrir, who also owned several islands that dotted the sea lanes by Hedinseigh. Unlike the jarls, the thanes seldom mounted ambitious military campaigns; their wealth was rooted in the land, which was worked by tenant farmers. From time to time they would become embroiled in skirmishes between the free peasant communities, or they would join forces in a sortie into Himinvagar, to which the rulers of the Sheltered Kingdom turned a blind eye, and rarely—very rarely—the retinue of some particularly foolhardy thane would accompany the jarls on a campaign to the distant south or east.

Be all that as it may, Hedinseigh awaited us, and we had to hurry. As it was, I could not guarantee Hagen's lifetime would be long enough to carry all my plans to completion, and to deny him peace in the afterlife I considered the most monstrous betrayal any Mage could visit upon his apprentice. Makran had done it time and again, but my own principles notwithstanding, one sight of the consequences was sight enough.

We pressed southward. The forests were behind us, while ahead the mountain bluffs of Alvland reared into view. Hagen, who had heard numerous stories about the beings who lived there, fixed his eyes on those peaks and never looked away.

I was always very careful in my dealings with the First-Begotten and their works, among which were the alvs, although there were almost none to be found in the human-inhabited lands of all four parts of Greater Hjorvard.

Those who remained, though, wielded dreadful powers, and would on occasion reach out an imperious hand to intervene in human events, always seeking to end warfare and bring peace to the land for the longest possible span of time. They had no great fondness for Mages but never openly opposed them.

For my part, the alvs had ever been a source of great fascination. In several instances, they could be very useful, all but indispensable. And they were always ready to help, though they never forgot to demand payment for whatever assistance they might proffer. They insisted on being paid in knowledge—I admit being at times amused by the truly childlike directness with which they tried to pry charms from me. They were invariably the charms the Council of the Generation had placed under seal of secrecy—how to waken dragons and command them, how to open the gates to the Lowerlands and gather powers there, how to enmesh a Mage in an invisible net and deprive him of his freedom...

Scattered trees nestled right up to the gray-brown slopes of the foothills. Immediately before us yawned a wide ravine that was almost a valley. It was easy to see the precise boundary of the alvs' lands—after some few hundred yards of lifeless clay and stone the slopes of the ravine were again covered with grass, but this was not quite the ordinary grass that grew elsewhere, being pale-blue in color. The ravine floor was thick with trees that also could be seen nowhere else—low-growing, they were, but with very thick trunks and broad, flared leaves of darkest green, something like maple leaves but twice the size. The beams made from those trunks never rotted and were very hard to burn, and were therefore greatly prized by the jarls and the free peasants as building material for their fortresses.

On outcroppings a good fifty yards above our heads, on either side of the ravine, stood two guard towers of bluish stone. Elegant and well-proportioned, their facades carved in lacy patterns, those towers looked nothing like real fortifications. Although the alvs no longer kept company with their creators, they still, all unawares, continued to copy their erstwhile mentors. Of course, the beauty of their structures could in no way vie with the masterpieces of elven craftsmen—with Silverheart, one of the elven capitals in Eastern Hjorvard, which had stood for long ages but been visited by only a scant handful of mortal men. I had been there once, and would remember that sight for the rest of my days.

The left-hand tower had a window that opened in our direction, and through it there came a quick blue glint, brief enough to escape the idle gaze of a chance traveler.

"What was that?" Hagen, instantly on his guard, bent and with an expert hand retrieved the shield that had been slung across his shoulder.

"They're asking us if we are worthy of the masters' attention," I replied, crossing my arms across my chest.

A true Mage never need say a word in order to accomplish his ends. Along with Orlangur and Demogorgon, Mages mark the Great Boundary between the light and the dark halves of creation, and a Mage acquires his power by turning the world about himself. A charm is merely a formality that is especially useful when working with beings made of other than inert matter.

I uncrossed my arms, and a faint reddish-orange ember appeared between my cupped palms, quickly extending into a pointed beam almost as tall as a man. That was my answer to the alv guards.

At first, I remember, Hagen was most impressed not by complex acts of genuine magic—a descent into the Lowerlands, the calling of the dead, and so on—but by such easy little sleights as the one I had just performed. For a long time I tried to explain to him that a Mage who can start a fire between his palms is just like a person who can curl his tongue into an O or wiggle his ears. There are many who can't do it, and those who can can't explain how it's done. And if they can't explain it, they certainly can't teach it to anyone else.

To be sure, I spent long enough enlightening Hagen on the doctrine of the Magic Fire, the primordial spark the Creator had breathed into our world even before the coming of the Young Gods. I told him how in every Mage there burns a fragment of that invisible fire, and that it can be given a multitude of forms; but to explain how exactly I had lit that little ember of mine…that I could not do.

Blue glints appeared in the embrasures of the right-hand tower. We were being welcomed and invited to enter.

And so Hagen and I crossed into Alvland.

CHAPTER III

FOR FOUR DAYS, GUDMUND, HAVING PARTED WITH FRODI, TIRELESSLY DROVE HIS HORSE eastward. The Vale of Brunevagar lay between two old, crumbled, densely forested mountains. Once, they had formed part of a mighty chain, one of Eastern Hjorvard's most majestic, though so long ago there had been no "Eastern Hjorvard"—it was all one vast land mass. That was before the First Day of Wrath, of which there now remains no evidence at all—all the humans living on Earth at the time perished.

While the Enfrenzied Powers raged, trackways of wind and water were changed, the continents moved, the Earthshield was rent with fissures, the waves of the World Ocean gushed into the fractures, forming new seas. The old mountains were ground down almost to their roots and great slabs of granite torn from their armored flanks, leaving their soft underbellies prey to the gently gnawing rain. But the spirit of those old hills—and old they were, in truth, for nothing in all of Eastern Hjorvard rivaled them in age except Hropt and Orlangur and Demogorgon, who belonged to all the world—lived on. It was likely for this reason the strange monastery far-famed among the First-Begotten had been founded in their midst.

All this Gudmund remembered on his journey. He had learned a lot from the tales told by his thane, whom the warriors respected not only for his good fortune in battle but also because at times he would rescue them all, or lay his hands upon some especially valuable spoils through use of his knowledge, which differed immensely from any Gudmund had ever heard of.

A younger son of a down-at-heel thane living on the frontier of the Sheltered Kingdom, Gudmund had left home long before, immediately after his mother's death and his father's remarriage. He had served as a guard for wealthy free peasants; then Fate had flung him into the Mercantile Republic, to

Haithabu. Famished, but lithe and fearless, he had passed through a meticulous screening to become a city constable. Then he had crossed paths with the thane, who was as yet no thane but simply Hagen.

Since childhood, Gudmund had had the kind of affinity for knowledge that was not frequently encountered among vagabond fortune-seekers. That, in time, caused Hagen to single him out from the rest, with the later approval of Hedin, the thane's enigmatic Teacher.

Now he was making fast for the monastery, knowing well this might signal an end to his service with Hagen—the thane did not forgive disobedience. But all Gudmund had to do was picture the face of the dying elf, the First-Begotten's eyes, and all his doubts, regrets and fears were gone. The elder brothers of the human race never lied to their younger siblings, so if an elf asked someone to carry a message, that message had to be conveyed, come what may.

Evening was gradually coming on. The area through which he traveled seemed to have been abandoned by humans long before, although a sharp eye could still make out, in the occasional clearing, old fields swallowed up by clumps of pine trees. There were also some semblances of roads, now become narrow trails—he was galloping down one such trail, bending low to his horse's neck.

At every step of his journey he had been tormented by uneasiness. What if that mysterious Darkling Rider was making in the same direction as he, and the purpose of the elf's commission had been only to prepare the monastery to fend her off? What if that strange, uncommonly dangerous wiccan was lying in wait for him now, having by some wizardry discovered she was being followed? He had no great hopes of overtaking his fearsome adversary. After all, Darkling Riders had richly earned their name, for on foot they could easily outpace someone on horseback.

Gudmund feared and hated wiccans. It was a legacy from his childhood, when he had become firmly convinced that witchery caused his mother's death. She had refused to give a crotchety and willful creature who had turned up at her door her last elegant gown, a memento of happier times, in payment for curing a murrain that, as no one doubted in the least, the wiccan herself had called down. The unwanted visitor eventually left, but not before whispering in his mother's face a spiteful-sounding yet unintelligible incantation.

His mother had shuddered as if struck, and a few months later had died of a strange illness none of the local warlocks could cure. Gudmund did not yet know that no one Darkling Rider resembled any other, and he spent no time pondering who might be this one's quarry. Whoever he was—and whether human or not—Gudmund would gladly stand with him.

He was saved by his ambusher's curiosity. A slim, almost invisible cord suddenly sprang out of the grass under his horse's hooves. The horse stumbled, and Gudmund somersaulted onto the ground; but at the last instant he happened, by some miracle, to mark a suspicious flittering in the underbrush and so took care to land on all fours. A head-over-heels tumble took him farther from the bushes than the would-be captor, who came flying from the thicket, had expected. It took two jumps to reach him and cast a throw-net at him, but by then Gudmund was armed with a short, thick, double-bladed dagger, the second blade arching out sickle-like from the crossguard. It looked like nothing so much as an ordinary boathook, except it had probably cost more than all the boathooks of Eastern Hjorvard put together because it had been forged by the craftsmen of Hauberk Mount. No blade made by human hand could have sliced through the seemingly fine but uncommonly strong cords of the Darkling Rider's net.

With a grinding sound, as if cutting metal, the knife made a long slit in the net. Gudmund ducked to one side and sprang to his feet, every bit as agile as his opponent. It would, of course, have gone ill with him had the Darkling Rider had her Fire-Bearing Chalice to hand; but she apparently needed a live prisoner capable of speech, so her fearsome weapon had been left in the bushes.

The wiccan tossed her shredded net aside. Her slim figure was wrapped in a dark-green cloak, tightly laced. In less than the blink of an eye, one of those laces was in her hand.

Gudmund unsheathed his sword and brandished it, intending to end this affair with a single strike; but the Darkling Rider made an astonishingly nimble sidestep. The lacing formed a loop around the wrist of his sword-hand, and a shooting pain forced him to drop his weapon, whereby he again unwittingly saved himself. The loop slid off, and he was able to spring aside.

Slowly, deliberately, she picked up the blade and silently advanced. The heavy sword lay comfortably in her small, graceful hand, and no one would have said that it was overly large for her.

Gudmund went cold. He had been disarmed effortlessly, and had nothing now but his hooked knife. He handled it splendidly, though, and his only chance lay in the element of surprise.

He swung his hand. The cunning gnomish artifact flew forward, glittering;

and as it did a fine chain unwound with a slight rustle from the hilt. The other end of that chain was securely grasped in Gudmund's hand. The knife was so made as to always fly point first and hook down. It had been aimed straight at the Darkling Rider's face, but she swerved aside and the blade whistled past her ear. Then Gudmund jerked hard on the chain.

The sharply honed dagger, hooked like an eagle's claw, bit into her shoulder, its bloody tip emerging through the torn flesh. Gudmund's lovely foe gave a shrill scream, her mouth contorted in agony: but even the pain did not cloud her reason. She plunged forward unexpectedly, slackening the taut chain, and knocked Gudmund's dagger backward and out of the wound.

Gudmund again tugged on the chain and the faithful weapon, seemingly of its own volition, leapt into his hand. Without a second's hesitation, he flung it again, but the Darkling Rider was not to be caught twice the same way. Wounded as she was, the dark stain rapidly spreading across her cloak, she shied away; and the beaked blade rasped into the ground, short of its mark. Still, she was clearly in no condition to launch a counterattack. Biting her lip, she turned and shuffled toward the bushes, holding her left hand against the wound and still carrying Gudmund's sword in her right.

The rapacious hook rustled ominously, cleaving the air as he swung it above his head, making intricate circles and figures of eight, all the while calculating how to strike the blow that would end this, once and for all. He had forgotten his opponent was no ordinary combatant, even one well-versed in all the tricks of the trade. The Darkling Rider had more powerful contrivances at her disposal.

She used the sword to parry the dagger one last time then abruptly drove the blade into the ground, hunched her shoulders, brought her elbows close to her body and held out her hands as if in supplication. A spherical shape appeared between them. Her face turned dead white, her eyes opened wide, and a dense, dove-gray mist billowed up from between those narrow palms. She was conjuring a charm.

But no Mage can perform sorcery at lightning speed—the less skilled the spellweaver and the weaker his powers, the more time it takes; that was why Gudmund had been met with a mere cord across his path. Evidently, the wiccan had been only a little ahead of him and had lacked the time to set an intricate magical snare, and the mounted warrior would easily have evaded a simpler charm.

Every movement is of great importance during a Casting. The Darkling Rider was utterly defenseless now, but she had counted the instants accurately, for Gudmund had to pull the hooked dagger out of the ground before he could throw it again. The deadly blade was heading for its target when the Lesser Sleepcharm began its work. Gudmund staggered, his eyes growing foolish and his legs buckling.

Had Hedin been there, he would have been able to see that the wiccan seemed to be splashing something grayish over Gudmund's invisible astral double, the very least of the astral Soulshadows. That Sleepcharm is simplicity itself, and transient, too; but it would gain her the few seconds she needed.

Hagen's warrior felt a sticky gray shroud flow over his mind. His legs refused to do his bidding, and he went down on hands and knees. The hooked knife lay useless on the ground some ten paces away. He still held the chain in his left hand but could not make that hand move at all. Sleep was beating him down. Before long his eyes would close…

The Darkling Rider tugged the sword from the ground, came up to Gudmund and was readying herself to stun him with a blow of the hilt to the head. Yet something was preventing her charm from taking its full effect—he slid along the very brink of an abyss of oblivion but had not tumbled into it.

All at once, he saw his mother's face, and the hatred that shook him then helped his soul cling to the narrow ledge above a bottomless chasm that stretched into the gloom of infinity. Somehow, he forced his right hand to obey him. Pressing it into the ground with an unseen movement, he managed to turn a tiny lever on the brazed cuff of his gauntlet and heard a slight click.

A shadow fell over him; the wiccan was close now. Just as the blow came down, Gudmund spent his last strength in one slashing stroke. The sharp, four-inch, three-faceted spike jutting from his gauntlet plunged into the wiccan's leg.

She let out a bloodcurdling shriek, and the charm broke on the instant. Fighting down a wave of nausea, Gudmund leapt to his feet, kicked his sword from her hand and again raised the hook that was once again in his hand.

At that point, the Darkling Rider judged it best to yield. This was a strange opponent, and one who could not be fought in the usual ways. She chose to retreat.

Gudmund had the good sense not to race after her. Sudden death might have been awaiting him out there in the underbrush, dealt by a tiny poisoned dart that came out of nowhere. So, hardly had the Darkling Rider disappeared from view than he took up his sword, bounded into the saddle and spurred his horse with all his might. Now every bend in the road, every bush might spell certain doom—he remembered well enough the Fiery Chalice that had wiped a whole ambuscade from the face of the Earth.

The elf was right, he thought. *The wiccan is on her way to the monastery, and is in hot pursuit. I'd give much to know the object of her pursuit, and I don't envy her quarry. All I can hope is to reach the monastery before she does. I did hurt her a little, after all.*

He continued on through the night, leading his horse to rest it. Fear would have kept him sleepless in any event. And as he went, the land around him began to change again.

Now, he was traveling amid the long, gentle slopes of venerable mountains, catching occasional sight of a treeless summit. The familiar spruces, pines, firs and larches were gone, their place taken by strange and august trees, very straight and uncommonly tall, like warriors frozen in battle array, their crowns reaching up to the clouds. The ground at their feet was deeply carpeted with moss, and even the birdsong here sounded nothing like the trills and warbles of any bird in Eastern Hjorvard. Gudmund breathed easier now. An ambush in such a forest, so clean and with such long lines of sight, was beyond the skill even of a Darkling Rider.

Even so, he was not alone.

From behind a tree trunk thick as a fortress tower, a youth in a dark-blue costume came nose-to-muzzle with Gudmund's horse. Spare and pale he was, with dark hair falling to his shoulders and equally dark, deep-set eyes. In his hand, he held a stave topped with a whimsical interweave of five, or maybe six, sharply tapered switches of wood, which, looked at straight on, resembled the rune *ajol,* which means "the beginning" in the language of the giants who ruled Hjorvard long before the First Day of Wrath.

The Great Teacher Hedin had once shown Gudmund those runes, saying, "Now they go almost completely unused. The Mages employ Feanor's Cipher and the humans have Merlin's new alphabet of sounds. Only the gnomes' secret tracts on the arts of the smithy still use the primordial runes."

The dark eyes surveyed Gudmund with an imperious gaze. Realizing he had reached his goal, Gudmund reined in and dismounted.

The youth, making not a sound but staring at the newcomer intently, pointed the tip of his stave at him. Gudmund was about to begin a prepared speech but was stopped short by the vigorously irritated gesture of a desiccated hand.

The confused warrior fell silent.

His captor stared at him yet half a minute more and then, still without a word, made a rapid gesture; and the stave's polished wooden switches came alive, lunging forward with the speed of striking snakes. Yet these were no snakes. Gudmund was a seasoned warrior and would have had no difficulty evading an attacking reptile; but now here he was, bound hand and foot in the blink of an eye and unable to move, his hand riveted to the hilt of his sword.

"What is all this, Iamerth scorch your hide?" a furious Gudmund roared, thrashing in vain efforts to loosen his bonds. "I have important business here!"

Paying not the slightest heed, the youth thoughtfully looked his prisoner up and down, scratched his chin and, apparently satisfied, raised the other end of his heavy stave and walked away, flourishing it as easily as he would a twig. Gudmund walked behind, continuing to emit surpassingly awful curses until he felt a sudden stabbing pain in his lip. The sharp tip of one of the switches that twined around him was busily trying to punch a hole there, with the clear intention of literally sewing his mouth shut. Gudmund was silent, horror clamping his throat, and the switch fell away.

I came racing here at breakneck speed, fought with a Darkling Rider, barely escaped with my life, he thought, wonderstruck. *Still, perhaps he's just a gatekeeper and gives the same greeting to all uninvited guests. But I've never seen such power as this!*

He could not turn his head, and all he could see before him as they went was the mossy forest floor. But they were soon at their destination. He heard the faint creak of opening gates, was carried in and set on his feet, and his bonds disappeared.

He quickly looked around. He stood in the corner of a fairly spacious courtyard that was surrounded on three sides by entirely ordinary single-story log buildings with all the customary windows and doors. Behind him were the gates, flanked by two such structures, and opposite, running along the gentle rise of the mountainside, was a long three-story edifice. Its frontage seemed hewn from the trunk of a gigantic tree by craftsmen with the artistry to present its innumerable inner rings to the view.

Gudmund could see nothing else that was strange or in any way memorable. The buildings were just buildings, as simple as could be, and with not a carved door casing or a decorated shutter to be seen.

There were four now facing him: the youth who had dragged him here with his peculiar stave; a young man with a sparse tuft of a beard, who was also wrapped in a thick dark-blue cloak and held an identical stave, but had a scrap of dark-brown polished wood on a cord around his neck; a bulky older man with a big belly, a double chin and a reddish nose, also with a scrap of wood hanging on his chest, but much lighter in color; and a very straight-backed, very wizened old man with an aquiline nose. His face was nut-brown, and he held not a stave but a thin twig. The scrap of wood at his neck was completely white.

"Listen to me," Gudmund began. "I come from afar. I have a great need to speak with the Preceptor. I have urgent news. And did you have to drag me here with such ill manners?"

"Your absurd rules are powerless in the domains of the Distant Powers, humanling," the young man said with airy unconcern. "And whatever you may have to say, we already know."

"A dying elf bade me make my way, no matter what, to the Vale of Brunevagar and to the monastery that stands there," Gudmund said crisply, staring hard at the old man on the assumption he was the leader of this little group. "I was to seek out the Preceptor of that monastery and warn him that a very cunning Darkling Rider is in hot pursuit of someone, had used a Fire-Breathing Chalice to exterminate an entire ambuscade that was lying in wait for her, and is now heading straight for this place. That was what I was charged to convey, and by the Perpetual Darkness, I deserved a better welcome than this!"

They were again looking at him as if he were a bothersome child. Then the fat one spoke.

"Whom do you serve?"

An innate wariness forced Gudmund to lie.

"I am a mercenary, a soldier of fortune."

The fat one glanced at the old one with "There, what did I tell you?" written all over his face.

"You lying worm," the old man said frigidly. "You are a warrior whose fealty is to Thane Hagen, apprentice of the Mage named Hedin. I read that in your thoughts. And the intentions of that Mage are too well known to us to let you go. To the pit with him!"

The eagle-nosed elder, no longer at all interested in the warrior, turned away.

"If you can read thoughts, then surely you can see I only wanted to help you!" Gudmund yelled, writhing in the tight embrace of the stave switches that again had him pinned. "I hate wiccans. I kill them soon as look at them. Stop!"

He would have had as much success appealing to the waves rolling in to the shore.

They dragged him to a corner of the courtyard. The planked walls slid apart on their own, opening on a passageway that angled down into the darkness. The youth disarmed Gudmund without haste then flourished his stave, for all the world like a housewife shaking a broom; and the warrior rolled down head over heels, sending aloft the blackest, most heartfelt curse he knew.

He came to himself in a cramped, dim little room with a tiny barred window high in the wall—the paneled walls, having opened to let him in, had promptly closed up behind him like living things. The cell held no furniture, no comforts, nothing but bare walls. After voicing a gratifyingly intricate array of oaths, Gudmund all but collapsed to the floor and sat there, his face buried in his hands and his mind a mass of confusion.

The elves would never have forged a friendship with scoundrels and torturers. Why, then, had he been tossed into this hole? Could it be they were allies of the First-Begotten yet enemies of the Teacher, Hedin?

But, knowing nothing of the Distant Powers, Gudmund soon stopped trying to understand. It was all to no purpose, anyway. *Since they didn't kill me outright,* he thought, *that must mean I can yet be of some use to them. Or am I to rot here for the rest of my days?*

Not an hour later, though, a commotion began up above that was noisy enough to penetrate even into his dungeon. First there was yelling; then a low, rumbling roar, followed by laughter that chilled his heart and almost stopped his breath—someone up there had just fallen under an unbelievably powerful charm. Even after that, though, the noise continued, with yelling, howling and squealing accompanied eventually by a hissing sound. As Gudmund watched, the gray light in his cell's narrow window turned crimson. A fire was raging out there, and he could not but know its cause, having once seen a Fire-Bearing Chalice in action.

The Darkling Rider had closed on her prey.

At that instant, may Ialini the Merciful forgive, Gudmund, for all his hatred of wiccans, felt the pleasure of revenge.

Meanwhile, the fire was spreading, the sounds of battle growing ever louder, and an acrid smoke crawled through the window. Gudmund began to cough, and might perhaps have slowly choked his life away in that pit had not lightning seemed to strike the roof above his head. The floor shuddered so hard he could not keep his feet. Above him streamed a billowing torrent of fire, flaming logs and planks flew in every direction, and the sky opened up overhead. Instantly, it was unbearably hot. Wrapping his cloak about his head, he ran from the burning ruins; and once clear, he looked around.

Half of the structures that surrounded the courtyard were already gone, replaced by towering piles of charred logs and roof-beams. The fire-gnawed gates had also fallen, and nearby, on his back, his arms and legs splayed, lay the youth who had met Gudmund in the forest, surrounded by all his weaponry. Evidently, he had been unable to part with it at the last. There was no one and nothing else in the yard, alive or dead.

Then, from the long three-story structure Gudmund had decided was the monastery's center came a heavy crash, wild cries and a staccato clang of steel. Tongues of fire and streams of smoke churned from the windows, though that building was most definitely not eager to burn. The wiccan must have broken through the defenses here in the yard, and now the battle had moved inside. The dead youth, he noticed, had no burns; like the dead elf, he seemed to be sleeping.

Gudmund unsheathed his sword and had his hooked knife at the ready in his left hand, but none of that told him what to do next. Caution and discretion demanded he make the most of his miraculous deliverance and be off in a hurry; but if, on the other hand, the Teacher had acquired new enemies, it behooved him to learn all he could about them. He hesitated a few moments longer, gazing ruefully at the splendid tree-studded titans that encircled the monastery. Then he sighed, took a more comfortable hold on his sword and strode decisively to the entrance of the main building.

He pushed the heavy doors, entered…and saw yet another body lying dead on the floor. The stave it had carried was almost completely incinerated, yet the charred switches still stirred. He went around it and moved carefully on, guided by the bellowing, whistling and howling.

He could not have said much about the decor of the rooms he passed through, for the fire had been this way. He saw broken, fire-blackened benches, cupboards and chests, and several times he found himself treading on the remains of ancient tomes.

On the second floor, the same scene awaited him, but to the left was a broad passageway leading into a spacious hall where the building's wooden walls had long ago been interlocked with the vaulted roof of a huge cavern. Gudmund glanced in, and at last looked on the fray.

It was a sight to behold. A slim figure in a cloak singed at the hem, with a Fiery Chalice in her right hand and a black curved sword in her left, faced some fifteen blue-clad opponents, among whom Gudmund recognized the eagle-nosed old man of recent acquaintance. Spells rolled back and forth invisibly through the hall, so powerful as to shake the walls and bring stones toppling down from the vaulted cliff face. The switch-topped staves kept trying to entangle the wiccan; but she was a blur of motion, slicing through them with her Black Sword or searing them with fire from her Chalice or halting them with a charm, all the while pummeling the monastery's defenders with freshets of flame. The old man raised his hands, conjuring swirling funnels to deflect the death-dealing heat.

Gudmund noticed that several of the blue-costumed soldiers held long silvery swords that glowed with a dim light. They tore into the streams of fire with ease, but against the black sword they could do nothing but throw off huge sheaves of sparks. He froze in place, mistrusting his own eyes. It was clearer than clear the wiccan had not used even a hundredth part of her powers in her skirmish with him.

Now, the Darkling Rider was trying something new, and to good effect. One of the swordsmen was caught by the stream of fire sent his way, the sword along with the hand that held it disappearing in a spurt of reddish-brown. A river of flame then seemed to burst from his body, flashing ghastly pale. The noise of battle drowned out the wild, thin scream; the body, torn in half, tumbled to the floor, and all that remained of the sword was its hilt, a smoking ember. The weapon was evidently proof against fire, but not when flames had taken the hand in which it lay.

Then the Rider was struck by one of the supple vortices raised by the old man, whom Gudmund had decided to call the Preceptor. The impact flung the wiccan to the stone floor; and with a triumphant yell, several of the monastery soldiers flung themselves upon her, their staves and swords at the ready. The Preceptor spread his arms wide in preparation for more magic; but the Darkling Rider, although stunned by her fall, rolled away and slew another of her foes with a deadly gout of flame. The floor where she had just lain exploded in a spray of blackened shards as a charm shattered the stone. By then, she was already back on her feet.

Gudmund could not understand what his erstwhile enemy was trying to do, but it did not seem she was fighting only for her life. She could always have retreated, but instead she was doggedly inching toward the cavern's dark depths, while the Preceptor and his brave boys desperately tried to halt her progress. Unable to fathom the sense, the goals or the reasons for this battle, he stood irresolute, not knowing what to do.

Meanwhile, the Darkling Rider's situation was growing more dire by the moment. A glancing blow from a sword made a bloody score on her left forearm only an instant before her attacker became a pile of ash. The

Preceptor spoke a charm that rained boiling oil down upon her; she tried to escape it, but some of the drops still fell on her face. Then Fat Man broke through the Black Sword's defenses and struck her fearsomely hard in the side with the butt-end of his stave. She gave a heavy groan and fell to one knee, and although she was still able to dispatch one more adversary, Gudmund could see that protecting herself against the magical onslaughts and replying to them with charms of her own whilst still continuing to flood all around with fire was sapping her strength

Although he had done nothing to give himself away, he was noticed at last when a trickle of liquid flame happened close by his hiding place. One of the blue-clad soldiers jabbed a finger in his direction, pointing him out to the Preceptor, then, grasping his stave in his free hand, hurled himself forward. Gudmund met him with the long chain of his hooked knife; thrown by his skillful hand, its unattached end wound around those pumping legs and the runner fell but was quickly up and on the attack again.

Accepting he now had no choice, Gudmund flung the beaked blade. The iron sank deep into the throat, the body jerked once and then stirred no more.

So, Gudmund was drawn into the skirmish willy-nilly, though the side he was on was one he would not have chosen for anything, had he been given a choice.

The Darkling Rider glanced at him, and he shuddered at the demented look in her eyes. With redoubled strength, she attacked again, forcing the monastery defenders back. Darting specks of light began penetrating deep into the dusky refuge under the mountain's lip; and there, where the light met the dark, Gudmund glimpsed strange greenish flares playing off the hundreds and thousands of delicate facets of what might have been a crystal of truly unlikely dimensions.

While he was wondering what it could be, the Darkling Rider had broken away from her assailants for an instant and was sending fire-red rills along the smooth floor directly toward the mysterious greenish flickering. Tongues of flame began to dance along the flagstones, and the light wrenched from Unbeing a huge green altar carved from a single, transparent, perfect gem such as Gudmund had never seen. Its depths hinted of the vague outlines of a very tall being draped in a long, loose robe—more than that he could not make out, because the stone was suddenly ablaze with a fierce green light.

Floods of unbearable brightness gushed down from above, forcing him to his knees. That light drained his strength and his will to fight. The floor juddered beneath him.

The Darkling Rider's contorted figure had almost disappeared beneath a mob of monastery soldiers. One of them knocked the black curved blade away with his sword just as she was raising it against him. A thick spiral of blindingly bright green light seemed to coil into the priest's back, and his weapon burned with the same fire. He struck, and Gudmund heard another groan; but then there were more spurts of red-brown flame, and the monastery's champion vanished in a maelstrom of fire.

The Darkling Rider dragged herself from the pile of bodies, holding a gaping wound in her side, her left hand clasping the Chalice tight against her. The Preceptor followed her for a few steps and gestured as if flinging a spear after her. Not knowing why he did it, Gudmund threw his trusty hook in the general direction of the spear, as if there had been a spear to see.

A wondrous flower bloomed in the air, a riot of fiery hues. Glistening, spattering drops of flame whirled on all sides, and the walls began to topple. Gudmund tugged on his dagger's chain, and winced at the blistering touch of the handle. The blade had taken on a strange greenish tint.

Dry, slim fingers grasped his hand. He looked down and met the wiccan's imploring eyes. They looked deep, deep, down into his soul and...

Who really understands the workings of a man's mind? He caught up his former enemy and, with all the speed at his command, dragged her along corridors and down stairways, hearing the howls of his pursuers at his back, across the smoking ruins of the courtyard and out through the gap where the gates had been. Flames burst behind them several times during this escape. The Darkling Rider was mustering the last of her strength to cover their retreat.

Once outside the monastery, Gudmund gave a piercing whistle, heard his faithful horse neighing in reply and felt a weight lift from his heart. But scarcely had he tossed the Darkling Rider into the saddle and leapt up behind her than the pursuers burst through the gateway. He spurred his charger, there was another eruption of flame behind them and off they went at a headlong gallop.

The vast trunks of woodland giants, immense green towers, flickered by, and he did not pull up until his weary mount at last began to stagger under him. An ordinary northern forest stretched about them, as far as the eye could see. There was no sign of any pursuit, if, indeed, there had ever been one.

Gudmund and the Darkling Rider sat staring at each other, and only now could he discern the terrible aftermath of the battle on her: five long sword-scores, her right side punctured, her cloak stiff and sticky with blood from a large gash, one side of her face cruelly burned and the other black-and-blue, her right arm almost immobile and her forehead deeply slashed.

They sat in silence, Gudmund completely bemused and the Darkling Rider thinking about…who knows what? Thane Hagen had been known to use the services of wiccans on occasion; they could, when they so wished, impart information that was truly invaluable. What Gudmund had to do now was find the words to ask her who she was, whence she came, whom she had been hunting, why she had attacked him and invaded the monastery.

He also needed to find out all he could about the monastery itself—why he had been bound and taken prisoner, what was the meaning of that crystal altar, and all the rest of it.

"Farewell, warrior," the wiccan breathed in an almost inaudible whisper, rising unexpectedly to her feet and clearly preparing to travel on alone, with all her wounds.

"No, wait!" Gudmund cried. "Have you nothing to tell me? What did that battle mean?"

A scarcely perceptible smile touched the Darkling Rider's disfigured face.

"It is not for you to question me, mortal. Rejoice only that I leave you with your life." She pointed the Fiery Chalice demonstratively at him, who went stock-still. The hooked knife was close to his hand, but even so, the wiccan would have had the advantage of him. "Be mindful, though," she went on. "The day is not far off when your masters will bitterly regret that the green stone remains safe in the Monastery of Brunevagar. And now, farewell!"

"But I rescued you," Gudmund said, looking directly into those vertical pupils. "Even a wild animal knows what gratitude is."

"You rescued me? But perhaps it was I who was at your back."

He was confounded. Then, with a few short steps, the wiccan was gone, disappearing into the underbrush—noiselessly, as was the way of her race.

CHAPTER IV

Brann led Hagen up into a clean, high-ceilinged room where the floor was strewn with soft, handwoven mats. He silently drew a heavy bench to the table and set out a wooden jug of beer and two earthenware tankards. The thane sat down, and Shrunkenhand, still uttering never a word, deftly unrolled Hropt's missive with one hand and began to study it with great care. Hagen waited patiently.

"So, you're off to send the Hound to sleep," Brann said at last, raising his eyes to his guest. It was only half a question.

Did Hropt say so in his letter? Or was that just a shrewd guess? Hagen wondered, and nodded.

Brann screwed up his eyes. "A dangerous how-d'ye-do. Have you ever been to Gnipahellir? No? 'Tis a terrible place. Sinister. Naught to eat there, naught to drink, naught but poison. And horrors aplenty, that have gathered in those parts down the ages. I don't know, I don't know…What business do I have there? And what will the wife say?" He glanced over his shoulder at the door, as if expecting his good lady to appear at any moment.

The thane raised an eyebrow. "What heed does a warrior pay a woman?"

"I'm no warrior," Brann replied dismissively. He seemed to be thinking hard about something. "Still and all, it's a fine blade."

Picking up Hropt's gift from the table with his good hand, he turned it this way and that, settling it in his belt. Hagen noticed he had placed it within easy reach of his deformed left hand.

Hagen decided to try another tack. "You understand what will happen if the Hound gets loose?"

"I do." Brann slitted his eyes again. "That I do. What I don't understand is why this is a job for you—why Hropt chose you, of all people."

Any who dared address the thane thus in Haithabu, say, or in Himinvagar, not to mention the lands of the jarls, thanes or free peasants, would have found himself cleft from shoulder to waist with one blow of Hagen's sword. Here…

Hedin's apprentice only gave a silent shrug and took a long pull of his beer, which he found to be excellent. Brann continued waiting in silence, clearly not satisfied with that reply.

"I have long been acquainted with the esteemed Hropt," Hagen said. "Quite recently, I had occasion to visit him again. He told me about the Hound's awakening, and counseled me to apply to you. Was he wrong?"

"No, of a certainty he was not." Brann stretched out a calming hand. "It's only that the path to Hropt's door is closed to many—I was but asking. No need to get your dander up."

"And have you been to Hropt's?" Hagen asked, squarely on the offensive now.

"I have," Brann responded, dipping his mustache in turn into his beer. He did not offer any details but, before Hagen could pose any more questions, spoke again. "To the Hound it must be, then! It'll be a famous foray." He gave a short laugh. "Well and good, Thane Hagen! You're a strange fellow, and I don't really know what you're about, but no matter. You may be young, but I can tell you've seen action. So, with the Forest's aid, I'll take you to Gnipahellir, and then we'll see. Your hand on it?"

"You'll take me to Gnipahellir, and what then?" Hagen asked, staring hard at Shrunkenhand. "I will do what I must with the Hound, but what of the way back?"

Brann's face darkened. "Ah, you're not a trustful sort. I told you—then we'll see. The Forest is none too pleased to have folk tramping back and forth along its Ways, like housewives to a well."

That was news to Hagen.

"Very well," he said coldly. "Take me to Gnipahellir by the Forestway. I need to reach the Hound with all haste."

"It ill befits humankind to meddle in wizardry," Brann grumbled. "But well and good, I say—the esteemed Hropt wishes it. So sit a spell, young thane. I have preparations to make."

The preparations were lengthy. Brann gathered a whole pile of sundry hunting gear and some clean clothing, faded from many washings. Then he lit a huge fire in the stove and began to cook a thick stew of pine needles and leaves. Dense clouds of steam rose from the kettle, and Shrunkenhand loaded all his equipment onto a wooden griddle and placed it in the thick of the acrid fumes. Then, after the infusion had cooled, he carefully smeared it all over himself.

"What are you blinking at? Come on, do as I do," he told Hagen, who had been watching all this with astonished eyes. "When you go a-visiting, don't you deck yourself out?"

The thane shrugged but obeyed.

Finally, when nothing more remained to be done, Brann turned to his guest.

"Now I'd best go and tell the wife. Wait here."

He strode toward the door, but before he could reach it, it opened in his face.

"And where would you be going?" The voice from the dark doorway was high-pitched. A woman's. "Here's a fine tarradiddle—stricken in years, he is, and still roaming the Forest like any thief, with the house in a shambles, the firewood almost gone, the well-sweep broke and a hole in the henhouse. Just wait till a fox gets wind o' that—but no, he must back to the Forest! And I'd dearly like to know who's got you flummoxed this time, you old gaby. Another o' them uninvited guests, eh?"

As the tirade progressed, Brann, cowering a bit and spreading his hands helplessly, gradually edged backward, as if to shield the thane with his body. Hagen slowly rose from his seat, half-throttled with rage. This howling hariden dared to question what he did and how he did it. Well, she would not be yowling long—if Shrunkenhand would not silence her then he, Thane Hagen, would.

There was no sign Brann was even capable of quieting his wife. All he did was mutter in a befuddled way and look with eyes full of guilt on that plumpish little body in her homely housedress with the sleeves rolled up. He hunched his shoulders around his ears while his wife continued peppering him with abuse, wrapped around a long and tedious litany of tasks that needed doing around the house and a narrative of her life, which had without doubt been forever ruined by this woodland ne'er-do-well.

Finally, seeing that Brann was not going to do anything constructive, Hagen intervened.

"Listen to me. This is business of the greatest import that cannot succeed without your husband," he told her, struggling with the urge to simply skewer her through the gullet. "But perhaps this will serve to brighten the few days of his absence somewhat?" Rummaging in his scrip, he drew out a silver brooch.

Shrunkenhand's wife eyed it dubiously.

"And how'm I to know you didn't wrest it from some doxy?" she snarled, glowering at him.

Hagen set his teeth, treating himself silently to a string of the very blackest oaths. What a milksop this Brann was, standing there like butter wouldn't melt in his mouth, as if to say, *Never mind me, she rules this roost.* How could any husband stand by while his wife mounted her high horse to rail at a guest? Even though Shrunkenhand did look shamed enough to sink through the floor.

"I swear to you by the torments of Niflhel," Hagen declared in somber tones, "that it was honestly purchased, in Haithabu."

Brann's wife gasped and clapped a hand over her mouth. An oath sworn upon the torments of Niflhel was inviolable. The most reckless rogue, the darkest soul in all of Hjorvard would never dare lie having once bound himself so, for fear of being greeted in the afterlife by a fate so bitter that, compared with it, death itself was but the merest of inconveniences.

The woman seemed to hesitate, swiveling her gaze from the brooch to Brann to Hagen. Then Shrunkenhand spoke for the first time.

"Hark you now, it won't be long—but five or six days to my return. And our guest must have my aid to find his way."

It was almost evening before the two travelers were able to quit the Shrunkenhand homestead. Hagen was fuming. Even after Brann's wife had agreed to take the brooch and let her husband leave, they had still to suffer the kind of interminable inventory of instructions to which little children are routinely treated. Hagen could not tolerate being lectured; even when his Teacher was explaining something new to him, he always worded it as though Hagen had made the discovery all on his own.

They led their horses at first, the forest around Brann's home being so dense as to make riding impossible. Shrunkenhand strode confidently due north, keeping the blaze of the sunset to his left. Hagen waited for the Forestway to begin, but nothing changed around them as they walked on.

The moon had already risen above the forest when they emerged from the dense tree cover into a small clearing ringed by young spruces. Brann pointed out a goodly stump in the middle of the open space.

"Bide there a while and hold the horses…" He attached a long strap to his animal's bridle. "…whilst I…do what is needful, as 'twere. Sit here, and mind there's no gawping at me."

Hropt and this one are two peas in a pod, protecting their skills more closely from prying eyes than any stack of gold, Hagen thought, but he made no objection, took Brann's horse from him and sat down on the warm, dry stump.

Brann moved behind his back and set to work, with much incomprehensible mumbling. The thane could easily have made out every word with a Hearing Charm, but he chose not to. For all he knew, Shrunkenhand might have sniffed it out and flown into a grand rage.

It was no short wait. A smell of smoke told Hagen Brann had lit a fire. The mumbling gradually grew more and more indistinct; and strange to relate, the cracking of the fire, the creaking of the trees in the wind and the forest rustlings were silenced, too. The clearing was shrouded in a gentle, heedful hush.

Then Shrunkenhand's voice, low and slightly hoarse, broke through the still air.

"Seems we're directed that way. On your feet and to horse!"

Hagen looked around. Brann stood, straightening his shoulders and clutching his right hand to his heart. A small fire burned soundlessly at his feet with a strange greenish glow; and although the wind had dropped altogether, a concentrated rivulet of blue smoke blew straight into a dark gap between the young spruces. The thane would have staked his life there had been no such gap when they first entered the clearing.

"That way," Brann said again in a hollow voice.

Hagen leaned forward over his saddle and stared into the opening, seeing nothing unusual out there, just a file of brownish trunks, moss and fallen needles. But it also held something ineffably deep, primordial, and yet simple. Here were none of the intricate constructs of the Higher Magic, the source of such pride for his Teacher and others of his ilk. This was, rather, a matter akin to the rising or the setting of the sun.

"Bestir yourself, sirrah! Move on, while the gates are still open." There was impatience in Brann's voice.

Hagen touched his horse's flanks.

A degree of disappointment awaited the thane beyond the Forestway gates. He and Brann rode along the most ordinary woodland track, although one quite broad, dry and easy to follow. Through the trees, they could see the moon, and the stars that were already spilling across the sky, and again there were the sounds of an ordinary nighttime wood. The trees thinned to the left as the track skirted a large mossy bog, a dark blot with high, wooded islands looming in the distance. And, try as he might, Hagen was unaware of the slightest sign that every step forward was taking him ten times farther than usual.

The moon that folk call the Wolfsun had clambered high in the sky before Brann ordered a halt.

"This is a baleful place," Hagen said quietly after a moment.

"You feel it, too? Aye, there are quantities of spirits abroad. They favor the Forestway. But worry not. We'll fence ourselves off—as best we can—and mayhap you'll add something unbeknownst to me."

Brann carefully chose a dry, mossy hummock, selected a branch and carried it around their temporary quarters, chanting. Hagen listened hard. It was not even a charm but a very simple, strange yet sturdy incantation; and Brann was intoning it with scant understanding of why he was doing so and what gave this defense its power. Hagen's Teacher had never told him of anything like this.

When he was done, Brann gave Hagen an expectant glance. The thane did not care to show all he was capable of—something there was in Shrunkenhand that made him wary, something that set this man apart from all his kind. Hagen had never felt the like of it before, and it disturbed him, as the unknown was wont to do.

So, Hedin's apprentice limited himself to the plainest possible Protective Square by borrowing a fragment of the might of the Four Eternal Winds. It was a charm known to many wizards in various forms, and Hagen hoped Shrunkenhand would see nothing odd in it. This was, indeed, an evil place, where the thane felt himself under the cold gaze of unseen eyes.

The Earth has a great many spirits; many are harmless, but others must be defended against, and by very powerful charms, at that. With that in mind, Hagen drew yet one more circle—a sensitive signaling circle—trusting that Brann would not notice it.

They lay down to sleep in the deepest gloom, the moon having been swallowed up by clouds that had scudded in from the north. Brann was snoring as soon as he flopped down upon his bed of boughs, but Hagen could not sleep. Unaccountable things were afoot here in the Forestway. He felt himself the center of the universe, the cynosure of the entire world. He seemed to be flying above uncharted lands, and every minute of his flight would have been hours in any other place.

The fire slowly sank, and he wrapped himself more tightly in his cloak. Gradually, a light, fitful sleep overwhelmed him.

He was awakened by a thin chiming somewhere in the very depths of his mind—his Protective Square had been triggered. But he did not stir. *One of the Fleshless is powerfully curious to know what we're doing here. Come closer, then. I've got a warm welcome for you.*

He felt no fear—his Teacher had explained to him many times how to shift in situations such as this, and Hagen had had a number of encounters with Devourers of Souls. He could not fail.

The being advancing on him made its presence felt with a deathly chill and a dimming of the reason. It had conquered Brann's incantation, albeit with great difficulty. Hagen sprang to his feet, straightening like a released bow-string.

He saw Shrunkenhand's circle glowing coldly green, and against that greenish luminescence a dark spot—blacker than night, blacker than coal, a rift in the gloaming. He was pounded by a stream of glacial power; multicolored circles swarmed in his eyes. This was a Devourer of Souls, indeed, but one of rare strength and ferocity.

Not wasting another second, he lashed out at it with a mighty spell he had long been holding in reserve.

Mages and humans are two different races, but some humans are talented from birth. Hagen was one such, and his Teacher had worked hard to develop those innate skills. Hagen could not have compounded any of the Higher Secret Spells on his own, of course; but in times of dire need, he employed those Mage Hedin had given him.

The magical expedient he used here was elementary but very potent. An onlooker would have thought he saw streams of flame converging on a black spot, and a pale, dead light shining all around. As if in pain, the spot convulsed once, twice, and disappeared, leaving only Hagen's Protective Square and Brann's Incantatory Circle, slowly fading.

Shrunkenhand raised his head.

"That showed him," he wheezed. "And I thought we were lost—he walked right over all our safeguards. That thing was a fright, and no mistake! What was it?"

"A Devourer of Souls," Hagen said gruffly, wiping away a drenching sweat and feeling insuperably weary. The spell had utterly enfeebled him.

"A *what?*" Brann was astonished. "I've never encountered such a thing in all my born days, though I've been treading the Forestway many a long year. Something's awry here. But how did you drive it off? Everything was aglow, ablaze…"

"Listen, let's sleep now," Hagen replied brusquely, preferring to leave those dangerous depths unplumbed. "I have the skill, and so that thing is gone. It won't be back. I burned it up. Now, draw your circle again."

Brann said nothing more.

The remainder of the night passed peacefully, and in the morning they set off again. The track curved around boundless mossy marshes, led along dry bluffs thick with pines and delved into damp groves of leafy trees. Hagen noticed that whenever their way became especially convoluted Shrunkenhand would pick up a twig from the ground, bend it almost double and carefully prop it against a tree trunk by the roadside.

Is he placing markers? he wondered. *But why would he do that?*

The answer followed fast. After several detours, the track suddenly disappeared. Brann tensed and raised his hand, silently signaling the thane to stop. Then he dismounted, leaned down and subjected something on the ground to close scrutiny. After a moment he sighed—with relief, Hagen thought—remounted and touched his horse's flanks, angling it slightly away from where the track had been.

At the next tree they passed Hagen noticed, resting neatly against its root, a broken twig that was clearly not there by accident. Evidently, there were places where the Forestway looped about itself, making it easy to lose the trail. But he could not have said if that twig was old or had been placed there just recently.

They rode almost in silence, exchanging hardly a word. Brann seemed gloomy and preoccupied, but Hagen attributed that to the events of the night and the difficulty of the journey. He himself was still looking for something to assure him of the wondrous qualities of the Forestway, of which he had heard so much.

That evening, the path again brought them to the edge of a bog. Between them and the broad, moss-carpeted expanse was only a narrow strip of young but sparse and withered trees. The setting sun flickered among the saplings.

Suddenly, Hagen believed he saw a human figure stealing along the edge of the swamp, keeping pace with them. He sensed the stranger's presence by the gleaming embers of the eyes, but when he turned around abruptly there was nothing to see. With a mental shrug, he urged his horse on; and the feeling that ten paces away, at the forest's edge, a spectral rider was cantering in step with him immediately returned.

"Brann!" Hagen drew Shrunkenhand's attention with a loud whisper. "There's someone here!"

"You noticed? Aye, the Eventide Companion's with us," his guide replied in the same whisper. "Don't be afraid. It's just a patrol sent out by the Master of the Marsh. They're harmless enough unless you attack them. Ignore him, and let that be an end of it."

Still, it was unusually early when they stopped for the night. Brann chose a strange place to rest—the bare summit of a high, wooded hill mounded with huge lichen-covered boulders and threaded with saxifrage. Hagen spent a long time eyeing it mistrustfully, not understanding why they could not go on, at least to those three pleasant-looking pine trees where, as he could feel even from a distance, everything was immaculate, and they could say "goodnight" and know that it would be.

He said as much to Brann, who shrugged and grumbled something to the effect that they would be at their destination the next day, so why make life difficult, since they would need every bit of their strength later. But Hagen was certain he was dissembling.

The thane paced the hilltop end to end several times, touching every stone. It was certainly an unusual place, but in what way he could not tell. There was nothing overtly menacing in their surroundings, but even so…

Even so…something infused the very air, something chill, clear and bracing that at the same time imparted the utmost clarity of mind. On top of all, tonight there would be a full moon.

"Fear not," Brann muttered soothingly as he tinkered with the fire. "'Tis a tried and tested place, a good place."

"But have you been here before? Have you spent the night here?" Hagen asked him.

Brann gave an odd smile.

"I have, of course. How could I not? There's no avoiding Shadows Hill, tha knows, when taking the Way northward."

Hagen's defenses went up. "Shadows Hill? What does that mean?"

"What puling lass are you, to quail at everything? So it is called, and I know not why. To tell you true, the esteemed Hropt himself styles it thus."

"I am no lass of yours, and you'd best watch your words," Hagen said coldly. "I am cautious because unclean things are loose in these woods, and without me, you'd have been in a pretty pass last night."

"Say you so?" Brann narrowed his sly eyes in that habitual squint. "And had you not been with me, mayhap no guests would have come calling."

Hagen gritted his teeth. Sad to say, Shrunkenhand might have struck very close to the truth if Hedin's apprentice were, indeed, a hunted man.

"These are all empty cavils," he said aloud. "I never have and never will fear anything or anyone, but I also have no intent to go out begging for trouble, an it please you, good sir."

Brann raised a pacifying hand. "Well and good, well and good. Hackles down, young thane. We needs must o'ernight here. And by noon tomorrow, you'll be at Gnipahellir."

The evening of the full moon was quiet and still, with suddenly clear skies from which myriads of tiny, fathomless fires gazed down. The pines creaked gently in the breeze, and the campfire burned down and went out.

Yet it was to be an evening of surprises.

Hagen had long ago learned the art of concentration, which enabled him to make for a goal with nothing else in his mind to distract him. Now he found himself plagued with thoughts that made him uneasy. Was his chosen path the right one? What part would his Teacher play in his life? What did the future hold? He was unsettled. But he could feel Brann observing him closely, and took care to let none of this show.

He and Shrunkenhand collected boughs for their beds and brought them to the dead campfire. The moon was shining full in Hagen's face, uncommonly bright, as it seemed to him. He almost had to squint his eyes against it. He threw his armful of branches down, turned…and froze.

He had two shadows.

He had two absolutely identical, completely distinct shadows, overlapping slightly at their point of origin, then diverging at an angle, as if two oil lamps burned bright behind him. But there were, of course, no lamps on Shadows Hill.

He beat down the urge to turn around, and instead looked harder at what he knew was there. One shadow lay utterly motionless, as it should, while the other was faintly fluttering, seeming to ripple from time to time. He carefully sank down onto his pile of boughs, and the shadows did the same. He felt no threat, though he was tense and chilled inside. He had never heard of anything like this, and owned himself at a loss as to what to do.

"Hey, Brann," he muttered at his companion.

"What?" The other leapt up, muddleheaded. He had evidently already been asleep. "Oh, two shadows. Aye."

"What is it? Where's it from? Is it dangerous? Have you seen this before?" Hagen blurted out in a single breath.

"What it is I know not," Shrunkenhand said matter-of-factly, settling back down. Hagen could see his powerful body had only the regulation single, normal, unstirring shadow. "But this is Shadows Hill, and so dubbed for good reason. There's no harm in it—you're simply being shown what sort of person you are, or so I think. Whoso mounts this hill at the full of the moon finds the shadows prankish. So, fear not. When I was first here on a night with a full moon I also had two shadows."

"What happened?"

"What do you mean, what happened? It was not to my taste. I felt a weakening in me. The Gods have deemed it meet that we have one shadow, not two. Then I tossed and turned as you're doing now—my dreams here in the forest were passing strange. And then I was sitting on the very same spot as you, and 'twere like I was stabbed by the thought—if this place ignites two shadows then perchance it will also serve to take the misrule away.

"So, from the feeling in my bones, I plucked a branch from that there bush and took to sweeping one shadow away, like a goodwife sweeping the floor. And it up and disappeared! From then on, wherever I be, I have had but one shadow."

"You swept your shadow away?" Hagen was startled. "But how did you choose which one to…aah…sweep off?"

"Same way. A feeling in my bones," Shrunkenhand replied. "One I didn't seem to care for, so that was the one I picked, and in short order, too. And forever after I have lived at peace."

Hagen licked dry lips. "But what changed in you?"

"What changed?" Brann thought for a moment. "Hard to say, but my life, as 'twere, has gone easy since. I began grasping at such as is seemly for a human, like all my fellows, and what is not human I let alone. For when I was young I would find myself…where I ought not to have been. As you see, I am hale and hearty to this day, for 'twas long before then that my hand…" He fell silent. His head drooped.

"And what would you have me do?"

"What would *I* have you do? Who can decide for you, humanling? You need to think hard, and then brush one of those shadows from you."

Hagen plunged into thought. A magic hill…that had suddenly endowed him with a second shadow…

"Brann, has anyone else who came with you to this place been given a second shadow?"

"No. You would be the first."

The thane focused his mind. He felt he was standing on the threshold of perhaps the most important step of his life. Strange powers, most likely the Distant Powers, had presented this mortal with an uncommon choice. What could that mean, to have two shadows?

Wait! To make a shadow, something had to be in the way of the light. That meant there was in Hagen, as there had been in Brann, something other than flesh and bone. Curious it was how that could be, how by removing one shadow one could dispose of that other inner essence, but what of it? There was no end to what could be expected from the Distant Powers, and now to be faced with a choice that would stem the disunity within by his placing a firm foot on one of the groundsills before him...

Perhaps so, or perhaps the riddle was no more than empty logic-chopping. It would be good to know what those two shadows meant. Two paths. What paths? He longed to speak with his Teacher, or even with Old Hropt.

Still, this was a terrible hill, a fearsome place. Haphazardly, in blinders and plain ignorance to change one's whole life with the sweep of a broom and never to cry over spilt milk afterward...

No, I'll leave it alone, Hagen thought. *Let it be for now. I'll tell my Teacher later, and see what he has to say about it.*

So lost in thought was he that only then did he notice Brann's eyes fixed on him in tense anticipation. *What a stare! He must be thinking that if he had relinquished a part of himself everyone else had to follow suit.*

"Why are we sitting here? Time for sleep. You yourself said we'll need all our strength tomorrow," Hagen said, as if nothing had happened, and settled more comfortably on his bough-bed.

By the moon's light, he saw the surprise flash across Brann's face, but no more was said. By sheer willpower, the thane forced those two shadows from his head, and he was soon asleep. Gnipahellir awaited them on the morrow, and nothing else mattered.

HEDIN

TWO RESPECTFUL BUT SHORT-SPOKEN ALVS LED HAGEN AND ME DEEP INTO THEIR LAND. Hedin Undardemolto—Bestower of Knowledge—they called me here, though this time I had come not to teach but so they could teach my Hagen. He was gaping, wonderstruck, at never-before-seen sights: the tall, slender, white towers; the silvery roofs; the fabulous gardens; and the peculiar machines the alvs had invented to scoop water from deep clefts and carry it to the filigree wings of aqueducts that brought the mountain torrents to all the lowland settlements.

The alvs did not grow cereal crops; they bartered astonishing fruits from marvelous trees for both grain and meat, since the country was covered end-to-end with orchards laid out on literally every scrap of fertile land. Many of those trees had been my payment to the alvs for their help.

They had inherited vast amounts of knowledge from the elves but did not themselves know what to do with it. They had no use whatsoever for history. A single tale preserved in the alvish chronicles—that of the Southern Outlanders' inexplicable incursion into Eastern Hjorvard—had brought me to the magic Door of the Lowerworlds, which was accessible to the Mages though not to them alone. There, I had deciphered the snaring charm that one of the Ancients had laid on it, and had left my own in its place. Now, when Hagen needed valiant and devoted warriors to mount a devastating onslaught, he would be able to pass through that Door.

For now we were guests of Alvland, and Hagen thirstily drank in such wisdom as he had never yet encountered. The alvs are great adepts, ceding only to the gnomes in the craft of metalworking and the building of underground chambers; but their palaces are far and away superior. They instructed Hagen on the properties of the elements that make up the Earth, taught him how to bring together those elements so as to end with a different combination having completely different qualities, and so forth. We spent an entire year in Alvland.

Then the time came to leave. My apprentice had made great progress over the past months. The sword in his hand seemed but a continuation of his body; he could beat back the alvs' best foilsmen. He had worked hard on the arts of magic, too, and could already manage some simple charms.

On quitting that mountainous land, we emerged onto an ancient, well-ridden highway that led from the Rogheim wolds to Haithabu, capital of the Mercantile Republic. It was my intent that the campaign to take back Hedinseigh should be launched from there.

Winter was drawing on. Though not so harsh there, in the far south of Eastern Hjorvard, it still brought hard frosts and even blizzards. All travelers and wayfarers begin looking for a warm place to lie low, and Haithabu in winter was almost twice as densely populated as it is in summertime.

As we came up on the thick, dumpy towers of Haithabu's city walls, Hagen's face silently twisted into a scornful grimace. What were these unsightly, spraddled things to the chiseled turrets of the alv townlets? I understood my apprentice's feelings but knew it would not hurt to enlighten him.

"Over the past hundred years, that fortress has withstood six or maybe even seven fearful investments," I said. "Haithabu has been stormed from land and from sea, and has never fallen. Those walls have stood against all manner of siege engines."

"Why?"

"Because the gnomes who laid those stones were thinking to make them durable, not beautiful."

The narrow, crooked lanes of that overgrown merchant town had clearly been laid at random. Almost every house, though, boasted a little store, a chophouse or a hostelry. The squares simmered with richly stocked markets selling wares from every nook and cranny of the known world. The Weaponry Market occupied a square of its own, as did the Cloth Market, the Grain Market, the Lumber Market, the Slave Market, the Ironware Market—the rows of booths were beyond number.

It was here, in the bubbling cauldron of a large town, that my apprentice would have to seek out those who would join him in his first assault on the fortress of the Sheltered Kingdom that stood on the island of Hedinseigh.

I had not, meanwhile, forgotten my last encounter with Sigrlinn or her strange words to me. I was long overdue for a visit, if not to Jibulistan then at least to the Castle of All the Ancients. Formally, the Council had nothing to hold against me, and no one would prevent me from putting a direct question to the Leader of the Generation.

But something kept me away. The Castle of All the Ancients was Merlin's domain, and the only place where he was stronger was on his own Avalon—I was the sole member of the Generation of late not to have succumbed to the urge to construct, somewhere in the Real or even in the Mid-Real, a visible token of power. I preferred to hoard my power rather than frittering it away on dead stone or wizardfire.

A number of times since my last visit to the Castle I had tried to invoke Sigrlinn, to speak with her through my Band of Erith, but never with success. Most likely, she was simply not in residence in the dazzling palace she had raised under the gentle skies of Jibulistan, the land made by Mage-hand and created by the combined forces of our entire Generation in the bygone days of our youth. There, too, in Jibulistan, was the Cerulean City, which Sigrlinn and I had so lovingly built.

Her silence surprised me. Time was when she had been content to remain in her palace.

No word came from the Council, either, which was also strange. Previously, the entire Generation had met to banquet in the Castle of All the Ancients seldom but regularly, and it was not an invitation to be slighted. I had been hearing of those feasts through all the years of my exile.

Then came the realization that they had simply decided to keep me at a distance from the common dealings of the other Mages. It smacked of the machinations of Makran and Esteri, but I cared not a fig for them. I was far more concerned by Merlin's enigmatic silence. What was keeping that great recluse so occupied?

While wandering the Earth during the ten centuries of my sentence, I had often felt, at the very limits of such senses as had been left to me, echoes of incredibly powerful and sophisticated charms conjured by the Leader of the Council of the Generation as they sped through the depths of the Ether. Yet now, when once again I had all my wits about me and had regained my strength and even acquired new powers, everything seemed to have gone dead.

But that, too, I dismissed, having no choice but to do so. Until my plan had reached a certain stage, I could not, in any event, stand against the combined might of the entire Generation. I determined to wait. That would be the first link in the chain—to force those who opposed me to act first, to show their hand.

We passed from one Haithabu tavern to the next, sitting at long tables and listening to the cacophony of voices. Here were fighting men employed by the jarls, most of whom over-wintered in Haithabu, where no questions were asked as long as the bills were paid when they fell due. They boasted of their exploits and the rich pickings they had found in the West. Here also were tenant farmers who had run away from their thanes, and the younger sons of wealthy free peasants come to seek their fortune in the Mercantile Republic. Occasionally, too, there would be a trader from the Sheltered Kingdom, holding himself proudly aloof from it all.

Dozens paraded before us, while we played to the hilt our roles of affluent merchant and young ward seeking a reliable bodyguard for a long and risky venture. We saw youngsters and men in the prime of life, worldly-wise fire-eaters and striplings who had just learned how to wield a blade, veterans of raids in all the four corners of Hjorvard and young sprigs who had left the comforts of home only the day before.

Little by little, the contingent took shape, for even as a babe-in-arms, Hagen had an astonishing flair for recognizing who could be of use to him. Among those who drifted in were the dour giant Frodi, and the brash and impetuous Gudmund, and the rest—Lodin, Knut, Isung. Reckless daredevils every one, whose foreheads furrowed in disappointment when they were told this was only going to be a trading expedition, and whose eyes blazed at the news that, in truth, we were off to probe the Sheltered Kingdom's soft underbelly with sword, fire and arrow. Each of them had left a memorable trail behind him—a murder committed during some pothouse fisticuffs, gaming debts that far exceeded in value the debtor's scant possessions, a daring robbery under cover of night.

Master shipbuilders constructed two swift dragon-warships to my specifications; armorers tirelessly forged coats of mail and other gear. The winter passed without a moment's rest; and during that time, Hagen—stubborn, fleet of foot and invincible in combat despite his youth—became a real commander, having learned my lessons well. He was readily obeyed, and discovered much about the art of command himself with no help at all from me.

The mustering of such motley cohorts was a common occupation in Haithabu during the winter, so none of the men there paid us the slightest attention. But the nomen…well, that was another matter. Late one afternoon, a glum goblin appeared—how it had gotten into the city remained a mystery, since a cruel death awaited it at every crossroads had any city guard discovered what it truly was. Yet it had somehow come through unscathed, and here it was, asking to be taken on.

"The name of great Hedin, Sage of Darkness, is held in high honor among the Nightfolk," it said in a quiet, husky voice, kneeling before me, "for that name belongs to the friend of him of whom we shall ever speak with much gratitude. There is little left to us. We hide in obscure, inaccessible places. Our life is bereft of meaning. That meaning we seek to recover."

"Where did you learn to speak so fair?" I asked in surprise

"It is said that my distant ancestor commanded the goblin armies of our father, Rakoth the Blest, and from him that goblin acquired the knowledge. Most has been lost, but some yet remains."

It took all my powers of gentle persuasion to convince it not to be over-hasty in joining Hagen's detachment. but instead to gather by degrees a force of its own that I could call upon when the need arose.

The goblin melted into the dusk, leaving me deep in thought. Of course, the Nightfolk knew nothing of my apprentice or of my plan; but being endowed from birth with a remarkable sensitivity to shifts in the Balance, they were anxious, though they could not have explained why. One of the scale's bright pans had dipped too low—or so I would have been told in my youth, although now I knew this was far from the truth.

I thought back to Sigrlinn's hints that something had stirred at the very boundary of the world, and the bearing this might have had on Rakoth. Maybe he was trying to shake off his restraints, or was at least regaining some awareness of himself, having had neither form nor shape for so long—so very long. One way or another, the appearance of that goblin at my door gave me roundabout proof that Rakoth had, indeed, grown restive, and that those who had once been his trusty servants sensed it.

By spring, Hagen had two hundred and eighty swordarms at his command, which was no great surprise, as the previous year had been a trying one for most of the jarls. Several of the coastal kingdoms to the west were suddenly in better trim than they had been of late, and experienced commanders were now in charge of the rearmed and moderately well-trained squadrons protecting the wealthy cities that had routinely been the target of raids mounted by the eldrings of Eastern Hjorvard. A drought was raging in the south, leaving many of the seaboard settlements deserted.

So, there were far fewer spoils to go around; and the first to go out looking for a larger share were, of course, the most venturesome. Heretofore, though, not one seawolf had so much as considered trying his luck in the Sheltered Kingdom.

The shipbuilders had finished our dragon-ships. Hagen bought the supplies we needed, and at last came the bright spring day when the waters of Haithabu harbor foamed white under the powerful strokes of our long oars. We were on our way to Hedinseigh.

It was Hagen's first sea-voyage, but it was as if he had been treading the narrow deck of a dragon-ship all his life—my apprentice had been an apt pupil. Night followed day and day darkened into night as we bore westward along the smooth slopes of shorelines fresh with the green of spring. Merchant vessels heading our way hurriedly changed course at the first sight of our black sails.

"But, Teacher, after we take the island, the troops will be expecting booty," Hagen said to me in an undertone one evening. "I don't know what my orders will be after the siege. To attack the mainland cities of the Sheltered Kingdom? Are we strong enough? We want the numbers to even make up three centuries."

"So says my apprentice!" I threw up my hands in mock horror. "Certainly, you're not over-supplied with men, so you must find a goal equal to your strength. It is all very simple."

Hagen pondered this, his eyes mere slits. "The Lesser Temple of the Sun in Erivag."

Inwardly, I was jubilant—Hagen had hit on the one correct solution—but aloud I said, "You think to carry the day against the priests with such ease?"

Hagen was eager now. "We'll strike by night. There are four gates, but we shall choose one to make our entry and go in without a sound."

"A fine plan. And how will you know where the best of the treasures are?"

He gave a fierce grin. "We'll find someone to ask who will answer true."

The dragon-ships had rounded the headland and were now running north. The wind having shifted, we took to the oars. Here, in the waters off the Sheltered Kingdom, the winds were persistently hard to read—the vessels of the Kingdom always had a following wind, but all others were left to struggle against gusty headwinds. I made a point of not intervening; there was no good reason to announce my presence to the priests of the High Temple of Iamerth in Vidrir's sovereign city.

At the end of a grueling week, we were rewarded with the sight of the scarped sea-cliffs of Hedinseigh rising from the water.

In the dark of night, when the moon was swallowed up by low clouds, the rapacious shadows of the dragon-ships made a hasty landfall. Farther inland, in the island's only accessible harbor, on a guard tower at the end of the breakwater, a red gleam blinked on and off, inviting us to run full-on into a chain stretched across the harbor mouth. The ships' prows had nosed instead into the rocky shore, and Hagen's men spilled silently over the gunwales. The tower door was locked; but from a little window down below, mossy with seaweed, the stout chain stretched, dipping into the waves.

The silence was broken only by the brief jingle of a grappling hook on a long chain as it bit into a ledge. One by one, the dark figures swarmed upward. The embrasures being too narrow to allow entry, short, thick crowbars went to work on the iron-sheathed roof.

A scarlet gleam blinked out an alarm from a chink in the tower, and was immediately answered by another in the depths of the harbor. A torch was tossed from one of the embrasures, followed a moment later by a shower of arrows. Hagen's men raised their shields, and the archers began firing back; but at that moment the roof gave, and drawing their swords, the attackers forced their way in. Soon I heard the ring of steel and the shouts of men.

Hagen was in the midst of it. He had been the first to leap onto the rocks leading to the fortress, the first on the roof, and now, I was sure, he was hewing and slashing in the forefront of the battle. Warriors should always see their commander in the thick of the fray.

Before long, all was quiet inside the tower. Hagen flung open the door and, standing on the threshold with bloody sword in hand, began issuing a flurry of commands, ordering some to work the heavy capstan that would reel in the chain and allow the dragon-ships into the harbor, others to storm the second watchtower at the end of the breakwater and the rest to return to the ships. Only a few minutes later, the chain had been retracted and the dragon-ships were past the first obstacle, the rowers pulling with might and main. For we all knew, at that very moment Vidrir's ironclad men were racing to the jetties, oxybeles, catapults and ballistas were being set up and cellars were yielding up heavy earthenware pots filled with liquid fire.

I sat motionless in the stern. Hagen was in charge, and I had no reason to interfere. For now, everything seemed to be following a script.

Pitch barrels were lit on the wharf; and in their light I saw people racing to and fro, several dozen archers at the ready and, more distant from the shore, the pikemen's dark, huddled ranks.

Unexpectedly, Hagen ordered his little fleet to come about. The ships separated and headed for the dim-lit, empty moorages. It was a risky maneuver, but it would trap all of Vidrir's valiants pouring out to meet us in the jaws of a pincer movement. Our archers let their first arrows fly, grapnels bit into the wharf, and Hagen's men sprang onto dry land.

My apprentice had reckoned well—Vidrir's warriors were a mass of confusion. The dense array of pikemen was peppered with arrows; one ballista was brought about, and the heavy beam with its sharpened, metal-encased tip was fired into the midst of them. The wall of shields scattered, and Hagen's men sent up a great cry and waded in.

When they were reinforced by the detachment my apprentice had sent to take the farther tower, that was more than the warriors of the Sheltered Kingdom could bear. Some threw down their arms and others ran away, while Hagen rallied his own contingent, which still had almost its full complement, and led it at a brisk pace inland toward the black walls of a small keep, scarcely visible against the night sky.

I followed after.

The keep was in a terrible state of disrepair, its moat silted up and the drawbridge mechanism so corroded as to be inoperable. The gates were bolted shut, but what defense was that against seasoned stalwarts who had successfully stormed countless of the prosperous cities of Western Hjorvard?

The low walls were easy prey to our grapples. The defenders assayed a barrage of arrows and even threw pots brimming with liquid fire, but Hagen's warriors flowed over the wall in five places at once, my apprentice again at their head. Soon the gates were opened to let the main force in, and a few minutes later it was all over. We had taken Hedinseigh.

To forestall his warriors' displeasure with their scanty spoils, Hagen explained to them that they had scaled but the first wall and that there was another to follow. Having herded the remains of Vidrir's forces into the castle dungeon and locked them up tight, we left the island. None could be prevailed upon to stay and guard it.

The whole of the following day we rowed for Erivag, a lonely promontory topped by the blue walls of the Lesser Temple, built by Vidrir's good grace. The terraced steps rose directly from the surfline; and on the plateau above, amid the serpentines of whimsically curved walls, were hidden the four entrances that would take us into the temple. I knew there were also at least ten even better-concealed entryways; but once again, I did not care to reveal my involvement at that time by battering down any secret doors.

The coastal waters of the Sheltered Kingdom were plied by tens, even hundreds, of vessels, large and small. We were on a course to the south, but even at that we could not avoid all encounters. Some time was spent emptying the holds of an ill-fated merchant ship into our own and scuttling the old tub; the master, captain and crew we bound and added to our plunder.

Toward evening we disembarked in the kind of wild, deserted place where the Sheltered Kingdom's temples were usually built, on the principle that human habitations were unseemly neighbors for the majestic sanctuaries erected to honor the Young Gods. In long single files, Hagen's warriors moved toward the distant temple. This time I went with them, in case the priests of Iamerth and Iambren had something more daunting in store than arrows and pikes.

We could see throngs of pilgrims passing through the temple portal to spend the night in prayer there and greet the morning light with solemn ceremony and hymns. The dusk was deepening. The human torrent flowing down the road thinned, the heavy doors were closed, and all that could then be seen were lights glowing in innumerable windows, for darkness was not permitted in the inner chambers of the Temple of Iamerth, Lord of the Sun's Light.

At last, in the clotted gloom, Hagen led his men forward. The warriors gathered silently on either side of the entrance, and my apprentice pounded on the gates.

Nothing happened for a long time. Then, finally, a tiny window opened up a crack and a gatekeeper inquired, in none too friendly tones, if the honorable pilgrims knew they had come untimely for today's prayers.

Hagen took to imploring the man, belaboring the fact they had nowhere to lay their heads that night and there was neither water nor shelter to be found in those parts.

"No, I cannot. 'Tis the law," was the porter's stubborn, surly reply.

"Then at least give us some jugs of water. We're dying of thirst!"

"You'd have me violate the Rule…but be it so. Wait here."

Hagen was no stranger to gratitude. The plump gatekeeper was not killed when he leaned out to proffer two large ewers, only stunned and dragged to one side. The water was not wasted, either.

Wiping their mouths as they ran, the men streamed through the narrow entrance. Several guards tumbled in confusion from the sentry-box, wielding wide, curved blades; Hagen ran the first through, and the rest were cut down by the warriors who followed after him, all noiselessly, speedily and without a word.

A broad corridor opened up before them, but it led to the huge public prayer halls. Hagen instead turned into an unremarkable side passage where a staircase spiraled steeply upward. I let them go; my task would be to draw out the priests. I proceeded on down the temple's main passageway.

It gradually broadened, adorned here with wall niches inhabited by motionless statutes. I felt their unseeing eyes fix on me with a dead and empty gaze. *Look, if you will, then. Look at me. You'd best not be looking anywhere else.*

A huge hall opened up before me, the first of an endless cavalcade—brightly lit, with snow-white walls of faceted mountain quartz that splintered the playful reflections of numberless lamps. The east side of the room was dominated by a statue of light green stone that showed mighty Iamerth, his hands extended in an expansive gesture, bidding the people to come to him. The statue's base was ringed by yellow-robed priests, their arms raised aloft, singing a slow, lilting psalm, while the multitude gathered in the hall fell to one knee and took up the responses...

I halted, somewhat discomfited. The temple masters had yet to pay me the slightest attention. Had I slipped their notice? True, I had performed no magic—that they would immediately have sensed. *Well, then, we'll wait.*

I turned and strode back to the narrow stairway up which Hagen had led his company, wondering all the while if I had erred in giving those priests too much credit.

There was the doorway. I began to mount the smooth steps. All around was deathly quiet and still, except for the pilgrims' distant, rhythmical chanting. The stairs led me to a narrower corridor on the second story, and there I saw a body. It was a temple warrior, complete with a sword that was daunting in appearance but inconvenient in combat. I knew that Iamerth's troops were never alone, which meant that the other had either run away or had been captured and was at that very moment leading Hagen's detachment to the treasury.

Still keeping my wizardry in reserve, I continued moving, as I hoped, into the heart of the temple. Everything was coming off, as it had in Hedinseigh, far too easily, somehow; and I was actually growing alarmed. Fate enjoys a good game of cat-and-mouse, and loves to seduce with the phantom of easy success.

The corridor began to branch this way and that, and arrows—crude daubs of something red—appeared on the walls. I took them as my guide. A corpse...another, with an arrow in its throat...a third sliced in two...a fourth with its brains beaten out, that being the work of Frodi's cudgel. Then I heard a faint and distant echo; blade was meeting blade somewhere ahead of me.

Not wasting a second, I rushed toward the sound.

By the time I got there the skirmish was over. A proud Hagen showed me the open door of a storeroom.

"We'll clean this out now and move on."

"No!" I exclaimed. "It's an ambush! Take only what you can carry and leave this place."

I know not why the thought came to me exactly as it did—everything had just been too easy for us that day. By flaunting their inattention and affecting to notice nothing out of the ordinary, the priests were seeking to lure us into a trap, and any minute now they would be closing off the exits.

Bent under the weight of sacks crammed with precious plate, fabrics and various adornments, Hagen's warriors galloped back the way they had come. I felt the touch of a familiar breeze. Chill, it was, and felt by no one else. Below and behind us a web of spells was being woven.

"Hagen!" I grasped my apprentice by the shoulder. "Try to escape using only your swords. Let them think you're common robbers. It would be best to keep my presence from them for now."

"I understand, Teacher, and shall do as you say," Hagen responded in a very serious whisper. He wiped off his bloody sword and ordered his men to prepare themselves.

The first blockade was by the stairway, where the corridor was barricaded by temple guards armed with the holy bows of Iamerth—huge, longer than a man is tall, their arrows designed to represent sunrays—accompanied by a dozen yellow-garbed priests. A dazzling light splashed into the men's faces, followed by a hail of long, yellow-fletched arrows.

With a frenzied roar, the detachment closed ranks, raised shields and lowered slit visors. Some had already fallen; but the rest covered the space between them and the temple garrison in one bound and began laying about them with their swords, axes and hatchets. The blockade collapsed like a child's sandcastle under a storm surge. The priests had no spells in readiness, having miscalculated the time they needed. But then again, how could they be experienced fighters if no one had ever attacked their temple before?

Then, somewhere at our backs, from the very depths of the temple, came a sound not loud but all-pervasive—the powerful, proud peal of a heavy bronze gong. I felt only a slight pricking at either side of my forehead, but many of the warriors fell to the flagstones, writhing in intolerable pain. Hagen kept his feet, although his face under the lifted visor grew whiter than chalk and his eyes briefly rolled in his head.

The stronger of his contingent helped the others up, and wasting no more time, we raced down the stairs.

"Faster!" Hagen yelled. "They won't strike again while it can still be heard!"

The tight spiral of the narrow staircase uncoiled beneath our feet. Down, down, down...

All at once the walls began to shudder, and shards of stone spattered in all directions; an icy, savage, howling wind blew full in our faces. There was a welcoming committee, made up, to all appearances, of the most adroit of our adversaries. Again—arrows, arrows and more arrows, a blinding, searing light and the walls and the steps trembling as under the tramp of heavy feet. A powerful magical blow was almost ready to fall.

I could sense the power of the Four Winds drawing together into a supple coil, could feel the invisible, swirling spasms that men call earthquakes crawling up from the bowels of the Earth. I was aware, too, of the approach of living beings from a Higher World—a rainbow glimmer, as yet visible to me alone, that heralded the opening of the door between the courses of the Real.

Lord Iamerth, in concert with his brother and companion, Iambren, Master of the Winds, had bestowed upon their priests and disciples a power of no small import for, other than them, only Mages were empowered to open the Door for the passing of another than themselves. That spell was one of the most closely held of all.

And this great might was being brought down on a small band of shameless temple-robbers.

My misgivings flared up once more. The temple employed at least five or six thousand guards—two dozen or more to each of Hagen's men. Why, instead, were such very powerful but also extremely dangerous forces being awoken to deal with a trifling handful of pilferers?

Something was amiss. Could they have been expecting me? They had let us march right in, pretending to notice nothing, and now...

But I did not yet sense any untoward presence. No Mage of my Generation had joined the fray. Nor was I aware of the use of any of the shifts to which only a Mage might have recourse in a magical duel. Still, I knew for a certainty this bore all the hallmarks of a certain mind. I knew because my memory was good, and I had no doubt that the stratagems had been precisely chosen, as if to remind me of the days of my rout and my capture.

I gritted my teeth. Up ahead and down below, I could hear Hagen's voice, a fearsome, unintelligible roar, as he led his staunchest and fiercest fighters in hand-to-hand combat with the temple guards. The clang of swords was deafening and the howls and groans most pitiful. And, to my shame, I still stood there shuffling my feet.

How could my enemies have known so quickly that I was there? How could I have missed the constant surveillance and have fallen, like a snared grouse, into a trap too simple to fool a village conjurer?

Hagen and his detachment, their ranks serried to resemble an iron hedgehog, were forcing the temple guards back in a maneuver that astounded even me. They were surrounded, and the temple archers were loosing arrows that no armor save that of gnomish workmanship could protect against at such close quarters. Only two or three dozen of Hagen's men were wearing such armor.

But my apprentice had found his way across his enemies' corpses to the gates, and there made a stand, while a huge accumulation of magical power remained still in abeyance, like an arbalest kept in reserve until the moment of gravest danger.

Or, rather, I earnestly wanted to believe it to be so, although every second was convincing me more firmly that it was not. I had yet to perform any magic at all, not even the simplest, so as to preserve the secret of my presence; but what was the point of hiding when a finger was being wagged at me, to let this naughty schoolboy know his mischief had long since come to the notice of his elders and betters? That was exactly how Sigrlinn had swept the regiments of my Empire of Night from the face of the Earth, leaving me casting about for the charms to counteract her. By the time I found them, my exile had begun.

But perhaps this time she was helping me—lending me her aid by giving me to understand I was under unremitting surveillance, so deftly constructed and woven from such subtly interlaced charms that I had remained utterly ignorant of it until the last moment, despite all my care and my much-vaunted ability to shake free from such overly intrusive attentions.

My racing thoughts were interrupted by the persistent pressure of a mind-message from Hagen: *Teacher, help! They're forcing us away from the gates!*

There was nothing for it—I would have to assist. However, since my apprentice needed to carry his second victory without the assistance of my magic, it was time for my sword and a body no longer in the first bloom of youth, which had served me faithfully these many years, to set to. I drew my blade, which was, of course, black—what other farewell gift could I have had from Rakoth?

"Have at them, men! Pile on, press hard!" I yelled.

They were slowly giving ground before the temple guards. The Black Sword made an arc through the air, knocking away the arrows heading straight for two of Hagen's men standing beside me, then sliced a temple warrior's curved ataghan in two and followed by smartly knocking another's helmet off.

We Mages are not permitted to kill mortals.

The detachment, emboldened now, easily dispatched the guards I had disarmed and drew ever nearer to the gates. In time, we reached them, with me covering the men's backs while Hagen gave short shrift to anyone who tried to block the path. Their booty sacks were still intact, and they carried out our dead and wounded, leaving not one behind.

I was last to quit the temple; but the moment I crossed the threshold, a power that had quietly been biding its time finally dealt the long-prepared blow.

It was spectacular. Unimaginable. Indescribable. All was again as it had been in the long-distant days of my rout. The sky blazed with a furious white light, the stars disappeared into the bottomless wells of crystal spheres, and a heavy, grating sound reverberated from the Earth as its dry surface cracked into long fissures that belched a suffocating black smoke. The wind blew from all four quarters at once, the air became suddenly dense, resisting every effort to tear through it, and overhead there burned ever brighter a shimmering glow as the Door between the courses of the Real swung open.

Yes, Sigrlinn, the Sheltered Kingdom is yours by right. I knew that and still I underestimated you—you or Merlin the Great himself. I remembered well what would follow. Hagen and his entire detachment had but minutes to live if I did not intervene—or find a way to take them from this place without resorting to my magic.

The ground began to split beneath them. Raising my eyes, I saw them feverishly lashing themselves together with belaying ropes. The buffeting wind made it hard for them to keep their feet, much less move a step in any direction.

A melodic crystalline chiming floated down from above, easily audible even over the wailing wind and the grinding sounds made by the unraveling and collapsing ground. A Door slammed open; and a warrior host, bathed in the light of spectral rainbow banners, advanced against us. The wind seemed to trouble them not at all, and the fissures in the Earth closed with lightning speed as they passed by.

Hagen let out a hoarse bellow, jabbing his sword toward this new danger. The forces flowing through the doorway carried long, thin swords with iridescent blades and smooth, very elongated wooden hilts. That was all they had—not a piece of armor among them, not a pike or a bow, but I was only too familiar with those death-dealing blades that ceded little to the enchanted Discs of Iamerth from the High Temple of Vidrir's kingdom.

Bows were useless—the wind brought down every arrow. The rainbow warriors drew closer, close enough now to see that there were male and female in their ranks, and that they were all tall with long, luxuriant hair. And as if that were not enough, another being sallied forth, this one from the temple. It had two legs and six arms, was girt about with gleaming yellow eyes and wore a loose golden robe. Its head was covered by a huge helm of scarlet and black, and it was twenty feet tall if it was an inch.

This was an old acquaintance, one of the keepers of Sigrlinn's palace in Jibulistan, adroit, cunning, skilful and brave. Yet she almost never used them in battle…

I had waited long enough. My sword all but leapt to my hand.

"Try to force your way through to the ships!" I called to Hagen as I sprinted past him. The wind that knocked the humans off their feet troubled me little.

I ran to head off Sigrlinn's minion, the zophar. There were only two possibilities—either the sorceress had decidedly changed her ways or those who were behind all this were trying to make me think this was her doing. If that were so, the zophar would be their last, best stratagem, intended to remove my last doubt.

The faithful servant of my erstwhile…ah…friend closed on me with its absurd waddling gait. In each of its six huge hands it held a long broad blade sharply curved at the tip, one Sigrlinn herself had designed. Seeing me, it made a strange noise, something like a muted groan of horror, but did not swerve from its path. Had it recognized me?

But zophars had never had any magical capabilities nor could they sense the presence of magic. They were excellent combatants, true warriors, but no more than that. And whose idea had it been to squeeze it into those ridiculous yellow vestments, like a temple priest? Yellow had never been one of Sigrlinn's colors.

Then we joined. All my thoughts, which are probably long in the telling, had come and gone in mere seconds. How those six swords whistled as they blended into one sparkling tornado above my head. How sorely the mercilessly cloven air groaned, how cruelly the tenuous bodies of the Ethereal creatures that filled the air—guilty of nothing and noways implicated in our brawls—were shredded. The yellow pupils brimmed now with insanity, and I immediately knew it to be becharmed. The charm was too complex for me to disentangle, on the instant; its fancifully convoluted currents of powers and energies at first sight bore the signature of forms similar to those Sigrlinn was wont to use, although I sensed also some almost indistinguishable differences. But there would surely be a better time for such inquiries...

I never did determine who had forged the zophar's six swords, but I must say they had made a wretched job of it. My Black Sword remained undamaged as it slashed through those blades like a sickle through ripe wheat, dropping the iron fragments one by one to the ground. The disarmed zophar simply stared with a dull, bepuzzled, entirely uncharacteristic gaze at its hands and the worthless hilts they still held.

I grasped one of the motionless, meaty arms, pulled, got a better grip, pulled again, and found myself level with a huge ear. The zophar made flaccid attempts to catch me, with sluggish movements that no way matched its recent swordwork. Apparently, the charm laid upon it was too narrow in its effect; one step to either side and it was lost, even though Sigrlinn had created the zophars to shift nimbly for themselves in completely unforeseen circumstances. They were clever, sly, quick-witted and would never, ever have allowed a foe to clamber up them, as if shinnying up a tree, to rap them hard slightly above and to the right of the ear with the heavy hilt of a Black Sword forged by Rakoth.

Without a sound, the stunned giant fell headlong, and I raced back to where Hagen's men were fighting off the assault of the rainbow warriors. They were having a weary time of it—already about half of them had slipped into the fissures, saved only by the ropes lashed about their chests. A mere three or four dozen—the strongest and sturdiest—could keep sword in hand and stand against the wind.

I saw Hagen join battle with the leader of the rainbow warriors, who was in the van. I saw the handiwork of the craftsmen of Hauberk Mount and a narrow iridescent slip that had passed through the ninety-nine crucibles of the Upperworlds clash and spring apart, shrouded in a rapidly dissipating puff of smoke. I breathed easier, sure in the knowledge that the gnomish armament had been worth the exorbitant sum paid for it.

Then I picked up the first stone I found on the ground nearby and hurled it with all my strength toward the spellbinding shimmering overhead.

There had been days when I floundered on scorching sands and bit my lips until they bled, in despair of ever gaining the upper hand over magical doors such as these. I had tried dozens—no, hundreds—of various spells against them, all to no avail. Rainbow warriors led by the lovely Sigrlinn had flocked through those doors, and my troops were no match for them in either strength or skill.

Much later, while perusing the alvish chronicles a mere six centuries ago, I had found my answer, which was as paradoxical as it was simple.

A certain army, the chronicle related, was besieging a certain city. The siege was already several months old, with the defenders steadfastly repulsing every assault, and the soldiery outside the walls was beginning to murmur. At that point, their leader—a prince he was, or king, or some such—ordered his sorcerer to make the city fall.

The sorcerer had, of course, received similar orders before, but all his efforts had been blocked by the city's own enchanter. This time, he cast the most powerful charm he knew, which was almost the end of him. The skies were breached; and unearthly warriors, their swords drawn, descended upon the city, which now seemed to be doomed.

Magic being powerless to stop them, a tower commander in desperation ordered a catapult brought forward and lobbed a heavy stone projectile right into that all-be-damned shimmering—upon which it disappeared, taking all its eldritch warriors with it.

That led me to a thought I at first dismissed as manifestly preposterous:— that the Door between the Worlds would close if struck by a simple stone. I then spent a not-inconsiderable amount of time looking for the incontrovertible proof that this was so, and finally, I found it. I had no idea if the other Mages of my Generation knew of this, if Merlin had this knowledge; but if they did not, then I had just handed them a priceless treasure, indeed.

For my tiny stone served its purpose well. The warrior ranks in their rainbow garb hesitated, stopped and suddenly began to beat a speedy retreat, melting into gleaming clouds that had sunk down to the very ground. Hagen and his men watched them go with astonished eyes. There remained only the gale and the sunken ground, but without my magic I could do nothing about that.

"Hagen! Can you move?" I yelled over the whistling wind.

His reply drifted back to me. "I can, yes, and some of the others, too, but not all."

"Go, then! Make haste—go to the ships! I shall stay."

My apprentice obeyed without a second thought. The four dozen men who were still afoot trailed after him.

The earthshaking vortices had turned the pen the winds had created for Hagen's detachment into a deep, broad pit whose floor was still sinking. Men were crawling up the slopes, clutching frantically at handholds that disintegrated in their grasp while trying not to lose their grip on the wounded and their sacks of booty.

But gradually the tremors began to slacken—some of the blind forces thrown against us had turned instead to Hagen and little group doggedly pushing toward the dragon-ships. The howling wind sounded almost perplexed as its might was stretched increasing thin, the force it could apply in any one place necessarily weakened.

All at once, whoever or whatever was directing this magical farrago seemed to hesitate, then left the main part of the detachment alone in order to go after Hagen, judging him to present the greater danger. The rest were finally able to clamber out of their fissures and pits.

"To the shore! Spread out," I ordered them. "At the double!"

The wind by now appeared completely confounded, sometimes gusting hard enough to knock us off our feet, sometimes entirely becalmed. The fissures serpentined toward us, but the men bolting for the damp rocks at the sea's edge bounded over them. The black sinkholes gave chase but could not gobble up their lively prey in one gulp.

Finally, one of the superintendents of those underground vortices recognized the problem and set them all to digging a deep ditch to cut us off from the shore. That at least made things easier for Hagen.

"To the left, close ranks!"

Again we had gulled both wind and earthquake. Again they were chasing us, allowing Hagen and his men to make a dash across the ground that separated them from the ships. The forces went after him once more, and then it was our turn to race headlong for the ships. Once on the shoreline rocks, the men jumped into the water, seizing hold of the beams that had been providently laid out for them. The strongest of Hagen's forces, who had boarded first, threw out lifelines to those still wallowing in the surf. The wind dropped, the monstrous tremblings shook no more, and it seemed that our unknown foes had admitted defeat. Even though the dragon-ships were still facing a strong headwind, that was nothing strange—for the coastal waters of the Sheltered Kingdom.

I was seized by an even greater doubt. Had I really been locking horns with Sigrlinn this day or was someone carefully aping her? Had it been she, the charm would have certainly been lifted from the onshore wind and the conflict would have continued out on the open sea. I knew that charm. Sigrlinn had been very long in weaving it, and it was her great pride, since she alone could lift or change it. It could hardly have been Makran or Esteri, though anything was possible…

No, probably it was Sigrlinn, all the same. Until I brought my wizardry to bear, the obscure would remain obscure. First, we had to attend to the wounded.

The oars rose and dipped. The rowers' hoarse voices lifted in an ancient victory song of the eldrings, raucously lauding their thane, as they were suddenly styling Hagen—bestowing upon him a title that was not yet rightfully his. Their spoils had exceeded their boldest dreams. The battle had, of course, taken its toll, but that was all behind them now. They had bested a wizard's wiles and they were on their way home. Already, they were instinctively calling Hedinseigh home.

We lodged in the island keep, although I could see how very vulnerable it was—a determined assault on it could be repulsed only with heavy losses. But there would be time later to build a better one.

Hagen was waiting for me, his eyes filled with reproach. Why had I not intervened? What exactly had happened after we stormed out of the temple? What was that horror in yellow, and how had I managed to lay it low? He had at least a hundred such questions.

"We were waylaid, Hagen," I told him. "One of my kin has been shadowing either you or me all the while. Not me, I think—I still flatter myself I'm not yet thoroughly blind and deaf, and I'd like to believe I would have known I was being watched. After we had our spoils in hand, they struck.

"But evidently we had thrown them off the track, too. They were probably expecting us to set about destroying the temple and torching the prayer halls, but all we did was empty out one of their storerooms.

"And the whole time, they were trying to determine if I was there. They sought to lure me into performing any act of magic whatsoever, however trifling, which would have played right into their hands. That was why I used my sword instead of my sorcery, and that was why I couldn't help you, my boy. But you acquitted yourself magnificently! And the companions you chose were worthy, too. Imagine, forty out of two hundred and eighty able to withstand the might of the four Halting Winds!

"But that's not all. Do you remember my telling you about the sorceress Sigrlinn? The one you threw mud at on the road out of Jol?"

The reminder was superfluous, for Hagen had never forgotten either that night or the lovely woman who had appeared to us in the pouring rain and tried to dissuade him from becoming my apprentice.

"So," I went on, "someone very much wanted me to conclude Sigrlinn was behind that attack, but…" And I laid out my doubts, ending with "Of course, it could still have been her, but I could not confirm it."

Worried, Hagen rubbed his forehead.

"What if they strike at us here on the island?" he asked gloomily.

"On the island? Let them and be welcome, for here I can answer them in kind. It's not at all the same as attacking the Temple of Iamerth."

I did not mention that Merlin might still deem this an upset of the Balance and apply his new charm of punishment—assuming, of course, that Sigrlinn had been telling me true.

"But why did they want you to think it was that sorceress?"

"I have no notion, Hagen. Perhaps the Mages of my Generation are again reordering their alliances for a real Magic War, of which I shall have much more to say when the time is right. Perhaps it is all somehow connected with a jockeying for position. The worst by far would be if Merlin had a hand in it. But usually I know the charms he conjures, while these I could not recognize at all. Enough of this, though. There'll be guests from the Sheltered Kingdom at our door presently."

"That's just what I wanted to talk to you about," Hagen responded, leaning over a map that had been brought in. "Will they be storming the port?"

I nodded. "That's the only possible way. Unless there's a secret path through the cliffs. You'd best—"

"I've already sent out a four-man horse patrol," he finished my thought. "I've ordered them to look for signs of a path to the sea and to inspect any suspicious caves. If they attack the port, we'll beat them off."

That we will, I thought, *provided there are no Discs of Iamerth to contend with.*

"I'm considering stationing four squads on the jetties," Hagen went on, but I raised a hand to stop him.

"You're experienced enough to do without any advice from me, my boy. But don't forget that our goal has never been for our two hundred and fifty swordarms to declare war upon the many tens of thousands under Vidrir's command."

Hagen bowed his head. "I remember, Teacher," he said. "What's needed is to extract from them the peace we seek, on our terms."

"Yes! Promise to return some of the temple valuables from your share of the spoils. Hammer home to them that they will gain nothing by embroiling the Sheltered Kingdom in a war with you."

"I'll make sure they know it." Hagen gave a slow smile. "I warrant I'll put the fear into those slugabeds."

"I doubt you not, Hagen. I shall leave you here alone for a while. I understand the risk, but too many strange things have happened of late and some of them I will not be able to puzzle out if I stay here. So, I must go on a short journey."

"I fear no one who appears here armed with only a sword," was Hagen's rather dour reply. "But what if we're set upon by those who almost made away with us when we came out of the temple?"

"Neither you nor your men can be killed by that wind or those cracks in the ground," I replied. "Have you forgotten one of the fundamental laws by which our Generation must abide?"

"Of course, I haven't!"

"Then if it all begins again, try to get out of the full force of the wind. And if a Door is about to open, you'll see a rainbow shimmer. What must you do to close it?"

"Yes, Teacher, you're right. Forgive me." Hagen bowed his head again. "I remember it all and shall do as you say. You can rest easy. And when you return, our banner will be flying over Hedinseigh!" Those high-sounding words were accompanied by a proud tilt of the head.

"I hope so. Keep your wits about you, now. The defenses should be in full readiness by tomorrow morning at the latest, because Vidrir's galleys cannot be here before then, even with a following wind. But…no, you'd better have the bulk of the work done before midnight. Whoever has come to the Sheltered Kingdom's aid might well loose the Bluewater Harriers to speed the ships on their way. So wait here for me, Hagen, and don't leave the island. Fare you well!"

"Fare you well, Teacher," my apprentice said, bowing and stepping aside.

I began to conjure a Charm of Transference—I had much work ahead of me, and, before all else, the Castle of All the Ancients awaited me.

CHAPTER V

WELL, THERE'S YOUR GNIPAHELLIR," BRANN SHRUNKENHAND SAID TESTILY.
He and Hagen stood on the margin of a low-growing, frost-thinned pinewood. The Forestway had ended. Hagen looked silently at the dismal, lifeless gray plain that stretched to the horizon, interrupted only in the far distance where his sharp eyes made out something that resembled a ridge of hills. There was not a tree or bush to be seen—only sky, and earth bare, rocky and colored by nothing but occasional clinging bands of silvery moss. The sky was marred by long smears of smoke welling out of the southwest. A smell of burning filled the air.

Shrunkenhand's reckoning had them at midday, but the sun was hidden behind heavy, smoky clouds; and in the foggy twilight that had the land in its grip, the thane could not say with certainty if it was really hills he saw out there at the very limits of sight or something else—clumps of very tall trees, perhaps.

He turned to his companion. "Thank you, Brann. I will not call upon you to go any further. You have fulfilled the first part of your promise. Will you wait for me here or shall we meet in another place?"

"I'm going with you," Shrunkenhand replied, following that with words whose meaning escaped Hagen at the time. "We set out together, and together we shall arrive," he said.

"And what purpose would you have there?" Hagen asked in surprise. "My intention is to send the Hound back to sleep and then retreat with all haste. What's the allure for you?"

"'Tis a wonder to behold, and I propose to behold it," Brann replied curtly. "Well, shall we be off, young thane? Or are we going to keep on lollygagging here? Now you'll be *my* guide, for I've never been far into these parts. I've always kept to the Forest."

Hagen nodded. "As you wish. I won't say I'm not glad of the company."

They spurred their horses due north, along the only route open to them. Gnipahellir was like a gigantic pit—all its roads converged on the Black Highway that would lead Hagen to the Hound.

An hour went by, and another, and another; and always in the same gray murk that neither thickened nor dissipated. They had not as yet encountered a single living thing. Even the spirits that had swarmed about them on the Forestway had disappeared.

"How dead it is," Shrunkenhand muttered, turning in his saddle to cast a wary eye around. "Never was there a place more dead."

"What are we lacking?" Hagen asked. "The fewer creatures we meet, the better. Or are you pining for the Devourers of Souls?"

But Brann had a ready argument against that. "Where a spirit shelters, 'tis meet for a man to be, sithee. But they say that where there are no spirits at all, humans will not long endure. Look lively, young thane, lest we both perish here not by the sword but by the Unseen Death."

"Away with your old wives' tales, Brann." Hagen frowned. "I've had a bellyful of those yarns over the years. There is no Unseen Death in Gnipahellir—its lair is far to the south. You'd need to cross the straits, and even then make many days' journey through uncharted deserts and forestland to reach its domain."

"Happen so," Brann agreed despondently.

They traveled on, Hagen calm and single-minded and Brann scowling and, the thane surmised, somewhat fearful.

Being far from the Forest makes him uneasy, 'tis plain to see, Hagen mused, then thought no more of it.

The sun apparently had no intention of setting; it seemed the day would go on forever. The thane knew that northern summer nights were short, but for there to be no night at all…

"What would you?" Brann gave a husky chuckle and licked dry lips. "Gnipahellir, young thane, is far further north than any populated land. And lucky we are that it's summer, for otherwise we'd freeze solid in an instant and that would be an end of it."

Hagen drew rein. "Well and good. We'll stop here."

Scarcely had they had time to set up their modest camp, in a narrow gully that was hardly discernible from a distance, when Hagen came to his first understanding of the words *Garm has awoken*, which until then had been no more than an ominous figure of speech to him. A furious, low-pitched snarling noise came from shallow subterranean caverns somewhere ahead of them, making everything around shake, judder, squeal and groan. The thane threw himself down and placed his ear against the cold ground, trying to determine the distance from their quarry. Brann just winced.

"And sure, you're ill-tempered," he said thoughtfully and for no discernible reason, "to be joggled about in the middle of the night and then kept from your sleep."

Those first rolling rumbles of sound were followed by others, all filled with a wild, bloodthirsty, frenzied hatred for all that lived and for whomever was keeping him—the great, battle-scarred Hound of Death—tethered, preventing him from feasting at will on the warm blood of the living rather than the loathsome, cold slop he sucked from the flesh of the corpses tossed his way. And for all the steadfastness of Hedin's apprentice, who had encountered no few horrors in his life, even he shuddered. He could easily imagine the fetters that still held the Hound bursting apart, a fountain of soil spurting up into the sky, and a monstrous head with burning eyes and eternally famished maw rising from a gigantic pit.

He shook off his nightmare visions. Brann stood alongside, his lips a thin line and his brows knit but his face calm; and Hagen felt an instinctive shame for being so—as he deemed it—weak.

"Aye, 'tis a lusty beastie," Shrunkenhand said with a hint of respect. "But I'd rather he'd slept on. 'Twould please me well to wish him sweet dreams."

Garm fell silent, and the thane and Shrunkenhand settled for the night. Their evening meal done, they wrapped themselves in their blankets, and Brann was soon asleep. But Hagen lay sleepless, the Hound's roar still ringing in his ears.

At first he thought he was dreaming it. Then, in a sudden rush, as these things always happen, his consciousness was invaded by a new sensation. It was a thin, mosquito-like whine at the very verge of human hearing. *Midges?* he wondered fleetingly, but in the next instant he was at the end of the gully, visor down, sword in hand and a small loaded arbalest on the ground by his side.

A long file of pale smudges was moving slowly across the plain, resembling nothing so much as the flicker of fireflies hovering over a marsh. Hagen then saw that each light was accompanied by a figure, vaguely white in the murk. In general outlines, the figures looked human, but they were blurred and they had no features. The procession was headed by someone tall and dressed all in gray and black. He could make out a sharp-pointed helmet and the broad blade of a strange weapon, bared and ready; and he was aware of the waves of strength that radiated from that being. Grim it was, and merciless, but at the same time indifferent to all.

The tall warrior drew level with the gully where Hagen lay hidden. He stopped and turned his head, leisurely, toward the motionless thane. Hagen felt a pair of mighty, invisible hands drag him from his refuge on the ground. A lunatic terror began pounding at the gates of his reason—*Up! Run!*

He grasped the slim stock of his arbalest, all the while realizing the senselessness of having done so, and determined, rather, to stay prostrate and still and let those cold hands go digging into the empty sand.

Next came the certainty that he really was going mad. In one moment he was looking at the end of the gully, at an uneven line of trampled sand and small stones, and in the next that picture was overlaid by another. He seemed to be rising to his feet while still lying on the ground. His heart was in an icy vice of pain; his mind was fogging...

Now... The thoughts came as in a fever. *How could I...That is Iargohor, Conveyor of the Dead...The Expeller of Souls...A charm! A charm...a charm...*

But before his memory yielded the spell he needed, his hand moved abruptly of itself and did the only thing it could do, which was aim the arbalest under the jutting brim of the tall black helmet, where there might be a chink that would be fatal to a mortal warrior.

No one had ever dared raise a weapon against mighty Iargohor, who had not come lightly by his title of Conveyer of the Dead. Age upon age, despondent caravans of souls unworthy of any other afterlife had dragged their way through the deathful fields of Gnipahellir to the dismal path of no return—the Black Highway and the road to Hel. On vanishingly rare occasions, living men ventured deep into Gnipahellir, but if they encountered Iargohor there he did to them what he was wont to do with all—he wrung their souls loose and carried them off to the bottomless pit of Niflhel.

The Conveyor of the Dead had once had a different name that no one now remembered. Mage Hedin had many tales to tell about how the youngest of the Young Gods had overstepped his bounds on the First Day of Wrath and had been dealt a severe yet just punishment by Iamerth, being first divested of his powers and of the richness of memory and then sent out to guide these doleful corteges.

Long, long before, Hedin, driven partly by curiosity and partly by sympathy for one who had also suffered at the hands of the Young Gods, had come to Gnipahellir and seen Iargohor but had been sorely disappointed. The Conveyor of the Dead had no interest in conversation. Instead, he reached out with invisible claws, as he did at every encounter with the living...

Hedin had raised a barrier of powerful Protective Charms, and the claws withdrew; but the Mage could not have said for certain whether Iargohor had responded to those wizardly boundaries or had simply understood that this was no common mortal.

The short, thick bolt struck a sheaf of sparks from Iargohor's armor. The dark figure staggered, and suddenly Hagen was no longer seeing two worlds at once. Iargohor stopped in his tracks, as if hesitating. Hagen went rigid, too, no longer even trying to call to mind his defensive magic. Only his hands moved, and not because he was moving them; they were moving in spite of him, hastily rearming the arbalest.

The gully was surrounded by a tightening circle of pallid, lifeless lights. The dead were waiting patiently. They had no reason to hurry. All that awaited them was something that amounted to eternity.

Iargohor strode toward Hagen, menacingly raising his longsword just like any ordinary warrior. All the thane could think to do was fire again.

There was a brief flash of light, and Hagen saw his first bolt already buried in Iargohor's body almost to the fletch. The Conveyor of the Dead stopped again, and seemed to stagger.

This febrile, insane scene was playing out in total silence, and Hagen had no inkling of what he was going to do next. He and his Teacher had yet to speak of doing battle with such a mighty servant of the Young Gods as Iargohor was still.

The tall figure with the fearsome sword took one more step forward, but this time with great uncertainty. Hagen again felt the touch of those stiff, invisible claws and hurried to conjure a Protective Charm. The fangs sliced into that misty but rapidly hardening defense like a cold knife into even colder butter, catching and seizing. But then Hagen loosed his third bolt, and the Conveyor of the Dead retracted his snares.

Iargohor turned, lowered his weapon and slowly passed a hand over his chest. The three shafts clinked to the ground, and that was the only sound that broke the thickening, burdensome stillness. In the silence of Gnipahellir, it resounded like the peal of a bell.

Paying no further attention to Hagen, the Conveyer of Souls, with a sweep of his sword, bade the dead follow him and strode on. Lacking the strength to move, Hagen watched them until they were lost in the shifting dusk.

Regaining his senses, he shook Brann violently.

"Ehhh, what is it? Time to turn out?" Brann mumbled sleepily.

"Rouse yourself, you slugabed!" the thane barked. "We almost went to Niflhel while you were sawing logs."

"But why not? That's where we're making for."

"Iargohor was here," Hagen said, very slowly and distinctly. "The Conveyor of the Dead. With his caravan. I suppose you've heard of him."

"Well, now!" Brann was genuinely surprised. "I know of him. I even saw him—thrice, mayhap—in my younger days, when I would stray farther into Gnipahellir."

Hagen goggled. "You've seen Iargohor three times?"

"What's so strange about that?" Brann shrugged.

"Then how is it you're still alive?" Hagen roared. "Iargohor wrings the soul from every mortal who crosses his path! How did you come out of it unscathed?"

"You say so?" Shrunkenhand seemed seriously baffled. "Wrings the souls out of them? 'Tis the first I've heard of that. True, is it?"

"Oh, believe me, it is," Hagen said venomously. "I shot him thrice with my arbalest and conjured a simple Spell of Protection, but I cannot think that's what stopped him. At least, he pulled out my bolts and threw them aside, with no visible wounds to show for it. Still, for whatever reason, he stopped and then went on his way. Can you explain that, you who've encountered him three times?"

"Perhaps he would have passed on by if you hadn't shot at him."

"No." Hagen shuddered. "My soul…was beginning to leave my body. A sensation not to be wished on one's worst enemy, not on this side of death."

Brann spread his hands. "I'm understanding none of this. There I was, sleeping, and felt nothing."

So, here's another mystery, Hagen thought. *What is Shrunkenhand's secret? Why did Iargohor not notice him? Maybe he's an immortal? But no, that's foolishness.*

"And one might ask, too, why he suddenly let you be, young thane, once he'd already started wringing your soul from you, as you'd have it."

Hagen made a gloomy, dismissive gesture. "Enough. We can think on all that later. Now we have work to do, and work that must be finished. Let's sleep a while longer, then we'll away."

WHILE GUDMUND WAS TOILING HIS WAY TO THE MONASTERY AND HAGEN WAS CONFERRING first with Hropt and then with Brann, Frodi was carrying out his thane's orders. He, too, traveled north, to the Roedulsfoel Mountains, seeking out the Keepers of Ialini's Veil. He, too, saw the sky shrouded in endless surges of smoke, saw birds, animals and other tiny denizens of the forests, such as Flower Maidens, fleeing the spreading conflagration. Once a fright of a mormath clipped past him. Frodi recoiled and raised his cudgel, but the nightmarish beast paid him no mind, being intent on ushering its two offspring to safety.

The hazy mountains that marked the boundaries of Ialini's Garden of the North came into view. Frodi passed through a broad, wildly overgrown valley along the banks of a brook, singularly unsullied, that filled the air with its soothing babble. He was a strong, bluff man, a fighter who rarely bent an ear to the music of water. Yet here he was, riding hour after hour as if in a trance so pure and resonant was the trilling of that shallow little stream as it slid over the many-colored stones that formed its bed. When he stooped to drink, it seemed to him the water gave off a faint, scarcely perceptible aroma, which he would have been able to identify had not all else around been rank with the smell of burning. When he raised his cupped, brimming hands to his mouth he felt he was holding a fine goblet filled with priceless wine, and the taste of that water he had no words to describe.

Everything else in the valley was a fellow to that brook. The gloomy spruces, lank pines and dismal gray mosses were gone, the slopes covered with such bushes, trees and grass as he had never seen, which in some ways seemed recognizable to a northlander but were also as different as could be from those of the north. He saw no thorny thickets or impassible wind-felled trees, no rotting piles of deadwood or dry, shed branches. Golden trunks bore downy crowns aloft, and the conifers were no prickly pincushions but instead sported long, soft needles and gave off a faint greenish light that could not be seen in sunshine but was impossible to miss in shade. Flowers too bright to be of the north made a whimsical contrast with the severe, straight lines of the tree branches.

Here, too, there was none of the seething, insane, endless, mutual devouring of growing, moving creatures that fills the forests of the south. There were fruits to eat—or more accurately, huge bulbous things with astonishingly tasty, juicy kernels beneath their scaly rinds. They hung everywhere, and he just plucked those he could reach.

Then he came upon a place where fire had eaten a disgusting bare patch in the luxurious carpet of green—charred skeletons of trees, bushes gnawed down to the roots, scorched grass. The fire had been brought down quite quickly, though, and the ashes had long cooled. Frodi, traveling by guesswork now, left the valley and made directly for Roedulsfoel.

The forests were even lovelier here, more majestic, the branches meeting high overhead in a coupling of gilded green, the leaves and needles intertwined into fanciful wreaths. Had Gudmund been there, he would have noticed the trees resembled the giants surrounding the mysterious monastery of Brunevagar—not quite as tall, though, and the life in this forest was incomparably richer.

Frodi did not have to travel by guesswork for long. A gust of wind brought the smell of fresh smoke, and he quickly turned his horse in that direction. Soon the air was gray, and smoky streamers came drifting through the trees. He saw a flash of fire and heard the crackle and roar of flame, punctuated by the unexpected sounds of raised voices.

Suddenly, thunder pealed, the forest trembled, and a cold blast of wind almost knocked him from his horse, sending blood-red circles flashing before his eyes. He knew nothing of magic but could recognize a charm when he felt one. Somewhere up ahead unknown adversaries were trading blows of wizardry.

At the very fringe of the fire, where Frodi was forced to draw up his cloak to protect his face from the intolerable heat, stood a handful of green-clad figures, not tall but well-made and graceful. They seemed to stand motionless, even though they were under assault from several dozen strange beings—gnome-like but even shorter, and every one of them hunchbacked and dressed in somber, dirty-brown, loose-fitting smocks.

All were aware that the Roedulsfoel dwarves knew wizardry, but the idea they could be brazen enough to pit themselves openly against the Keepers of the Veil would no doubt not have occurred even to a Mage—with the exception of Hedin, of course.

The dwarves were fighting with glum, bitter determination. Though ignorant of the wizardry in that battle, Frodi was certainly competent to judge their skilled use of slingshots and bows. The four Keepers were deflecting the bolts with sudden gusts of wind, but they could only dodge the heavier stones.

While three held off the dwarves' concerted onslaught, one worked at something under the cover provided by his comrades. Before long, the heavens opened, and the tongues of flame were drenched by a torrential downpour, while two earthbound whirlwinds burst out of the forest and began blasting the burning boughs and branches aside.

The flames hissed, and steam billowed up. The sheer wall of magic rain fell only two steps away from Frodi but not a drop ever touched him. Meanwhile, one of the whirlwinds eddying around the blaze danced up to the crowd of dwarves and sent many of them flying. Those it missed took to their heels, squealing and cursing.

The four in green crossed their arms across their chests, bowed their heads and soundlessly departed, seeming to float over the charred, hummocky ground. Frodi could discern no movement of their robes to match the rhythm of their steps.

"Hey! Tarry a while!" he yelled to them, stepping from his hiding place.

They stopped. Now he could study them more closely—slender bodies, narrow shoulders, elegant hands. But their faces baffled him—neither male nor female they were but something between, beardless and mustacheless, with mild features and smooth, unwrinkled skin.

Hagen would immediately have begun trying to recall if his Teacher had ever mentioned such creatures and, if so, whether he spoke of them as friend or foe. Frodi knew nothing of such high matters and did not even bother to wonder about the creatures' gender. He simply pressed his right hand to his heart and said, with a bow, "Greetings to you. Would I be looking on the Keepers of Ialini's Veil?"

"The very ones." The reply was courteous but cold.

"Then know this!" And Frodi, without once drawing breath, rattled out all his thane had bade him say.

When he was done, the green-clad quartet eyed him in silence.

"And what follows from what you have said?" one of them asked in a melodious though not womanly voice.

"What follows?" Frodi was taken aback. "I don't know. I was only ordered to warn you. That I have done. And what follows from my words is for you to decide, not so?"

"What would you do?"

Frodi said the first thing that came to his mind. "I would try to quench all the fires in your forests. Perchance change the course of the winds, so they would not carry the smell of burning to Garm."

The Keepers of the Veil huddled to discuss this. Frodi waited patiently.

"Very well, messenger," one of them said at last. "We have heard your words. You shall be our guest this day. You are in need of rest, and your journey home will be long, for the sea is far from here."

And why, dragon devour me, do they suppose I'm on my way to the sea?

Long he followed them, through forests more lovely than any he had ever seen. Over low knolls and though shallow dells, Ialini's Garden stretched for dozens of leagues; and no mortal ever born could remain indifferent to its beauties, to the bright, clean colors, to the flowers and leaves—scarlet and silver, sky-blue and dark-green—to the crimson trunks and gilt canopy with its enchanting honeyed scent. One could not have said which bush had the most exquisite flowers, which tree the most majestic form or the most delicious fruits. Green clouds of dense foliage twined into flower-bedecked garlands. There was an astonishing sense of measure and order in this forest that in no way impinged upon the freedom of all its living things, for Ialini the Merciful could not abide either duress or bloodshed.

Their path forded crystalline rills, where rosy waterlilies swayed in stone basins nestled in the bosom of the transparent waters. Birdsong accompanied them all the way. It was impossible to believe that this lush land bordered on Gnipahellir, the dismal kingdom of death.

At last, the winding path led them to a round dale whose floor was mantled with tall, soft grass and studded with solitary bushes. Around its edge was a wall of trees, their branches interwoven overhead. It was the forest's own reception hall.

The stars might have descended from the night sky and settled into crystal spheres of dew, to light the hall with their silvery glow. The bushes' leaves and flowers shone with all the colors of the rainbow, yet muted and dim. The grassy green turf served as a table the Keepers quickly set with wooden goblets and platters of fruits and nuts. Frodi could have sworn that never had he tasted nor would he ever taste food so good, while what he drank there far outstripped all the renowned vintages of the lands of men.

"You see the beauty of Ialini's Garden?" one of the Keepers quietly asked him, as he sat there stunned by all the splendor.

"Beautiful and astonishing it is, indeed," Hagen's warrior replied through a mouthful of food. "I have never seen the like."

"Nor shall you," the Keeper assured him. "All this was created by Ialini the Merciful—she whom you, in your folly, oppose, like to the dwarves we had to scatter before us this very day."

A nut lodged in Frodi's throat.

"We oppose Ialini? What foolishness is that? My thane himself sent me here. Would he have done so had we been at odds with you?"

"He is not at odds with us, nor we with him. By our nature and by the mandates of Ialini the Merciful, we are enemy to no one. Even the dwarves who burn our forests we never kill."

"And why not?"

"The Lady Ialini could never bear that any living creature should shed a single drop of blood at the hands of her servants or in her name. She has no need of fields smoking with the blood of innocent victims. We wreak no harm upon anyone, not even the most vicious foe who attacks her Garden.

"But I digress. The thane whom you serve is well known to us, as is his Teacher, Mage Hedin. That Mage it is who opposes our Lady, and it pains us that such strong and courageous men are to be found among those who serve the Sage of Darkness, for their prowess we sorely need in our struggle against another evil, a true evil."

The fervent speech left Frodi almost completely bemused. He frowned, knit his brows, rubbed his forehead once, twice, coughed, but could not find the words he sought. His strength had never lain between his ears. One thing only he understood—these wondrous strange Keepers had something against Thane Hagen, a man revered by all his warriors, and against the thane's Teacher, too. And this news had to be conveyed to them without delay.

"But why in…Why are you telling me all this?" he finally forced out. "A fine thing to say—my thane set against the Lady Ialini!"

"Not directly, but he is against her even so," his table companion continued softly and earnestly. "All the evil comes from your thane's Teacher. To him you are nothing—dust by the roadside, an ant or a fly that one can swat away at a single stroke and then forget it ever existed. The title of Sage of Darkness is not given for naught. Think on this, warrior: Why not stay here? In your heart—a heart no longer weighed down with villainy and brigandage— you have already come to love this place and are not averse to living here and becoming one of us, to protect and multiply its great beauty, following the purpose of the Lady Ialini."

Frodi grasped his temples. "Your prating's enough to make my head spin. You speak badly of the Teacher, you try to affright me. Your words are ill-intentioned, Keeper!"

"My words cannot be ill-intentioned," the Keeper argued gently. "We are enemies to no one on this Earth. Were Mage Hedin to come here we would not lift a hand against him, unless he tried to harm our forests. But even if he did so, we would do battle with his actions, not with him. The most we may do to him is take him prisoner and send him away, far away from our bounds, doing him not the slightest harm and leaving him alive and well at the end of all.

Now do you understand? Think on't, for the call of Ialini's Forest is strong in your heart. Stay with us, become one of us, I say to you again."

The aromatic air was making Frodi's eyes dazzle, but his seasoned warrior's instincts were already warning of danger. From that moment on he only pretended to be drunk and unsteady, while in truth he was imperceptibly checking his weapon and settling it more comfortably. Yet it seemed that the polished grip of his beloved cudgel lay in his hand by chance.

For all that, though, a wave of anguish swept though his heart. How good it would be to stay forever in this land of fairytale, guarding it with body and soul against all dangers, to visit this forest palace every day, to drink the water of these springs, to breathe the scent of these flowers. Forever to forget the backbreaking, deadly toil that is the lot of any man-of-arms whose task is to lay the groundwork for victories to come.

Then the enchantment disappeared, as if blown away on the wind. He heard the creak of a dragon-ship's oars when all the rowers are bearing down as one on the wooden sweeps of a manmade sea-beast going athwart the foe; the grating of his sword's steel as it pierced an enemy's armor, to emerge crimsoned with another's blood, drawn in honorable combat; the thane's brusque commands that wheeled his small, ironclad detachment about to face a new threat, as always at exactly the right moment, neither too soon nor too late; and the quiet voice of the Teacher, Mage Hedin, by the large fireplace in the hall on Hedinseigh's long winter evenings, regaling all who cared to listen with marvelous tales of Hjorvard's days of yore, as if weaving a wondrous fable.

"Time to be away." Frodi rose, unable to resist a last, farewell draught that drained his goblet to the lees. "As you yourselves said, the sea is far off."

He whistled for his horse and began to saddle it.

"You refuse, then?" the Keeper said slowly, with a sorrowful shake of the head. "Well, I expected naught else. Your error shall be clear to you yet, but then it will be too late."

"Maybe I will rue it." Frodi shrugged. "But man has many causes for regret. It's not important whether I will or not." He was already tightening the girth.

"We have warned you," the Keeper said, staring full on him with transparent greenish eyes. "We have warned you, which means that we have warned your thane, and his Teacher, too. Ialini the Merciful does not want another war. We bow to her will, and more than that, we also hate all war and any violence whatever, and we believe the day will come when they shall molder away, leaving not a trace on the Earth."

Frodi could only shrug again in reply to such grandiloquence—he could not chop logic with a Keeper so well versed in the arts of rhetoric. Gudmund, his friend and familiar, would probably have known what to say. Gudmund could read, after all, and was a man who knew much, while Frodi was just the son of a village blacksmith from a free peasant village down by the coast and had never in his life pondered such matters. Thinking always set his head abuzz and caused a prickling in his temples. He was far more at home whaling on someone with his cudgel.

The moon had risen, and the smooth, well-worn path made travel easy. Frodi had left Roedulsfoel behind him before dawn, burying forevermore in the depths of his memory his yearning for the loveliness that would never be his.

Hagen's warrior had a long journey ahead of him to the Unavagar coast, to the poor fishing village in those savage parts where he planned to wait for Gudmund. It never even occurred to him that his friend might not return.

At a turn in the path, his horse shied back and whinnied in fear. Frodi patted its neck to calm it and continued on, unaware of the squat, dark shadow that had slipped out of the bushes to tail him.

HAGEN LOOKED AROUND SULLENLY. IT WAS THE SECOND DAY HE AND BRANN HAD TRAVELED through the Gnipahellir wilderness. To east and west the Endmost Mountains loomed. The travelers were making for the wide mouth of a mountain valley that gradually narrowed into a distance that was empty, dry and dead—a wilderness of nothing but reddish soil and gloomy, dark-gray scarps.

Ordinary mountains are scored with a myriad crevices and dotted with the creeping grasses that obstinately strike root in the lower cliff faces. There are signs of streams that once tumbled down the slopes; there are washouts, gullies, ravines. But these mountains were like castle walls raised by a massive hand. There was none of the smooth easing of foothills—no, these mountains, rather, were grim bastions reaching abruptly into the sky. The stark bluffs shot upward for thousands upon thousands of feet to end in sharp spear-tip summits.

These were the Endmost Mountains, and what lay beyond them only the Mages knew. Not even birds dared cross the boundary marked so clearly by those peaks, which had been established by the Young Gods in times immemorial after the First Day of Wrath.

Hagen also knew what lay hidden behind those forbidding hulks, because his Teacher had spoken of it often. The other face of the Endmost Mountains was washed by a sea that was eternally fettered by ice. A white wilderness stretched to the Encircling Ocean, a black ring of endless ebb and flow that girded the plane surface of the world. In that ice nothing lived—not the white sea-bears nor even the seals that were common farther west. These were the domains of Ialven, Steward of the Bitter Cold, Commander of Blizzards and Sacristan of the Snows.

By order of Iambren, Ialven's older brother and Lord of Winds, when winter came to Eastern Hjorvard and Iamerth went to gaze down on the southern half of the world, Ialven would open his gigantic chambers of ice. Iambren's winds would liberally scoop out the cold and the snow stored therein to whiten the fields and groves of Hjorvard, and give repose to the Earth's womb and to Iathana, guardian of its fertility and older sister of sweet Ialini, Mistress of the Green World.

Ialven's own amusement was to fashion innumerable adornments from ice floes and blocks of snow, layering one upon another and subjecting their perpetual windings to the most intricate of rules. It was from him, the story goes, that people in ancient times had learned methods of calculation more complex than simple addition and subtraction, for time was when Ialven would often go a-roving, especially in the summer months when his storehouses were secured by an immense lock of wizardry.

Those days were gone; Ialven had lost interest in the world around him. He was engrossed now in the abstract realm of numbers. He cared no more for humans or their affairs, and seemed to have forgotten how hard he used to work to find an application for a rule or law he had discovered. Numbers, which owe allegiance to no gods, Young or Old, had in the end imprisoned him, and now laws of numeration embodied in fragments of gelid water—laws so complex the Mage had yet to be born who could comprehend them—went plodding through the endless icy wastes of the Outer Sea.

All this Hagen told to Brann as they journeyed on, but Shrunkenhand listened with air of sneering doubt. It all smacked too much of fairytales to him. The thane had expected his tale to be greeted with rapt attention and open-mouthed surprise and was somewhat irked by the sardonic reception, though he tried not to admit as much to himself.

"Folk have no business meddling with such things," Brann said at last, with a dismissive gesture. "Gods, Mages, miracles—to my mind, there's your life and your human affairs that you're born to discharge. We needs must drive away the unliving, to be sure, and for that a man wants a good head on his shoulders and some knowledge of his foe. But 'tis bootless to get caught up in the affairs of those nomen. That only ends in you losing your own self."

Hagen elected not to dispute this. Just because his companion knew the entrance to the Forestway and would perhaps again be needed soon, that did not earn him the right to an attentive hearing, so he let him chatter on. He, Hagen, had enough of a job to do—he and his Teacher both. A great and prodigious one, and a part of that job was to send back to sleep the Hound that had woken up so untimely.

Hagen instinctively laid his hand on the flask of poppy juice Old Hropt had given him.

"Where's the way in?" Brann's question steered the conversation away from the uncomfortable topic. "The mountains will close in soon, sithee, and still no gates to be seen."

"We've yet to clear the first picket manned by the sentinels of the Black Highway," Hagen said gruffly. "So keep your voice down. Their hearing's sharper than any dog's."

Shrunkenhand screwed up his eyes. "You're going to fight 'em?"

"You don't fight such as they," Hagen replied, gruff as before and very little inclined to conversation. Those giants could appear at any moment, and here was Brann prattling on about nothing!

"Fear not." Shrunkenhand gave a sudden grin, as if reading the thane's thoughts. "There's no one for a league around. Beyond that, alas, I cannot tell, but when 'tis closer I am never wrong. I've had several occasions to test it."

This was another unpleasant surprise.

"How do you do that?"

"How does a fish sense the rain? Heed the Forest. It has that and more to teach."

Brann urged his horse forward, and a mystified Hagen followed after.

For a league, or maybe a league and a half, they did, indeed, travel unmolested. The valley became a narrow ravine drowned in darkness, and the path angled downward, beginning the descent to the Threshold of Niflhel. Yet it was Hagen who first noticed the giant, having conjured a Hearing Charm to detect, in the distance, the heavy tread of a minion of Iaeth, morose Lord of the Underworld. Iaeth's expansive domains were home to the souls of cowards, faithless husbands and wives, seducers male and female, and others who after death were found unworthy to ascend to any of the glittering Upperworlds—to the Eye of Iamerth.

"When the Young Gods divided up the world," Hedin had told his apprentice, "they were long in deciding which of them would take ownership of the erstwhile kingdom of Hel. None wanted to rule there, although whoever was lord of those dead souls would be mighty indeed. First they thought to cast lots, then they decided to watch over Hel in turns, with only Iamerth the Fair abstaining from this arrangement, but that only worsened the disorder there.

"Then Iaeth volunteered. He had grown weary of the Young Gods' tumultuous life and sought some secluded place for thought and abstract reflection. So, to him was entrusted the surveillance of Hel. From that time he has been known as the Pensive God, although what he can be racking his brains over all these millennia escapes me entirely."

The giant could not have been an inch under twelve feet tall.

"Now, there's an ugly sight!" Brann observed, eyeing it as it trudged along the path. "I've never seen so much iron as he's carrying. And what d'you suppose they've got to defend themselves against out here?"

Hagen shrugged and again motioned to Shrunkenhand to be quiet. The thane had a tight grip on his arbalest, although he knew there would be no sense in using it. The only thing that could kill a Warrior of the Black Highway was a particular weapon such as was once crafted by the Ancients for their own unknowable purposes. Hedin had spent more than one decade puzzling over their secret and was close to success. Meanwhile, the sword at his apprentice's side was excellent for dispatching humans and wizards, Darkling Riders and gloomy kheddees, for striking trolls and dragons dead on the spot, and capable even of divesting a Mage of his bodily shell. It was, however, as useless here as a blade forged not by the spectral hammers of the Ancient Southern Gods but by a tipsy blacksmith-in-training in some free-peasant smithy.

The giant was ironclad to a fare-thee-well—a horned helmet draped with a scaly camail that hung down to the middle of its chest, a closed cuirass with sleeves and skirts of mail, chausses for its shins and vambraces for its forearms, and on its feet articulated iron sabatons of improbable size. In one hand, it held an iron club, and in the other the kind of small triangular shield swordsmen use in single combat.

It was breathing hard, pulling the air in with nostrils so broad they seemed to be turned inside out. Something had disturbed it; it was making lowing sounds and swiveling its head from side to side.

Brann calmly watched this horror approach with his customary thoughtful squint. Hagen, too, did not take his eyes off it as he drew from the folds of his clothing a short tube and a tiny pouch filled with a caustic black powder. Shrunkenhand looked on, intrigued.

A sudden change in the wind's direction put them upwind of the Sentinel of the Black Highway, which gave a menacing roar, raised its club and dashed toward the rocks that were their hiding place.

"It's scented us," Brann commented with supreme composure. "What shall we do now?"

"You'll see," Hagen murmured, raising to his lips the tube charged with the black powder.

The tramp of feet and the snorting was loud now, and very close. Two goodly hands in mail gauntlets grasped the edge of the rock then, above the granite spur, appeared a keg-sized helmet. Even through the darkness of the narrow visor slit, the giant's eyes could be seen, glinting red.

Hagen leaned forward, placed the tube as close to the visor as he could and blew hard.

With a roar that easily rivaled one of Garm's growls, the giant began to whirl about, dropping its shield and club to clutch at the air with its great paws. Then it started tearing its helmet off.

"That'll keep it busy for a good long while," was all Hagen said.

They worked around the wailing, howling giant and went on their way.

"Handily done," Shrunkenhand said approvingly. "Killing to no purpose is not to my taste."

Hagen cut him short. "Let's wait and see what comes next."

What came next was a cavern, which began when the sides of the ravine drew together until they almost met, making a tall black arch that curved overhead. Beyond was a wall of impenetrable darkness.

"How are we going to see our way when we brought no firebrands?" Brann wondered.

"Enough of your belly-aching. We'll find something better."

The horses balked at the cavern entrance. Hedin's apprentice raised his right hand and whispered a few words, and a shining bluish sphere appeared on his palm. It was one of the first charms Mages taught their wards.

"I've heard talk of the Threshold of Niflhel," Brann remarked in a low tone. "'Tis a cavern like any other, though a big one, to be sure."

"Death saturates everything here. Surely you can feel that?" Hagen hissed through his teeth.

He was already being assailed by a nightmarish torrent of insane visions. Beyond his lightsphere's narrow reach, the eyes of thousands upon thousands of creatures, both disembodied and corporeal, were fixed on them with a hatred greater than words could express, every one seeking the oblivion that would come from drinking deep of their hot blood. How could Shrunkenhand not feel it? Hagen was having to exert every ounce of strength to hold at bay a spasm of fear. He felt as if he were plunging headlong into his own grave.

The horses' hoofbeats no longer echoed around them, the cavern walls being too far away for the sounds to reach. Scarlet pinpoints of eyes flared in the gloom ahead, and unseen wings rustled above. Whatever flew on those wings was almost grazing their heads.

Shrunkenhand nodded toward the gleaming crimson eyes.

"You're in fear of them, young thane. Square yourself, now! You're a man, and humans are always stronger than the unliving. They reach us through our fears and uncertainty."

"You've never piqued the interest of the Devourer of Souls," Hagen retorted hoarsely.

"A singular member of the unliving it is," Brann said stiffly, "created especially to do what it does—and may that creator be accursed! But this place...this place is but their birthright."

"Whose birthright? What nonsense is this?" Hagen, drenched in cold sweat, spoke with difficulty. "I understand none of this."

Brann was eager to explain. "This is the homeland of the unliving. Gnipahellir and this cavern are their rightful domains. What surprise, then, there are so many here? And one more thing I'll tell you. Those of the unliving that feast on human flesh do not dwell hereabouts. There's naught for them here."

He was cut short by a fearsome, roaring din. The ground shook and shuddered, and the thane's horse gave a pitiful whinny and went down. Brann hurriedly dismounted before the same happened to him. Close by there was a collapsing, a splitting, a crumbling, and a hot, stinking wind blew in their faces. Garm was wide awake still, and in good voice.

The noise subsided, and they continued in silence.

It was gradually growing lighter; before long, they could even make out the ground beneath their horses' hooves. Hagen extinguished his sphere—too soon, as it turned out, for something instantly dropped onto him from above. Claws hooked into his armor and sharp teeth tried to bite through his hauberk's dense steel weave. Brann came to the rescue by slicing the thing in two with his little double-bladed hatchet.

The wraiths, too, were closing in; the thane could not see them, but he felt their clammy touch, and his brain clouded over in response. He hurriedly rekindled his wizardfire, adding some Protective Charms for good measure.

"Now are you persuaded?" he gasped at Shrunkenhand.

"Of what? That winged bloodsucker attacked you, not me."

"Mere chance!"

"No," Brann sighed. "And you'll come to believe that yourself soon enough."

They were journeying blind now, descending deeper and deeper underground; and before long they caught up with one of Iargohor's processions, this one traveling without its Conveyor. The pale, glowing figures trailed along the only road left to them—to the Hound's lair and beyond, through the Great Gates to the abyss of Hel.

Leaving those straggling ghostly files behind, they came at last to a place where it was almost as light as a summer's eve in Hjorvard. Even larger caves seemed to lie ahead, and they gave off a terrible stench.

"We're close to the Hound's lair," Hagen murmured.

The wraiths and other creatures, winged and earthbound, still followed hard on their heels. Some loathsome, hissing thing stirred on the ground. Finally, their horses became completely unmanageable; they jibed and refused to take another step forward.

"Hold this," Hagen said, thrusting his reins at Brann.

"Where are you going?"

"The lair's behind those rocks. I need to get up close. Must I explain everything?"

Shrunkenhand did not reply.

Hagen scrambled through the palisade of jutting rocks, accompanied by a swarm of hideous creatures, the living remnants of Garm's horrible feasts. Writhing, scuttling, hobbling, putrid, they maintained a wary distance but kept pace with him, and thousands of greedy eyes held him fast. He must perforce set up a magical defense; but the charms drew down his strength, and each stride was shorter than the last. His sword was unsheathed and ready, even though it could do nothing for him now. All his hopes rested on the little flask in his left hand.

He had almost reached the ridge of rock when the Hound lifted its head and gave a peevish growl, sensing the approach of a stranger. Topping the jagged line of granite fangs was a slate-black muzzle, white eyes, apparently blind, and a gaping maw the color of blood and fire. Garm had fared well on the corpseflesh he was fed here in Near Niflhel—the Hound was as big as any edifice ever built in Haithabu or Birka.

The white eyes without pupils stared at the motionless thane; then came a growl that pitched Hagen to the ground. Choking in fury, the Hound heaved against its chain with all its might. Living! This one was living!

All the vile creatures that had been dogging the thane's steps hurled themselves on him at once, sinking their teeth into his armor; and revulsion overcame fear. He leapt to his feet, sweeping his sword in a broad arc, and the rocks were spattered with the black blood of any that were not fast enough getting out of the way. His lightsphere had long ago gone out, and his protective barriers were weakening—for Hagen, after all, was not a real Mage but just an apprentice, albeit a very diligent one.

The Hound wheezed, strangled by its chain. Those white, demented, seemingly sightless eyes never left him, not even for an instant. Hagen could now see the whole huge brown body, the gigantic claws on the monstrous paws, and the pile of bodies scattered around the bloody pit that was its jaws. There was a veritable mountain of mutilated corpses.

He had only a hundred paces still to cover, and cover them he did, though it drained him entirely. Claws and fangs stabbed at him, and he thrashed about him with his sword. The Hound's chain was as taut as a drawn string; Hagen could see long black fissures serpentining across the wall that held the chain rings—the restraints seemed about to give way at any moment.

At last he was there and with a fling of his arm sprayed the flask's contents onto the cold, torn human remains that lay under Garm's snout. The Hound bayed rabidly in his face, and the last thing the thane remembered was a horrific fetor that dimmed his mind.

He collapsed, spreadeagled and strengthless, onto the pile of cadavers.

HEDIN

THE MILKY MIST THAT HAD SWIRLED THICK AROUND ME A FEW INSTANTS BEFORE SLOWLY dissipated. The Charm of Transference had done its work, and I was near the Castle of All the Ancients. Near enough, anyway, since that Charm never brought me to precisely the right place but only into the approximate vicinity. Sigrlinn had always been better at it than I, who had never managed to achieve a precise transference.

The pillar and the castle that crowned it looked now like a Mage's dark stave with witchfire burning atop. By an odd conceit of its builders, the Mages of the First Generation, the castle could take on any color, and that day it shone like a lit candle set by unknown spellcraft inside a diamond.

The air of the Middle Sky grew dense about my feet, forming a solid but invisible path that led all the way to the castle's filigreed parapets. How long it had been since my last visit! Outwardly nothing had changed, but what awaited me within?

I strode to the balustrade that encircled the castle. I had failed in my attempts to speak with Sigrlinn using the Band of Erith because she was again away from Jibulistan. There, too, she had me baffled—why was she treating the Band like a toy, leaving it in her apartments instead of keeping it with her always? Any Mage could speak with any other at will, as long as they both had the Band within reach. I was never without mine.

If conversation with a Generation member proved impossible using the Band, the only other way was to come in person to a special hall in the Castle of All the Ancients.

I passed by the Council doors. It was at this very railing I had stood on the day of Hagen's entrance into this world in the godforsaken and human-scorned village of Jol. I had crossed this very threshold on my way to the

Sphere of Lots.

Something drew me into the Council Hall. I had no business there—all I wanted was to speak with Sigrlinn, but there I was, pushing open the door.

The hall was empty—as it should be—except for one, who sat in his rightful place, calmly watching me with cold eyes: Merlin the Great, Leader of the Council of the Generation.

I almost recoiled. What was he doing there? But...

"Hedin, Sage of Darkness, greets the Leader of the Council and bows before him." Someone inside me, a cordial someone, had delivered the phrase demanded by protocol.

Merlin rose, tall and lean as any stork, and inclined his head in a crisp nod of his own.

"Merlin accepts the greeting of the Sage of Darkness," he replied, meeting my tone and meticulously following the canons of the Ancients.

I own I was only playing for time. Had he been expecting me? Or was he in the Council Hall by chance? He had previously preferred his beloved Avalon over the Castle of All the Ancients, but much could have changed during the thousand years of my exile.

Merlin waited, his eyes still on me and his face beginning to betray the slight irritation I knew so well, which came when he was distracted by trifles from matters of importance.

His frigid voice broke the lengthening silence. "You have business with me? Speak, then!"

"Yes, I have business with you." I had suddenly decided on a daring offensive. "I have heard rumors that one of the cornerstone laws of the Ancients has been changed, and that the Council is now entitled to punish a Mage with Unbeing. Is that true? And if it is, why must I hear of it in passing, and not at a Gathering of the Generation, as is proper?"

"Well, well!" Merlin smiled, not at all surprised—at least, not outwardly—by either my words or the knowledge I had gleaned. "I see banishment has agreed with you, Sage of Darkness. You have become a devotee of the law, excelling even the Leader of the Council himself in this. You, who used to set those laws at naught and broke all you could."

"That is no answer," I persisted. Something prevented me from meeting Merlin's eyes; I began to raise my head then suddenly lowered it again, as if in fear, and continued looking at the floor. "It is my right, as a member of the Generation, to ask you such questions."

Merlin nodded. "Indeed, it is. And here is my answer to you, Sage of

Darkness. I will say you neither yes nor no, because, although you may demand a reply, nowhere is it written that I am obliged to answer you. I hold that you have not yet earned that right."

It was an outright affront, a challenge, a slap in the face. Call it what you will, the essence of it remained the same.

"Is it a duel you want, Merlin?" I asked, hastily surrounding my thoughts with all conceivable barriers, although I had not yet felt the Leader of the Council attempting entry into my mind.

"A duel? " Merlin stretched his thin lips into the faint semblance of a smile. "Challenge me, then, if you wish."

This convinced me yet again that I still grasped nothing of his intentions. Had he insulted me deliberately, in full confidence of besting me in honest single combat, stripping me of my apprentice and sending me into exile again? Or did he really believe I had not yet fully expiated my prior transgressions?

Be all as it may, the hour of my encounter with Merlin had not yet struck. That I knew, and so only shrugged as my first reply.

"No," I said then, trying to make my voice a model of impassivity. "Even if you were to call me out, Merlin, I would not give you the satisfaction—if satisfaction it be."

I closed the Council Hall door behind me.

They all seem to be in agreement here, I thought as I made my lonely way along the balustraded walk. *In agreement and trying to confound me. What can Merlin want? He never does anything without good reason. On the other hand, we're all so accustomed to seeing some deep meaning in his every word and deed, he could now be making use of our superstitious circumspection. Maybe his intent is to set me at odds with myself, causing me to err and act foolishly, and then to extract from the Council a sentence of death or of eternal imprisonment, such as was meted out to Rakoth.*

Enough of Merlin, though—he had not been my purpose in coming here.

Soon I came upon another wide, intricately carved and encrusted door, this one on my right, and I pushed it open. It gave onto a whorl of stairs that led upward to the castle library and the Mages' personal apartments. Each of us had a suite of rooms in the Castle of All the Ancients, one of the secrets of which was that it could always accommodate all comers.

My chambers had long been vacant. Once there had been no question of entering a Mage's room in the owner's absence, so none of us had secured our doors with locks either real or magical, but perhaps that, too, had changed. Time was when our rooms in the Castle of All the Ancients were the best hiding place of all; and since serving my apprenticeship with Old Hropt, I had kept there something that might serve me well now, with a new Mage War in the making, though it would be useless if that war turned universal and shifted to the Astral Plane.

The spiral staircase brought me to a wide corridor with windows looking out on the castle's inner courtyard. I did not have to think where I was going; my legs remembered the route, even though I had not passed that way for more than a thousand years.

I turned the silver door-handle, which moved gently under my hand; and narrowing my eyes without meaning to, I stepped in, greeted by the faint but familiar—painfully familiar—odor of my home, which no amount of airing would ever remove.

Everything was the same. By the window that took up an entire wall, three armchairs crafted of ancient tree stumps, a gift from the woodland trolls, made in the days before they ran wild; an oval table in the middle of the room; in the corner, a stand holding swords and spears, arbalests and helmets, the blades giving off a matte gleam as if cleaned only yesterday; the same books on the shelves, penned or collected by me. All was as it had been, and it did not even seem that much time had elapsed, for there was no dust anywhere.

But was everything really safe and sound? I had thrust completely from my mind the memory of some possessions I had left there once. When young, you often do something not knowing why, out of sheer curiosity, and later your creations unexpectedly take on entirely unanticipated qualities.

In those days, though, I had had help from Rakoth and Merlin, and Sigrlinn, too, had given me aid. Afterward, those artifacts had long left my mind—I remembered them only during Rakoth's First Rebellion, when it was already too late. With them, the One Laid Low might have been able to hold out a little longer, yet they could not have saved him. Later, when I began to pursue my own designs, I had need of them only in the latter stages, for earlier I could not have risked drawing attention to myself in that way.

But I never did bring them into play, for Sigrlinn had called me out—the rest of the story is known to all. When my exile was over, I was all taken up with Hagen and was quite certain my handicrafts would not have escaped the notice of the Council, and of Merlin above all. I could not imagine they would have survived intact all this time.

My mind had gone on a new tack over those ten long centuries, one that put me in no particular need of them. So, I had chosen to show no interest in whether they still lay where I had left them, for fear of rousing untimely suspicion.

I went over to my desk, which was the massive trunk of a gigantic sequoia cleft in two. It looked as though I had left my work but a few minutes before and had now returned—a scatter of instruments, burners, utensils, a few alchemical treatises. I silently counted to ten and opened one of the drawers.

And was not one whit surprised to find it empty—yet another of the Laws of the Ancients had fallen. However, I was, ridiculous as this may sound, already becoming accustomed to it.

So, Merlin had been cleaning house here, and perhaps he was not the only one to have been rummaging in my rooms. But, no, he would not entrust my legacy to anyone else, as he knew well enough what danger might lurk in the most ostensibly innocent magical playthings. Merlin the Great deserved the name, because he was never, ever wrong about when to delegate a task and when to set to it himself.

The Laws of the Ancients were toppling one after another. I had been taught that those Laws provided the undergirding for the World Balance— violate them and havoc would surely follow. That was not so, after all. Or maybe the Young Gods had changed the limitations placed upon us, and only Merlin was as yet privy to this.

But wait, I told myself, the inviolability of our private quarters in the Castle of All the Ancients is not a law but only a custom unswervingly observed over the millennia. An Astral Messenger may be sent to induce the Lords of the Hallowed Land to change the world, but in order to change a custom reputed to be invulnerable, one has to change oneself. Merlin has changed. What is the Generation to him now? What are its unwritten laws and traditions? Just so much empty noise? Or is he piously convinced that he has been acting for the greater good?

I really had no idea.

But I could not tarry there long. Since the room no longer held anything I needed, I left it—backing out, for some reason—and pulled the door closed. My apartments could wait until I had more time to spare.

I proceeded down the corridor to Sigrlinn's apartments. Before I went to the Hall of Words to call her forth, etiquette required me to assure myself she was not in the castle.

Her door seemed woven of the finest petrified lace, of crystallized spider webs. Instinctively afraid of harming such magnificence, I knocked loudly on the doorjamb with the hilt of my sword, Rakoth's gift, and—wonder of wonders—the door opened, with a soft, melodious peal of invisible bells. The mistress was in residence.

My heart began quivering in agitation as I entered, but that was a disgrace to me and I would have no truck with it. We were to speak of serious matters, and to combine that with sweet—or even bitter—memories I knew for certain would be the greatest of follies.

I entered a small suite of rooms all decorated in blue and green. The floor was covered by a soft carpet the color of sea-grass. A convolvulus wound across the walls, almost completely covering the stonework, and every available spot was filled with flowers and plants, small palms and oddly dwarfed pines. Sigrlinn sat by the window, wearing a dark-green gown. A tropical vine wreathed her feet, and several books lay nearby. She raised imperious eyes to me.

"Greetings, Sage of Darkness."

"You're the second today to call me by that long-forgotten name, but no matter. All health to you."

"Really? Who anticipated me?"

"You can't guess? Merlin, of course."

She frowned for a second and placed a finger against her temple, as if in deep thought.

"But I'm sure you aren't here without good reason."

We were playing a strange game. We both knew that, and each knew the other knew it; but still we persisted, keeping our own thoughts closed up tight. I could most likely have broken through her defenses but could see no purpose in doing so yet. If Sigrlinn had really been warning me on that previous occasion, trying to caution me and thereby to save me, I should at least attempt to keep her neutral.

"No. But I did want to see you," I replied. And that was the truest truth. "To discuss some business with you, and just because—"

Her eyebrows arched. "Business? This is the first I'm hearing of business between us."

"There you err. Many years ago, you warned me that Merlin had acquired new rights and powers. You were afraid I might rouse his ire and that he would set in train an unknowable mechanism of destruction. So we now have a common cause, that being to keep me alive, although I still don't know what moved you to save him who was once your enemy."

"I'm under no obligation to justify my actions to you!" she replied, a little more tartly than was necessary for the game we were playing. "And if you are so bent on knowing then consider it a whim of mine." She looked defiantly into my eyes.

I seized the advantage. "Don't stop at that. What happened next?"

"Nothing happened." She shrugged, but again she was trying to feign indifference and failing, which was strange to me. Sigrlinn could masquerade as anything she wished, and only by dint of penetrating several layers of false thoughts could one understand what was really in her mind. "A not particularly astute Mage with a boy for an apprentice chose once more to challenge an invincible foe. My patience was strained to the breaking point."

She fell eloquently silent.

"What does that mean?"

"You must find your own way out, Hedin." She turned away. "I told you then, on the road, and now I can only repeat myself—I have no desire to be banished on your account." Her voice had become dry. "And if you dare rake up the past, I swear by the Moonbeast I'll call you out in a trice!"

I saw then what I had never seen in my life—Sigrlinn's lips were trembling.

"Forcefully spoken," I said slowly. "Very well. I'll find my own way out, but tell me this—out of what? And, by the way, why is your Band of Erith always where it ought not to be instead of under your hand?"

"To reduce the distractions," she said curtly.

I shook my head. "You conduct yourself no better than a petulant lady-in-waiting at some mortal court. Answer my one question, and I shall not disturb you again."

"I won't," Sigrlinn said coldly, rising from her chair. "Not for the sake of the future, nor even for the sake of the past. I won't answer, Hedin!"

"Then you'd best dispatch this body of mine with your own hands," I said. "Because if I don't find my way out, no one will envy my end. I wonder what you shall do when I am no more."

"You've been living with the conviction that I existed for you and you alone?" She gave a frosty laugh. "My affairs and my apprentices are as much mine now as they have ever been. Do not flatter yourself that anything has changed, Sage of Darkness."

A chill ran down my spine. I realized she was speaking the pristine truth.

"Very well. I shall shift as best I can," I replied. "But at least tell me how matters stand in your Sheltered Kingdom. Do you not tire of it?"

"How matters stand?" She screwed up her eyes. "So now at last we have the reason for this entire conversation."

"The reason?" I spared no effort to make my surprise sound natural.

"One of the temples has been attacked," she said airily. "That comes as news to you? Or does your apprentice not warn his Teacher of his brazen plans to assail a sanctuary of the sun?"

"What makes you so certain it was my apprentice?"

"Almighty Creator! Hedin, you try my patience." She leapt to her feet, her face flushed with wrath. "You thought he would not be recognized?"

"Recognized?" I was astonished in good earnest now.

Sigrlinn sighed.

"I do not understand why I am still talking to you. I should have set you out of doors at once."

"But you didn't," I remarked. "What rumors are abroad concerning my apprentice?"

Sigrlinn was beside herself again. "I swear by the Great Lords of Night, Hedin—you have grown intolerable! Your apprentice robs the Temple of Iamerth in my Sheltered Kingdom and here am I, deep in long, respectful dialogue with you. I don't know what possessed you to thrust your head into the lion's mouth, as mortals say. Merlin is furious, think on that. Though I cannot know what the Council of the Generation will decide, there is nothing I can do. Ialini's mercy is great, to be sure, but…"

"Ialini, you say? So all this grandeur is her doing?" I nodded at the forest flourishing in the corners of the room.

"That is none of your concern!" she snapped. "I will not be questioned like this. You had best go. I did too much for you as it is, on the day the temple was attacked."

I took my leave with a silent bow.

Back in my own quarters, I all but flung myself into one of the trolls' armchairs and tried to bring some order to the welter in my mind. That had been an odd conversation, indeed, but what did it mean? What had Sigrlinn been trying to achieve? And what was actually known about our raid on the temple in Erivag?

One thing at a time. Sigrlinn had said that my apprentice, not I, had led the attack, and had been recognized. Was that possible? Entirely possible—Birka and Haithabu always abounded in spies of all stripes. Hagen might have been observed with me there—or even earlier. But an agent could only have known my apprentice by sight if he already knew me, so how would Hagen have been seen among those attacking the temple while I was not? That could not be. Either both of us were seen and recognized or neither of us was.

Assuming someone in the temple knew Hagen by sight but not me—or did not notice I was there—then Merlin and Sigrlinn, or even the Young Gods themselves, had to be employing incompetent informants; and I knew that such was not the case.

At the end of it, during our skirmish at the gates and later, I had stayed in plain sight all the while, even though I used no magic, which meant the Council could not officially accuse me of misconduct. Who could have seen Hagen but not me?

One possibility was that I had, indeed, been spotted, but since I had conjured not a single charm, they had decided to call it an unauthorized action on my apprentice's part, using that as another—and maybe the last—warning to me. No. Now I was just hiding behind idle fantasies—and for what?

But wait, I thought next, *what if neither Hagen nor I was seen? Why, then, would Sigrlinn be toying with me? And what of those insinuations about the Council of the Generation? And why have I not heard a word on that from Merlin?*

His position as Leader of the Council gave him particular ties to Iamerth, whose temple we had treated so very disrespectfully. Merlin could, of course, know all but still be keeping his silence if that sat well with his own unfathomable plans. And what did Sigrlinn mean by the last thing she said, that she had already done too much for me that day? Had her zophar really been a sign to me, a sign I had failed to understand? And now she could not— or did not wish to—speak of it openly in the castle?

Maybe she had been ordered to dispose of me and had carried out those orders in so perfunctory a manner as to ensure I would come out of it unharmed. That would explain why all the might of the Halting Winds, even in concert with those subterranean vortices, had been insufficient to overwhelm my apprentice.

If all that were true, then Sigrlinn had been intimating to me I was under constant surveillance, and of a kind that, with all my skill, I could neither avoid nor even sense. Well, there were ways of verifying such things.

The dismal thought then occurred to me that the question I had been wrestling with—who had set in train that magical attack at the Lesser Temple in Erivag that almost took the lives of my apprentice and his entire detachment—still remained unanswered. I had not been given a single direct indication, only oblique hints. So, then, I would continue the search but would continue it elsewhere.

There were times when, willy-nilly, I had to thank Merlin and my judges for condemning me to so long an exile. It had given me time to return to the roots of all, to make my own pathways that, if they had ever been known, had long ago been discarded as superfluous.

Our world is not a single entity. It consists of a multitude of lands with gates between them that only Mages can open. Those other lands are inhabited by beings far more powerful than we in one respect or another, and one appropriately skilled can make use of their unique capacities. It was my intent to go to the Lowerworlds, and to a strange race that lives there whose special talent lies in the sensing of charms. They are appallingly punctilious, and maintain the most detailed annals—to what purpose, I have never understood. I had discovered those beings before my exile, after which the Gates of the Worlds were long closed against me.

Now, I could again exercise the rights that had been restored to me, and my first task must be to determine exactly what had been brought to bear against us that day in the temple.

I left the Castle of All the Ancients with the aim of putting as many leagues as possible between it and me. At length I found myself in a narrow ravine amid fanciful mountains, none of which was of any interest to me. After a pause to allow the whirling in my head occasioned by the lengthy Transference to ease, I began by degrees to open the door to the secret way. Soon I was looking into an undulating cloud, a haze of dim rainbow hues. I swaddled myself in my cloak, checked the free movement of my sword in its sheath and stepped forward. The Gates of the Worlds swallowed me up.

Strange and savage landscapes flickered before my eyes—it was as if I were being carried along on the powerful current of a swift-flowing river. I could, of course, have pried apart the layers of the Real and slipped between them as I had in the Castle of All the Ancients on the day of Hagen's birth; but then it would have been child's play for any Mage to follow my trail. The opening of the Gates could have been discovered, too, but after my rapid Transference to the very ends of the Earth that would have tasked even Merlin.

When the torrent that carried me finally loosened its close embrace, I stood on the brink of a brown cliff, a bottomless scarp that fell away from my feet; far, far below, the brown wall disappeared into a surging, bluish mist. From crevices in the rock grew low trees with very thick trunks and branches, gnarled like crawling snakes, and long, spike-tipped brown leaves. In the depths of their foliage were large, unblinking violet eyes, watching me.

A second before the swift, scaly body lunged, clicking jaws that bristled with teeth, I said a Charm of Deflection, and with a wild scream the creature tumbled into the chasm. I rubbed my temples. Everything that lived in this world was skilled in wizardry. A mere mortal, mighty warrior though he be, or an insufficiently expert wizard would meet a doleful fate here.

I wandered long on tangled paths through that brown mountain forest, aiding myself with Protective and Way-Opening charms. Finally, the thickets ended, the last toothed serpent made a snapping strike at my shoulder and, squirming, toppled to the ground, its insides seared away. A broad valley opened up to me, wreathed in fog with the outlines of spired buildings looming vaguely through it.

I had never had the time I needed to study that world; all I knew were the paths to certain power centers, and one of those lay before me.

I descended a gentle slope, plunging into the dank billows of fog. Something resembling a roadway appeared beneath my feet, and I walked along an endlessly changing path that was never the same two times together. An alien power drew me on, and I strode toward it as toward a beacon no one else could see.

The paved way ended; before me was an opening densely packed with impenetrable gloom. I stopped, unsheathed Rakoth's sword and slashed at the screen, narrowing my eyes as I did so. A light so bright as to border on intolerable spurted at me, and with one hand protecting my sight, I walked into it.

In huge transparent spheres hanging from the ceiling glowed condensed Ether, the World Substance that preserved within itself the traces of anything ever done by every living thing. The master of this strange place could read, by the slightest changes in those glowing vessels, the spells we spoke in another world. I had long sought the way to this being, had patiently tried to understand its language and to find out what it might need so I could later strike a bargain with it.

However, while it helped me with a will, it refused any payment. All it would say, and mysteriously at that, was that the day would come when it would need my help in earnest, and each time it had me swear an inviolable Mage-oath, binding myself by the blood of All the Ancients that I would then do whatever it wished that was within my power. I did not like that. I apprehended some artifice in it, but I had no choice.

In the corner, beyond the merciless circle of light, something stirred. A long shadow, angular and malformed, moved toward me. I felt the cold touch of another's thoughts and, as I always did, shuddered inwardly. I could never accustom myself to that.

I briefly stated my business, which was to determine who had been doing wizardry—and how—in such and such an area of the World of Magic, which was what those hereabouts called Greater Hjorvard.

— *First reaffirm your oath,* a dry, icy, inhuman voice grated in my mind.

I had to raise my right hand and recite the words it needed to hear. Only then did the shadow move to the glittering repositories of the Ether and stand before them.

May the Moonbeast rend me if I understood how they did it—all my efforts to puzzle out the wizardry they used had come to naught. I did not belong to their world, and could only be glad the Creator had rendered them forever incapable of opening the Gates of the Worlds.

Dark veins suddenly began to show in one of the spheres before which the writhing shadow stood, branching and forking into an intricately intertwined web. I sensed the pulsation of the massive force that enshrouded the sphere, and took an involuntary step backward, because the being was working its ways with a potency that exceeded all of Merlin's capacities many times over. How had the masters of this land acquired the art of questioning the Ether and understanding its replies? Too many lacunae were gradually being revealed in what we had been taught, for all that we had sallied forth from the Castle of All the Ancients convinced we were in possession of all the world's secrets.

The creature's vigil at the repository went on and on. The black web surrounded by a white glow changed, now growing until it filled almost the whole sphere then all but disappearing. I waited patiently. The master never erred—I had had numerous occasions to test the truth of its words—but this time it was clearly procrastinating.

After a period of time nearly twice as long as usual, the sphere suddenly flared so bright I hardly had time to throw up a hand against it. The shadow started back, as if in fear, and slithered toward me.

— *I release you from the oath you swore today,* it grated. *I can say nothing. All has been most artfully concealed. He who wrought the wizardry had knowledge of us. I do not even know how many conjured the charm. They took care to confound it all, so that none of us living in this place could comprehend it. They had knowledge of us, and of how to conceal their sorcery from us. Therefore I release you from your oath on this occasion.*

I admit being once again bewildered, and astonished beyond all measure. Nothing like it had ever happened to me before. Still, I had no intention of giving up so easily.

— *I will swear you another oath,* I said, *if you will tell me true all that you felt, at least, and if you will confide to me your thoughts on who could hide the end-points of his spell in such a way, and on the knowledge he must have had of you to succeed.*

— *Very well,* replied the voice in my mind. *Repeat the oath and I shall tell you what you ask.*

After I had done that, it continued.

— *First, the practitioner of that wizardry must know that we exist and that we maintain annals of the sorcery performed in the World of Magic. Second, he must have power over the Near Ether, in order to distort beyond recognition the traces of the charms conjured in it. And third, he must be able to create Mage-images, to make it appear to us that the wizardry is the work not of one but of a countless multitude.*

Only an inconsequential portion of their strength was thrown against those whom they wished to destroy, with far more being expended on hiding the end-points. That was likely why the one conjuring the charm did not achieve his purpose, having too much to attend to at one time. And I shall say also that this was not the doing of those whom you call gods. We are well able to feel them. They almost never hide anything, and their deeds are as different from the deeds of your kind as the attack of a fanged beast differs from the bite of an insect. Such things are not pleasant to your ear, but they are the truth.

I jumped in briskly.

— *So this was one of my kind?* That was better than naught. At least then I need not fear direct interference from one of the Young Gods.

— *I cannot be certain,* the voice scraped. *I cannot. The defense was so unusual. None of your kind has ever yet achieved the like, for it requires other powers. You are not able to roil the Ether.*

I had to acknowledge to myself the truth of that.

Though our conversation continued, it did not give me even one tangible clue. The master was unable even to say if one of "my kind"—meaning of our Generation—had entered their world. But at least I had, as yet, been the only one to open the Gates of the Worlds.

I brought to mind the images of all the Mages of the Generation in succession, realizing immediately that Merlin alone was capable of turning the Ether to his own ends. Even so, I needed at least indirect evidence that it was so.

— *I have already said that I detect none of your kind.* The disgruntled creature would settle on none, including the Leader of the Council of the Generation. The circle had closed.

— *But that is of no import,* it said at the last. *Since I could not answer, go seek the solution from Great Orlangur or his brother, Demogorgon. They can tell what others cannot.*

It might as well have advised me to take my mystery to the Creator.

The Gates of the Worlds opened, the familiar rainbow radiance surrounded me, and a few moments later I stood again on the solid ground of the world that was home to Hagen and me. I returned having learned almost nothing.

Had I crossed paths with something completely new? No. That simply could not be.

Good enough. Though morning may not be wiser than evening, as Hropt was wont to say, thinking is best done with a clear head—and, I might add, even better done among one's own folk.

A Charm of Transference hurled me all the way to Birka. From there I would have to sail to Hedinseigh, the island being too small to guarantee a safe landing rather than a plunge into icy water a league or more from the shore, and there was nothing at all enticing about that. I preferred the deck of an agile dragon-ship.

The jarl who offered me passage for a small sum was on his way to Himinvagar. When I told him that one of the Sheltered Kingdom's islands had been taken by seaborne marauders, he was at first speechless then wanted to know about the gallant in command. I tried to satisfy his curiosity while at the same time turning to, as any good shiphand should. I had no doubt whatsoever that within the month my apprentice would be well supplied with a fine batch of new recruits.

The still-unseen Hedinseigh announced itself with a column of smoke rising high above the island. The rowers hastily armed themselves. The jarl first balked at putting in to the harbor, and I had to almost double the fee for my passage. Our eyes told us to expect the very worst, but inside I was calm, and certain Hedinseigh had held firm. One of the small advantages to being a Mage was the ability to know much ahead of time, although we could not explain whence that knowledge came.

My presentiments did not deceive me. At the harbor mouth, still smoldering, their charred catwalks and bronze battering rams helplessly nudging into the gray bulk of the breakwaters, were the hulls of five of Vidrir's galleys; and the breakwaters by the watchtower were thickly littered with the bodies of ironclad troops from the Sheltered Kingdom. The dumbfounded rowers eyed the carnage as they slowly edged the dragon-ship closer to the wharf. I crossed my arms and kindled a wizardfire so my apprentice would not, in the heat of the moment, scuttle this vessel, too.

Hedinseigh harbor went into an uproar, and I could only smile to myself as I paced past a hastily assembled honor guard of five dozen, worn out after fighting all night—I, who had presided over parades of squadrons many hundreds of thousands strong.

Hagen strode rapidly to meet me from the far flank of his formation and made a dignified obeisance. It would not be until later, when we were alone, that, waving his arms and bobbing up and down like a child, the words falling over each other, he would tell me all about Vidrir's seaborne attack. For now, he continued playing the part of the victorious leader of a gang of seafaring daredevils who had done what was, to all appearances, the impossible.

"Welcome to Hedinseigh, Teacher," he said, bowing low.

I learned that immediately after my departure, my apprentice had chosen prisoners to send to Vidrir as couriers bearing an offer of peace. There was no reply—or, rather, the reply was brought by ten of the Sheltered Kingdom's battle-galleys. Hagen met them with ready-armed ballistas and catapults, targeted on every last one of the multitude of buoys he had placed before the harbor mouth. Hollow clay shot filled with liquid fire set two of the galleys alight far outside the breakwaters, but still some of Vidrir's men were able to land near the watchtower guarding the mechanism to raise and lower the chain that closed off the harbor.

They were greeted by bowmen and arbalesters concealed on hanging stages and rafts on the other side of the breakwater. Three more galleys caught fire in succession, and those who fell from the decks and moles were dragged by their heavy armor to the bottom of the sea. The attackers sounded the retreat betimes.

"Did you contrive to discover who struck us by the temple, Teacher?" he asked me when his tale was done.

I gave him an account of my adventures, changing just a few details here and there so as not to sap his strength with fear. I had faith in Hagen, but it never hurts to be careful. It was not for him to know that the Lowerworld clairvoyant had assured me time and again the assailant had been someone utterly unknown to me.

"In fine, we learned little," I concluded. "Like as not, the Sorceress Sigrlinn had no part in it."

I was alarmed, unpleasantly and unexpectedly so, to see Hagen's tense face brighten visibly.

"If not she, then who?" he asked, more animated now.

"Most likely Makran and Esteri, perhaps with some help from Merlin," I replied slowly, still distracted by what I had just seen. "But that will not affect our plan. Stay the course."

Our situation remained extremely uncertain and entangled in all things but one, for Vidrir acted exactly as I had foreseen. After his failure against Hedinseigh, he sent intermediaries to sue for peace. That was his way—if he did not succeed by force of arms, he would try to get his way by guile. So, he invited Hagen, with all his people, into his service, and argued his case long and hard.

Hagen carried himself splendidly. Lofty and surefooted he was, while at the same time managing to convey by hints and asides that he was not at all averse to the offer. Finally, when a price that suited both sides had been decided upon, he received the title of hereditary thane, Hedinseigh became his domain and in return, he bound himself to swell the ranks of Vidrir's army when the call came, to protect the seabord from pirates and so on and so forth.

All this came about because Vidrir was still unable to prove that the assault on the Erivag Temple had been Hagen's doing.

The Sheltered Kingdom's fleet withdrew from the island, and Hagen released every single prisoner, who expressed themselves greatly surprised by such good treatment. The first—the smallest and simplest—part of my plan was complete.

CHAPTER VI

AGEN'S RETURN TO CONSCIOUSNESS WAS A SLOW AGONY, RACKED WITH SPASMS OF
vomiting. Someone was washing his face, lifting to his lips a warm, bitter
liquid that brought some ease and plunged him back into the profound
healing oblivion of a sleep that shielded him from the pain. Gradually, the
nightmare visions of Niflhel's monstrosities gave way to a gray pall; and then
the thane saw an iron-hued sky louring above him, felt the warmth of a
campfire on his side, and heard Brann Shrunkenhand's calm voice.

"Well, you got fair knocked about, young thane! I tell you true, I never
thought to see you hold up under that—'tis few enough can bear the breath of
Garm. But you're a strong un, upon my word! Where were you raised?"

"What of...the Hound?" Hagen's voice was husky.

"Slumbering peacefully. What else was he to do after a draught of Hropt's
cordial?"

"I...have to see for myself." Hagen tried to get to his feet, grimacing with
the effort. Shrunkenhand almost had to force him back down.

"Where are you off to in such a hurry? Back through that filth? It's thrice
worse when the Hound's sleeping. I didn't haul you out so you could poke
your neck right back into the noose!"

"Then why did you?" Hagen said raggedly. He was still having difficulty
speaking.

Brann seemed momentarily embarrassed.

"You don't think about that when you're dragging a dead weight," he
snapped.

"But still I have to return to Garm," Hagen said, in a quiet tone that
brooked no discussion.

Shrunkenhand set his jaw. "There's no arguing with you. Know, though,

133

that I won't go back in there. Go alone, if such be your pleasure," he grumbled. "I'll conduct you to the gates, young thane."

This time, though, they were not confronted on the road. The giant they had blinded had vanished, and his brethren stayed out of sight. The travelers passed through the ravine without incident.

At the black arch of the underground gates, Brann pulled up.

"I shall go no further," he said, looking Hagen hard in the eyes. "Nor should you, eh?"

From anyone else that last would have been an appeal, but Brann made it sound like a threat.

"Brann, I never explain my intentions, but this time I will try," the thane replied, meeting the man's gaze. "I cannot present myself before Old Hropt without having seen the Hound sleeping with my own eyes. Do you understand? It's not that I mistrust you. I simply have no choice."

"How powerfully your second shadow draws you to the darkness," Brann said quietly and very distinctly. "You kept it...and now you pay."

Hagen shook his head wearily. "I don't understand you. When I come back, you shall explain that to me. Fare you well!" And he was off again into the gloom.

Even with the lightsphere and the wizardly defenses, constantly renewed, the thane was hard-pressed to reach the Hound's lair alive. The attack launched by the vile brood was three times more frenzied than before— Hagen's sword was soon stained to the hilt with dark blood, yet they showed no inclination to retreat. He fought his way through, saw the huge head lying listless on the pile of corpses and the wrinkled lids over tight-shut eyes, heard the monster's steady breathing, sighed with relief and wheeled his snorting horse around.

And immediately reined back. A soft greenish light poured into the cavern ahead, forming a lustrous arch. In that arch appeared the shapely silhouette of a human figure.

He knew who it was, and prepared himself for battle. His precious Sword of the South glinted silvery-blue as it flew from its sheath, like a fish leaping in a waterfall. He tried to spur his horse into a gallop, but the poor beast was beyond mastering and, with a frantic whinny, reared instead of plunging forward.

Hagen leapt from the saddle. He saw, could feel, that all the hideous things around him were gone, as if swept away by the wind. With no more hesitation, his sword at the ready, he advanced on the shining arch.

"Once a clump of mud, now cold steel, Hedin's Apprentice?" The melodious voice was pitched a little lower than normal for a woman. "Stop there. I have done nothing to harm you. Lower your sword, calm yourself, and let us talk. Will you do that?"

"What is there to talk of, Sorceress Sigrlinn, Green Witch?" Hagen asked hoarsely. "Let me pass. I must be gone from here."

"Have you not dreamed, through all the long years of your apprenticeship, of meeting me again? You were a boy then, but now you have grown, while I...believe me, I have not changed."

"Step aside, O Long of Life," Hagen said with a somber sense of impending doom, propelling the sounds from his throat by sheer force of will. He understood these were empty words, but to yield without a fight was more than he could bear. Something stronger than shame, pain or death—the bitter pride and inexplicable obstinacy that come over a man in times of extreme, unavoidable danger—was urging him on.

"I recognize Hedin's teachings there." Though the sorceress's face was still shrouded in darkness, he heard the mockery in her voice and knew her lips were twisted in scorn. "Better death than the shame of captivity, strike first and then see what happens, and so forth." She sighed. "So familiar! Familiar, believe me, and utterly bereft of interest. He repeats himself. He cannot conceive of anything new...I pity you, humanling."

Hagen made no reply. He was forcing his way though the snare the suddenly very thick, viscous air had become. He knew he must not answer, and instead pressed on toward the arch.

"You are silent," Sigrlinn continued. "Yes, you are proud, bold and strong. You have given up everything for power and for the chance to rule. But the price is beyond your ability to pay."

"I don't understand you." He thrust the words out, knowing full well he should not speak. "What price?"

"The price for your thaneship, for the legions you have mustered, for the throne you so desire, for the kingly mantle you may one day wear, if fortune wills it. You will spill rivers of blood to satisfy your Teacher's vanity, and I dread even to think what will become of you beyond the pale of death. The Gods are wrathful, Thane Hagen. Beware their retribution!"

"Your menaces are wasted on me!" Hagen roared, oddly comforted by the very noise he made.

"Yes, I know," the sorceress replied with a hint of sorrow. "And that is why I want to suggest to you a way of escape, out of respect for your valor."

"A way of escape? My first escape shall be from this place!" He spoke in a crow-like caw, his throat so dry it seemed to be cracking. "Begin by not blocking this way, and then talk to me of all else."

He realized, of course, that he had erred, for challenging a Mage to feats of eloquence is but time wasted; yet he could not hold his tongue.

"I can grant you your desire, I fear, only if you accept my conditions," Sigrlinn said in harsh tones.

The air around him became as dense as hard-packed snow.

"And what are those?" The arch was close now, but those last steps were difficult beyond belief.

"You shall leave your Teacher and go with me," the sorceress said, each word falling like a shard of ice from her lips. "I shall take you with me to the Castle of the Mages, which we still call the Castle of All the Ancients. You shall stand before Great Merlin's throne and, by the agency of an Astral Messenger, shall beg the Young Gods in person for their mercy and indulgence. Ialini the Kind of Heart, Mistress of the Green World, will intercede on your behalf, for I have in the past done her some service. You will be pardoned and your fate will be separated from those of other mortals.

"You cannot even imagine how great a distinction is offered to you in this. In all the long history of the Mage Generation, only two before you have been vouchsafed the like."

"If I am not the first, I have no taste for such honors," Hagen interrupted. The air was grudgingly giving way before him—he had discovered that forward movement was easier if he held his sword with the cutting edge perpendicular to his chest, slicing, as it were, through that invisible barricade.

"It is not an honor. It is fate." Sigrlinn spoke no less forcefully than he. "It is not for you, mortal, to contend with destiny. Even we Mages submit to it, as do all other creatures, living and unliving. You shall leave with me, or you shall not leave at all."

"You are violating the Law of the Ancients!" Hagen cried out. "No one is entitled to make free with another's apprentice."

"Nothing on Earth is immutable. Even the Laws of the Ancients change," Sigrlinn said softly. "Or…they are changed when the preservation of the old code begins to imperil the World Balance. You have no escape, no choice. I would not wish to force you by brute strength, although it would cost me nothing to bind you and take you with me."

"Save your threats, sorceress!" There were not many more steps to go, but they were far harder than the last few feet between him and Garm had been.

"Powerful as you are, you can tie me but never subdue me."

"That remains to be seen," Sigrlinn purred.

In a secluded apartment, surrounded by silks, velvet and gold, before the cozy crackle of a fire and with a goblet of good, crisp wine in hand, those words—and the tone in which they were spoken—might have had the desired effect. In a gloomy ravine, amid the swarming nightmare spawn of a world of dead things, they did to Hagen what a red rag does to a bull. He who had never lost his composure in combat, who had always fought with well-considered precision, lurched forward, his eyes blinded by a bloody mist. The explosion within swept away all thoughts, all reason. He saw only the elegant silhouette against the greenish glow and trembled with a hatred stronger than any he had ever known.

Sigrlinn may have been prepared for that attack, but if she was, she had underestimated her opponent. The Sword of the Southern Gods flared, shearing through the invisible barriers; and in an instant the thane was at the lustrous arch and driving into it in what swordsmen call a deep lunge.

The sorceress sprang aside as the blade ripped through the hem of her light cloak—Hagen had not given her even the fraction of time the strongest Mage needs to conjure a charm. The second swing of the sword clove the arch's right-hand support, and it instantly disappeared. An animal instinct for the only way out, which his studies with Hedin had strengthened, flung Hagen into the impenetrable gloom that hid the door to safety in the land of the living.

As he ran, he whistled as loudly as he could for his horse with the full understanding he was giving away his position; but without a horse he had little chance of getting by the horde of bloodthirsty brutes assailing him from all sides. His trusty mount was almost immediately snorting beside him, smashing its hoof into what must have been, judging from the sound, the skull of something foul that happened to be in the wrong place. Hagen bounded into the saddle; he knew Sigrlinn would very soon be summoning up all her arsenal of magic.

He made no attempt to surround himself with barriers of wizardry, which would have been useless against a true Mage. Not even able to light his path with wizardfire, he gave his horse its head to find the way.

Through the clatter of hoofbeats on stone, Hagen's ears were subtly attuned to the approach of monsters emboldened by the absence of light; he had not been aware of such sharpness of hearing while on the way to Garm. The sword whistled, slicing the air to right and left; a rapid hiss gave way to the crunch of flesh and bone, and another foe would breathe no more.

But why is she holding back? he wondered in amazement when he saw the opening, gray before him. He was almost there, and Sigrlinn had not tried to stop him.

She chose her moment well. The horse collided with an invisible obstacle, stumbled and went down, giving Hagen almost no time to dismount safely. There was a breathy sound that seemed to come from dozens of husky throats, and spectral gray nets appeared from behind the rocks. Shifting as if handled by artful yet unseen fishermen, they blocked his only path.

In a sudden, swift movement that was hard to dodge, the intricate interweaving of gray ropes—he still could not determine if he was facing living creatures, wraiths or real nets wielded by ghostly giants—was upon him. Revolted and exasperated, he swung his sword in a glittering half-circle, gashing the webbing that seemed so alive; and it recoiled, buckling and creasing as if in pain. One of the ropes split apart, and a gleaming red smear spread slowly down his blade.

Slipping between the torn edges before they could bind together again, Hagen was hurtling toward the door when he felt the soft but improbably powerful blow of a fist on his back. He was flung to the stony ground, and heard a wild neigh, an almost human cry of horror. His horse was caught in the nets.

Would that I knew if the Law of the Ancients that forbids a Mage to kill a mortal by his own hand or by magic still holds, he thought as he struggled to his feet. The shock had sent everything swimming before his eyes, but his sword was still in his hand.

The nets advanced on him again from three sides, but this time, having realized he could be seen in both light and darkness, he lavished his life force on a Firecharm. A fiery tornado began to swirl around the thane, the roaring wall of flame rising almost to the roof of the gigantic cavern and flooding out in every direction.

It was a rare—a very rare—Mage who entrusted that magic to an apprentice, it being imparted only to the most able among them. Hedin had taught his ward the spell—one of the closest to a real Greatcharm—for use only in the direst extremity, as the last of the last expedients, when all other methods of defense had been exhausted. The fire consumed the life of the mortal who conjured it up as easily as it would dry grass; so while that mighty wall of fire might transform all foes, seen and unseen, into ash, it could not be made to rage for long. Every new moment maintaining it could cost a man his life.

Hagen escaped before the flame died down. Once through the gates, he fell into the arms of Shrunkenhand, who was keeping an anxious eye on the darkness that had again thickened behind the thane's back.

"What sport was that?" was all Brann had time to say before, with a frenzied whinny, Hagen's maddened horse came pelting out of the gloom, having escaped, by some miracle, with its life. Hagen caught the reins in a death-grip.

"Ride on!" he said in a rasping whisper. "Ride, or we are done for! Both of us! Ride on, I say!" And he mounted and gave his horse its head, not caring whether Brann was following or not.

He was.

They rapidly closed in on the dour ravine of Gnipahellir; then the mountains began to draw gradually apart, retreating farther and farther into the distance. They were aware of no pursuit, but Hagen, under no illusion the Firecharm had dispatched all his foes, wondered what Sigrlinn would do next.

The powerful sorceress had more than enough ways to stop them. Were those living nets the best she could do? She could—and he knew this for a certainty—have drunk up all his strength and turned him into a motionless block of wood. She could have taken the movement from his legs, the sight from his eyes. She had not. Why not, if she had been so set on abducting him?

And what of my men? he thought glumly. *If there has been a watch on us since we left the shore, they could have been captured after I sent us on our separate ways. I can only hope Gudmund has not rushed headlong into some venture, that Frodi has kept him from any foolishness.*

But look how it all draws together—first that wiccan with the White Blade and the Disc of Iamerth, then the Devourer of Souls, though that last could have been mere happenstance. Besides, he proved weaker than I, and they should have considered that. Then, last of all, Sigrlinn. But if all this is the work of one mind, why even speak with me, who was to have been cleft in two by the Disc of Iamerth at the Living Crags? Something very complex is afoot...I need to meet with my Teacher, as soon as ever I can and crabbed though my way there may be!

"...and it was burning behind you something fierce!"

Hagen realized Brann had been talking to him all the while.

"Yes, I had to fend the monsters off with fire," he replied carelessly, as if he conjured a Firecharm every day of the week.

Brann looked askance. "Only the monsters? Would you had witnessed yourself come flying out of that cave! I've seen corpses look better. Who did you meet in there, young thane?"

"That's none of your affair," Hagen muttered gracelessly. "Keep your distance from that, Brann. It's my war, not yours, so stay clear. They'll aim at me but it'll be you they hurt, and care not one whit if they do."

"A pretty walk I've had on the Forestway," Brann griped back. "Well and good. If you want to hold your peace then hold it. I don't need you to tell me that a man has no business meddling in such things. Know, though, that I shall cross ways with the esteemed Hropt yet, and shall hear all from him. I daresay your dealings with the Strong Ones go well beyond sending that there Hound back to sleep."

"What will change if I tell you? You'll not stand on my side. Maybe you'll even act against me. Why, then, should I tell you anything that can hurt me?"

"Suppose it's not to be with you or against you, but to shield others from harm?" Shrunkenhand asked point-blank.

"Suppose it is?" Hagen replied morosely. "I've already told you, I won't say anything that can hurt me."

"I swear to you by the Gates of Niflhel that I'll undertake naught against you while you trouble not the guiltless and leave the innocent in peace!" It was a solemn oath, albeit a little theatrical.

Hagen just stared. "You'll undertake naught against me? And who are you to say so? A king? A lord? A wizard? How, exactly, do you propose to judge me?"

"I'm no king," Shrunkenhand said—wearily, Hagen thought. "I'm no lord, never was and never will be. As for how I shall judge—until your warriors set peaceful villages afire, until people are driven to market like livestock, until coastal pirates, sailing under your flags, put trading towns to the sword...until then, expect no evil from Brann Shrunkenhand."

"I shall remember that," Hagen replied calmly. "I shall remember your words, Shrunkenhand. And I shall also remember how you helped me, and saved me by dragging me from Garm's lair. Now enough of these lofty matters. It's a long, hard ride to the Forest, and we may well encounter the Conveyor of the Dead again."

But two days passed, and they reached the borders of Gnipahellir without incident. Brann wasted no time at all lighting his fire and seeking the entrance to the Forestway.

The Green World—ever faithful, untouched by treachery and living by its own laws, which in some respects agreed with, and in other respects diverged from, Ialini's own precepts—silently opened up its secret pathway to the two travelers. Only then could Hagen breathe somewhat easy, for he hoped it would be no simple matter for Sigrlinn to find him here.

Then Brann unexpectedly reined in his horse and sprang to the ground. Hagen tensed and with his second sight glimpsed pale green eyes under the roots of a moldering stump. It was a tiny woodland sprite, like the one who had called him and his Teacher enemies. But what was Brann about to do?

Shrunkenhand unstrapped a dark-brown wooden flask from his belt, opened it and poured out a few drops of pungent liquid. The stump was immediately swathed in a cloud of whitish-green dust, and with a quiet sound of escaping breath, it disappeared, leaving only a scorched patch of ground.

Hagen was startled. "What are you...? Why...?"

"You don't tell me everything, nor shall I you," Brann responded, his face sullen and hard. "I shall say only that I have no fondness for such as hope to wait out the time beneath a stump, like a grouse under a spruce in a rainstorm."

And he would explain no further.

"Will we be going by way of Two-Shadow Hill?" Hagen asked his guide.

"I don't know, but like as not the trail won't take us there," Brann replied, with what Hagen thought was a hint of sadness. "You refused once, and who knows when the Forest will give you another chance?"

"Is it really the Forest that decides, not you?"

"Yes. It leads us as it will. All I do is follow its signs. I can only guess the turns the path will take."

Little need be said about their return journey. Sundry spirits crowded around their evening campfires, but the Devourer of Souls stayed away; and they came safe at last to Shrunkenhand's solitary dwelling, where his wife was working in the vegetable patch. Catching sight of the returning warriors, she laid down her bundle and straightened up, arms akimbo. Even from a distance, she looked primed for battle.

Brann's mood darkened. He pulled up his horse and turned to Hagen.

"Farewell, then, young thane," he said, in some haste. "Go your way and mind you don't forget to greet the esteemed Hropt on my behalf if you see him."

He turned his horse and rode toward the gates. Hagen watched him for a few moments then shrugged and flicked the reins. He had decided to go back to the Living Crags.

DUSK WAS FALLING AS HE APPROACHED OLD HROPT'S HOME THREE DAYS LATER. A DIM

141

light flickered in one of the windows of the long facade, and Hagen's heart began to pound at the sight—that could only be his Teacher's wizardfire.

But he did not permit himself to knock until he had tended to his horse. The door opened at the first rap, and on the threshold stood Mage Hedin.

"Teacher," the thane breathed, dropping a respectful bow—a habit he could not break, no matter how often he was upbraided by a Mage who cared naught for such tokens of deference.

Hedin's hard, strong hands were on Hagen's shoulders; and for an instant, the Teacher clasped his apprentice to his chest.

"Come in, my boy," he said in a low voice. "We have much to discuss."

"Step in, wayfarer, step in!" Hropt boomed behind Hedin's back. "Step in and tell us all, but first you shall taste my smoked venison, pickled mushrooms and ale."

"And everything else that's in your cellars, Hropt," Hedin smiled. "I know you'd never permit a weary traveler to begin a long tale without a hearty repast. Very well, have your way, although I'll tell you outright that these are taxing times and every hour could be precious to us."

Hagen, Hropt and Hedin sat at a long table set with bowls and pitchers. The host began by draining a half-bucket-sized tankard of dark ale.

"So, you sent the Hound back to sleep, Hagen?"

"Yes," the thane mumbled, his mouth crammed full. His was a disconnected story, because Hedin and Hropt kept saying "Enough, enough, that can wait. Now, eat" and then would promptly begin showering him with more questions. Hagen gave them all the detail he could, noticing how his Teacher flinched at the mention of Sigrlinn.

"I must see that," Hedin said bleakly. "With your permission?"

"Of course, Teacher," Hagen replied.

The Mage looked closely at his apprentice for a moment or two then raised a cupped hand in which a blue light trembled. The magic fire moved closer to the motionless thane, closer and yet closer, until it was all he could see…

When he came to himself a few moments later, the wood in the fireplace had settled only a little and the supply of beer on the table was as generous as before. Hropt sat with his huge fists resting on that giant table while Hedin, his lips tightly pursed, paced rapidly to and fro, his head lowered in thought.

"We must return forthwith to Hedinseigh," he announced, once Hagen was fully recovered. In that short time, the Mage had decanted from Hagen's memory and seen through his apprentice's eyes all that had happened by Garm's lair. "It's far worse than you think," he continued. "I don't know—

yet—if Garm's awakening was an accident. The dwarves of Roedulsfoel have loosed fire in Ialini's Gardens before, but previously the Hound paid no mind. Now, with that Darkling Rider…"

"Aye, and where did she get that White Blade, I'd like to know," a morose Hropt interjected. "Those rascals have never before been able to lay their hands on weapons of magic."

Hedin turned to him. "If Hagen is not mistaken—and I am sure he's not—we have dealings here with someone's apprentice. A golden thread in the shadows of her mind—there can be no mistake. But that would be unprecedented! No Mage of our Generation has ever selected an apprentice from that brood. The Laws of the Ancients do not expressly forbid it, but…"

"They have eyes like carrion crows," Hropt mumbled. "It was my error. I was inattentive. Some human picked up wizardry from the giants—the real giants, the first-born, far and away greater than the giants of today—and that was the end of it. Before you could turn around, there were your Darkling Riders, ready-made."

"It no longer matters whence they came," Hedin said, after patiently hearing him out. "The wiccan who was killed by your Stone Sentinel was someone's apprentice, and her Teacher was influential enough to inveigle the priests of Iamerth into giving her a holy Disc, and a White Blade into the bargain. To inveigle from the priests of the Sheltered Kingdom…" He bowed his head and was silent, lost in thought.

"Your Generation has entirely taken leave of its senses, Hedin," Hropt broke in. "In bygone days I would have told them to go to Mimir's Well, find favor with its Guardian and seek his permission to drink the Waters of Wisdom. They are destroying themselves, you mark my words, Mage!"

"I am trying to put distance between myself and them," was all Hagen's Teacher said.

"War has not yet been declared," the thane remarked. "Otherwise, why did they let me go? It smacks of a last warning. The Laws of the Ancients are falling one after another."

"Yes," his Teacher responded, "and that bears Sigrlinn's hallmark. Ah, sorceress, sorceress…I would rather venture out alone against all the forces of the celestial realms than try to divine your whims and schemes. But who, in the name of the Moonbeast, could have dared initiate the Darkling Riders into the High Magic?"

"What would it change if you found out?" Hropt argued. "Do you know how to skirt the Law and fight another Mage to the death? And are you certain that you would prevail?"

"If you're not certain, you don't give battle," Hedin shot back. "Besides, I don't want to kill anyone. That's not my way. Such vulgar, dirty dealings are for the weak and the cowardly, who try to drown their own cowardice in the blood of others, We were confined when our powers were not as great as they are now, and out there…" He jabbed a finger eastward. "…they know that very well. Yet they issue no challenges. It's strange…although, if Merlin really has brought about a change in the Laws of the Ancients then the game will have no rules.

"I can understand but little from what took place in the cavern. That was Sigrlinn's very best snare, Hagen—those living nets could have entangled you in an instant, and even your sword would have availed you nothing had you encountered them in an ordinary world. Spells, it seems, weaken in the vicinity of Niflhel. So, you were not let go. You made your own escape, seizing the one chance you had.

"But to capture another Mage's apprentice, without sending a challenge by the Castle Raven…By the All-Creator, all the canons have been flung aside! And by Sigrlinn!" He clasped his head in his hands and seemed to shrivel into himself.

Hropt rose and awkwardly rested a heavy hand on the Mage's shoulder.

"Why grieve over the past when it cannot be changed?" he said in a hollow tone. "You must think about what to do next. If nothing is presently limiting your power…"

"I cannot even be sure of that!" Hedin exclaimed. "Maybe there's a secret trap of Merlin's hidden in all this. He could have sent an Astral Messenger, gained himself a temporary respite from the rules and used that to make me violate them myself. An unconscionable gambit but an effective one. All I have to do is break, in my ignorance, a Law that is still in effect—the Ancients knew how to punish! And those Laws have been so compiled and so ratified that my magic is impotent to discover which are still in operation and which have been discarded."

Then there was silence, which Hedin eventually broke.

"And there is much more to consider. I must wonder about the powers of Brann Shrunkenhand, if even Iargohor, Conveyer of the Dead, has no dominion over him. Have you aught to say on that, most esteemed Hropt?"

"I have but one explanation, though I fear it will not please you," the Father of Hosts replied. "The simplest would be to assume that Brann is being helped by one of the Ancient Powers or even a Distant Power, but I'll warrant

144

'tis not so. His spirit…"

Hedin cast a rapid glare at Hropt, lightning-swift, but what Hropt said next was quite strange.

"His spirit can probably go stock-still, like a wild beast in a thicket when the hunters are on the prowl."

"And what about that Two-Shadow Hill? It was he who made me go there," Hagen chimed in. "Where could that second shadow have come from? And how can one of them be swept away, like any trash?"

Hedin and Hropt exchanged glances.

"'Tis said that Two-Shadow Hill has from time immemorial been consecrated to the Distant Powers," the Mage replied. "Perhaps the two shadows represent the two Principles within you, the human and the magical; and to brush one away, to efface it, is, in Brann's mind, to divest yourself of one of those two antagonistic Principles. Though if you ask me, brush as you will, nothing will actually disappear. You are simply making a choice. Brann is convinced that he is just an ordinary man—although, to be sure, he's a great deal more than that.

"But we can spend more time on Brann later," Hedin concluded. "Now we must be on our way. Hedinseigh is not close at hand, and all your men, Hagen, have probably already been long on the road. Since we have no time to waste, we shall travel by way of a Transference. Go now. Your horse must be ready."

After Hagen had closed the door behind him, Hedin looked at Hropt reproachfully.

"How could you think to say 'his spirit is free' in my apprentice's presence? Does he need more confusion than is already his? And how sure are you of that?"

"How else can you explain why the Conveyer of Souls lacks the power to wring his soul from him?" Hropt replied. "There is only one explanation—Brann's spirit is free of fear. He owes allegiance to no power. He is his own man. Death has supremacy over him, but the Soul-Banisher does not. I know not how he achieved that, who taught him, but like as not he learned it all himself. Think on that, Hedin—a mortal, a human, capable of doing that which only Mages could once do."

Hagen's Teacher rose. "Well and good. I shall reflect on that at a later time. Now we must away. I am forced to begin sooner than I wished, but if they strike first then all is lost. I'll be throwing away the fruits of many years of hard work."

"I have never asked you this before, but now…" Hropt looked the Mage in the eye. "Will victory be yours? Or…?"

Hedin gave an almost imperceptible smile. "Save your conjectures, O Most Worthy of Honor. No matter what, I doubt you'll understand me. For you there are only two results—victory or death. Deem this…a scouting expedition."

And with those words, the sorcerer left, closing the door behind him.

"He's about to upend the whole world and he calls it a scouting expedition!" Hropt shook his head and poured himself more ale.

ALTHOUGH HEDIN TRIED HIS BEST TO HAVE THE CHARM OF TRANSFERENCE BRING HIM AND Hagen as close as possible to Hedinseigh, they were instead hurled far to the south, into the Mercantile Republic. The Mage glanced at the crenellated walls of Haithabu, at a loss as to what to do.

"I have never misjudged so, not even during my own apprenticeship," he muttered. "Well, there's nothing for it but to enter the city. Tomorrow, when I have my strength back, we can try again."

They found lodgings for the night. Hagen subjected all the locks and bolts to a careful inspection, since his Teacher did not want to use a wizardly defense that would give away his whereabouts to other Mages.

"Damnation!" Hedin mumbled as he settled into his narrow cot. "The Nightfolk must be roused, and there's no way to send them word."

"Teacher…" Hagen began, but the Mage waved it away.

"Later with your questions—later. On Hedinseigh. You'll have much to do there. Make the most of the moment, let nothing occupy your mind. Sleep."

But that sleep was an uneasy one. In the dead of night—in the witching hour, as the country folk say—when all the tavern's lodgers and servants were deep in dreamless slumber, a bolt of heavy, forged metal shifted and slid slowly through its loops, moved by an unseen hand. The door opened silently, and on the threshold of the quiet inn appeared a figure swathed in a green cloak with a black curved sword secured at its waist. Hedin's apprentice stirred restlessly, but the Mage heard and felt nothing. He was journeying afar, in the formless Astral Realms.

The Darkling Rider sped up the stairs, to the corridor that led to the rooms. Then she proceeded more slowly, halting for an instant before each door.

An icy wind blasted into Hagen's dream; he gave a low growl and awoke. All was quiet, but the anxiety, once aroused, persisted. His Teacher lay on his back, arms crossed, and his breath seemed stopped. Realizing that he was not to be reached, Hagen quickly but without undue haste examined his armor and weapons. An enemy was close by, and that was a fact requiring no magic to discern.

The Darkling Rider stopped outside their room, removed from the folds of her cloak a round object bound in a cloth and unwrapped it.

Hagen thought to stand to the right of the door, which opened inward, so he could strike his first blow in the very doorway; but then he checked himself. That decision had come unsummoned, and if the intruder had anything better to hand than an ordinary sword or lance...

So, he stayed where he was, and watched the wall against which he had been intending to stand slashed open by a glittering white Disc he recognized only too well. Iamerth's deadly weapon sliced through the thick planks as if they were nothing, pierced the wall three times and then disappeared, not to be seen again. The thane heard the culprit's light footsteps. The deed was done so why hide anymore?

Hagen collapsed onto the bed in a cold sweat. Then, hearing the footsteps recede down the corridor, he hurried to the window and pressed his face against it.

The Darkling Rider came out into the open, stood at the tavern door, looked around and unhurriedly strode away.

The thane uttered a few words to undo the Charm of Nightsight and clenched his teeth in fury. No one had wanted to kill them. They had just been made to understand that he, at least, could be killed at any moment. He did not close his eyes again all night; and at daybreak, when his Teacher moved and came out of his trance, he quickly told him all that had happened. Hedin said nothing. He eyed the three neat slits in the broad planks and silently clenched his fists.

"How many more warnings must they give us?" he hissed. "Now I'm sure that we were not tossed this way by accident!"

A second Transference brought them far closer to Hedinscigh. They engaged a longboat in a fishing village and, tacking hard against a headwind, struggled toward the island. Before long they could see the jagged summits that gnomes had made into fortress towers topped with saw-toothed crowns. They were being watched from the embrasures, Hagen knew, by dozens of sharp, attentive eyes.

Soon the port came into view, with three dozen dragon-ships moored in readiness by the jetties, the stone enclosures concealing catapults and ballistas aimed at the harbor's narrow neck, and the warriors scampering down to the wharves. Hagen was cheered by the sight of his stronghold, but the Mage's mood remained bleak.

The thane and his Teacher were greeted by much shouting and beating of swords against shields. They passed through the gates and entered the courtyard of a castle neither of them recognized, those same gnomes having rebuilt it into an impregnable citadel. The bastions soared two hundred feet into the air, and were overtopped by the battle towers. Covered galleries and subterranean passageways stretched out to every little fort on the shoreline; and in the interior, flocks still grazed and grain still grew.

There on the wharf, Hagen asked if his men had returned and, being told that they had, commanded they be brought to him immediately. In quarters high in Hedinseigh keep, surrounded by compact tiers of defensive magic so no one could eavesdrop on their conversation, the five warriors who had been with him two weeks previously gathered. The sixth was Hagen, and the Mage made the seventh.

Lodin and his company had little to tell. They had reached the assigned place uneventfully, found the gnomish weaponry already delivered, inventoried it several times and conveyed the precious freight safely to Hedinseigh. The tales of Frodi and Gudmund, though, took longer, for Hedin was constantly stopping them, questioning them, asking them to recapitulate. He was interested in the slightest details, and especially in those of Gudmund's adventures.

"You disobeyed my orders," Hagen told him sternly and then, having received from his Teacher a sign that went unnoticed by the rest, continued. "But I excuse you—once and nevermore!—for the sake of the news you bring."

When the door closed and the five—laden with lavish rewards, and Gudmund best rewarded of all—were gone, Hagen turned to his Teacher, his brows knit in anger and his eyes glittering.

"Master, we can wait no longer. We are beset on all sides and have been left in no doubt of that. I think Ialini herself has had a hand in it. And wherever she is, you'll find her royal brothers, Iambren and Iamerth, too! Would that not be the source of the White Blade, and the Disc from the Temple of the Sun?"

The Mage nodded. "Your reasoning is sound. Yes, it is time to begin. The story told by your men has made much clear to me. Judging from the great similarity between the two Darkling Riders that crossed paths with you and with Gudmund and Frodi, they were obviously taught by the same hand. Which hand that was is not important to us at this time, and I do not care to guess. Perchance Makran. Perchance Esteri. Perchance some other member of the

Council who feels no great amity for me. Perchance Merlin himself stands behind it.

"All this we shall puzzle out, but not now. I'm even glad that the Distant Powers have intervened, although that almost cost Gudmund his life. The Distant Powers are nothing if not capricious. They have a very, ah, uncommon understanding of the Great Balance, if one can even call it an understanding.

"We were taught that the Great Balance was the keystone of the world and all its ways, though I do not now believe that to be so. The Distant Powers do seem to hold the Balance sacred—their interference has always been unforeseen and unpredictable. As yet, we do not know what put the Darkling Rider on the trail that led her to the monastery, though I have heard tell it is the training ground for splendid warriors who are well capable of destroying whatever does not accord with the views of their preceptors, while the preceptors themselves derive their dogmas from revelations granted by the Distant Powers. Who knows, perhaps they took issue with he—or she—who taught those fey wiccans."

"Then the residents of that monastery could be our friends?"

The Mage shook his head. "Unlikely. They, too, have declared their enmity to us, so what are our hopes of coming to terms with them? Contact with the Distant Powers is very dangerous, even for a Mage. To speak free, Gudmund could disappear at any moment and I would be unable to help him. They are as adept at revenge as the Ancient Ones are at punishment."

"But what of that strange band that joined forces to face the Darkling Rider—elves, wood gnomes, even a kobold and a troll?" Hagen asked. "Try as I may, I can make neither head nor tail of that."

Hedin shrugged. "I'm not the Creator, why ask me? Clearly, though, 'twas the elf that brought them together. All the other nomen—except the most evil-minded, like the mormaths—bow to them. The trolls may be bandits and sometimes even eaters of human flesh, but they are in mortal fear of the elves.

"And the First-Begotten would not be what they are if they could not pass beyond the skyline, to see and hear there far more than is ever revealed to men. The elven strongholds in Eastern Hjorvard owe much of their very survival to the support of the Distant Powers. The Young Gods are, I believe, frankly afraid of the elves, for they are, after all, the Children of the Creator Himself."

That surprised Hagen. "And humans are not?"

The Mage raised a soothing hand. "Of course, you are. But He created the elves himself—with His own hand, you might say, although He certainly has never had any hands. The finishing touches to humans were made following His intent and under His Eye by the Young Gods, who had not yet taken it into their heads to invade this world and assume governance over it.

"But there are races on the Earth…" Hedin lowered his voice to a whisper. "…that the Young Gods and the Old Gods and even the Creator Himself leave to their own devices."

"The Mages. I know." Hagen nodded. "You've spoken to me of that many times."

Hedin responded only with an enigmatic shake of the head, and no more was said on that subject.

They went back to discussing the current situation; and after a while, the talk turned again to Gudmund, whose account still seemed incomplete.

"Why did they attack him?" Hagen asked. "That was utterly senseless. He had brought important news, a warning of impending danger. Before flinging such a courier into a dungeon, I would have weighed everything most carefully."

"This from my apprentice?" Hedin frowned. "They knew everything they wanted to know in the first few seconds, but were too self-assured to give the tidings their due importance. The Distant Powers, and maybe Merlin, too, had condemned us as violators of that infamous Balance, and the game was up."

Hagen flushed, ashamed of his error.

The Mage leaned toward him. "Think no more of that. Difficult times begin for us on the morrow. Milord Hjorleif has eased our way a little, hard-won as that advantage may have been. How many did you lose in Himinvagar?"

"Eight, before a ninth fought through to Hjorleif's counselors," Hagen replied. "But the result made the losses worthwhile. I was delighted to hear that the forces of Himinvagar had crossed Vidrir's frontiers."

"Crossed them or not, how much longer will they be able to avoid giving battle?" Hedin questioned. "I have helped them as best I could, visiting bad weather and night frights upon Vidrir's army.

"But enough of that. Is your plan the same as before?"

"No. I had to make changes on intelligence I received." Hagen reached for a bundle of maps and unrolled on the table some that showed the interior of Eastern Hjorvard. "Several new outposts and fortified encampments have been discovered—here, here and here." They leaned over the map together.

And in the watches of the night, the clouds that covered the moon suddenly, as if obedient to someone's behest, opened up over Hedinseigh. Assembly bells sounded in the towers and bastions, oil lamps flared into life, and the walkways thronged with detachments in full battle gear, appearing from nowhere on the instant. There was no flash of sword, no clanking of iron as Hagen's men loped with a lithe, wolfish stride down to the dragon-ships. The day for which Hedin had prepared so long had arrived.

HEDIN

I, HEDIN, SAGE OF DARKNESS, ACKNOWLEDGE TO MY SHAME THAT AFTER MY conversation with Sigrlinn and my encounter with the Diviner of Charms, I was greatly disturbed. I had sworn no oaths, made no vows; and no one could compel me against my will to continue pursuing my intentions. Why not abandon them before Merlin came fully into his new rights? But I knew well enough that to abandon my Plan would be to repudiate my own self. My very existence would lose purpose and meaning.

So, I rolled up my sleeves and set to work as if that battle by the temple had never taken place. A few successful forays across the sea to Western Hjorvard quickly won Hagen renown as the most successful commander among the many, and the one who was, to boot, the most open-handed with his men. The other jarls met with failure after failure, which were, of course, partially my doing—I kept all their enterprises under constant surveillance, and each time contrived to frustrate some major union in the making or send such foul weather against their ships that they had to return home with nothing to show for their pains. On rare occasions, too, I resorted to prophetic dreams, which I sent to the defenders of the towns of Western Hjorvard, their sorcerers and soothsayers, thanks to which almost every attack launched by the jarls was repulsed. A mere handful were left to boast of their successes, and first among them was Hagen.

I did not help him in battle, though. His dragon-ships struggled as mightily against the squalls and headwinds as did the others'. He was met by steel-plated detachments of heavy cavalry and ironclad foot soldiers; his shoulders and those of his warriors bore the very same brunt of the bucketsful of boiling water or hot pitch upended upon them; his chest was equally a target for arrows and rocks. He took the towns not by magic but by valor, and also by a knack for sober calculation that never ceased to amaze me.

Whenever possible, he would forgo the bloody assaults and the nightmares of wholesale pillage, and he conducted himself not like a crude trespasser moved only by thoughts of booty but like a reasonable and courageous king intent upon creating a new state. After taking a town, he first promised the inhabitants all manner of liberties and privileges, and pledged to free them from the extortionate levies the barons were wont to impose on the borderlands between some of the kingdoms, both great and small, of Western Hjorvard. He also undertook to protect them against the incursions of the other jarls, and that had the best effect of all.

Meanwhile, building on Hedinseigh continued apace. Mountain gnomes labored day and night on its walls and bastions, turning the cliffs that encircled the island into a complex system of unassailable fortifications; and endless files of people began streaming to my apprentice as Hjorvard's best fighting men gathered under his banners. Within three years, his army had grown from two hundred and fifty swordarms to sixty-seven hundred. New dragon-ships rolled one after another off the shipways, and gradually Hagen began gathering to himself not only Western Hjorvard's hitherto uninhabited islands and its regions devastated by internecine conflict but parts of our Eastern Hjorvard, too.

The first to feel his iron fist were the free jarls. It never came to all-out warfare; but once he had given two or three of the more recalcitrant among them a good thumping, the rest were only too ready to grant him his due respect. Now no major campaign took place without him, and he almost always led them. Many of the jarls began to seek out opportunities to enlist in his service, those being both the weakest and most inept and, strange as this may sound, also the most wily and farsighted.

Beyond the lands of the jarls lay a string of free-peasant communities, which required more subtle methods. Hagen had control over a sizable share of the maritime trade, of which the sons of the soil stood in dire need. The Mercantile Republic's moneybags, outraged by this unceremonious encroachment upon their commerce, dispatched couriers to the Sheltered Kingdom.

This perturbed Hagen not in the least. He had been scrupulous in his service to Vidrir, being the first to present himself at the musters and bringing the most dependable, numerous and well-armed contingents. We had even had occasion to fight alongside the Sheltered Kingdom when the wild nomads of Rogheim joined forces with the pirates of Southern Hjorvard to test the strength of Vidrir's swords.

The lightly armed mounted archers brought by the pirates from the shores of the southern mainland crushed the forward line of Vidrir's foot soldiers by throwing them into confusion under a barrage of arrows and then spearing them. But they were broken, like an ice-floe against a rock, when they collided with the tight formation of Hagen's pavisers. The Hedinseigh forces held the center; and thanks to them, Vidrir was eventually able to carry off the victory.

Then came the time of Ilving.

My apprentice had long cared little for women, regarding them as no more than playthings for men and a treat to be enjoyed after a victory. On our first visit to Haithabu, I had made it my business to conduct him through all the circles of vice, which he partook of without interest, almost as if in duty bound, and for a long time thereafter forgot about the coarser pleasures of the flesh. For a long time, but not forever—only until he met Ilving.

Her father, a jarl, had stood out against my apprentice longest of all, doggedly endeavoring to resist the inevitable. With the four ships that remained to him after an unsuccessful raid on Western Hjorvard and a mere five hundred men, he issued a challenge to Hagen, observing all the formalities demanded by the ancient punctilio of those who roam the sea. With that alone he won my respect—and, let it be said, Hagen's, too.

I remember an overcast, blizzard-tossed winter evening when it was a rare man who would have ventured out onto open water. The sentries caught sight of a foreign dragon-ship with numerous torches secured to prow, sides and mast and a bell tolling on the deck. Two of our patrol boats, each half as big again as the intruder, immediately came alongside and readied for boarding; but its crew showed no inclination to fight, declaring instead that they were envoys to the esteemed Hagen, Subjugator of the Sunset.

Then an old warrior with white mustaches that brushed his chest and a dark, almost nut-brown face weathered by the winds and salt air of all of the twelve seas of Greater Hjorvard stood in the castle's main chamber and uttered slow words that brimmed with scorn. He accused Hagen of betraying the sacred freedom of the maritime militias, of entering into pacts with the repugnant warlocks of the West, of wishing to be slavemaster to all, etcetera and so on and so forth. This envoy concluded by calling Hagen out to a duel.

"I should grind you into dust for such impudence," Hagen replied, in equally measured tones. "Even your rank should not protect you. Be glad, then, that I do not fight old men. But tell your jarl I shall come to the chosen place at the appointed time, and I shall be alone."

He kept his word, not even allowing me to accompany him, although of course I followed the engagement from a distance. Gradually, Hagen forced the elderly jarl behind a small outcrop, out of sight of the retinue that had accompanied him—which included the old diehard's flaxen-haired daughter—and only then displayed his real facility as a swordsman. Finally, using one of my favorite tactics, he knocked the sword out of his foe's hand and lowered his own blade.

"This battle is without purpose," he said calmly. "It is dishonorable, since we are unequal. You do not know who taught me to fight. So, I offer you an honorable peace. I know that you will pridefully refuse, and that you do not fear death. But think of your men and of those who inhabit your lands. They are in your charge, if your title of ruler counts for anything at all. Let us sheathe our swords and announce our decision to end this foolish squabble. I shall do nothing to harm you, provided only that you swear by the Eternal Torments of Niflhel not to rise against me."

I know not what the disarmed jarl was thinking about at that moment—maybe his daughter—but a month later he was welcomed with honor to Hedinseigh. My apprentice suggested an alliance, and before long I noticed that Hagen was spending more and more time in the east, in the domains of his erstwhile enemy. The third time, he returned with a face like a thundercloud. I looked him in the eye, and he colored unexpectedly and told me all.

As I listened to his heated, incoherent tale, so unlike his precise, smooth speech when discoursing on campaigns, sieges and affrays, I thought sourly that in this, where he seemed to crave my advice and help the most, I had nothing that could help him. Nothing, that is, except my own bitter memories.

The jarl's proud and willful daughter had bewitched him in truth, and without the slightest knowledge of magic. Most likely she had but gently and diffidently offered him what I could never give—namely, sympathy and compassion.

I knew naught of how matters progressed between the two of them from then until their wedding, which was celebrated in lavish style in Haithabu, midway betwixt the domains of Hagen and those of his father-in-law. Shortly thereafter, Hedinseigh had a new mistress.

At first, she feared and avoided me. My apprentice and I were amused by her fear, but I also took steps to overcome it, beginning with quiet conversations and with the folk tales she enjoyed so much. Then I presented her with a few rare trinkets, gave her some valuable advice—little by little, she warmed to me and no longer shrank back when she glimpsed me coming down the corridor.

Ilving took the entire domestic management of Hedinseigh securely and commandingly into her small but strong hands. She engaged countless servants and kept a strict watch over them, and the rigorous life of a fortress on a constant battle footing changed completely. Kitchen gardens flourished, herds multiplied, and there was fresh milk, curds, cheese. But in truth, all the changes would be too long in the telling.

I observed my apprentice's genuinely intense attachment to her. More important, though, I discerned to a certainty a depth of feeling he kept hidden from all others, and I could not but envy him somewhat.

Meanwhile, some astonishing events were in train among my fellow Mages. I had expected the magical assaults to continue on the island we now occupied, yet from the day of my return to Hedinseigh after my meeting with the Diviner of Charms no one had so much as laid a finger on us. We were opposed in nothing we did.

Then I turned to one of the darkest sides of the knowledge acquired during my exile, however, I discovered something of extremely unpleasant import to us.

Far to the east of Hjorvard, beyond the Iron Wood and the wolds of Rogheim, beyond even the Nomar Mountains, are great expanses of desolate, reeking bogs. Those deathly, quaking wastes stretch for dozens of leagues around, veined with the dark- and light-blue ribbons of tiny streams and rivers. There are no humans there, and almost no animals and birds.

It is this place to which the oldest and wisest marsh trolls—those with teeth ground down to the gums, long-lived in spite of human spears, elven arrows and gnomish axes—sometimes go, for a repose that gently eases into death. Most trolls are dull-witted enough, but even among them are some ancient clans standing jealous guard over the secrets of an uncommon magic they hardly ever employ. An odd and mystical magic it is, too, as mystical as the very origins of their grotesque and gloomy race.

They have mastery over the Slow Water, as they are wont to call it, which is not the rotation of the world around oneself from which the Mages derive their power. It comes, rather, from the strength imparted by the marshwater, which roams on its unhurried course, offering shelter to thousands upon thousands of small lives as it goes. That strength, channeled into the Real, is their magic.

Untold eons ago—probably in the very first hours of Creation—sparks from the Flame of Creation touched the newborn, fresh-wrought bogs and, as they snuffed themselves out, imparted to those bogs their share of the might the Creator had invested in them. For long, long years, none of the Wise Ones knew of this. But when at last the Ancients penetrated down to the very essence, it was only to discover that nothing could be changed. Instead, a macabre prophecy was made known to them. Should anyone take it in mind to wipe from the face of the Earth the last troll, the doomed creature's final word would, in turn, wipe away the entire visible world. On some strange whim, the Maker had chosen not to divest the trolls of that power.

Yet it must be said that they were wise in their use of it. They never strove for authority or riches but were content to enjoy the security the power gave them, since it placed anyone who dared hunt them in great jeopardy.

During my exile, the trolls had helped me in word and deed; by degrees, and guided by their cloudy hints, I found my way to their cherished, swampy retreat. There was revealed to me the Magic of the Slow Water, which is powerful, lugubrious and not as benevolent as it might be. I had kept it a close secret, but now its hour had come.

The trolls had long been perfecting the art of knowing when they were being shadowed and of confounding their pursuers, and I had learned much from them. The only thing stopping me was that the Magic of the Slow Water animates powerful and ancient beings that otherwise are found sleeping in those Lowerworlds some call the Great Marshes. Under thick layers of moss and bizarre plants never seen in our lands, which spread in a dense carpet over small warm lakes, those remarkable creatures—the Masters of the Slow Water—live. It is to them that the practitioners of such wizardry must appeal, asking to share the sharpness of their sight, which gives them the ability to see through worlds.

But, once roused, they are racked with a terrible hunger, and whoever awakens them must send them food. The trolls had transformed entire villages into charnel houses to make good the debts incurred in escaping the great troll-hunts that would still occur from time to time.

Yet the Magic of the Slow Water goes beyond that, for the flowing waters also commit to memory your foes' reflections. A pursuer need only appear for a moment in a droplet of dew, and the water will remember it.

The Magic of the Slow Water is a component of the titanic Magic of Water, which is itself part of the boundless Elemental Sorcery that has long been kept secret from us. Rather, it is vouchsafed to only the closest confederates of the Young Gods, and to trolls, gnomes, kobolds and other beings such as they.

Slowly and carefully, then I began my search. I took care not to wake the

Marsh-masters by first proceeding along the common waterways. Though, perhaps, something may have caught the eye of a bug rising momentarily from the water, or perchance a reflection glistened in an overgrown oxbow, or somewhat there was that other creatures living those quaggy fens espied...

There was emptiness all around, and that very emptiness gave me no peace—I could not have been left wholly alone. The trail might be old and faint, but a trail there must be. Surely, those who kept me in their sight could not hide themselves so well as to be proof even against this component of the Marsh Magic. Would I finally have to awaken the Seers of the Marsh?

My decision was long in the making and my payment long in the preparation. It was no simple matter to collect great herds of livestock from various worlds—and that was only the half of it, since the toll also included human flesh. The trolls unhesitatingly took the straightest route, but for me it was a knotty conundrum. Some of the mortally ill acceded to my request, on condition I made their families rich.

Their death was quick, quiet and painless, coming as they slept; but then I had to win for them a happy afterlife. It is not easy to deceive Iargohor, but deceive him I did, thereby increasing my indebtedness to the Young Gods. By that time, I had lost count of the divine precepts I had violated.

All the lengthy and laborious preparations were at last complete. I had piles of animal carcasses, and I had my people, who were to depart this life only at the very last moment as they stood before the monster's gaping maw—but I had plunged them into blissful slumber so they saw and heard nothing. I sent all those requisites over to the other world and began to weave an intricate web of spells.

Then came the revelation. I gazed through the eyes of a being that dozed in the mire yet could see right through the world. It was a painful thing—I had a terrible desire to blink, but the eyes that were now mine had no lids.

What I saw were the fanciful folds and furrows of the Real hovering, so to speak, over the place where Hedinseigh lay. I say "so to speak" because in point of fact they were under and over and round about, but a mortal observer on the island would have perceived them as being up aloft.

In those folds nestled several strange figures, each unlike the next. The first I recognized, albeit with some difficulty, as one of Esteri's White Warriors, who were at once servitors and fighters, much like Sigrlinn's zophars but somewhat less carefully made, as befitted their mistresses' skills. The three others were, at the moment, unknown to me, although I was immediately aware they were endowed with such wizardly power as I had never seen a servitor possess.

I also had no trouble discerning the invisible threads, concealed with care from all mind-gazes, that led away from the web hanging over Hedinseigh to the layers of the Mid-Real and to those who had mounted guard over me. Every movement I made was instantly known—but to whom? To Esteri, like as not, and almost certainly to Sigrlinn and Merlin, too, for the Archmage of the Generation must surely feel the need to stay abreast of what the unrepentant mischief-maker was about.

The scaly residents of the marsh also answered another question for me. I had wanted to know when that web of unsleeping vigilance had first been stretched over Hedinseigh, and discovered it had been deployed shortly after our attack on the Erivag temple—which meant the Council must still not have a shred of real evidence against me.

Nor was it especially troublesome to guess what those spies who hid themselves so well from each and all were anticipating. I was certain now that Merlin needed only the slightest pretext to make away with me, and that he had been in search of it since the day of my return from exile. He alone had the power to create such folds in the layers of the Real, and to secure those pleats with charms. The Archmage was biding his time, not taking his eyes off me even for a moment.

But I was still unclear as to Sigrlinn's role. What was her part in this story? She had joined Ialini's retinue to some purpose, even though two more different personalities would be hard to find anywhere. I was dimly aware that my once-beloved was acting on a plan; but was I its target, or was she, rather, pursuing goals of her own of which I was unaware?

I discovered also that all the temples of the Young Gods in Eastern Hjorvard were rapidly increasing their complements of guards and enlisting more and more soldiers. I did not need the help of the Diviner of Charms to sense the growing concentration in the temples of the nethermost magical powers that lay at the priests' disposal.

Are they intending a move against Hedinseigh? I wondered. *Doubtful. The temples have never been military establishments. Yet all that happens in our world once happened for the first time.*

Meanwhile, Old Hropt was not sitting idle. Deep underground, the gnomes, who still submitted to his will, were busy day and night forging weapons. They had remained loyal to the Father of Hosts, who had awakened them to life in the unimaginably distant days when the Young Gods were not even a twinkle in the eye. Whole mountains of swords, shields and helmets were held ready in safe places; for ever since I had realized I was being watched, I had made an effort not let the scope of our preparations become common knowledge.

Merlin knew there had been little to distinguish my previous apprentices one from another—they had all been warriors and kings, founders of principalities and of empires. He was probably expecting something of the kind from me this time, too.

Perhaps, he might be thinking, Hedin will try to seize the free-peasant territories and the Mercantile Republic, which is likely enough, since he already has the lands of the jarls in his grip. But once he impinges on the Sheltered Kingdom—which he must, of necessity—then the Mages and Sigrlinn, who triumphed over him once before, will go to war to stop him. He will not be able to stand against the entire Generation. Eventually, going down in defeat and in desperate hopes of saving himself, he will inevitably unleash forces in violation of the Laws of the Ancients—the Great World Balance, that is—at which point, nothing will prevent me, Merlin, from doing away with him. Order will be restored.

I made not the slightest effort to resist the watchers. Since my rousing of the marsh monsters had escaped their notice, let them go on thinking I was oblivious to it all. The changes on Hedinseigh should come about gradually; then, when they were finally seen for what they were, it would be too late to mount a meaningful response.

AS THE YEARS WENT BY, I CONTINUING RE-ESTABLISHING MY BONDS WITH THE NIGHTFOLK. All the remnants of Rakoth's dark armies, which had scattered and gone to ground in secluded and distant corners of this and several nearby worlds, had to be reassembled. In old gnomish pit workings, goblins stirred. Kobolds, created once upon a time as a counterweight to the gnomes, who themselves were maintaining their neutrality, went to secret caches to retrieve carefully hidden and much cherished weapons that bore the runes of the Dark Magic of Metal. The harrids restrung their bows, and even the woodland kheddees—to say nothing of the trolls—felt life returning to them.

My apprentice, meanwhile, was thriving. His force now numbered ten thousand swordarms, Ilving had borne him a son and many of the lands of both Western and Eastern Hjorvard, weary of living in lawlessness, were openly calling him their ruler and pressing him ever harder to take the crown. For his part, he did what was fitting—answering them with vague allusions and avoiding giving either a direct refusal or a direct acceptance.

Those years, which sped by so fast, I remember now as a time of true happiness. I worked hard, forging deep into the secret layers of Elemental

Wizardry so that, when the time came, I would be ready to meet the Young Gods on my own terms. Their powers, after all, were not boundless, for only the Creator is all-embracing. His Children, whoever they be, are only a part of the world he created, and no part can surpass the power of the whole. The Young Gods might have crushed the Ancient Gods who ruled the Mageworld before them, but not even they were an equal match for all of Nature.

That is why, in addition to my studies of Elemental Sorcery, I also persevered in my search for the way to the Axes, to the Pillars of the Third Power of our World. To Great Orlangur and Demogorgon, whose kingdom encompassed all: the Real and the Mid-Real, the Astral and the realms of Eternal Gloom, all the innumerable worlds and High Heavens, and even the Stellar Boundaries. Together, they ruled omnipresently and ubiquitously; they ruled, but did not govern.

No one knew their purposes or desires. They had no need of temples, reverence or genuflections. They existed in and of themselves. And were the whole world to disappear the very next day, they would endure. Truth be told, they were the entire mainstay of that infamous Balance. Sometimes, they helped those who contrived to petition them, but sometimes not. No one could understand why they decided as they did.

I would have been mad to count on help from the Spirit of Absolute Knowledge and the Spirit of the Congregate Worldsoul, or to construct any plans thereon. None could expect that of me, and if all came to pass as it should...

But before closing in mortal combat with the denizens of the Hallowed Land, I had more—much more—to do. Hagen had his duties, too. He would ultimately have enemies, inhuman enemies, to confront, and for that he would need a sword made by hands more powerful even than those of the gnomish adepts.

To that end, I had long kept watch on a certain distant, sultry land that lay amid the wild virgin forests and yellow plateaus of Southern Hjorvard. A strange place it was, and one where the Young Gods were of no consequence. During my exile of ages I had trodden every path of Greater Hjorvard, and can say with certainty that there and nowhere else, through some unknowable whim of the world's new rulers, were preserved inviolate, alive and still in possession of their powers, the Ancient Southern Gods. Hardly had my wanderings brought me to those parts than I sensed their magic, coarse as sackcloth, congealing in my way.

In that place, trees never seen in Eastern Hjorvard dipped their long-leafed branches in the black waters of forest rivers. Singular beasts—furry lizards, hairless wolves and many-headed snakes—settled their scores in a murky green mist of dense foliage, lithe vines and impenetrable thickets. In the midst of the forests, and at a respectful distance from the rivers, were settlements surrounded by farmland. The people there stayed well away from those rivers, for the somber waters swarmed with sharp-toothed connoisseurs of human flesh. Instead, they used ditches fenced off with thick wooden palings to irrigate the fields.

Every village, furthermore, had a clear view of The Mountain, as the locals called it. Crested with a white crown of eternal snow, the great gray hulk looked down with silent scorn on the teeming life at its foot. And in The Mountain's stone innards roosted the harsh old power that ruled those lands.

To its broad gates streamed long caravans with provisions, goods and files of slaves. Under those grim vaults were performed rituals so repellent my pen falters in describing them. There the dismal echoes, weakening gradually as they carried, bore through passageways and galleries the last howls of victims stretched taut across the altars as their lifeblood drained away under sacrificial knives.

The god that ruled here found his strength in human suffering and fear—so unlike Hropt he was, though their provenance was the same. The Father of Hosts had preferred to see his entire kingdom, his entire realm, fall rather than to seek salvation at so vile a cost.

The inhabitants of that land were not eminently hospitable. In the first village into which I strayed several sturdy and well-fed militiamen set upon me, felled me to the ground and bound me, after which they began to question me, alternating their inquiries with the blows of a whip. I did my best to show them how much it hurt, since what powers the Council had not stripped from me still sufficed to keep the scourge a fraction of an inch from my body. Eventually, it transpired that I was declared a vagrant traveling without permission issued by some district commandant; and having so heinously violated the law, I would have to be taken to The Mountain.

When the villagers heard my sentence what I read on their faces was undisguised joy, but I did not hold them to blame. After all, this odd and dangerous stranger was taking the place of a sacrifice chosen from among them. The lot could fall on anyone—friend, wife, neighbor, mother, child...

I determined not to resist. They placed a heavy yoke on my neck and attached it with a short chain to a longer one on which, like a bunch of berries, were already strung fifteen or so despondent individuals destined, like me, to be sacrificed to the bloodthirsty Lord of the Mountain. Looking into the eyes of most of them, all I saw there was brutish horror; only a few of those eyes still flashed with unquenched fury and the will to fight.

The caravan got under way. We passed through a rich and abundant land whose soil yielded three harvests a year, and whose inhabitants could have flourished with far less effort than was required in the rocky ravines of my own Eastern Hjorvard. Yet poverty reigned everywhere, and I was very soon aware of its cause. So much—so very much—was swallowed up in The Mountain's insatiable belly. The most anyone could dream of attaining here was to become a menial in the great shrine—a guard or even a caretaker—since those who were so employed lived off the fat of the land. That this entailed treating compatriots and kinsfolk like cattle seemed to concern few of them. Certainly, malcontents were reported to the authorities swiftly and with a right good will.

But for the most part, the locals occupied me little; I was far more interested in The Mountain and its mysterious Master. It was not so much his nature that intrigued me, since all the Ancient Gods are essentially of the same origin, but what powers he wielded and what had enabled him to stand firm against the Young Gods. At the time I knew nothing of the fearsome rituals that were performed in The Mountain's underground vaults.

Then it was that I, Hedin, Sage of Darkness, first understood how little I deserved my title, for there were opened before me depths of darkness and the means of deriving strength from that darkness to which, even were I on the very brink of death, I could never have recourse. They would entail the something worse than death that was already covertly stalking the demented Master of the Mountain.

In due course, our caravan reached The Mountain's first long spurs, which extended out on all sides. The condemned shuffled on in listless silence with drooping heads. Meanwhile, I was doing all I could to portray myself an ordinary mortal—I wanted to see as much as possible and understand it, to find the answers to my questions before this provincial god realized the fish in his net was too large and overly eager to use its teeth.

All the roads leading from distant parts of the country flowed together into a great, dusty square before gigantic gates that dwarfed those of the temple in Erivag—those would have seemed but a pitiful picket had they been transplanted there. Behind those gates loomed a darkness pierced by crimson and blue firebolts, which exhaled swirls of suffocating yellow smoke. A hot, dry wind carried the smoke into the throng that filled the square, but no one even dared wipe away the streaming tears.

Guards wearing full-face masks and apparently not at all troubled by the smoke strode through the ranks, brandishing spiked cudgels and keeping a close watch on the crowds congregating under their cold gaze. A mere sneeze or a cough resulted in the unfortunate blasphemer being seized by his own neighbors in misfortune and smartly handed over to the guards who, turning a deaf ear to his heart-rending cries, would hastily thrust him into the darkness behind the gates.

We stood long in the baking sun before someone in a yellow robe—plump and imposing, although nicely caked with dust—appeared, accompanied by eight guards. Sticking out a scornful lip, he jabbed randomly with his finger at several of the sentenced, including me. There were five of us. Three promptly collapsed into the dust, squealing and drooling. One—powerfully built, olive-skinned, bearded and clearly a native of the northern reaches of Southern Hjorvard—clenched his fists and gave a low growl of irrepressible fury. He would have flung himself upon the yellow-garbed swagbelly had not the latter prudently increased the distance between them, measuring to a nicety the length of the chain that held the captive fast.

We were led through the gates. The thick-witted power of the Master of those parts weighed heavy on my temples, as if a stake lay on either side of my head and on each ten strong men were pressing down with all their might. My normal sight was insufficient to show me either the walls or the ceiling of the tunnel down which we passed—there was nothing but billowing darkness shot through with those firebolts and wan flares. A powerful rumble would now and then resound overhead as the earth trembled, and still those poisonous yellow vapors rolled toward us.

The three who had lost both their hope and their wits were dragged bodily by the guards. The olive-skinned man walked under his own power, wheezing, his teeth bared. I myself was shouting, so as not to seem conspicuously calm.

The preparations for the ritual were lengthy. We were led through halls lined with rows of heated cauldrons full of smoking, seething liquids, strange aromatic oils and other substances I could not then name. One of my four unwilling companions died on the spot, to the accompaniment of envious gazes from the rest.

I shall not describe the excruciating cries of those plunged into the huge copper cauldrons by the guards or tell how they were dragged out, only to have charred brands touched to their scalded bodies, for their tormentors' greater amusement. I so wanted to use even the smallest part of the combat magic that had been left to me, but I restrained myself, for something of greater importance lay ahead. I was beginning to see through the vague, turbid cloud to the heart of it all.

What followed was more foul and repulsive yet. I shall not record here what they did to the women, for no parchment ever made could support the telling of it. They gave them to be defiled by...not even by other humans, but by...

No, it does not bear remembering!

We were brought at last to the central hall. The Master of the Mountain was giving a fine show, putting every effort into his indescribably colorful fireworks, but I was not watching them. My eyes, instead, were fixed on the tall black throne at the far end of the room, which looked tiny when viewed from the entry door.

A figure sat there, making slight, almost indistinguishable movements. It seemed to be wreathed in hazy smoke, and I could not get a clear view of it, try as I might. A huge plaza strewn with sand lay at the foot of the throne, and to the left and right were two similar courts, but smaller.

In general, there was nothing supernatural on view here. These were all most ordinary—and not particularly imaginative—tokens of power, strength, and barbarity. But I went cold and my hair stood on end when I understood in time the reason for that endless succession of bloody sacrifices, for this horrific scene of slaughter that was unfolding before me.

Great lizards trampled the people underfoot. Thin, but very hungry, snakelike things with scarlet maws lapped at the blood. Gigantic mills turned, the stone circles and sharp-toothed gears moving with deliberate slowness. The blood was, in truth, flowing in torrents.

At first I was too startled and stunned to understand any of it, but a few seconds later I began to look at that hall with other eyes, inhuman eyes...

I saw a light, greenish mist streaming from mouths unhinged by torture and gaping in a silent scream. I knew what that was: it was suffering, horror, and pain issuing forth. It rose like steam over the melt-water in an icy lake; and flying creatures with large leathery wings, invisible to the naked eye, caught it in huge pellucid sacks as it reached the ceiling. Once their sacks were full, they disappeared into passages set in the far wall.

Yet even there I could follow the monster's winged minions as they came to the place where the blood of the tortured flowed through countless troughs, and dropped there those massive bladders filled with inexpressible human sorrow and despair. Other beings, with many hands and as many eyes, then set to work boiling the human blood over a slow fire and infusing it, in huge transparent vessels, with the emanation of human suffering. This mixture was stirred until it thickened, and was finally served up in huge goblets to the Master of the Mountain seated there on his throne.

He drank it off, and for a time the blinding fire in his four eyes burned intolerably bright. Slaves, guards, executioners and victims began to shudder, the walls trembled, the very bowels of the Earth quaked. The god had received a new influx of strength.

Yet there was in that hall another focus of might—a true focus that had no need of such shoring. In a stone crevice to the right of the throne was wedged a shortsword of blue steel that radiated waves of steadfast, unyielding power. One glance was enough to satisfy me that neither gnomes nor Mages had made it, that it was, perhaps, the handiwork of someone who had ruled here before the coming of the Young Gods.

The power with which that weapon was invested resembled not at all that which I had encountered in the renowned magical swords of my youth, maturity and exile. There was something indescribably peaceful in that sword; it had been forged with no dark thoughts of revenge or conquest. The hands that had crafted it had reveled in their art, or so it seemed to me.

And one other understanding came to me then. There it was, my future apprentice's weapon I had been seeking so long on his behalf.

Meantime, I was shoved ever more insistently toward the huge mill, whose bloodstained stones had already made short work of three fellow prisoners. The fourth, the swarthy stranger, stood alongside me emitting muffled growls and wildly rolling his eyes.

Still I used no magic. I simply snatched the spear from the nearest guard, knocked him aside with the shaft then snapped the yoke from about my neck as easily as if it had been made of straw. I flung the guard who hurled himself on me between the slowly rotating millstones. Next, I freed the olive-skinned man, signaled him to follow me and quit that torture chamber with rapid but steady strides.

Our flight went unremarked—too many people were groaning, howling and cursing their fate for the yelp of a second guard to be heard above the dreadful din. Before those in charge realized what had happened and sent out pursuers, we were at the gates.

It was the battle of the Erivag temple to the life, for we were, as later, set upon in the very gateway. I was entitled to kill, being temporarily divested, as it were, of my title of Mage; and I was as adept in the clutch as I had ever been. I slashed and hewed with pleasure, to my heart's content, grateful that our adversaries were not armed with bows. Leaving seven or eight bodies behind us, I and my involuntary companion burst out into the square before the gates and were rapidly lost in the crowd.

THE DECADES PASSED; MY EXILE WAS OVER. MY PLAN WAS COMING TO FRUITION, AND IT WAS time for Hagen to take up a sword that was worthy of him. He must perforce gain it himself, must lay his own hand on the weapon clasped in stone. The most I could do was serve as a brief distraction for the Master of the Mountain, whose power, though very great, was all concentrated in one place—in constant readiness, it seemed, to rebuff an attack from the Young Gods.

A Charm of Transference took me, Hagen and three thousand swordarms to the square before the gates. The cloud of yellow dust had not even settled before my apprentice's light-haired, light-eyed warriors—giants in comparison with the local inhabitants—had formed themselves into a tight wedge formation and launched their assault.

The Master of the Mountain had no way expected this. He was prepared only to deflect a magical attack, and his guards were proficient only against unarmed men. Their pitiful attempt to hold us off at the gates cost the lives of three dozen of their bravest, but Hagen's men—some of whom had fought at the Temple of Erivag—held their formation and pressed on.

The defenders of The Mountain came howling from side passages, only to perish under the swords and arrows of Hagen's warriors. We crushed a second blocking force at the entrance to the main hall, and when the blunt head of the formation emerged, its armor glinting, from the broad tunnel's black opening the room fell suddenly silent. The guards, the executioners and the tortured froze into immobility, their mouths agape, staring at the fiendish thing, all arms and legs and bristling with pikes and swords, rapidly bearing down on them.

It gave me great pleasure to set Rakoth's sword to hacking through the mechanisms of those grotesque mills. Wraiths of my creation raced about the hall. Thin threads of wizardfire flowed upward to strike at the winged gatherers of human torment. The Mountain's guards who charged me were knocked off their feet by the invisible waves of Ether I sent surging out in every direction. I had set in train all the combat magic I knew, and never had I felt more free; yet not one mortal perished at my hand.

Hagen, meanwhile, slaughtered everyone who stood in his way as he made directly for the throne.

The Master of the Mountain leapt to his feet, opened a great, yawning mouth that suddenly looked exceedingly large and spewed forth a long stream of blue-red flame. Burning everything in its path to ashes, it stretched all the way to me; and I thanked my stars that the riskiest part of our scheme had come off so well, because the time might now be too short to strike anew at this Ancient God.

I met the flame with a shield woven of darkness and turned it back, sending it flowing off, unextinguished, to various quarters. Whirling columns of smoke soared aloft, screening Hagen's detachment from sight. My wraiths had served their purpose, for now the Master of the Mountain had determined that I was his chief adversary.

Hagen was already racing up the steps to the throne—alone, leaving all his men below to contend with a swarm of guards sent from their hiding places by The Mountain's ruthless Master to be butchered. They would have to be held back with naught but ordinary swords.

Only then did the Ancient God deign to pay attention to the little human figure closing in on him. The hall rang with horrid laughter that could as well have been the cackle of a gigantic bird. The Master of the Mountain drew himself up to a height that exceeded Hagen's twice over and raised an immense cudgel.

Then, for the first time, I saw our enemy clear. He was almost eighteen feet tall, but his body looked like a ghastly, putrefying jumble of bones bedecked with scraps of flesh and pullulating with diminutive creatures that might have been beetles or ants. The huge, hairless, elongated skull was adorned with round blue-black eyes that had neither whites nor pupils and a long thin-lipped mouth—it was a loathsome, sickening sight.

Yet this god had once been beautiful, merry and carefree, had roamed the lovely southern forests, frolicking in the sparse woodland glades with those who lived there, had marked the succession of rainy and sunny days, sending drying winds or moist sea breezes as the need arose. The tiny villages at the forests' edges probably set up chapels in his honor and decorated his likeness with flowers in due season. He was good then, or at least not evil.

And what had he now become? A frightful monster prepared to exterminate all life in his own land in order to live but one day more—and for that the Young Gods were to blame.

The god's cudgel rose and fell, sending up a spatter of stone from the shattered steps. Hagen swerved aside and slammed his blade into the Mountain Master's hideous leg.

I had been waiting for that instant to deal a blow of my own. All the might I had drawn together gusted out at once, and the world reeled around me so rapidly everything swam together. The god's mouth opened again, and a stream of flame was already gushing toward my apprentice—our enemy preferred to forego more refined forms of magic.

Then the invisible arrow I had loosed found its target.

Through the hall's roof, grown suddenly transparent, all The Mountain's layers now a crystal casing, a Dragon of Time baring innumerable teeth gazed down, its eyes burning with the pure light of the deep sea and its huge mouth stretched into a smile that was the stuff of nightmares.

Hagen was instantly forgotten. The startled god raised his head for just the time it took for my arrow to reach him and for Hagen to wrest the Blue Sword from the grip of those stone jaws.

When my arrow hit its mark amid a great scatter of orange sparks, the god flailed his arms and staggered with an odd squawking sound, something between a groan and a cry. His throne blazed, the stone melted and flowed down in a stream of dazzling white. The Master of the Mountain was backed up against a chasm, teetering on its very brink.

I froze, knowing this was the deciding moment. I had not succeeded in bringing him down, and had no strength to strike again.

But Hagen kept his head. His newly acquired sword glinted, a lightning flare amid the flashes of crimson light. Then he was wrenching the blade, still unstained, from the Ancient God's thigh.

A harrowing cry of feral pain made the walls sway and crack. Hagen struck again, and the Master slumped sideways, his right leg severed. He shuddered once, twice, clutched the wound, which was oozing dark blood, and pitched over the chasm's edge.

The shrill cry died away in the depths, smoke streamed from fissures, and my apprentice gave the command to withdraw.

The Master was not, of course, dead—gods do not perish at mortal hands. The two of us together might have been able to finish him off, though I felt even so there was still too much power in him. He no longer had a body, but soon a disembodied Spirit, even more bloodthirsty and merciless than before, would settle itself on a restored throne in the heart of The Mountain, unless before that the Young Gods—or Merlin—seized their chance to make an end of it.

That was how Hagen came to own the Blue Sword, whose fame very quickly spread through all four regions of Greater Hjorvard. I devoted quite a lot of time to that blade. The gnomes of my acquaintance simply scratched their heads over this weapon forged from a metal unknown to them. At first I thought of the Gifts—the metal stones that fell to Earth from time to time—but the upland craftsmen disabused me of that notion.

So, I left that enigma unresolved, and occupied myself instead with the sword's magic, which was, I discovered, labyrinthine in the extreme. There was the Ancient Magic of Metal, with which I was somewhat familiar, and—I knew not why—also the Magic of Stone. The rest of it I could not decipher on the fly, and I lacked the time to work long and painstakingly on untangling that complex web of charms.

We had many more adventures, but they all involved affrays with humans or other mortals. My kinsfolk, the Mages of my Generation, maintained an utter silence. Hedinseigh remained under observation, but no actions were taken against us. I tried again to speak with Sigrlinn, but in vain—the Castle of All the Ancients was deserted, as was her palace in Jibulistan. Indeed, my Band of Erith seemed to have gone deaf and blind, leaving me unable to speak with any Mage. I sensed a noose around me, drawing tighter and tighter as the time grew ever more short.

But the steps of my plan were being accomplished one by one, and I needed to be patient only a little while longer.

It was then I received word from Hropt that Garm had awoken.

HAGEN HAD DONE RIGHT; THE HOUND HAD TO BE SENT BACK TO SLEEP BEFORE THE YOUNG Gods made their appearance in our world. A pity it was that, after all he and his men had endured, we would now have to begin immediately, but once Sigrlinn raised her hand against my apprentice, all the prohibitions and codes of honor were cast aside. We could delay no longer, although my arsenals of magic were not yet fully stocked. There was no choice. If we did not strike the first blow, if we did not throw our enemies into strength-draining confusion, we would certainly be annihilated.

The bells of Hedinseigh sounded the assembly. The men settled on the dragon-ships' polished benches. Hagen slid the Blue Sword into its sheath and bowed before me in farewell. We were about to lay siege to an entire world.

PART THE SECOND

CHAPTER VII

THE HEDINSEIGH FLOTILLA WAS STILL IN SIGHT OF THE ISLAND WHEN THE MOON WAS gathered up in the hairy paws of night. The following wind gave way to a headwind, and surging swells came pounding in from larboard. The wind blew more fiercely by the minute. The crews struck sail, and all took to the oars.

Hagen clambered onto the carved prow of his flagship and settled there, on the grinning snout of some fabled sea monster. His helmsmen were running almost blind, relying solely on their excellent knowledge of the local winds and currents, while he, aided by a Charm of Nightsight, peered endlessly into the darkness, his sword, unawares to him, drawn half out of its sheath.

How many of us will they allow through? was the importunate thought stirring at the back of his mind. *All our artifices have surely long been known to them, and they are toying with us still.* He was ready for anything, and would not even have been surprised to see the waves part and the Worldserpent itself rear up above the swells.

"Come down, your honor!" the helmsman cried, straining to be heard. "The sea's too rough! Come down!"

It being unwise to test the patience of troops setting out on a bold and dangerous foray with a vainglorious show, Hagen slid down from the wooden beast's scaly neck onto the deck, allowing the charm to weaken. *The horizon's empty. If a blow is coming, it will come, like as not, from below the waves or from on high. We have most certainly been noticed.*

But thane he was and thane he would ever be—a seasoned commander of maritime campaigns, ever watchful that the rowers' reliefs reported timely for duty and that no one missed his turn to sleep.

By morning they were approaching the shores of the Sheltered Kingdom. The sea was barren, rough and stormy, and the sun was still submerged in dense gray clouds. The dragon-ships put into a small inlet that was somewhat protected against the waves by a scarp jutting far out into the sea.

The men sprang into the shallows, and the ships pushed off again. Hagen swiftly led his four-thousand-strong detachment away from the shore toward the dark-green wall of trees that lay behind the flat, narrow strip of sea cliffs. A vast throng of feet silently scaled the granite slopes, leaving not a trace behind. They could have penetrated far inland before any human detected them or any dog caught their scent.

The day slowly caught light over the Sheltered Kingdom's forlorn and rocky shorelands as Hagen's men filed toward the forest in double time. When they were close to the treeline, Lodin, marching alongside the thane, shaped his hand, placed it against his mouth and made several shrill, jay-like calls. The piercing sound sank into the silent green wall, and after moments that seemed interminable to Hagen, they heard the reply.

Lodin turned to his commander. "The Nightfolk are here, my thane."

Century after century, the detachment disappeared under the dense shroud of the forest. Soon the plateau was empty, with no memory left of the army that had so recently disembarked.

IN A TINY GLADE ENCIRCLED BY AGE-OLD PINES, FOUR BEINGS MET FACE-TO-FACE. TWO OF them were human—tall, in dark armor, with long, straight swords; the one who placed himself a little ahead of his companion wore his sword across his back, the hilt jutting up over his right shoulder.

The other two could have been taken for human only from a distance. They looked like gnomes but stood slightly taller and were less thickset. Their arms were long, hands almost touching knees; and their long greenish locks escaped from under low brown riveted helmets. They were dressed in crudely fashioned black-dyed oxhides, and curved, lavishly serrated ataghans hung from their broad belts.

These were goblins.

The leader bowed. "We greet the esteemed Thane Hagen, apprentice of the Mage great in wisdom, Sage of Darkness, who is friend to our Father," it said, its voice a hoarse blare. While not well-favored, its face was at least not brutish, as are those of others of its kind. No fangs sprouted from its mouth, and its fingers ended in nails where others had claws.

"I have brought them all." The leader's round head wagged, indicating the forest at his back. "Four thousand, all who wished to fight. We are ready."

"Excellent," Hagen responded. Hedin's lessons had stripped him of the squeamish fear that almost all humans feel toward goblins. "We have little time, and will have to march all this day and through the night. We shall not wait for stragglers. We have no carts. There is no place of refuge in the Sheltered Kingdom. If we are defeated, then better for us never to have been born. Have you explained that to your forces? Do they understand?"

"They do," the leader rumbled. "They do. These are such as wish to quit their hiding places in the forests, where they are hunted like wild animals. We desire to found our own small domain somewhere in the distant reaches of Hjorvard and to live there, at last, as others do. Here are those who have rejected our Father's terrible gift, and have no taste for human flesh. I, Orc, have spoken and you, esteemed thane, have heard." This was a proud goblin.

"Orc? A strange name—it is the name given to all of your kind in Western Hjorvard," Hagen told him.

The leader smiled. "And how is that strange? Humans have forgotten that in the language of our Father, who once ruled all of Western Hjorvard, the word *orc* means neither more nor less than *free*."

"I see. And the others of your tribe? The rest of the Nightfolk?"

"All who have not run forever wild are ready. And may this be the last war between us and the humans—we also want to live."

"This war is not between you and the humans," Hagen said sternly, looking at the goblin with grim eyes. "It is a war between those who prefer to live as slaves and those who would rather die free. We are issuing a challenge to the Young Gods, who were the undoing of your Father—to them and to them alone—and we are battling their minions, be they men or nomen. Good it would be if you were to explain that to your forces as we go. And now, forward! Send out your patrols. From now on there shall be no rest. Remember, we wait for no stragglers."

Avoiding the well-trodden paths and traveling instead through back-country ravines and byways choked with downed trees, Hagen's force moved speedily northeast, making straight for the Sovereign City, capital of the Sheltered Kingdom. No one fell behind, since Lodin had chosen his hardiest men for this campaign and it seemed the goblin chieftain had done the same. Hedin's hand was felt resting on them all, for as they marched on his apprentice encountered not one—not even the most diminutive—wood sprite or any other of Ialini's minions. The thickets seemed dead.

"This troubles me," Frodi grumbled to Gudmund, who strode along at his side. "'Tis an evil silence. How much longer will they bear our presence here?"

"You croak like any raven," Gudmund sneered. "Just be glad that we're covering ground."

But Frodi only muttered disconsolately to himself.

Evening drew on and night fell, and still they continued, marching past tree-trunks that crowded together to form an impassable wall, fording streams, leaving quiet woodland pools behind them and giving a wide berth to the few villages that nestled under the forest canopy. It was not until dawn tinged the sky to the east with green that Hagen at last allowed the haste-driven armies to halt.

Men and goblins sprawled silently and haphazardly onto the grass. The thane had brought them to a deep gully, its slopes thick with bushes and a brook murmuring along its floor.

"'Tis...peaceful...in this place," Orc said in surprise, loudly sniffing the air. "As we marched there was something...sensible of us...all around. It was as if someone I could not espy, try as I might, was watching us. But here..."

"That's why we stopped here," Hagen replied. He had settled on a green hummock beside a slightly raised patch of rather withered turf. He peeled back the grassy lid and plunged his hand deep into a dark narrow opening in the ground.

"Step aside, gentlemen," he said loudly.

Lodin, Gudmund and Orc promptly found somewhere else to be, and Hagen slowly drew out a begrimed little bag. The harrids had done their best—no one could have carried Hedin's amulet farther into the Sheltered Kingdom than they.

"And now we rest," the thane said carelessly, tucking the bag into the bosom of his shirt.

The valley seemed littered with corpses. Eight thousand warriors were spread across it, a living, breathing carpet. With every hour that passed, the amulet over Hagen's heart, at first almost burning hot, would grow cooler. When he no longer felt its warmth at all, that would mean their cover was gone and in a few hours, at most, news of them would reach the field headquarters of Vidrir, who had moved eastward to hunt down the overweening Hjorlief and his army. Or maybe the priests in Sovereign City and the Mages who were aiding them—Sigrlinn, for one—would settle their own scores with this insolent invasion even before Vidrir's return. Hagen shuddered at the very thought of the Disc of Iamerth.

As the sun still worked its way to the zenith, he ordered his army afoot. The last stage of their march was ahead of them, and by evening they must be at the Sovereign City.

The forest had thinned to small copses that lurked on land unfit for tilling, and in little dingles. As far as the eye could see now there was nothing but fields, pasturelands, meadows, roads, granaries, farmsteads and villages. And people—people everywhere. Forward, though, while the amulet of the Sage of Darkness still retained its strength!

The long column poured out of the woodland's dusk. They could now have been easily seen by spirits, had they not been well free of the thickets where the Fleshless held sway. But from human eyes they were hidden—for the time being, at least.

They skirted the meadows to avoid any unwanted encounters with villagers, who would not enjoy colliding with an army traveling under a cloak of invisibility. They traveled as fast as a galloping horse, looking neither right nor left and holding on to their weapons to silence the clang of metal. Their route took them by two small towns; and then, as the afternoon sun was beginning to slide toward the western horizon, they saw before them the gigantic towers and bastions of Vidrir's capital.

All this while Hagen kept his silence, marching with lowered head and deep in thought. His centurions and chiliarchs had no need of constant prompting, and that left him free to consider his next actions. To that point, everything was proceeding exactly as prescribed by his Teacher's plan, and what troubled him was not that but rather Hedin's words of farewell.

"You go in haste. You cannot wait to give battle," he had said, his stern eyes fastened on his apprentice, who was unaccountably discomfited by that direct gaze. "Your love of warfare I know. You have never been defeated, and that may have spoiled you somewhat. I feel that you hold yourself to be invincible.

"Yes, you're handy with a sword, and you imagine that you have no equal among mortals. But that could be your undoing in Vidrir's capital. Understand, they who await you there are not the petty kinglings of Western Hjorvard nor the well-nourished temple guards of the south. In the Sovereign City, you will no doubt come upon other Mages' apprentices, and that I fear more than aught else. I have done my utmost to pass on to you all my weapon-craft, and you, alas, have invested too much trust in your blade. The Sheltered Kingdom has swordsmen of equal caliber to send against you. And some there are in this world more adept even than the Mages against metal playthings such as your sword. I mean the Young Gods—the Sheltered Kingdom did not come lightly by its name.

"You must stifle your pride, for the danger is not to the army, which is superior to the Sovereign City's defenders, but to you yourself. Have no doubt that when you and your men engage, the priests will very quickly determine who leads the attack and will send against you the very best at their command. And you are so sure of your preeminence that you may become careless."

I promise you that I am taking great care, Teacher, Hagen thought. *I have eight thousand swordarms at my back, and am needful not to myself but to them. So let me rather be supposed a coward than rush pell-mell where I'd best not go.*

"My thane!" The rapid whisper was close by his ear. Lodin's face was slick with sweat and alarm filled his eyes. "Belike we'll soon be seen. Look there, ahead!"

By the road stood a neat gray two-story house of well-dressed stone. Near a gateway in the fence stood a tall, thin old man with a long, fine-featured face. He wore a voluminous gray cloak and leaned on a stave. He glanced about him in agitation, as if looking for something, biting his lip anxiously.

A device on the front of his house struck Hagen's eye—a device he knew only too well and hated just as much. Big, bold, scarlet, it was the crest of the Wizards' Guild of the Sheltered Kingdom. The Wizards' Guild of the Sheltered Kingdom was an association of warlocks whose knowledge derived from revelations made to them by the Young Gods. Not one of them, of course, could vie with a true Mage, but all were capable of pulling a Mage's apprentice up short.

"Damnation!" he said, his voice husky. He could feel the amulet against his body cooling ever faster as the enchanter's rapt attention rapidly sucked the last strength from Hedin's handiwork. The cloak of invisibility still shrouded Hagen's forces but was about to disappear at any moment.

Out of the corner of his eye, he noticed Gudmund readying his trusty hooked blade and was scarcely able to grasp his warrior's wrist in time. The thane's furious eyes and compressed, bloodless lips were more eloquent than any words could be. Gudmund quickly lowered his weapon.

Hagen gave the sign that meant "Forward, at the double."

To be as close as might be to the city gates and there be spied by a wizard! Now he would have to tarry here and play spoiler with this accursed old gaffer, who had chosen the worst possible time to get in the way. Brusquely ordering Lodin to take command, he made directly for this new hindrance.

The warlock slowly raised his staff, the white carved knob at its tip unhurriedly tilting until it pointed straight at Hagen, who stopped short at five paces' distance from the old man. The amulet was so cool it could hardly be felt. In feverish haste, Hedin's apprentice wove a Sleepcharm, but knowing the folly of investing all his hopes in that alone, he engaged another course of his mind and there raised a Darkcharm, which was yet another of the Greatcharms.

The sorcerer still held his staff on the thane, while with his left hand he made an intricate pass. The amulet's strength was gone, and Hagen, having risked himself long enough, struck the first blow.

There was no time to waste, for people were already gawking at the wizard. The gray head trembled and bent to his chest, the wrinkled lids closed, and the hand that grasped the staff suddenly lost its firmness. He staggered like a drunken man.

One of the onlookers gave an alarmed cry, and several of them sprinted forward. Hagen could sense their fear and their desire to be of help— evidently, the enchanter was loved and respected in this village.

His astral double was already dimming, enmeshed in the charm Hagen had conjured; but the hands that supported the limp body seemed to imbue it with new strength. Leaning on those who had come to his aid, the wizard made a mighty effort and stood upright.

His lips moved, and the thane instantly felt the air thickening around him. It was an artless piece of gramarye, but he had no time for a magical duel. His enchantments had helped him see the unseen.

That morning, in the valley where he had dug up the amulet, this charm would have been too feeble. Now it could well suffice to strip the curtain of invisibility from the entire army, which was still on the march at his back, the goblins' forged pattens tramping through the dust. The vanguard of the detachment under Lodin's command had made good time toward the city, but not yet good enough. They were no less than a league from the gates, and the army itself stretched almost a league from end to end.

The sorcerer was himself again. He gave an imperious sweep of the hand, and that simple but effective charm at a stroke drained Hagen's amulet of the last of its warmth. The curtain of invisibility fell away, but not before Hagen had conjured a charm of his own—the Great Darkcharm.

Impenetrable darkness surged up before the gates of the capital—a dense, inky-black murk in which no one could see his hand before his face. The people cried out in shrill terror.

And so we are discovered, Hagen thought. That blot of gloom at the city's very gates could hardly have escaped the notice of the temple priests.

He raced off after the trailing ranks of his army. Ahead of him, he heard the clash of steel and the fighters' frenzied cries. He overtook one century after another, running in the gray twilight that lay within the cloud of darkness he had unleashed, which was blue-black to the outside eye.

The goblins were excitedly talking over each other and jostling for a sight of the battle already raging up ahead. The guards at the gate held their ground, and the clanging of swords in action filled the air.

One of the most important elements of Hedin's plan—to penetrate the Sovereign City unnoticed—had failed.

Now we shall have to clear our way by main force, Hagen thought pettishly.

But by the time he reached the huge gates, Lodin had dispatched their defenders; a jumble of bodies lay scattered on the paving stones, and bloody weapons were everywhere. Hagen felt his temper rise—his troops' sacrifice in overcoming this first obstacle had been great. Unacceptably great. They had laid down two lives for every three taken, a prodigiously high price.

"They had good men posted here," he said, nodding at one of the Sheltered Kingdom's dead.

"Yes. And we lost thirty, my thane, although we were armed both with bows and arbalests," a morose Lodin replied, approaching him. The chiliarch was breathing hard, and sweat streamed from under the close helmet with its raised visor.

"Take up the dead," Hagen said in a hollow tone. "Forward, then, and may the aid of—" He broke off. Beyond the gates, a bright light flooded the capital's clean, paved streets, that being where his screen of darkness ended. In it, striding rapidly toward them, were several priests of Iamerth, followed by a mass of pikemen.

Hagen raised his sword, roaring out a wordless battle-cry. He had but seconds to fend off this new assault.

In tight formation, an iron snake, the troops flowed behind their commander. Hagen did not have to glance back; he heard the hundreds of feet marching in lock-step behind him. Fate had bade him lead them into this battle, and lead them he would.

When no more than ten paces lay between him and the priests of Iamerth, one of them raised his hands in a majestic gesture and spoke words full of menace.

"Halt, you wretches! The wrath of the all-powerful Sun and of his Lord, Iamerth the Most Fair, shall burn you to cinders if you so much as set foot on the holy ways of the Sheltered Kingdom's capital. The Perpetual Darkness shall be your home, and the Dragons of Time shall devour your souls, for such sacrilege as this renders you unworthy of any other afterlife!"

I'll warrant there's a Disc of Iamerth under that mantle, Hagen thought. He slowed his pace, and Lodin rushed ahead. In one bound, he covered the distance between himself and the priests, and out came his sword.

Had he been met with any weapon—sword, ax, dagger—he would have easily parried the blow. Instead, the priest made a languid movement with the fingers of his right hand, and Hagen's seasoned chiliarch fell headlong.

All of that took only a fraction of a second. The thane came out of his torpor, and his forces burst though the open city gates, rapidly filling the gate-court, fighting in the towers and across the battlements. Meanwhile, the goblins howled in the rear, demanding their share of the battle.

The Blue Sword's cutting edge was pointed right at the head of the foremost priest, but he peacefully crossed his arms over his chest as if to say, *Have at it, do your worst.*

Even though Hagen was entering this single combat in a full suit of burnished steel armor and with a visor covering his face, he was in no doubt the priest had recognized him, and in that he was correct. He saw the eyes of Iamerth's chief votary grow round in astonishment and his mouth fall open, and heard him call to his fellow-priests, pointing Hagen out to them.

Then Hedin's apprentice felt the hostile power that was gathering somewhere in front of him stir, aroused from its sleep by his very presence, and he realized a magical duel was about to begin. This was coming far sooner than he and his Teacher had reckoned it would; their assumption had been that he would be able to surmount that first barrier armed only with his sword.

His centurions were rapidly deploying their squads into the side streets. Vidrir's pikemen stood firm, and battle was joined in narrow alleyways, in confined courtyards, on roofs—indeed, wherever a man could stand and brandish a sword.

But while Hagen's warriors, tempered by many campaigns and affrays, and well-tested in hand-to-hand combat, gradually began pushing the defenders back, the way down the city's broad and spacious main street was still blocked by the priests of Iamerth, supported by Vidrir's heavy infantry, a solid wall bristling with steel lances.

On the run and as fast as ever he could, Hagen surrounded himself with a protective circle sufficient to guard him against the simple combat charms that were the normal currency of lesser priests and wizards, while at the same time readying his own magical offensive. He could not, to be sure, turn the entire world about himself, as a true Mage could. He could only work with the residuum of a rotation a Mage had already brought about. However, since at any second at least one of the Magic Race was performing such wizardry somewhere in the world, human warlocks and their ilk were never in want of that remnant power.

Hagen struck out with the sudden, booming might of a cyclone when it drops its first ravening tentacle down to the ground, and was immediately enveloped in a fearsome blast of heat. He seemed to have been flung into the red-hot heart of a working forge, and a gilded sheen, intolerably bright, filmed his eyes. The priests of the Temple of the Sun had broken through his defenses.

But too late. Only an instant before the frenzied flame they had called down from the heavens to turn the thane to blowing ash struck, his cyclone caught the priests up and tossed them about. The bodies, orange robes aflutter, were flung down onto the pavement, up against the walls; and there they lay, improbably bright spots plastered against the gray flagstones. The only one still standing was the Chief Votary of Iamerth, but even he had kept his feet only at the cost of halting the gush of death-dealing flame he had been sending in Hagen's direction.

Every movement of his scorched body caused hideous pain, but the thane, gritting his teeth, struggled through those last few steps and, with the last blast of his cyclone, struck the final blow. He saw the priest blanch, saw his last desperate attempts, in the grip of the whirlwind, to hold back his enemy for even an instant longer. He failed. The Blue Sword sliced the air, and the orange-mantled body was cleft in two.

Hagen looked into the shadows of that fading mind and saw there a broad saffron strip with the tiny golden vein that distinguished an apprentice of one of the Young Gods. Then the pain felled him.

A moment later, he was engulfed in a wave of his own men. "The priests have killed our thane, death to them all!" someone cried. The bodies of the servants of the Sun that still held the glimmers of life were hacked to pieces; then the men fell upon Vidrir's pikemen, who had been looking to retreat.

Hagen opened his eyes. The pain was unbearable, but still he raised his lids, causing Gudmund and Knut, who were leaning over him, to howl in wild delight, "He's alive! Our thane's alive! Forward!"

Although every movement brought a flare of pain to Hagen's blistered body, filling his vision with multicolored circles, he stood up. Forces more powerful than suffering were driving him on, and he could not have stopped even had he wished to.

Though he had not tried to still his agony with charms, all at once he felt strength and calm flowing into him, as if someone very powerful had raised to the lips of his astral double a goblet brimming with a restorative made of stars.

Thank you, my Teacher, Hagen thought as he rose to his feet unassisted.

"Praise be to all the powers, our thane is hale!" Knut called out.

"Hale—hale, indeed—so enough of this huddling here!" Hagen roared. "Onward!"

It was certainly time for him to join the fray. Vidrir's pikemen had retreated only a few paces, and the street was strewn with Hagen's dead and wounded. The long pikes struck true, and many a coat of mail had not been strong enough to withstand them. He took a firmer grip on his Blue Sword, and with a veteran fighter's soft, slightly splayed gait advanced on the wall of enemy shields.

"Our thane is with us!" The mighty cry rolled through the ranks, rallying Hagen's men. They pressed forward, shoulder to shoulder.

Orc and his goblins had caught up, meanwhile, and stones broken from walls and pavement began to fly. Arrows soared, quivers emptying apace as the short black bolts loosed at point-blank range pierced hauberk and brigandine and punched through helmets. Vidrir's warriors dropped to the ground, but the rest closed ranks over the fallen.

A gap had opened between the two forces, which the thane was first to cross. An arrow from the enemy's rearward position broke against his gnomish visor as, armed only with his sword and wincing from the burns—more bearable now but still raw—he closed with the dense forest of pikes arrayed against him.

A notched tip capping a long shaft deftly wielded by a strapping pikeman flashed in his face. The Blue Sword responded in a dim flicker. The movement was slight, indistinguishable to the eye, but the head of the pike was gone and its owner was left holding a useless pole.

Before three more pikes could strike at the place where he stood, Hagen was already upon the row of enemy shields and saw that between the ventail of his immediate adversary's tall, tapered helmet and the body armor a narrow slit had opened. Knocking aside the blade raised in defense, his sword plunged in, slicing through the upper rows of links; and before the ranks could close again, Gudmund was by his side, parrying a blow aimed at the thane, who then stuck down another.

Hagen's warriors streamed behind their commander, bursting through the breach. The odds were equal now, and the superiority of his troops in hand-to-hand fighting was beginning to tell. Vidrir's pikemen could still turn the battle if they were to disengage, pull back smartly and reform their wall of shields. That they were trying to do, but instead their formation broke and their retreat turned into a panicked flight. Hagen's men followed close, tearing through the last small, scattered knots of opposition, and with a triumphant roar penetrated deep into the city.

Resisting the temptation to pursue, Hedin's apprentice instead dispatched fresh centuries to the aid of those still pushing down the side streets. His detachments, though thinned, were still strong enough to cut through the remnants of the city's defenders. They converged on the High Temple of Iamerth. Fires were breaking out along their route.

As far as Hagen knew, the way to the city center was wide open—he was marveling at how easy it had been when the long-expected unpleasantness finally began. Arrows, pikes, stones and even heavy kitchenware began raining down from second- and third-story windows. A flagstone suddenly turned under the feet of the man running at Hagen's side, and he disappeared into an avid, bottomless blackness. Two massive granite slabs soundlessly moved apart in a nearby wall, and slingshots fired hefty clay missiles through the gap.

Other hiding places just like it were revealed all along the army's way. Armed men appeared, seemingly out of nowhere, fired their arrows or flung their darts, and the stone walls slid shut. A breathless messenger panted his way to the thane to report that subterranean galleries had opened up and the detachment left to guard the gates was under attack. Hagen's troops were surrounded.

Nor was that the worst of it. The men would have been able to shift against an enemy normally armed, but the temple priests had recovered from their earlier defeat and were back in the fight. Not that any of them had taken to the streets again, but something glinted from the pinnacle of the temple. A broad white circle of light fell on the paving stones at Hagen's feet, and the granite began to smoke.

He stopped his men in time and, as the ashy circle cooled, ordered them to break in the doors and windows of the nearest houses while they still could. He was one of the last to take shelter, and could only watch as three goblins left in the open became three little piles of gray ash.

Hagen sent runners to the other chiliarchs, racking his feverish brain for ways to counteract this new threat. He knew his rearguard was battling Vidrir's ironclad troops, who were swarming up from under the ground. The enemy was storming the gates. The five hundred or so humans and goblins holding them were putting up a desperate fight, but, step by step, were being pushed from all sides back toward the gate towers.

Up ahead, dozens of small orange-robed figures emerged onto the temple terraces and stood there, motionless, while again something glimmered from the top of the temple's great bulk.

Breaking down walls and edging their way across roofs and through courtyards and attics, Hagen's men moved forward once more as the townsfolk's arrows hailed down onto their backs. Hagen saw an old woman toss boiling water right into a soldier's eyes, and though promptly hacked to pieces by his comrades, she was not alone.

The farther they penetrated the city, the more bitter and desperate the resistance grew, with wild skirmishes playing out in narrow corridors, cramped courts and low-ceilinged garrets where there was room enough neither to swing a sword nor to protect a fellow soldier. The inhabitants of Vidrir's capital had armed themselves with axes and oven forks, pokers and kitchen knives. Hagen's men were hit from behind with billets, had furniture dropped onto their heads, and everything in their path that would burn was set alight. In reply, they killed every living thing, even the cats and dogs that greeted the strangers with bared fangs and unsheathed claws.

Grand as the army had been when it entered the city, the chaotic street fighting had not so much melted as scattered it. Small detachments scuffled here and bogged down there, some encountering stronger resistance and others coming upon richly stocked stalls and stopping then and there to divide up the spoils. So, by the time Hagen came level at last with the great square before the Temple of the Sun, he led few more than three hundred men; and there was no time to delay the assault until the laggards caught up.

He looked around from his vantage point on the roof of a house that was burning along one side. Before him stretched an endless array of multicolored roofs under billowing clouds of smoke. In the distance, he could make out the gates, over which the standard of the Sheltered Kingdom yet flew—but upside down, as a sign his men still held the gate towers and were protecting the route out of the city.

And there stood the temple, the sun glittering on its polished buttresses and its translucent crystalline columns made of solid blocks of mountain quartz, purchased for an untold sum from the gnomes of Northern Hjorvard by Vidrir's great-great-great-grandfather. A gigantic step-pyramid, it reached high into the sky, its colonnades stretching, wing-like, to wide-flung terraces. Hundreds upon hundreds of priests were there now, motionless and mute, gazing down upon the mettlesome but scant few who had burst onto the

Temple Square.

Hagen knew they could not long stand there in full sight—he had either to beat a retreat or lead his three hundred in a desperate, all but hopeless assault. He was not sure he could wait for the rest of his troops, who were at that very moment fighting their way through the fiery confusion behind him, warding off endless attacks from armed civilians and the remnants of Vidrir's forces.

He was brought out of his agonizing uncertainly by the silent flare of a circle of Temple Fire hitting close by. In his black armor, he had apparently drawn no one's eye, but five of his men, caught unawares, were incinerated without a sound and with lightning speed. To remain there would be madness, and in the thane's mind, the only way to fight magic was with magic.

So, gathering his strength for the second time that day he recited a Great Darkcharm. Shapeless scraps of gray mist cowering in the corners of a broad square still awash with bright sunlight—that was the best he could do. This close to the temple, no earthly magic could vie with the might of dread Iamerth. The Darkness had retreated before the Light, for this was the kingdom of eternal Day.

I should have known, he thought sourly, though his Teacher had never told him anything about the priests' terrible weapon. And of a certainty, they still had something even worse in store.

"What are your orders, my thane?" Orc brayed into Hagen's ear. "All is clear behind. My lads are guarding the way to the gates, but I have ordered them brought up here. If we triumph we will find our own way out. If we are laid low there will be no withdrawal."

"Where are the other detachments?" Hagen asked bleakly, surprised by his own chagrin that the goblins, inferior to his men in weapons and training, had still reached the temple before the balance of his own forces.

"They will be here soon, esteemed thane," the goblin chieftain replied. "Which is to say that fifteen hundred of them are no more than fifteen minutes distant. They are meeting no further resistance."

"Very well. Proceed as we agreed earlier. Take your position on the north side of the building to await the signal, and tell your men to lie low. They are discharging invisible fire from the temple."

The goblin bowed, and tramped and clattered its way down the disintegrating staircase. For a few moments, Hagen was alone.

"And to this you have come."

The voice behind him was familiar, albeit unexpected, and full of an inexpressible, indescribable bitterness. Bitterness, hurt and vexation there was, but no wrath or towering rage.

He whirled around, the Blue Sword, weapon of an Ancient God, instantly in his hand. It alone, being proof against the enchantments of the Mages of this Generation, could save him now, for it would be bootless to contend with Sigrlinn in the sorcerer's art, even though he had once contrived to slip away from her under cover of an impenetrable Firecharm.

The sorceress stood by a shattered window, both hands resting on the sill. She was looking at the floor and unhurriedly gathering together the shards of broken glass with the toe of a fine green leather slipper. A long dark-green gown enveloped her slim frame, and her wondrous hair rippled across her shoulders and down her back. Unarmed she was, and seemed to have been called abruptly away from a festive board.

Hagen had always been bewitched by this fey beauty, even though he was firmly assured she was his teacher's enemy, which meant she was his sworn enemy, too. She had tried to capture him, he had fought against her with all his might and would have killed her in the heat of battle had he been able; but now all that fled from his mind. He saw only her eyes, deep and wise and brimming with reproachful sorrow. No matter who might have assailed him at that moment, he would not even have raised his sword, such peace there was in that intent gaze.

"You poor, you foolish child," she said, her voice low. "To this you have come, despite all the warnings. How hard I tried! I so wanted you to understand at last the colossal and invincible power you dare to defy. And you did understand my warnings, but this is the conclusion you have drawn from them." She sighed again and shook her head. "It was folly for me to try to stop you in the cavern at Niflhel, and I beg your forgiveness for that. Will you grant me your forgiveness?" And she raised her sweet eyes to his.

No Mage has ever begged the pardon of a human. Hagen knew that, somehow, but was surprised to find himself believing she spoke true.

His throat closed. He was tongue-tied. He wanted to reply and could not, and the only thought in his mind was that all was now lost and he was forever doomed.

"So, you don't forgive me?" she persisted gently.

Hagen did not reply. His hand was tight on the hilt of his sword, but he did not draw it from its sheath. No, he could never bring himself to harm her, no matter what his Teacher said.

"You are silent," she said thoughtfully. "And that, indeed, is your right.

Have your way, then. You will now hear what I have to say. I hope that some of it, at least, will stay with you.

"What, my child, do you think is the purpose of this great war, in which you are no more than one of thousands upon thousands of wordless, drawn weapons that must fulfil their task and then perish? Do you know that you differ in no wise from any ordinary sword or javelin? You were promised greatness and power, and so, like a mormath possessed by its thirst for blood, you have visited war upon your own kind, whose only guilt was that they desired to live in their own way and not as seemed well to a Mage named Hedin. You are seized by the delirium of power, you dream of your own empire, but I say to you that there once was such an empire. From the Iron Wood and Rogheim to Hauberk Mount and the place that is now named Haithabu it extended, and Hedinseigh was its heart.

"You imagine the walls protecting your island to be powerful and indestructible, but I tell you they are but a poor likeness of the gigantic bastions that formerly rose over Hedinseigh. They soared up to the very clouds, and a numberless army stood guard both day and night. By fire, sword and fear the master of Hedinseigh ruled, or I should say his Teacher ruled—the Mage hight Hedin.

"His ill deeds are incalculable. If one were to pile, each upon another, the skulls of those undone by the Empire of Night, for such was the name of that realm, they would form a mountain that towered as high as the Castle of All the Ancients, the peerless Pillar of the Titans. The tears shed by mothers, wives and daughters would cause the Great Sea to overwhelm its own shores and flood all the land.

"The Mages' patience was finally exhausted. We declared war on Hedin. I was the one who declared it, as you, I believe, know well. But your Teacher once loved me." Her voice fell to a whisper, then rose again."And later, when our paths diverged, he, driven by jealousy and vengeance, endlessly opposed all my undertakings. He found a strange pleasure in it. I created, he destroyed. The Empire of Night occupied almost all of Eastern Hjorvard, and had I and the other Mages not intervened it would have occupied the rest.

"But it fell, and we sent your Teacher into banishment. That was the most we could do to him. I hoped that, after experiencing for himself all the burdens and misfortunes of mortalkind, he would bethink himself; but I was wrong. He only grew harder, and when the time came for him to take an apprentice—I know not why, but the Lot fell strangely. It sent him you, a born warrior and conqueror, decisive and unbending. And he has been using you, using you until he can use you no more, and now has sent you to certain death, because no one has ever succeeded in storming the capital of the kingdom that is under my protection.

"Yet I pity you. I pity you and all the unfortunates whom you are drawing with you into the pit. I shudder to think of the afterlife that awaits you. Listen." She stretched out her hand to him. "It is not too late to make all right. I do not threaten you. That would be ill-advised. Instead, I appeal to your good sense. Surely, you have told yourself in the depths of your soul—even if not daring to speak it aloud—that you are going to assured doom. You are an experienced warlord. Are you struck blind? In but a few days, the entire might of Vidrir and his magical legions shall descend upon you—in a few days, hours or minutes, depending upon your next actions. The Sheltered Kingdom's army can be here in three or four days, but even before then the priests will make answer.

"The temple has no desire to wantonly slay the innocent humans and goblins that you have deceived, and therefore has not shown all its power. Beware, though, lest it loose that might upon you, holding nothing back. Call off the assault, before it is too late. Gather your men and lead them from the city. No one will stand in your way. None of your warriors will be punished. But to you…

"To you, Great Merlin, Leader of the Council of the Generation, extends the choice of a noble portion in life—to become his apprentice and helper in far, enchanted Avalon or, if you prefer the lands of mortalkind, to follow me and take from me such knowledge of the world and Creation as Hedin, Sage of Darkness, much as he might wish it, could never give you.

"So, now I have said all I wished to say, and the decision is yours." She drew herself up, touching the windowsill with the tips of her long, elegant fingers.

A messenger thrust his head into the room. "My thane, the chiliarchies of Berd and Frear are here!" he blurted out, then caught sight of the motionless sorceress and stood rooted to the spot, his mouth hanging open.

"In a moment," Hagen struggled to say. "That will be all."

He felt only desolation and weariness—an unbearable weariness of existence itself, which had suddenly become quite meaningless. He was not looking at Sigrlinn, and did not see her determined efforts to catch his eye. He had a decision to make. Should he assent or not? Should he lead his men away from the temple or cleave his Teacher's former companion in two with his sword?

Indeed, he had a very great deal to do, but could neither move nor even utter a sound. Sigrlinn had spoken, but his mind had grasped nothing. He remembered the words, but none of them had meaning. The effect came not from what she said but from her own self, from her very presence. In those instants, Ilving was not even a memory.

Again there were heavy footsteps on the stairs, and Gudmund, Frodi, the chiliarch Berd and Orc burst into the room. The goblin's stocky body was unexplainably nimble; its eyes were starting from their sockets and its lips flecked with foam. A frenzied roar erupted from its gullet as it lunged at Sigrlinn, brandishing a bloody ataghan. Gudmund, meanwhile, was whirling his trusty hooked knife overhead.

Sigrlinn gave them the mildly displeased look adults reserve for mischievous children and raised her hand in a perfunctory gesture.

"No!" Hagen cried, understanding his faithful comrades were about to be transformed into something that would trouble the sorceress no more. In an effort to forestall her, he finally drew his sword and flung himself upon her like one full mad.

So close was he that a simple, lightning-swift Sleepcharm could not have stopped him. He was driven by a strange despair. Only a moment before he had not been able even to think of raising a weapon against her. Whatever was forcing him to do so now had addled his wits.

Of course, he never closed with her, for the Blue Sword was met by a pale-scarlet strip of flame that surged from Sigrlinn's right hand. Neither human nor gnomish steel could have withstood that encounter with wizardfire, and any weapon forged by mortal hands would have been split in two; but the Sword of the Ancient God held firm.

Sigrlinn was thrown back by the force of the two blades meeting. Hagen, too, was knocked off his feet, but she had the worse of it, pitching over the windowsill and plunging down with a cry. He raced to the empty frame and looked down into the courtyard but saw no one—Sigrlinn must have hastily opened the doors to another world, and some time, at the very least several hours, must elapse before she could find her way back.

Breathing hard, he cast a wild look over the warriors at his side.

"We shall wait for no one else," he said in a cracked, surprisingly lifeless voice. "We storm the temple at once, and I shall lead the charge."

HEDIN

THE LAST DRAGON-SHIPS CAST OFF FROM THE JETTIES IN HEDINSEIGH HARBOR; HAGEN'S flotilla was away to storm the capital of the Sheltered Kingdom. I stood for a long time watching them go from the very top of the keep. I had much to do now, for the army needed a Shield of Invisibility that would last them at least until they reached the amulet the harrids had hidden for me at the forest's edge.

I in no way deluded myself our plan would go off without snag or hitch. The charms I proposed to use in protecting my apprentice were my own, developed through long years of wandering; and those who were tracking me would not at first understand what I was doing, although Merlin and Sigrlinn would be immediately aware I was performing sorcery. I cared not if they knew, if they tried to understand. It was even to the good, for while they were trifling with me, Hagen would be well on his way.

But the strike against the Sheltered Kingdom was only a small—albeit important—part of the grand scheme. I leaned over a model of the world on the table before me that showed Greater Hjorvard entire, all its four parts, with its mountains, seas and rivers, forests and towns. Looking closer, I could make out a file of diminutive ships sailing from Hedinseigh to the shores of Eastern Hjorvard, under cover of a thin, misty curtain. Whilst I retained my composure, the charm would hold.

On to other things. I placed the Band of Erith about my head, concentrated my mind and called up Hropt's image. The Father of Hosts was quick to respond.

"'Tis time," I said. "Go now."

"Ah, the long wait is over!" His face was menacing, his brows knit. "The gnomes and the others are ready—the humans of Rogheim, the creatures of

191

the Iron Wood and their herdsmen—all. We march now, and Vidrir shall never return to his Sovereign City again."

I shook my head. "Don't gloat out of season—the battle is not yet won."

My conversation with Hropt over, I turned back to the table but found myself gazing at the ceiling as fear stirred within. Would there be time to loose the avalanche before Merlin launched his own assault and spoke the sentence of death that had perhaps already been laid upon me by a hastily assembled Council of the Generation? But I could not peer inside the Castle of All the Ancients until Hagen's cover had ceased to function, for that, sad to say, would divert the strength I needed to bring him safe to the Sovereign City.

Soon, very soon, our Archmage would be struck all of a heap! In just a little while, in only a day's span, we would finally to be able to settle all the misunderstandings between us in the only creditable manner—in single combat. But first, he would be amazed to hear through the Young Gods' Unslumbering Eye that Old Hropt, last of the Ancient Gods of Eastern Hjorvard, had ended his voluntary retirement in the Living Crags and was now leading a force many thousands strong he had composed from almost naught—from the scattered remnants of the Nightfolk, from all who were at odds with Vidrir, from any who had been aggrieved by the Sheltered Kingdom or had always taken issue with whatever authority. And Hropt's army was making rapidly for Vidrir's borders. That would give Merlin abundant food for thought.

I paced my apartments. Hagen, Hropt...now my third ally. A sphere surrounded by an aura of fire hung in the air. The dim shadow in its center was the Diviner of Charms.

— *The hour of which we have spoken has come,* I told it in my thoughts. *Are you ready?*

— *Yes, if you reaffirm your oath,* it said, as it always did.

— *You shall receive the souls promised to you,* I replied slowly. *This I swear to you by the Mage's Inviolable Oath.*

A light breeze blew on my cheeks, and immediately a huge sense of relief overcame me. The Diviner of Charms had lifted from me the effort of keeping the window between our worlds open.

— *The chief of your kind has conjured a Viewcharm,* it told me almost immediately. *It is aimed at your habitation.*

— *Very well. When there is more to tell, inform me at once,* I responded.

A Viewcharm! So, the Archmage's minions had been quick to pass on the news. But all was exactly as it should be. Merlin was alarmed, and his first thought was to find out what was occupying the second greatest firebrand and rebel—second only to Rakoth Brought-Low—of his Generation.

All I could do now was wait.

The hours passed. Hagen's dragon-ships were approaching landfall, and Hropt's contingent was on the march. I stood motionless over my living facsimile of the world that instantly reflected every event transpiring in the Great World. It was well worth all the time and effort I had spent on it.

"Cease, Sage of Darkness!"

It was an unfamiliar voice, low-pitched and sweetly melodic, a strong, lovely female voice. I sensed in it a hidden power so great as to make all my art seem mere buffoonery.

Then there was silence. I waited, tense, but there was nothing more.

— *What was that?* I asked the Diviner of Charms.

— *I know not.* My scout was panicking, writhing in a sudden access of fear. *It is wholly new to me. And it combines the work of your kind and of those who stand above you.*

Had the Diviner not spoken so, I would have been certain I had just heard the voice of Ialini, coming to me from the realms of the Hallowed Land, or perhaps from her temple in Greater Hjorvard, where she spent much time. More warnings? Or was Merlin trying to dupe me? But why? If he already knew all, why had he not convened the Council? Had he decided to act alone? I understand none of this…

I cudgeled my brains fruitlessly for a while. My Charms of Knowing were unavailing, and not because they were coming up against any barriers. No, they were working, but were telling me nothing. It was as if the Great Void itself had turned to face me. Nor was the Diviner of Charms able to help, even after it had shaken off its fear. All I could do was pay no heed to those strange words, though they sank deep into my memory.

Meanwhile, Hagen's force had met up with the goblins and was passing unseen through the forests. Hropt, too, was squandering no time—his faithful gnomish guard had crossed into the Sheltered Kingdom, cutting off Vidrir's westward line of retreat, while the Rogheim horsemen and the denizens of the Iron Wood moved in from the opposite side.

Morning broke, and still I had encountered no opposition. Merlin's tireless gaze was ever fastened on Hedinseigh, but he contented himself with that. All the other Mages sat idle, too, and I was at a loss to know why my very boldest and most optimistic expectations had been so readily vindicated. I had been ready for far greater resistance.

Hagen had safely reached the amulet cached by the harrids; I felt the power

I had invested in it begin to flow outward. On the little world spread across my table, his army, looking like nothing so much as a miniature column of ants, moved on under the gray curtain of my Charms of Invisibility.

Again I waited, from time to time asking the Diviner of Charms if anything had happened; but it seemed the Mages, one and all, as if on command, had ceased weaving their enchantments. There was not the slightest trace of them to be found in the pearly currents of the Ether that was invisible to mortals. That very silence spoke eloquently to me of the unparalleled tempest that was soon to come in its stead.

Whilst I still could, I repeatedly checked all the defenses I had prepared, since every single one of those countless magical snares would have to work as intended.

I grew alarmed when Hagen neared the walls of Vidrir's capital. I suddenly sensed his disquiet and then, through a hastily conjured Viewcharm, saw him grappling with the wizard. Before I could help he set in motion an enchantment that identified him—and me—as easy as winking. I did not blame my apprentice for that—he had really had no choice. It was myself I faulted.

But after Hagen cast his Darkcharm, the ensorcellments flew so thick and fast the Diviner was hard put to say what they were and call out their creators' names fast enough.

The entire Council of the Generation was all atwitter. Merlin had swung his piercing gaze to the Sheltered Kingdom. Makran and Esteri, my inseparable enemies, and many, many others were in a great fret. Only Sigrlinn's voice could not be heard in the cacophony, the Diviner told me.

I smiled. It was all going as expected, and even falling too close to my projections. The Sheltered Kingdom was what kept the Mages safe. After shattering my Empire of Night, they had dedicated the Kingdom to Iamerth the Fair and had sworn that the Young Gods' sway over the Earth would ever be inviolable. The Kingdom was their guage.

I did not know at the time what, if any, repercussions that oath might have, but I did know the Young Gods were honored especially highly in the Sheltered Kingdom, and revered there with unremitting zeal. *Probably,* I thought, *that is much to the liking of the Lords and Ladies of the Hallowed Land.*

— *They are all looking at you!* my Diviner shrieked—if I might so describe it—into my mind. I should, though, have expected no less; my companion had always erred on the cowardly side, and only my promise of a rich reward could ever have tempted it to go against the gods.

For a while, I felt nothing. Then, the wind howling through the weather vanes' iron supports fell silent, and clouds began to scrabble toward the sun, careful to skirt its fierce brightness as their fleecy billows filled the sky. Soon the blue of the Aer had undergone a malign and frightening change as downy torrents of dark-gray clouds, marbled with light, began a monstrous dance over Hedinseigh. Amid all that unanticipated roistering the sun shone on, calm and triumphant; and not one cloud dared darken it, as if Iamerth wished to see all for himself, in the tiniest detail.

— *The Gates of the Upperworlds are opening,* the Diviner announced. *And of the Lowerworlds, also,* it hastened to add.

That, too, was no surprise. Since my kinsfolk in the Generation had nothing new to throw against me, they were now responding to Merlin's call to arms and gathering their enchanted forces from all of the world's courses. Some were humanlike, others were not; some had reason, others did not. They were armed with swords, fangs, horns and other implements of destruction. They killed with a glare, belched fire, exhaled a suffocating smoke—I was constantly amazed by the variety of means for waging the most grievous and bloody wars employed by the Mages of my Generation, for all that they prated on unendingly about eternal peace.

So, our wait was over. Hagen was racing down the broad streets of the Sovereign City to the temple, while Hropt was outflanking the Sheltered Kingdom's army and should close with it no later than the evening of the following day. All was going according to the plan. Could I have overestimated my adversaries?

— *How many Mages are opening the Gates of the Worlds?* I asked the Diviner.

— *Only two,* it replied dejectedly. *The two who have always sought to harm you.*

— *Makran and Esteri, I'll be bound. But why have the others fallen silent? Even Merlin is no longer watching Hedinseigh. And what, in the name of the Moonbeast, is occupying Sigrlinn all this while?*

The answer to my question was quick in coming when the sorceress began speaking to my apprentice. Like a man stung, I raced to my model of the world, but it was too late. I could see them and hear them but could do nothing, for Sigrlinn had enveloped the setting for her talk with Hagen in a defense impervious even to subtle gramarye. With my newly acquired power I could have ground the building itself to dust, but I would have pulverized Hagen along with it.

Listening to Sigrlinn's silver-tongued speech, I trembled as in a fever, and slowly, step by step, began to weave wizardry so black, so devastating, that it could instantly bury my apprentice and his temptress. I called to him with all my might: *Hagen, hold fast! Throw off this weakness. You have in your hands a sword feared even by the gods!*

Perhaps, somehow, my appeal broke through the veil of alien wizardry, for Hagen seized his weapon at the very last second, when almost all my hope was gone.

Sigrlinn, her fiery blade at the ready, had accounted for every little thing but one. Her one weakness was in not knowing that the Blue Sword drew its strength from the valor and fury of the one wielding it. Hagen's frenzy helped it bear up against her.

The rest of it could not have gone off better. As she fell, my once-beloved had perforce to open the Gates to another world so as not to be smashed to pieces against the paving stones. That done, though, she would have been able to return in a matter of minutes; so, I employed the ancient knowledge of the black creatures I had encountered underground in the unpeopled and forgotten mountain towns of the far south and began opening ever more doors before her as she tumbled through the layers of the worlds. With all my might, I accelerated her fall, sending my lovely enemy ever deeper into those far reaches where time itself holds no authority over the fabric of the world, and forcing her to spend her strength in futile attempts to slow herself down. That was wizardry she could not counter.

A powerful urge emanated from the farthermost, darkest corners of my mind, where memories of the pain and despair of my last days in the Empire of Night lay buried. I wanted to destroy her physical body, turning her into a fleshless spirit that would long pose no threat to me. But I quailed at the thought. I could not do it, because as eternal as the bitterness of my defeats might be, no less eternal were the memories of the bliss I had known in the Cerulean City, which no one could ever take from me.

So, I merely dislodged Sigrlinn from the field of battle. To be sure, hardly a day would pass before she would be clambering from the abyss into which I had cast her; but meanwhile, Hagen would be relatively safe—were it not, of course, for the might of the temple arrayed against him. What had Sigrlinn said about the powers it was holding in reserve?

Be all as it may, my apprentice stood at the very gates of the Citadel of Light, that being the grandiloquent name used on occasion for the Sovereign City's temple, while the tempest raged on over Hedinseigh. The crush of black clouds dipped lower and lower until its edge almost touched the surface of the sea. Lightning bolts, blindingly bright but bringing no thunder, flared here and there between their shaggy bulks. The Diviner saw the Gates into our world yawning wide, and, marching through them, the serried ranks of an alien army. And it felt two Mages rapidly approaching my island.

But why only two? Merlin was still sitting on his hands, and had been doing so long enough to rouse my suspicions. What was in his mind? What if he was conjuring up an Astral Messenger? That was a very complex enchantment when approached by the avenues the Leader of the Council of the Generation was wont to tread. If that was where things stood, I was in dire straits and needed to act now.

So, then, we won't wait to be attacked. Our first courier goes out now to Makran and his lady friend!

I closed my eyes, stopped up my ears and saw the gigantic, magnificent, breathtaking Sphere of the Worlds, glittering with colors beyond description. On it—our world, a tiny sparkle that was at first almost indiscernible among many hundreds of others but grew rapidly larger, until it was no longer a sparkle but an assemblage of diminutive translucent spheres, silvery pearls laid one within another.

In its depths, another light appeared. That was the moon, and I centered my thoughts on it. The dispirited, lifeless plateaus and mountain ranges swept past, superseded soon by the Innermoon, a wondrous world of night filled with beauty and mystery. There, on a long agate-and-black bluff looming over a steel-gray sea that so resembled our northern ocean, stretched the lanky body of the Moonbeast.

All had ever named it so, though none knew its origins or its true name. Ancestor of the Mages, some said. Right Hand of the Creator, others relayed in a whisper. Scion of him before whom thought fails—of Great Orlangur, or maybe of his brother, Demogorgon. There was much idle chatter, but no one knew the truth.

Nor, for that matter, did I, but that was of little import. Glad was I now that I had sought the comradeship of the Moonwolves! Glad was I that I had wandered the sorcerous ravines of their land, a land replete with magic more ancient than that of Mages or elves, more ancient even than the Elemental Magic, for the gramarye at the Moonwolves' command had arisen in the first hour of our world's existence, when night first entered its precincts.

In my vision, I hastened ever closer to the enormous gilded opals of the Moonbeast's eyes. Its furry lids closed, trembling, then opened again; and I dove into the depths of those great brown pupils. Now I was seeing the world through the eyes of the Beast.

It is simple to say and the description may be brief enough, but even my approach to the Lunar Overlord required me to craft a gauzy web of charms, to pass along a path, closed to all outsiders, that even the Moonwolves traverse only once in their lives, when they leave the Earth and become one with their forebear. To be, albeit briefly, such a Wolf—not in body, which would have been far simpler, but in spirit; a dying Moonwolf fallen in honorable combat, for to them only is opened the way to the Innermoon, hidden from human eyes that see only a dead world of stone and rock.

So now, stripped of my bodily shell, which sat motionless in my apartments in Hedinseigh Keep, I entered the domains of the Moonbeast. I looked down on the Earth through endless expanses, narrowed my eyes and clearly saw both the Gates of the Worlds flung open, and the legions passing through them; also, floating majestically amid the demented roil of clouds, two shadowy figures in billowing dark-gray cloaks.

How self-assured they were, that malevolent pair! They sensed at their back the might of the entire Generation or, at the very least, the support of Merlin. Why was I so sure of that? If the Archmage had been constantly watching me and observing my preparations for war, he would hardly have limited himself to a mere two Mages who, for all their hatred of me, were far from the strongest of our kind.

I could not believe that all my new knowledge, so unlike that which is usually vouchsafed to young Mages in training, had remained a secret to him. Could he possibly have decided an old weapon would suffice to settle with me? That would have been most unlike him. Where was his much-vaunted perspicacity?

But enough conjecture. Now those two will know what is meant by the Magic of the Moonbeast!

Unseen hands reached out to grasp thousands upon thousands of slender, crystal threads—to the Great Harp on which Night plays its towering melodies. Deft fingers separated those strings from their frame, and they became tentacles that extended far into the immensity of the Mid-Real. From their tips flowed a myriad tiny blue and silvern stars that turned to dark-blue and black and drifted earthward in thickening torrents, in clouds that might have been a heavy snowfall. Gradually, that gleaming throng took on the appearance of four clawed, predacious paws that stretched toward the two Mages, who were blithely on their way to collect a victory that seemed so easy.

At first they noticed nothing—nor, indeed, would I have; but then both my mind and theirs, probably at one and the same time, were invaded by an eerie and unnatural hush. The Great Harp of Night, now by my will a fearsome weapon, had fallen silent, and with it all the sounds that are always with us, shielding us from the maddening, maniacal roar of the distant but indomitably mighty swells of Chaos.

But before that awesome, droning din reached our bourns, I had to make the best possible use of the time allotted to me.

The two Mages, discerning the approaching danger, hurriedly stood back to back, and in their hands flashed swords of spectral flame, green mottled with blue. The occult creature's grasping paws neither recoiled nor retreated, not even after Makran sliced off a claw, which promptly turned into a shower of tiny black stars that returned to the tentacular strings of the Great Harp whence they had come.

But what good were two plain blades of fire against a far mightier primeval magic? I saw one of the paws tear through the flaming fan of Esteri's defenses, scatter and cover the sorceress with a glittering blue-black mantle. A raging maelstrom swirled over the place where Makran's companion had recently stood. A rift in the fabric of Reality swallowed Esteri up, and her partner followed only a moment later. And it all happened without a sound.

I had made a clean job of it, and could preen myself a little. They had not understood what they were contending with and had tried to fight it off, although their true recourse should have been flight, whithersoever and far, far afield. They would be long in extricating themselves from the deeps to which the Magic of the Moonbeast had consigned them—far longer than it would take Sigrlinn to escape from the Lowerworlds.

The task still remaining was, or so I believed at the time, the easier of the two. I had to make away with the armies that had already invaded our world and close the Gates between the two expanses.

Slowly, carefully, turning the world about itself, I began to abandon the Moonbeast's body and mind. The Harp's strings returned to their places; and at the outermost point of my range of vision, I saw a dark, gigantic hand, seemingly woven of a close compaction of nocturnal gloom shot through with starlight, touch those sorcerous strings. Music of ineffable beauty—inaudible, alas, to us—again filled the Worldsphere.

And I was back in my tower on Hedinseigh.

— *What news, Diviner of Charms?*

— *The Gates of the Worlds are still open. The warriors still march.*

Powerful sorcery is being made on the Pillar of the Titans, but so many spells there are that I cannot determine outright who is conjuring and why. They are for the most part Defensive Charms, and very strong withal. Many of your kind have gathered there.

— *And those who are stronger are higher than us?* I asked nonchalantly.

The utmost silence.

I grew pensive. What more was needed before the Young Gods and Merlin would act?

My brown study was rudely interrupted by a determined pounding at my door. I drew back the bolts, and Gerder, the chiliarch left in charge of the Hedinseigh garrison, burst into the room.

"Teacher, an enemy fleet without equal is approaching the harbor. Huge, three-masted vessels with five banks of oars. They're hurling fireballs and loosing streams of flame that set the very stones alight, and the walls are coming down. We have been knocking and knocking but could not rouse you. What are we to do? It's a long-range bombardment, beyond reach of our catapults."

"Withdraw your men to where the fire cannot touch them, Gerder," I said. Though my voice was calm, I was no way certain we would be able to hold the island now. I had, of course, already considered such an outcome, but only when matters came to an extremity, and we were far from that. "If they begin to disembark, do not engage them hand to hand. Bury them with arrows. I will deal with them in a moment. That will be all."

The chiliarch hurried away, and I looked at the image of Hedinseigh Bay on my model of the world. In such close proximity to the focus of its creator's power, the model showed not only those I had becharmed but also other sorcerous forces and armies.

What I saw was tens, hundreds and then thousands of proud, splendid vessels made of precious rosewood, their carved sterns adorned with gold and enormous gems and their prows rising high above the water like the slender necks of swans. Sturdy rams sliced through the waves, whipping them into foam. Each ship did, indeed, have three masts, rigged with purple lateen sails. The great oars rhythmically rose and fell.

I could make out the weapons platforms and the odd-looking trebuchets mounted on them, whose complex nexus of levers and pull-rods at intervals dispatched silvery spheres that flew toward our fortifications, trailing fire. The guard towers on the breakwaters were already burning—not from the inside but from without. Tongues of flame hungrily gnawed at stone walls that had once seemed impregnable. Fortunate it was that Gerder had already moved away from the areas of greatest danger, which it was now senseless to defend.

Well, now. Though Mages are not entitled to kill mortals with wizardry, or even with their own hands, no one will say that I cannot stop them from bombarding my island. We will begin with a little wind.

I already suspected that if matters went very ill with me some of my charms would be ineffectual, especially those intended to command the elements, which, as everyone knows, have their own masters and suzerains among the Young Gods. But never before had the wind, Iambren's servitor, refused to heed the bidding of my magic. I tried again, using my most powerful charms and even amplifying them with a special assemblage of fortifying enchantments—all to no purpose. I could not raise the faintest breeze.

The blaze fed by our enemies' mysterious missiles crept toward the shoreline bastions.

More of that would be too great a risk, I thought with a brief, involuntary frown.

Meanwhile, my heart had turned cold at the thought that I might have been somehow rendered entirely powerless. So, partly to test that theory and partly because I wanted to be done with this once and for all, I recited a Firecharm. That was a piece of combat magic that had always served me well.

It was a sight for sore eyes, that wall of fire leaping from the water up to the very stars, scattering the clouds and devouring them. The flame encircled Hedinseigh, and the hostile fleet with it. I drew the humming curtain toward me, and the ring shrank inward. The captains on board those enemy ships had no choice but to order their crews to the oars and to have them bring the vessels in closer to the island.

Hagen had done well in promoting Gerder to chiliarch and in entrusting Hedinseigh to him. Immediately, the catapults and ballistas spoke their piece, striking in the grid pattern to which they had been adjusted long before; and their accuracy was a most disagreeable surprise for the raiders. Unsupported by Makran and Esteri's magic, what could they do?

Beaded with sweat, I continued forcing the rose-colored vessels in to shore with that surge of fire, before the assailants' minds cleared and presented them with the understanding the defenders could have no reason at all to be peppering them with stone shot and clay pots full of liquid fire if they had access to a mighty Firecharm. Before long, as many as a hundred vessels were crammed together at the harbor's narrow mouth, with not a drop of water to be seen between them. They jostled each other, breaking their oars and snapping their rigging, while I kept tightening that ring of fire, bringing ever more ships to their fresh-dug grave. So crowded were they that some were forced into the harbor and up toward the jetties.

I must give them their due, for they fought fiercely—I had not expected them to show such valor; but the desperate onslaught of those tall warriors in helmets sumptuously crowned with peacock feathers was dashed to pieces like a heaving wave against a cliff. Hagen's men, timely deployed and with their longbows, slingshots and arbalests at the ready, gave them a proper welcome.

The stone projectiles from the castle's ballistas and catapults smashed through hulls, holed decks and downed masts. Our two largest trebuchets speckled the air with stones the size of oxen, which stove through the upper decks, breached all the lower decks and ended by punching out through the bilges. Seawater gushed in through the huge holes, and the crippled vessels sank one after another.

In all the disorder, it was actually impossible to miss. Packed together as they were, and unable to maneuver, our enemy's floating palaces were facing their doom, and their crews were not slow to realize this. A human flood swept over the crippled decks, the warriors jumping from ship to ship. Some fell overboard and were crushed between the vessels; but the rest, in spite of all, kept making for the land, preferring an honorable death by the sword to a watery end in the sea's cold depths. I could not even offer them terms, as I was unsure of the world from which the wizardry of Makran and Esteri had summoned them.

The ships that had fared better still hurled their strange incendiary missiles at us. I saw that the squadron was not yet completely masterless, since an order had been given to concentrate the fire on the nearest portside bastion. Soon, streams of melted granite flowed along the jetties, and Hagen's men were forced to withdraw from their positions in the tower, the heat having become so great no one could even come close.

The footsoldiers' attacks were repulsed time and again by spates of arrows, slingshot balls and arbalest bolts, but still the embattled tower could not hold. Amid the flames appeared an immense black fissure that split the wall from top to bottom. Gerder ordered our catapults to target the vessels bombarding it, but too late. Before the enemy trebuchets fell silent, committed to the deep along with the ships that carried them, the burning bastion exploded from within with a dull roar like subterranean thunder, and crumbed into a pile of glowing debris surrounded by pools of molten stone.

I had reckoned that once the vessels showering the bastion with missiles foundered the unknown commanders would turn and run, but that was not to be, for the remaining ships began firing on the blazing ruins again. These globes, though, were stuffed not with heat but with cold. Within a few minutes, the red-hot streams had chilled and become stone again. The enemy warriors were quick to attack, then, even though the fire had consumed almost half the ships, a good third of them had been broken and sunk by our catapults and the rest were in the path of the fire and therefore doomed. The attackers were left with no alternative but to prevail. The fiery ring was still closing in on them, although I was holding it back with the last of my strength.

Down below, amid the ruins of the bastion, Hagen's men, following Gerder's strict instructions, met the enemy with bows and arbalests instead of hand-to-hand combat. Our ballistas continued methodically spewing their death-dealing projectiles, plain and incendiary. The trebuchet crews had been bidden to keep to their business; no matter what the result of the battle on the wharves, they were to continue sinking and burning all the ships they could before our forces were obliged to withdraw into the fortress. Those manning the catapults were also working with a will.

The feather-helmeted warriors began plying their bows, but the defenders of Hedinseigh remained under cover. Soon, the remains of the wharf were bestrewn with bodies in ornate armor, their gorgeous feathers wallowing in ash and dirt.

Unable to hold the spell any longer, I let the wall of fire go out and even from my high vantage point could hear the cries of surprise. Now Gerder would have an easier time of it, as some of the attackers would certainly return to their ships in hopes of saving even a few of them from the flames.

Once I had caught my breath, I decided to attempt something else, something I had rarely tried before. I wanted to sow fear and uncertainty among the assailants, but illusions are not, in general, my forte; and if there was but one wizard with the enemy forces, however great a bumbler he might be, he would easily be able to dispel any hex of mine.

I remembered conversations I had had in the Temple of the Unseen, recalled its residents' masterly skill in calling down upon a careless traveler unbearable fear or a fatal diffidence, even if their target was a wizard immune to fear or a great warrior. The Magic of the Unseen was simple, and strange it was that none of my Generation had happened upon it on their own. They did use it, but on single opponents—two, at most; and I was disinclined to employ untested charms on hordes of enemies at once. Yet there was also no purpose in trying to sap their courage with ordinary charms intended to manage humans and known to any Mage, for I had felt the strength of the defenses drawn up around the attacking fleet the moment it appeared.

I was on the very point of invoking the enchantment when the Diviner of Charms broke its silence.

— *The chief among your kind is conjuring a Charm of Transference. He is preparing to make his way to the place you call the Sovereign City of the Sheltered Kingdom.*

Damnation! I had not expected that to happen so soon. The plan had been to rivet the attention of all the Mages on Hedinseigh, and thus give Hagen the chance to complete his task in the Sheltered Kingdom. But all had been going awry since Sigrlinn had spoken with him; and though Merlin had long sat idle, he knew well enough the source of the greatest threat to his beloved Balance, and was hurrying now to the Temple of the Sun.

Very well, then. There was nothing for it but to use a charm I held dear that would work on the Archmage only once and no more, for even with its element of surprise, a skillful Mage could defend against it effortlessly. In a manner of speaking, it put a spoke in the Transferring Mage's wheel, sending him to a place diametrically opposite to where he wanted to be and scrambling his brains to boot. It was a trick that would work only with help from the Diviner or its ilk, since it depended on knowing to a nicety the progress of the Transference.

It worked. Never again, of course, would Merlin permit himself to be hoodwinked in that manner, for only vigilance was required to prevent anything of the sort happening a second time. But for this once he would awake some hours hence with a pounding headache, having slammed into barren cliffs at the farthermost tip of Southern Hjorvard.

My four greatest enemies being out of commission for the while, I was presented with a brief respite. I could rest a little before launching the second attack, which would, I hoped, be more powerful, and impressive enough to pique the attention of the Young Gods at last. Before Merlin and Sigrlinn could return to the action, the avalanche of my making should be all-encompassing and ineluctable.

Now, what is afoot in the Castle of All the Ancients? I placed the Band of Erith on my head.

I saw the familiar Council Hall. Merlin's chair was empty, as was Sigrlinn's place; and Makran and Esteri were not present, either—I noticed several doleful faces among their friends. The rest of the Council members were in attendance, along with a multitude of other Mages. The hall was in an uproar, filled with the babble of awestruck and bewildered voices, with everyone asking everyone else what to do.

"Look, there he is!" someone cried, and the hall instantly fell deathly silent. As one, they turned to face me.

I was, I own, somewhat taken aback. Had I been there in body I would no doubt have been most uneasy, but Hedinseigh was as yet beyond their reach.

"And what, exactly, is the trouble, kinsmen?" My surprise was almost unfeigned. "Why am I suddenly of such great interest to you?"

"Why, madman?" howled Shendar, a Mage of the Council and one of Merlin's underlings. "You ask why—you who have set our entire world on the brink of destruction!" His face was crimson, and tiny droplets of spittle flew from his mouth. "What, thanks to your good works, is occurring at this moment in the Sheltered Kingdom? Or have you forgotten that it is our common guage to the Young Gods? That while the Kingdom stands inviolate, while the towers of the Sovereign City soar aloft, the affairs of our Generation will be ours to conduct? Or perhaps you are unaware that should the Sheltered Kingdom fall the Young Gods will dispatch us where previous Generations of Mages have also gone, never to return? What have you done in the Kingdom, madman?"

"If I have done anything there, why do you all linger here, wringing your hands, instead of departing thither to restore order?" I jeered back at him.

"What sense would there be in doing that now," Shendar shrilled, "when all is ablaze and the sword wanders unrestrained through the land, when the altars in the lesser temples have been cast down and the prayer halls desecrated? The fate that awaits you shall be more terrible than Rakoth's." He bared his teeth in a spiteful grin. "That we have settled. We have just combined in dispatching an Astral Messenger to the Lordly Thrones. Tremble now in expectation of their judgment!"

"You speak fine words, but to what purpose?" I broke in. "Their meaning escapes me. Instead of trying to set all to rights in your beloved Sheltered Kingdom, I repeat, you have wasted your precious time sending a Star Messenger. Why so?"

Shendar did not reply at once. "Because…" he hissed after a long, hate-filled silence. "Because when we received the news it was already too late. Those who had tried to stop you depended too much on their own strength, and that was their undoing. See what your apprentice is about in the Sovereign City!"

And I saw.

CHAPTER VIII

"W E STORM THE TEMPLE AT ONCE, AND I SHALL LEAD THE CHARGE." HAGEN SAID AGAIN, gathering the leaders of the recently arrived detachments about him.

All were silent, having already learned of the priests' fearsome weapon, from which there was no escape. That empty, smoothly paved square before the temple, where there was no cover—how many lives would it take?

"Surround the temple entirely," the thane instructed. "And spread the ranks as thin as possible."

Not one warrior in this battle could be allowed to see his commander's true state of disarray. Hagen's officers hastened away to convey his orders, certain beyond question that their thane, in his wisdom, had thought everything through and foreseen all. In truth, though, Hedin's apprentice was cruelly racked with uncertainty, and did not know what he must do.

Since his Nightcharms had failed, he would have to resort to Daycharms. A Firecharm would, of course, have been most reliable of all, but Hagen knew he would not be able to maintain it long enough. By the time his men were at the temple walls he would be dead.

He hurriedly cast his mind over every single spell he knew, and recalled a Viewcharm that revealed the outlines of shallow-dug underground passages. Long, long ago, under his Teacher's guidance, he had made such a charm, in the days when they were paying frequent visits to the mountain gnomes.

What if there are galleries hidden under the city? There could well be—it's impossible for the Temple of the Sun not to have a secret passage in case of emergency.

The charm was simple and quickly done. The stones paving the square gleamed blue as Hagen looked on, and—oh, joy!—below them, like a tangle of fiery snakes, the outlines of an entire labyrinth emerged into view. One of its corridors, from the looks of it perhaps the broadest of them all, passed right under his present hiding place.

"Hey, my fine fellows!" he called to the two hundred men who were sharing his refuge. "A pit must be dug...just here. Ransack every room for crowbars, axes and shovels, and hop to it!" For if our time runs out, the fire will take us all, he told himself, though he did not, of course, speak those words aloud.

There was no one to be seen on the vast open expanse before the temple with its snug encirclement of houses, some partly burned, others partly demolished by investing forces keen to barricade themselves behind as much broken masonry as they could collect against the terrible flares of Temple Flame that were striking the ground intermittently. The priests still stood on the terraces, silent and motionless as any graven images.

While the space around the temple might seem tranquil enough to the eye, the ear could sense movement, and plenty of it—the measured march of ironclad footsoldiers and shouted commands, shrill but unintelligible. The din of the distant battle had subsided somewhat, Vidrir's pikemen having been forced from the gates by the timely arrival of Orc's goblin detachments and two of Hagen's chiliarchies. All that noise and tumult drowned out the sounds of the hasty digging that was creating a broad pit upon which all Hagen's hopes now rested.

The men had turned all the houses in the neighborhood upside down in their eager search for any earthmoving implement and now were stubbornly gnawing, mole-like, deep into the rock-hard, unyielding soil. The flat stones paving the courtyard had been pounded to dust, and by Hagen's estimation they must be almost upon the vault of the underground passageway.

His mind turned to the temple priests. *I know you're waiting for me to come dashing headlong across the square, so you can thwart me. Wait on, then, and more power to you!* He was full aware, though, that even worse might await him in those underground passageways. What if there was Temple Fire down there, the same as on the surface? For a moment he even vacillated. But, no—an open attack would be certain death to for the entire army.

The crowbars hit on thick stone.

"This will anger you, Honorable Thane, but you must have boring tools sent for." The familiar bass voice was Orc's, who had returned with his troops. "This stone looks to be surpassingly solid, and proof against any crowbar."

"You're right," Hagen agreed, and hastily ordered that the tools be brought.

The tunnel vault proved resistant to all efforts, and it was not until a large iron borer was uncovered somewhere and brought in that matters went more briskly. Soon, they broke through and dropped ladders into the broad, square opening.

They were all astonished to find the corridor well-lit—evenly placed apertures set into the walls held transparent membranes that gave off an even, gilded light. Down the wide, dry tunnel before them, a barely perceptible breeze wafted, carrying the scent of precious incense.

With all possible speed, Hagen's men poured into the cavity. He left almost a third of them above ground, to keep watch on the temple and the gates and make the priests think the invaders still intended a surface attack. Hedin's apprentice was taking a desperate risk, but could see no other way.

They marched in combat array, with drawn swords, armed arbalests and well-stocked quivers, the shield-bearers ever ready to cover themselves and their comrades with large, iron-sheathed shields impervious to pike and arrow. At Hagen's side were Gudmund, Frodi, Knut, Berd and Orc, the goblin chieftain having insisted on placing a select hundred of his bodyguards in the van of the assault.

They moved in silence, with only the echo of their steps rebounding from the barrel vaults to be heard. Hagen counted the paces; the square was large but it could be crossed in a matter of minutes. Finally, he calculated, they were below the temple, having met not a single living thing on the way.

The tunnel began forking in a bewildering fashion. Hagen, navigating by memory, left marks on the walls, but how could he be sure which passage led to the surface? The charm was silent on that point.

"Break into single files and keep each other in sight," he ordered. This, too, was a risk, since the interior entrance to the underground crypts was probably guarded, and a single file might not be able to break through.

But luck stayed with him. Not a quarter-hour passed before a scout reported that a stairway leading to the surface had been found.

An alarming thought darted into Hagen's mind. *It's all just too easy, too simple. Are we walking into a trap, perchance? Neither warriors nor priests in the passageways, these shallow tunnels...How could they have nothing in store for an enemy who might find his way into these galleries?*

As the tail of the besieging forces made its way underground in the courtyard of a dilapidated house on the other side of the square, Hagen was already mounting smooth, brilliantly polished steps, noting that, while the tunnels were bathed in a gentle golden glow, the way ahead was impenetrably dark. He turned a corner and came up against a blank gray wall. The stairway had dead-ended.

Frodi let out a savage roar, but Hagen knocked on the wall with the hilt of his sword. Behind it was a resounding emptiness.

"Break it down!" he ordered curtly, and instantly the dozens of crowbars and drills the provident ones had brought with them bit into the stone. Hedin's apprentice did not even try to open the door—if door there was—with Charms of Destruction. His skill with them being imperfect, he feared bringing down the vaults onto the heads of his men in the process.

The soft sandstone gave way easily—the barrier was not thick—and soon the thane was the first to break out into a bright and spacious arcade that was as empty as the subterranean crypts behind him. He immediately recognized the place, and knew he was standing beneath the temple's lower terrace. From here, a passage spiraled through prayer halls to the Chamber of Altars, the Sheltered Kingdom's holy of holies, and thence to the repository of the Discs of Iamerth.

He would now have to bypass the Chamber, find his way to the Discs, master them and only then return to the Chamber. What was to come next he banished for now from his mind, although of course his Teacher's plan had been elaborated in the most exacting detail and was well known to him. *All in good time. Forward!*

At a rapid pace that was almost a run, he led his men through the empty gallery topped with a high, arched ceiling and richly decorated with fanciful statuary.

Around the first corner waited orange-robed priests.

The arrows of Hagen's bowmen flew faster than the Protective Charms of Iamerth's votaries. Bodies fell to the snow-white tiles. Not one of two dozen was left alive, but the last of them had managed to raise the alarm; and the entire temple rang with the sound of running feet. Soon, though, all was again silent, as if the Servants of the Sun had only performed some complex maneuver and come again to a standstill, waiting for the enemy to approach.

The Ethereal courses above the temple promptly filled with torrents of magical power—or, as the Teacher would say, with the smell of primitive spells being cast.

Hagen's army went into a jog-trot. The thane could feel the rage amassing in his path, and in the farthest depths of his mind there stirred an ancient fear that Hedin's teaching had not fully eradicated—the fear of the Young Gods into whose sanctuary he had just intruded uninvited. It was a clinging, enervating fear, as persistent as one of those odious little pusscats the Mage's apprentice hated so.

He steeled himself, reached out with the sensitive, unseen fingers of spells and, with a barely suppressed cry of pain, was quick to pull them back. An intolerable agony had burst into his mind. Traveling, as it were, along the bridges of his magic, it thrust thousands of needles under his nails, rending his ears, forcing his blinded eyes from their sockets...

Hagen halted his sorcery, and the pain ceased on the instant. *Good enough. We'll rely again upon our swords, as they did in olden days.*

The thought was scarcely gone when, directly beneath his feet, he noticed a stone that protruded from the floor just slightly more than it should. At the bidding of a powerful instinct, the thane drew his foot back and, looking up, saw barely noticeable fissures in the ceiling. Had he but touched the suspect tile, a pile of stones would have come crashing down on him from above and flattened him.

That was only the first in a whole series of ambuscades that were not all avoided with such facility. The corridor was blocked by grates that abruptly swung out of the walls; the floor tiles unexpectedly turned underfoot to reveal deep pits lined with palisades of sharpened spikes. Enduring its losses, Hagen's detachment forged stubbornly on. It had now penetrated deep into the temple but, since destroying that first blockade, had encountered no opposition.

Then the murderous string of traps was behind them, and the corridor was rimmed with doors, all locked up tight. The thane felt no need to break them down, since he was on the temple's main thoroughfare, which led straight to the Altar Chamber, and the time had not yet come to skirt around it, as his Teacher had instructed.

The gallery's walls and ceiling were covered with thin plates of amber-colored stone; enchanted, they radiated a soft, dim light. Niches held quiescent statues of lovely women and mighty warriors. Made of pure silver they were, with precious stones for eyes, and some of the goblins began to grumble, their gaze greedily fixed upon the priceless, undisturbed booty. Orc restored order with a few loud and angry words.

Hagen listened hard to what his senses were telling him. There could be no mistake—the priests were in hiding and were permitting him to move unchecked so as later to have done with him once and for all.

Of a sudden, the corridor widened to right and left as the amber walls began alternating with columns of gold, and high, silvered thresholds led into two vast prayer halls with flowers sprouting straight from the floor, each sporting a variegated blossom the size of a grown man's head. The entire ceiling was taken up with gigantic representations of the sun. In the far recesses two huge crystalline windows faced east and west, where the morning and evening vigils were held. The walls were decorated with vivid frescoes and mosaics inlaid with gems and gold, silver and emerald plates that represented the acts of Iamerth and his victories in hand-to-hand combat with Rakoth the Merciless, Great Lord of Gloom. Hagen smiled, noting how the priests' imagination had inflated one Mage's defeat in a struggle with a far more powerful enemy into an equally matched battle between two divinities.

"Orc!" he called. "I want you and your troops to make sure that no stone is left standing here."

"That we can do." Orc beamed, and with a rattle of armor and weapons, a thick brown torrent of goblins flooded the prayer halls while Hagen led his own men on, hearing behind them wild cries, crashing noises and a great din. As pillagers went, Orc was a past master.

Beyond the first prayer chambers appeared a spacious room, veritable acreage under a roof supported by three rows of very tall columns of white marble. This was the priests' inner sanctum, and here Hagen found his way blocked in good earnest.

The far end of the hall was suddenly stained orange; and only he saw, amid the layers of altered light, the rapid movement of figures appearing from side doors with long staves in their hands. The Priests of the Sun needed no other weapon.

"What tomfoolery is this?" Gudmund muttered, uncoiling the chain of his hooked knife.

"Bowmen at the ready!" Hagen barked as the strip of orange light began to crawl toward them. He was anticipating a magical assault and was ready to deflect it, should the need arise, with a Firecharm.

The veil that covered the approaching priests was scarcely within arbalest range when he gave the command to fire. A dense swarm of short black bolts flew, drowned in the orange radiance; and no one, not even Hagen, could tell if they had hit their marks. The veil congealed, and at first it seemed he could make out a body falling, but then his second sight failed him.

"Have at them!" he roared, seizing his sword. "Bestir yourselves, Children of Darkness!"

The archers and arbalesters needed no encouragement. Like mechanical manikins, they were already loosing arrow after arrow into the bright veil as it made its unhurried but inexorable approach. Nothing, it seemed, could slow its steady progress. It was as implacable as Fate itself.

A stern voice, resounding under the high, vaulted ceiling, said to them, "Woe unto you who have intruded into this temple! Drop your bows, throw down your swords and break your pikes, for your lot has been decided by the celestial court, and accursed you shall be from everlasting unto everlasting, as long as the Thrones of the Powers shall stand—"

"Attack!"

Hagen's battle cry split the air, and his forces went forward to meet their destiny, pikes bristling from behind a solid wall of shields. The archers continued their hail of arrows, and out in front, protected by a shield bearer on either side, strode Hagen, the Blue Sword burning bright in his hand. He counted off the distance and the time, for he knew that even a short-lived Firecharm would demand all his strength and leave him bereft.

The orange cloud and the black wall of burnished steel moved ever closer. Hagen heard his army's morose footfalls behind him, saw out of the corner of his eye the black stubble of pike tips, and could not understand why the masters of this place still held back. One short burst of Temple Flame and nothing would have remained of his cohort, not even ash.

Or are the priests afraid to use that weapon here in the ceremonial halls? The thane remembered how the stone walls and walks of the city had burned and melted when touched by those fatal tongues of wizardfire...

Bright surges of light came without warning, scorching the eyes and dazzling the warriors even through the narrow slits of their sallets. The light thrust and buffeted like a strong wind, yet it did not burn. The men felt their armor grow hot, but nothing more, the aim of those dispensing the fire having evidently been to blind the attackers and rest at that. The fierce golden radiance swallowed up even the swath of orange that covered the priests advancing on them.

Raising their shields, lowering their heads and helping themselves on with some choice oaths, the Hedinseigh ranks did not break stride.

"And you shall be accursed from everlasting unto everlasting..." the nasal voice under the ceiling proclaimed once more.

Then, at last, Hagen struck with the Firecharm he had long held in readiness. The fire flapped its ruddy wings between the ranks of white columns, roaring and twisting into supple whirlwinds. This was a simple, living, human fire that shriveled and cremated all it touched, yet could it do the same to that orange radiance?

His calculations had been correct—the death-dealing heat slashed across the outer limit of the orange mist, and while his plumes of fire lasted but a second, that was enough. That accursed orange veil disappeared, and with it the blinding glow. His men saw their enemy clear, and with a triumphant bellow threw themselves into close combat.

Hagen had squeezed all he could from the priests' brief moment of confusion. It seemed that a powerful, serried formation trained to strike as one hand would instantly crush the priests, who were not even protected by armor and whose only weapons were their long white staves; but the servants of Iamerth were not, in truth, defenseless against the unrelenting steel.

As if enveloping them in an amber cloak, there appeared about the head and shoulders of each a dazzling white sheen, similar to that which had just filled the hall. The sharp, stinging rays again clutched at the eyes of Hagen's men through their narrow eye-slots. The orange radiance, once dispersed, did not return. Instead, the priests' bodies suddenly came apart, splitting into spectral doubles, completely indistinguishable one from the other. Long pikes speared the empty air, for there was no way to know which was a living man and which a mere apparition wrought by wizardry. Hedin's apprentice knew no charm to dispel this enchantment.

Hagen had never been so intoxicated by the frenzy of battle—he was, after all, fighting in the enemy's most cherished citadel. With a deep sigh of release, his flanks covered by his faithful shield-bearers, he lunged forward, his Blue Sword held at arm's length. With no time to raise his staff in defense, the votary of Iamerth fell, cleft from shoulder to waist. Like maddened snakes, the black pikes stabbed from behind the wall of shields. Not allowing themselves a moment's ease, the archers and arbalesters worked their weapons.

It was a whistling vortex of death before which nothing could stand, but the priests spun and swiveled, nimbly evading at the last moment the seemingly undeflectable blows. Then they would strike out with their staves, splintering the pikestaffs like kindling. Where stave-end met shield, a broad pool of molten metal would run down; and if their white lightning bolts broke through the first line of defense and hit a soldier's helm, he would fall with a muffled groan, his face scarred with terrible burns.

Yet, although the priests of Iamerth were agile and quick, although three-fourths of the blows dealt by Hagen's men found only fleshless phantoms, the thane's army was still pushing the enemy back before its all-too-solid wall of shields.

Hedin's apprentice did not give those with a taste for hand-to-hand combat—such as Gudmund and Frodi—their head. No one broke ranks; the order of battle was strictly observed, with alternating intervals of fighting and rest. The thane was in the very thick of the fight, and his sword was causing thorough devastation among the priests, although his shield-bearers had already twice had to replace their disabled shields.

The Blade of the Ancient God sliced unceremoniously through the white staves that so easily parried ordinary weapons. Several times, the priests thrust hard and swiftly enough to reach the thane's armor, but the craftsmanship of Hauberk Mount kept its promise—the metal glowed almost red-hot, which was enough to scorch the leather jerkin below the chain mail until it hissed and cracked, but the murderous heat never touched Hagen's body.

Even so, each such strike that slipped through almost knocked the thane off his feet—and this was a man famed for his hardiness and for his skill in parrying blows deft enough to break through any defenses.

Step-by-step, step-by-step, forward, forward, come what may. Each row of white columns left behind was a mark of success, bringing them ever closer to the golden gates at the other end of the hall that must give out onto the terraces where, in a place of deepest concealment, the Discs of Iamerth lay.

And why have they not been used? That would have put us almost beyond saving. And where is that mysterious Darkling Rider with a Disc of her very own?

By degrees, they forced the priests from the hall. Hagen was the first to break out onto the open terrace, discovering it to be a good fifty feet above ground level. The surviving priests withdrew to the sides, while the thane turned right onto a rising spiral of terraces. His squires took up new shields.

The Hedinseigh forces were streaming with blood and treading through it, the red drops splashing up from under their iron-soled feet. The temple's defenders were perishing—they were outnumbered, they had no bows. One priest was equal to any three of Hagen's men, but still they lacked the strength to hold him back. Hedin's apprentice reached the first turn, rounded it…

And saw running toward him a tall, very thin priest whose flowing white robe bore the likeness of a crimson lightning-bolt across the chest. His left hand was extended and the right raised shoulder-high, the open palm level with his ear.

Some of the more fleet-footed arbalesters drew up and sent hefty iron shafts in his direction, but the old man caught them easily with his left hand as he ran, and flung them to the ground. Then he threw out his right hand, as if pitching something heavy from his shoulder.

A sixth sense, an instinct for danger, doubled Hagen over an instant before a bright ball of fire pierced the air where he had stood. The flame sliced instead into the close ranks of warriors behind him. Someone let out a short scream.

Once again the air was rent with arrows, not one of which so much as grazed the priest, who in turn tossed another handful of invisible fire at Hagen. The squire who screened him saw his shield incinerated, both his arms disappear, together with the armor that covered them, and his coat of mail melt; the warrior died without a sound, deeming it unseemly to flaunt his agony for all to see.

Hagen understood that here, on this narrow terrace—maybe fifteen feet wide but not an inch more—one skillful fighter could halt an army, if none equal to him in strength could be found. He shied away as the hand of destruction swung forward again, heard the thump and clang of an armored body falling behind him. Only then did he pounce.

A finger's breadth more, and the priest would have been out of range of Hagen's lunge, but as the blade's sharp tip inscribed a second crimson stripe across his chest he staggered, and the thane's second blow—upward, into the throat—finished him.

That was the last of the clumsy attempts to halt his progress by single fighters, no matter how adept. He was no longer tested. The temple understood his strength, and now had no alternative but to ready its last strike, which would be invested with all the might the votaries of Iamerth could muster.

What had misled them into delaying, rather than mounting a display of strength from the very outset? They knew well enough this was no simple mortal adventurer, for the most reckless daredevil ever born in the four regions of Greater Hjorvard would never, not even in his wildest dreams, have conceived of attacking the High Temple of the Sun. The priests' last doubts should have vanished when Hagen used his Firecharm; the temple always dealt fittingly with rivals expert in magic, and had never suffered such losses as on that day.

It's as if they've taken leave of their senses, Hagen thought.

The terraces continued to spiral upward. No one blocked the path; not a single arrow nor even a crossbow bolt flew toward them. On and on they went, the way uncoiling before them, until it widened out to twice its previous breadth, forming a half-moon that contained five granite pedestals, each crowned with a crystal cube. In four of them the much-sought-after Discs of Iamerth peacefully lay. The fifth was empty.

There, the High Priest of the Sun stood in haughty solitude, his hand resting on one of those cubes. Barely a moment passed before a second figure came around a corner, causing Frodi and Gudmund's jaws to drop in unison. It was a Darkling Rider, very much like the one who had confronted them and full sister to her who had perished in the skirmish with the Stone Sentinel, the apprentice of…whom? Held between her slim pink hands was the faint glimmer of a small white light, and Hagen went cold. *Must I now engage in open battle with the bearer of a White Blade?*

They were but two facing a force of many thousands, yet those two had power enough to outmaster any army. What cared they for the secrets of formation, flanking maneuvers and strike? What need had they for legions and cohorts? Each of them was an army entire, and stronger than any human force. Workaday swords could never overcome them, and well they knew it—hence the High Priest's scornful smile, the unpleasant curl of his thin, bloodless lips. Meanwhile, the Darkling Rider stood calmly to one side.

What could save Hedin's apprentice now? A Firecharm? But no, the priest's hand lay on the crystal cube. Hagen would fall to the Disc of Iamerth before the charm was done. With all his being, he felt that the other was waiting only for him to make the slightest movement, seen or unseen; and a second after that, the Disc belonging to Sun's Suzerain would find its mark.

The priest slowly drew back his hand, fingers raised. The crystal receptacle opened with a light chiming sound, whereupon the temple master arrogantly crossed his arms on his chest. He knew that no matter how fast Hagen's conjuring he would be faster. He was certain.

The thane noticed a tiny movement to his right, by his knee. One of his men had thrust his heavy pike too far forward, placing the shaft square under Hagen's hand. Driven by a sudden impulse, he seized it.

Those watching from the side, mystified as to why the thane did not dispatch those two at once, saw only a sudden strange contortion of his body and a rapid flickering through the air.

He put his all—every long year of arduous training—into it. His throwing stance was one never seen before in the history of warfare, and the pike flew faster even than a arbalest bolt. Forged by Hedinseigh's best smiths, well-tempered, jagged and already primed with the taste of enemy blood, it struck the priest full in the chest.

The man was instantly shrouded in sparkling golden dust. Like a cloud it was, fine and iridescent, and the thane's pike disappeared into it.

But not without trace, although never a scratch appeared on the priest's body. He was flung back from the crystal cube, and the Disc stayed in place. The temple master slammed against the parapet. He let out a throaty sound, his head fell back, and twitching, he slid slowly down, though his eyes were open and fully sensible.

Hagen then made the mistake of ordering his men to advance while he darted toward the open, glittering cube, for that was when the Darkling Rider, who had been motionless, entered the fight. His worst fears were realized— the light in her hands was, indeed, the embryo of a deadly White Blade, a sorcerous sword from the World of Shades and the Mages' favorite weapon. In an instant, it became a long, sickle-shaped cutting edge that extended smoothly from the slender hand holding the invisible hilt. The wiccan strode toward the running men and raised her arm to strike.

At once, the terrace was almost deluged with blood from the cloven bodies. The White Blade lengthened to a good ten feet, and all who came within its fatal range were already dead men, saved by neither armor nor armament.

But on the way, the Darkling Rider's sword hacked through a stand on which a Disc of Iamerth lay in its transparent container. The crystal cube broke, and the will of Fate cast the fearsome artifact of the Young Gods, glittering dimly, at Hagen's very feet.

Several arrows had pierced the wiccan's breast; but with a hoarse laugh like the cawing of crows, she adroitly snapped the shafts protruding from her body and began laying about her once again. The priest, meantime, was gradually regaining his strength and trying to rise, his wiry brown hand outstretched. The Disc on the open pedestal from which he had been thrown by that well-wielded pike began to tremble, as if eager to be in its ruler's grasp.

Hagen held the Disc at his feet to the granite with his sword, all the while feverishly trying to recall the charms his Teacher had named as sovereign in such a pass, which was truly the most extreme of extremities. The thane saw the Darkling Rider raise her White Blade to strike once more, and understood he would have but a second to live if he did not find a way to master that other Disc. What heretofore had seemed unthinkable, impossible, was now the be-all and end-all.

Again narrative becomes too slow to describe as it ought all that now transpired. Events collapsed in on themselves, thoughts and decisions rose unbidden from incalculable depths. Though Hagen truly had much else to think of, it seemed he was all at once looking down from a mountain pass upon a flourishing valley. He saw the Discs being made, the sun transformed into a giant furnace in whose heat the wonder-weapon for the most faithful of its servants was born. He heard the Words of Power that were spoken over all.

That was when he understood that this barrier was too great for him to surmount. He could not bend to his will the Disc in its crystal cube, no matter how great the danger urging him on. So with all his mind he reached out to the one at his feet—the only one with which he could even hope to succeed, because it had been sent to him by Fate. The others he could not so much as come near, not while they still lay in their sparkling boxes.

The Disc pinned down by the Blue Sword twitched like a living thing, as yet unable to break free. The White Blade in the Darkling Rider's hand began its murderous run. Like one bewitched, Hagen watched as that ribbon of purest white flame came ever closer, leaving a trail of corpses that had been the most trusty and valiant of his men. He seemed entranced, bound by unseen trammels that were broken, when the White Blade was a mere ten feet from him, by a fierce desire to live—a desire that of a sudden commanded the Disc, simply and wordlessly, *Forward!*

The grayish plate obediently broke free and, before Hagen even had time to be surprised, clashed with the White Blade in the middle of the terrace. Those two ancient implements, the one elongated, the other circular, created in the unimaginable depths of time before time was yet measured—those two guardians of the power of sunlight were worthy adversaries. Never before, never since the Days of Creation, had a Disc of Iamerth and a White Blade of the Mages met in combat.

And where Light collides with Light, Darkness must of a certainty appear.

It was not long in coming, and its approach was as stupendous as the stately progress of its immemorial enemy. From the place where Disc met Blade, heavy billows of thick, inky blackness splayed out, greedily devouring every ray of light. Hagen was knocked off his feet by the black wave that swept over him, and he kept a grip on his sword only by dint of a desperate effort that almost tore his muscles.

The Disc toward which the priest was reaching remained in position.

In an instant, all was silence, sounds drowned in the dense black. The thane saw nothing except the blue of his blade, but even that did not dispel the gloom, seeming, rather, to render it all the more impenetrable. Hagen could not discern the positions of his warriors, could not see where the Darkling Rider was or what she was doing. His chest was being prodded by the rough hand of a cold wind, which was first to penetrate the dark toils and carried with it the mournful wail of inhuman voices.

Evening gave way to night. Over Hagen's head, stars were slowly coming out. Stupefied, he stared around him and saw no one—he was alone on the empty stone terrace. No, not alone, for far off there lay a man, his head buried strengthlessly in the crook of his arm. Only very recently he had been the Temple's High Priest. He did not stir, and the Disc toward which he had been reaching was still on its pedestal, under the open crystal lid. Oppressed on all sides by the mighty onrush of Darkness, Iamerth's weapon had become a simple cold circle of metal. Hagen felt its powerlessness, and knew that it was now or never.

He caught up the Disc and hastily chained it to his belt. Next he had to be done with the priest. He took a better grip on his sword and advanced upon the prostrate form.

There was another figure moving, barely perceptible, in the gloom, at the very limits of sight. The Darkling Rider, deprived now of her terrible weapon, was casting a charm—Hagen could see her hands moving as she did so—but he was no longer in dread of such sorcery. Darkness was a cloak of protection to a Mage, and here, in a manner unfathomable to him, lay the center of its power. So, although unaware of this, he felt no fear, for all spells and enchantments were impotent—unless the spellcaster bore the title of Sage of Darkness.

He felt a chill, like an icy current in a warm river, slide across his body, but nothing more. He knew this enchantment—it should have taken all his strength and paralyzed him—but he was protected by the Darkness.

The wiccan halted, and he heard her reedy, gasping cry, for all the world like that of a surprised child. He strode closer to the priest, who had raised up on one elbow and was looking at him, maddened horror in his eyes.

"Have mercy, O Most Mighty!" The words issued from the temple master's throat on a gush of blood. "Have mercy, for is it worthy of the valiant Hagen to kill an unarmed man? How much honor will he find therein?"

"Redeem your life!" the thane spat, not taking his eyes from the Darkling Rider who, the charm having failed her, stood stock-still clenching her now-useless little fists.

"How shall I redeem it, O Hagen, Thane of Hedinseigh?"

"You shall tell me how to command the Disc of Iamerth!" Hagen said, raising the lambent tip of his sword to the priest's throat.

On the thin lips of the servant of Iamerth appeared a feeble grimace that he no doubt had intended as a scornful smile.

"Then I shall die this very moment." The priest turned away. "They are protected by superior powers. I have nothing further to say. Strike me down if such is your wish."

Hagen frowned. "Then answer me this. How is it that one such as she..." He nodded toward the wiccan. "...has possession of that Disc? Who placed it into her hands? And how was that permitted by those...superior powers?" He was gibing at the priest now. "Speak, then!" The sword tip pricked the throat of the supine man.

The priest looked askance at the Darkling Rider, who had approached quite close—looked on her with fear, Hagen thought—and finally spoke.

There had appeared in the temple a white sorceress of Ialini's retinue, one invested with the particular trust of the Heavens. And the Gods had said to him, the Keeper of the Discs, "Deliver Iamerth's weapon to her apprentices, for the Balance of the World is in jeopardy and this Disc will help restore it with but a sprinkling of the blood of a few mangy sheep."

He had acceded to the will of Iamerth the Most Fair. He had entrusted one of the Discs to that sorceress's apprentice, and was astonished to discover that she was a Darkling Rider. He had no heart for it, but durst not disobey.

There it was—Sigrlinn was teaching her wiccans the Higher Magic. Hagen knew enough to understand that it was impossible. Time out of mind, the Darkling Riders had kept to themselves, busy with their evil sorcery; and the Laws of the Ancients, of which his Teacher had spoken so often, had placed the strictest prohibition on teaching the secrets of magic to that brood for, even when they destroyed, the Mages strove to create, through their apprentices, something new, while the Darkling Riders could only destroy.

So, behind all those attempts to kill him, from the very first, Sigrlinn had stood. Hagen was pierced—he knew not why—with pain. First she had sought to obliterate him, then to win him over; but why had she stopped trying after that first failure? Why the long, obscure conversations in the Niflhel cavern and here in the Sovereign City? If she had been tracking him so closely, why had she not killed him sooner, if such had always been her goal? Why, being so aware of all his movements, had she allowed him to force entrance into the city and reach the very temple itself?

Oh, Teacher, when did I need your counsel more?

The thane set himself at risk then by turning to the wiccan, who still stood a little distance away, making no effort either to conceal herself or to attack him.

"Does he speak true?" he asked "Answer me, and you shall leave this place without let or hindrance, whole and unharmed. This I swear to you by the name I bear—I who have never lied, not even to my bitterest enemy."

"Why such a need for grandiose words?" the Darkling Rider responded in a quiet, tired voice. "None of us shall leave this place. Can you not see that? The Darkness has swallowed us up. We are within it, and ours is not to cross that boundary. So, do not threaten me, thane. You did not vanquish me in honorable combat. You were saved only by a miracle. Therefore, I shall not answer you."

Her words returned Hagen to reality. Why was the huge terrace completely empty? Where was his army? Where, at the end of all, were the bodies of the dead? Where was the way out, and—more importantly—whither did it lead? He looked down, but all was plunged in gloom.

"Take me to the Chamber of Altars!" he ordered, glaring ferociously at the priest. "And hop to it, before you're run through!"

The priest crawled to his feet, keeping a wary eye on Hagen's sword, and had taken the first step when the Darkling Rider sprang. He had expected no less of her, based on his long studies of the stratagems and subterfuges of her kind. A step to the side, a half-turn and a strike with his sword—in Hedin's way, downward from the right, to hit just above the ear—and the wiccan went instantly limp.

Hagen bade the priest bind the unconscious body, watching close to see that the knots would hold.

"Now take her across your shoulder, and we go," he said in a voice that brooked no dissent.

The priest hurriedly hoisted the dead weight, grunting with the effort. They moved along the deserted stone terrace and turned into a broad passage. Darkness reigned everywhere; everywhere they encountered only emptiness and silence.

The priest's feet barely moved, and he was muttering something to himself. Hagen listened, but the words seemed to have no meaning.

They passed the priests' inner sanctum and began to mount a broad spiral staircase, still unable to see more than four paces ahead. The staircase was long—fifteen hundred steps by Hagen's count. Finally, they came to a spacious court before two massive stone doors covered with artful, intricate carvings. Panting, the priest stopped, and gave the thane the imploring look of a hunted creature. In that broken being there was not a trace of the erstwhile pride and power of the master of Iamerth's temple.

"Do not enter there," he wheezed, propping the Darkling Rider against a wall. "Do not trespass, weapon in hand, against the gods. They are far stronger than you can imagine, than even your Teacher thinks! For this insult to the temple they will, in their wrath, sweep all from the face of the Earth, innocent and guilty alike. They will turn your Hedinseigh and the Sheltered Kingdom to cinders."

But Hagen was adamant. "They will turn the whole Earth to cinders if I do not enter," he replied. "Open the door. Did you not once have charge of this place?"

Trembling all over, the priest began to slide the heavy bolt. Hagen stood at his shoulder, sword at the ready in case it occurred to the Servant of the Sun to do anything foolish. Behind them, the wiccan groaned and shifted in her bonds.

When the bolt was fully drawn, Hagen tugged on its handle, which was carved from a solid piece of stone. The door did not move. Out of the corner of his eye, he caught a spark of malicious triumph in the priest's gaze.

"Open it!" He was breathless with rage, and the point of his sword danced at the priest's throat.

"I cannot!" The servant of Iamerth gathered all his courage and looked Hagen full in the face. "A key is needed, and there is no key. You can kill me, but that will not help you."

"A key, you say?" The thane tore from his belt the key he had found on the Darkling Rider killed at the hand of the Stone Sentinel by the Living Crags.

The doors opened, and the crevice between them was flooded with an unbearable, withering light. The Darkness could find no way into the Chamber of Altars, symbol of the Young Gods' authority and might. The priest shook from head to foot, unable to take even a step despite the sword tip in his back and the blood that trickled down. Hagen gave him a hard push; and he flew forward, stumbled against the threshold and sprawled on the floor, his hands across his eyes. Hagen then closed his visor and stepped through the doorway.

Below a crystal dome stood seven tall altars of white marble, set between golden columns. Each was elaborately carved, and on each certain objects lay. Directly opposite the door was the chief among them, the altar of Iamerth, Lord of the Sun's Light. It was higher and wider than the rest, and the air above it seemed to burn and flow. This was the source of that bright glare.

Hedin's apprentice strode across the hall. Thousands upon thousands of voices called to him, asking, enjoining, begging him to stop. He did not listen, did not even wonder whose voices they were. He bore down upon the Altar of the Sun, mentally calculating exactly where he would strike.

A strong, slantwise blow, just there, will cleave it to its foundations. At that moment, he was, unaccountably, in no doubt he could do it.

He passed Ialini's altar with its living maple wreath and scattered leaves, the altar of Iambren with its straw fan—these were the emblems of the Young Gods, their guages to the Sheltered Kingdom. For some reason, they had been very important to those who had placed them there, but what that reason was Hagen did not know and neither, for certain, did his Teacher.

Seven altars, seven emblems. Six already lay in Hagen's scrip, and he was making for the last when a wave of dry heat hit him in the face and the radiance that hovered over the white stone began to reveal the outlines of a stern, manly face with eyes of the purest white light.

Into his sanctuary, to the place where Hagen stood, Iamerth himself was descending.

HEDIN

D o you see?" The low, wistful question came from the gentle Felostei, who never engaged in warfare and whose apprentices had always been renowned practitioners of the healing arts. "Do you see what you have wrought? The Darkness is swallowing up the Temple of the Sun. The most ancient and dismal prophesies are coming to pass. The gods will descend to Earth. The hour of reckoning is nigh…" She hid her face in her hands and turned away.

With rising amazement, I had watched that patch of impenetrable Dark as it crawled over the temple. Whence had it come? And where was Hagen? I could see his army, the perplexed chiliarchs trying to restore order against all odds, and the few surviving goblins huddled together, gaping at the spreading cloud of gloom with crazed hope in eyes that glowed red. Hagen was somewhere within, under a shroud impervious even to my sight. What had he done? In the name of almighty Orlangur, what?

I must have cried those last words aloud; and as if in reply, I heard a quiet, husky bass voice that seemed to resound from underground, and its might was near as great as the Earth's very deepest foundations.

"He struck Light against Light," the voice said. "He opened the door to the Dark. But that is to the good. There cannot be eternal day on Earth, for she, too, needs rest."

That voice turned everything in the room upside-down. The vision of the Castle of All the Ancients flickered out, leaving only the outlines of the temple and the upper tiers of the courses of the Dark that shrouded it. The Diviner of Charms was in an apparent catalepsy.

The voice had set my every sinew atremble—not from fear but because my entire being responded to it, though not by my will.

"Great Orlangur…" I said slowly, still not believing what had happened. My mind was about to explode into a jumbled swarm of thoughts, but the Spirit of Knowing foreran me.

"I have been following you with interest, Mage," the voice intoned. "Do not stop. Continue. Nothing has happened to your apprentice…yet. He has cloaked himself with the Pall of Darkness that rushed in when the gates were opened to it. The fabric of the Real has been torn, and the Distant Dark, the gloom from the far boundary of the Great Chaos, has burst upon the very heart of the Well-Ordered. The Young Gods will soon begin to act. I feel their movement. Demogorgon, my brother, is also watching you—remember that. I hope you will understand where your duty lies. And now, farewell! Expect an attack on your island."

I was so shaken, it was hard for me to reach my chair. Never before had any of the Mages of my Generation been granted the honor of conversing with Great Orlangur. The Spirit of Knowing bowed to no one. He stood on a par with the Creator Himself and had not hitherto, to my knowledge, openly intervened in the affairs of our world.

But what has happened? How can the tear in the Real, with all its likely ill effects upon our Hjorvard, be mended? And what can be done with the Gods, if they come at us from the Hallowed Land? We worked so hard to send the Hound back to sleep and prevent it from drawing their attention untimely— could all our labors have been in vain? And what was meant by "Demogorgon is watching you?" What duty must I discharge? What does the Congregate Spirit of Earth—he who gathers up into himself the souls of all creatures that depart the fleshly life, the brother of Orlangur, the second of the Pillars of the Third Power, as the pair are called—expect of me?

At the very least, I had been given clearly to understand that the Third Power was more inclined to help me than it was to gaze on impassively as events unfolded. The Young Gods would have much to think about when they learned the Spirit of Knowing had deigned to speak with me!

Rousing myself, I hastened to restore my connection with the Diviner of Charms, and found it still deranged. Never a model of courage, it had been thrown into a raving panic by the voice of Great Orlangur, and was cursing everything in creation—itself, me and this entire undertaking that would inevitably exact its price. I had to deplete my strength to place it under a Steadying Charm, which I did with a right ill grace, before I could prevail upon it to do anything at all.

Meanwhile, there was mayhem all around. The battle still raged in the near approaches to Hedinseigh, the besiegers' ships ramming each other ruthlessly in their efforts to escape the conflagration that had consumed two-thirds of their fleet. A fresh attack must already have begun since, in their haste to find favor with the Young Gods, Shendar and company had set the might of the Castle all the Ancients astir.

The clouds that had all but congealed around the island began gradually to part company and crawl away in pitiful tatters, their retreat as inglorious as the finale of Makran and Esteri's assault. Iamerth's visage had touched the horizon, and the sky above the island grew dark. The skirmishes in Hedinseigh's bastions were subsiding; Hagen's men were mopping up the last pockets of resistance and taking prisoners, whose fate would not be an enviable one, dependent as it was upon the mercy of their captors. Even were they to flee, they had no hope of finding their way home, those homes being far away in other worlds.

From the eastern edge of the Exalted Dome, as the Wise Ones sometimes call the sky, from the already dim horizon, a miniscule point of light was making straight for Hedinseigh. It grew by degrees, becoming a golden cloud; and a few minutes later, glancing through the embrasure, I saw that it consisted of thousands and thousands of tiny glittering crystals.

I turned to the Diviner.

— *What do you hear?*

— *A great sorcery has been performed,* it replied, sounding weak with fear. *Your Generation has united. They have opened doors and given entry to a famished, slumbering power. It is empty within. It desires to be sated, and its food is you and your might. And it will bolt me down besides!* it added, almost tearfully. *They drive it on. They imbue it with ever greater...ever greater impetus. Your Pillar is all befogged...*

So, Shendar's best recourse against me had been the Hungering Stars, for such was our name for them. This was an ancient, well-tested weapon used by the Mages of prior Generations many a time to settle scores with the headstrong. That living cloud had seen the light of day in my lifetime, too, when a wizards' rebellion was put down in one of the human kingdoms—an engrossing and edifying story to which I shall return another time, it being too long in the telling.

They had also tried to use it in cowing Rakoth, before they knew his true strength and when Merlin still had every expectation of shifting for himself, without the help of the Young Gods. That was the one and only time the weapon of the Ancients had proved powerless against a Mage of our

Generation. The Hungering Stars, for all their ability to engulf, to suck dry a spellbinder's very soul, were shattered like breakers on a cliff, confounded by the titanic bulwarks raised in their path and fashioned of a concentration of Darkness's own essence.

Rakoth repelled the attack, and much strength did it cost him. When the might of the Castle of All the Ancients, where Merlin ruled, clashed with the onrush of ancient Darkness, celestial spheres were torn out of place, tens— nay, hundreds—of worlds sank into starry conflagrations, the waves of flame that rolled through the Real turned a countless multitude of living beings, both fleshed and fleshless, to ash. Even the invulnerable Dragons of Time numbered their losses. The great shudder that racked All That Is left only three places unscathed, those being the Hallowed Land where dwelt the Young Gods, the Castle of All the Ancients where the Mages' combined efforts kept it at bay, and Rakoth's black stronghold in the depths that lay far below the lowest of the Lowerworlds.

When designing my plan, I had, of course, given due attention to this threat. Rakoth had countered it with brute strength where, in fact, cunning was called for.

There could be no doubt Shendar had aimed the Hungering Stars as precisely as a Disc of Iamerth would be. I was their target. Yet the Stars possessed reason, and would never be deceived by a trick as simple as that employed by my apprentice to evade Iamerth's weapon in the ravine on his journey to Old Hropt. Neither powers derived from the turning of the world, nor the Magic of the Slow Water, nor any elemental magic at all could stop them. They hurtled directly toward the spark of my mind, determined to snuff it out forever and intern me within my own madness.

The Diviner of Charms keened and wailed, until I ordered it to be silent if it valued its life. When its whimpering quieted and I could settle my mind, I looked at my model of the world and saw the flock of fiery raptors closing in, speeding now over the seas of Near Hjorvard. The Castle's envoys could be met by fire and water, stone and steel; but all those they had overcome more than once. All those they knew.

Very well, then, the time had come to test the worth of a contrivance I had devised for just such an eventuality although, unfortunately, the opportunity to try it out in practice had never yet presented itself.

I turned again to techniques of ancient wizardry thickly coated with the dust of undeserved oblivion. Dizzied by their own power, the Ancients had created much of this, whose import even they could not grasp; and those priceless secrets had lain neglected for many millennia. Even the all-knowing Merlin had never come upon much that was revealed to me in the ages of my exile, so great was his scorn for the wretched, self-taught wizards of humankind. Not one of those wizards, mind you, had command of pure knowledge—I was long in winnowing out the grains of truth from the preposterous accretions of later commentaries.

In the far reaches of Western Hjorvard, on islands lapped by the Girdling Sea, I heard a strange legend of one who governed birds of flame. Such legends are rife in all corners of the world, and at first I paid the storyteller no great heed. The tale was of a wizard who roused the ire of celestial powers that called down upon him birds of flame and burned his fortress all away. He, though, not only survived but was even able to drive those birds into abysses so deep they remained there still. This was followed by commonplaces to the effect that, ever since, they had been burning the Earth from within as they struggled to the surface; and when they did, the end of all would be at hand.

At first I listened only with half an ear, until I came to see how strongly the description of those "birds" called to mind the Hungering Stars. I began to make careful inquiries.

A great deal I could tell of how I slowly penetrated to the essence of those events that had transpired so very long ago, struggling my way to the truth, rummaging in ancient manuscripts, as the fable gradually began to take on flesh. By comparing fragmentary sources and slighting not even the most fantastic, I understood the story was of the fractious apprentice of a Mage of an Ancient Generation. No milksop he—there was no easy way of destroying him. So, the luckless Teacher appealed to the might of the Castle of All the Ancients.

The Hungering Stars burst forth from their long captivity, but the apprentice proved he had not wasted the time spent in training. He let them burn his fortress, but scarcely had they turned upon him when he deftly shielded himself from them behind barriers consisting of tiny windows into other worlds. The Stars would have detected the opening of ordinary doors, but these windows the wizard opened so fast, so skillfully and so imperceptibly the Castle's raptors disappeared one by one into abysses deep beyond knowing.

My quest for the way to open those uncommon windows was quickly ended, though, when I realized our usual methods were powerless here, the Ancients having wisely hidden some of their creations from us. Our familiar charms that drew their strength from the turning of the world would offer no protection against the Hungering Stars.

That caused me to ask a question that was absurd on its very face: Could the Ancient Ones be intending one day to return?

Nor was any component of the elemental magic, or of the wizardry of the celestial spheres, of help to me. I toiled and moiled, assaying the most crack-brained remedies and not even neglecting the shamanry of the savage tribes. There it was that I found my solution.

The alvish chronicles again came to my aid, by making mention of a strange tribe with the wayward habit of wandering among islands separated by stormy, almost unnavigable straits. Prompted by a higher instinct, like that of a good hunting dog, which told me there was something unsavory there, I hurriedly made for the easternmost tip of Southern Hjorvard. There, under a fecklessly blue sky, on the shores of warm, overgrown lakes teeming with fish, I found at last what I had sought so long.

In the heyday of their might, the Ancient Ones had lavishly shared their secrets with chosen mortals, and had left behind them many strange tunnels between diverse courses of the Real. The wizards of that tribe had found their way into the Lowerworlds, happening directly into the realms of the Yellow Scorpions. Those intelligent, voracious and exceedingly dangerous beasts have always known how to surmount the barriers between the worlds, and Hjorvard's only salvation against such a disaster lay in the bulwarks raised by the Ancients for that very purpose in days of old.

But having once encountered the Scorpions, the wizards were able to speak with them for a fee customary among creatures such as they, that being the sacrifice of other human beings. From the Scorpions they learned how to use little windows that opened and closed on the instant, as the need arose. The secret lay in the Scorpions' stingers, which, as it were, cut through the Real and then promptly stitched it up again. For the needed power, the Scorpions drew, strange to say, upon that same turning of the world, but their manner of using it was wholly different.

Lacking the time to descend to detail, I knew only that the island wizards owed their mastery of that art to the dry stingers from dead Scorpions—laid low by causes natural or unnatural—their Teachers gave them. I forthwith armed myself with a collection of such stingers and, after several unsuccessful attempts, now conceded nothing to those unnamed wizards in the skill of smartly ripping through the Real.

Being now prepared for my encounter with the Hungering Stars, I was able to turn my mind back to Hagen. The temple was still in the grip of the Darkness, and nothing seemed changed from the outside. Then the Diviner of Charms convulsed in a soundless cry.

— The Great God is entering your world! The Great God is going to the temple!

My insides went cold. Iamerth! Convinced of the danger, he had set dignity aside and was on an urgent mission to save his citadel in the Sheltered Kingdom from the unlooked-for incursion of Darkness!

I saw the sky over the Sovereign City run through as if by a gigantic sword, which split the slab of blue and gave a stupendous view onto the abyss of the far Mid-Real. There, against a black background sprinkled with a polychrome of wandering lights, the glittering Gates of the Hallowed Land formed a gold pyramid whose apex reached up into infinity. An iridescent glow at the pyramid's base resolved into a gorgeous butterfly, its fluttering wings eager to carry it to Earth.

The Diviner of Charms was able to show me all this as long as I was strong enough to hold its craven fear in check. Only it was capable of discerning Iamerth's advent into our world; as yet, no one else had become aware that the Creator's vice-regent was descending. So, all had thus far proceeded in accordance with my calculations—the Mages were occupied with Hedinseigh and the gods with the Temple of the Sun in the Sovereign City. The time had come for me to implement the next stage of my plan.

But first, before setting off on that long and arduous path, I gave flesh and substance to my astral double, hanging around his neck an amulet I had created long ago, similar to the one given to Hagen. My double would remain here to distract my enemies' attention and cover my absence.

My insentient likeness stirred and reached out a hand to take from me a dry scorpion stinger—all it could do was stand against the Hungering Stars. Magical power would gush from it in torrents, for I had not stinted in that; and it would occur to no one that Hedinseigh had been left masterless. For me, though, it was time to drop down to the Verge of the World, though not before I was certain Hagen had come safe out of the temple—with a Disc of Iamerth or without, I cared not.

I made a sign to the Diviner. Again I saw, in all its beauty, the majestic and mysterious Godspath, along which the gods make their rare journeys from the bourns of the Hallowed Land to the lands of mortals and immortals. Leading from that pyramid of gold directly toward me ran a narrow, glimmering pathway that wound across the backs of the formidable Beasts of the Mid-Real, kindred to the Dragons of Time except that, unlike them, they had unresistingly entered the service of the Young Gods.

The abysses that separated the Hallowed Land from the populated worlds are immeasurable, and the way between them lengthy and hard; but the diamond trail formed by the Beasts' backs brought the Young Gods across that distance with great speed. I knew then that in the Chamber of Altars, which was Iamerth's most likely goal, his image must already be appearing. If my apprentice had not yet riven Iamerth's altar nothing could save him now. I could not reach him, not while he remained under that impenetrable shroud. Once again came the bitter understanding that my title—Sage of Darkness—was no more than empty noise, for I knew not how to break through that wherein, by universal repute, my sagacity lay.

— *Hurry, the cloud of creatures from your Castle draws near!* the Diviner croaked, and that was bad, indeed. I could not cast Hagen to the mercy of Fate, nor could I jeopardize my entire plan by remaining in a fortress under attack by the Hungering Stars. But what if…?

I pulled the Band of Erith down on my brow.

"Hropt! Answer me. It is I, Hedin!"

"Ho! 'Tis long since I was so gay!" a mirthful voice roared in reply. "We have those cowards of Vidrir's on the run like the carrion they are. We have scattered them, and now I hunt the ruler of this sorry Sheltered Kingdom."

"Leave him be. We have other business to hand. Take you to the Sovereign City, and give your Sleipnir the spur!"

"The Sovereign City? What has happened there?"

"Iamerth is coming to his altar, and the temple is shrouded in Darkness…" I brought the Father of Hosts abreast of events as quickly as I knew how.

"How long have I awaited this hour and those words," Hropt broke in, his low voice so full of hatred even I was horrified. "I shall be glad of a meeting with him."

That alarmed me. "Never think of attacking Iamerth! Don't forget that for now he is beyond our reach. Help Hagen, if help be needed. The Altar of the Sun is still intact."

"Have no fear," Hropt responded. "My steed shall carry me to the city in a twinkling and come what may I shall find your apprentice in the temple."

With that we bade each other farewell.

— *You risk losing your soul, Mage!* It was the Diviner of Charms, reminding me the Hungering Stars were drawing near.

On my model of the world's sphere, I saw the swift flicker of a little star. Looking closer, I discerned the tiny figure of a rider galloping through the air on a golden-maned, eight-legged stallion. Hropt had tarried not at all, and was already making hotfoot for the Sovereign City. A silvery flame twined among Sleipnir's slim legs; he sped faster than a bird flies, faster than the wind, faster even than any arrow.

All the same, I was soon certain the Father of Hosts would be too late, since the rainbow butterfly of Iamerth's astral plume had already reached the ragged edges of the ugly blot of Gloom that had swallowed the temple.

Yet they reached the Sovereign City at the same time, Hropt and Iamerth, and what happened next I did not see, for the Hungering Stars were upon Hedinseigh. I had left it too late to make my escape, and all that now remained was to wrest the Yellow Scorpion's enchanted stinger from the hands of my double and try to match my skill in digging pitfalls in the very fabric of the Real with that of the nameless wizard who had shared with me the secret that might possibly save me.

I felt unseen fingers touch my hand and cling there. They were the probing, tentacular feelers of the beings called Hungering Stars. I struck out almost blindly with the stinger, as if it were an ordinary sword, reciting the needed charm by rote. The alien touch was immediately gone, and I hurried to the open windswept observation platform at the very top of the tower.

Hoarse cries of alarm were already rising from the baileys and bastions in the fortress below. I heard the centurions and squad leaders cursing their men into position and preparing to loose an answering volley of arrows, because the Hungering Stars already soared over Hedinseigh like vultures. When any of them shot out a sudden sprig of fire that struck a cliff or fortification, the stone erupted in blazing fountains. The people milling below were of scant interest to the foul brood set upon me by the Castle—they wanted me and me alone—but in their hunt for me they could not avoid destroying all around.

I saw a scarlet streak trace obliquely across one of the corner towers, saw the tower's top shudder, cant slowly sideways and collapse. I was quick in retaliating.

In the twinkling of an eye, a hazy line appeared directly ahead of the fleet pack of Stars, resembling nothing so much as a shaggy, heavily knotted cable fashioned of a tight weave of clouds; and I was struck by a wave of icy cold. Another rift in the Real had opened, revealing for an instant a gap of densest blue, and several dozen of the Castle's predators disappeared full tilt into that fathomless pit.

The scorpion stinger began to crackle drily as it gradually heated up. Only its first owners knew how to invest it continuously with power; I would have to make away with all my assailants before the stinger became ash in my hands.

I was, of course, immediately recognized. The hordes of Hungering Stars, throwing out tentacles both visible and invisible far ahead, raced toward me. Cliffs were furrowed by a searing plow, the ancient pines carefully preserved by the gnomish fortress-builders burned. Bridges and galleries came crashing down, riven by gigantic swords of flame; streams from springs high up on the mountainside boiled and disappeared in clouds of steam.

Meanwhile, my apprentice's warriors were putting up a valiant resistance with arrows, pikes and bolts. Even catapult missiles flew aloft, only to vanish in quick red-brown flashes, for the heaviest boulder could not, alas, harm the Hungering Stars.

The world was breaking apart around me, whirling in an insane kaleidoscope of colors. The stinger in my hand, hot now, sliced the air; and a long gray cleft barred the way of the Stars racing in from the east. Their rear ranks swerved aside in time, but a good two-thirds of them sank without trace, the edges of the Real closing over them.

Yet a far greater number still hovered everywhere over the island, making ruins of all below. As fast as ever I could, I flung open before them windows into other worlds. To north, west, south, west again, east—I struck out on all sides, whirling like a child's top.

My enemies were not at all interested in being quietly butchered. Instead, they promptly changed their tactics, stretching into long, thin files and forming an immense funnel that whirled high above. I was hard put to sever the unseen cords tearing my mind to pieces, and to add to the misfortune, my defense of Hedinseigh was keeping me pinned down there. If I vanished, the Hungering Stars would simply follow me—as soon as they had incinerated the entire island.

The sharp end of the glittering funnel above the fortress stabbed into me now, and the rifts in the Real that had thinned the Stars' ranks were no longer eating them up in their tens and hundreds. Indeed, I was lucky if four or five disappeared at a time.

The stinger began to burn my hands. In all the turmoil, I had forgotten to furnish myself with something as simple but necessary as a pair of gloves, and I could not waste time conjuring even the simplest Chilling Charm, my time being fully occupied in finding the strength I needed to split the fabric of the Real.

The Hungering Stars tightened the noose around my observation platform, circling faster and faster, merging into a single glittering ribbon of fire. Their razor-edged rays reached out to me, blinding my eyes, delving into me as they lunged toward my mind and sending sharp jolts of pain coursing through my body. That body was on the brink of surrender—sweat streamed from my chest, my forehead and my temples, and my arms were growing leaden.

The battlements close to where I stood flared and melted, the stone flowing down in fiery torrents. Gerder's face poked through the trapdoor opening, covered with soot.

"Great Teacher, the fire is too much for us!" he cried. "Where we snuff it out, it flames up again presently."

"Take refuge!" I yelled back. "Let it burn! Save the men, not the stones!"

Gerder vanished, and I saw then that a thin, blue haze was beginning to rise from the stinger in my hand. There were far fewer Hungering Stars now, but I already knew my weapon would be gone before I could finish them all.

I became a fusion of fury, fear and pain, and most likely was not even in my right mind. Never had I achieved such heights of sorcery, never had the world's power poured into me so freely, and never had I felt so acutely impotent. The plan had miscarried, and I was now faced with the destruction of my physical body and the nightmare internment of my soul.

Some half a hundred Stars, evidently impatient of the delay, were making directly for me, leaving almost no time to raise the smoking stinger in defense. A monstrous, rumbling laugh of victory rolled over me; I was toppled by an avalanche of light, and a fearsome heat enveloped my body. Still, I contrived to shield myself with one more fissure in the Real.

I dealt that blow by instinct and, not knowing why, accompanied it with a Charm of Constraint, a simple spell known to many Mages that deprives an opponent of the strength to move. When I opened my eyes, I saw the never before seen. Fettered by my artless spell, trembling in a kaleidoscope of hot fire on the observation platform's melted flagstones, lay a sharp-rayed Hungering Star.

The entire onrush had disappeared in the abyss that yawned before us, all except this one—this wondrous, fiery being whose secrets, whose provenance, were probably known to Merlin alone. I knew the Hungering Stars were intelligent beings, but had no idea of their language. Besides, forcing my captive to speak was the least of my worries just then, for I was still under attack.

The thought quickly gone, I raised my head and saw that my adversaries had fallen out of formation. Their gigantic funnel had disintegrated; the Stars were in utter disarray. I would have sworn they were panicked, had I thought them capable of such a feeling.

I glanced around for the Yellow Scorpion's stinger that had fallen from my hand and saw a tiny pile of black ash where it should have been. That sight, I remember, did not so much shake me as throw me into a wrenching paroxysm. The destruction I had opposed with all my might now seemed inevitable. I cried aloud, begged I know not whom for I know not what. Shame came later—much later.

I cannot say my will easily won the upper hand—even regaining my feet was a struggle—but, surprisingly, my soul had not left my body, nor was my strength entirely gone. None of my fears had come to pass. The Hungering Stars still swarmed above Hedinseigh—not many now, about two hundred—but they were biding their time, neither attacking nor retreating.

There I stood, my knees weak, my arms slack and my mind disordered. I cast my eyes hither and thither, seeing smoke rise from the charred stones below, and the imprisoned Star writhing in its invisible cage at my side. Still I stood, not knowing what to do. It had been long since my mind had failed me so, my thoughts refusing to serve me and my memory offering nothing.

Something had clearly happened to the Hungering Stars. Could they have called off their attack because one of their fellows is in my hands? Risky enough to assume that, but nothing better presented itself at the time.

I examined the Star more closely. Its fire had faded a little; and its hot, hazy substance was shot through with short, quivering maroon waves, like the rise and fall of a panting chest. I carefully began to feel it out with Charms of Knowing woven into intricate and refined combinations, my first aim being to reach the intellect of that creature, understand its goals and its language and, perhaps, attempt to speak with it.

I own that I was emboldened, and had almost come to trust in my conjecture that whilst I had that captive Star by me there was nothing to fear.

The Charms of Knowing began their leisurely journey to the Star, which seemed to shrink back in fear. There was a brief hissing sound. Rays that burned with the sun's heat jumped out at me, only to break against the bars of the magical cage. My spirits rose—the might of a solitary Star in no way compared with the combined strength that came from their ability to fortify each other. I could protect myself against any one of them with ease.

Charms of Knowing are subtle and astonishing instruments, which slowly penetrate into the essence under study. They require time and constant reinforcement. They may run up against insuperable obstacles raised by some other wizard, but never are they altogether powerless.

Never until that day. My entire arsenal of Knowing was exhausted in a meager quarter-hour, and all I had learned was that the Ancients were very adept at concealing their secrets within those places most likely to be explored by those who would follow after. They had foreseen the eventuality of someone capturing a Star, and had securely hidden all the approaches to the forces that ruled it. Even so, intentionally or not, the Star protected me. I sensed a disturbance in the magical Ether so powerful I did not need the Diviner of Charms to detect it and understand what it meant.

The Hungering Stars were in communication with their confined comrade.

I hurtled down the stairs.

— *What is that?* I cried in my mind to my spectral aide.

By way of reply, it only mumbled. Then I saw the crimson characters athwart the window opened into its world. This was the cipher of the Ancients, the serpentine whorls invented when that world was in its infancy.

I felt rather than heard the answer.

— *The letters I know. But they are combined into nonsense, or to speak more true, they are combined into nothing at all. Wait. Perhaps I can unlock this riddle...*

— *How long?* I asked tersely. Time was passing, and I still had to discover Hagen's situation and, if nothing terrible had happened there, to give him a new commission before I set off for the Lowerworlds.

— *A day, or mayhap two,* the Diviner replied serenely, paying no heed to my hoarse yelp of laughter.

I returned to the observation platform. There, all was as before. My adversaries held sway over the island, the Hungering Star quivered in its cage...and I still did not know what to do.

My confusion lasted but a few minutes more. Then I was assailed by a powerful disharmony, a chorus comprising dozens of discordant voices.

"Release our brother, Conqueror, release him, and we swear never to harm you!"

A sigh of relief burst from me.

"Release him with all speed, Conqueror," the Stars implored. "He is weakening. He fares worse by the minute. Release him, and by the blood of your Creator from which we are made, we shall swear allegiance to you."

"You swear to obey me?" I cried, doubting not I would be heard and understood. "You will serve me and fulfill my behests?"

"No, O Conqueror, that we cannot do. We are under interdictions older and stronger than any other in this world. We cannot go against our own nature."

"Whom do you serve? What interdictions are these? If you are intelligent beings, who infringes thus upon your freedom? Join with me, and I shall not only release your brother but shall also return from the abysses of the Mid-Real the remainder of your kin! I alone can fetch them thence. And if you stand with me, I promise to liberate you from all and any interdictions and charms laid upon you by the Ancients. Choose, then—freedom with me or servitude in the Castle of All the Ancients!"

"We thank you for so saying, Conqueror." The words resounded with an everlasting sorrow. "We thank you, but we must decline. No Mage may quash the charms upon us, for they were laid by the gods themselves in the youthful hours of this world. We cannot submit to you and renounce our obedience to the Castle."

"Very well. Then take a solemn vow. Swear—one and all!—by the blood of the Creator never to take the field against me and to do me no harm—neither me nor my body nor my soul—nor to deprive me of freedom or sentience." I had recited an intentionally exhaustive list, so as to leave the Castle's servants no loopholes and prevent them from considering the expedience of taking me prisoner for my own good.

The Hungering Stars pulled up, as if on command; and then they spoke their plangent vow—and most impressive it was, I must admit. The fire they shed flooded the sky, its rays intersecting; the gigantic letters of the ancient alphabet came and went, forming into words that embodied the most profound and primordial concepts, the root of roots and the foundation of foundations.

When they were done, not a doubt remained in me.

I next took the vow of the imprisoned Star; and the flaming sphere, once freed, swept upward and was gathered in by its kin. Then, the Castle's servants streamed away, back to their abode in the east.

I hurried back down to my model of the world. It was time to know what had befallen my apprentice and what in general was happening in the Sovereign City.

I began by trying to penetrate the dense curtain of Gloom with help from the Diviner of Charms, but in vain—not even its preternatural hearing could catch so much as the slightest echo of the sorcery being wrought there. The blot of Darkness remained motionless, Iamerth had disappeared, and Hropt was nowhere to be seen.

Nor did the Band of Erith answer to its purpose. No, if I wanted to break through that pall of Darkness, I would have to do so bodily.

To that point, good fortune had been my constant companion, but now it seemed to have turned its back on me in high dudgeon. Having drawn that profound philosophical conclusion, I began conjuring a Charm of Clearing, one of the most powerful I knew. I had frittered away some considerable time on that before something else occurred to me that caused me to curse myself roundly and in the choicest of terms.

Why was it that the Darkness had not dissipated when the very Ruler of Light made his appearance? All for naught I had wrested Hropt away from business that was undoubtedly of greater importance. For naught I had panicked, in my failure to understand from the very outset what was as plain as the nose on my face—that the Young Gods were paying less attention than I had expected to all the misrule we had created. The Lord of the Hallowed Land had merely sent down into the world of wights one of his astral bodies so he could see all, as it were, with his own eyes and maybe put the fear into those jackanapes while he was about it.

Vexed, I smacked myself on the forehead, hard. How could I have missed that? I had fallen into the crudest of all imaginable traps!

My self-flagellation would doubtless have continued longer had it not been for the Diviner of Charms. The Castle of All the Ancients was showing signs of life again—gates to other worlds had been opened, and not just by Makran and Esteri this time. Hedinseigh was now under assault from human warriors, which was bad enough, and from spirits, too, which was far more dangerous. I could not believe what it told me.

— *The Children of the Shadows are coming! The Disembodied are coming!* it shrilled, and began gabbling the names and clans of the inhabitants of distant, mystifying worlds and lands where the mind is not always enfleshed or has lost its crude bodily form. Those trackless expanses where death and destruction roam at will have always provided the Mages with their most fearsome, most ferocious, bloodthirsty and unreasoning helpmeets.

Those spirits, on a tireless hunt for human blood and human minds, are monstrous vampires far more terrible than the human dead that are at times unearthed from their graves by pernicious sorcerers. They are much stronger and more dangerous than the spirits of our Earth; and only the Devourers of Souls, which are their close kin, could possibly vie with them. Long, long ago, the First-Begotten had fought long, fiercely and gloriously against the Disembodied when they invaded our world; and the wounds of those battles, burned into the plains in the far west of Southern Hjorvard, were yet to heal.

I had only just begun to think on how best to meet this new threat so as to cure them forever of their appetite for visiting our world when the Diviner sensed a new wave of spells emanating from atop the Pillar of the Titans.

— *Beware, these, too, have been sent after your soul!* it cried, and then proceeded to rattle off something that at first made no sense. *With eight and eleven winds... Thwartwise the spate through seven Worlds... into the domains of the First Intent... the Crystal Harp of Morning... its strings drown out the hurricanes... oil calms troubled waters...*

It continued in this wise for quite a while, but by then all was clear to me. What my brothers of the Generation proposed was neither more nor less than to break the connection between my wizardly—my Magely—essence and the body that contained it. They had commanded freedom for the savage might of the eight ordinary winds that shift the great bulks of Aer in our world, and had added to them the eleven magical winds that shake the boundless masses of the all-pervading Ether. Those immense forces were flowing now into the formless gray realms of the Astral, to create there a new substance—an Astral Assassin that could call nothing its own except that which its masters had instilled into it. It was being summoned for the sole purpose of killing my astral double, of severing the cables that brought together the wonderful amalgam of essences that in common parlance, short and sweet, is called "Mage."

The only good thing about an Astral War is that it can kill no one who knows naught of it; all for whom the word *astral* is but an empty sound will remain safe. Their doubles are invulnerable, for it is impossible to slay a specter not endowed with the knowledge of its death.

I hastened to raise defensive barriers, which was not the work of a moment. The Mages of my Generation were stealing from me one priceless minute after another, and I still did not know what had happened to Hagen.

CHAPTER IX

HEDIN'S APPRENTICE STOOD ROOTED IN THE CHAMBER OF ALTARS, WATCHING THE gradually forming visage of the Master of the Sun's Light—Iamerth the All-Powerful, first among the Young Gods—who now descended in his own person into his temple to bring order there at last. Hagen's sword dangled listlessly from a flaccid hand. The death-dealing Disc lay inside his shirt, forgotten. There remained but a few steps between him and the altar, but why take those steps? He was too late; all was lost, now and forever. His soul—the soul of a man redoubtable in battle, who ran mad at the sight of blood and never numbered the enemies arrayed against him—was overwhelmed by a resignation more irresistible and a despair more debilitating than any he had ever known. He was not blinded by the light, not scorched by the blazing heat; but his strength was abandoning him, melting like ice in the sun, and he was not even alarmed.

The bearded face above the altar, with its unnaturally regular, fine-cut features and smooth, shining skin, unwrinkled and unblemished, that resembled nothing so much as a thin layer of incandescent metal—the face of Iamerth—had at last taken on flesh, and the outlines of neck and shoulders began to fill. Hagen could not look away from those eyes without pupils that glowed with a white fire. They seemed to burn through him, incinerating his very soul.

But deep within him, a hot, griping pain was born, grew stronger and pushed him forward, toward the white altar. The Blue Sword began to rise, albeit indecisively, in readiness to strike.

On the altar's smooth surface lay a transparent sphere of mountain quartz, a tiny facsimile of the sun. This was Iamerth's emblem. If it cannot be removed then at least it must be broken, Hagen remembered.

But the apparently unseeing eyes of the god drilled into him, and he froze, as if entranced.

In the glinting interlace of sharp-tipped rays, Iamerth's powerfully muscled shoulders at last appeared. A clenched bronze fist thrust through the air as though to reach inside him; and it was that fist, and the threat it augured, that roused Hagen from his stupor. A hoarse, inarticulate oath broke from his throat, the Blue Sword flew shoulder-high, and he leapt forward. Now he was by the altar.

A transparent flame enveloped him. The pain was intolerable, and he sprang back with a wild cry. The god looked a little more intently at him but, on some inscrutable whim, still did not kill him.

Hagen tore off his helmet, which was burning his skin beyond bearing, and threw it aside. Tears rolled unnoticed down his scorched face. With a desperate effort, he raised his sword again.

Then, at his back, he heard a familiar voice he could not be hearing—the voice of Old Hropt.

"Stand aside, my son!"

Scarcely had he recoiled from the altar when there was a scarlet flicker. It was the Father of Hosts' trusty spear, hurled to begin the settling of scores with the one who had subjected him to such indignity so long ago. The ochered crimson shaft blazed as it flew—even the metal tip burned—but before turning into a cloud of fine cinders, the weapon struck the transparent sphere of the emblem and flung it from the altar.

There was a dull roar, as if a huge cliff had collapsed. The floor shuddered, the walls trembled, and black fissures raced across the polished stones. Iamerth's shriveling gaze bored into Hropt's chest; but the ancient leather armor, worn as it was and patched in many places, did not even smoke.

Old Hropt gave an unexpected laugh and drew his Golden Sword from its pellucid sheath.

"And you were all but roasted by that shabby counterfeit," he said, still smiling and pointing at the image of the god, incomplete and now hanging motionless over the altar as if all its life-force had abandoned it on the instant. "Yes, it was daunting." He made directly for the altar. "I allow I, too, was afeared when first I came. Yet 'tis but the image of Iamerth, not his own self, Hagen. Come you here. We have a job to finish. Take the emblem and stow it, and then help me hack apart that stone."

He gestured at the altar with the tip of his golden blade.

Hagen tried to take a step, and hissed malevolently at the stabs of pain from his burned hands and feet. Wincing, moving with bent knees like a clumsy marionette, he made his way toward Hropt. A strange languor still held him, and even the unexpected appearance of the Father of Hosts had not been enough to dispel it. He was wickedly racked with pain; and although he was no stranger to suffering, on this occasion an exquisitely skilful tormentor had struck through to his inner being. The agony blinded him and permitted him to think of nothing else. His reason had been submerged in a bloody, fiery mist, and memory itself was drowning there.

"Shake a leg, there!"

Hagen's strength and the wizardly gifts so carefully fostered and nurtured in him by Hedin rose up against the pain. The burns covered his body, the inert substance that was the very lowest form of the Great All That Is, but the magic, unscathed, took charge.

The Mage's apprentice stood close by the altar now, and Iamerth's simulacrum still moved not at all.

"With me, my son—one, two, three!"

The two swords, one blue and the other a gleam of gold, fell as one onto the altar's white surface. There was a sharp, high-pitched grinding sound, almost a shriek. The steel plunged deep into the stone; and the image of the dread sun god opened wide its uncanny eyes, but no blast of fiendish heat followed.

"He will do nothing." Hropt grinned behind his thick mustache. "Because the emblem is unseated. By the way, don't forget to pick it up."

Still grimacing with pain, Hagen struggled to the emblem lying amidst a web of black cracks that fissured the floor. Straining, he lifted the smooth, very heavy sphere and put it away.

Their first blow had driven two deep, straight cuts into the monolith, about a third of the way from top to bottom.

"Together, now!" Hropt breathed.

Their second blow shook the entire temple. All Hagen's deftness and accuracy was needed to find the narrow crevice left by his first swing, but this time, the swords passed two-thirds through.

Somewhere above their heads, a sharp, imperious cry resounded, like the scream of a huge bird of prey; and there was a chiming sound, as of crystal plates being pushed apart. Hropt glanced upward, and his expression turned uncommonly ferocious, even bloodthirsty.

"A fine encounter, I swear by the Wells of Elivagor," he rasped. "'Tis long since we last met...Sentinel of the Hallowed Land!"

Hagen recalled to mind what his Teacher had told him about those Sentinels. The Winged Giants, who were no more aware than the Yellow Scorpions of the boundaries between worlds, had been created by drear Iardoz on his best of days. Greatest of soldiers within the frontiers of the Well-Ordered, whose bounds are laved by Chaos, only twice had they quit their post at the thrones of the Young Gods—first when Rakoth's Black Legions approached the Hallowed Land and again when the remnants of the Rebel's forces, driven into the worlds' darkest crannies, were repelling with rare obstinacy storm after storm, assault after assault, and all the might of the Mages of Merlin's Generation was not sufficient to dispose of them. Sigrlinn's zophars were their pale and distant likeness; but they, even endowed with six rather nimble arms, were no match for the creations of the Young Gods, who had received their wisdom and their creativity from the hands and the intellect of the Father Everlasting.

"Only a magical being may overcome your Pall of Darkness," Hropt told Hagen, looking intently upward and motioning strangely with his sword, as if determining the best trajectory to the ceiling. "No human could find the way. Yet what poltroons they are! They never enter into honorable battle face to face but always send one of their mindless creatures. That winged spindle-shanks—don't go after it with your sword, now, Hagen. Your blade is good, but the steel of the gods is better. Leave it to me. Let's see what there is in me yet."

He drew a gusty breath and straightened his powerful shoulders, throwing out his already bulging chest.

"But the gods must…move on their own account," Hagen said in a scratchy voice, picking up his cooled helmet and donning it. "So says my Teacher."

Hropt nodded vigorously. "Yes! Except that when they begin to act we will then know the limits of their powers. That is why we're here. But before they come at us, we must be done with this altar."

On the third blow, with a resonant, almost melodic, crackling sound, the stone fell apart. The temple rang with a heavy groan full of inexpressible agony, as if unknown executioners were slowly dragging the sinews from a living being. The cracks that had come when the emblem hit the floor began to widen rapidly. Iamerth's image vanished.

Then, overhead, hovering under the ceiling in a gleam of orange light, appeared a great eye no less than three feet across and a good foot high. Unwinking, it stared straight at Hagen, who, for all his courage, could hardly keep his feet. Such wrath boiled in that gaze, and behind it was such truly invincible strength as to leave no room in the mind for any thought other than the panicked shrieks of the instinct for self-preservation.

"They want to see the performance through to its end," Hropt hissed maliciously, knitting his brows. "They have naught to burn us with now, but they have resolved to witness the Sentinel of their Throne breaking our backbones."

He cast a rapid glance at Hagen, blew hard on him, and with his right hand made a motion of tossing something loose, like sand. Hedin's apprentice immediately felt his tormented body, brutally burned twice that day, again flooded with strength, a veritable freshet of strength, as the pain receded once more.

The Father of Hosts gave a small, satisfied smile. "That's better," he said. "The temple's tumbling down. That winged thing is breaking the roof in, I know not why. But unless we want to be buried in the rubble, we need to be gone from here, and smartly, too," he added with supreme serenity. "And that we cannot do until we have dealt with that envoy of our great and mighty Young Gods, to make them understand at last that we are not to be trifled with."

Slivers of transparent crystal that wizardry had made as solid as granite crashed down from above, and through the gap thus formed surged a blinding light. *How many more times?* Hagen wondered. *Their every appearance begins with fireworks.*

Then, onto the pile of transparent shards, gently descended an amazing being only Hropt, among those then living on the Earth, had ever seen before, and that only in the unbelievably distant past. So splendid was it that Hagen stopped short, struck to the very heart, for this being was pure might, pure power unadulterated by passion, malice, hatred or desire.

About fifteen feet tall, the Sentinel of the Hallowed Land held in either hand a short iron rod. The long white wings sprouting from its back were tightly folded; the large green eyes below two perfectly arched brows were calm and held no signs of wrath. Powerful muscles rippled, scarcely discernible, across its lovely naked frame. The Sentinel of the Hallowed Land wore not a stitch of clothing, and its body was sexless.

"By the will of the Almighty Ones, you shall part with your flesh and may your souls answer for your sacrilege." The florid words fell from a finely drawn mouth with even, snow-white teeth. "Approach and grasp these handstaffs. If you do so of your own accord, in repentance and shame for your misdeeds, you shall perhaps meet a gentler fate."

"Away with your nonsense," Hropt growled, and in his voice Hagen heard the tempestuous rumble of battles fought when the world was young and the Father of Hosts led his legions in the desperate fight against the new masters from Without. "Come you hither and try to take my soul!"

For some moments, the Sentinel of the Hallowed Land stood motionless, its head tilted slightly, seeming to listen. Then, it resumed and with a light, resilient step moved toward Hagen and Hropt, as if in obedience to an order issued from afar. The iron rods, now crossed over its chest, glistened with quick greenish sparks; and its face held a thoughtful, almost sad expression ill-suited to one entering a fray.

Battle was joined. The servant of the Young Gods flung forward both hands, aiming the rods, dagger-like, at Hagen and Hropt. The speed of the attack beggared the imagination. Hagen saw neither the beginning of the movement nor the rod hurtling toward him. His view suddenly filled with a dim greenish glitter that was immediately replaced by a bright blue beam of light angling across that stupefying radiance.

Yet the hands of Hedin's apprentice, faster than the mind that ruled them, raised his sword; and the artifact of the Ancient God held firm. The soul-snaring rod was stopped.

Hagen, though, was tossed across the room, against the opposite wall. As he rose, he saw Old Hropt—unyielding, legs seemingly rooted in the stone floor, dented sword held aloft—mount his own offensive. The golden blade slid through the narrow space between the two rods, and the point plunged into the Winged Giant's flesh. A grass-green liquid oozed thickly from the wound; but the servant of Iamerth, its face betraying not the slightest hint of pain and its attention not at all distracted, again raised its outlandish weapons.

The thane came out of his daze and once more was full of fight. He hoisted the Blue Sword and darted silently forward. Carelessly, not even looking his way, the Winged Giant swung the rod, and Hedin's apprentice again sprawled headlong. Stretched out on the polished tiles, he felt with his entire body the convulsive jolts that rolled through the floor. A fissure lengthened, widening beneath him, as the temple continued to collapse, and scarcely was he on his feet again before several panels tore from the wall and fell where he had been lying.

Hropt was working wonders with his Golden Sword. Never in his life had Hagen seen such skill—not even in his Teacher, whom he had believed to be the world's best swordsman. The Father of Hosts was girt about by a rustling wall of gilded glimmers that time and again warded off the Winged Giant's attacks. The celestial warrior's belly had already been slashed deep four times by Hropt's blade, and its haunches, legs and feet were smeared with that strange green blood, if blood it was.

But we cannot outlast it, Hagen thought. *Hew this one with an ax, it will care naught for that.*

Old Hropt, though, showed every sign of having a plan of some sort, for he held his ground, not giving an inch and fighting as if the greedy maw of a bottomless chasm yawned at his back. Then he flew forward in a frantic attack, only to fall back a few paces again. Hagen could at first see neither rhyme nor reason to it. Then he understood that Old Hropt was slowly leading the Winged Giant in broad circles, to where the crystalline sphere, Iamerth's emblem, had lain after being knocked from the altar.

At last the celestial sentinel's back was to Hagen, and the thane rushed forward, his sword atilt. But he was stopped—nay, he was almost nailed to the spot—by a low and indescribably menacing sound, midway between a growl and a roar, from Hropt.

"Be still! Do not meddle!"

The thane obeyed, and right timely, too, for at that very moment the Chamber of Altars was invaded by a multitude of temple priests led by the High Priest Hagen had so rashly dismissed from his thoughts on entering the heart of the Sheltered Kingdom's Great Temple. Alongside the High Priest strode the Darkling Rider. He would have to bar their way single-handed.

In his scrip lay seven powerful magical objects—the Divine Emblems— but they were of less use to him than seven cobblestones, which at least he could have pitched at his attackers. Then he saw the High Priest and the wiccan beginning to cast a spell, and knew he must forestall them with one of his own.

The artless little charm knocked the tiles from under the feet of the priest and the Darkling Rider; but in the same instant all the other, lesser priests, working in concert, pelted Hagen with what felt like a pile of invisible sacks filled with soil. His knees began to buckle and his legs to tremble under a weight beyond belief, at which point he realized the floor was giving way beneath him and he was passing through it—not through cracks between the tiles but through the floor itself. He was being forced into another world.

Engrossed in his combat with the Winged Giant, Old Hropt could offer no help. Desperately trying to hold on, Hagen considered his last resort—to summon up a Firecharm, which had rescued him once already during that long, long day. But time was not on his side; he realized the Real of another world would have closed in over his head long before his enemies would shrivel into ash under the surge of that magical flame.

Instead, help came from an unexpected quarter. He seemed to feel an immense hand pushing him upward. Like a diver who had touched bottom and was returning rapidly to the light and the air, he shot through the spectral layers that bounded the Mid-Real.

When his feet were again on the marble floor of the Chamber of Altars, he glanced down—only once, but that single glance almost cost him his reason. There, in a greenish twilight that swirled like a monstrous, impossible cloud, he encountered the intent gaze of two huge, unblinking eyes, each with four pupils.

The eyes of Great Orlangur.

They blazed, they burned a path into the very essence of his humanity. All the depths of Hagen's memory lay open to the Spirit of Knowing, who was ever mindful to demand and receive due payment for his assistance.

The eyes dimmed, the Gates of the Worlds closed. The thane again stood in the middle of the quivering Chamber of Altars, in the very heart of the Temple of the Sun, which, already shaken to its core, lacked the wherewithal to withstand in addition an appearance by a Pillar of the Third Power. The invisible fastenings that secured the enormous stone blocks and columns burst as the collapse of Iamerth's stronghold proceeded apace.

Now Hagen's body, every iota and atomy of it, was flooded with a fearsome strength as cold and calm as the eyes of the great Spirit that had endowed him—a mortal, and therefore almost beneath the notice of the gods—with their sight. He could not grasp the roots or sources of that strength nor did he know what charm was required to direct it. He was aware only that he had to leave that place; and that the Great Dragon, whose motives and actions were unintelligible to mortal and god alike, had for some reason presented him with a chance of survival.

The High Priest and the Darkling Rider had regained their feet, and the silent crowd of lesser priests drew closer, arms raised in conjuration. Hedin's apprentice threw forward his right hand, turned palm outward as if trying to shield himself from them all at once. The gesture was that of the priest on the terrace who had loosed arrows that burned with his own inner fire.

Fire did not descend from the higher circles of the world and rush in under the unsteady vaults of the Chamber of Altars. The Earth did not gape and swallow up the temple entire. Lightning did not strike. Indeed, all that happened was that the High Priest's acolytes, to the last man, vanished, as if evaporating into thin air; and the wiccan and Iamerth's chief servant were slung into a corner. At the very limit of the supernatural vision bestowed upon him, Hagen spied a rainbow glimmer dying away as the Gates of the Real, opened to let the lesser priests of Iamerth pass through the impenetrable canopies of Darkness that swathed the temple, closed again.

He could not, however, allow himself to muse long on what had just happened. Picking up the Blue Sword, he strode over to the Darkling Rider, determined to tolerate her no longer.

"You wish to kill me, Apprentice of Hedin?" she said in a husky sigh, licking parched lips. She stood motionless, looking him in the eye as he approached. The High Priest, meanwhile, was in full scuttling retreat, hunched over and whimpering feebly, trying all the while to hide behind the Darkling Rider's back.

Hagen did not reply. Behind him, he heard Hropt's sword clanging against the Sentinel's iron rod and the Father of Hosts' muffled roars, while his opponent fought on in silence. By all the rules of magical warfare, the thane should now imprison his adversaries and, by any means whatsoever, including torture, extract from them all they knew and then execute them, or he should kill them on the spot.

Instead, Hagen, as if stopped suddenly by an unexpected thought, wordlessly motioned toward the door with his sword.

The priest did not need to be told twice, but the Darkling Rider hung back.

"I shall remember this, Hagen," she said quietly.

"Without high-flown words is all I ask," he said indifferently, turning from her. The new awareness engendered in him by the Great Dragon's gaze could not deceive him. The wiccan would not attack.

And, indeed, she did not.

Meantime, Old Hropt, by dint of judicious withdrawal and sundry evasive measures, had led the tenacious Winged Giant on an elaborately tortuous journey across the Chamber. By the time Hagen turned back to them, their battle had moved directly behind Iamerth's altar.

"Are you ready?" Hropt, still intent on his task, called to the thane. "Come closer to me, and mind your head!"

In a charge upon his stubborn enemy, the Sentinel of the Hallowed Land stepped on the very spot where the emblem of the sun had crashed to the floor. Suspicion most likely came then, but too late.

With something between a gasp and a lusty cry, Hropt thrust his golden blade with all his strength into the very center of the radiating web of cracks.

Hagen sensed that the strike came coupled with a very ancient, crude, unrefined but exceedingly powerful charm constructed according to rules unknown to him. Hropt's sword plunged into the floor, as if the surface were made not of the strongest stone but of thin pine planking, and in that very instant, an abyss yawned beneath the Winged Giant's feet.

Tiles showered down, and awnings, ceilings and walls crumbled, sending clouds of acrid rock dust wafting into the air. Through a veil of dust, Hagen had a momentary glimpse of the Sentinel unfurling its mighty wings in a frenzied effort to hold fast, and a veritable cascade of debris crumpling and breaking them, turning them into grotesquely inverted clumps of matted feathers bedaubed with that odd greenish blood.

"Jump!"

Hropt's wild bellow drowned out even the din of toppling masonry. The Father of Hosts stood by a breach in the wall, the door having already disappeared under a heap of fallen stone. Hagen raced toward him; and as he did so, a column came down behind him. The floor was quaking now. Hropt grabbed him by the hand and stepped through the gap.

In a glance down, Hagen saw not a confusion of broken beams and blocks but a limitless, blue-black ocean. They were already falling when he produced a Braking Charm, such as had saved his life several times, but the speed of their precipitous plunge did not change. Hropt was shouting into his ear, but the words were unintelligible; and Hagen realized this fall was lasting far longer than was needed to carry them from the summit of the temple to the ground. He could see nothing in the impermeable blackness that surrounded them, felt only Hropt's iron grip on his wrist and was deafened by the whistling of the wind.

As they continued to plummet, face first, he assayed another Braking Charm, then a Charm of Nightsight, but all to no avail.

Scraps of Hropt's words drifted toward him: "Don't try...worth...the well...

Charms are worthless in the well? Is that it? Hagen wondered. *But what well, Iamerth scorch my hide? Is this the way through the worlds? Where are we going? How did Hropt open this path? And where's the Winged Sentinel?*

Faster and faster they sped through the layers of gloom, the onrushing stream of air burning their faces, and their eyes closed for all that they tried to keep them open. Hagen finally acknowledged himself at a loss to understand what was happening to them, and efforts to inquire of Hropt came to naught, for the skirling wind took the words and whisked them away.

Then a bright white bolt of lightning split the darkness. It burst alongside with a fierce flash and booming roar, and was followed by a second that singed Hagen's helmet. The next of those fiery arrows would take them both.

"Orlangur!" Hropt's howl tore though the violent screech of the wind.

Something moved in the encompassing darkness as shapeless tousles of gloom began to come together in solid courses and close above them. When the third lightning strike flashed directly overhead, Hagen turned to see rings of darkness stifling that streak of blinding, fiery light in their irresistible embrace.

The Flame of the Hallowed Land had been kept from them.

But who works so hard to defend us? he wondered. *Surely not Great...*

With that, their fall was over. One moment there was swift movement, the driving wind biting into face and eyes. The next Hagen felt his feet firmly planted on soft moss under soaring vaults drenched with a strange, greenish light that were lost in the thick mist gathered above them. Hropt stood alongside, adjusting his armor.

"Where are we?" Hagen ground out. "What was all that?"

A smile of morose satisfaction spread across Hropt's bearded, scarred, bewrinkled face.

"We are where no mortal has ever been, save Sigurth, son of Sigmund," he said quietly. "I, too, have never before entered this place. These are the domains of Great Orlangur."

"I knew it!" Hagen exclaimed. "But how...?"

"I opened our way with a charm he himself taught me," Hropt murmured, his eyes fixed on the far distance. "Once, I fervently implored him to save not me but those who had trusted me and for whose lives I answered. However, he did not heed my prayer. Instead, he returned to me the gage I had given to Mimir—my eye, from the depths of the Wisdomwell—and taught me the charm. 'Do not oppose the Harmony of the Spheres as it takes its course,' he said to me then. 'Wait, and remember that the day is coming when, in the time of your direst need, the charm I instill in you now shall revive of itself, and lead you to me, both you and he who shall be your key to my door.'

"I remembered all that only now." The Father of Hosts gripped his head in powerful hands, his face contorting. "All those memories abandoned me then, by his will. But why—*why*—did he not help me then, who helps me now?"

"That you have not yet understood, Ancient God of a young world?" The voice was calm and deep. A vortex of green mist appeared on a low rise some fifty paces away then lifted and rippled away, gradually revealing the long coils of a majestic golden body. Thus the Great Dragon—Orlangur, the Spirit of Knowing—manifested himself to them in all the beauty of his material form.

When his huge eyes, each with four pupils, rose to meet theirs, Hagen staggered back and dropped to one knee, for no mortal can withstand the gaze of that Great Spirit, Pillar of the Third Power. Indeed, those who merely kneel before him rather than swooning dead away can be numbered on the fingers of one hand.

Even Hropt, the indomitable Old Hropt, Father of Hosts, strongest of the Ancient Gods who were the first masters of the world, bowed his head low, being incapable of confronting the Essence Manifest.

"No, I have not yet understood," he replied, his voice hoarse.

The Dragon was silent. Along the head crowned with a bright coronet ran waves of green mist, passing and vanishing, so that he who commanded them never looked twice the same. Now he had a human torso, arms and face but a long dragon's tail in place of legs and, outstretched above his shoulders, mighty wings. Orlangur's human mien was neither male nor female, the virtues of both having merged into one aspect, wherein the manliness of the features and the muscular power sat easily with the long, thick locks and the softness of the face.

"You are all much enamored of devising great hierarchies for the powers ruling this world," he said. "Tell me, Hropt—during the ages when you ruled Hjorvard, who was stronger than you?"

"Fate, Destiny, most assuredly," the Father of Hosts replied, forcing the words from his throat. "We lived in expectation of the hour of Ragnarok, foretold to us by the prophetess."

The perplexing questions continued. "And who stands above Fate? Why were you predestined to fall, and humbly consented to await your end?"

Hropt, at an impasse now, said nothing.

"Why have you dinned it into your head that Fate is all-powerful? In truth, in our world none is all-powerful. Not the Young Gods, not I, who am named the Spirit of Knowing. Not my brother Demogorgon, not even the Creator Himself, nor the Lords of Chaos who oppose Him. Only one is truly all-powerful, but he resides outside the bounds of the assemblage of worlds known to me, and I shall say naught of him."

The Dragon's manner of speaking was abstruse and convoluted, and the intent of this conversation was a mystery to Hagen.

"And all this I say, O Hropt, Lord of Asgard, to make you understand that there is no being who may make free with your portion in life. There is the

Great Harmony of the Spheres, there is the compounding of inert matter's myriad diverse forces and aspirations into the one truly invincible Equilibrium. Those there are who call her Fate.

"You and your cohorts lack the strength to turn aside the spearhead of the Equilibrium so as to usurp from the Young Gods dominion over this world. Neither I nor my brother intervenes in the natural course of events when the strongest is prevailing, for that would contradict the Harmony of the Spheres of which but now I spoke. So it has been these many eons.

"But no more. Now I will help you, until due time and not in everything. Ask me no questions. The answers you must seek out yourselves."

Great Orlangur bowed his head as if in farewell, and was engulfed in a sudden thickening of the billowing green mist.

Before either Hropt or Hagen had time to be surprised by these events, they were sucked into a black funnel that appeared abruptly and hung in the air a few paces away. Then they were borne aloft. The sensation was actually pleasant, like lying on a sack stuffed with eiderdown; but the wind was howling and whistling again, and they could not say even two words to each other.

These millstones of the Great Powers will end by grinding me to the finest flour, leaving not a trace behind, Hagen thought glumly as they traveled through the well.

They were ejected onto the square before the temple. The wind was still on the instant, and a granite pavement was beneath their feet. Immediately before them, where the Temple of the Sun should have been, a huge, shapeless cloud of impenetrable dark loomed like a vast black cliff to the very boundaries of the sky.

Close by, in a bleak encirclement of Hagen's men, stood a dejected crowd of priests, their hands bound on top of their heads. The High Priest and the Darkling Rider were nowhere to be seen, and Hagen spent some moments looking warily about him. *What if they heave into view around the corner, and bring that Winged Giant with them?*

As quick as his first survey of the Temple Square was, though, he could not help but note and commend his chiliarchs' efficiency. Despite his disappearance, his men were out in full force, some tending fires under huge field cauldrons and others leading files of Vidrir's disarmed ironclads.

All the commandants he trusted and held dear stood a little apart in a tight circle, discussing something. To judge by their faces, their conclave was concerned with nothing more important than the guard-duty roster, but Hagen knew his chiliarchs could be debating only one thing—what to do next—and praised them in his mind for their self-control.

Then he and Hropt were noticed, and the martial discipline fell apart in a commotion of jubilant cries and much banging of swords on shields. Soon they were completely hemmed in.

"The thane! Our thane! He has returned! He's stronger than the Darkness!" the men shouted.

"'Tis time I was gone, my son." Smiling, Old Hropt laid a hand as heavy as carven stone on Hagen's shoulder. "Try to recount all to your mentor in the finest detail, for I must away. There is much to do and I cannot tarry here. Oh, yes—I have a Winged Giant's rod for you." The Father of Hosts showed him the deadly thing, wrapped in a rag. "I'll keep the other for myself. Take care, now, not to touch it with your bare hand!"—for the thane was reaching out to it—"It will drink your soul and cast you so far hence even the Great Dragon himself will not be able to recover you. Farewell! I shall answer your questions later."

And before Hagen could stop him, Old Hropt lightly elbowed his way through the press of astonished men and goblins and buoyantly strode away, disappearing as instantly as if he had turned an invisible corner. A few moments later, the welkin rang with the neighing of a powerful steed carrying its rider through the air, the two becoming one in a rush of speed.

But surprise was a luxury Hagen could not afford, not with thousands upon thousands of men, goblins, harrids and kheddees awaiting his order. He cast his eyes over the crowd about him, realizing he owed them at least a few words.

"The deed is done, and you have fought a battle more gallant than ever was fought on this Earth!" he cried. "You did not fear the temple's flame, you conquered the enchanters who served it, you did not retreat in the face of certain death, and you overcame death itself. The Darkness sought to swallow me, but I trod its paths and have returned. The deed is done, warriors of Hedinseigh! Before us lies the way home. Even the gods themselves could not stop us! Generation after generation of bards shall sing of your exploits. Seize the gold and silver of this city, and let us go home."

His answer was a thunderous roar of exultation from the warriors who thronged the square.

"Chiliarchs!" he barked. "Have your centurions lead a block-by-block search. Overlook nothing. Bestir yourselves, Children of Darkness!"

The once-disorderly mob underwent a rapid transformation, churning and eddying as men and goblins hurriedly divided into their squads of ten and proceeded one after another into the maws of the streets.

Then there began the rapid but systematic stripping of all the Sovereign City's valuables they could lay their hands on.

Hagen was left alone with the chosen few: Berd, Frear, Gudmund, Orc, Frodi and three other chiliarchs, and Knut. Only Lodin was not present, and the thane's eyes darkened when they fell upon that empty space. Knut noticed, and grasped what was in his commander's mind.

"He lives, my thane," he said. "He lives but...it is right ill with him. The priests' fire has sore afflicted him. Perhaps the Great Teacher..."

"I swear by the cavern of Niflhel and the chain of Garm that I shall do my utmost to bring Lodin back to Hedinseigh," Hagen said, his voice hard.

They were waiting to hear his story, but since no one dared be first to ask what had happened to him, Hagen instead began to question them on the events that had transpired during his absence.

He learned that when the Disc of Iamerth had met the Darkling Rider's White Blade on the terrace of Iamerth's Temple and the Distant Darkness had gushed through the crevice in the courses of the Real upon the Citadel of the Sun, an unknown force had flung all of Hedinseigh's warriors far from the temple precincts. Some felt their heads spin, others found their eyes growing dim, but none could remember how it was they found themselves on the square, outside the cloud of Darkness. Yet in a trice, thousands of men and goblins had been safely transported there.

The battle in the city had by that time quieted, the remnants of Hagen's detachments having forced Vidrir's ironclads into retreat. The ominous cloud of Darkness hanging over the city had finally broken the defenders' spirits, and they began to yield.

Following the immutable law of Hedinseigh, the prisoners were treated mercifully, disarmed and let go whither they would, with only the commandants being held for questioning. All the city's warehouses, arsenals and treasuries had fallen safe and sound into the hands of Hagen's warriors. Already wealthy men, they were now finishing the job by gathering together all the gold, silver and precious stones there were to be found in the city.

A strong guard had been posted on the outer walls and gate towers, and the chiliarchs had determined to search for Hagen and wait for him one more day before fighting their way back to Hedinseigh.

"We were greatly concerned for you, my thane," Knut said, looking Hagen in the eye. "No one knew what had happened, whence that Darkness had come that covered you up, what was your fate...and we were, I own, prepared for the worst."

"I am not to the Darkness's taste." Hagen smiled.

It was the plain truth. He was, indeed, not to the Darkness's taste, although it had not yet really tasted him. But that was not important. For now, the thane did not want even his best comrades-in-arms to know about the Sentinel of the Hallowed Land and all the rest of it.

After the chiliarchs had made their reports, there was silence. Hagen could not but acknowledge they had done everything necessary during his absence; the army was ready to depart at any time.

He took up his theme again. "There is naught more to be done in the temple, for the Darkness did not stand in my way there. As I now understand, it did expel everyone else, but I went where I was to go and took what I was bound to take."

He touched the scrip that held the seven emblems, seeing the fear that flickered in their eyes when they heard this news. Every one of them, in the depths of his soul, was expecting the retribution of the Young Gods to fall upon them at any moment, even though they had not lacked the courage to challenge them, for the power of the regents of this world was rarely made manifest in everyday life, while the Great Teacher—their name for Hedin—wrought wonders almost every day.

"And that doughty man who accompanied me is my Teacher's friend and ally. He came to my aid when he saw the Darkness cover everything and determined that we were faring poorly," Hagen concluded with only a slight transgression against the truth.

His chiliarchs seemed satisfied with this explanation, having learned to trust their commander entirely and implicitly in all matters magical.

As the thane issued the necessary—albeit most particular—instructions and informed himself on certain details, he was all the while beset by a disquiet that grew by the minute. Could his Teacher, his truly Great, truly wise Teacher, have misconstrued? The Mage was expecting that the Young Gods would seek to punish those who had desecrated the grandest of their temples in Eastern Hjorvard. He awaited their retribution, and was ready to repulse it.

Instead, there had come only Iamerth's astral double and a Winged Giant, and that could mean either the plan was fundamentally flawed or that neither the sanctuary nor the emblems were by any means as important to the Young Gods as Hedin and Old Hropt had judged them to be.

HEDIN

I WAS DEEP IN THOUGHT. SO, MY KINSMEN HAD NOT ONLY OPENED WIDE THE DOORS into our world to beings that had no place here, dooming many a land to destruction and their inhabitants to an agonizing death, but had even decided, on their own account and in Merlin's absence, to direct an appeal to the Young Gods, itself an action without precedent. I had suspected all along they would not rest content with the dispatch of that Astral Assassin and was not surprised when, after a scant few minutes, the Diviner of Charms began a measured recitation of all the twists and turns of magical power accompanying the appearance of an Astral Messenger, whose purpose was to carry it across the vast abysses of the Mid-Real that separated the Hallowed Land from other spaces of the Well-Ordered.

Our Worldsphere was not such a very large islet, as islets go, in the shoreless oceans of the Great Chaos. If the Mages of my Generation were pursuing two ends at once, they must surely lack confidence in the success of either. Certainly, Shendar's word would hardly count as high in the eyes of Iamerth the Most Fair as that of Merlin.

— *The Spirit legions have crossed the bounds of your World*, the Diviner told me.

The season for reflection had run its course. Now I would have to exert who knows how much strength to halt that incursion, while simultaneously determining how to endure an Astral War and what to do about the Messenger. Now was the time to employ almost all I had prepared against just such a predicament—almost all but not all, since I must also discover what had happened to Hagen and Hropt.

I had to acknowledge to myself that my plan was beginning to run askew. Although I had counted on a prompt reaction from the Young Gods when the

High Temple of the Sun was attacked, the Hallowed Land was maintaining an incomprehensible silence. I could not quit Hedinseigh for Vidrir's capital to investigate on the spot. By founding my stronghold on an island I had unwittingly restricted myself, even though an island was by far the easiest to defend against attack.

In the meantime, nothing at all had changed in the Sheltered Kingdom's seat of power. The huge, motionless cloud of Darkness still hung over the temple, hiding it from view. My apprentice's chiliarchs were ordering their troops and holding their positions, plainly marking time until their thane's return. I would have given a lot to know what Iamerth's astral double was about in the Temple of the Sun, and what welcome Hagen and Hropt had given it—assuming the Father of Hosts had found his way to my apprentice.

Astral beings can be neither destroyed nor even harmed by ordinary weaponry, and can be combated only with powers called forth from the Astral Plane. I could challenge that manifestation of Iamerth's handiwork in our world, but only if I were physically present in the Sovereign City.

— *Why do you delay?* the Diviner yelped. *Are you struck deaf? They are coming for your soul!*

It was time, then, to show those of my kin who had sent the Disembodied swarming into our world that Hedin, Sage of Darkness, still had some tricks up his sleeve. Being themselves unpracticed in the Elemental Magic, they would surely be bewildered by it.

On several past occasions the Disembodied had burst through the boundaries of our world, and after each such invasion once-flourishing and densely populated states had been left desolate. All that lived—men and nomen, animals, plants, fish, birds, even insects—perished every one, their earthly remains serving as temporary containers and food for the malevolent spirits to whom this bloody feast was a pleasure like no other. In the distant days of my apprenticeship, I had marveled that the Young Gods did not have done once and for all with this affliction, did not put a stop to the Mages' willfulness and their inclination to lose all sense of measure when it came to settling scores.

Neither then nor since had my question been answered. So, I had stopped cudgeling my brains for naught and instead began studying those fearsome incursions. The long hours poring over ancient alvish chronicles were well spent, and left me in almost no doubt that a way to stop those spirits was there to be found, for the elven lords of Southern Hjorvard had once beaten off the Disembodied, had even driven them from our world.

I fell to unriddling this enigma of the First-Begotten, inspired more by the thrill of the chase and my contrary nature than aught else. All the rest, convinced the Disembodied were invincible, squandered extraordinary effort on finding ways to dominate them—no one tried to understand how to resist them.

I succeeded in tracking down the old masters of the Ancient Magic, those wizards who had fumbled their way to the governance of such Elemental Powers as the aforementioned Magic of the Slow Water. Great were the pains and long the hours required to amass the great miscellany of intelligence that had been scattered to the winds, and cautious the experiments I conducted, all within the bounds permitted by the Young Gods and Merlin. Now, while I could not claim to have mastered all the secrets of the Disembodied, I could at least hope the surprises I had in store would not sit well with them at all.

I had to do what was to be done before that numberless swarm, whistling like a biting wind through scarped cliffs, made landfall, while it still poured across the frontiers of the Real into our world. Oh, would that those Gates now thrown wide before them could be slammed shut with a simple stone!

The Diviner applied itself to unfolding before me, like the riffling pages of a book, the tangled windings of the only spells that could have opened the Gates to our world and let those wretches in. The might being expended on breaching the Real was a wonder, indeed. The Pillar of the Titans was likely shuddering from summit to base.

My facsimile of the Worldsphere now had a brownish tinge. I strode to the window and there saw the world outside was darkening rapidly, its contours becoming indistinct, as though the air were choked with dust. The sun had grown dim, and the wind had fallen as if snarled in fine, dark webs.

The Mages of my Generation had already been obliged to abandon their illusion that the Hungering Stars, the dog pack they had turned loose from the Castle of All the Ancients, could not be beaten. The time had come to lay to rest another of their fables.

The world around me was frozen in place; no ordinary Mage-magic could help me now.

My mind roamed the limitless wastes of the Astral Plane, seeking to use keys long lost from our world to open hidden doors and free slumbering forces born when the first living creature came forth herein. They are not terribly ancient, those forces. They grew as life now attired in flesh won—step by step and by dint of unbelievable exertion, torment and sacrifice—its place under the sun. Not one of those exertions, whether ending with success or with corpses piled high in horrific burial mounds, ever really went to waste. The measureless torrents of life's agonies poured into the sinkholes of the Mid-Real and there, in time, took on visible form, becoming Entities. Demogorgon the Unconquerable, Spirit of the Congregate Earthsoul, was their father.

All false humility aside, this was one of my true masterpieces—to seek out the paths to those beings, to learn their language, to find the charms that would invoke their aid. Being the quintessence of the suffering experienced by the living in the course of colossal catastrophes, one of their main callings was to protect Life. They hated the Disembodied, if they—neither Spirit nor Enfleshed nor purely Astral Beings—could be said to hate.

Merlin knew of them. He knew, but he had never tried to exert his power over them. He probably supposed none of our Generation would be able to do so, either. And how correct he was.

But I was not trying to *command* the Children of Demogorgon. I knew they could be useful, even invaluable, in one—and only one—instance, that being the invasion of our world by the Disembodied. I had readied a Charm of Bestirment against just such an eventuality.

When the gray realms of the Astral Plane came into view, I worked a simple piece of wizardry to create a slew of astral doubles whose task was to proceed to the furthermost bounds and, with subtle charms particular to each of Demogorgon's creations, awaken them from their long sleep. There, outside the precincts of this world, where familiar concepts and common logic lose their meaning, I looked upon the world of the Astral Plane, and although this place should be home and hearth to a Mage, I was unnerved. It is not easy to see though hundreds upon hundreds of eyes at the same time, in entirely different directions, missing nothing and ready at any moment to respond to an unanticipated threat.

Soon, very soon, Merlin would be recovering his senses, and Sigrlinn, too, was no doubt well more than halfway along the difficult trail that led up from the abysses to which my will had consigned her. I must not dwell on Hagen, because any unrelated thought of that sort would place my own creations at the ultimate risk.

Feeling the legions of the Disembodied approaching, I urged my envoys on. My strength was fading like water seeping into sand, but I could not fail.

Then came the moment when all were at their assigned destinations. I let out a slow breath. My mind was no longer painfully divided.

"Slumberers, arise!" I called to them in their language.

My power, expelled from a multitude of vessels, slammed into the veil of sleep behind which the wits of the Children of the Congregate Spirit were hidden.

And I collapsed to the floor like a rag doll.

A murderously unbearable pain sucked, vampire-like, into me. It contorted me, tore me, twisted me, turned me into a lifeless heap of rude meat and bones. I felt that every sinew of my living body was being pulled from me, one by one.

The Diviner's horrorstruck voice brought me to myself, and I struggled to rise as before my eyes swirled a fanciful whirligig of pale dimming visions of distant worlds, the trackways of the Real and the Mid-Real. I pushed myself up onto one knee.

— *What is happening? What are you doing?* the Diviner wailed. *All the world is turning inside out!*

Having finally succeeded in beating down the jumble in my head, I glanced at my model of the Worldsphere. What I saw sent ice coursing through my veins.

The Disembodied were not loitering in the farther reaches of the inhabited lands. They were not distracted by the bloody banquets to be had in the far more densely populated territories of Western Hjorvard. No, the spirit armies were making straight for Hedinseigh. They split the sky above my head.

But that was not all I saw, for not only were the layers of the Real bending and parting but there was also a strange trembling above, at the upper edge of my model. I had never in my life seen the like. Then my ears were filled with a deep bass droning, like hundreds upon hundreds of querulous voices chorusing some baleful warning.

I essayed a return to the Astral Plane, but once my magical sensibilities had carried me there, I found myself all but blinded and deafened. The gray expanses were gone, and in their place were frenzied, rampaging, motley fountains of raging liquid flame. I was stunned. Never had I seen such gramarye there, or heard such a mighty fanfare, as if from hundreds of thousands of triumphant trumpets. For the briefest of spans, out of the corner of my eye I noticed a manifold movement, fleet, slithering and astonishingly silent amidst all that thunderous din.

For an instant all was still. Then the sky above Hedinseigh split like an overripe fruit under a heavy hand. A deafening blow flung me from the Astral Plane and back into my body, and my tower shuddered to its foundations.

I could only watch the battle unfold and do what I could to shield Hedinseigh from destruction.

— *What have you done?* the Diviner cried in horror. *Not even ash will remain after this!*

"Instead of standing there screaming, why don't you tell me what is afoot?" I replied hoarsely, completely forgetting in all the tumult that it could not hear words, only thoughts.

It overcame its fear—in itself no small feat—and went back to work, shouting out confused and disconnected scraps of information. It, too, had never before witnessed such truly universal powers in conflict, and was hard-pressed to make out even a small portion of what was transpiring.

It spoke of waves of quenching spells cascading down upon the advancing spirit legions, of the magical clamps that braced, in a manner known to neither of us, the frayed firmament over our heads, of the spirits' countermeasures as soon as this new turn of events became clear to them. My skin was numb with cold, even though I could recognize only a fragment of their sorcery, so horrible was the frigid, sepulchral chill that emanated from them, so frightful were the abominations at their command.

Something unimaginable was, meantime, taking place over the island. Day gave way to night, the stars rolled across the velvety blackness of their spheres like tiny crumbs of silver, the crystal domes of our world shattering, one after another, into a myriad minuscule shards. The fabric of the Real was giving at every seam, the Earth groaned, and the walls of my fortress trembled but still held, for I was reinforcing them magically, and all my strength was going into those Repelling Charms.

I learned from the Diviner's reports that the Children of Demogorgon had not yet closed with the Disembodied, but were laboring to shore up the shuddering layers of the Real and thus prevent the spirits from bursting into our world. I could guess why—any act of murder must be repulsive to the Defenders of Life, even in the most extreme of necessities.

May Iamerth scorch my hide if I knew how that battle was being waged out there beyond the white-hot verge of the empyrean. The magic of Demogorgon is probably the most secret in the world, and cedes but little to the enchantments of the Creator Himself. Even the ways of Great Orlangur were more intelligible to me.

For all that, the onslaught of the Disembodied had weakened, mired down in unexpected obstacles, and I could breathe again. Then, since I scarcely needed to concern myself with what was to follow, I hastily shifted my attention to Vidrir's capital.

My eyes lit upon the cloud of gloom above the temple at the very moment the Sentinel of the Hallowed Land was folding its magnificent wings and sliding smoothly into the darkness, as if diving into a pitch-black, night-mantled sea.

Accursed be Material and Immaterial, fire and water, stars and worlds! After all my disruptions, the Young Gods had seen fit only to send down one solitary Winged Giant! And, adding insult to injury, that nimbus of Darkness was firmly lodged between me and the site of the battle, assuming there was anyone still there to put up a fight.

But as soon as that last thought crossed my mind, I took myself to task, because had Iamerth's likeness—his double—already brought order back to the temple there would have been no need to dispatch a Sentinel who served at the very foot of the Fiery Throne. That must mean my apprentice and Old Hropt were still alive and at work.

I was, I own, ready to kick up my heels when that simple little fact came to me. Now was the time to make my own journey to the Sovereign City, while the Children of Demogorgon held the Disembodied at bay and the Castle of All the Ancients had gone still, the better to hear the most delicate modulations in the clangor of that unexampled affray.

Hagen could not, of course, stand alone against the celestial warrior, Blue Sword or no Blue Sword. Given more time to explore, I would surely have been able to better equip my apprentice, perhaps even with something from the arsenals of Chaos; but we had been forced to begin untimely. Yet Old Hropt had not been born yesterday, either; I knew the Father of Hosts was master of some surpassingly powerful combat magic, strong enough to lay low all save possibly a Young God…or my own self, who had studied it through and through.

All the while, in the demented sky, the tatters of night and day continued their frantic dance as giant blades of fire clashed and flew apart. The stars were altogether gone, and against the black canvas of the exalted sphere that was their home innumerable pale spots thrashed wildly. I even thought at times I saw the vault of the sky bend, as if ready to split apart at any moment.

The Diviner was completely befuddled by torrents of charms and magical disturbances that meant nothing to it, and I was beginning to lose the thread of its unavoidably incoherent reports when suddenly I sensed that, in a single instant, everything around me had changed.

The change was not good. It was the malign breath of December's chill blasting the blossoms of May, a powerful current running a ship against rocks treacherously hidden in the briny foam.

A portion of the power that strove for the universal and total destruction, leveling, obliteration and annihilation of distinctions and of motion, a portion of the lugubrious principle the Creator had instituted as a grim but essential tool of renewal, had erupted into our world.

This I knew immediately, even though I had never before crossed paths with the Disembodied. My heart sank at first, and a shameful panic almost overwhelmed me. Then came the understanding that the defenses mounted by the Children of the Congregate Spirit had not broken down, but that one of the Disembodied had, rather, chanced to slip through that barrier.

I leapt out onto the gallery that girdled my tower. The scene revealed when my magical vision and my ordinary eyesight came together was a view to behold. From horizon to horizon, the sky blazed. Even the sun had disappeared in that flaring ferment of fire.

— *It is coming!* the Diviner shrieked.

But I had already seen for myself a misty gray speck approaching and growing rapidly larger. I had not been mistaken—one spirit had broken through and now, brimming with a horrid lust, descended meteor-like upon the world below, deeming it defenseless prey. My ears were torn—lacerated— by the shrill, unbearable scream of a hideous mind.

The gray spot began to look like a spreadeagled figure with arms and legs wide-splayed. Closer and closer it came, and a surge of deathly terror rolled over all on Hedinseigh. I heard their despairing cries, for few could withstand the horror this Spirit brought.

Then, for the first time that whole, wild day, I felt hatred, the kind of heavy, heart-gnawing hatred that clouds the eyes with a crimson mist and lays the hand on ax or cudgel at whatever risk to life and limb. The thing streaking down on us, howling sickeningly with bloody anticipation, was made to kill and knew—wanted to know—naught else. The guilt lay with those who had let it into our world. With them I would settle later, but for now...

For now, I had the Disembodied to contend with.

The world obediently turned full circle. I was suffused with new strength, and only the shortest of moments thereafter I raised aloft a tissue of pale-green fiery threads, time-tested weapon of the Mages. The ravening grayish thing plunged like a stone into the waiting net. There were swirls of glaring green, a sharp pain tore through my temples, and the webbing disappeared as if licked away by a giant unseen tongue.

What I heard next was distantly reminiscent of gloating laughter.

Oho! Long had the Mages passed from one to another, in hushed tones, implausible legends of the supernatural power of the Disembodied. I had placed but little credence in those tales. Now I knew my doubts had been ill-placed.

For my second blow, I used all the strength the Creator had bestowed upon me. The spirit was seized by rings of greenish fire that destroyed everything in its path, even the air. That was a thrust it could not fully parry, yet though its approach slowed, it did not stop.

The Diviner was beside itself with fright—again, yet again. It fancied it saw the spirit reaching out to it even though, for all they might wish it, the Disembodied could not open the Gates of the Worlds without help. I must say, though, that had the Diviner been in that room with me I would not have deemed its fears unwarranted. My body grew slick with the sweat of unseemly, craven fear.

And then the solution came of itself. A brief charm, conjured lightning-fast, turned that howl of triumph in the skies into a horrified wail.

A Higher Charm it was not, to be sure. I had done the simplest thing I possibly could—I gave the spirit a body. Magical transformations such as that a Mage learns at the very beginning of his life's journey.

Even so, I realized I lacked the strength to stop the entire squadron of the Disembodied. The spell was simple enough in form, but I felt the world around me was about to come off its invisible axis.

The spirit had what it had always wanted, and now plunged toward Hedinseigh's expectant ragged cliffs. There was nothing it could do. On solid ground and with a tolerable amount of time to spend, it could probably have extricated itself from the vessel I had given it, but its time was dwindling fast.

I followed the gray figure with my eyes as it tumbled helplessly head over heels, slammed into a smooth scarp with the dry sound of a branch snapping in the wind and slid down toward the hungry, endlessly raging surf. The horrified howl broke off. The body was dead, and the spirit was imprisoned within it—not for long, if truth be told, but I was not sitting idle, either. Another spell sent granite blocks crashing down from the perches they had occupied through the ages to raise a grave truly fit for a king, and I proved sorcerer enough to fetter the spirit in that tomb.

I felt its despair, savage and boundless, and knew then I had acted aright. Fire flared in the narrow confines of the burial site, turning to ash the body in which I had immured the spirit, welding shut the few crevices that remained between the rocks and imprisoning that fiend for good and all.

Only then could I wipe away the copious streams of sweat. I had seen easier work, I must say, than combating one of the Disembodied, and especially one endowed with such powers.

And still the battle continued beyond the verges of our Reality. The Diviner was again reeling off some of the charms employed in the fray—such as it was able to identify, at least. The stockpile of magic being expended was impressive, and could have occupied my entire Generation unceasingly for ages on end; but I had no part in that conflict, so turned my eyes again to Vidrir's capital.

At first glance, nothing had changed—the same cloud of Darkness over the temple, my apprentice's forces now restored to order by their chiliarchs. Then, from under the impenetrable black curtain, came a heavy, reverberating rumble, the sound of a wholesale collapse. It grew, and as it did, the people on the square cast alarmed glances at the murky cloud, backing away from it for safety's sake.

I fastened, fiercely and with all the wizardly sensibilities at my command, upon that accursed curtain beneath which I knew Hagen and Old Hropt—the two beings closest to my heart in all the immensities of the universes—were in a fight to the death with the Winged Giant. Scarcely had I begun my assault when I sensed the presence, close by the temple, of a colossal Power, shedding so bright a magical fire I narrowed my eyes perforce to avoid being blinded by it. It was situated simultaneously in the Real and the Mid-Real, and it was as immobile as I, in tense expectation.

Great Orlangur had deigned to betake himself to the Sheltered Kingdom.

The Dragon of Knowing doubtless felt my unseen presence on the instant but gave no sign of having done so. What was his purpose there? Could he have been watching Hagen?

Suddenly, there was outright confusion in the temple. The Spirit of Knowing began to depart down the uncanny byways of the Mid-Real, followed—to my horror—by Old Hropt and…my apprentice! The Sentinel of the Hallowed Land had disappeared almost without trace and the rumble of collapsing walls was stilled.

Almighty Ancients, what does he want with them there? was the only thought in my mind. But, since no one had ever yet been able to track the Great Dragon, I did not even try. Orlangur knew what he was about, and would countenance no murder. My apprentice was not in danger—or so I hoped.

The ill-assorted trio passed out of sight; and I, at a loss as to what to do, again focused my mind on the skirmish between the Disembodied and the Children of Demogorgon. It would have been bootless to vie with the Golden Dragon, to flail around, to shake the Worldsphere needlessly with charms that were prepotent to a Mage but of no account to the Spirit of Knowing.

The two Powers brought together by my good offices continued their quarrel. Although it could still go either way, Demogorgon's troops had still not resorted to killing but instead bent ever more effort to strengthening the skeleton of the Real. The spirits, too, did not try to drive their adversaries back, either because they lacked the strength to rout them or for some other reason. I did not understand even a tenth part of the course of that magical battle and could discern only its general contours. The system behind it was a mystery to me.

No matter. Given time, we shall puzzle it out, I thought by force of habit cultivated during my age-long exile…and then upbraided myself for my blithe optimism. *Who knows if I shall live to see another dawn?*

With nothing better to do, I used the Band of Erith to translate me to the Castle of All the Ancients.

Panic reigned in the Council Hall. Shendar sat by Merlin's empty throne, his head in his hands. All in attendance were talking and shouting at once, and none could understand how I had contrived to fend off every attack on Hedinseigh.

"Merlin does not respond! Let us try again, in concert!"

"Why are the gods silent?"

"What plot has he hatched, that Hedin? Should we perhaps offer terms?"

"Fool! The Temple of the Sun is lost, the emblems are gone, and soon we shall all be consigned to Unbeing if we do not have done with him!"

"Yet why has he wrought all he has wrought?" the gentle Felostei asked, her voice low and thoughtful amid the general uproar. Those big, wide-set eyes the color of violets were fixed on me but seemed not to see me, and I was pierced to my soul. To her I no longer existed, having become no more than the true image of a blind, raging hurricane that wanted taming.

"Soon you shall know, Milady of the Healing Arts." I could not hold back— I had always been more kindly disposed to Felostei than to the rest. She had tried to defend me, even after my defeat and imprisonment, when the triumphant Sigrlinn had brought me to the Castle to be judged by Merlin and the Council.

"It is to me you speak?" The fine black arcs of her brows rose in the slightest degree. "In vain, Hedin. Once I fancied that you were unjustly persecuted, that your punishment was too grave. Now I see I was wrong. You should have either gone unbanished or been treated as Rakoth was treated. You have destroyed the whole world, have been the undoing of our entire

Generation!"

No other Mage in the Council Hall was paying any attention to her, even with the Band of Erith on her head. Why not? Did they not sense me?

"Why do you alone hear me?" I asked my sorrowful interlocutrix.

She shrugged her narrow shoulders. "Your Band is behaving most oddly. Only one who understands the Silence can hear you, and the others are too agitated to feel their surroundings as they usually do. But I shall speak to them of you later. Why did you begin this war, Hedin? Would you depose Merlin? How can you? Do what you may, you will neither deprive him of life nor confine him."

"Your intelligence is irreparably antiquated," I replied. "Be not so hasty in your judgments. You can see that my exile has taught me something."

She nodded wanly. "I can. But what of it? Know, Hedin, that you shall have to make an end of me, too, if you ascend Merlin's throne at the cost of his life. I have always feared the Darkness and Unbeing, but to give the quietus to your tyranny—and you can never be other than a tyrant and a murderer—to overthrow your dominion, I will go to any lengths."

"You cannot," I said in a strangled voice, not immediately grasping the meaning of those words spoken quietly, sadly and without the slightest hint of affectation or posturing. She always told the truth. "Or is it…is it that you wish to begin a new Generation?"

"'He who comes after me will be stronger.' Is that not written in the books that Merlin compiles for his apprentices? That is what you fear, Hedin." She spoke more slowly now, as if coming to a long-awaited realization. "You stand in abject terror of Unbeing and the retribution that follows after. And so there is nothing you will not do to…to preserve our Generation and, if you succeed in that, you will then seek to bring down the Young Gods themselves, I know not by what means.

"But hear me—that shall not be. I shall bear a child who will be the first of a new Generation, and will find a way to be done with you. And if to that end I must be away ere then, so mote it be. The world will make shift without me, and without you, for that matter."

"You cannot decide at a stroke for all," was the best I could manage.

"For all?" She gave a pallid, all but unnoticeable smile. "Even the most courageous and wise among them have taken leave of their wits. I think Sigrlinn would have been of better help here than I, yet she chances to be absent. So, Hedin, you may know that I have always preferred humankind above my own brethren. The Creator intended the Earth to be the habitation of humans and the First-Begotten, and all else that lives and dies there. Mages are a departure from that primordial plan, an error of history. Your doings have once again convinced me of that. But…I have nothing further to say to you. Let the others hear you out." And she clapped her hands.

At that distance, I could do nothing to block the effect of such a simple, swiftly conjured charm. The entire assembled company could see me now.

All was again as it had been on my previous appearance here—the noise in the hall immediately stilled, replaced by a strained silence; and while no one would look my way, there could be no mistaking the universal and utter contempt that emanated from them all.

Shendar wrenched his hands away from his face, and I was taken aback. Only a moment before I had thought him broken, crushed by the news of the most recent miscarriage in the storming of Hedinseigh; but I had been cruelly mistaken, for the rawboned face of Merlin's retainer betrayed only a malicious joy. He did not look perplexed at all.

"And so you show yourself," he ground out through gritted teeth. "Look well, then, and remember all, for never, I'll warrant, shall you come to this place again. The Astral Messenger has reached the Hallowed Land, and our lords and masters have lent a gracious ear to our insignificant petitions. I fear that an unpleasant surprise awaits you. The Young Gods are greatly angered, O Most Worthy Hedin, Sage of Darkness!" And he stretched his bloodless lips into a forced grin.

"And what of your pledge to the Masters of the Hallowed Land?" I retorted, affecting to be blithely unconcerned by any of this. "Have you purchased your own manumission at my expense?"

Shendar was angered now beyond measure. "We have driven a mangy sheep from our midst!" he howled. "You are stripped of the title of Mage of our Generation! You are outside the law, Hedin, and your apprentice, too! And as soon as we have received all that we are to receive from our suzerains, your very memory shall be erased!"

"First you must reach me, you braggart," I replied calmly. That calm, as the Moonbeast is my witness, came hard, especially after hearing the words of Felostei, which, try as I might, I could not dismiss from my mind.

"Fear not. Those who are commanded thus by our lords and masters, the Young Gods, shall reach you," Shendar said, grinding his teeth in spite.

A memory came, unbidden, of the far-distant years of our apprenticeship. At that time, it had seemed to me we could become friends, because we were forever embarking together on the most unlikely and risky adventures in sorcery of our own devising, including some that were extremely dubious. But my erstwhile partner in those many and sundry escapades, who had once held no secrets from me, was now ready to erase me from the face of the Earth. Very well. Everything is in flux, everything changes, as one of Merlin's apprentices would have said.

"And when is that momentous event to take place?" I asked with derisive disdain, looking him in the eye.

"In the fullness of time," he snarled, then suddenly threw up his hands in the familiar gesture of Expulsion. "Wrack and ruin shall be yours henceforth, outcast!"

I made no effort to resist, preferring to let Shendar think I lacked all control over him and his fellows, ensconced there in their impregnable—as they still deemed it—Castle of All the Ancients. Once again my gaze roved over the walls of my apartments high in the Hedinseigh keep.

The battle between the Disembodied and Demogorgon's handiwork had been gradually receding. The children of the Congregate Spirit were confidently pushing their adversaries back, driving them into the distant corners of the Mid-Real. The Diviner still diligently recorded all it could of the charms being conjured—or, more precisely, not it but its Ethereal spheres. It had sworn to me it would decipher this mosaic and render it into a form accessible to me in due course.

My enemies had played every card in their hand, and neither the magical warriors from other worlds nor the Hungering Stars nor even the reputedly invincible Disembodied had bested me. The Castle's arsenals were almost exhausted. I had answered their Astral Assassin with a no less Astral Defender. The two of them would circle forevermore around my original double, or would come together in one brief clash in which the champion I had created would have every advantage, since I knew all its foe's magical constituents, thanks to the Diviner of Charms.

A brief lull in the war of wizardry ensued, allowing me to shift my view back to Vidrir's capital, and my heart leapt with joy when I saw Hagen and Old Hropt, their feet firmly planted on the paving stones, standing before the temple in its shroud of Darkness and looking skittishly about them. Even the Father of Hosts resembled little the stubborn harum-scarum I knew so well. Great Orlangur had not detained them long, and I must determine what he had said to them and in general why they had been needful to him.

Important as that was, though, it could all wait. It could wait because of what Felostei had said to me.

A superseding of Generations can come about for various reasons. The gods might be angered at the old Generation and transform all its Mages into puny elemental sprites that live on forever as custodians of acorns or stewards of anthills, or exile them to the far layers of the Real. Or they might gather them in, elevating them to the Hallowed Land.

Mages may also depart by their own doing, as it was before the framing of the Law of the Ancients, which forbade and rendered impossible the murder of one Mage by another. Wars reaped a rich harvest in those days, until at last a Wise One constituted and actuated the Charm embodying that law, one of the greatest Charms in the long history of wizardry—which now, by all appearances, the Young Gods themselves had abrogated.

And there was one more way, which, if my information was correct, had happened only once before, that being when Mages began giving birth— actual, physical birth—to others of their kind, as humans or elves do, when they begin bearing children. If but one such infant were to see the light of day, the entire Generation would be doomed, and the Mages would die of a mysterious plague that sundered the tenuous astral bonds linking the physical and spiritual principles in them.

The only Generation to have departed in that way had left us a detailed discourse on the subject, yet the provenance of succeeding Generations, our own included, still remained a mystery to us all, the all-knowing Merlin included. Felostei knew well the doom that stalked us, and had not spoken lightly. And given how inflexible I knew her to be, I could not but acknowledge her threat had struck real fear into me. There really was nothing to stop her. For the sake of her own hazy and arcane principles, she would, with the utmost serenity, dispatch into Unbeing both me and our entire Generation, and would herself depart into that eternal night with the gentle sigh of one drifting off to sleep after labors long, hard but well discharged.

How could I stop her? To keep her under constant watch would demand too much of the strength that was sorely needed elsewhere. What if I made the others privy to her intentions? A sterling idea. What was the likelihood of my kinsfolk electing to march off into the Darkness on the whim of one of their number who had arrogated to herself the right to decide who would live and who would not?

Yet Felostei could easily disavow the charge, and again I would have neither the opportunity nor the strength needed to plead my case before the bar of judgment in the Council Hall.

Not least of all, why did those ill-omened Masters of the Hallowed Land yet delay, if the Astral Messenger had reached them long before and they, if Shendar was to be believed, had "lent an ear" to what he had to say?

Here, my musings were interrupted by a sharp rapping at the window. I turned and saw, sitting on the sill with angrily ruffled plumage, a blue-black Castle Raven wearing a crimson ring on its right leg. This told me I was being called out to a duel forthwith. On the ring was one short word, inscribed in the ancient curlicues of the Primordial Runes, whose meaning was *Merlin, Archmage of the Generation.*

CHAPTER X

HAGEN LED HIS ARMY FROM THE PARTLY BURNED, PARTLY DEMOLISHED SOVEREIGN CITY. His men stepped out with right good cheer—their losses had not been great, and their booty was plentiful—and the thane heard cries of praise rising from the marching ranks. The mysterious temple—now a towering mound of debris still swathed in that cloud of Darkness—they left behind them.

The emblems of the gods lay meekly in Hagen's scrip, the destruction of the temple seeming to have caused them no harm. He had followed to a nicety the design he and his Teacher had laid out, and all that remained was to return to Hedinseigh.

He lifted his head and looked westward, toward the far horizon. He spied, at the very edge of the sky, faint glimmerings, feeble as faraway lightning but sufficient to alarm him all the same. There could be no mistake—unknown enemies had mounted a wizardly attack upon his Teacher's island. Maybe the Mages of Hedin's Generation were on the offensive, or maybe it was the Young Gods themselves.

But then, the latter's conduct was now, as ever, beyond his ken. They had allowed him to storm the temple, had left their servants without aid or succor, had done almost nothing to prevent him from seizing their emblems. A Winged Giant they had sent—he ran a hand over the fearsome staff, wrapped in a scrap of cloth, he had thrust into his belt—and that had been the whole of it. His Teacher's expectations had been wholly other. *And what shall we do now?*

The answer to that question was quick in coming. Not far from the Sovereign City, a familiar figure in a threadbare cloak stepped from a roadside coppice and hurried toward him; Hagen, caught unawares, cried out in relief and joy. It was his Teacher.

The Mage seemed greatly aged, shrunken, enfeebled. His eyes had sunk into the jutting frame of their sockets; his face had a blue tinge and was scored with deep wrinkles Hagen had never noticed before. The skin sagged, hanging in dry folds under the chin and over the cheekbones, and there were enormous swollen veins on the backs of his hands.

The Mage clasped his apprentice in a hasty embrace.

"Save your questions until later, my boy. You must away with all speed. The gods have still not taken to the field against us, but Merlin, whom I was about to overturn, has returned and issued me a challenge. I have very little time. We must hurry. Prepare for a translocation to Avalon—I will conjure a charm to bring you close as may be to Merlin's stronghold, but the last few miles you must cover on your own. I cannot tell you those miles will be easy and pleasant. Set against them, the Temple of the Sun will seem but child's play."

"That I must doubt," Hagen sighed, turning over in his mind all the reversals of the raid on the temple. "Teacher, such things I saw…"

"Tell me, then," Hedin demanded, casting a preoccupied glance at the sun. The long—implausibly long—day was coming to an end; the rim of that scarlet disc scarcely showed above the horizon. "Tell me, but quickly. I still have much to do." And he squeezed the thane's elbow lightly, encouraging him.

Hagen's tale, though of great consequence, was soon told. He spoke of the Disc of Iamerth and the emblems of the gods and the Staff of the Sentinel of the Hallowed Land that stole souls. The sorcerer's face remained impenetrably closed, his lips tightly compressed and a deep crease across his brow. From time to time he gave an almost imperceptible nod, as if finding confirmation of his own thoughts in Hagen's words.

"Permit me to see your spoils," he said quietly.

Placing Knut temporarily in command, Hagen moved to the verge of the road with his Teacher, and Hedin spread his cloak on the ground. Hagen slowly unpacked his trophies—the milky-white Disc of Iamerth with a chain passing through an opening in its center; Ialini's green bough; Iambren's fan; the scoop of Ialmog, Ruler of Waters; the black hatchet of Iaeth, the Pensive God and Great Lord of the Dead; the belt of Iathana, Lady of Unreasoning Creations; the lamp of Iavlatha, Guardianess of the Stars; and, finally, the crystalline sphere of Iamerth, Lord of the Sun's Light. After the emblems of the Young Gods came the Winged Giant's Staff.

The sorcerer bent low over the mysteriously glittering hoard. Hagen, reverently silent, felt his Teacher weaving Charms of Comprehension and sending their unseen fingers to touch the plunder. The thane was bursting with pride. What he had done, no man had ever done before; he had laid hands on all the seven great emblems that, in the universal certainty of all wizards and warlocks, contained much magic. The hard lessons learned during the affray in the Chamber of Altars had tempered his ardor, though. What if he was correct in his suspicions that the emblems were by no means as important to the Young Gods as all their subjects were inclined to believe?

Several minutes passed, and Hagen waited patiently, until at last his Teacher sighed and leaned back, spreading his hands.

"I'm nothing if not bewildered. Either all these…" He gestured at the emblems spread out before him. "…are not what we thought they were, or my dotage is upon me."

Hagen drew himself up.

"Teacher," he said in a strained voice, "when we left Great Orlangur, I wondered how the Young Gods could have allowed me to seize their sanctuary so easily. One single Winged Giant, and already we had the emblems. Where were the celestial hosts? And I, blasphemer that I am, remain at liberty to walk the Earth, which does not gape and try to devour me, as it did by the Erivag temple."

Hedin slammed a fist into the other palm in furious despair.

"Damnation! I should have foreseen this. It was a trap, my boy, a trap, and we both tumbled into it. The emblems contain almost no magic. I have assayed them by every means at my command, encountering no resistance but also seeing no wizardry there save the very simplest, such as prevents one from fading or causes another to shine, which any village spellmonger could easily cast. It was a snare. We swallowed the bait, but where are the jaws that should now spring shut?"

"But, Teacher, Iamerth's emblem cleft the temple's stone floor with one blow, and then Hropt brought down the Sentinel of the Hallowed Land in that very place. And the Staff and the Disc—can there be nothing in them, either?"

"In them there is something," an exasperated Hedin conceded. "I sensed there what I expected. And Iamerth's emblem has a heft to it that I understand little enough but is no way wizardly."

Never had Hagen seen his Teacher so hopeless, muttering inarticulately, his fists clenching and unclenching convulsively, his eyes flashing fire. The outburst was short-lived, though; and by dint of great effort, Hedin came again to himself.

"Yet none of this countermands Merlin's challenge," he said in an even voice. "Be all as it may, a battle there must be. I shall seek to give you power over that Disc, since you manifestly have the strength now to hold it in submission."

The conjuring was lengthy. The tail of Hagen's army had long disappeared around a distant bend, and still the Mage knelt over the Disc, sweat beading his temples as many-hued glints ran from time to time along the fearsome weapon's edge.

Finally, he lowered his hands with a sigh and slowly rose.

"It is done," he said, with a strengthless exhalation. "Test it on yonder pine. Apply a Displacement Charm, then a Dispersing Charm, and finally a Questing Charm to bring it back. Your thought will aim the Disc, but its flight you must support yourself. Usually, it draws its direction from the sun, but now, you understand.... and I admit I have no time to seek out other sources of power. That would likely take several days."

Hagen obediently did all his Teacher had bidden him do. He imagined the distant pine to be a giant in disguise, and...

The Disc rose abruptly from the ground, and the thane hastily applied the first two of the three charms he had prepared. A bolt of swift white lightning split the air and deeply notched the tree trunk. Then, suddenly, to the astonishment of them both, the tree was gone, and in its place was a real giant, who keeled over with a heavy groan.

The Disc had sliced him almost in two. Dark blood flooded the grass, his big round eyes rolled, and a cudgel easily the length of a wagon shaft fell from knotty fingers.

"My word!" The Mage whistled. "That I did not expect." Then his voice rose almost to a shout. "Hagen, halt the army—now!"

Hagen had not even had time to think how he was to do that when all around him dimmed, only to clear an instant later. He and his Teacher stood in the very midst of the army.

But they were too late.

The mighty oaks and elms growing on either side of the narrow road that had stretched the Hedinseigh forces out a good mile had one after another become terrible red-eyed giants brandishing huge clubs. Attired in leather armor and caps sewn with plates of bone, they rhythmically swung their cudgels, rumbling in full-throated satisfaction at the sight of humans and goblins writhing in agony.

Knut had kept his head and greeted this unlooked-for threat with a hail of black-tipped arrows, but the giant in the vanguard of the attack, although resembling nothing so much as a porcupine with all its quills standing on end, seemed troubled not one whit by that. His dark cudgel rose and fell, striking down human or goblin with every blow. Hagen saw his pikemen drop back, closing their ranks up tight and reaching for the giant's legs with their pikes as the massive club crashed down and rose again, each time revealing three bodies motionless on the ground.

A supple vortex of rage invaded the thane's mind, and a red mist clouded his eyes. His warriors were perishing, and he, their leader ought to be in the forefront, in the place of greatest danger. The Blue Sword leapt to his hand; he hoisted the glittering blade and darted forward with a hoarse cry. His Teacher could do nothing to hold him back.

The men of Hedinseigh took heart at the sight of their commander, and promptly rallied behind him. Any assault led by their thane would, they fervently believed, necessarily turn the tide of battle.

A fountain of soil spurted up as a gnarled cudgel plowed into the ground close by him—the giant had missed only by a hair's-breadth. The thane threw up his hands, fetching his troops up short.

"Pull back!" he roared. "Pull back, and down swords!"

Five or six giants had surrounded the head of the army, their clubs working like flails on the threshing floor and already stained black with blood. Hagen crept close to one of them. With a hiss, the Blue Sword plunged up to its crosspiece into the monstrous brown foot. He wrenched the blade out, and dark crimson blood bubbled from wound—which, however, immediately crusted over, stemming the flow. The giant roared, and Hagen was very nearly flattened by his cudgel.

Then, mentally berating himself in the choicest of terms, he grasped the Disc of Iamerth.

The colossal club was closing with his head when the Disc bisected the body of the giant; only a bolt of white lightning could be seen piercing the air as the weapon returned to its new master. A second giant, staring in astonishment at his dead companion, gave a sudden, piteous howl. The ground reared up around him, and he disappeared, the sound of his wails fading rapidly as if he had fallen into a well of unknown but most considerable depth. Hagen knew then his Teacher had not been idling the time away.

The rest of the giants bolted; and Hagen was already aiming the Disc at one of those broad backs but thought better of it. He sickened at the slaughter of fugitives, preferring to meet his foes honorably, face to face.

It took no little time to reassemble the scattered squads, bind up the wounded and give the dead a hurried burial. Hagen watched his Teacher's face grow grimmer with every passing minute.

"Only imagine—Ialini's woodland giants!" the Mage said in an undertone when the army at last moved on. "Whose plan could it have been to send them into battle? They are servants, builders, porters, but surely not warriors. The zophars in Erivag and now these…" His voice trailed off, until at last he was immersed in thought and communed only with himself.

They marched together, teacher and apprentice, at one with the army of Hedinseigh, which was smaller now but still a formidable force. As they went, Hagen questioned the Mage on what had transpired after the Castle Raven had brought Merlin's challenge.

"My first thought was that the duel would begin forthwith. I could not even remove the ring from the bird's leg, so hot was the metal with the sender's wrath," Hedin said. "So, I sought to speak with the Leader of the Council of the Generation, and succeeded in doing so, although previously he had favored me with scant attention. 'When shall we meet and with what weapons in hand?' I asked him. 'Whenever you wish, Sage of Darkness,' he responded, and I was surprised, for the one demanding satisfaction customarily insists on a swift settling of scores.

"'What does this mean, Merlin?' I asked him then. 'You do not wish for a speedy resolution?'

"'Who could take pleasure in wiping from the face of our world one of his own kind?' he gibed. 'I am on Avalon. Since I acknowledge how fruitless it would be to expect a visit from you here, I suggest that you proceed with all speed to your precious Hedinseigh. Close the circle of your defenses around the keep as you may, so mightily have you labored over those charms. Hasten to Hedinseigh, and there all will become clear to you.'

"'And where is your much-vaunted Astral Messenger?' I asked him then. 'Where is the fearful retribution to be meted out to me by the Young Gods?'

"'I am that retribution,' he replied, bombastic as ever was, and thus he ended the conversation. And I came quickly to you, my boy. The decisive moment has arrived. The plan will now either fail utterly or we shall continue to…hold fast yet a while, until all turns to our advantage. And so, Avalon awaits you."

The army was marching beneath a cloudless starry sky. Hagen, his head lowered unbeknownst to him, heard his Teacher out, fearing to utter even a word.

"And now," Hedin said, "tell me about Great Orlangur."

Hagen's story was not lengthy. The sorcerer listened most attentively, nodding now and then, what he heard seeming to confirm his own conjectures. When Hagen was done, Hedin laid a hand on his shoulder.

"The Third Power has never before openly intervened in the affairs of our world," he said. "I am loath even to guess what the end of this may be. Now the Distant Ones shall surely make answer—I yet cherish the hope they will see fit to grapple with the Mistress of the Darkling Riders, but who can speak with certainty on the intentions of the Distant Powers?

"Your tale has given me much to think on, but now it is time for us to go our ways. Yes, I know your army is tired, and burdened with booty and the wounded, so I shall send you first elsewhere than to Avalon. You shall spend a day and a night in a far, secluded place where you will, I trust, be beyond the grasp of either Merlin or Sigrlinn. There you may rest and catch your breath.

"You will leave the wounded and your spoils in that place, from whence you shall immediately pass on to Avalon. I shall open the Gates and hold them open for a certain length of time. As I have said, you will be one day's march from Merlin's castle, since I lack the power to bring you closer. And thereafter…you know all. Our every hope is invested in your success," the Mage added, lowering his voice.

Hagen made Hedin a slow, deep obeisance, feeling at that moment only a bitter unease coupled with the almost complete certainty he was parting forever from his dearest friend, his Teacher, his only guide in a world of extraordinary complexity whose true framing is divulged to a mere handful of mortals. Hedin was his source of knowledge of that world, without whom he, who feared no human foe, would be left alone to face great wizards who could in an instant consign him to bottomless pits where death would come as deliverance.

Hedin touched an unyielding hand to his apprentice's bowed head—carefully, as if with misgiving—then pulled away, stepped back and said quietly, "Gates!"

Before the army spread the rainbow fan of a door opening between worlds. Hagen was the first to stride into the broad passageway, with the rest following after. It was as always—all around dimmed, leaving nothing to see but motley streamers stretched along either side of the unseen path like sleeping snakes.

For a mile or more behind the thane marched his army, the crude weight of its gray, brown and dark-green armor and armaments mingling with the delicate interplay of the layers of the Mid-Real that shimmered about them. The men no longer sang or even spoke, for only their most seasoned centurions were familiar with a crossing such as this. The rest, though somewhat daunted, believed in their thane and followed him without demur.

Some of the younger men, trying not to break stride, strove to touch the unseen path beneath their feet. Hagen saw what they did, and knew their fingers would encounter nothing but a hard, smooth glassy surface. Perhaps they were progressing across a celestial sphere, perhaps this was all but an artifice for their eyes—he knew not, and it seemed of no importance to a thane preoccupied by the imminent rallying of his troops for the storming of a stronghold in comparison with which all their adventures in the Temple of the Sun would be a mere bagatelle.

So lost in thought was he that he did not at first notice that the rainbow glister was gone, and their heavy, cleated boots were submerged now in soft, tall grass of a delicate green that gave off a faint and pleasant perfume akin to that of the spring meadows in Eastern Hjorvard. He did not at first hear the birds whistling one to another, or the joyful hubbub that broke out among the men when they again saw the loving light of a sun that was bright but not pitilessly, scorchingly hot.

The army was in a secluded valley that opened to the sea. Across the slopes scrambled dark-leafed trees with sleek brown trunks whose dense, leathery foliage was unknown to Hagen. Their tops were sharpened pikes and the spaces between them were wreathed with thorny vines that bore large pale-pink flowers. Bees hummed, and the surf quietly pounded the shore. All was peace, and for the first time in many days and weeks, his sense of danger told him nothing threatened them in this place.

"Ha-a-alt!" the command rang out. "Pitch camp!"

Yes, it was quiet here, and serene, and seemed safe; but even so Knut set up double patrols, and the sentries looked and listened in good earnest to the slightest dithering in the bushes or the creak of branches rocked by the wind.

The hours passed, all remained calm, and the army gave itself over to deep, heedless rest. Some slipped off to bathe in the warm sea, others lay down to sleep on soft mattresses of grass; and only the most bellicose among them still tended their swords, running their sharpening stones up and down, up and down the cutting edge.

This luxurious night, full of tangy odors carried on the breeze from the depths of the shoreline forests, with unbelievably large stars against the black velvet of the sky and soft rustlings in the thickets—would his warriors ever see another such? Or, for that matter, would he?

By sheer force of will, Hagen forced himself not to think how many more of the men who followed him fearlessly through fire and water would never return to the grizzled Hedinseigh crags that were home to such as had found Eastern Hjorvard too oversupplied with people for their liking.

Dawn broke, and the warm waters received hundreds, even thousands of strong male bodies accustomed to the cold steel-gray swells of their native seas and now luxuriating in the novel caress of water dappled with sunlight. Then axes rang out across the surrounding slopes, in a hasty effort to lay in stores against the coming siege.

Hagen bided his time. He noticed the men looking at him askance, as if to say "Well it would be to delay our orders to move out." And he postponed as long as ever he could, but when the sun had overtopped the zenith and begun its leisurely descent to the horizon, he at last gave the long-awaited command.

His eyes—the eyes of an experienced military leader—could not be deceived; the troops prepared with an ill grace. They came grudgingly into formation, casting dull-eyed glances about them. No one was ready to leave this cozy valley.

"Brothers!" Hagen cried. "I know that it is well with you here. I promise you that, when our business is done, we shall return and shall then be able to fetch a proper breath. But is it now fitting for such swords as yours to sleep in their sheaths? Our enemy, though half-defeated, is still strong. He must be dealt the final blow. He will try to send you astray, wrap you in a deceptive fog of wizardry, but you must pay that no mind and follow only my commands. Trust in me, who has never in any way deceived you. You fought valorously at the temple, and long shall each of you be hymned. You did not tremble in the face of sorcery, did not tremble before the very gods themselves. Surely, then, you will not now permit this treacherous weakness to get the better of you. Forward, for the glory of Hedinseigh!"

No sooner had the rattle of sword on shield abated, no sooner was the rumble of answering cries stilled than a gray curtain composed of thousands upon thousands of pearly threads of fog descended over the sea. Silence fell on the instant, and Hagen waved his sword in a silent order to follow his lead.

The army soon formed a long swath along the spectral boundary between the worlds in order to reach uncharted Avalon all at the same time.

The crossing was but momentary. In the course of one short second, the thane's face was plunged into a cold, slightly viscous slurry that floated in midair; then, his eyes were spattered with merry sunlight fragmented through thick dark-green foliage. He seemed to feel the ground sliding out from under his feet, so unexpected, so intoxicating was the perfume of the forests that flowered eternally on Avalon's shores.

Hagen recognized not a single tree, not a single herb around him, for everything was whimsically changed in accordance with the odd caprices of the master of those parts. The tree trunks seemed tightly interwoven with a multitude of cables; the greenish bark was ornately adorned with agate. Yellow veins inscribed every leaf with a subtle, intricate design, and the heavy corollas of crimson flowers drooped languidly amid the branches.

Then, from the thickets in their path emerged the black head of an ant— an ant, that is, the size of any wolf. Hedin's apprentice had time neither to seize his sword nor to raise his shield against this denizen of Avalon heading straight toward him, fleet-footed and silent.

Gudmund came in time to the rescue. He had set foot on the soil of Avalon with his hooked knife at the ready, and now he flung it with little understanding of the nature of this new foe but knowing from its movement alone it was too fast not to be dangerous. The sickle-curved hook cleaved the insect's armor-like shell, separating its head from its body.

"A warm welcome to Avalon, this," Frodi said gruffly, taking a more comfortable hold on his cudgel.

The haze that marked the way back was gone from behind them. Hagen's army stood now on the packed sand by the surfline, where the waves rolled in to break at the edge of the gently sloping shore. A mile away, above the forest's green foam, brownish crags rose, vaulting upward to the very clouds, a giant staircase fit for a colossus. A featureless beach stretched to right and left, and the sea here and there revealed damp black teeth of stone that were the tips of underwater ridges.

Avalon was in some ways greatly reminiscent of the lovely land they had just quit, not without regret, and yet it was also very different. There was something elusive, incomprehensible, abroad here. The trembling of the air over the warm cliffs was different somehow, suggesting to the thane an elaborate dance of mysterious, diaphanous beings, the daemons of an aerial ocean. Even the sand beneath their feet held riddles; scooping up a handful, Hagen saw that every grain varied in color from the next, in a gamut that ran from inky blue to a deep ruby-red.

The slain ant lay, sinister and black, on the shore. The thane gave Gudmund a grateful nod, which seemed, however, to go unmarked, for Gudmund was examining the carcass, his face a picture of unfeigned grief. Before Hagen could question him, he straightened up.

"I have done wrong," he said, his voice dry and cracked. "No one merits death here. Perhaps he was not attacking. I have deprived him of life on an empty suspicion."

"What would you?" Frodi barked at his friend, grasping him by the shoulder. "Had you not killed it, it would have killed you. Those chops could bite through armor, I'll be bound!"

"I have done wrong," Gudmund said again, hearing nothing. "On this island no one merits death."

As if in confirmation of those words, the ant's last resting place suddenly shone with a scattering of tiny, fiery stars. The outlines of the carcass disappeared, followed shortly thereafter by the lights themselves. On the sand lay the body of a young woman dressed in the simple homely frock of Eastern Hjorvard.

Gudmund grew horribly pale, and his hand clutched his hooked knife.

"I have killed my own mother," he said tonelessly and suddenly, with all his strength, made to thrust his blade into his eye.

He would certainly have taken his life had Frodi's cudgel not forestalled him by crashing down on his helmet when the glittering blade was but a finger's breadth from his pupil.

There was a discordant muttering in the ranks.

"This is a hex!" the thane cried, with the realization that fear could in a matter of minutes turn his magnificent forces into a herd of mindless beasts seeking salvation in flight. "This is Avalon, the island of guile! The enchanter of these parts has wrapped Gudmund in a fog of wizardry. We must loiter here no longer. Forward, for Hedinseigh!"

But while his voice still resounded, it was swallowed up by one more powerful than any human's, proceeding from the very bowels of the Earth. The hollow, rolling roar came from under their feet, making the ground tremble. Hagen's men looked about like cornered animals, raising shields and pikes that were useless now.

The roar became a deafening din, the land was seized with violent tremors, and the many-hued sand on the shore suddenly shot up to the sky in fanciful fountains, then fell again, streaming down the cliffs' gray slopes. Mighty mountain walls punched through the yielding layers of sand behind them, sprouting up through the ground like a grate rising from a castle floor. All along the shore, as far as the eye could see, the smooth bluffs towered one after another, reaching for the clouds and darkening the land.

Then there was utter silence. The rocky walls moved no more, seeming to have been there for long ages, their faces showing not the slightest fissure or handhold. The road to the sea was cut; the only path open to them led to the island's interior, where lay their goal—Merlin's residence.

Hagen hurriedly ordered the troops to move out. The sight of those cliffs raised high above had shaken their courage, and many were only now beginning to understand how awe-inspiring was the foe their commander challenged.

"It is but an entryway that has been closed to us," the thane cried, though not giving much credence to his own words. "Had he been able, he would have rained those rocks down upon us. Do not lose heart. We shall prevail!"

Once the eyes and arrows of clandestine patrols had been dispatched ahead and to either side, the army moved away from the shore, Frodi carrying Gudmund's insensible body over his shoulder. They plunged into the thickets. Everything here—the grass, the bushes, the trees—seemed unfamiliar, primeval, never before seen by human eye. Hagen's men, extended willy-nilly into a long column, passed along a narrow, ill-defined trail—almost a footpath—trodden out by someone amid the virgin groves. They encountered not another living being, and try as he would, Hedin's apprentice could detect no magic in his surroundings.

The outlandish forest was soon behind them, replaced by low yellow-leafed bushes that clung to a brownish, terraced slope. Shields and bows at the ready, Hagen and his bodyguard carefully breasted the ridge, and saw below them, contrary to all their expectations, a picture of bucolic calm.

Trees rimmed the fields and clustered in dark copses; drays and small wagons, horsemen and foot travelers plied the cart-tracks; and there were none of the cliffs Hedin had led Hagen to expect. And, although the Teacher had said Avalon was not notable for its great size, hilly plains extended into the distance, disappearing at last into the horizon's bluish haze.

The thane raised his hand abruptly, bringing his followers to a halt. He was overtaken by a familiar feeling of obscure alarm, as if he had just tumbled headlong into an open trap. He did not believe his own eyes—there could be no peaceful vale here. He was, like as not, behexed! But why? Was it to drive them mad, since Merlin was ostensibly forbidden by the Law of All the Ancients to murder mortals, even those who attacked him?

Hagen concentrated his thoughts, seeking again to understand if some hidden enchantment lay before them—and again failed. If there were charms here, it was surely beyond his power to unweave them.

Yet you cannot continue holding your army at a standstill. How much longer will that disagreeable forest at your back suffer the presence of uninvited guests? The words were spoken by a soft, insinuating voice in his mind.

The thought then came to him of itself—he must move on, and pass through this intervale with all speed. He lowered his hand, and the army went on, forming into a wider column on the march.

The road dipped behind one hill, another, and yet another, circled a small field and brought Hagen's men up against a low wattle fence, such as was found in any free peasant village. The thane heard inarticulate exclamations of surprise from the troops behind him as they goggled in astonishment at this entirely unremarkable settlement, which resembled any of thousands that thronged the southwestern border of Eastern Hjorvard. Not a man there had not seen such hamlets countless times, and many had grown up in one. But how, they wondered, could this village be here, on the sorcerous island of Avalon, famed far and wide for its bewitching beauty and allure?

'Tis a glamour, no more, Hagen thought, gritting his teeth.

He kicked at the fence, half-expecting his boot to meet no resistance and pass straight through, but instead he encountered a firmly seated stake that did not even tremble at the impact.

If a Mage so wishes, he can bring solidity even to an apparition. Yet still something held the hand that was ready to rise and send the army on. Too finely detailed was this vision of Merlin's—and that it was no more than a vision, Hagen had no doubt.

While he pondered thus, the village had noticed them. A woman gave a heartrending cry, and frightened younglings wailed in chorus. A man darted out onto the stoop of the nearest house, bow in hand and the arrow already nocked.

The village was in a great commotion. Hagen watched livestock being driven away, and women running, clutching in their arms whatever of their worldly goods they could snatch up and dragging their children after them. The thane held back as some fifty hastily armed villagers scurried to take cover behind granaries and barns, their bodkin-tipped arrows poking out, ready to fly. He gave no orders, even though his most trusted chiliarchs were beginning to whisper to each other in alarm, nor did he speak after one of the villagers, unable to restrain himself any longer, loosed an arrow that one of his men took full in the face. Despite the rumble of indignation, despite the calls for vengeance and blood, Hedin's apprentice kept his silence. Something was urging him forcefully to order a retreat. He did not know why.

After that first arrow others followed, felling two goblins and one human.

The thane raised his hand and pitched it forward.

It was the signal to attack. With a roar, the men bounded over the fence, easily crushing all who tried to stand in their way.

"We cannot linger here. We depart, now!" Hagen cried at last.

One end of the village was already afire. A stray arrow broke against his breastplate, but he paid it no heed, knowing he must not allow his army to become bogged down in this wretched wick, accursed by all gods, Ancient and New.

Hagen's word was still law to every last one of his men, so the iron snake slowly wended away from the destroyed settlement. The wind carried the faint blare of horns sounding the alarm in neighboring thorps, and here a small, tight-knit handful of the village's hardiest defenders was trying to break out of a goblin encirclement. Orc's stalwarts had them pinned down, and were mocking them heartily, secure behind horn-plated armor and good chain mail looted from the Sovereign City's arsenals.

Before Hagen could intervene, one of the villagers managed to injure one of the scoffers with a woodcutter's long-handled ax, and the incensed goblins promptly attacked.

"Enough!" Hagen bellowed. "Be done, you wolfspawn!"

The goblins unwillingly disengaged. The few human survivors, not believing their good fortune, took to their heels. One, however, did not run, instead falling back slowly. Hagen caught only a passing glimpse of him before he disappeared behind the corner of a granary, but that one glimpse sufficed.

Dark and Light, moon and sun—what, in the name of the Creator, is Brann Shrunkenhand doing here?

"Take that one alive!" Hagen barked, and a contingent headed by Frodi raced to obey, but not in time to prevent Brann from vanishing into thin air.

At that moment, the glamour began to melt away, as any hex must; and the place around the men of Hedinseigh was transformed before their eyes. The valley, with all its seeming comfort and ease, disappeared, and in its place a black wasteland unrolled like a gigantic tablecloth, its scorched surface sending up clouds of fine dust around the boots that tramped across it.

Another spectacle? Hagen wondered, by now firmly convinced all they had seen on Avalon hitherto had been conjured up by Merlin. He did not for a second believe the lifeless barrens before them had real existence, and thus it mattered not how they crossed them, since all roads on Avalon would lead to Merlin's palace.

Suddenly, the sun was very hot. As the army plodded glumly toward the horizon, Hagen's only care was to prevent his troops from marching in circles.

This did not, however, continue long, for there was a trembling at the very edge of the visible horizon; and something came racing toward them. Hagen hastily mustered his men into battle array, and not a moment too soon.

A horde of ants streamed at them from all quarters, legs working busily and rending jaws agape. This was Merlin's army, and no one yet knew if it was real or an illusion.

The shield-bearers closed ranks, the pikemen thrust their weapons forward, the arbalesters spanned their bows, the archers picked out their first arrows—and Hagen lowered his visor and bared his Blue Sword. The Hedinseigh army, surrounded on all sides, formed a closed circle, a maneuver it completed only thanks to Hagen's foresight in ordering it timely done. The brutish attackers met an iron wall that gave every appearance of being impregnable.

The first dense swarm of arrows, arbalest bolts and slingshot missiles flew. The first wounded ants rolled on the black sand, instantly disappearing under a succession of scuttling feet. The pikes struck, running the brown bodies through; the poleaxes, hand axes, swords and daggers rose and fell, rhythmically doing their bloody work; and a caustic smell filled the air.

The Blue Sword had already brought down three of the beasts. Hagen hacked and slashed with a cold heart, at the same time attending, as always, to what was transpiring around him. Within the first few minutes, he knew the battle was lost.

A solid, rustling carpet of insects, too numerous to count, stubbornly advanced toward the deadly glitter of thousands upon thousands of human and goblin blades, toward the jagged pike tips, toward the hail of arrows. There was something spellbinding in that living wave, in the stolidity with which its six-legged monads parted with their lives. They had no fear of death.

Step by step, Hagen's men were driven back. Even Rakoth's Titans in the days of the Great Wars could not have withstood that onslaught; and, for the first time in his life, Hedin's apprentice, with a sudden pang of despair and a strength-sapping bitterness, acknowledged that he no longer knew what orders to give.

Yet all eyes not otherwise engaged were fixed on him, full of hope and faith; and his warriors never doubted that no danger, however unforeseen, could possibly best their commander.

In any other battle, he would long since have issued the order to regroup in preparation to break through the enemy ranks, or if the opposing forces were very strong, he would have reinforced his defenses as best he could and tried to hold out until the piles of dead bodies cooled the enthusiasm of those coming to take their place. Neither stratagem could be effective here. The ants knew neither fatigue nor fear, and their numbers seemed truly beyond reckoning.

Hagen's sword had taken off the forty-sixth ant-head—he was tallying his victims, though he knew not why—when all around abruptly changed, as it had done so many times before. The attacking ranks fell into disarray, the ants began blindly casting about, and the assault by the terrible guardians of Avalon upon the wall of shields broke off all at once, save for the ones and twos that stumbled upon the Hedinseigh forces, only to meet their end on the instant. Still, this could no longer be called an attack.

No human or goblin even had time to feel duly surprised before the grim landscape began rapidly to pale, fade and blur, and the stir of ants became transparent, the tree trunks and grass showing through their bodies. A few moments later the morose black wastes and living carpet of rapacious insects were no more—they had vanished, melted, dissolved away, and the army of Hedinseigh was on a narrow road in a dense, fanciful forest, its vanguard already in the thickets at the forest's edge.

Hagen's raised hand brought them to a halt. He was bemused. *Why did Merlin stop working his spells when his servants were about to achieve their purpose?* he wondered. *And how could he allow the apprentice of his implacable enemy to stand where I am standing?*

Up ahead, girt about by a festive wood, gaily green, he saw a snug clearing, one side of which descended smoothly to a river at least half an arrow-flight wide. In that clearing, deep in bushes bearing huge, unimaginably colorful and fragrant roses such as he had never seen, stood an elegant three-story mansion crowned by three turrets with finely chiseled spires. White were its walls, and its windows were set in dark scarlet frames. A blue-and-gold-striped flag fluttered above the roof.

This was the place. Provided only that what lay before them was not yet another glamour, Hagen stood on Merlin's threshold.

HEDIN

My APPRENTICE'S ARMY PASSED ENDLESSLY THROUGH THE GATES OF THE WORLDS, NOT knowing what fate awaited them on the other side; and I was, I own, a little ill at ease in the knowledge that most likely only one would come out alive, and that one would be my own Hagen. *Avalon is what it is, and Merlin is what he is*, I thought, and I did not delude myself so far as to believe his attention would be engrossed in me and me alone.

And yet...and yet...

My plan was cracking at every seam. I had hoped to rouse the Young Gods to action by sending Hagen to storm their High Temple, to raid the Chamber of Altars and seize its every last emblem, those magical objects reputed down the ages as more mysterious and less attainable than aught else in the entire world of Eastern Hjorvard. I had supposed that, in all the uproar, the Young Gods would simply have no time for me; and I would have been able to slip away unnoticed to the Netherside of the Worlds, where for ten centuries Rakoth had languished in baneful confinement.

Such had been the first part of my plan. Throughout my exile, I had, unceasingly and by all methods available to me, gathered intelligence on the fate of my Rebel. I spurned not even the wildest fabrications or fables, for concealed in each of them, come what may, was a grain—albeit only the merest scintilla—of truth.

Long—very long—was my pursuit of every detail of the path to Rakoth's dungeon, but always some part of it evaded me. The sole certainties were that the Netherside of the Worlds lay beneath the Power Vertex, and that there, fettered to an invisible cliff by enchanted chains, hung Rakoth, discarnate. His prison was surrounded, as legend had it, by "seventy times seven savage lands" filled with vigilant turnkeys set there by the Young Gods. Of some of the beings guarding the prisoner I knew all, or almost all; on most I had only scraps of information. Then there were those of which I could say nothing, having failed to discover even their names.

I was sure I would not be allowed simply to amble up to Rakoth's cell, for the Young Gods kept a stricter watch upon him than over the Hallowed Land itself. I needed to distract them, but in such a way as to arouse not even a shadow of suspicion. Let them believe that Mage Hedin craved power, coveted the magical emblems, but nothing more. My purpose in arranging that bloody and, in all essentials, unnecessary attack on Vidrir's Sovereign City had been to wrest Rakoth from his incarceration under cover of the resultant mayhem.

I had waited for the Young Gods to reply and, as it turned out, waited in vain, since that entire magnificent temple had been a counterfeit. The Masters of the Hallowed Land had gazed serenely on my travails, had smiled at Hagen's foolhardy assault—and not once had all the might of the Young Gods been flung against me. They had not sent their chief reserve force—Rakoth's jailers—into battle. Instead, I had been forced to grapple with Merlin and the other Mages of my Generation, to sacrifice my apprentice's army by pitting mortal warriors against the wizardry of Avalon; and now, at the end of all, I would still have to ride roughshod to Rakoth's prison, with little hope of doing so unobserved.

A mounting despair whispered that there was no further reason to hide. Better I should use all my strength to make one speedy push through the layers of the Real. To do so, however, would be to sign my own death warrant. Instead, with great deliberation, I began my changes, again calling upon the Magic of the Moonbeast and the aid of the Great Harp of Night. Thus I hoped to escape the unwelcome attention of my kinsfolk on this occasion, at least— though that hope could not, of course, extend to the Young Gods. Only two creatures in all our world had ever warred openly against them and knew perhaps something of their capabilities. One was Old Hropt. The other was the Ancient God of the Mountain, whom I had stripped of the Blue Sword that now belonged to Hagen.

But not even Hropt could speak to the possible results of enlisting the Nightharp's help in combating the Young Gods. That experiment would have as its subject my own self.

After I had passed through all the stages of the Great Transformation, before my eyes appeared the indistinct outlines of the Great Harp. Its astonishing harmonies gently infused everything around me, dissolving the world in their chords; and fantastic shapes began to stir in the flowing lilac mist.

I gave the wondrous instrument free rein.

Unknown hands and an unknown mind had, in the unimaginable depths of the Earliest Ages, created it, given it life and endowed it with a complex soul racked by conflicting yearnings. The Moonbeast alone, in the course of long centuries of silent quest, had come to understand what it could do. Now, through the Moonbeast, that knowledge was also mine.

The Harp's sounds spread across the fabric of the Real, changing it as easily as the potter's hands that knead the willing clay, and I assisted it in the smallest possible way. A vast funnel began gradually to draw me in, and the iridescent flickering gave way to a view of an azure sky mottled with airy, translucent clouds. I looked down and saw land far beneath my feet. I was walking through the sky of another world.

I had, of course, visited these environs of the world of Greater Hjorvard before, but they differed little from the landscapes I knew so well; and the beings who lived there were not in the least warlike and were entirely unschooled in magic, to boot. I had, therefore, disregarded them. I now knew that to have been a woeful error.

The Gates of the Worlds, thrown open to me by the Harp's mighty refrain, were on the point of admitting the Mage named Hedin into the subsequent course of the Real when the ground suddenly began speeding toward me. Like one in the grasp of a pitiless giant, I floundered helplessly in the air, finding nothing to lay hold of. I dropped, the wind wailing in my ears.

It cost me little effort to understand what had gone amiss. Below, close to the ground, slowly circled four winged beasts that in some wise resembled dragons but with human heads and faces. The gangling bodies had in addition to their two legs two arms, also human in appearance, and two clawed paws that seemed expressly made to tear living flesh. The beings soared around a thin column of smoke that rose from a blue valley between two rows of hills.

Something very powerful was pulling me toward it, invincibly.

I understood then that in the short seconds remaining to me before the moment of impact, I would be unable to divine the charm laid on me and even less to counter it with one of my own. *But since a pressing invitation has been issued, why should I not accept it?*

The world around me broke into a demented dance, as it had when the Hungering Stars were storming Hedinseigh. I did not attempt to protect myself, and I did not try to regain power over my undutiful body. Instead, I accelerated my fall to the bounds of the possible, until I became a fiery meteor streaking across the sky.

With a hoarse cawing, the dragon-like beasts moved to intersect my path, their heavy wings beating.

The ground was rapidly approaching. The winged beings tried to block my way but too late, for I had already turned my whole self into a narrow blade of hot fire, had extinguished all my thoughts, had closed down every sense but sight. My body sliced like a flaming sword through an unprotected flank, and the wounded beast gave a shrill croak and fell away.

In the fragments of time left before I rammed into the ground, I struck a final blow, imbued with all the might of the world that turned about me. That blow could do my foes no great harm; but the chains that bound me disintegrated, and I was again my own master. Now I could attend to those overgrown crocodiles with wings.

They had been powerless against me while I was a fiery sword; but now that I had again assumed both body and mind, they could make away with me in a matter of moments if I waited for them with folded arms.

One of them lolled on the ground, its leathery wings clumsily outstretched, but the other three were making toward me full tilt, sculling through the air with all their might. They gave every indication of being far less rational than the Hungering Stars, which had at least pulled up when required to choose between winning a victory paid for with the life of one of their own and beating a retreat. These dragon-whelps seemed to know only one feeling—hunger—and to see in me only food.

Their first onslaught almost cost me my mind and my soul. I extemporized some sharp blades of ice and plunged them into the broad chest of an approaching monster, but it did not even tremble. In the very image of a lizard catching a fly, its long transparent tongue flicked toward me with lightning speed, and I had to spend my precious strength in an equally brisk evasive action. I conjured phantoms to throw them off the scent, but they seemed gifted with a peerless instinct for what was magic and what was not. Another sticky tongue unrolled with a dry, snapping sound close by; and while eluding it, I noticed another gray fillet tearing toward me.

There was no time to either escape or becharm it, and the Black Sword of Rakoth sprang of itself into my hand. The broad blade was for an instant wreathed in a transparent crimson fire that brought to mind the glow of the Great Bonfires of Rakoth. Then, with a light hissing sound, it sliced right through that menacing tongue.

Its weapon gone, the fanged monster flapped aside, making strident hooting sounds; and at first I thought I was done with it. However, it soon recovered and again began circling above me as if waiting for something to happen, while its two companions attacked me together.

A charm threw up a wall of flame from ground to sky in the monsters' path, but they flew through it as if it were not even there. Another spell surrounded me with black shields woven of impenetrable gloom. They were innumerable, those shields. The beasts pawed through them, used all their bodily might to shatter them; but more kept appearing in their way. So it would continue—until my strength was gone.

Breaching my wall of shields was costing these servants of the Young Gods dear, yet they persevered against my desperate resistance. Oozing green blood, and with broken claws and deep wounds on backs and flanks, they somehow stayed aloft.

I was struck through by a chill fear and the foretaste of a fearsome end. I had used all my most powerful spells, to no avail. I realized belatedly that the Young Gods had prepared their helpmeets for precisely such duels as this, and that whichsoever charms I conjured would be expected from any who might seek to free the Rebel. Unfortunate it was I had not come to that realization earlier.

At the last moment, when even I believed my end inevitable, I made one last attempt to save myself. All my remaining strength I directed toward the Great Harp, seeking to open a way out of that world, even though I knew these creatures were well able to follow me wherever they listed. This I should surely have done at the very beginning, but I had given myself too much credit and my opponents too little.

The misty vortex of the opening Gates sucked me in with not a moment to spare, and I disappeared from that layer of the Real, leaving those horrors behind me, roundly cozened.

A bleak world woven from mantlings of gloom greeted me. I had, in my unseemly haste, slipped through too many courses of the Real, laying a trail so clear and well-defined that should anyone, however sparingly adept in wizardry, take it into his head to ascertain where Mage Hedin was and what he was about, the inquirer would have had his answer in no time.

That instantaneous eruption had at least served to greatly reduce the number of guards I might encounter on my way to Rakoth. Yet the most important among them, safe in their boltholes in the Great Netherside, would now no doubt have clear and certain indications as to who was coming their way, and with what end in view. Still, the jailers I had just encountered surpassed in strength all the rest of Rakoth's guards taken together.

The charm that bound the Harp and forced it to do my bidding had dissipated, and my madcap flight through the worlds ended. I stood at the very edge of a gigantic cliff of blue-black rock shot through with countless blood-red veins. Ragged clouds sped through the sky in smoky whorls. I saw neither sun nor stars, for all was steeped in a gray overcast. Far below I heard the swashing of an unseen sea, with only an occasional cresting wave, a tiny white strip of foam, emerging from the gloom to break against a rock.

The brink of the precipice sloped gradually down into an ash-gray valley dotted with black-leafed bushes. Far, far away, the dark at the distant horizon hinted at the contours of mountains soaring into the sky.

I had begun to work on another charm when suddenly I sensed a powerful opposition holding my hand as in an iron vice, and the charm died aborning under that crude onslaught. From the remote mountains, across the valley's dark expanse, a white spark flew toward me, gleaming brightly against the gloomy background of black rocks, its sharp rays biting into the ground, sending up slender shafts of fire that spread amid the boulders and marked its path.

There was no time to speculate on who or what it was. Instead, I hastened to raise magical bulkheads against it while at the same time reestablishing my power over the Harp.

But the airborne thing was too fast for me. A terrible blow the like of which I had never felt swept away all the tiers of my defensive charms. A myriad burning needles penetrated the minutest parts of my being, and from my chest tore a hoarse cry that sounded very distant to my ears. Then came the despair...

Half-insensible, I fell prone on the rocks, yet I still would not believe this was the end. That I refused to acknowledge! Overcoming the pain, I unsheathed the Sword of Rakoth. Come what may, far better an honorable encounter than a coward's death.

Sharp awls of white flame circled leisurely about me in a blindingly bright cloud. I could have sworn the thing was grinning malevolently at me, eyeing me askance as I squirmed on the rocks like a cur put to the knife.

Malice brought strength. I rose on unsteady legs, holding the Black Sword before me with both hands, and immediately sensed a growing pressure. I was being forced backward, toward the precipice behind me.

That was when I leapt.

I discarded the remnants of the defensive charms that were draining my strength and put my all into that one short bound. The tip of the Sword from the World Beneath, the Sword of Darkness, slashed into the dazzling, snowy radiance. A wild howl shook the rocks and flung me down again, but the image burst and disappeared in a tempestuous flash of serpentine black fire. There, standing on the charred ground before me, was a woman.

"Sigrlinn!" I rasped, too weak to say another word.

She came toward me. "You were expecting Iamerth?" she asked harshly.

"What are you...? Why are you here?"

I rose on one knee, my sword again at the ready. She gave a scornful smile.

"Your own strength no longer suffices?" She raised a sardonic brow. "Fallen into friend Rakoth's debt, have we?"

"Come and take what you want, if you are able," I grated. "Allowing that anything of mine is needful to you."

"Can you suppose I have so little to occupy my time?" Again that scornful grimace. "Then, listen, Hedin. The Council, Merlin and I are out of patience. And not we alone, I must tell you. The Astral Messenger has reached the Hallowed Land, and we have received the verdict of our lords and masters, the Young Gods. Iamerth the Most Fair has declared your penance. If you submit and throw yourself upon his mercy, he has promised to forbear. If not..."

She spread her hands.

"And pray do not squander the time in high-flown refusals. I already know well enough you will never yield, and I have said all this at the request of Ialini the Merciful. I am here to stop you. You confounded all, even me. No one ever knew you were planning a foray to the Wellspring of the Worlds."

May Great Orlangur damn me if I know aught of this Wellspring.

"But that is madness on your part," she continued.

I could not but be made suspicious by this excess of words. At our previous such encounter, when all my armies and bastions and every tier of my defensive magic had been destroyed and we had met face to face like this in our last single combat, she, as I recalled, had not dawdled a minute more than necessary.

"Even so, you shall not master the powers of the Wellspring. Neither Merlin nor I nor any other Mage, present or departed, is equal to that task. Only the gods may enter that bubbling fountainhead and command its might. But you would have annihilated All That Is—except the Hallowed Land, to be sure—with your clumsy meddling. And so..." She strode toward me.

I had come to myself somewhat as she spoke, having sought to make the best possible use of the unexpected respite. If she did not obstruct the action of the Harp—and she would not if I conjured my charm while at the same time somehow drawing her attention—I would be saved. I would leave her behind in this world; and before she overtook me again, I would have done everything possible to be at my destination. *First, though, let us try to win a few more seconds…*

"So, the Archmage, the Leader of our Generation, Great Merlin himself plays the caitiff?" I asked in the most natural voice I could assume. "He refuses to meet me in single combat?"

"A Mage's passions and enthusiasms are but a Mage's passions and enthusiasms, no more," she replied coldly, her face a mask of stone. "The behests of the gods are above all. Merlin has abandoned his prior intentions."

Time now to go on the offensive.

"And why does he not make use of his right to punish with Unbeing those who violate the Balance? The Council would surely have supported him."

"That is none of your concern!" my once-beloved broke in. "And you have delayed me long enough. Only for decorum's sake, I ask again—Will you yield?"

I shook my head. My adversary shrugged and, holding on her face that same look of weary indifference, raised her hand breast-high…

Great Orlangur must have been with me again. Even before Sigrlinn's charm began its work, I knew for a certainty I would not be able to render it harmless, nor would I be able to reestablish my mastery of the Harp and thus quit this world. Someone had imbued her with truly prodigious might, greater by far than Merlin's. My only hope lay now in my sword.

Again, for the merest sliver of time, my sword-strike overcame her wizardry. I seemed caught up as in a gust of wind. All the bitter memories, all the weight of the seemingly endless millennium of my exile, all the gall of that inglorious defeat, all the hurt of orphaned emotion—the only radiant emotion I had ever felt—all this flowed together and flared out in the streak of fire the Black Sword of Rakoth traced in the air, slicing through it downward and to the right.

In my worst nightmare, I could never have seen myself raising a hand against Sigrlinn. Time was when nothing had been more important than denying a foe the chance to inflict injury while leaving him unharmed, the Generation's Code of Honor being still strong and the Laws of the Ancients unwavering. Now, everything had changed. I understood that the coming battle would be fought as between two humans—to the death.

She had no time to defend herself. The green fire that streamed from her hand could not stop the Black Sword of Darkness; its blade was descending upon that elegant, unprotected neck when my mind seemed to explode.

I saw the shore of a quiet woodland lake planted with whimsical trees, under the balmy, bright-blue sky of Jibulistan—the silver-blue towers, graceful and slender, that vaulted up from the far bank; the broad stairway running down to the water's edge. We stood in a boat steered by a zophar and gazed upon our creation, while Sigrlinn's servant, with rhythmic beats of the oars, propelled our little craft toward the river that flowed from the lake.

Our Cerulean City was complete. We had given it to our helpers, one of the tribes of Jibulistan; and now we were leaving, returning to the greater world. We had thought then that thus, hand in hand, we would pass along all the magical paths that would be our lot in life.

Time would show how cruelly mistaken we were.

That brief flash of memory was sufficient to stay my hand and parry a blow that had seemed ineluctable. The blade's black lightning drew back.

We stood motionless. On her face there slowly dawned an expression I had long forgotten as, surfacing through the ruthless strength that overlay it, something rose from deep within. Before me now stood not a proud, tight-lipped victrix eager to smite and punish but almost the Sigrlinn I had once known, the Sigrlinn of Jibulistan and, before that, of the Mage School in the furthermost reaches of the Real.

She did not ask why I had done what I did. She understood.

We faced each other, stock-still. For an instant, I fancied she was wavering, that the images arising from the depths of memory had in some way affected the part of her unspoken plan that called for me to be put out of the way. But once again I was grievously mistaken.

Her eyes narrowed. The momentary weakness had passed, and the business of bygone years troubled her no more.

"In the name of the Council of the Generation..." she began, raising her hand.

Return to Hedinseigh! The thought flashed like lightning. *Return and take the fight to Merlin, since you wish it so greatly!*

The message was swift beyond belief, and had been carefully hidden from any in the Castle of All the Ancients who might be observing our meeting. Sigrlinn did wish me to go back. She wished to keep me from Rakoth and from that Wellspring of hers. But she also needed me to continue my duel with Merlin.

Sigrlinn, Sigrlinn, lovely enchantress—what do you really want?

She believed she had entirely closed off my way down to the Netherside of the Worlds. And, true enough, I would go no further without the aid of Great Orlangur.

I sensed the unseen presence of the Spirit of Knowing, and a cold voice spoke in my mind.

— *She has been sent by Merlin, but seeks to deceive him. The Archmage has ordered your capture, but she has determined only to halt your progress here.*

The raised hand lowered. The charm she had conjured had activated the immense powers the Council of the Generation had invested in her, and it was as if Devourers of Souls in their legions had seized hold of me. I seemed to see those faceless gray figures stretching out their long, fleshless hands toward me.

So, I conjured a charm of my own, and speedily, too; and on the sheer precipice of that nameless gray world again began the magical duel that had been interrupted ten centuries before.

A complex charm I had created during my exile, one that adopted the magic of Western Hjorvard's Wizards of the Sea and drew its strength from the tireless movement of waters, engaged the eternal fury of the sea spume boiling below us to hurl back her ghostly squadron.

— *Have done!* Again Great Orlangur spoke to me. *You deliver yourself into her hands!*

Sigrlinn's face blazed with intemperate ire when she saw the power of the great sea fling away the spirits she had summoned. Before she could strike another blow, I employed all the power of the tempestuous swells that raged in those unknown seas against the frame of this world, strengthened a hundred times over by her magic-making.

Like ocean waves that strive ceaselessly down the centuries to break through indestructible sea-cliffs, the charm opened a road away from that place. To Sigrlinn it must have seemed I had disappeared.

Again a demented swirl of worlds, of skies and lands, of seas and valleys, of clouds and mountains, of creatures reasoning and unreasoning. On I traveled, broaching nightmare realms inhabited by such creatures as would never appear even in the course of the most exquisitely horrible brainsickness. Scarcely had I appeared in their course of the Real before they rushed at me in countless throngs, but the might of the Nightharp, freed by the magic of the Moonbeast, drove me on so fast that, to my own surprise, not one of Rakoth's jailers could hinder me.

I had lost count of the expanses that lay behind me, and only the increasing trembling of my black blade gave me any hint we were approaching the Netherside.

There I found a fine welcome. Merlin or the Young Gods had finally perceived what I was about, and had thrown all they could into the battle. I faced legions of gray phantoms, the shades of dead wizards compliant to the gods and almost as adept in wizardry as we Mages—Devourers of Souls, such as roam the World of the Dead but stronger by far; fire dragons with neither wits nor intellect, since the price exacted from their creators for their ability to spit fire capable of consuming my very magical self had been to see their dragons relieved of all acumen; demons, the strongest of Rakoth's erstwhile warriors, captured in other universes—powerful necromancers who derived their powers from Hel itself. These last had probably been lured by the promise of forgiveness and salvation from the eternal, intolerable torments to which they had been condemned by the victors in their triumph.

This was the last boundary drawn by the Lords of the Hallowed Land. They had apprehended that my goal was not the Wellspring, whatever that was— *and I must one day determine if it is but another trap*—but the friend who had been sentenced to indeterminate confinement. They had understood, and had emptied out their arsenals to prevent me. All that now remained was for them to enter the battle themselves.

And so we came together—a Mage whose physical form was no longer in its first flower of youth, wearing a threadbare cloak and with long black sword atilt, and a numberless army that stretched from horizon to horizon. I knew there was only one course of the Real separating me now from Rakoth's dungeon. Never before had any Mage, save Merlin, penetrated so deep into the lower reaches of the Worldsphere.

While they did not consider me easy prey, they were decidedly sure of themselves. I knew not who ruled in that sunless, starless World of Darkness, but I did know he had given his helpmeets a truly deranged instruction—to take me alive.

The dragonfire could burn away any charm I conjured, the gray phantoms could fetter me with their own wizardry, the Devourers of Souls craved to possess my very being, and the captured demons, their nooses good and ready to ensnare my body and its astral doubles, sought me as coin with which to purchase their own freedom.

When that great horde began to move—with a roar, a scream, a cry, a groan—a blinding white stripe slashed across the black vault, a sharp beam of light pointing out to that infinitude of creatures their sole, their only goal.

Me.

This was the moment for which I had prepared so carefully and so long. Now was the time to test all the ruses, subterfuges and charms I had readied against this darkest of hours, since I could not, to be sure, have put them to the proof earlier.

A Charm of Transference, which came off well, unlike many of its predecessors, carried me into the very thick of the fight, close to where Orlast, largest and strongest of the race of dragons of the Wizardry-Consuming Fire and evidently named with a nod toward Great Orlangur, plied the heavy air with broad wings. The Black Sword of Rakoth trembled with the power that pervaded it as I made liberal use of the world's motion. The blade flickered faster than lightning, faster than light and thought itself, its movements indiscernible even to me. The ungainly Orlast wheeled to face me, but the sharp black edge easily pierced horny armor impervious to any other weapon, plunged in to the hilt and struck the heart.

The crimson blood gushing from the wound almost knocked me off my feet. Brown wings beat spasmodically one against the other, the misshapen head fell back, but I was already gone and did not see Orlast's end.

I had next to shear through snaking nooses with another rapid charm from Moonbeast's store to send the three swiftest Devourers of Souls about their business with insides burned away, and to turn four ghostly sorcerers to ash with the jolt of a Lesser Firecharm.

Once again, as in the battle for Hedinseigh against the Hungering Stars, the conflict had become a funnel with me at the tip, while those sundry legions pressed on toward me to put out at last the light that burned fierce within me and so vexed the self-styled masters of this world.

The surge of hostile charms seemed about to tear my soul to shreds. For a few moments, I fought against it, trying to hold it back like a dam restraining a heavy snowmelt. Then, when the wizardry was endowed with such might as to exceed the bounds of my strength, I reverted to an ancient principle of the human soldier's art, which no Mage of my Generation had even thought to study—victory from retreat.

By dint of a few magical strikes, not strong but precisely aimed, I turned the entire flood of sorcery aimed my way into a lithe vortex that circled me. Its energy I directed downward; and as I had reckoned, it outmatched in strength the vaults in this ultimate course of the Real. I dropped through before my dumbfounded enemies knew what I was about.

And no wonder! They had, after all, obstructed all the Magic of the Great

Harp with such care and such zeal. But it was too late, and the vaults of the Last World closed above me. The Young Gods' efforts to close Rakoth's prison up tight had turned against them, for their helpmeets could not on their own, without the aid of the Masters of the Hallowed Land, enter into the Fallen Mage's place of internment. Iamerth was only too well apprised of Rakoth's skill in turning the reasoning and unreasoning alike to his purposes.

Still not believing I had made good my escape, I rose to one knee, looking around as best I could.

The Netherside of the Worlds—a fearsome land bereft of light, joy or life, containing naught but belts of flowing matter held blistering hot, as they ever have been, by the forges of Iardoz. Nothing would it offer to human sight, but I looked upon it with other eyes.

I stood on the surface of a crimson river, a dense layering of chimerical waters that oozed slowly away into the uncharted gloom. I was wrapped about by protective magic that kept the heat from me and prevented me from tumbling into the scalding depths.

What remained now was to reach my friend with all possible speed, before the Young Gods or Merlin could appear in this place. So, I began my search, bringing to it every power, every capacity at my command.

Had it not been for those long years of work, those years of blindly straying through the endless labyrinths of the Higher Magic, I would never have found Rakoth. Only a previously devised system of spells served to uncover to me the ember of his mind, barely glowing beneath the black spans of that cavernous world.

Little else remained but to take myself to him. I began to prepare a Transference (with care, now, with care...), but hardly had I completed the linkage of spells in preparation for spinning the world around me when the blackness ahead was torn by a torrent of gilded lightning, a din stung my ears and tongues of leaping flame formed into a familiar figure, now draped in a cloak made of a myriad of white sparks, tiny facsimiles of the creation I had riven with the Blade of Rakoth.

"Death tarries no more!" the figure proclaimed, raising its right hand and bending like a drawn bow.

I had time neither to reply, to defend myself nor even to back away. Evidently, Sigrlinn's original plan—the one that saw me grappling with Merlin—had failed, and now my undoing was upon me.

The white-hot flesh of this world was carrying us smoothly into the unknown blackness, and for the first time in my many centuries I found myself on the very brink of that fearful precipice below which the Ocean of Unbeing rages. Such power there was in her that neither the Black Sword nor the Spirit of Knowing himself could help me now.

Yet she was nothing more than the tip of an arrow loosed at me by Merlin—or so my mind told me. That knowledge brought no relief.

Then everything abruptly changed—I had never seen aught like it, and Great Orlangur grant that I never will again. The Netherside gloom was split by four giant columns composed of greenish, gleaming spirals. The power that flowed from them knocked me to the river's hot, supple surface, where I lay motionless, watching those green spirals enclosing Sigrlinn on all sides like a boa constrictor coiling around its prey. The blow she had directed at me encountered instead one of those gleaming columns. The green spirals flashed crimson, some crumbed into black ash, the column cracked and collapsed, but meanwhile the remaining three had closed over her head...

She cried out, I suppose. I saw a mouth torn open in a silent howl, but heard not a sound. Her hands were bound up in an abundance of fine green threads. Then she was snatched upward and disappeared, together with her sinister abductors, and all was gloom and silence again.

I was benumbed, too weak to move. There could be little doubt that had been an interference, universally unanticipated, by the Distant Powers. I remembered Gudmund's tale, the skirmish between the Darkling Rider and the servants of the Distant Ones, and the dim intimations that none other than my once-beloved was teaching the rudiments of magic to the wiccan race. I really could not be surprised by what I had just seen.

Still, little as I wished it, I felt I could not leave matters thus, that I was obliged, whatever the cost, to wrest Sigrlinn from the hands of the Distant Ones, to grant myself the opportunity to square all with her myself at some later time. My first instinct was to speed away in pursuit of the unintentional saviors that had made off with her.

Instead, shivering from head to toe, I forced my thoughts back to finding the path to Rakoth.

My mind wanted no part of what had just occurred. Sigrlinn was my sworn enemy, and I had no right to allow sentimental memories to drain my strength. I should have been rejoicing that the Distant Powers had delivered me from a powerful opponent. But, though duty and conscience compelled me to waste not a second in freeing Rakoth, still I wavered in treacherous indecision, squandering precious moments.

Good sense at last prevailed. Having conquered my agitation and the trembling of my hands—itself no easy matter—I at last completed the Charm of Transference that carried me to where I needed to be.

It was hot—very hot, as stifling as any blacksmith's forge. Torn from the surrounding dusk by a morose, dark-crimson light that came from nowhere, six wooden posts hung in the void, forming an elaborate enclosure around a space that might have contained something faintly reminiscent of a naked Magesoul, highest of the Mage's Astral Bodies.

That soul did not glow. It had no clear contours. It was mind and only mind, divested of every last one of its material vehicles, disincarnated and left with naught but unending suffering.

Again I stood, stunned and startled by the despair imprisoned within those cumbersome shafts. I felt, of course, all the might of the charms laid upon them—the work of Merlin's hands—and I knew I need only touch but one of them to release the energy that had been accumulating there for a thousand years in an explosion the Netherside itself might not withstand.

Well, now, Sage of Darkness, there is no way back for you. You are a malefactor who has dared defy the Young Gods, and the war between you will not end until one side holds the field alone.

Slowly, slowly, the thick knot of spells I had prepared to free Rakoth began to uncoil. Little enough it would be to break through the stockade that held him, for I must also restore to my friend the body that had once been his.

The moment had come to resort to the most proscribed of all the sources of power forbidden to a Mage. No mere wizardry was strong enough to tear down Merlin's spells, which were so cunningly woven as to require decades of deciphering. But from time immemorial there had existed in our world one other fount of power, firmly denied to us by the Laws of the Ancients. It was the Power of the Increate Chaos that lay without. That was the only Law I knew how to outflank, and never mind that I had yet to put that learning of mine to use.

Rakoth and I had found a crabbed and circuitous path of charms long, long ago, during our earliest dealings with the Darkness, that seemed to suggest the way to us of its own volition, and right obligingly, too. But the Rebel never did make use of that knowledge, not even on the day when he took his final fall. I knew not why.

First, then, to the Astral Plane…the creation of a double…a turn of the world that makes of that double a spectral battering ram to destroy the barriers. Back I bring him to the Netherside…and now, onward to the bourns of Chaos!

I was wittingly leading my double to perdition. The cost to any other would have been great beyond belief—at the very least, a terrible demise of the physical body and eternal torment of the soul in the afterlife—but a Mage of some adroitness and with a certain knowledge of wizardry's farthest frontiers could avoid that fate. My double's sacrifice would open to me the sources of a wild, unbridled strength from the darker side of a world given material form.

I did not have long to wait. No, heavy footsteps did not rumble beneath me, nor did bright glimmerings light up the black span of the sky. Instead, all my being was transfixed, feeling the unseen threads of an utterly alien self reaching out to me across the Creator's Barriers. At their first touch, I vested all my strength in one short, sharp jolt. My double silently vanished, and the threadlike feelers immediately drew back.

For several very long moments nothing happened. Then I advanced the second course of my spells, like a captain in the heat of battle throwing his reserve regiments into the fray. I waited for yet a few more excruciatingly endless seconds, and then…

All my feelings, both of human and sorcerer, rose up against me at once. I was battered by a cataract of visions from Chaos—colors, sounds, images, astral mirages, traces of powers and charms, reflections of Ethereal tempests, mirrorings of the Indestructible Flame the Creator had once brought to bear in overcoming the prior masters of All That Is. Another fragment of time, and I would have run mad under that spate, were it not for a third tier of wizardry I had prepared to reflect them back.

It began to work by itself, lopping off the death-dealing outgrowths of Chaos and molding the narrow channel of power that would bring me all I needed to free Rakoth.

It was not long before the results made themselves known. Waves of raw power beat imperiously against the elegant structures of the charms protecting Rakoth's place of internment, and the polished edifices of the Higher Magic could not stand before that frenzied offensive. I myself was almost torn apart, and there could be no question of profiting from that flood of energy for any length of time.

The wooden shafts around the imprisoned Mage burst into a natural, living fire and immediately dissolved into invisible motes of ash. The solid ground beneath my feet began to buck, and thousands of unseen but powerful gullets disgorged a soul-riving howl that churned beneath the domes of the Netherside. In one short instant, I was shown the entire megalithic Pyramid of Worlds, all the way up to my own Hjorvard; and every one of those worlds was in the grip of a massive convulsion. Mountains fell, rivers burst their banks, forests flared, multifarious beings became crazed and fell upon each other.

The shock caused by the incursion of Chaos into the World of the Well-Ordered gradually quieted, of course; and the more numerous the courses of the Real that lay between any world and the Netherside, the weaker was the effect of that ruinous surge. I knew that Hjorvard had gone almost unscathed.

But at the time, that concerned me little. Rakoth's prison had collapsed, and in the encompassing darkness I discerned again the feeble outlines of his naked soul. It was, however, still in a state of Unbeing, adrift in an ocean of tormenting visions and apparitions.

By an effort of will that almost cremated my mind forever, I severed the channel to Chaos. I had ready the spells that would give flesh to the prisoner's soul. There was the seed of a new body, too, the very likeness of the old one that had been committed to the flames on the day of his chastisement.

Some time passed in reconstituting from the Great Elements a new vessel for Rakoth's soul. I proceeded without thought, following designs rehearsed a hundred times over. Soon, I stood over the supine body of a powerful man in the flower of his strength, tall and with a luxuriant shock of wavy blue-black hair. A straight, slender nose, a strong and prominent chin, thick brows meeting over the bridge of the nose, rather generous lips...

For a moment, I looked for faults in my creation and, finding none, prepared for the final stage of my sorcery—my magical appeal to the soul of my friend.

"Awake! Awake! Fire has consumed the toils that bound you. You are free. Again this splendid, romping world awaits us. Again we are to taste the sweetness of boisterous battle. Our foes are strong, but we are more than we were. A great war seethes within the bounds of the Well-Ordered, and how can it be fought without you, O Rakoth the Rebellious?"

Carefully, with the finest threads of Ether, I stitched up the innumerable bonds between Rakoth's soul and his new body, the ones so crudely severed by the victors exultant a thousand years ere then. All my art was brought to bear, all without exception. Questing Charms revealed the bonds still unrestored, and I united them, fusing together that astonishing conflux of strength and sense that once had been a Mage, and one of my Generation's most powerful.

Long did this continue, until at last the outlines of the imprisoned soul entirely melted away. Mentally, I wiped the sweat from my brow. The work was done, and it remained now only to say...

"Arise and walk!"

At that point, all my strength abandoned me; and I could only stand and watch, swaying, as the eyelids trembled and opened to reveal those deep, black eyes, the bewildered eyes of a man roused from a long and heavy sleep—eyes in which thought still slumbered. The fingers moved, then, and the muscles of the chest tensed...

Rakoth rose up on one elbow.

"What happened to us? Where am I? Hedin!"

His eyes flared with delirious joy, and I felt a weighty burden of memories that chafed the very soul sinking irrevocably into the gloom.

But before I could reply, to say nothing of moving, I sensed, up there in the world of Hjorvard, the escape—or deliberate unchaining—of truly fearful forces whose nature was beyond my knowledge and even my suppositions. The danger was a stab of pain that tore the veil from my eyes, and I saw Avalon and the birth there of a scorchingly bright beam of Power that reached through the abysses to the Pillar of the Titans, was reflected by some strange sorcery from the walls of the Castle of All the Ancients and plunged precipitously downward. It encountered no obstacle. It swept through the worlds, tearing and burning with its brute strength the very fabric of the Real as it went. The Dragons of Time shied away from it in horror. In its wake it left a strip of Absolute Nothingness, of Unbeing, of Utter Nullity, and it destroyed innocent lives without number that happened to cross its path.

It was aimed at us, at Rakoth and me.

No power there is within the bounds of the Well-Ordered strong enough to parry this blow, I thought. *Merlin is visiting upon us the punishment of Unbeing.*

Those short instants when Death was speeding toward us I squandered in a frenetic, desperate search for deliverance, but my terror-stricken mind offered nothing other than to resort to the aid of Chaos. While I had broken the channel that fed me with strength, its traces still remained in the Great Ether. With the undiluted, unreflecting despair of an animal thrashing in a trap, I tried to revive that connection and draw again upon the inexhaustible energy of Chaos.

I reached out to those forces as a man dying of thirst strives toward the salvation of water. I stretched with all my being, unsparingly, yet found nothing but the pitiful remnants of Chaos's might lingering still in the channel I had dug.

Meanwhile, an unbearably shrill shriek, as from a huge steel bar running across a gigantic pane of glass, was growing louder, the air was heating rapidly and an odd light, yellow and lifeless, was all about us. Rakoth, up on one knee now, glanced quickly upward and understood all.

I raised aloft a shield hurriedly woven from the forces of Chaos. Before disintegrating into a scattering of tiny black crystals, it held Merlin's deadly weapon back for a second, deflected it a little. But not enough.

Rakoth sprang to his feet. Though his eyes still seemed bedimmed, there blazed in them already the fierce, morose fire I knew so well. Even in so short a span of time, he had called upon the residuum of his former might, upon all who bided yet in the world's most distant, most secret corners, patiently awaiting his return.

And his summons was heard. I sensed the supple surges of his strength, as once it had been, hurtle out to meet Merlin's arrow, felt the Firstborn Gloom and the Light Anew Created entwining in such a battle as none had ever seen. Rakoth encompassed the ray of swift light with hordes of black wings, clouds of denizens of the night, doing his utmost to turn it aside. The Rebel's face was distorted with the fearsome exertion, as legion upon legion of strange beings burst up from under our feet, immolating themselves in their effort to weaken, for however brief a time, the Young Gods' blade of destruction.

I understood then how terrible a foe my friend had been to the Masters of the Hallowed Land, as I also understood that his rebellion had been doomed from the outset. The gods had had power enough to scotch any attack made directly upon them. That is why gods are gods.

Even though Rakoth fought furiously, the time came when he could do no more. His eyes were suffused with blood, and when he turned to me, I read in them a torment so great I recoiled before it.

"I am done. Crouch down. And..."

Like an automaton, I obeyed, and none too soon, for Merlin's weapon was upon us.

The world grew murky in my eyes, and an intolerable, indescribable pain tore me apart and darkened my mind. But in that last second, I sensed Rakoth was conjuring a charm of colossal strength—and no defensive charm, either, but one full of a prodigious hatred begotten by the knowledge that this was the end of all.

CHAPTER XI

W HAT HAGEN SAW WAS NO VISION. HE ASSUREDLY FELT THE GREAT WIZARDRY THAT invested the nearby walls, and fortunate it was Avalon's power was at that moment preoccupied with events transpiring far away. Merlin had not, of course, failed to notice this brash incursion into his lands; but he was evidently, for reasons yet unknown, holding to the Law of the Ancients that forbade a Mage to kill mortals either by his own hand or through spells.

Hagen wasted no time, but issued a brief command that sent two centuries of his best and most resourceful warriors forward. They tramped across flowerbeds and through rose gardens with impunity. Grapples were flung, hooking onto cornices and window frames, and glass tinkled down, also bringing no response. The armor-clad troops broke down the ground-floor doors and disappeared one after another through second-story windows, and still no defenders—if any there were—appeared.

Hagen grew tense—this silence foretokened a trap. Obedient to his rising alarm, and far sooner than he had expected to, he unsheathed the Blue Sword and led four handpicked centuries forward. Knut was to bring the rest of the army in behind them.

The first wave of attackers had vanished soundlessly into Merlin's castle as if swallowed up by some great beast. Hagen was the first of the second wave to cross the threshold, and found there...no one and nothing.

There was a spacious foyer, elegantly appointed with furniture of dark, water-seasoned wood. They could have believed themselves in the reception hall of one of the Sheltered Kingdom's dignitaries rather than on a wizardly island rocked eternally on the waves of the World Ocean. In the corner, warm as the day was, a stove gave out a cheerful heat.

Hagen looked around, holding his blade at the ready, and, seeing nothing to pique his suspicions, quickly crossed the foyer, making for the wide doors on the other side of the room, his men following. They left the ample antechamber behind and, passing through an inner door, came upon a wide staircase with two doors on either side of its foot. Hagen sent several squads through each door, and himself raced up the stairs. This was not his first intrusion into a stranger's palace, castle or town; he was well accustomed to both swords and wizardry, and had neither cringed nor retreated before the Disc of Iamerth.

But here no one yet had barred his path. And nowhere was there a single dead body.

He had mounted the first flight of stairs, his warriors marching in step behind him, when a new sound obtruded into the measured trudging of iron-shod feet—a disgusting, damp, chomping noise. Hagen spun around as if stung. The stairway behind him was empty, and something—something with wings and a huge maw sown with sharp fangs—was swooping down on him, flying in utter silence, its beating wings seeming to pass through the air rather than push against it.

Faster than mind could think, his hands did what was needed. Finding itself discovered, the horror swerved aside, but the Blue Sword was swifter. One leathery claw-tipped wing was sheared off, and the thing crashed to the stairs, flailing convulsively. Hagen queasily prodded the misshapen body with the toe of his boot. It seemed to be all mouth.

But this one brute could not have bolted down every last one of my warriors, he thought, bedazed. *And if it had, there would be blood...bodies...weaponry.* He listened hard, and heard nothing. Outside, his warriors, all discipline, awaited their orders.

But why, by the almighty stars, is it so quiet here, in Merlin's home—not a cry, not a weapon's clang, not a footfall? Could they really have all been swallowed whole?

The answer soon presented itself when all five doors on the floor below swung open and a flood of loathsome gray-green creatures, the veriest replicas of the horror he had just hewn down, gushed toward him.

The air filled then with the glitter and rustle of whirling, murderous steel. The Blue Sword struck right and left, slicing through the freakish bodies amid spurts of pungent, dark-brown blood. Sundered wings and paws slapped against the walls, but otherwise the things died without a sound, their creator having evidently deemed vocal chords too great a luxury.

Absent the supernatural skills he had learned from his Teacher, he would never have been able to fight his way down the staircase and across the foyer to the porch. Once he crossed the threshold, all the monsters that still lived halted as one and hung in mid-air, their wings feebly quivering.

"Hold your positions!" he cried to his men, with no more thought of concealment. "This I shall do alone."

My warriors would never betray my confidence by allowing themselves to be devoured, every one, by these beasts of Merlin's, without offering the slightest resistance, he thought. *That being so, there is wizardry here—but wizardry that will, perhaps, have no power over a Mage's apprentice.*

Wiping his blade automatically, Hagen strode resolutely back over the threshold toward those gaping maws and clawed, winnowing wings. Next, he must again cross the foyer and go up the stairs.

But the beasts had clearly learned some cunning in the meantime, for now, in groups of seven and eight, they assailed him from all sides, descending steeply upon him and endeavoring to fasten on his legs. Hagen believed armor crafted by the masters of Hauberk Mount to be more than a match for teeth, but these beasts were manifestly armed with something stronger than mere jaws.

Plashing through pools of sticky blood and across carcasses that fell apart under his heels like rotten meat, he struggled to the staircase. Streaming with sweat, he reached the top of the first flight, and swayed there in exhaustion— he, Thane Hagen, whose sword would work for him untiringly through day and night. His back against a wall, he dismembered another dozen, until at last one approached him furtively and took him by the leg.

The floor yawned beneath him. He seemed to fall through ceiling after ceiling that parted in his path. The world around him was changing; he was being drawn into a fearsome abyss. Yet his head and hands still obeyed him, could still continue the fight, and with a final effort his sword sliced the ravenous mouth in two...an instant too late.

Suspended between two worlds, he now understood that the maws of Merlin's winged warriors were made not to tear and rend bodies but to serve as portals to a cavity in the Real, where all the men of Hedinseigh who had been first inside the Archmage's home were held captive. By some miracle, Hagen still clung to the very edge of his course of the Real. Something unseen—something that emanated from the very depths—was supporting him, and the abyss was not yet strong enough to overcome that sustaining strength and suck him in.

His first thought was that the Spirit of Knowing had again come to his aid—*What greater assistance could I expect?*—but he promptly dismissed that idea, since he had not here felt even a thousandth part of what he had experienced in the grotto of the Great Spirit.

A Delaying Charm, then?

He had conjured the simple spell unwittingly, and it held him up. Merlin's horrid beasts still circled above his head like giant bats, the Action Charm that moved them having evidently made no allowance for such a circumstance.

He gingerly essayed a Displacement Charm, which had the desired effect, causing the sinister abyss to loosen its avid embrace. Merlin's greedy-gut army was caught by surprise when, whistling rapaciously, the Blue Sword sliced through another half-dozen of its warriors at once, and Hagen broke away and swept up the second flight of stairs.

He smashed a window and its transom with sword hilt and vambrace, leaned over the sill and cried to his men, "There are winged beasts here. Allow none to pass through. Overlap shields. Attack! Bowmen forward!"

Then he spun to greet another wave of Merlin's servants.

The blade of Hedin's apprentice, it must be said, did not labor in vain. The entire staircase was covered by a repulsive carpet of dead beasts, and the number of the living was noticeably decreased. Then Hagen heard his footsoldiers, on the attack at last, roaring with one voice. He found a moment to glance behind him and saw men and goblins moving forward in good order, covering themselves on all sides with their shields. The archers had arrows at the ready, and piketips glittered farther to the rear, prepared at any moment to rise up in a deadly palisade.

The warriors of Hedinseigh closed on the building in good order, employing battering rams on either side of the front door to widen the entrance. No one hindered them, the stones gave way with unexpected ease and the first ranks, in formation, strode inside.

Again Hagen's ear caught the faint, loathsome rustle of hundreds upon hundreds of wings as Merlin's raptors swept through the second-story doors and down the staircase to meet this new threat. He began to ply his sword with redoubled energy, and there came from below the bowstrings' harmonious song, the short whistle of arrows and the slapping sound of beasts falling lifeless to the floor.

There was now a veritable deluge of winged creatures, so dense as to displace the air itself. The passage to the right of the windowed landing where Hagen stood was thick with them; and as good sense indicated that the main enemy was to be found where the resistance was greatest, he might have next been expected to gather all his strength and push through that right-hand door.

Any other mortal commander would probably have proceeded thus, but the Sage of Darkness's apprentice, unceasingly working his sword, wondered instead if it might not be a trap. *What if Merlin is now sitting most serenely somewhere in the opposite side of the house—if, indeed, he even still remains in his castle?*

Giving way to a sudden impulse, he darted to the left, hurriedly slamming the finely carved oaken door shut and bolting it. The winged maws, outmaneuvered, beat witlessly against the barrier thus created, but on the thane's side of the door there was not a foe to be seen.

He could draw breath now and look around. He would never have bested Merlin's servitors without his warriors—their attack and the sacrifices it had entailed had more than served their purpose.

He stood in a comfortable room—evidently a library, with walls lined with folios bound in dark leather. In the far corner was another door, low, arched and hung on long, strong hinges.

Behind that tight-shut door great wizardry was being made. Magnificent powers intertwined there in an unimaginable dance, twisting and whipping in silent fountains of spectral flame. Hagen sensed the presence of astonishing, unheard-of beings that bowed before their Overlord to receive his orders and scurried away. Without a shadow of a doubt, Merlin was there.

The thane listened hard. Through the door he had just entered, he could hear the sounds of battle on the staircase as the Hedinseigh footsoldiers forced their way upward, step by step. He hesitated. *Would it not be better to wait for my people, especially since Merlin clearly cares nothing for them now, even were they to raze his mansion to the ground?*

Then, the bookshelves along the far wall came to abrupt life, sliding sideways to reveal a narrow well-lit passageway. Hagen sprang aside, panther-like, his sword held ready. He felt the approach of a living being, one furnished with both reason and strange powers—or, at least, inhuman powers.

A tall, straight-backed, lean old man with an aquiline nose and a sprig of mistletoe in his hands strode into the room, his indifferent gaze gliding over the dumbstruck thane.

What business has a preceptor of the Distant Powers' cloisters here? Hagen wondered in astonishment.

"You seek an audience with Merlin?" the odd newcomer inquired coldly, turning his back to Hagen.

"I do, and I shall go in first!" Hagen declared in a haughty tone that was unexpected even to him.

But the preceptor showed not a flicker of interest. He simply continued on to the vaulted door and grasped the ornate metal handle.

In less than the blink of an eye, Hagen had bounded to the side of the stranger, laid a powerful hand on his shoulder and turned him so they were face to face. There was, however, time enough to feel surprise, and to wonder what he was doing. Never had he allowed himself such foolishness in hand-to-hand combat, for close proximity gave his opponent an easy chance to upend him by the simplest of means and with no magic whatsoever.

The floor lurched out from under Hagen's feet, and the doorjamb canted rapidly toward his face. It took all his skill, and an effort that tore at the muscles of his stomach, to avoid the impact. Even so, his head hit the wall so hard that everything swam before his eyes and he almost let go of his sword.

But the old man was not content with that. The thin sprig of mistletoe was suddenly alive; its shoots lengthened and flung themselves at Hagen, well prepared to bind him much as their fellows had trussed Gudmund by the monastery in the valley of Brunevagar.

But this preceptor faced a man armed with the Blue Sword, weapon of an Ancient God. Neither he nor Hagen knew—only Mage Hedin suspected—that this sword had been forged for precisely such an encounter in times of old, when the Distant Powers had first entered the bourns of Greater Hjorvard. Cold those intruders were, and foreign to the bright and merry life of that world, and thus began a long struggle waged by the Ancient Gods, the first real masters in those parts.

Hagen had heard nothing of the fearful battles fought in both the spectral worlds and the entirely real valleys of Southern Hjorvard, where the sword he now held had worked wonders on the field of honor. He was unaware of the years spent and the effort expended by the unknown craftsmen of the Ancient Gods who created that blade, of the knowledge of the nature and intentions of the Distant Powers they had invested into its mysterious blue metal. The Sword had long awaited its hour, and that hour at last had come.

The blade was a living thing. Hagen was dragged forward by a mighty force. He lunged hard, through no will of his own, his arm describing an unthinkably rapid half-circle, and the floor was besprinkled with mistletoe shoots.

Now it was the turn of the astonished preceptor to start back. He was only a servant of the Distant Powers, and knew no more than Hagen the true history of their arrival in the world of Hjorvard. He had never expected any weapon, however uncommon its properties, to overmatch his Living Stave.

Thane and preceptor stood motionless, facing each other. Both were breathing heavily, neither seemed to know what to do next, and only Almighty Time can tell how long that stalemate might have continued had not a heavy battering ram begun to pound at the door to the stairway. Hagen's men had at last reached the bolted door and, spending little time in thought, had proceeded as was their wont.

The preceptor cast a glance behind him, taking his eyes off Hagen for a moment; and the thane made a rapid leap, understanding that another such chance might never present itself. The Blue Sword flashed in another forward lunge.

Hagen was, however, contending with no ordinary mortal. The servant of the Distant Powers moved but slightly aside, and the hissing blade only slit a fold of his cloak. Hagen was immediately hit in the chest with a hot billow of air, most unexpected in this place, that threw him against the wall opposite.

The door cracked and shuddered now under the ram. The walls on the hinge side were crumbling, and it was clear this barrier would soon be no more.

The preceptor hesitated as the door, its hinges broken, crashed to the ground. Hagen's men rushed into the library and arrows flew, but the bewitched passage was already closing behind him. The warriors of Hedinseigh shrank back despite themselves, but to their credit quickly mastered their momentary confusion.

"The whole ground floor is ours, my thane." Berd's voice was hoarse. "We have destroyed more flying things than we can count, but they come from every crevice. On this floor…" He gestured behind him. "…we have yet made little headway."

"Very well. Place this room under guard. I shall go through that door. Berd and the rest, follow me, bows at the ready."

Leaving a dozen men and a few belated goblins in the library, the thane carefully turned the handle of that low vaulted door. The well-greased hinges made no sound, and it opened with surprising ease.

What met his gaze was a spacious chamber awash with soft gilded light. The commodious room was empty except for a rectangular block of marble in the center that could have been an altar for worship or sacrifice and, standing alongside it, deeply pensive and staring fixedly at his feet, a tall, spare man who greatly resembled a stork. His arms were crossed over his breast.

Hagen recognized this person immediately, having often seen the

Archmage of the Generation in spectral scenes created by his Teacher.

"Defend yourself, Merlin!" he exclaimed, advancing fast with sword atilt and his men thronging behind him.

Several long strides carried him to the Leader of the Generation, who turned and eyed the warrior closing on him with a cold, fastidious curiosity. Scant instants had passed since Hagen crossed the threshold of this room, but all his livelong days he would remember the scornful look in the Archmage's eyes, which was such as might be bestowed upon an entirely repulsive but fascinating reptile. And Merlin gave not the slightest attention to Hagen's men.

A quivering shook the marble altar at that moment; a muted roar—the sound of gigantic millstones put back to work after a long winter's rest—reached the thane's ears, and Merlin leaned over the stone. Hagen's Blue Sword was upraised, ready to lay low any obstacle in its way; but the Mage, his eyes never leaving that marble surface, made a squeamishly dismissive gesture with his left hand as if shaking something unpleasant from his fingers, and Hagen slammed full on into an unseen but very hard barrier. He saw stars, and struggled to keep his balance.

The Thane of Hedinseigh could not know that at that very moment his Teacher was fighting his way to the Netherside of the Worlds and to Rakoth's prison, destroying as he went all the magical impediments Merlin had thrown up. He did, however, have an inkling of how effortful Hedin's struggle must be, and he understood for a certainty, without knowing why, that he must draw the sorcerer's attention from his accursed pedestal even if it cost the lives of all his men, and his own into the bargain.

He ran his hand along the invisible wall before him, finding it smooth and cool as a windowpane. *It will be proof against any human blade, I'll warrant,* he thought, *but that need not prevent me from trying.*

He stabbed at it halfheartedly with a short dagger, which glanced off as from a thick block of ice. *But this is mere human steel, and I have better to offer.*

The gnome-blade struck visible sparks from the transparent barrier and plunged into it to almost half its length. Hagen shook his head in bewilderment.

The very reason for magical barriers is that they be impregnable to any weapon. But this...this is like wood—ordinary, if very sturdy, wood that turns some arms aside while allowing better weapons to penetrate.

Having spent long enough in thought, he brought his Blue Sword down hard on that transparent wall. The blade was instantly swathed in a sparkling white flame, there was the sound of a huge chest filled with crystal slivers tipping over and spilling its contents onto a stone floor, and the sword, after coming full circle, returned to its former position.

He stretched out a hand. The barrier was gone.

Simple. A good deal too simple, he thought, holding back by sheer force of will a body only too eager to attack whilst one of the goblins—the bravest or perhaps the most foolhardy—dove, howling, into the circle left by the vanished barrier.

There formed instantly above its head a small but well-defined snow-white funnel that rotated like a thing gone mad. Waving its arms aimlessly, the goblin was snatched up from the ground, dropped its ataghan, gave a hoarse cry…and was dragged up to the ceiling, where it disappeared in a thin flash of cold white fire.

Hagen's warriors drew back, horrified. Had not the thane been there, they would no doubt have promptly betaken themselves as far as might be from that hall, that house and that damnable Avalon.

"Mages do not kill mortals by their own hand or by wizardry!" Hedin's apprentice cried in a frenzy, sensing their indecision.

Their implicit trust in their commander calmed the men somewhat. The goblins went on muttering, though, until Orc, with some well-aimed smacks and rich language, restored relative order.

Merlin still stared fixedly at the stone. His hands rose slowly to his face, as if he had scooped up water in them and wanted now to rinse his eyes. He was readying himself to cast a Greatcharm.

Too frantic to think of anything better, Hagen unsheathed one of the dirks he always kept at his belt and threw it hard, aiming for Merlin's head. Dropping down from above, the hungry mouth of the unnatural whirlwind sucked in the small steel plaything as ravenously as it had just devoured living flesh.

A pretty pass! And what, in the name of Great Orlangur, are we to do now? We could level this entire building to the ground and that would likely trouble Merlin no more than a gentle breeze. O mighty Spirit of Knowing, if you yet care how this tale shall end, give me but a hint!

And a solution offered itself immediately, though not through the aid of the Pillar of the Third Power. Hagen had merely allowed himself to be caught up in the heat of battle, and now took himself sternly to task for his unpardonable heedlessness. How could he have forgotten about the Disc of Iamerth?

The Arch-Enchanter continued performing slow passes before the mysterious altar, and some of them Hagen recognized. Merlin was imbruing the charm he had made with the molten metal of Great Powers lavishly drawn from sources beyond the thane's understanding, and Hagen knew with every certainty that the magic-making was close to completion.

The pure-white, glittering Disc eased into its new-minted master's hand. Hagen sensed the fearsome weapon's unreasoning readiness and its unquenchable thirst to kill—it cared not whose life it took nor whose blood it drank. It had parried a blow from the White Blade, but could it visit any serious harm upon a true Mage? And why, for that matter, was Merlin the Great serenely allowing Hagen to stand there, in full sight, flinging a variety of sharp objects at him and fretting him in general?

A sixth sense, an instinct for hidden danger, was doggedly warning Hagen of a trap. *The only questions are—where and what?*

All at once, the building trembled from its foundations to the spire on its roof, and a cold shudder ran through him. Something terrible was taking place. A chill fear strode imperiously into his mind, suffusing it, removing every last shaft of light, enveloping it like a sticky gray mist…

Through the doorway behind him stepped a short, swarthy girl with two long braids the color of a raven's wing trailing down her breast. Her eyes modestly lowered, she came on, disregarding the thane's dumbstruck troops. Yet he sensed keenly the threat that emanated from her, and moved to cross her path…but too late.

The tight black braids unwound, and a living waterfall of hair flowed along that solid little body, wrapping around it like a second cape. When that cape flew open, the faces of men and goblins were lashed by the buffeting gusts of an icy dead wind, a wind from the Worlds of Ice, from a fearful sinkhole, a rift in the fabric of the Real. *That sinkhole*, thought Hagen, paralyzed with the terror of what was to come, *is somehow connected to the cavern in which my warriors who were engulfed by those winged maws now languish.*

Except that this maw was larger by far.

My whole army, like as not, is in that abyss by now. It was a horrifying thought. So that was why the Archmage had not responded to all their clumsy sallies, which were less able to harm him than a single mosquito might injure a man snugged in a cloak. Merlin had been waiting for the army to enter the house.

The entire army? How can this little dwelling accommodate thousands upon thousands of warriors? But why should it not? And what if Merlin has laid upon them some ostensibly harmless charm to make them march, detachment after detachment, into the trap, assured that they were following their commander's orders to the letter?

You shall requite me yet, accursed wizard, for your guile! Hagen swore to himself, and those few words sufficed, having signaled death for many who had dared cross his path and had been able at first to harm him in some way.

The hurricane roughly dragged men and goblins, clutching desperately for a handhold, into that gaping black gullet. The warriors fell, rolling over and over and trying with all their might to get a grip on the smooth floor, but in vain. The most faithful centurions, the most seasoned chiliarchs, the wildest hellions—all those whom Hagen prized so greatly—disappeared one after another into that awful belly.

He was alone.

The wind grew stronger, was fierce enough now to wipe Merlin's well-appointed home from the face of the Earth; but Hagen stood, looking into that narrow crevice in the fabric of the world, unaware he held his ground only because he had unwittingly thrust the Blue Sword between two floor tiles and had its hilt in a death grip with his right hand, while the left still grasped the Disc of Iamerth.

When the hurricane began to dislocate his fingers, Hagen flung the Disc. He flung it like any other weapon, but his hatred fueled it. The handiwork of the Ancients trilled a brief paean of victory then removed the head of the being before him—no tongue would name it a person, far less a woman.

But the blood that spurted up was a dark scarlet, the brains were gray and the last cry was plaintive and piteous. The body fell, the fearsome maw closed, the wind was stilled…and Hagen felt upon him then the furious glare of the Archmage, who had at last discarded his mask of conspicuous calm. The thane noticed with malicious pleasure that Merlin had not completed his Greatcharm.

The Disc of Iamerth—gleaming, clean and white—returned to the thane's hand.

A mighty voice rolled beneath the high ceiling. "You have killed her, you thing of naught, you pitiful puppet in the hands of a madman and destroyer! You have killed her, so now bid farewell to your life and your soul, for I shall send you to a place where—"

Not caring to hear more—or, rather, understanding that speed was his only salvation—Hagen replied with a death-dealing bolt of white lightning, with the undeflectable Disc of Iamerth. He directed it, however, not at the enraged enchanter, who stood in place, his arms aloft, but at the marble altar, having only now detected the carefully disguised oceans of Power that lay hidden within its elegant stone. In mere instants, Hedin's apprentice created in his mind an image of that sacrificial altar, and again reflexively recited all the needful aiming spells.

If Merlin's power did extend to this weapon of the Young Gods, he surely had no time to exert that power. With a piercing, grating squeal, the Disc sliced into the marble. The house was racked with a shudder stronger by far than the last, and this one not wrought by the will of the Archmage who was master here. Once embedded in the altar, the Disc plunged into it, trailing a fiery spoor. The power that had slumbered in the stone tossed and grumbled like a brown bear roused from hibernation, and the floor beneath Hagen's feet was seized with a powerful trembling.

Merlin's long, rawboned face was a picture of unconcealable horror. Seeming to forget his enemy's brash apprentice, the Archmage watched, his hands dangling impotently, as the black fissure across the altar's surface grew ever wider—the Disc was gone from view and was now finishing its task in the depths of the stone.

Hagen's eyes met those of the Archmage, and the way Merlin looked upon him struck icy talons of death into his very soul. He knew that for destroying Merlin's plans, he had earned an answering blow and should perhaps even prepare to die. Still, he knew his intuition must be true and that by striking at that marble altar he had deprived the Leader of the Council of the Generation of a very, very important—perhaps even a crucial—weapon. Maybe in that way, if in no other, he would be of assistance to his Teacher. In that way, if in no other...

Pale as death, Merlin turned toward Hagen, who was rooted to the spot, and the Archmage appeared ready to throttle the thane with his bare hands. Slowly, as if stuck fast in dough, Hagen raised the hand holding the Blue Sword to defend himself.

"Now, I swear by the torments of Niflhel, I must perforce violate the Law of the Ancients," Merlin hissed, a cobra preparing to strike. "But first I shall tell you this, you worm! Your Teacher has resolved to crown himself prince of this world. Belike, though, his portion shall be naught but Nothingness, even should he get the best of both me and the others. And now you go to the judgment of Iamerth!"

Hagen knew enough about the Charms of Transference to apprehend he must shift from that spot with all speed. It would be no complex matter for the Archmage to hurl him into the unimaginable remoteness of the Hallowed

Land, but in order to do so, Merlin must lay his enchantments not on the thane's person but on the place where he stood.

Chips of stone sprayed up, as they had from the black floor of the cavern where the Darkling Rider came to blows with the servants of the Distant Powers. A splinter struck Hagen's helm, leading him to give thanks to his Teacher for all he had learned—had he moved an instant later or been an inch closer, he would now be facing a flight through the abyss and an appearance before the limpid eyes of the dread Sun God.

Very well, you braggart of a wizard, a game of tag it shall be!

But Hagen had underestimated Merlin, for the Archmage was weaving invisible nets around him too quickly to allow him to stay still for even an instant. Again and again he had to move and move fast, zig-zagging around the room to deprive Avalon's lord of the opportunity to take close aim while also trying not to cross the line beyond which the whirlwind hiding up in the rafters might swallow up him.

Merlin pursued him mercilessly, but quickly recognized this mighty warrior would not soon tire and that, thanks to Hedin's teachings, Hagen could sense his unseen snares and avoid them. So, the Archmage suddenly abandoned that stratagem and instead fastened upon the darting figure a heavy, fixed glare. Any other mortal might well have run witless under that unblinking stare. This was the only charm that could place Hagen in true jeopardy.

Although still busy ducking and dodging, Hedin's apprentice felt a strange change inside. All at once, he very much wanted to drop down on all fours and howl.

It was a Charm of Transformation, used by Mages wishing to rid themselves of a tiresome encumbrance, to make of it something that could hamper them no more—a block of wood, a bird, a flower, or a fish. For, while they could not take a man's life, they could perfectly well change his body.

Although it could be laid upon any living being, this was a spell rarely used in wars of wizardry, since it required not a little time to complete, even for such an uncommon adept as Merlin. And Hagen did not know how to defend against it. His frantic efforts to deflect it were brushed aside as effortlessly as a storm wave sweeps away a leaky raft.

The enchantments crept into his mind as he continued darting to and fro, trying to come within sword's reach of Merlin, his face drenched in blood and tears. He knew all was lost, that he would not survive for even half an hour as a bedraggled gib-cat—he would simply be throttled by the first of Merlin's servants who happened by.

Teacher! Teacher! Help me! Where are you?

Silence. And who could know if his desperate appeal had even broken free of that enchanted isle and found its way to the Netherside of the Worlds?

His legs were buckling, his arms visibly shortening, his hands losing their grip on his sword; and under his garments he felt a thick, rancid fur growing through his skin. His jaw began to protrude, pushing against his lowered visor...

But his mind was the last to change, as if Merlin was mocking his victim, making certain he would remain fully aware of his nightmare changes until the ultimate moment, when the mind became that of an animal, human only in its memories and in the searing, unbearable pain of all it had endured.

Teacher! Oh, my Teacher! Orlangur! Damnation!

Simpleton! Use the Disc! It was the sound of tocsins, ringing in their hundreds.

Through the veil of blood that clouded Hagen's eyes, he saw the marble altar slowly, almost reluctantly, fall into two halves, and the Disc speed back to the hand that had sent it. Somehow, he forced his fingers—already stumpy, bent, all but unbiddable—to grasp it. And so high did his hatred burn he did not even have to aim—the glittering circle tore itself from his hands.

A fine net flared golden in its path, a net woven of sunrays, for the Weapon of Light could never have been halted by Darkness. Blindingly white, as if made of purest snow from the most inaccessible mountain summits, the Disc sheared into that gilded gleam. There was the sound of dense, sturdy sailcloth tearing, and its movement slowed; but the threads quickly burst in a shower of scarlet sparks. In a matter of seconds, the net was cut.

Those seconds were all it took for Merlin to regain his strength; but to do so, he had to countermand the Charm of Transformation. The fearsome heaviness disappeared, and Hagen was himself again. A few short, foxy-red hairs fell out of his gauntlet.

The sorcerer threw both his hands forward, stopping the Disc between his palms less than an inch from his face. There was a hissing sound, and his hands were wreathed in steam. Then the Disc broke free and hit him between the eyes. A thunderstruck Hagen watched his death-dealing weapon, most powerful of all creations of the Light, come flying back to him, leaving a bloody vertical scrape on the bridge of Merlin's nose—and nothing more!

But the Archmage had won that victory at a cost. His temples were beaded with sweat, and the self-assurance had disappeared from his eyes. He spoke no more maledictions, issued no further threats, having understood this fight could not be taken lightly—it is not easy to best an adversary with the Disc of Iamerth in his hands.

Yet for Merlin, this marked only a brief postponement of his final, unavoidable triumph, for what mortal, even one armed with a wonder-weapon, could prevail over a Mage? The Leader of the Council of the Generation had many resources at his disposal, while without that Disc from the Temple of the Sun, Hagen would long ago have vanished from the world.

Hagen realized he must not permit the sorcerer to gather his thoughts and his strength. He knew not what would come of this battle and was not, truth to tell, much interested in that. His army was lost, he was alone, and not even his Teacher could help him retrieve his warriors. So, he would belabor this wizard with the Disc until his hands and mind failed him, and then, what would be would be. *Perhaps by then my Teacher will be here...*

And belabor he did—hatred lying heavy on his breast, not a thought in his mind, seeing nothing but Merlin's gaunt figure. Time and again he sent the Disc hissing through the air, giving the sorcerer no time to compose a charm of even the slightest complexity. Always it was parried. *This is truly a great wizard,* Hagen said to himself with grudging respect.

Sometimes long, agitated, tentacle-like hands with nimble fingers rose through the floor to clutch convulsively at the Disc in mid-air. Sometimes a blue mist thickened unexpectedly before Merlin's face, stopping the Disc like a featherbed checking an arrow's flight. Sometimes he knocked Iamerth's weapon aside with his bare hands. Yet each time his body sustained a new wound that seeped blood, each time he groaned in pain, and never could he gather enough wizardly strength to strike back.

They circled each other around the hall, Merlin trying to draw Hagen into the ambit of his magic while the thane was ever mindful of the need to stay as close as might be to the door, for safety's sake, even though it offered him no path of retreat.

Merlin seemed to be weakening. His clothing was soaked with blood, and he left a crimson trail on the floor. His heart crazed and raging, Hagen flung the Disc furiously, finding his target each time; and still Merlin bore the blows, having nothing to counter them.

He is yielding, that thrice-accursed warlock! Sweet, is it? Take this, then! And this! And this! Hagen's eyes burned with a wild flame. A raving madman now, he brimmed with an unquenchable thirst to kill. He did not know how, but kill he would, by each and every black god!

There was a murmurous rustle behind the open door that led into the library. This boded nothing good, and Hagen sprang across to the window so he could keep the doorway in sight without taking his eyes from Merlin.

That one movement, simple as it was, saved his life, because at that moment a many-legged, fire-breathing kreytar waddled into the room, followed close, as if in fear of coming late to the carnage, by the gigantic ants whose acquaintance he had already made.

Merlin gave a roar of derisive laughter.

So! While Hagen had been enjoying his trifling revenge, the wizard, although under constant attack by the Disc, had found the strength to call upon his servitors. Caught by surprise! Caught like a fresh-faced, thick-pated sneak-thief in a halfpenny store! The thane was choking on his fury.

The kreytar had by now hauled itself over the threshold and was clumsily turning its grotesque, doleful snout toward him. He knew well the manners and habits of those beasts, since the gnomes often employed them to tunnel through especially solid rock faces. Kreytars, though easy to train, were signally pacific, and no one yet had found a use for them in battle. Their appalling appearance and ability to spit fire notwithstanding, they could not abide quarrels among those they served; every falling-out rendered them immediately useless, able neither to eat nor to sleep, and afflicted them with grave maladies.

Most likely Merlin has dealt handily with that problem, Hagen thought, dodging at the last moment a stream of fire that passed a hand's-breadth from his head and set the windowsill and casement afire.

He cared not at all to kill the unfortunate beast; for all the fury under which he labored, that wrath was directed against Merlin and Merlin alone, not against his servants. But there was nothing else for it. Dodging another gob of fire, he brought his gauntlet down hard to break the head of an ant that happened near then made an unusual, upward sweep with the Blue Sword, plunging its well-tested blade into the kreytar's soft, broad throat.

The anguished beast cried out in a voice that was wholly human. The hideous, green-scaled body jerked once, twice, and was still, a wisp of smoke drifting upward from its mouth.

Swarming past the prostrate carcass, the ants came at him now in such numbers as to render them invulnerable to the Disc. He took a more comfortable grip on a sword-hilt that was warm in his hand while still moving from place to place as fast as ever he could, so as not to fall prey to Merlin's nets.

The Disc had returned once more to its owner but could not be thrown again until Hagen's attention was freed from those damnable ants that wanted nothing more than to knock him off his feet and chew through his throat with their powerful jaws, in blithe disregard of his excellently crafted gnomish neckpiece. No doubt about it, this was Merlin's one best chance.

His arms were suddenly heavy, his feet seemed rooted to the floor, and his head slumped strengthlessly to his chest. This charm he recognized. It was a Greater Sleepspell, and how could he, a mere mortal—albeit an Enchanter's apprentice—vie in wizardry with the Archmage of the Generation?

Through veiled eyes, Hagen watched incuriously as the Blue Sword slipped from his right hand and rang on the tiles. He fell to his knees, while somehow maintaining his grasp on the Disc of Iamerth.

The ants had him tightly surrounded, their dire crescent-shaped jaws working, their long legs pawing impatiently at the floor, their eyes glittering like red-hot embers. In the grip of an unconquerable drowsiness, Hedin's apprentice gazed vacantly at those frightful, silent ranks.

No! Arise! Have I so misjudged you?

The voice, a voice of fearsome power, thundered inside his skull. It was the voice that had earlier told him to use the Disc. For an instant, Hagen was looking upon himself—a broken man, humbly awaiting retribution on bended knee, and already preparing his appeal for mercy...

Then he saw the burning towers of the Sovereign City and his men, fighting to the death with those whom he, their commander, had called their enemies, and all willing to die on a word from him.

And the goblins—persecuted, cornered, their very existence long a curse to them, and left now without a shred of hope.

And his Teacher, mournfully shaking his head...and Ilving being led to a slave-market somewhere in Southern Hjorvard...

He began to fight. No, he did not emulate the Archmage in weaving charms and countercharms, seeking to purge his astral body of the Elixir of Sleep by the usual wizardly expedients. Instead, with tenfold strength, he forced himself to remember all his madding, frenzied life, a life full of combat and battle, its every moment committed to a perilous game played against inhuman, unearthly powers one hundred times stronger than he, to remember all with whom he had fought and all with whom he had reconciled, those whom he had loved and those whom he had hated, that which he had taken and that which he had given. He strove desperately to drag himself from the soft, sucking mire of sleep into which Merlin the Great was determinedly pushing him.

The ants waited. Merlin waited, too. He had already begun to weave a Charm of Removal, to further his intention of bringing Hagen before the bar of the Young Gods in the Hallowed Land, where the Thane of Hedinseigh would find neither aide nor advocate. Hagen was waiting also—for Merlin to draw nearer.

It cannot be said that human memories alone had entirely outmatched the magic, but at least his mind was no longer floating away and his left hand—the hand that held the Disc—was again his to command. Merlin, seemingly oblivious to all this and busy with his enchantments, came ever closer…

Little more than five paces away from the kneeling thane, he stopped, as if troubled. He was ready to pronounce the last words of his Greatcharm, had raised his hand in a majestic gesture of Power and Command, when Hagen, with a sharp flick of the hand, again flung the Disc of Iamerth.

The Archmage was left with no time to fend off the entirely unexpected blow—he was already imagining this pitiful mortal laid low, wholly in his power. After all his efforts, the last thing he had expected to see was the swift sheen of a fleet-flying Disc.

But he would have been no Archmage had he been snared on so simple a lure. He had always in store several charms for an extremity such as this.

The Disc of Iamerth whistled through emptiness. Merlin had disappeared without trace from his Sanctum of Spellcraft, had simply dissolved into the air.

At that moment the ants attacked.

Although the sorcerer had abandoned his Sleepcharm, Hagen still felt its effects. He defended himself languidly, wielding his sword with a heavy hand. The Disc crossed the room end to end several times and then slowly, as if guilt-ridden, zig-zagged back to him.

The thane fought deliberately and silently, husbanding his strength; and this stood him in good stead when the ants were joined by his old acquaintances the flying maws, which burst into the room as soon as the Archmage had vanished. Again his broad blade hissed, cleaving the air. Hewn asunder, the horrors toppled, their bodies first covering the floor then forming growing heaps, which rose higher and higher until Hagen was waist-deep in them.

But in a matter of seconds he realized he was losing. Merlin's creatures, both airborne and earthbound, were attacking from all sides. The Blue Sword was working miracles, but increasingly, the ants were able to force their way through its glittering screen and seize onto his legs. His blade was cutting the winged brutes down mere inches from his body, and he sensed that before much longer his fight would be over.

It was, like as not, the despair that made him see how both the winged things and the ants were as like to their fellows as egg to egg. Then could not the Disc of Iamerth be given them all as a single target?

Fate would allow Hagen very little time to test this idea. After only a moment's hesitation, his mind aimed the Disc at his winged foes and his left hand hurled it.

The result surpassed all his expectations. As if on unseen wings, the Disc swooped through the air, sundering every one of the hideous creatures in two. Neither claws nor teeth could save them as the Disc swept past the gaping mouths, each time escaping being drawn into the pit of destruction. The air was far less congested now, even though reinforcements still came winging through the open door, only to share the fortune of their fellows and add new bodies to those already littering the floor.

Now the thane could beat back the ants. Step by step, he forced them toward the doorway, his sword whirling ever faster. Soon he was close enough to reach the handle, slam the heavy door and slide the thick bolt home. The Disc was still flitting above his head, finishing off the last of Merlin's flying servitors.

Hagen carefully moved away from the locked door. The ants gnawed frantically at the other side yet without, it seemed, much hope of success. The jaws rasped and ground, but all to no avail.

Hardly had he caught his breath and begun thinking what to do next and how to retrieve the Disc of Iamerth, still enthusiastically exterminating its adversaries, when once again, at the far end of the hall, Merlin appeared. Paying no heed to Hagen, he ran to his cloven marble altar. He leaned down, took one of its halves in his arms and, straining, set it upright again, then turned to the other half. He was in fearsome haste, looking neither to left nor right—and with good reason, for at that very second, in the Netherside of the Worlds, Mage Hedin was destroying Rakoth's place of confinement, sending a shockwave rolling toward Eastern Hjorvard.

It must not be said that great destruction was occasioned thereby. The floor merely shook, the door handle rattled, and charred pieces of windowframe fell to the ground. While Hagen did not know what exactly was taking place, there came to him the firm conviction his Teacher had achieved his end.

Where now was all of Merlin's restraint, the stolid patience with which he had borne the Disc's assault? His were the burning eyes of the most terrible spawn of Darkness, intoxicated on human flesh; and no sooner had the weapon of Iamerth halved the last of the flying things and returned to Hagen's hands than the Archmage struck back.

The safekeeping of his apartments seemed to concern him not at all as all the air around Hagen exploded into flame, tossing him backward. With a roar, the walls and ceiling came down in billowing clouds of brick dust. A heavy roofbeam fashioned from several thick steel bars fell close by, shattering the stone floor beneath it. Hagen was trapped under a pile of debris, but managed to remain conscious by some marvel, despite the fearful pain. His fate now was to watch what Merlin did, since he could move neither arm nor leg.

The Archmage, meanwhile, seemed to have lost his wits as he bounded to the wall and slammed his fist into a panel that visibly differed in no way from the rest. A secret compartment yawned, and from its black depths Merlin drew a tall glass vessel with a tightly seated lid, rather like a large wine jug except that it blazed from within with a gilded light. He wrenched at the lid, but it did not yield; so he slung the precious—and so it must have been, for otherwise he would not have concealed it so carefully—vessel to the floor.

Shards flew far, and tongues of fire, golden as sunrays, danced across the stones. His arms raised prayerfully aloft, Merlin fell to his knees amid those flames, as if in supplication, and remained so as his garments and hair caught fire, declaiming loudly in a language unknown to Hagen, who understood nothing until Merlin cried out, with inconceivable power and passion, "Iamerth!"

Despite the pain fogging his mind, the apprentice of the Unruly Mage felt cold claws of horror tear through all his being. He sensed then that this did not presage the advent of a mere likeness.

The answer was immediate. From the flame rose the tall, handsome figure of a powerful, half-naked man that glowed unbearably bright. The kneeling Archmage shuffled backward, uttering a single brief phrase, and that with difficulty.

But the visitor was evidently well aware of what was afoot, for he answered with only one short word—short it was, but sharp as an executioner's ax and every bit as deadly. The Mistress of Eternal Perdition herself had entered that room and had charged that word with all the intolerable chill of her halls of torture.

The tongues of flame subsided at once, and the resplendent figure disappeared, leaving Merlin lying motionless on the scorched floor. But he was soon on his feet again. He limped in unsteady haste to a marble altar composed now of two halves propped up against each other, leaned against it with both hands and began to cast a charm.

Never had Hagen seen sorcery invested with such titanic, such dreadful forces—forces he could not even name. From beyond the distant bounds of the world they came at Merlin's call, submissive to his power. He yoked them together with adamantine bonds, and each of those powers was singly capable of turning all of Eastern Hjorvard to ash.

Gradually, the sorcerer's hands molded a gilded sword that hung motionless in the air. Several times he lost his thread and had to begin all again, while at the same time wrestling with the chief tool of his magic in its state of disrepair. It was not long, however, before the golden blade was ready, and Merlin's next spell took almost no time at all.

The floor by the altar began to reveal a vision of some indescribably awful place. Hagen saw a dark-haired man rising up on one elbow and, standing beside the man, his Teacher. Before the thane could even rejoice that Hedin apparently still lived, Merlin spoke the last word of his Charm in a voice of thunder. The golden sword turned in the air and plummeted toward the image of the Unruly Mage, and so powerful was that spell it sent rafters, bricks and beams tumbling down onto the pile of wreckage under which Hagen lay buried.

But the thane felt none of it, for he knew now the Archmage had loosed at his Teacher an arrow from which there was no escape, which signified that he, Hagen, had failed to carry out Hedin's last behest, had not been able to protect him during his struggle in other worlds. The shame, pain and bitterness of that terrible loss, which was now inescapable, shattered the mind of the Thane of Hedinseigh, and he found the haven of oblivion.

HEDIN

I OPENED MY EYES, MY WITS RETURNING TO ME AT A STROKE. BUT IN TRUTH—THE thought came of its own accord—far better they had not. The pain was that of being sliced into tiny pieces by thousands of keen-edged knives, there was a buzzing in my head, and I had the strength neither to rise nor even to move, but only to shift my eyes a little.

Rakoth lay prone, his face buried in the crook of his arm. Only then did I remember what had happened to us, and I was measurelessly astonished— how could I still be alive, after being struck by Merlin's Sword?

Rakoth stirred and groaned. His powerful hands pushed against the resilient, oozing lava as he tried to rise. I saw his pallid, bloodless face, his dark, half-demented eyes. Then his body convulsed, and with a hollow cry of pain, he lowered his head. He must be suffering more than I, having borne the brunt of the Sword's evil power.

I sought again to stand, this time with signal success for, after several failed attempts, I at last managed to keep my feet. With a gait more halting than I would have wished, I approached my friend.

"Rakoth," I said quietly, laying a hand on his shoulder.

"Hedin!" The Fallen Mage's voice was a hoarse, low rumble, and his eyes glowed again with a mad fire, for no torments could ever divest him of his fierce thirst for battle. "Hedin! And so, by the Great Darkness, we live, it seems."

"We live," I said, forcing out the words. "We have endured—have endured, do you hear?" My strength was returning by the second, and growing within me, striving for an outlet, was a wild, primeval joy such as I scarcely remembered, which far surpassed even the delight I had felt in the Castle of All the Ancients when an apprentice had again been mine after those centuries of exile.

"What now, brother?" Rakoth thundered, rising to his feet. "I always believed the day would dawn when you would come. And now, I think, we shall have a bonny brawl. Will you permit me to stand by your side?"

I could be nothing but struck by how fast the Rebel had come to himself and was again ready for combat.

"We return now to my fortress on Hedinseigh," I said. "But you're right— the brawl will be bonny, indeed. I've already run afoul of the Young Gods for seeking to bring you away. I had hoped..."

It was Rakoth's turn to touch me on the shoulder. "Put that tribunal from your mind. You were in many ways right in trying to dissuade me from the Rebellion."

I hastened to break a silence that threatened to become uncomfortable. "But somewhat has been done, even in your absence. Now we will not meet the Masters of the Hallowed Land empty-handed."

"And Merlin has found something to regale us with as well," Rakoth observed, squaring his shoulders. "What was that horrible thing, pray tell?"

"Whatever it was, I'd say Merlin was prevented from engaging all its might against us," I replied, sensing a faint glimmer of light. "My apprentice must have striven mightily to prevent the Sword from striking us in full strength."

"And stoutly done!" Rakoth gave a grim smile. "Well, and should we not be gone from here?"

I nodded, readying the first in my store of Charms of Return.

To fight one's way down to the Netherside of the Worlds is far more difficult than to ascend from that place, just as an experienced diver, who must carry a considerable weight on his descent into the depths, will surface with almost no effort.

"There's a hearty welcome already awaiting us in the nearer worlds, I'll warrant," I remarked. "I'll counter it as best I can, while you conserve your strength."

"I should say not!" Rakoth was indignant, his eyes again glittering in anger. "You'd have me stand and watch?"

He has assuredly changed not in the least.

With a simple piece of sorcery, a turning of the world about me, I took us through the roof of the Netherside to the place where the countless legions of Rakoth's jailers had mounted their assault on me. I would have given much to traverse it without a second's delay, but that, alas, proved impossible, for I had never happened upon the appropriate spells and sources of power. The Young

Gods' martial menagerie teemed here like fish in a hatchery, and there were more of them now, it seemed, than on my previous visit.

Those howling, hooting hordes bore hard down on us.

"Lend me a sword, Hedin!" Rakoth called, seeing I was about to use my magic. "Now they shall see what I am still good for."

I tossed him my weapon. Magic was still my own preference, but Rakoth could infuriate those monsters to such an extreme degree as would serve to reinforce the effect of any charms I might cast.

He gave a jaunty whistle and plowed into the battle, with one stroke removing the head of a sizable fire-breathing dragon. I neither saw the blade's glint nor heard the air riven, so swift was that blow. He might as well have waved but a hand holding only a sword-hilt, applying unknown enchantments to separate the monster's grotesque head from its misshapen body.

A bloody free-for-all began around the Fallen Mage. I, meanwhile, was patiently collecting all the hatred being hurled at us. During my exile, I had noticed that an enemy's fury can serve as a source of power—provided, of course, that the appropriate transforming charms can be found. It had cost me some pains, but now I could calmly reflect back the magical blows directed at us and, with only a slight turning of the world, knit me a net to catch the anger of our foes. Since I had employed a similar procedure on my way down, I could not use exactly the same method again, for my adversaries had learned their lesson and were no longer inundating me with torrents of crude magical power that could quite easily, given the desire and the appropriate skill, be turned to a use apt to catch any enemy by surprise.

So, Rakoth worked his sword whilst I wove my net of charms and waited. My friend allowed not one of the beasts to break through to me, and that gave me the liberty to spend a second or two mulling over the future. Magical techniques developed in the distant past and learned by heart did not require the constant intervention of my mind.

To all appearances, Hagen had stirred up a grand hurly-burly on genteel Avalon. Something also told me he was still alive but that I had to hurry if I was to deliver him from there in good time.

What was that charm cast by Rakoth an instant before the Sword of Merlin had struck us? I had never heard its like, and the more I thought about it, trying to recall even its most general contours, the more sinister and inscrutable it seemed.

By this point, Rakoth's recklessness had literally driven the foes surrounding us to distraction. Their fury and hatred washed over us, my stores of power were overladen, and it was time to leave. I called to him.

Giving his sword not a moment's ease and not turning his back, he retreated to join me. I grasped him by the forearm, and we soared upward, leaving the servitors of the Hallowed Land astonished, perplexed and infuriated behind us. Like two shooting stars, we sped through the worlds. Thousands upon thousands of eyes sought us, thousands of wagging tongues conveyed the tidings of our appearance, thousands of ears heard the tidings, and the owners of those ears hastened to broadcast the dreaded words: *Rakoth has arisen! Rakoth is coming!*

Of me there was no mention, but vanity has never been among my shortcomings.

How much time would Merlin need to craft another death-dealing Sword? I could only entreat Fate to let us meet it not on our journey, where there could be no salvation, but on Hedinseigh, where preparations had long been in place for the most fearful of magic wars. The one unknown in my equation was the Young Gods, but I could not know the limits of their powers until I engaged them openly. There was no way back; the bridges were burned. I had returned the Rebel to the world, and now the result was ordained—the only victors would be either we two or the Young Gods.

The rising torrent of power that carried us pierced through course after course of the Real. The pursuit—if any pursuit there was—had long been left behind, and I could only wonder at the ease with which we had made our escape from the Dark Worlds that lay below all. The charms were all but exhausted, only their last layer, in the parlance of the Mage, remaining—that entire sequence of interrelated enchantments that have a single goal but attack that goal, so to speak, from various sides. *We can withstand one more hard-fought battle, if the servants of the Young Gods overtake us*—Merlin's minions I feared not at all—*but after that, all the way to Hedinseigh, we can look for help from no quarter. Unless the Great Orlangur is moved to mercy...*

The pleasure of that serene flight was ended, of course, all too soon, when we were caught on a nameless world and surrounded on a barren, hilly plain under a grime-gray overcast sky. Up in the clouds glided flying lizards, huge winged shadows that every now and then dove earthward, deftly picked something up in their long jaws and again soared aloft.

Our shoulders suddenly bore thousand-pound weights. Someone had calmly, confidently swallowed up all the energy I had stored for the way ahead—too calmly and too confidently, though, for suspicion to rest on the Archmage.

Rakoth understood all on the instant, and replied to my helpless shrug with a grim smile.

"So, they come at us—a little earlier than I would have liked, but so be it. I shall show them they buried me too soon."

Again he took up his Black Sword, running an affectionate hand down the blade.

"I'm glad you kept it safe, Hedin my friend," he said warmly. "It pleases me, I own, that my gift was not without its uses. And I promise to return it as soon as we're done with those swag-bellied ruins." He tilted his head at the dark hordes of sundry creatures advancing on us, filling the plain below and the sky above.

"There is worse than this," I said, glancing around. "These we shall shake off, but after that…"

"Ah, you foresaw it." He smiled. "Of course, how could you else? What shall I do, now—stay close?"

I gave a short nod. The time had come to unseal a cache of power I had prudently established in a world not far distant. Where exactly it was I did not know, and that was of no consequence. What mattered was that I could use that supply of might to hold the beasts of the Hallowed Land at bay until we could be gone, in our last leap between the courses of the Real.

When the circle had closed around us, and the diversity of spirits, demons, dragons, Servitors of the Elemental Forces and on and on and on was but a few hundred paces distant, while the air grew glacial in anticipation of a final stroke of wizardry, I set my own reserves in motion, freeing colossal forces I had gathered over long years, one jot at a time. They would have been greater, those stocks, had not the accursed Hound forced us to begin unseasonably.

The sky around us changed color, the clouds seeming to flare up from within and only the patch above our heads remaining untouched by the flame. As if stirred by a titanic spoon, the clouds began to circle faster and faster until they became a veritable whirligig. The wind started up a frenzied drone.

The tail of a prodigious tornado dipped down from the sky, sucking me up along with the Fallen Mage. I had opened the Gates of the Worlds with a Greatcharm, and we were on our way.

"Bravely done!" Rakoth shouted in my ear, right hand fisted and thumb cocked. "But what next?"

Darkness. Light. Stars. World succeeded world as we sped ever onward: but the hue and cry was at our heels, and I sensed they were gaining and would be upon us before we could reach Hjorvard and the Hedinseigh stronghold.

We had left the Gray Worlds behind and were very close to our own when I saw Rakoth bite his lip.

"We are outrun," he murmured.

"Then we shall fight," I replied in like style, all the while feverishly seeking a way to avoid that fight.

You are not outrun, impetuous Mage. It was the rich, powerful bass voice of the Spirit of Knowing, and through the murk of the Mid-Real there shone upon me eyes with four pupils apiece.

"Abysmal Darkness!" a stupefied Rakoth rasped. "What is that?"

He had, of course, immediately sensed the close presence of an immense Power that differed strikingly from anything he had encountered heretofore.

You are not outrun, but be prepared to leave Hedinseigh. Your apprentice is in distress. He has fought famously and has supplied me with much invaluable intelligence that has assuaged my hunger and has greatly gladdened me. Therefore, I say to you, hurry! He lies in Merlin's palace, insensible but not yet inanimate, crushed by crude stones. As for these, worry not. I shall put fear into them, but beyond that you must shift for yourself. Farewell! I am certain we shall meet again.

I know not what the Great Spirit did then, but suddenly I felt the pursuit break off.

"What was that? *What was that?*" Rakoth had seized on me like a tick, and as I explained it to him and he shook his head in admiration, the sky closed for the last time over our heads and I saw, far below but clearly distinguishable—Hedinseigh.

"There's precision for you!" Rakoth remarked respectfully.

From this vantage, it was plain to see how my fortress had suffered from the fireballs loosed by the fleet of warriors in feathered helms, and from the fiery blades of the Hungering Stars. Many of the bastions had collapsed, and almost all the watchtowers had disappeared without trace; but the keep stood firm, and while it stood, Hedinseigh would abide.

"Whose master stroke was this?" Rakoth asked in surprise as he joined me in surveying the fortress.

"There will be a time for tales later," I cut him short. "You will remain here whilst I go and rescue Hagen. Belike he has fallen into a trap."

Rakoth raised an astonished eyebrow. "You'd leave me with the keys to your Protective Charms?" he asked.

And that was, indeed, cause for wonder, since the Protective Charms that guard a Mage's residence are the mystery he holds most dear.

"I have no secrets from you," I replied. "I leave now for Avalon. You shall stay here and keep up the defenses. It's not likely they'll begin before I return. Meanwhile, move up into this world everything subject to you."

"Rest easy on that score," the Rebel assured me, his eyes flashing with triumph.

We were in the fortress's main bailey now. Gerder, who had been in command during my absence, sighed in frank relief.

"All is well, Sire Hedin," he reported.

And, indeed, the fires had been put out, the prisoners set to work—the indefatigable chiliarch having immediately begun to patch up the most dangerous breaches—and the troops rested and fed, while the armorers hurried to replenish the stores of arrows, pikes and projectiles and replace dented and cracked shields.

Dismissing him with a nod, I went up to my apartments with Rakoth following after. I briefly introduced the Rebel to the Diviner of Charms, and they found matters to discuss while I verified for the last time all the magical snares and screens of sorcery I had placed around the fortress. We could withstand a first assault, but on more than that I could not rely.

Having hurriedly conveyed to Rakoth the essence of my preparations, I took to weaving a suitable Charm of Transference and was ready to depart when the Diviner suddenly took fright.

— *From the place you call Avalon a sorcerous arrow has been launched!* it yelped. *The greatest of your wonder-workers has directed it toward your island!*

Bravo! Bravo to you, Merlin. Not for naught are you the Leader of the Council of the Generation. An instant apprehension of events, and all's done!

"I shall try to stop it," Rakoth said, thoughtfully screwing up one eye as if aiming a bow.

"Rather, muster your forces, call on all you can," I replied, trying to dissuade him. "There is worse than this—this is but a test."

"Well and good, then, I shall away to muster." Rakoth went into a corner and began casting an intricate spell.

The Diviner had latched, like a woodpecker clinging to a pine, onto the fiery blade that sped toward us; and half a minute later I knew all I needed to know. Merlin had made of Avalon a gigantic pump that was avidly sucking strength from the natural circulation of magical energies, and a subtle mesh of sorcerous guides and wizardly forms was transforming the fragile masses of fearsome forces into a weapon of dread.

It was but short work to determine the system of enchantments used to secure that current of Fire, and then to make my counterstrike. Although my spells were no match for the might with which Merlin's Arrow was endowed, the elemental magic to which I resorted was distinguished by its ability to parry blows many times stronger.

The clusters of sorcery that bound Merlin's Arrow, teased out by my spell, disappeared; and within the gray murk of the Mid-Real bloomed an extraordinary flower of fire, that being the high revel of flaming spirits disenthralled, rejoicing in a modicum of freedom before new charms were cast to commit them again to the morose business of destruction.

On Hedinseigh, of course, we saw and heard nothing—neither firebolts in the sky nor thunder beyond the horizon—all such events took place outside the bounds of Hjorvard. We did feel a powerful jolt that shook the island's cliffs to their foundations and brought down several damaged towers.

Merlin's Arrow was no more, but he could be in no doubt of my understanding it had been no more than a probe. He had known I would fend off his first attack, and had only been pushing gently against the fences that surrounded Hedinseigh.

"Well done, well done," Rakoth said, breaking momentarily from his labors.

I glanced at him. The Fallen Mage's face glistened with sweat, and mounds of powerful muscles rolled and rippled along his naked arms—the Rebel's magical systems greatly favored the use of his own bodily strength, reflected in sorcery. The air around him gave off a dull luster, and numerous flame-red streaks had converged in a complex design at whose very heart, like Great Night's opening eye, there gradually appeared a spot of Darkness, perfectly round.

Rakoth was breaking through to the deep-seated strata of the Mid-Real, where hid those of his faithful servants who had survived the retribution of the Young Gods and had neither disavowed nor abandoned their former master. Employing the magical might of Hedinseigh, my friend was stubbornly reasserting his authority over the dark precincts of the world that lay beyond the Young Gods' long reach and had always been his source of strength—and his error, by vesting his hopes in little but brute might and his countless hordes.

Now, through the narrow corridor he had opened between the worlds, he sent a Power Missive that told of his return; the Children of Darkness who heard it would rise up from their depths. Though it took all his physical and magical energy, in a few hours he would again command legions of those beings the Darkness eternally engenders in its unending hostilities with the Light.

Those First Principles are diverse in size and import, and none may be named all good or all evil. Their color, too, is no more than a symbol. Absent Rakoth's firm hand, of course, the Nightborn could never have acquired all the capabilities for combat, but those with which they were equipped by nature were not to be scoffed at, either.

Meantime, the Diviner had fallen silent, not because all at once no sorcery was being performed within the bourns of the Worldsphere but, on the contrary, because time was needed to puzzle out the endless skeins of spells being cast in Avalon and the Castle of All the Ancients and the world of Hjorvard, too.

I myself was much exercised by thoughts of the servants of the Distant Powers, wondering if they had decided to intervene in earnest, deeming this moment opportune for remaking reality to suit themselves, or if they had carried Sigrlinn off only because of her squabbles with their helpmeets. Much here was unclear to me. Why had my once-beloved locked horns with the Distant Ones? On what uncharted pathway of Higher Wizardry had they met face to face, with neither side willing to give ground?

But there was no time for guessing games. I had to hasten to Avalon.

I bade Rakoth farewell with a strong, silent handshake, words being superfluous at such a time. A moment later, a Charm of Transference hurled me toward Merlin's home.

I cannot claim I had foreknowledge of all possible dangers. Rakoth would withstand even a concerted attack by our whole Generation, but should the Young Gods descend into our world a few minutes would be more than he could bear alone. Magical bastions take decades to create, and to initiate any other person, even a Mage, into all the subtleties involved in commanding them was simply impossible in so short a time.

While still journeying along the paths of the Mid-Real, I sensed that up ahead several layers of defenses, raised hastily by Merlin, awaited me. The Archmage could hardly know my destination yet, for I had closed up my thoughts behind an impenetrable curtain, the very same whose secret I had so feared to divulge to Merlin at the beginning of the events described in this volume. I doubted not but that the Leader of the Council of the Generation was bending all his skill as an Enchanter to divine what was in my mind—those plans and intentions I had never even entrusted to any becharmed hiding place. And, by the Darkness, a glorious prize would await him should he contrive to break down my defenses. Such thoughts would earn me a slow and agonizing death. But then again, I had known myself condemned from the moment I dismantled the walls surrounding Rakoth's place of internment.

The first obstacle I encountered was intended by its framer to hold back anything that sought a way to Avalon, be it magical or corporeal in nature. Once, many centuries ago, I had collided with something similar and at that time could only butt my head against it, blankly and to no benefit whatsoever. Now, I was simply amused by the clodpate I had been then, who would wade into a tussle without having first learned how to give as good as he got.

As soon as I felt a hurdle approaching from afar, I hastened to effect a Supreme Transformation. *Since light will pass through the obstruction, we shall make ourselves a particle of light.*

Here it should be noted that even the most adept of Mages are reluctant to invoke a Supreme Transformation, it being a charm of improbable complexity that demands vast outlays of strength, is susceptible to the most unexpected influences and depends at times on so much happenstance that he who works such a Transformation, be he three times a Mage, may find himself entrameled in its consequences until the old stars blink out and the Creator comes to light the new.

It requires combining and maintaining in a steady and strict balance the four Great Foundations of Fire, Water, Air and Earth; the eight Lesser Foundations of Stone, Wood and the rest; and the one hundred and twenty-eight Minor Foundations whose enumeration would be out of place in this chronicle, and then becoming one of those Foundations. This is not exactly simplicity itself, since every last little component of one's being must be brought to a state of pure Foundation, after which one must proceed from the lower Foundations to the Supreme and so forth until there remains only that which mortal philosophers call Substance.

It is needless to recount how much time I had spent rehearsing that Transformation in its most infinitesimal details. When developing my plan, I had, of course, considered the possibility I would have to break through magical barriers, and had spared no effort in amassing a suitable arsenal.

The world around began twinkling with a fanciful polychrome of sorcery; and for an instant, I was deprived of sight, memory, the sense of touch and all other human and magical characteristics and became a particle of pure energy, speeding with a myriad of its own kind through a screen drawn across the path of inert matter. Once through that obstacle I was myself again, for there is nothing more dangerous than to remain long in any phase of a

Supreme Transformation when at the slightest disruption in the balance of forces you will perish beyond recall and fade away, leaving neither trace nor memory behind.

I stood on Avalon's sod, the Black Sword at the ready. The entire clearing between the thickets and Merlin's home had been trampled by hundreds upon hundreds of heavy boots and pattens, the house door was stoved in and the windows broken, yet there was not a body in sight. Hagen's army had made forcible entry, but what had happened afterward?

Although the Diviner of Charms was not at my side, I did not need its help to feel that in the damaged house before me taut cables of enchantments were being woven. Merlin—no idler, he—was gathering his forces to strike another blow. Like Rakoth, he was calling his servants from all the world's bourns, on occasion directing instructions to those who remained in the Castle of All the Ancients. He was also searching for Sigrlinn. I could even discern her name, so powerfully did he call to her. His gaze scoured the expanses of sea and land, broached the oceans of the air, but all for naught.

For several minutes, I simply stood and listened. *How can he not have sensed my presence? Or is this just a cunning trap?* There was no wizardry barring entrance to the house, not even the most artless, which was not at all in Merlin's character. Yet I had no choice. If Hagen was alive, he was most likely in that building—and I did sense the faint beating of his heart. I called to my apprentice, but he did not respond; either he had lost consciousness or Merlin's magic was preventing him from hearing me.

I drew a deep breath and cast a Charm of Invisibility, which would, to be sure, offer no protection against an Archmage but would at least deliver me from having to force my way through row after row of his helpmeets. Then I strode across the threshold, and immediately felt the shuddering in the foundations. Merlin was offering Hedinseigh a return engagement in the art of parrying fiery arrows. My only hope was that Rakoth would resist the temptation to arrange a magnificent firework display to tickle his own fancy, and would instead softly stifle the strike somewhere in the Mid-Real.

Inside the house, disorder reigned, yet it was not the havoc that might be expected after a bitter siege but only a slight disarray that smacked of deliberate inattention. No more blood or bodies than there had been outside—not even, thunder strike me, not even a nick in the furniture!

I judged it best to go back outside and circle Merlin's castle at least once, and behind it I at last found unquestionable traces of a battle. The roof of one of the wings had caved in—roof beams, tiles and all, and above one of the windows was an unsightly black half-moon of charring. There, and only there, would I find Merlin—and my apprentice.

Suddenly, and very close by, I felt Hagen's labored, infrequent breathing. He was, no doubt about it, insensible; and now I knew why Merlin's Hall of Spellcraft had lost its roof. My prescience had not betrayed me—my apprentice had fought like a lion, and through his valor had prevented Merlin from pouring into his Sword all the power he had originally intended to invest in that fearsome weapon.

I ran up the scree of brick and beam fragments, grasped the sill of a third-story window, pulled up and found myself in the Hall of Spellcraft, or what was left of it.

Greatly as I wished it, I could not recall how many ages had elapsed since last I was here. Directly facing me was the white marble altar, now cleft in twain, that was known to all Mages of my Generation as Merlin's White Stone—his own personal handiwork and the acme of his magical art. With its aid he commanded the movement of magical power in all the worlds of the Great Sphere, and myriads of beings born of magic submitted to the sovereign biddings of that Stone. Now, though, a thin black crack ran down Merlin's miraculous artifact from top to bottom, and the two halves of the mass of marble were simply leaning up against each other.

To my left, where the entry door should have been, loomed a heap of broken stone, roof joists, paneling and suchlike refuse. Around the pile sprawled dead ants, Merlin's renowned servants, their heads bearing the traces of frantic blows from a sharp, heavy blade. When I saw a kreytar's feet protruding from the debris I understand why there were two large burned spots on the opposite wall and what had set the windowsill afire—the kreytar had spat fire, but its adversary had been too quick for it.

And there, under the stones, beside the kreytar's scaly snout, lay my apprentice...and he was dying.

Merlin the Great was there, too, leaning over the Altar of Spellcraft.

I extended a hand holding the ring I had taken from the Castle Raven's leg, the one inscribed *Merlin, Archmage of the Generation* in the flaming curlicues of the Primordial Runes.

"You called me, and I have come, O Challenger!" Such was the formula prescribed by ritual for a magical duel.

Stooping, ghastly pale, Merlin did not at first look at me; and when he did, bombast such as "You did not expect me on Avalon? You looked for me to cower in my hideaway on Hedinseigh?" became unbefitting. All that was unimportant now, and was so because, a few paces away, Hagen's body was exuding the last drops of life. I would have to crush the never-defeated Merlin before I could drag my mortal from under those blocks of stone.

Merlin, too, understood that the time for words and niceties was past. Before I could even blink an eye, he struck his first blow—fleet, unexpected and sly. Evidently, he also had spent his time profitably, and had several delightful surprises in store for me. However, he had failed to reckon that ten centuries spent amongst humans and other of the Lesser Folk outweighed a hundred millennia ensconced in the Castle of All the Ancients. He did not know what it meant to fight for one's very life.

His reasons for allowing me in were clear, for the closer the enemy the greater the chance that a sudden, well-planned attack will succeed. My body began to tremble and was bathed in a copious sweat, moisture leaking from every pore. Such is also the lot of all astral bodies, save that there it is not sweat that leaks away but the life force itself. Merlin had summoned the Great Elements, one of the mightiest and most toilsome components of the Higher Magic, to which he had devoted centuries of persistent study. If I did not stem that torrent, I would within a few minutes be deprived of all my strength, would not even be able to walk; and it would remain only to bind me with the appropriate charms and fire a fatal arrow into my heart.

But there was yet more magic-making coming hard on the heels of the first, for Merlin could not put everything into one charm. The floor tiles grew soft and suddenly slid upward, embracing my legs like fawning cats. Earth, second of the Great Elements, was preparing to swallow my physical body as soon as the life force had left it.

Before Fire, too, could bring its strength to bear I myself called on its aid, for I did not know how to contend with this sorcery of Merlin's—or, rather, I did know but lacked the time, which is in essence the same thing. All I could do was try to break the subtle Ethereal connections he had made with the Entities of the Great Elements. That complex sorcery was coming so easy to him because the Young Gods, Masters of the Elemental Magic, were at his back.

In the few instants remaining to me, I did the one thing I could do, which was to strike out with a Firecharm powerful enough to set the Mid-Real, the Astral Plane and even the rivers of the World Ether ablaze. Under the Hall of Spellcraft's partially collapsed roof, a new sun flared. Taut streams of bright reddish-brown, all-consuming fire burst out in every direction, like the swells of a mighty ocean whose frenzied onslaught is capable of destroying walls and toppling towers. The waves of flame swept away the walls that still stood and tore the roof to tatters, and I knew those fiery serpents could press on and on, shredding the fabric of the world, stretching out in gigantic rivers of flame. Only by dint of much effort did I keep them from me and from the mound of rubble that was Hagen's impending sepulcher.

The rampage of that wizardly flame was short-lived, though, for even I lacked the strength to sustain so universal a blaze longer than a minute. The first things I saw through the subsiding vortices of flame were the Altar of Spellcraft, snowy-white as ever, and the Archmage, gripping it tightly with both hands. The flame flowed harmlessly off him like water from the body of a swimmer emerging from the sea. On this I had not reckoned, even though I knew well enough that here on Avalon Merlin could deflect any stroke of magic consisting only of brute strength.

But not even the Leader of the Council of the Generation could protect the charms he cast from the fire's frenzy. They melted away, and Merlin and I stood face to face once more. Were it not that the Hall of Spellcraft had been utterly destroyed, our first skirmish could have been said to have ended in a draw.

For long moments, we looked at each other in silence.

He was not expecting that I would turn my back to him so abruptly and, instead of trying to finish him with some cunning piece of sorcery, would employ an artless little enchantment to scatter the pile of wreckage that covered Hagen's body.

The Archmage collected himself, and was already returning to the offensive with a charm of his own. I, meanwhile, scooped the unconscious Hagen up in my arms, seized his sword, he having never relinquished his hold on the Disc of Iamerth, and, tarrying not another second, decamped, slipping away from under Merlin's very nose and leaving him howling in an access of rage. The Gates of the Worlds opened before me and slammed shut again, and I was standing on Hedinseigh's soil.

"Tell both men and goblins the thane has returned, and his army will soon follow after," I tossed at Gerder as I ran by.

I knew naught of the fate of the warriors who had gone forth with my apprentice, of course; but, having seen neither blood nor bodies, I surmised Merlin had most likely herded them into the depths of the Worldsphere. If such were the case, that was no great misfortune—with the help of the Diviner, we would seek out the lost and bring them back, if time but allowed.

I flew up to my apartments at the top of the island's keep. Rakoth met me on the way, glanced silently into Hagen's face and just as silently offered a shoulder to share the load.

"You weren't long on the job," he observed in a tone of admiration. "There's no recognizing the cautious Hedin. He hazards and he wins. Will miracles never cease?"

"Better help me preserve Hagen's soul," I retorted anxiously.

And this truly was the time to effect that rescue. The gnomish armor had held firm, there was not a single wound on my apprentice's body, and yet life was leaving it. I felt traces of wizardry there, cast a glance at Rakoth, met his gaze and knew we were thinking the same thing—that Merlin had not overpowered Hagen but had managed to implant in him such a revulsion for life that his soul was in haste to part with a body whose injuries were by no means fatal. Aiding that enchantment's success was the heavy burden that had lain on Hagen's heart in his last seconds before losing consciousness—the sense of duty unfulfilled.

Untangling that finely wrought web of cunningly laid spells was tiresome work. Rakoth could only sigh and stand helplessly by—such undertakings as the unraveling of charms laid by others, which required magic-making of fine-grained exactitude, were not among his talents.

"I repelled the second arrow," he told me when I finally let out a relieved breath after having discharged the last of a complex cascade of countermeasures. "There was nothing to it—I raised one Darkshield and was done. There was not even need for a second."

"He was testing us," I murmured. "Or perhaps…perhaps he was simply distracted by his own need to prepare something other."

The deadly black despondency that had stripped my apprentice of his desire to live was gradually retreating. For want of anything better, I had simply recovered all his very best, most pleasant and cherished memories, restoring from Unbeing people, events, colors, aromas and forcing it all into his devastated and beclouded mind. Also, I did all I could to draw from his body every loathsome trace of his conflict with Merlin. Before long, Hagen opened his eyes.

"Teacher!" The word burst from him, and a treacherous moisture dampened my lashes. "I did not…So, we live?" He all but bolted upright on the couch.

There being a lull then in the Magic War, I acquainted Hagen in all possible detail with everything that had happened to Rakoth and me. The Fallen Mage bowed ceremoniously to my apprentice, who then began his own tale. I saw a measureless surprise in Rakoth's eyes. He could not believe this mortal had engaged as an equal the Archmage, against whom he himself—the Overlord of Darkness, with all his innumerable troops—had once proven powerless.

"I am indebted to you for my salvation," he said solemnly when Hagen fell silent. "I swear by the torments of Niflhel, which are naught in comparison with what I was made to suffer, that although my debt to you can never be repaid, I hope the opportunity will arise for me to discharge even a portion of it."

"Have no fear—the war isn't over yet, and we shall all have more than sufficient opportunities to save each other," I remarked.

"Great Darkness, why do they delay?" Rakoth growled, grasping his head in his hands. "I weary of waiting!"

At that moment, the Diviner began to bombard us with his commentaries on charms cast by our enemies, so fast we were hard-pressed to assess any one of those magical terms. Something strange was in the wind. While earlier, the Castle of All the Ancients had simply called upon the Hallowed Land through a hastily cobbled Astral Messenger, without success, they were now hurriedly mustering all the forces they could find.

Again the Gates of the Worlds were opened, again enchanted legions marched the land, plied the air, swam the oceans. Great heroes of battles with the Darkness awoke in their tombs, and appeals had even been sent to the Distant and Ancient Powers, urging them unite and shatter the Sempiternal Evil, as they loftily styled us. And answers had come, but the Diviner could not understand them.

Yet Merlin was idle, which greatly surprised and alarmed me. At this time, he should have been on his way to the Castle of All the Ancients, from whence he could send a real Astral Messenger speeding to the Godsworld, could direct the efforts of the other Mages of our Generation, could breathe life into all the stores of his own magic. Yet he did nothing, mired there in the wrack of his Avalon; and the Diviner discerned not the slightest sign of any sorcery being made there.

Neither did the Young Gods show themselves, though the denizens of Niflhel were stirring, sharpening ancient rust-eaten swords whose hilts were made of the bones of the dead and impregnated with corpsebane. The carrion-eaters scented rich pickings. The divine Ialven was all attention, too, having been distracted from his endless sport with building blocks of ice. Preparations for war were also underway in the elven strongholds, while the alvs remained as yet unperturbed.

In the meantime, Old Hropt was pressing hard on Vidrir's slowly retreating army. Hjorleif of Himinvagar had suddenly turned back, evidently troubled by the warnings from his court wizards, and blood-red banners flew from the spiked flagstaffs of the citadel on the Isle of Brandeigh, lair of the Black Mages. All understood the world order was teetering, and were preparing either to defend what they owned or to seek an alliance with one who possessed more than they.

But we who were to blame for all that upset were, strange to say, left in peace, and that allowed me at last to pose my question to Rakoth.

"By the by, what was that charm you cast an instant before we were struck? I have never encountered its like. You were able somehow to weaken Merlin's Sword."

"I?" Rakoth's surprise was genuine. "I cast a charm? I remember nothing, but doubtless if you say it was so, then so it was." He wrinkled his forehead, searching his memory, but soon admitted defeat. "No, nothing comes to mind. It's probably been knocked out of me. But you can ask..." He nodded at the Diviner.

— *Yes, he did what has never been done,* my invaluable counselor replied. *None in my world had heard of any such thing, but all almost died of fright, although they could not explain whence came that sudden fear. Behold your spell!* And before us flared a long series of fiery runes.

Busy at first with trying to decipher them, I did not immediately look at Rakoth; but when I did, my gorge rose. The Fallen Mage's hair stood on end, and his demented eyes ranged aimlessly across the walls of my apartments. Then, with an unthinkable effort, he mastered himself and spoke in a hoarse, hesitant voice.

"It is the end, Hedin, the end of all! I have summoned the Unnamable into our world."

The floor gave way beneath my feet, and my mind grew murky.

"Damnation!" Rakoth's dismay was beginning to cede to anger. "Merlin's Sword effaced my memory of those last moments. When I realized I could not deflect that ruination from us, I was seized with a terrible despair. I was no longer myself, and knew only that we would decay, would rot away, would disperse amid the waves of Chaos, and nothing would remain of us—not even an afterlife would be ours. And the rage rose in me, and I thought: Then may the victors also perish! And I spoke the spell.

"I created it in the time of my strength, when I commanded almost all the secrets of Darkness and had divined how to open the gates to...to It against which none may stand but the Creator, and which will now devour all—space and time, matter and magic, the World and Chaos together with their suzerains. Eternal Nothingness will reign.

"And no one—no one—can cast It out! There is simply no such strength, not even in Orlangur and Demogorgon."

He sat on a bench rocking back and forth, his hands about his knees and his gaze aflame with volcanic fire.

I carefully touched his forearm.

"You despair oversoon," I said, but my voice broke and the words came out in a repellent, stifled wheeze. "All is not yet lost. We still live. And if we must call the Creator, then call Him we shall, may the Darkness take us all!"

"That it will, and soon enough," was Rakoth's grim prediction.

"Only if we let it," my apprentice said, coldly and calmly through gritted teeth.

"Yes," I sighed. "If we let it."

Rakoth was long in mastering the blind rage that suffocated him; but when he was finally calm again, we sat all three at the table. I sent word to Hropt, charging him to come with all speed to Hedinseigh. While waiting for the Father of Hosts to arrive, we put our heads together.

PART THE THIRD

CHAPTER XII

SWICK-SHOO, SWICK-SHOO SANG THE BLACK WHETSTONE AS IT SLID UP AND DOWN THE long sword made of strange blue steel. *Swick-shoo, swick-shoo.* No other weapon could so much as scratch the blade and it scarcely ever dulled, but for Hagen the sharpening ritual was a sacred duty.

So, there he sat, sharpening his Blue Sword, as he always did before a battle. A day had passed since his Teacher had brought him out of Avalon, and now the two Mages, Rakoth and Hedin, were busy looking for Hagen's troops, who had been consigned, every last man of them, to a frigid, gulping abyss by Merlin's perfidy and guile.

They had discovered a terrifying sinkhole in the Reality of their world—a starless, sunless place of ice and fog where dismal, almost brainless creatures wandered in the gloom amid towering clumps of standing and floating ice. Merlin had sealed the entrance to those murky realms up tight with Powerspells, whose whimsical curlicues Teacher and Diviner were teasing out, while Rakoth prepared, in case all else failed, to break in by main force.

The warriors, sailors and other residents of Hedinseigh had been told nothing of the lost army's fate.

"They live," Hagen had assured them all. "They live and soon they will be with us again." No word of his could ever be doubted. Once the thane said it was so, then so it was.

The Diviner, too, had much of interest to recount, having finally come to grips with the sorcery evolving on the Pillar of the Titans. The Young Gods had commanded an end to Hagen's Teacher, and even sweet Ialini had ordered her servants into the fray. The Masters of the Hallowed Land were furious with Merlin for having allowed Mage Hedin such latitude and having sent only Sigrlinn, sorceress of Ialini's suite, to tame the brash warlock, even though

Sigrlinn herself was presently at war with the Distant Powers and no one, not even Ialini herself, knew how that could profit her.

By tacit agreement, neither Hagen nor his Teacher nor Rakoth spoke at that time of the Unnamable. The two Mages had conjured long, the Rebel deploying vast swarms of astonishing vassals to the farthest reaches of the Worldsphere and Hedin creating astral scouts and dispatching them on the long journey through the gray domains of the shades. Those there were, too, whose destination was the Mid-Real. The Diviner, meanwhile, untiringly cast about for the slightest changes in the flow of the world's magical energy. None of them—not Hedin nor his apprentice nor even the Diviner—believed the Unnamable would defy all their efforts.

"There are not nor can there ever be such things as all-powerful beings!" Hedin said, pounding a fist into his palm. Hagen had never seen him so distressed. "That would run athwart the Creator's intent. There were barriers keeping that wretched brute from entering the bounds of Chaos, and of the Well-Ordered, too. If we can raise again such barriers as once there were, we can halt it."

"Perhaps. Yet the charm I spoke not only roused It from eternal sleep and called It into our world but also made a path for It through the fabric of the world," Rakoth objected. "Well does the Darkness know that, having once passed through those barriers, It will never stop until It has devoured all the world, and Chaos along with it."

"Be it so!" Hagen's teacher exclaimed. "But what means will It use to destroy All That Is? By making it a part of Itself?"

"Hold there, hold!" The rumbling voice was that of Old Hropt, who had spurred his eight-legged Sleipnir hard in answer to Hedin's call. "My head's right giddy for want of good ale. Come now, my friend, let us begin from the very beginning, or I shall never be able to help you. I've heard something of this creature, surely I have, but only rumors—altered, bobbed, and at tenth hand. Tell all from the very beginning, and leave naught out. We shall all give ear, sithee, and it will be easier then to think."

Proud Rakoth looked askance at the Father of Hosts, irked by his unceremonious tone; but the former Master of Asgard, having seen many a look worth two of that, paid it no mind.

And the Fallen Mage began his tale.

"Long, long ago, when the Mages of our Generation were passing through their harsh apprenticeship under the stern eyes of the Ancient Ones, who at that time had not yet finally quit our world, we were all first told of the

Unnamable. What or who that was our mentors did not say, for they were most unwilling to touch upon that subject in their discourses. The young sorcerers learned only that, somewhere beyond the precincts of Chaos and the Well-Ordered, at an unimaginable distance from the boundaries of our Worldsphere and behind a barrier no feeling may conceive and no word or concept may describe, lay Nothingness. And within that Nothingness there is Something."

"I understand none of this," Hropt muttered. "If there is Something in Nothingness, then the Nothingness cannot be nothingness!"

"Chaos and the Well-Ordered, for all their seeming dissimilarity, are somewhat akin in basics," Rakoth continued, casting another irritated glance at the Father of Hosts. The Rebel did not like to be interrupted or to have his word called into question. "In both there is inert matter, light and movement, in both there is a multiplicity of magical forces. But Nothingness is so named because it contains none of that. None, and there's an end to it. No being from our world could remain whole there.

"And in those domains, if one may call them so, resides the Unnamable. The Ancients tried to understand what It is, with markedly little success, but did determine that It is rational, improbably and indescribably powerful, and racked by eternal hunger—not, to be sure, hunger as we understand it. Like beings from the realms of Chaos that are capable of devouring the fabric of our world—the World of the Well-Ordered—the Unnamable swallows up the components of the Real and all else, and once It seizes upon a tidbit of alien matter no power may stop It. With each particle swallowed, Its power grows, much in the way of the denizens of Chaos."

RAKOTH, HEDIN KNEW, HAD BEEN VASTLY INTERESTED IN ALL THIS, EVEN IN THE LONG-distant days of their youth, when the inconceivable Nothingness and its mysterious denizen had first captured his imagination. Many centuries later, when he became Overlord of Darkness and acquired the keys to treasured storehouses of power and knowledge he imagined to be boundless, Rakoth had returned to his old fascination, already dimly wondering how he could turn it to his own benefit.

His dream at that time was to find a way to set the Unnamable upon the Hallowed Land, though to the Fallen Mage's great regret, he never did. Yet he had doggedly pursued his investigations, carefully studying the nature of the barriers that partitioned Space. Before long he ascertained that here the Creator had done Himself proud, for those bulkheads were more powerful yet than the renowned buffer raised against the onslaught of Chaos.

But even the Creator had ultimately been bound by the great law whereby the harder the object is, the more fragile it will be. The indefatigable Rakoth had come to know that by bringing together the magical powers of the spirits of interstellar Darkness and purloining a fragment of the aimlessly squandered energy of Light, he could create something resembling a giant battering ram capable for a brief moment of breaching those bulkheads.

All that done, Rakoth finally contrived to weave an astonishing charm that no Mage would have scrupled to rank among the Consummate and Most Occult. He then stored that spell against the rainiest of days, swearing that should he ever face an inevitable and inglorious end he would use his secret weapon and, by threatening his conqueror with all it portended, would force fortune to smile on him again.

Yet at the very last moment, when all his strongholds had fallen, his armies had been scattered, his most loyal comrades-in-arms had perished or been imprisoned and the legions of the Young Gods had overrun his citadel, Rakoth wavered. He did not doubt the knowledge gained through such grueling toil; he firmly believed that by pronouncing those fateful words he would doom to destruction the entire world and all who dwelt in it. It was that he suddenly realized he lacked the will to perform that truly monstrous act. He hesitated, most unexpectedly remembering the myriad living things that had not even a notion of the bitter war being thunderously waged within the bourns of the Worldsphere.

The thought caught him entirely by surprise. Prior to that, all creatures, be they reasoning or unreasoning, were to him no more than soulless instruments, and he could ruthlessly dispatch them in their hundreds and their thousands to certain death if prompted by military necessity or whatever else. But on that occasion he had delayed, losing precious seconds and giving the Young Gods' guard—the Winged Giants and Sentinels of the Hallowed Land—time to surround and capture him.

Still, all must have its limits, and seemingly interminable torments of incarceration end. Freedom had come, had come unlooked-for; and when Rakoth knew he would again have a body and that his prison would be ground into dust, he most likely took leave of his senses from the sheer joy of it. Then, when he realized certain death bore down upon them in the form of Merlin's Sword, he ran full mad, the last restraints collapsed in his mind, and he spoke the black words of perdition to All That Is.

"'Tis not to the purpose, though," Old Hropt frowned. "Better we should speak of what has held the Unnamable outside our boundaries."

Then the sorcerers and the Old God began to converse in the language of Higher Magic, so recondite that even Hagen, who judged himself by no means a dilettante in matters wizardly, was soon lost, for what was taking place at the Bounds was truly impervious to human understanding. Time itself was maddened. The Darkness and the Light were perishing together; and there was nothing, no power at all, that could break those barriers down and allow a bodily entity to leave the world of men and penetrate their realms.

With help from the Diviner and the annals of wizardry of all ages past, recorded in its Spheres of Ether, ancient Charms of Knowing were called up and sent by Rakoth on the long journey from the Dark Citadel to the bounds of All That Is, punching through the world and through Chaos, too, and returning.

The conclave was lengthy.

"If Merlin has not yet understood what is happening, he will, of a certainty, be disturbed," Hedin said. "The Young Gods, too. Damnation, it has ever been my intent to force them to act, and if the Unnamable does not stir them, there will be nothing left for me but to crawl on my knees all the way from Hedinseigh to the Hallowed Land and crave their pardon!"

"But why would you have them act before we ourselves were ready?" Rakoth objected. "The Darkness has long healed its wounds. Its strengths are greater than ever, but against the Hallowed Land, all that will, I fear, avail us...nothing." And he gave a wry grin.

"We're forgetting about Orlangur and Demogorgon," Old Hropt reminded them. "That pair is a perplexity to us all. How can you be sure they lack the strength to prevail over the Unnamable?"

"It would, indeed, be well if the Spirit of Knowing were here," said Hedin with a nervous smile and a rub of the hands. "He's been appearing almost daily of late, but then, at the most interesting moment, he suddenly vanishes!"

"And what of the Distant and Ancient Ones? Can they possibly stay aloof?" the Father of Hosts asked. "I doubt they have a place of refuge outside the bourns of the Well-Ordered. If the Distant Powers have carried off that Sigrlinn of yours, maybe they will stand with us."

"To thwart the threat from the Unnamable I would join even with Iamerth himself and all his brotherhood," Rakoth announced, right joylessly.

They then moved on to consider going in search of the Axis of the Distant and Ancient Powers, touching on the charms that might grant them admission to those secret regions.

Hagen had seen his Teacher's face fall at the very mention of Sigrlinn's name. But why speak of Mage Hedin? The thane, too, had to admit to himself that, had he had been free to do so, he would, in spite of all, have already been off to rescue the sorceress. In his rational mind, he understood that her capture should be cause for rejoicing, as it had removed one of his Teacher's most powerful enemies from the fray; but still his innermost self—not his heart, which belonged to Ilving, but his innermost self, that deep, dark, cruel place imprinted forever with the image of the most seductive of all Greater Hjorvard's women, mortal or immortal—whispered on and would not be done.

The final decision was that Hedin and Rakoth would begin by weaving and dispatching to the Bounds a whole legion of Scouting Charms that would warn them as soon as the Unnamable sought to penetrate the precincts of the Well-Ordered, while Hropt and Hagen fought their way down to the Icy Abyss where the troops that had stormed Avalon were confined and deliver them. The Unnamable was all very well, but no one yet knew if Rakoth's Curse had had any effect, while the war was a certainty.

The Young Gods were alive and well. The Mages in the Castle of All the Ancients were busily preparing for the final combat. Missives were being sent to the Lords of the Ancient and the Distant Powers. There would be no shifting without elven magic, and Hedin was preparing to call upon his devoted alvs—without hope of inciting them to take up arms against the Young Gods, of course, though help in dealing with the capricious and unpredictable Overlords of the Distant Land they surely could provide.

For the rest of it, Hedin's plan was to remain unchanged. There was simply no choice, for if they threw all their forces against the Unnamable, only to be destroyed by the armies of the Young Gods...

An appeal to the Spirit of Knowing and his brother Demogorgon would be bootless; they would intervene only if they deemed it necessary, and no prayer had ever yet moved them to action.

Then, at the very end of the conversation, Old Hropt said, with a sudden frown and an unwonted irresolution in his voice, "And what of the Isle of Brandeigh? What if we were to—"

Rakoth's eyebrows shot up. "Brandeigh? Even I gave them the widest berth! Have you forgotten who they are?"

"Not I. But the Unnamable threatens all, even the servants of Chaos."

Thus Hagen, to his surprise, learned that Brandeigh, an isle of the worst repute these many millennia, was actually the domain of the ablest helpmeets of Chaos, and the Black Mages were their name—although they were, of course, no Mages. There was a channel through which the masters of Brandeigh drew power from beyond the verge of the Well-Ordered, and so well fortified it was that even the combined might of all the Mages of a single Generation had never been enough to sever that accursed navel-string. Yet the Young Gods had left the servants of Chaos in peace, to the mystification of Hedin, and of Rakoth and Old Hropt, too.

"I'd as soon not clash with the legions of Chaos into the bargain," Hedin said, and he shuddered in disgust, as if eyeing something loathsome.

"I fear we shall have to choose—all the world and a war with Chaos or universal destruction without the least hope of victory," the Father of Hosts argued, furiously tugging his beard. An alliance with the masters of Brandeigh evidently held no great allure for the erstwhile Lord of Asgard, either; but the appellation of Most Wise he had enjoyed in his day had not been won by slighting in time of need even the most unimaginable sources of support.

They decided, though, to leave Brandeigh's fearsome proprietors for the greatest extremity, when the Unnamable had begun slinking into the precincts of the Well-Ordered. Something greater than a revulsion that defied explanation kept the Mages Rakoth and Hedin from countenancing such an unnatural union—and that something Old Hropt could in no way be made to understand.

Then, when Rakoth had gone out onto the observation platform to greet the first detachments of his servants as they arrived at the island from the distant courses of the Real, and the Father of Hosts had been taken by a desire to quench his thirst with a couple or three mugs of good ale, and Hagen was left alone with his teacher, the Mage gave an unexpected laugh—although that laughter, it must be owned, was mirthless, indeed.

"Here's a wonder! Before we know it, we'll all be swallowed up by Nothingness, yet still we sit, debating how we are to master Merlin! But the greater wonder still is that if we do not continue trying to master him he will certainly master us, and the Unnamable be hanged!"

"Teacher, can it really be that all our spoils from the Temple of Iamerth are of no use to us?" Hagen asked. He was still nettled by the idea that treasures gained through so much work and so much blood were—all, of course, except the magnificent Disc that had saved his life on Avalon—good for nothing.

"I have hopes only of the staff you and Hropt took from the Sentinel of the Hallowed Land, and nurture vague suspicions regarding Iamerth's emblem," the Mage admitted. "Either the rest are the most thorough shams, of use only to dupe the priests and the unfortunate inhabitants of the Sheltered Kingdom, or there lies hidden in them magic that is inaccessible to my mind. But the time is short. Seek out Hropt, for you had best be on your way at once."

"First I must visit Ilving," Hagen murmured.

The sorcerer gave a brief nod and, already in the grip of his own thoughts, strode rapidly to his apartments. The thane followed his Teacher with his gaze then set off to his wife's quarters.

They had parted but recently—only five days before, as the time was marked on Hedinseigh—and it would have been unbecoming for the highborn daughter of a jarl and spouse of the mighty Thane of Hedinseigh to throw herself on her husband's neck after so brief a separation. Therefore, Ilving was propriety itself, but Hagen could read her true wishes in her eyes even as, attended by her ladies-in-waiting, they exchanged the phrases befitting such an occasion.

Then followed...much else, and it was only with the greatest difficulty he tore himself away when Old Hropt came, with much stamping and clearing of the throat, to stand outside the door.

"Rakoth's forces are here, and a sight they surely are," the Father of Hosts told the thane in an unaccountably low voice as they proceeded through the citadel's passageways. Hagen was in full armor, the Disc of Iamerth hanging at his right side. Hropt had strapped on his renowned Golden Sword in its transparent sheath, the wonder-weapon making an odd contrast with the huge sheepskin coat in which the Old God was muffled. With the loss of so much of his power, he had begun to feel the cold as sorely as any mortal.

A guard saluted the thane with his sword then quickly raised a thick steel grille, and Hagen emerged onto the broad parapet that ran around Hedinseigh Keep. From there he had an excellent view of the spacious bailey, which was usually full of people hurrying about their business. Now, though, that vast paved space was host to entirely different beings.

Only in the most ancient granite blocks, remnants of the foundations upon which the new towers and bastions had been erected, still lingered a memory of the days when Hedinseigh had been the proud capital of the puissant Empire of the Night, and its flagstones had frequently borne the weight of guests much like those now present.

On a stone dais in the very center of the bailey stood Rakoth, wearing a cloak scarlet as a tongue of subterranean fire. Hagen was transfixed, staring in amazement and even some confusion at this person with whom he had been peacefully conversing only a few hours before, and who had given only the faintest signs he was no mere mortal, albeit one strong of body and with a commanding gaze. The Rebel had undergone a striking transformation, and now Hagen could easily picture the Fallen Mage in those distant days when his regiments had dominated almost the entire Worldsphere and had stormed the Hallowed Land, and their chief had been proudly styled Lord of Darkness.

Though the air was still, Rakoth's crimson cloak trembled, as if a mighty hurricane gusted through it. His mane of splendid blue-black hair under the tall helmet resembled a diadem woven of gloom itself. His powerful arms were raised in imperious welcome. The commander was greeting his troops.

And still they came. The air groaned under the beat of powerful wings, sickle-shaped claws left deep grooves in the indestructible granite, and the eyes of creatures inconceivable save in the most fearful nightmare burned with a wild fire. Age upon age, the gloom had nursed them tenderly in secret dens, and now, knowing neither doubt nor hesitation nor even fear of death, they were again ready to hasten into battle on the wave of the hand of him who stood now before them in a scarlet cloak, the dark wreathing his head.

Other detachments tramped through the air. Beings resembling humans, armed with round shields and huge cudgels, marched in under banners bearing blood-red eagles; and great ape-like, loping, shaggy things that recognized no weapon other than their own paws, while arrows fouled in their thick pelts and swords broke against their steely skin.

There was a slithering of many-headed snakes; and detachments of shades that swallowed their enemies' souls, turning them into pitiable, helpless dolts; and demons from other universes, like those that had tried to block Mage Hedin's way to the Netherside; and many, many others, in great numbers and in a plethora of shapes and forms. Their bodies eclipsed the sun, and day became dusk. Hagen, astonished as he already was, became even more so when he began to ponder how this swarm would fit into his stronghold's bailey, which, although quite expansive, could never...never...

The answer was not long in coming. The first of Rakoth's warriors to make landfall took their places in the bailey while the rest were...pulled into them. Long chains of beings folded up, concertina-like, and soon the Rebel stood before a vast throng of individual weird and wondrous creatures, not one of which resembled any other and whose diversity would require mountains of parchment to describe.

Hagen turned to the sentry, who was eyeing the strange assembly with great surprise but with no fear.

"Does it not affright you to have such fine fellows as your allies?" Hagen asked him.

"No, my thane," the warrior replied gamely. "After one look at them, all our enemies will turn tail without a fight! But then again," he added more softly, "I would not care to neighbor with them forever."

Hagen nodded. "Good. You may resume your duties."

And so it should be. His reckless daredevils, with their taste for the boldest forays, would eschew no horror if such a union augured victory, but after the battle they would become ordinary mortals again and their natural fastidiousness would return.

The skies over Hedinseigh had cleared. Rakoth was about to address his servants, and Hagen and Hropt went on their way.

They left the citadel and skirted the outer walls, where glum prisoners toiled to stop up with rubble the charred gaps left by the seaborne ballistas and the Hungering Stars. Unlike Hagen's men, they had been frightened beyond measure by Rakoth's muster, and now their guards were engaged in the exhausting task of bringing them back to order. Since the thane had issued strict instructions not to treat the prisoners cruelly, the warriors of Hedinseigh were achieving their ends more by threats than by the scourge.

Passing through the portside gates, Hagen and his companion took a narrow path that led along the walls and struck off into the island's interior, then turned again onto a slim track that wove among great boulders to the edge of a sheer precipice eighty feet above the raging surf. Taking a small leather pouch from his pocket, Hropt shook out onto his palm a piece of amber only a little larger than a hazelnut.

"Whilst you were canoodling with your wife, your Teacher gave me this." The Father of Hosts deftly tossed the nugget up and caught it again. "It is a key. It will hold the Gates open until our return. We will be met there by such as serve Merlin, of course, so your Sword and your Disc will have work aplenty. Are you ready?" he asked in his booming voice.

Not waiting for a reply, he flung the amber over the cliff's edge, roaring out a wild charm in a language unknown to Hagen.

The amber flared in the air, a fiery trace following after like thread from a needle. It was as if a giant unseen pen of fire were scribing a luminous slash across the twilight sky.

And that slash floated toward them, still gleaming.

"Jump!" Old Hropt cried when it was almost upon them. "Jump, and aim well, or your Teacher will never gather you to him again!"

Hagen unwittingly glanced down, to where the swells surged in from the broad expanses of the deep, dashing with eternal, unquenchable hatred against the cliff's indestructible fangs and spraying the rocks copiously with white foam that could have been the blood of a brave but foolhardy hero of the sea.

"Jump, then!" Hropt's bellow stung like a lash, and the thane leapt forward, gritting his teeth and fixing his eyes on that narrow golden stripe.

A gust of freezing wind struck him in the chest, bringing with it a whole flock of ice-needles, sharp as arrows, that blinded him for a moment. He was flying into a bottomless chasm, with impenetrable blackness all around and no sound in his ears but the shrill, spiteful wail of a wind that chilled the very soul.

But it was soon over. Something soft enfolded his body. His fall slowed, and then he felt the firm ground under his feet and snow covering him from head to toe. Alongside, snorting and shaking himself off, Hropt brushed the white flakes away with disgust.

"I hate the cold," he said, by way of explanation.

They were on a dismal snowbound plain studded with blocks of ice upended as if a frozen river had broken and begun to flow here. The endlessly eddying wind had swept the snow into great drifts, white snakes streamed along the ground, and a multitudinous flight of white gnats fluttered down from the low, gray clouds. There was not a tree, not a bush to be seen, not even snow-blown. The White Silence, a wordsmith apprentice of Felostei's would have called it, had he been amongst the living at that time.

"Where to?" Hagen asked Hropt, turning his back to the wind. He had not an inkling of how to find his men in these snowy wastes.

"Climb that clump of standing ice, and we'll see what we can see," the Father of Hosts said, leading the way to the closest one, which was also the tallest, being at least four times a man's height.

Hagen had thrust his gauntlet's gadlings into the stubborn ice when he heard behind him an incomprehensible rustling, quite light and barely discernible over the howl of the wind. His finely trained reflexes flung him aside in the very same moment as a furious roar from Hropt and a repulsive hissing sound reached his ears.

Hedin's apprentice could not but be well accustomed to the most unexpected encounters in the Wizardworlds, so he was not at all surprised to see, rising from a scattered snowdrift, a terrible horn-plated head with a large toothless maw. This was an ice-snake, and ice-snakes crush their prey between bony gums, thus having no call for the fangs other predators use to tear and rend. Hagen thought he saw a rational mind behind those yellow eyes, and remembered what Hropt had said about Merlin's servants in those savage parts.

The Father of Hosts, backed up against the ice floe, seized his Golden Sword, but the beast showed no fear of it.

"Wretched spawn of the Jotnar!" the Lord of Asgard suddenly snarled full in the fiend's face as it drew near. "I killed your ancestors when this world was yet young, and I commanded them! I know you, descendent of Frok! That white spot under your nostrils was burned by my sword into your ancestor's snout, and at my bidding all its descendents have borne that same brand. Do you remember what I did to your forebear? Do you wish the same for yourself?"

The monster cocked its head drolly to one side, as if listening. The speed of its attack had patently slowed, although the snow behind it still boiled like a spring freshet as the last coils of its long body caught up with the rest. Hagen watched them carefully out of the corner of his eye. He was suspicious of any movement, and he could not understand why Old Hropt was tarrying so instead of dispatching their attacker.

It was the thane's suspicious nature that saved them, for he noticed something under the snow moving toward them with disquieting speed, and hoisted his Blue Sword just in time. The ice-snake's log-like tail collided with the blade, almost knocking it from the thane's hand. The steel snagged in the scales that covered its body but could not break through the stout hide; and Hagen fell into the snow, his strength and his excellent balance failing him for once. The snout, sown with large horny plates, made a downward plunge, the jaws gaping…

Old Hropt promptly thrust his sword into the snake's mouth, reinforcing the strength of the iron with the power of a crude and ancient spell. It seemed to Hagen that invisible wedges followed the blade into the wound. The flesh and bone of the monster's head were torn apart, and the skull split in two, sprinkling the snow around with dark, fetid blood.

But Hagen's senses, honed by the peril, also caught a trace of alien wizardry. The two yellow eyes, still with that alarmingly rational look in them, were raised up from the pile of bloody debris as by an unseen hand and pressed into the ragged flesh of the long body that writhed in agony. In an instant, the glittering yellow spheres had grown into place. The blood still spurted, but the unknown spirit that ruled this being was not yet ready to yield.

The beast was wondrously robust, and its armor-plating resisted even the enchanted swords wielded by Hagen and Hropt. They were surrounded by airborne clumps of snow, their feet slopped through dark-brown puddles, and clouds of repugnant steam rose from the huge wound where the snake's head had been. Yet still the powerful rings kept trying to crush them to a pulp. The Mage's mortal apprentice and the immortal Ancient God were left with nothing to do but hew and hack at flesh unprotected by scales, jabbing at those two eyes that brimmed with burning hatred.

Hropt, trusting in his enormous strength, stood deliberately still when the awful thing fell upon him. He allowed himself to be encircled, with the intent of reaching one of the eyes with his sword. But the deadly clasp tightened, the blade dropped from his suddenly strengthless hand, his face crimsoned, his breath came shorter, and his eyeballs began to bulge from their sockets.

Hagen sprang onto the rings that held the Father of Hosts like a vice. Then, pushing off, he flew upward, and the Blue Sword struck slantwise, slicing through both of those monstrous eyes.

A frenzied but impotent groan, very like a man's, came from the inert coils of the headless body, and the ice-snake collapsed onto the snow and lay motionless.

Hagen struggled to free his companion from that terrible embrace.

Hardly had Old Hropt come to himself and caught his breath before he was bending over the two pools of yellowish slime that were the remnants of eyes.

"This is the handiwork of an enchanter," he said with certainty. "I know these sweet beasties well. As a rule they are circumspect in the extreme, and inasmuch as they possess the rudiments of rationality, they can sometimes be made to understand that it is better not to fight but to go each his own way in peace. This one, though, was possessed by some spirit—you drove it out when you cleft its dwelling places. But I do not envy your men if they have already encountered a creature such as this."

The silent Hagen morosely wiped off his blade with snow. He was thinking of his promise to his warriors that they would soon rest again in that lovely place where they had spent the happy day before the siege of Avalon, of his assurances to them that Mages do not kill mortals with their wizardry. Sinking under a hot wave of shame and bitterness, he groaned through painfully clenched teeth. The reckoning he would sooner or later present to Merlin—or die in the attempt—was now of unparalleled size.

The Father of Hosts had meanwhile wasted no time in finding his sword in the snow, and had begun trying to rip open the snake's skin from the inside.

He turned to Hagen. "Some help here! If you make yourself armor from this, you need fear no weapon, be it made by man, elf, gnome or troll. As I hear tell, even the Soul-Banishing Staff we wrested from the Winged Sentinel cannot best it." He touched the staff, which was carefully wrapped in a strip of oxhide and tucked into his belt.

It was good advice, and Hagen took it; but even with both of them together it was work, indeed, to strip off a good-sized piece of that unyielding skin. Old Hropt nestled it in his satchel, and they went on.

"I do not think our way will be smooth even now," Hropt muttered after a while, stopping and peering into the distance. The horizon was still shrouded by the falling snow, and no spell known to Hagen could penetrate that veil.

"Don't try. You'll only squander your strength," Hropt told him "Though none have fortified this place, the snow here was made to reckon with one with your powers. Belike Merlin has made of it a prison for human wizards."

Hagen did not fully understand that last remark and wanted to ask about it, but before he could the Father of Hosts grasped his arm.

"Up ahead! Look!"

They had come unawares to the edge of a vast hollow, whose gentle downward grade began at the spot where they stood. There was not one clump of ice on those slopes, and when seen from a distance, the entire hollow was shaped so perfectly as to resemble a gigantic snow-white bowl.

Yet the spectral glimmering of that mantling of snow was broken by a black mass moving at the very bottom, and through the sporadic blasts of snow, Hagen saw men and goblins.

"Hropt!" It was probably the first time in his life that joy overcame his good sense. He was about to dart forward, but the Father of Hosts had a firm grip on his shoulder.

"Are you blind?" he roared, pointing to the hollow's opposite flank. "See there!"

And the thane saw, and a heart that had never known fear stood still.

Within the low, swirling clouds was a sudden, strange, circular movement, as if a huge funnel were forming there. The powerful evil wind tore at the curtain of clouds; and an eye, dark and unfathomable, gazed out at Hagen. Behind the clouds lay darkness, and none could tell whence came the pale, crepuscular light that spilled from under that gray veil.

A swift green spark emerged from the Dark Eye, followed by another, and yet another, in a luminous dark-green rain that fell on the sinuous snowdrifts. The snow began to melt, sending steam billowing up. The endless deluge of green sparks grew denser, merging into lines that curved into long spirals, and soon a gleaming column extended from clouds to land. No great intellect was required to understand what this was.

The Distant Powers were on the march.

The description of their Columns of Might, which had saved his Teacher's life and snatched up the lovely Sigrlinn, was fresh in Hagen's memory. *But why are they here? Could they have come for my warriors?* He was compelled, as an honorable commander, to stand with the vanguard of his army, absent any way of escape. He could not leave his men in the hands of Fate a second time.

"Now we show a clean pair of heels!" Old Hropt rasped. "We must go. There's naught more for us to do here." Plucking in despair at his beard, he had pulled out a good handful of hair. "We are no match for foes such as these, Hagen. Let us away before our Gates close against these Powers!"

"Go? Not I!" Hagen shouted in reply, throwing the heavy hand from his shoulder. "If death there must be, I shall share it with them." He jerked his head frantically toward his warriors.

"Fine words, you luckless lackwit!" roared an infuriated Hropt.

Hagen would hear no more. He was already racing down the slope, unsheathing his sword, his soul flooding with the long-awaited zeal of battle that intoxicates, clouds the mind and brings a pleasure sweeter and more subtle than any other known within the bourns of the Worldsphere. The thane ran, almost flying, hardly touching the ground—fortunate it was the snow had not settled deep on the slopes—and the Blue Sword shone with menace in his raised hand. A cry burst from his throat, but the wind caught the words up and carried them away so he could not even hear his own voice.

And behind him stamped Old Hropt, cursing explosively as he ran.

The army, milling aimlessly in the snow, noticed them; and the exclamations of astonishment, alarm and, finally, delight fell on Hagen's ears despite the wind. Paying no heed to the mysterious gleaming pillar descending the opposite slope, the great multitude of warriors shambled toward their commander.

The thane did not know what he would do the very next moment, although usually he planned every foray, every siege, every campaign to the last detail and acted on impulse only in exceptional circumstances. That tightly woven column of green spirals harbored an obscure threat, but he advanced upon it without so much as a thought of the danger it might pose.

By now, even the rearmost ranks of the warriors of Hedinseigh had learned their general had appeared. Hagen dove into the thick of the crowd.

"The thane! Our thane! He has come!…We always knew!…The thane!" rang out on all sides.

Working their elbows manfully, his chiliarchs, along with the indefatigable Orc, the goblin chieftain, pushed through to him.

He wasted no time. "Everyone over there!" he shouted, indicating the direction with a nod. "Every one of you get as far away from those columns as you can! And prepare for battle. Hop to it, now! I know you're cold and hungry, but if we do not prevail this day we shall all perish beyond recall, and worms shall feed not only on our bodies but our souls!"

His audience shuddered as one. Never had they seen their usually imperturbable thane in such a taking.

A panting Hropt slammed into Hagen's back then stood, shaking his head from side to side and struggling to speak while men and goblins filed away behind them. With amazing speed that set their endless hours of despair in these snowy wastes at naught, the warriors formed a wall of shields and readied their bows, arbalests and pikes.

"That will never do," Old Hropt said with a gusty sigh. "Take your army away, Hagen. I'll hold 'em back. They'll never o'ermaster me."

But Hagen knew well enough the Father of Hosts was lying, with the best of intentions and only to save him and all the rest, and was preparing to make a last stand here. The thane could not explain whence came that certainty, but perhaps it was that he could discern in Old Hropt's eyes something that sat strangely on the Ancient God—a deathly, almost human heartsickness and a foretaste of doom.

"No," he said, "we stand together." And, turning, he called to Knut, "Lead the detachment out, following those tracks of ours. There, where they break off, is the door to Hedinseigh."

The chiliarch gave a hurried nod and led the weary, harried, frozen and famished troops away with all the speed of which they were capable. Yet they went unwillingly, stopping every moment to turn and look back at the two small figures that grew ever smaller as they strode to meet an unknown danger.

The first to break ranks was Frodi, and after him Gudmund, who had by then come to himself again, and Isung, and several dozen more of the bravest and strongest in spirit. They were joined by some half a dozen goblins, with Orc at their head. Knut yelled and cursed them all roundly, but to no effect.

Hagen, of course, noticed the blatant disobedience to his orders, but there was nothing he could do about it. He and Hropt were closing on the green column, from which suddenly, one after another, tall, faceless forms began to emerge.

Horrible they were, not because of their hideous appearance or the cataclysmic magical power they exuded but because they were entirely alien to all things living and unliving—even to that bleak and icy world. They were toweringly tall, and they truly had no faces; instead of nose, brows, mouth, eyes, chin, Hagen saw only a bare, flat surface that could have been chiseled from stone. Each finely made and evidently strong body was wrapped in a cloak-like aura. He noticed no weapons.

He did, however, mark something else that pulled him up short in astonishment, wrath and despair. At the head of one contingent of those strange beings, in the very heart of the Distant Ones' formation, marched Sigrlinn.

HEDIN

I HURRIED, ALMOST RUNNING, DOWN A CORRIDOR OF THE HEDINSEIGH CITADEL TOWARD my apartments, where the Diviner of Charms awaited me. The poor thing had almost swooned dead away when it learned the whole truth about the Unnamable.

Back in my tower, I removed some protective charms and opened a cunning and carefully concealed lock. The gnomish mechanism operated noiselessly, and the stone moved to reveal a small secret compartment where I had stored the seven emblems Hagen had taken from the Chamber of Altars. I thoughtfully removed them all—Iambren's fan, Ialini's bough, Iamerth's smooth, glittering sphere...

The thought that had come to me while I spoke with Hagen was, in sum and substance, simplicity itself. The Young Gods would not be guilty of the slightest negligence when it came to holding their power inviolate—I remembered still the speed and precision with which they had determined what was afoot during Rakoth's First Rebellion, when he was storming the Hallowed Land and was closer to victory than ever before. The Fallen Mage had been counting on catching them off their guard, had taken all conceivable and inconceivable precautions, but still could not keep himself safe. The Young Gods had uncovered his scheme, and had prepared a worthy welcome for his Dark Army, while Rakoth's single-handed attempt to penetrate into the precincts of the Hallowed Land had ended in his escaping by the skin of his teeth.

But once we had agreed the Young Gods might overlook anything at all except an encroachment upon their authority, the only assumptions remaining were that either the emblems would bring ruin to whoever might steal them or served other purposes—maybe the masters of the Hallowed

Land could now see and hear everything that transpired around me—or the Creator's First Servants had created an artful forgery, good for nothing but...

Yet the temple had collapsed after Hropt knocked Iamerth's emblem from the altar with his spear. That was when the destruction had begun.

I had reckoned the Young Gods would be forced to move against Hagen and me as soon as my apprentice's army had taken Vidrir's Sovereign City by storm and Hagen had laid his hands on the Disc of Iamerth.

They had done nothing.

Our skirmish with Merlin was neither here nor there, because the Young Gods would never have left the Archmage entirely alone to counter any serious threat to their power.

I thought on this long and hard. *The Diviner would have me believe the gods are incensed and their chastisement will be dreadful. Could their weapon of choice be these outwardly sham emblems?*

There, I hesitated. Was I strong enough to destroy the renowned emblems, which were—or so the Ancients had taught us—the focus of the Young Gods' strength and authority in the mortal world?

I decided to begin with the chief among them. Iamerth's dark-agate sphere rested in a pile of marble shavings on a plinth by my desk. A forgery? A hostile eye at the very center of our citadel? Or the focal point of great forces impervious to my understanding? *The riddle must be solved, and solved now. The Unnamable we may leave for the nonce, until reliable intelligence comes.*

With the greatest of care, I sent a whole squadron of my Charms of Knowing to assault that crystalline stronghold, seeking any—even the tiniest and most negligible—loose end I might grasp to unravel the whole tangle.

Show me what you can do, you accursed gewgaw! Something there is in you that split a stone floor to a depth of four feet or more!

I waited long and, as I was to discover, in vain. As with the Hungering Star, even the most refined Charms of Knowing proved impotent, having been woven by a mere Mage who was no god. This was only to be expected; I had been prepared for it. But we were on Hedinseigh for good reason. Here, hard by the focus of my might, I had better to show.

I had the time to spend, and while Rakoth held forth to his legions in the bailey, I worked without respite. The Magic of the Moonbeast came again to my aid, for either its Overlord felt something akin to an interest in me or was simply willing to help the first to speak into its mind and dispel its hundred thousand years of solitude.

On the desk between my hands a comical little shrew-like beast now scurried to and fro, poking its glistening black nose everywhere. As the gods would hold, I had committed a great sin, for only they are permitted to create life. That was one of the allegedly inviolable Laws of the Ancients, but I had tossed that absurd prohibition aside and was sensing no opposition, much less retribution.

The little creature whose creation had swallowed up so much of my power was able to see the inner essence of things by viewing them with the Moonbeast's sight. Not even the secret, interlaced magical powers that are generally able to parry Charms of Knowing could hide from those small, glittering eyes.

The beastling scuttled up to the emblem, sniffed it and, in a diverting and entirely human gesture, touched it with a paw. A sudden white light flared in the depths of the agate sphere, like distant lightning, but my little spy showed no fear. It made a leisurely circle, peering at the globe first with one canny eye then with the other, as if weighing something. Was abruptly still, seeming to have found at last what it was looking for and jumped—right into the stone. It ran off, then, into the black-curtained distance, along serpentine paths that led to a tall, dark mountain behind which flaring lightning raged.

I soon lost sight of it, and all I could do was wait.

So, Iamerth's emblem, whatever else it might be, was no forgery—in that at least I had made no mistake, which itself was cause for some pride. Or would have been, had all this come about in the course of a trifling magical contest during the creation of Jibulistan, when our entire Generation was united, like arrows in a single quiver.

Meanwhile, all was quiet in the World of Magic as the armies of the Castle of All the Ancients drew ever nearer. Evidently, the first rather feeble assault had been the handiwork of Makran and Esteri alone, but now whole hordes bore down on us. I was unconcerned, since the Legions of Darkness could hold them at bay for as long as was needed.

And still Merlin sat idle, and the Hallowed Land was maintaining an enigmatic silence.

Once the Diviner, startled, told me an unexampled act of sorcery had been performed—to all appearances, by a mortal—on the midnight side of Eastern Hjorvard. The Diviner understood nothing in it, and could only show me a runic inscription. I, too, was bemused. I saw wrath in that spell—wrath and a call to action—but whither was directed the unknown wizard's appeal I knew not.

I turned back to Iamerth's emblem and seemed to see a strange picture in its depths—a distant landscape with a mountain that loomed over All That Is, a thin thread of a road running from behind its flank. My beastling was somewhere in that uncharted world. What did it see?

The Diviner was glued to its Spheres of Ether, in expectation of some marvel to come, but my little scout did not return and we caught not a trace of wizardry. Only those white lightning bolts still lit the narrow crescent of sky over that mountain in miniature that lay deep within the emblem.

I belabored my brains to remember where I had seen that astonishing place before. The mountain's contours looked more like the work of human, elven or gnomish hands than the result of rollicking water and wind. Improbably sharp, they resembled giant swords forever embedded into the mountainsides and awaiting their hour. I could make out five of them.

Dim scenes, long forgotten, rose from the lower reaches of memory. My mind's eye glided along the very edge of a deep but not bottomless chasm. Clouds floated just above my head; and down below, on the floor of that deep vale, I could discern houses, meadows, fields, even people and cows—a peaceful, populated land it was...

Yes! And to the left, above a low ridge of hills, was that summit, lording over all! The same mountain I saw now in the crystalline emblem. Sigrlinn was with me then, and someone else—Makran? Or Merlin himself? It was during our apprenticeship with the Ancient Ones. But what did it all mean? What was that world beneath our feet? Why that strange mountain? And why were we there at all? I did everything I could, applying even powerful charms to rouse the memories, but all in vain. My own mind had turned against me.

There was a tiny movement on the road from behind the mountain. My beastling was coming home. That it had found its way so easily into the sphere was not surprising, for what barriers in the fabric of All That Is could stop a being crafted from scraps of Light stitched together with threads of Darkness? It was, after all, entirely possible my eyes were seeing only the emblem's false and fraudulent form, and that it was in actuality a most complex combination of diverse magical forces twisted into rings and wound into vortices. The little thing had simply sought out a cranny between them and squeezed through.

As my messenger approached, I tried to center my thoughts again on what I had seen. The emblem, then, was no sham, but either resembled a gate into some secret world usually barred to humans and Mages alike or contained the imprinted reflection of that place. Why had Iamerth seen fit to place this likeness into an emblem destined to reside in the temple? And whence came those memories that had revived in me when I saw the silhouette of that mountain? And never forget the emblem might also, even now, be betraying all my secrets to the Young Gods or maybe throwing wide the gates of Hedinseigh to welcome in their helpmeets.

Of course, my suspicious nature then sent me on to other thoughts, one of which was that, somewhere within the bourns of the Great Worldsphere, there might be a hidden place to which—who could know why and, for the nonce, who could care?—to which Mages came, or to which they were brought, at the very beginning of their life's journey. And when the visit to that—aah, call it a sanctuary—was over, all memories of it were diligently expunged from the surface of memory and remained only in its remotest depths, from which no spell could ever raise them.

And what if it is...the Wellspring of the Worlds? Sigrlinn had mentioned it, either with a view to trapping me into revealing my true intentions or in the serious supposition that I could make my way there by main force. At the time, her words had roused naught in me but an idle, passing surprise—there were, to put it mildly, far more pressing matters at hand—but now I sat motionless, trying desperately to extract from my memory even the slightest shred of intelligence about a place to which I had betaken myself as a callow apprentice.

The Wellspring of the Worlds, the Wellspring of the Worlds—was it perhaps the source of the might with which the Young Gods had invested the Sheltered Kingdom? But then how could Hagen have taken possession of the emblem with such ease? I would never believe the Young Gods had simply been careless when they dispatched from the Hallowed Land one solitary Winged Sentinel to defend the temple. But, then, what channel of Power was this, that could be uncovered neither by commonplace spells nor by special spells of my own nor by any particular spells fashioned by Rakoth for that purpose? If the Diviner saw no sorcery being wrought by that emblem...

Yet, were I to assume the emblem's powers were so well hidden that no effort of ours could bring them to light, then in truth I knew nothing of magic or wars of wizardry or the Young Gods themselves. They should already have intervened several times in accordance with my plan; but the Hallowed Land was letting all pass, not showing its strength and thus not imparting to me any knowledge of that strength.

Being in a complete muddle by then, it was almost with relief I felt a light touch. The weightless beastling had hopped smartly onto my arm. I stroked it carefully with my index finger—it was making a faint but satisfied snuffling sound—and with a small, short charm I became one with its memory.

A ROAD PAVED WITH ANCIENT, CRUMBLING STONES LED AROUND A SHEER CLIFF-FACE THAT soared to unimaginable heights, the summit scraping the very sky. Lightning glimmered, silently illuminating that sky with spectral white light as might shine through a burial shroud. The road was edged with gnarled oaks, clearly planted by a deliberate hand, for they were all the same age and placed at precise intervals. The branches were garbed in dark foliage and filled with strange life, for many-armed things with tails, tiny heads and huge eyes set above flat snouts leapt from bough to bough. Now and then they sent up a wailing chorus, addressing in an unknown language the creature that ran along the road and through whose eyes I saw all. Something there was of menace in their wailing, but even more of warning. Or such was my understanding.

The roadside oaks ended suddenly when the road came up to the foot of the mountain. My creature lifted its gaze; the rocky, dark-gray slopes swept upward—lifeless, bare, unfissured, bereft of any hint of vegetation. It was an unbroken gray monolith. Then the creature's attention passed on, to a shaggy layer of clouds.

There was no sense of enclosure, no feeling of oppressive confinement as in a cellar or underground vault. It was not at all like the Netherside. Behind the clouds, the beastling's second sight saw sky, stars whose constellations looked odd to me and a black infinity of airless spaces. It seemed like any ordinary world from the Great Sphere's endless array, but I was in no doubt the similarity was only outward, because my envoy was still inside the emblem.

The beastling set off again. It had as yet encountered not a trace of the magic that could have enclosed this world within a small crystalline globe. Even when it crossed the emblem's bounds and looked behind, it could see the narrow track running away into the distance and the even rows of oaks to right and left—but no magic.

Above its head was one of the facets that so resembled a blade. I had not been mistaken—it really was very much like a sword. I could have sworn the cutting edge was honed to such inconceivable sharpness it could even split a mote of dust that happened to fall on it, or a feather shed in flight. The stone blade, straight as could be, ascended aloft and was lost in the clouds.

My beastling surveyed its surroundings thoroughly then scurried on. Behind the mountain was a broad valley whose borders rose smoothly to the horizon, where narrow strips of woodland fronted cliffs that mounted sheer to the heavens. Through the valley flowed a quiet rivulet; and there was a fine, prosperous village, far and away superior to those in Eastern Hjorvard, except possibly in its southernmost reaches. Two-story houses flanked clean log-paved streets, and people in sturdy clothing went unhurriedly about tasks common to the inhabitants of thousands upon thousands of villages in all the great diversity of worlds.

Evening was drawing on. Lightning still flared above but seemed not to disturb the locals in the least. Nor, for that matter, did it trouble my little proxy, which sped like a hunting dog on a fresh-laid scent, having sensed at last the presence of magic true and strong.

Skirting the village unremarked, the little beast hastened on to a tall oak standing apart, so old and mighty that no oak of Greater Hjorvard would dare take its place alongside for fear of seeming a mere seedling in comparison. It was an oak for the ages. And from among its roots, each of which was broader than the body of a horse, gurgled a spring.

So that's it, I thought, dumbstruck, watching the water bubble in its broad stone bowl with a multicolored shimmer, the billowing steam glistering from within. Spilling over the lip of the bowl, the water bathed the oak's roots and soaked into the ground.

By the Wellspring, on a root polished to a gleam, sat an old man of enormous stature dressed in a simple dark-blue cloak and holding in his right hand a staff so white it seemed made of the purest mountain snows. Ever and again he scooped up a handful of water and flung it skyward, bringing forth another flash of lightning, which he did, I thought then, to allay his boredom or for his own amusement. He was thin, raw-boned, gray-haired, and his hands looked brown; but there burned such a fire in his eyes the gods themselves might envy the strength in that old body.

My little spy took to nosing around the Wellspring, disentangling the intricate mass of highly complex charms that held this truly great interweaving of wizardly forces in balance. All the enchantments fed upon the Wellspring's strength, but whence it derived that strength remained a mystery to me.

Yet I understood the crux of it. Before me was the legendary Wisdomwell and its master, Mimir. That was a name young Mages learned at the very beginning of their instruction, from the very first ballads they heard and tales they read. But all those ballads told that at the bottom of the Wellspring lay the Lord of Asgard's pledge—more simply put, Old Hropt's right eye. Great storms had ranged over the world since that time, lands had changed their aspect; and the fearsome pledge had come back into the possession of the Father of Hosts.

Nor had the Wellspring itself remained unchanged. As my little agent circled that stone bowl, it gradually began to outline for me the astonishing cluster of primordial energies that flowed into the Earth here, bestowing some of their might upon the Spring on their way. The gigantic, indescribable, unimaginable Power the Creator had laid in our world at the beginning of time, and which had since revolved within it, adopting a numberless multiplicity of forms, was here being used to replenish the might of the Young Gods.

All that would, of course, have to be rigorously proven. Complex calculations would have to be performed, and the systems of transforming spells employed here would have to be studied in detail. My proxy was conscientiously collecting all possible intelligence, and gladly would I apply myself to the task—but later, at my leisure. Now, there was something of greater importance.

Iamerth's emblem was connected in some way with the Wellspring. What did that signify?

As if in response to my unspoken question, the beastling carefully approached the edge of the stone bowl. The Sentinel of the Well, whistling into his thick white whiskers and lighting up the sky with one lightning bolt after another, seemed not to notice.

I was looking now at the water's seething surface. Through the bubbles that rose and burst, the bottom could clearly be seen. There lay seven emblems, neatly arrayed—seven exact copies of those that had fallen into our hands and which the Young Gods had not rushed to rescue as I had expected they would.

The veil fell from my eyes. I gritted my teeth to hold back a groan of scalding shame. *We have been duped, duped like children, and now the Masters of the Hallowed Land are probably shrieking with laughter at our clumsy efforts to call them out.* It was clearer than clear to me then that the real emblems, the links between each Young God's Essence and those inexhaustible stores of Power, lay there, in that hidden place, accessible to neither Mages nor mortals where we young wizards, heirs to the gramarye of the Ancients, had been taken once and once only, for what exact reason I knew not. Perhaps somehow to commune with the great magical energy that permeated all the world.

The Temple of Iamerth that had fallen so unexpectedly to my apprentice contained only a copy of Iamerth's emblem, though it was directly connected with the true Stone of Power. Even the copy could probably endow the temple priests with wizardly abilities, but then and there I sensed squarely that it had another purpose also. I had no proof, but could not question my intuition.

Through that copy, the gods could at any second send a flood of murderous might from the fathomless Wellspring to Hedinseigh, turning to ash the entire island and all that lived there. And of course, they could see and hear all that transpired here.

Yet there they had erred. They had not considered, not even for an instant, that I might be able to puzzle out the complex system of defensive spells or that my envoy might find its way into that bewitched sphere.

But then... why have I not been destroyed? Perhaps they don't know that my spy has paid a call on Mimir? Or are they playing a game so subtle as to defy my understanding? Or are we, Mage Hedin, mistaken after all—could we be shielded here from the Wellspring of the Worlds' fierce fire?

By an effort of will suppressing a chaotic swirl of thoughts guided by neither rudder nor sail, I tried to recall Sigrlinn's exact words. She had said something to the effect that only the gods may enter the Seething—or some such epithet—Fountainhead, and that if I were to do so, the whole world would tumble into a cavernous pit.

I knew then I must go a-calling on Mimir, whether he welcomed me or not and whatever the cost.

Who knows? Perhaps there, at the bottom of that stone bowl, lies our only chance of halting the Unnamable. I did not doubt Merlin and the Young Gods already knew what was happening, and for that reason alone had left us in peace. Most likely the present threat was too serious for precious time to be wasted in bringing two presumptuous Mages to heel. Perhaps Merlin would, in due course, again turn his gracious attention upon us, but for now the gods were clearly occupied elsewhere. They had not even troubled to call off their faithful servants, who were mounting a foredoomed assault on Hedinseigh.

But maybe the endless squabbling among the Mages is to the gods' advantage. The thought was sudden. *Could that be why they are in no hurry to settle with us? A pike in the pool, as they say, keeps the carp alert. Or is it that Mages who are busy fighting among themselves can never unite and dethrone the Young Gods, much as they themselves dethroned the first masters of this world, Old Hropt and his fellows?*

I clutched my head in my hands. Once I had deemed myself master of such maneuvers, had prided myself on my ability to achieve all through guile rather than brute force—unlike Rakoth, with his constant reliance upon the size and might of his armies. I had prided myself as a practiced hand, while in truth I was a pitiful novice who must learn the art of warfare from the real adepts.

But what should I do with the emblem? Fear prompted me to dispose of it with all speed—to stow it aboard an old decommissioned dragon-ship that would be towed far away from Hedinseigh on a long line and scuttled on the high seas. The Young Gods would hardly expect me to divest myself of such a treasure, certain as they were that I prized the emblem as a priceless trophy.

And there was your plan's weakest point, I told myself, *your assumption the Young Gods would intervene and thus allow you to unriddle the sources of their power and the applications of that power. That, with this in hand, you would then be able to fashion a defense and know what was needed to breach their armor. But they have not yielded, have not swallowed the lure.*

Indeed, I had come upon one of the roots of their might by simple chance, and belatedly. Meanwhile, though, Rakoth the Rebel, Rakoth the Fallen Mage, was free, and sooner or later the entire Hallowed Land would descend upon us. If, of course, the Unnamable did not devour us all first.

I poked my head through an embrasure. Rakoth was still issuing orders to his legions, like a little boy playing with a new box of tin soldiers. Belike it would be best not to let him in on all the particulars of my discoveries. The time was not ripe, and he was hot-blooded and quite capable of racing off on his own hunt for the Wellspring. But Old Hropt must generally know the way there, though the Young Gods could have shuffled the courses of the Real like a pack of cards since the days when the Lord of Asgard ruled the world of Hjorvard and Mimir's Well could be reached by one traveling on foot.

I had at my disposal one other form of magic I had not yet applied in this war. Very powerful it was and, sure as Fate, mortally dangerous to anyone rash enough to employ it. It was the Magic of the Dragons of Time.

No one had ever seriously studied those mysterious creatures. They were to most a given—eternal and immutable, a peculiar whim of the Creator, Who had created, for reasons known only to Himself, the Great River of Time that surges unceasingly from future to past and had submerged them in it. Yet they, like any other sorcerous Being—a troll, say, or a unicorn—had their own magic, which may be studied but whose use...

Aye, it had been for me a toil, but as in many other difficult straits when the classical magic we were taught by the Ancients proved powerless, I was, strange to say, aided by my exile. It was nothing less than striking, the diligence with which the Ancients had narrowed the scope of the wizardry accessible to us. Had they foreseen our propensity for bickering with the Young Gods?

Since a whole saga could be written to tell how I tapped into the secrets of the Dragons of Time, I shall limit myself here to a brief excursus.

I had sought out the sanctuary of a very ancient people who, for untold ages, had bowed the knee to Almighty Time, whose incarnation they saw in the mighty Dragons that lived in the Great River. For hundreds—for thousands— of years, amidst the snowbound mountains and plains of Northern Hjorvard, that people had slowly forged a keen blade of wisdom. Its wizards and priests had more than once reached a place of enlightenment, raising themselves up in their mind's eye to the Astral Plane and beyond, as far as the Great River itself, where they watched the Dragons frolicking in its waves. Little by little, they learned to communicate with them, and not only recorded all this diligently on scrolls but also carved it in stone, in the very deepest crypts of their temple in the rocks.

Then one of the Ancients—or Merlin or maybe even one of the Young Gods—bethought himself and vented his wrath upon those audacious mortals. Fire, water and terrible demons of fire, from which there was no escape either on or beneath the Earth, devastated their tribe; and earthquakes carried all to completion by collapsing the galleries carved into solid granite. The parchments were lost, the rune-engraved slabs shattered and buried under great mounds the victors deemed impregnable. Satisfied, they departed.

But two families of that unfortunate people were left alive, having been far from home by chance on that day. When they returned, the injured and dying, before breathing their last, told them how the holy place had been destroyed; and those survivors swore a sacred oath they would find a way to exact retribution. From that were born, lived out their lives and sank into darkness many generations of the Guardians of the Holy Runes, as they styled themselves; and one fine day, I happened upon them.

Laborsome it was to dig down to the very deepest, most secret galleries, for the spiteful spirits of the Earth installed there to guard that place were unyielding, obstinate and had strength enough.

I spent close to twenty-five years reading those shattered pages, and at the end of all did not become Overlord of the Dragons of Time, that being reserved to the Creator alone. But something of their magic I did learn to employ.

It was in very truth a terrible skill, somewhat resembling Rakoth's ill-starred curse that had called the Unnamable into the world. Having once broken free of the unseen chains of wizardry that bound them, it would have been mere sport for the Dragons to make dust of the Worldframe—indeed, of All That Is—with their fangs. So, I was withholding them until the decisive moment, the crisis I had dubbed in my mind "the storming of the Hallowed

Land"—which now, seemingly, could not take place until I had first clawed my way to Mimir's Well.

I had no desire whatsoever to use this last resource. For all anyone knew, the Dragons of Time might at last need be called upon to halt the Unnamable, but I could in no way be certain the same spells could be applied to them twice with equal results, and it would take years to compose and test new ones.

I was much troubled, too, by the strange sorcery discerned by the Diviner that had, it said, been made by some mortal wizard. Also, two things in Hagen's tale of the battle on Avalon had alarmed me more than aught else, for the simple reason that I could not explain them. The first was the unlooked-for visit of a servant of the Distant Powers to Merlin's abode. The second was Hagen's unexpected encounter with Brann Shrunkenhand. Plainly, that rendezvous had been arranged by the Archmage himself, but to what purpose?

I suspected Brann of supporting one of the parties in this conflict, but which? He could with equal success have served Merlin or Sigrlinn or Orlangur or Demogorgon or the Young Gods, and why not the Distant or Ancient Powers—or Chaos itself through the agency of the warlocks of Brandeigh? There had to be a reason why he had slipped unharmed from the claws of Iargohor, Conveyor of the Dead, and had brought Hagen away safe, too.

That the Leader of the Council of the Generation had willed my apprentice into combat with one who had but recently been his guide did not sit well with me at all. The Diviner had yet to make good sense of all the charms Merlin had brought to bear when the legions of Hedinseigh had set foot on the soil of Avalon, having had much else to concern itself with; but I felt that effort must eventually be made. *Until your warriors set peaceful villages afire I shall be no enemy to you,* Shrunkenhand had told Hagen, and a village *had* been set afire, albeit only one and through the fault of Avalon's enchanter. But did that mean Brann was now one more to contend with, and would soon begin enlisting human troops in Hjorvard?

I did not for a minute doubt him capable of that.

The Diviner drew me from my perplexity, and I was almost relieved to hear that the armies of the Castle of all the Ancients were closing on Hedinseigh. This time, though, my kinsfolk had come, too, having likely learned something from the failures of the Hungering Stars and the Disembodied. Very well, then—it was time to send forth Rakoth's legions.

I did not know if the Castle had already received the news the forces of Darkness had gathered and were ready to fight.

Yet, this time I hesitated somewhat, for the Mages had thrown against us not only monsters and manikins made by their art but also simple mortals called from other worlds, unfortunates worthy only of pity. I cared not at all to raise a bloody abattoir by my fortress walls—I, too, had learned lessons from the fall of the Empire of Night.

I knew I must separate the humans from the monsters, which latter I would have no hesitation in destroying. My intent was, with as little bloodshed as possible, to drive the humans from the field of battle. I thought of the never-to-be-forgotten stone that had closed the Gates of the Worlds on the day of our attack upon the Lesser Temple of the Sun in Erivag...

"Rakoth!" I called low.

"Here!" a powerful voice replied. The Fallen Mage appeared in the middle of the room, draped in his famous crimson cloak, the one he had worn during the desperate siege when his regiments had broken though the last barriers between them and the Hallowed Land, only to be crushed at its very threshold.

"Deploy your forces," I told him, reviving my model of the Worldsphere with a spell. "Our guests are on their way." And I quickly told him my plans.

Rakoth nodded. "Good. I must say I don't understand why we are putting our soldiers at risk so as to separate or isolate those...But let it be. This is your island, and I shall do as you say."

"Then hurry!" I tilted my head toward my model, even though the approaching armies could be seen just by looking through the window.

Although the sun was already dipping toward the horizon, there were a good six hours of daylight left to us, for the summer nights are short on Hedinseigh. The clouds had disappeared, as if in fear of the battle to come; and the serene afternoon sky sprawled overhead like a panther at rest. There were black dots and dashes on the horizon—vessels plying land and air, carrying numberless hordes gathered by the Castle Mages from worlds both adjacent and remote. I sensed my kinsfolk's presence, although they had not as yet shown themselves. Evidently, they were busy preparing their first attack.

Rakoth left to disperse his regiments, while I sent for the chiliarch Gerder. I ordered him to conceal all the humans and goblins in the underground chambers and to stay well out of the battle. After dismissing him, I went to Ilving.

Fear lay buried in those deep eyes, but jarl's daughter and thane's wife as she was, she listened impassively to my cautions. Then she said sharply, "It does not befit a wife to flee from the danger to which her husband is subject." She turned away from me. "I stay, and so does my son. That is my last word, wizard."

An amiable word it was not, but I understood why. She was afraid and was trying to hide her fear from all, and from herself first and foremost.

"As you will." I inclined my head to her. "Then, as the wife of a thane—"

Again she cut me short. "I know where my duties lie. Fear not. All the women and children remaining in the fortress shall be safely hidden in the crypts, but such as know how to bind wounds and care for the injured shall be sent to the aid of my husband's warriors. I shall accompany them."

I nodded again. This little woman had a firmness of spirit my apprentice's most rakish hellion might have envied.

I left, and made my last rounds of the fortifications before battle was joined. They had honorably stood during the first siege, and I did not doubt they would hold this time.

But then, from somewhere deep within floated a vague presentiment that we were fated to be besieged again after this; and an icy wave seemed to wash over me at the thought. An ill omen it was—so ill it took me a few minutes to dispel the blackness in my mind.

Files of warriors were descending the long stairways into the safety of chambers hidden deep underground within the strong stone bones that underpinned the island. Their arrows and swords could not help Hedinseigh against the forces now readying their decisive assault. Those who instead would fight under my apprentice's banners were, in their hundreds and their thousands, rising into the air, crawling across towers and bastions and diving into the shoreside waters.

An exhilarated Rakoth directed the complex torrents of his creatures, in his element once more, euphoric, without a thought as to how this all might end. No torments or sufferings, no defeats, not even the most cruel, could change him. He had, unfortunately, learned nothing.

But time passes, and still there is no sign of Hagen and Hropt. With alarm, I returned to my sanctum of spellcraft and asked the Diviner for the latest news. There was none, not a trace of sorcery, not even in the Icy Abyss that presently held my apprentice and the Father of Hosts. That alone was cause for suspicion. Could they have found nothing there to oppose them?

The little beast I had made of Light and Darkness scampered up and nudged its nose into my palm. *You have done well, little one, and your creator forgot all about you,* I thought ruefully. *You have earned a name. You shall no longer be a Mage's plaything, and shall become your own self.* Raising my right hand and covering the beastling with my left, I intoned these words:

"Henceforth and forever, I name you Hervind, which means 'He who is everywhere.'"

Then I cast a spell.

The newly baptized Hervind flinched under my fingers, and then I sensed a hot flow of gratitude streaming toward me. When a magical being receives from its creator a name of its own, it gains its freedom. Nevermore would any charm, including my own, force it to do aught it did not want to do. It had its own magic now, which a sorcerer would have to learn in order to exert authority over it.

"I will make a request of you," I told my fresh-minted assistant. "There must be a return to the world of the Wellspring. An exploration of the road. An understanding of what Mimir does there. What people are they who live in the village by the Seething Fountainhead? And what are those strange, sharp facets on the mountain on the way to the spring? They strongly call to mind gigantic swords embedded in the mountainside. Find out all that if you can, please."

The response was a feeling, silent but unmistakable. *I shall do all or molder away. Doubt me not, Master.*

Two hops brought Hervind to Iamerth's emblem, which still lay in its marble base. Then he disappeared into the dark crystalline depths.

Now, if Merlin must hold his silence, and the Hallowed Land, too, we shall busy ourselves with those who knock at the door uninvited. I unsheathed the Black Sword and almost ran up to the observation platform.

My place was, in truth, not there. I should have stayed close by the Diviner, in order not to miss a single stroke of wizardry; but, for the first time in my life, instead I cast caution to the winds, so eager was I to behold the majestic and enthralling sight of those hordes deploying to engage in deadly combat.

Wherever I looked, the entire horizon, from one end to the other, was crowded with approaching enemy vessels. Soaring in the spaces between them, with an occasional flap of huge wings, were things that resembled dragons but were a little smaller, less powerful and did not breathe fire. Even higher, above the slender masts and scaly backs, was a disorderly fluttering of smaller creatures that looked from my vantage point like a swarm of black dots. Something was tumbling in the waves beside the ships' prows; large bubbles burst on the surface of the water, as if marking steady breathing in the depths.

My kin were also near; I sensed their presence. They had come together somewhere behind the main forces and, like me, were sending out from there the long, sensitive feelers of Scouting Charms.

My Generation, then, had thought better of calling me out to a purely magical duel. Though their first siege had failed, they had again gathered their legions, were again prepared to send out living flesh, to form it into a suicidal battering ram and throw it against the barriers and screens of fangs, claws, sickles, saws, pincers and other keen-edged weapons employed in abundance by the fosterlings of Rakoth, erstwhile Overlord of Darkness.

It was an alluring, an intriguing sight, and I was tempted to stay where I was and simply watch—a neutral and impartial witness of a gripping, if bloody, spectacle.

Dismissing those importunate thoughts, I returned to my apartments.

— *You will never assemble enough souls to pay me fair,* the Diviner grated in my mind.

— *Let us first live till the morrow,* I replied wearily.

All at once, I distinctly sensed myself being summoned in the wonted way, and hastened to don the Band of Erith. Shendar's familiar words I heard then, thunderously delivered and bitter in their flavor, anent immediate surrender, punishment, vengeance, order in the world and on and on. I had heard it all dozens of times before, and now did not even much try to comprehend his meaning.

When at length he had said all and fell silent, I gave him my reply.

— *There is naught new here, Shendar. I had hoped you would have something of greater interest to offer. I have long cared nothing for any of your doings. Have at it. Begin your siege, if you wish, and remember that if you fail...*

At that I stopped, pulling myself up in the nick of time, for I had almost blurted out Felostei's secret intent. They should instead go on thinking they had time aplenty, and that there was nothing to stop them from organizing yet another assault if this one did not come off—else they would, I feared, fight now like mad things.

Not waiting for a reply, I tore the Band from my brow.

The Diviner again gave voice.

— *Sorcery! Sorcery in the Icy Abyss! He whom you style Hropt has conjured a very old charm, a Charm of Rending, Riving and Rupture!*

So, there it began. It was, for all I knew, possibly better for my apprentice to bide in that inhospitable place, tackling first one monster then another—he and the Father of Hosts together would surely prevail—than to be with us here in the thick of this fray. Were he at hand, my kinsfolk would stop at nothing to kill him.

There came from without the strange sound of thousands upon thousands of living beings groaning dolefully and piteously, racked by agony. Soon, though, the noise died away, slowly dissolving into a low, rolling growl that closed in menacingly from all sides, like the muted rumble of distant thunder. Unable to resist, I thrust my head outside.

A blinding-bright light was flooding the motionless sea, as if Iamerth were trying to burn up everything, leaving not a shadow behind. The Mage-vessels moved ever faster toward the island, gaining speed every instant, while the winged creatures kept pace. I had also expected to spy, somewhere to the rear, the Sentinels of the Hallowed Land, but they were as yet nowhere to be seen— indeed, their masters may not even have deigned to dispatch their servants into this battle.

I did, however, catch sight of numerous old acquaintances that had sought to block my way to the Netherside. *Only let them not summon the Disembodied,* I thought, with a pang of fear.

But those evilsome spirits would hardly have resolved so soon on another incursion, not after having been so recently trounced by the Children of Demogorgon.

The numberless horde was flocking, rolling, swimming, flying full at us, a multitude of magical shields covering its vanguard against the chance I might flout the Great Law of the Ancients by daring to slay mortals. It was likely with that in mind the commanders of the Castle forces had drawn up formations of mortals alongside those of monsters to which that prohibition did not apply.

I saw Rakoth, contrary to his byname of Fallen Mage, soaring proudly aloft on the back of a wondrous beast with astounding emerald feathers, a short powerful neck and long paws ending in scythe-like claws. The creature had no wings, and I could only marvel at the speed with which the Rebel was regaining his magical powers, it being far from simple to compel skyward a being born to walk the Earth.

The defenders of Hedinseigh were in position, a few circling above the island while the remainder stayed within the protection of the fortress walls or skulked in the depths of the sea. Rakoth did not intend to attack first—rather, he was drawing our foes into the offensive.

So, the first blow dealt to our defenses came from my kin. The Diviner let out a sudden yelp, and I felt a terrible pressure upon me that grew with every second. The air above the fortress seemed to have turned to stone, and my shoulders sagged under the immeasurable weight of mountain ranges. Through the bloody murk that filled my eyes, I tried to read the runes the Diviner obligingly displayed for me, endeavoring with all speed to find the spell's tender spot.

Then, in the Spheres of Ether there appeared the utterly unbelievable. A magical battle had begun to play out in the Icy Abyss, too, and the Diviner cried out three short words.

— *The Distant Ones!*

Before I could think what to do, I had also recognized the presence of Sigrlinn's incomparable magic-making. *Are they in league now?* I wondered.

Then, outside the walls, thousands upon thousands of horns sounded. The Mage Army had launched its assault upon Hedinseigh.

CHAPTER XIII

A T SIGHT OF SIGRLINN, HROPT FIRST GOGGLED IN SURPRISE AND FOLLOWED THAT WITH A protracted stream of the blackest imprecations. The sorceress, wrapped in a long green cloak, came slowly on, staring straight ahead. She must have seen Hropt and Hagen, yet her lovely alabastrine face changed not at all, as if she had been suddenly blinded or was engulfed in darkness.

"She it was who led the Distant Ones here," Hropt roared. "Alone they would never have found the way. They are hunters after souls, and your army is their quarry.

"Much idle chatter have I heard about them, but I believed none of it," he continued more calmly, seeing that the Distant Ones were making extremely slow progress toward them. "It is said they catch people and separate body and soul, like our Devourers, and make of those souls something even I durst not speak aloud. I did not believe it, for sure I did not, and now I see the error of my ways."

The Distant Ones—those twelve faceless figures—continued their leisurely descent, Sigrlinn ambling among them like a sleepwalker or one in the grip of a powerful charm. Hagen was left in no doubt as to the intentions of these beings, since they were making straight for him and Hropt.

"Belike she herself is a prisoner, and under enchantment," he argued. somewhat uncertainly. "I would pay dear to have that wiccan with her Fiery Chalice somewhere close at hand."

"The last thing you want to do now is call on a Darkling Rider's aid" was Hropt's testy reply.

They stood side by side, swords drawn, waiting for the enemy to come to them. Hagen's army was already climbing the slope opposite; only Frodi, Isung, Gudmund and a few others hung back in the middle of the hollow.

"Tell me, Hropt, how are they to be stopped?" the thane asked brusquely, not turning to look at his companion. He was unable to tear his eyes from the figures' slow approach. Something soulless there was in their movement; it seemed the motion not of living beings but of lifeless machines, like catapults or ballistas.

"You have a Disc of Iamerth at your belt," the Father of Hosts replied. "If that doesn't stop them, nothing will. Our swords are quick, but a Weapon of Light is what it is. Do not allow them close."

Hagen's hand obeyed unwillingly. As if lifting a heavy load, he unchained the Disc from his belt and fixed his eyes on his enemies' rearguard as he prepared to recite the spell that would decide all.

All at once, an entirely unexpected and wholly alien thought stabbed him: *Why should the first offensive be mine?* Never before had such doubts assailed him on the field of battle; he knew for a certainty that he who does not deal the first blow will be given neither time nor opportunity to answer an enemy strike. He had always followed that artless principle, and success had never slighted him—not among the tall turrets on Western Hjorvard's windy plains, nor upon the hot hills of the South, nor amid the standing ice of the Northern Continent.

Only here, in the otherworld of the Icy Abyss, watching beings that differed in every way from the Creator's Elder and Younger offspring move toward him, had he ever hesitated. Something prevented him from loosing the death-dealing Disc, from being the first to spill blood. Perhaps they might yet part in peace?

"Why do you delay?" the Father of Hosts snarled. "Throw the Disc!"

"They have yet to do us any harm," Hagen argued, surprised by the sound of his own voice. It was as if someone else—a puppetmaster behind the curtain of a traveling show—were speaking through him.

"And when they do, it'll be too late," Hropt promised him. "What ails you? Hagen!" he roared in a voice so inhuman even the Distant Ones halted for a moment. "Hagen, rouse yourself! It is an enchantment! It is Sigrlinn—curses upon her, world without end!"

The sorceress in the emerald cloak responded in no way to that frenzied howling, although she could not but have heard it, were she in full possession of her senses.

Hropt shook Hagen by the shoulder hard several times, as if that could avail against wizardry, then, wasting no more time, mounted his own attack. A once-dread charm rang out again. In times past, it would have turned mountain ranges to dust, would have boiled the very seas away to an arid wasteland, but now it only melted the snow under Sigrlinn's feet.

Hropt gave the hollow, hoarse gasp of a mortally wounded beast, seized his sword and ran to meet the Distant Ones.

A malevolent, warlike roar rang out at Hagen's back. It was the goblin chieftain, the fearless Orc, who brandished his curved ataghan of burnished steel and raced after Hropt, his momentum drawing the others on behind him. Gudmund was already spinning his hooked knife on its long chain above his head, Frodi raised the cudgel he had moments before dropped into the snow. Only Hagen remained in that strange stupor, unable to move arm or leg or even to call upon his Teacher.

The Distant Ones' column, that whorl of transparent green spirals, suddenly reared like a striking snake, and its open mouth hovered over Hropt. The Golden Sword, whistling, clove the air, making contact with the outer spiral, striking a sheaf of luminous grass-green sparks from it and splitting it open. Streams of translucent flame the color of verdant young leaves spurted from the cut, and the column jerked spasmodically like a creature severely wounded. Hropt brought his sword up again but was knocked off his feet, almost like Hagen in his skirmish with the ice-snake; and the Father of Hosts rolled down the slope, sending up a cloud of powdery snow.

The Distant Ones had made no effort to intervene. The column straightened and was still, but something was clearly amiss. The sinuous spirals rotated yet, but were less orderly now, and shudders rippled across the gleaming pillar.

Snarling, spitting and muttering, Old Hropt struggled to his feet. His sheepskin coat smoked and was charred in several places where the green spirals had touched it. There the Father of Hosts stood, looking not in the least daunted, his shoulders hunched, drowning in his shapeless coat, his arms hanging loosely.

The Distant Ones came on more quickly now; and as if pulled by invisible ropes, Sigrlinn, too, lurched forward. Her escort left no tracks in the snow on that rapid descent; only the sorceress was trailed by an uneven chain of dark indentations made by her small feet.

The scene that followed etched itself forever into the memory of Hedinseigh's thane. The stooping Hropt suddenly straightened and cast off his ridiculous sheepskin to reveal a broad, double-edged throwing knife with two diverging blades. With a quick flip of the hand, the weapon flew at the sorceress.

The Old God and Lord of Asgard was not, of course, relying altogether upon mere rude weaponry, for the blade was enchanted. Hropt had likely kept it with him through the long millennia of his life, and had laid the spell in the days when the Aesir ruled the world.

Sigrlinn did not even try to evade it, much less raise any defensive charms against it; the Distant Ones did all for her. Four tall figures in filmy green cloaks dissolved into the air and an indistinguishably brief moment later appeared in front of her, shielding her with their bodies from that fleet blade.

Though the long years, Hropt had retained the incomparable skills that had been his as warlord of Valhalla. His knife flew with the speed of Thor's famed Mjolnir, puncturing the neck of one of the Distant Ones, passing right through and...disintegrating in a puff of black ash that settled slowly onto the snow.

The body in its vaporous green cloak slowly bent double; and Hagen, still stupefied, waited for it to fall. Instead, it straightened, albeit with apparent difficulty, and continued on its way.

The green figures had returned to their places and were again marching forward—intractably, inescapably, inexorably.

But Hropt did not yield. His sword atilt, he strode toward a Distant One on the far flank and swung his arm.

Struck unexpectedly in the chest by an unseen hand, Hropt toppled onto his back. The Distant One leaned unhurriedly down, and a greenish radiance began to flow from it to the supine body. For a few seconds nothing happened. Then, the Father of Hosts gave a sudden, ear-stopping yell, a wild cry of pain and of horror more inexpressible than the Ancient God had ever known.

"Ha-a-a-gen!"

Only then did the thane come out of his trance. To that point, he had been looking on indifferently, immersed in a slumbrous haze and lacking the strength to counter the charm he sensed was on him. Hropt's cry gave him unlooked-for strength, and he began trying to defend himself against that hostile wizardry. At first sluggish and unsure, then with growing fervor, he applied techniques of the highest refinement he had studied diligently in times past, his Teacher having taken the greatest care that his apprentice should always be able to carry the day against wizards and shamans of any tribe, human or alv. The enchantments laid upon him were neither strong nor artfully woven, and from the powerful sorcery being conjured throughout the wider world there was strength to be had. Hagen made good use of that rampaging flow of magical energies.

But the charm, though inartful, was robust, and the thane was pierced with a cruel pang when he bent to draw from the river of wizardry. Still, though wincing and hissing with the pain, he was able to pull himself upright and recite the Bracing Charm.

A sharp, invisible knife sliced and sundered the gray snares of impotence and indifference, the torpor vanished, and his hand flashed toward the Disc of Iamerth.

Nothing could hold him now. He was himself again, and a familiar cold hatred surfaced in him, which did not hamper his aim or his ability to parry a blow but made his body swift and obedient. The spectral white lightning of the Sun's Disc rent the air and the flying streamers of snow.

Though Old Hropt believed Sigrlinn to be their prime enemy, Hagen aimed at the warrior that leaned over the prostrate Ancient. The thane had seen what happened to the Father of Hosts' throwing knife, even though its owner was protected by mighty combat charms of yore. The wizardry of the Time Before Time, when the world was young, was powerless over the Distant Ones, they having appeared there much later, after the Young Gods had laid hands upon All That Is.

The Disc of Iamerth sliced into the Distant One's head with a sharp, ear-splitting grinding sound; and it seemed to Hagen that the death-dealing circle had struck not flesh but stone. Throwing up a spray of fine green dust, quivering and shuddering, the Disc began slowly to dive into the body of the being Hagen had, for want of a better name, dubbed a Distant Warrior. It was much as when the Disc had delved into real stone, in the ravine hard by the Living Crags and in Merlin's hall of spellcraft on Avalon.

The smitten servant of the Distant Powers froze in place, and Hropt took the opportunity to roll aside, leap to his feet and swing his blade.

Ringing, the Golden Sword rebounded from the Distant One's stone neck.

Hagen at first fancied the remaining eleven were paying no attention to any of this. The Disc had split the mysterious being's head in two; one of the halves came away and fell into the snow. The glittering circle was then free to speed back to the thane's hand, but its flight was suddenly halted as the air rapidly thickened, making breathing impossible and tearing the lungs from within with a dull, oppressive pain. This was the sorcery of the Distant Ones, and Hagen knew no defense against it.

Old Hropt's mind, though, had yielded a valuable memory. In his comfortless wanderings after the destruction of all his world, his cohorts, his Asgard and its gods, Sleipnir's master had passed down many a strange road; and although he had not gleaned as much priceless knowledge nor as many magical devices as Hagen's Teacher had in his own roamings, he had come upon the Distant Ones. As luck would have it, he was now able to recall something that would serve well in the present plight.

Drawing himself up, the Ancient God threw aside his sword. The dense, poisonous fog the air had become seemed to do him no harm. He seized up the half-head sheared off by the Disc, which now resembled nothing so much as a simple, smoothly chiseled block of plain greenish stone, and, groaning with the effort, flung it at the shoulder of the nearest Distant Warrior.

Old Hropt himself probably did not fully foresee all the consequences of that desperate act. No one had ever pondered the inner import of the name "Distant Powers," and even Hedin's refined intellect had been satisfied by the explanation that it signified only that the bearers of those powers had entered this world from far away, from the furthest confines of Chaos.

Fragments of the Distant Powers must, I dare say, keep a due distance between them, Hagen thought briefly as he watched the long greenish body, flung back by Hropt's fearsome blow, sailing off in a smooth arc, even though the Ancient God's bizarre weapon had never touched it.

The rest of the Distant Ones probably then shifted their sorcerous powers to restraining their kinsman's backward flight, for the air instantly cleared and the terrible stifling disappeared without trace. Hropt's blow had the additional effect of weakening the unseen toils that bound Sigrlinn. The sorceress's eyes suddenly opened, their burning gaze meeting the thane's.

"Hagen!" she cried, then gave a hoarse gasp and jerked forward, as if under the lash of an invisible whip.

The body of the Distant One beheaded by the Sun's Disc began slowly to rise. It moved like an automaton, but with far greater ease. Before Hropt could turn, the green figure slammed into him and knocked him off his feet, and the two adversaries were swaddled in an impenetrable green shroud beneath which the Father of Hosts could be heard howling wildly.

Hagen lingered no longer. He felt out the lengthy, unseen threads along which the Power flowed to direct the headless body and hold Sigrlinn in rigorous captivity and aimed the Disc once more, this time not at the nearest Distant Warrior but at those ethereal conduits for an alien wizardry.

The Disc seemed to cry out, in a voice loud and human, as it cut through those sinister navel-cords. There was a flash, the droning sound of invisible strings bursting, and the weapon returned to him, its glittering surface marked now with dark spots of charring. The half-decapitated stone body collapsed on Hropt, pressing him into the snow, but the malevolent, putrid-green glimmer had disappeared, and the Father of Hosts could move again.

The sorceress darted aside—a doe breaking free of her tether—as green lightning wound into a wondrous spiral burst over the combatants' heads.

Now the Distant Ones were seized with urgency. They were fronted by three adversaries, any one of whom could outmatch their small band, but the faceless warriors had not come idly by their reputation for possessing the most enigmatic powers to be found in the Well-Ordered. The column of green spirals was moving again, clearly making for Hropt, who still floundered trying to throw off the crushing weight of that stone body. Sigrlinn was surrounded by a roundelay of dancing green sparks; and although the fire went out before reaching her, again her arms drooped listlessly, leaving her unable to conjure even a single Assaultcharm.

Meanwhile, the eleven remaining Distant Warriors rushed at Hagen.

A faceless giant that had pulled two steps ahead of the rest slowly bent double, its chest split asunder. The Disc returned to Hagen's hand, and he prepared another strike; but the snakelike living column, wound about with spirals, had reached Hropt, who lay clumsily about with his sword, which he had by some wonder managed to retrieve from the trampled snow. The blow went aslant, the blade glancing off harmlessly, and even Iamerth the Most Fair could not have foretold what would have happened to the Father of Hosts in the next moment had not the Distant Forces' weapon encountered first the fury of Hagen's Disc.

There was a clap of thunder as deafening as the peal of a colossal tocsin, the greenish entwinement trembled feverishly, and fiery green blood flowed from the gashed spirals. Breaking at the point where the Disc had sliced into it, the column collapsed, burning to black ash the ground that for an instant showed beneath the snow.

But the Distant Ones were unmoved. Invisible iron fists hit the thane hard in the chest, tossing him backward. Everything went murky as he fell, but his fingers still kept a rock-hard grip on the precious Disc.

The fallen thane's men came to his aid then, the long-legged Isung colliding full on with a rapidly advancing Distant Warrior. His sword, gnome-made though it was, broke against the stone head, and the shock threw him down on one knee.

Isung, that paragon of strength, would have risen, had he been contending against man, goblin, elf, troll or kobold; but he was facing a Distant One, and the paltry flesh of a piteous mortal held no interest whatsoever for a creature of stone.

The thane's hair stood on end. For the first time in his life, he knew a crushing, enfeebling, invincible horror that invaded the very depths of his mind, draining his strength and his will to fight. From the Distant One's unseeable throat burst a deep-chested growl alongside which the roar of a feeding lion in the torrid deserts of Southern Hjorvard was but a gentle lullaby. A green ray from the Distant Warrior's brow touched the place where, beneath an unmarred hauberk, pulsated a living human heart. From Isung was wrung a short, stifled howl, and he collapsed onto the snow. The outlines of his body seemed to wear away, to dissolve—or perhaps Hagen only fancied it so?—and over the chest of the fallen man there slowly rose a dim light, like a butterfly with wings of fire. The wings fluttered once, twice, and the butterfly was taken up by that green ray, which was quickly gathered back into the Distant Warrior's head.

The Warrior made an indescribable muttering sound, low and querulous yet somehow satisfied, sharply straightened up—and Hagen was struck so forcibly that all his bones cracked, and for an instant he fainted away. He would have sworn on oath he had seen the soul of his faithful companion-in-arms consumed by an unknown being the means of whose own dispatch was yet moot, and that the devoured soul had strengthened the Distant Warrior many times over.

Not eleven now but ten tall stone creatures bereft of faces moved on the thane. The eleventh, its chest riven, still sat on the snow but was already beginning to stir. Sigrlinn was locked in a frantic struggle with the green dust that beset her and would not let her be. There was no help to be expected from her.

The apprentice of Mage Hedin might well have seen his end that day, had it not been for Orc. The goblin chieftain feared nothing—not elves, nor Mages, nor gods, nor humans. All he desired was to save his tribe from utter destruction, and the Thane of Hedinseigh was his only ally on the entire vast and inhospitable Earth. Orc would rather have diced himself into small pieces than allow Hagen to perish before his eyes.

Two Distant Ones were already leaning over the prostrate thane when the redoubtable goblin appeared alongside.

"Beware! They wrest souls from bodies!" Hagen rasped, trying to return the Disc of Iamerth to obedience.

"So they may, but goblins have no souls," came in hollow tones from under the low helmet.

The burnished steel ataghan flew up and swept down; and as the dark, glittering blade flew to its target on the Distant One's neck, the long history of that sword flashed before Hagen's eyes. The last of the blades forged by Rakoth's smiths in his halcyon days, it had somehow survived the universal upheaval after the Young Gods' victory, which included their search for the weapon that had been crafted within the Dark Boundaries. The ataghan had passed from hand to hand among the goblin chieftains of Eastern Hjorvard like a great and peerless relic, and it was never used. Only Orc, in preparation for the campaign against Vidrir's capital, had dared unlock its carefully chosen hiding place out in the fens.

The powerful enchantments the Lord of Gloom had laid upon the blade awoke then to life. Rakoth had woven there a great many murderous spells, employing all his considerable talent, and had then forgotten how, or had been simply unable, to repeat his masterwork.

The ataghan split the Distant One's neck in twain as if it were made not of stone stronger than any on the Earth but of yielding flesh. When the blade had done its deed, it flared with a pallid, poisonous flame and became a sprinkle of black ash.

The green, soul-wresting ray slid along the goblin's broad chest, but to no avail—Orc did not even sway. In that instant, Hagen at last brought his Disc back into play.

As another Distant Warrior slumped to the snow, he rose. Old Hropt had contrived to free himself. Like a hunting dog, the Ancient God sniffed the frosty air, and Hagen knew why—he was searching for traces of Rakoth's charm that would bring death to the Distant Ones.

Now the Disc of Iamerth whistled through the air with the speed of raindrops in a storm. Giving the enemy no time to recover, Hagen coldly, cruelly brought down every last one. They were not dead, though. Life clung to all but two—the one Orc had beheaded and the other Hropt had hit with the fragment of head. The rest were moving, trying to rise; these were not the convulsions that preceded death but were sensible and purposeful.

Meanwhile, the shining that surrounded Sigrlinn had faded away, and she it was who first came to herself.

"We must away with all speed—soon there will be hordes of them here! To your feet, Hagen, to your feet. Take up that goblin. At a dead run, all of you! Be gone from here!"

"Should we not first block their way?" Old Hropt asked, his voice hoarse.

Sigrlinn's fierce eyes flashed; she shook her head.

"The charm is too strong. I secured it so well it would take even me several days to destroy the passage from the Distant Ones' abode to the Icy Abyss. But enough of this prattle!" She stamped her foot. "We must run like the wind!"

"Presently." And Hropt again tried his sword against the neck of the Distant Warrior killed by Orc. This time his blade did not betray him, and before long Hagen and his companions were hastening away from that accursed hollow, leaving behind them the two truly dead bodies, each hacked into several large pieces.

They ran along the broad strip trampled by the army of Hedinseigh, and already had reached the crest of hills opposite when there was a savage glittering behind them, as from myriad green lightning bolts striking the ground.

"Don't look back!" Sigrlinn cried, forestalling Hagen's desire. "Do not turn your head! It is an invasion, and we cannot stop them! Quickly, before they sense our escape from this world!"

She would not allow him to slow his pace or turn around.

There followed a maddened race amid jutting blocks of ice. Hedin's apprentice felt the back of his neck crawling with an unmistakable foreboding that death was bearing down on them. He seemed to see the hollow they were quitting, but the snow had disappeared beneath a solid torrent of faceless warriors with bodies of stone...

In the wind-ravaged air immediately ahead of them burned, even and calm, the gilded light of a fine thread stretching from land to sky that marked the Gate into their own world. the world of Greater Hjorvard.

"Faster! Those curs will be upon us any moment!" the sorceress cried, with a glance behind.

Goblins and men strode one by one to that golden line and disappeared, until soon only three—Old Hropt, Hagen and Sigrlinn—were left in the Icy Abyss. Hedin's apprentice, still not trusting the enchantress they had rescued, approached the golden thread last, behind her, his Blue Sword at the ready.

A warm sea-wind touched frosted armor, the unbroken brightness of Hedinseigh's sky burned overhead; and towers, their outlines painfully familiar, rose to right and left. Hagen and his companions stood in the spacious fortress bailey while the last of the warriors they had delivered proceeded through the wide-flung gates of subterranean shelters.

But a harsh, ear-piecing wail came from all around beyond the walls, and Hagen unerringly recognized the sound of trumpets sounding the attack. A swift winged silhouette flashed across the sky, and Rakoth waved a greeting from his flying charger, his scarlet cloak undulating behind like a scrap of flame. Across the bailey toward Hagen and the rest ran Hedin—and pulled to a dead stop, as if he had come up against an invisible barrier, when he saw Sigrlinn.

Far less than an instant had passed before the air around him trembled with powerful defensive charms accompanied by forces gathered in readiness to strike an incinerating blow. Hagen could judge the measure of his Teacher's speed.

So could Sigrlinn.

"Powerfully and adroitly done, Hedin." She gave a wry smile that stopped short of her dark and wrathful eyes. "But I do not propose to vie with you today—unless, of course, you are resolved to test yourself."

The Mage directed at her an openly appraising glance then turned away, not favoring her with a single word, and put his arms around the shoulders of Hagen and Hropt.

"I am happy you have returned." His voice shook. "You had a hot time of it?"

"Right cold, I'd say," Old Hropt muttered. "Those Distant Ones nearly did for us all."

"Very well. We'll go up and talk." Hedin nodded toward the top of the keep. "Come along. Soon enough it will be…rather noisy here."

"And she?" Hagen tilted his head toward the sorceress.

"She? Don't concern yourself with her. Her power is almost gone."

"You could have kept that to yourself," Sigrlinn observed with cold rage.

"After you almost killed me in the Netherside?" Hedin asked point-blank, but the sorceress held his gaze, and only smiled scornfully.

Their conversation was again interrupted by the roar of numberless horns, and Hedin hastily ushered them all indoors.

"The Mages of my Generation tried to turn the air to stone," he remarked with the hint of a smile as they mounted the spiral staircase to his apartments. "That gave me some little trouble."

"And how did you shift with that?" Sigrlinn inquired venomously.

Hedin stopped. "There is something here I do not understand. Do you expect me to tell all these things in your presence? I have some wits left to me yet. And do not think me deterred by your present defenselessness. I remember well how it was." His cheek twitched, and he turned away.

They went up a few more flights in silence, until the Mage unexpectedly halted before an entirely unremarkable stretch of wall.

"After you." He stepped aside with ironic courtesy. "Fear not, it is for but a short time. I am no Merlin, and it is not my habit to torment and torture."

The masonry hazed and dimpled as they watched, and the mighty hewn blocks melted into the air, revealing an arch and, beyond it, a small windowless room lit by the even glow of magelight. The floor and walls were draped in rich dark-scarlet rugs, and on the table Hagen saw an elegant silver bowl holding fruit.

"Bide a while here." The sorcerer repeated his gesture of invitation, while Sigrlinn flayed him with a furious glare. How could she, the Generation's second in strength after Merlin, be abducted like some slack-jawed village wench by such as styled themselves Distant Ones, and then be locked away by her own erstwhile lover? Yet, having no choice, she passed silently into that chamber, which more closely resembled a prison cell, and the wall closed after her.

Hedin was long twining complex Protective Spells about the entrance; and when at length he was done, he led Hagen and Hropt on up the stairs.

"Well it would be if she saw the Diviner into the bargain," he said testily.

Hagen, however, was not calmed by this. He had already guessed the army of the Castle of All the Ancients was investing the Hedinseigh fortress. A bitter battle lay ahead, a magical duel. *And what need have we of that sorceress in our citadel, who can calmly cipher through all the skeins of defensive enchantments set about the island? Though, indeed, she cannot simply be sent home.*

"Teacher, are you sure she cannot get out?" He could not hold the question back.

"I am. The Distant Ones have deprived her of almost all her powers. She is capable now of only the simplest charms and control of the most negligible forces," the Mage replied. "But the enchantments I have laid upon her would suffice had she fallen to us in the flower of her strength. In order to be again the Sigrlinn she was, she must find her way to her palace in Jibulistan, and elsewhere, too. However, I will do my utmost to keep her here as long as suits me."

By THE TIME THE THANE HAD ENDED HIS TALE, THE THIRD SIGNAL FOR THE ENEMY ATTACK was sounding without the walls.

"Such dawdles they are," Old Hropt remarked, rising and settling his sword. "I must own that, bone-chilled and weary as I am, I would be not one whit averse to another fight. 'Tis long since I grappled so gaily!"

Hedin shook his head at those youthfully spirited words. "Hropt," he said, "it is time to hie you back to your army in the Sheltered Kingdom. Our warriors there have been overlong without a commander. Here both your sword and mine are powerless. And if it comes to fisticuffs, then better we should throw ourselves into the mouth of a monster of Chaos or the craw of the Unnamable Itself."

"I've never understood that in you Mages." The Lord of Asgard shrugged his powerful shoulders. "If you ask me, death on the field of honor is sweeter by far. When blades are whistling all around and bodies are falling, your death, if ordained, comes easy and unremarked. Strange it is that I must say this to you! No, I remain here. Nothing will happen to the army. I have given all the orders that were needful. The gnomes were preparing to return to their mountains and the horse-herds of Rogheim to their plains. The goblins, trolls and humans remained, but I found for them a tolerable refuge."

Hedin shook his head again but gave Hropt no argument, while Hagen could not conceal his delight. Hropt's hastily mustered detachments had done their duty, and could now disperse and take shelter, but with such a fighter as the Father of Hosts close by, this battle was already half-won.

Their placid conversation was interrupted in a most untoward manner when something with four leathery wings and a terrible mouth sown with fangs appeared at the window and lisped, "They advansss."

"Go down, Hagen." Hedin raised a heavy gaze to his apprentice. "Your swords will not be needed soon—and, I hope, not at all."

"I must see it," the thane retorted, lowering his head stubbornly and gainsaying his mentor for perhaps for the first time in his life. How strikingly unalike was that proud warrior then to the beggarwoman that Fate had made his mother.

The Mage hesitated, and conceded.

"Only do not hinder me," he instructed. "Stay near, so that if need be…"
He did not finish the thought, for from outside the narrow embrasures came a howling, a roaring, a whooping of thousands of voices; the light of day was dimmed, and firebolts of many colors began capering madly along the edges of the sky.

The Mage turned hastily to the Diviner, while Hagen and Hropt, not exchanging so much as a word, raced up the narrow staircase to the observation platform.

The top of the keep, sharp as a dragon's fang and towering high over the island, afforded a sweeping view. The dense belt of enemy vessels massed on the horizon had begun to move. It arced and crept toward them, and, though some ships were faster than others, nowhere was there a break in their formation. The countless throng of humans devoured sea and sky, and the winged legions of the Castle of All the Ancients reached almost to the very sun. The thane saw Rakoth slant swift through the azure in his fiery cloak. His detachments still held their position.

The Generation's forces were near enough now for the observers to make out the details of the ships' rigging. The vessels resembled those that had mounted the unsuccessful attack on Hedinseigh some days previously—tall they were, steep-sided and many-masted, with rosy sails. Filling the gaps between them moved long yellow galleys towed by huge sea-beasts, whale-like but with webbed flippers, enormous tusks protruding from their mouths, and sharp, high, bony fins. Through the air floated astonishing constructions with immense rhythmically beating canvas wings, some harnessed to giant eagles. Even higher soared small dragons, winged wolves and other beings assembled in haste by their overlords to die in a bloody battle whose purpose was unknown to the vast majority of the warriors that marched under the banners of the Castle of All the Ancients.

Fear, an icy serpent, slithered into Hagen's heart. Never before had he faced such a force. How many could Rakoth have brought? And could his servants stand against the combined might of an untold multitude of worlds?

The Mages pitilessly drove their condemned vanguards to the slaughter—in an effort, as Hagen understood, to ascertain the strength of Hedinseigh's wizardly defenses. His Teacher, however, would not be hurried, even as the battle lines came ever closer.

The Mages broke first.

Behind the rear lines, within the gloom that ringed the horizon, arose four bright, ruddy-red spouts of flame. The regiments of the Castle of All the Ancients hastened to move aside, giving way to the fiery giants. The flame rose to the very heavens, and was lost in the firmament's blinding glare. Hedin, whose favorite weapon had always been a Great Firespell, now had to counter creations fashioned of that same element but even more mighty. Hagen distinctly felt the massive wizardly power bestowed upon those scorching columns coming on from north, south, east, and west.

Yes—the thought intruded unbidden—now we surely shall have a hot time of it. And Hagen's mind was suddenly filled with his son and Ilving, that proud spouse who had chosen not to quit an island doomed to a cruel siege.

The spouts had passed the enemy regiments' battle formations and were rapidly nearing the shoreline, their tips swathed in billows of steam. At the zenith, directly above the island, a gigantic dark-gray funnel began to form, and its tail, ready to suck up all the detritus, slowly descended on Hedinseigh.

The Teacher still did nothing, but Hagen knew how deceptive the wily Mage's silence could be.

Rakoth quickly moved his flying regiments as far as possible from that fearsome tail. Though it was still distant from the Earth, Hagen could already feel the air flowing fast across his face.

Then the Mage made his response, but did not try to match his opponents' rivers of fire or ocean swells. Hagen guessed his Teacher was striking, as he always had, at the most vulnerable spot of any Assaultspell, that being the magical clamps that held its forces securely together. Like Merlin's blade of fire flaring away futilely in the Astral Plane, all four of those menacing spouts became shapeless pools of liquid that burned across the water. Hagen, of course, realized none of that would have been possible without the Diviner— the secret weapon of he who was a terror to all infatuates of that deadening Balance.

The same fate overtook the funnel with the gluttonous mouth. Hedin had breezily parried the first magical blow, and Hagen knew then their enemies had already made a fatal error in trying to conquer Hedinseigh by degrees. Had they sent the Hungering Stars and the Disembodied in a concerted attack, the citadel could not have stood.

The remains of the fiery spouts burned down and went out, and the armies of the Castle of All the Ancients resumed their advance. Hagen was unpleasantly pricked by the awareness it was all too sprightly and too swift. After a failure such as they had just suffered, the Mages ought by rights to have halted to regroup. Their adversary had repulsed their first onslaught with ease, and that had unsettled them not at all. The Castle detachments continued approaching the Hedinseigh shore as if nothing had happened, and the thane was hard put not to bring up his arbalesters and trebuchet crews, so great was the temptation to meet those enemy ships with a hail of stones, arrows and spears.

All at once the air before the citadel walls filled with a bluish glimmer like a thick, soft fall of strangely tinted snow, bringing from Hedin a reaction far quicker than before. Hagen realized the Castle Mages had concocted a toxin to smoke Rakoth's servants out of hiding. It must have been harmless to people but lethal to the handiwork of Darkness—unless the Mages were no longer respecting the Law of the Ancients that forbade the murder of mortals.

"A rare go, Hedin!" Hropt, who was also observing the battle with bated breath, said in his husky voice. "That's the ticket to purge the poison."

For the sea around the island seemed to boil, looking to Hagen like rain falling upward as particles of the briny deep rose to swallow the bluish flakes then settled in a downy black froth over the pebbles on the shore.

"I envy no one who breathes that in," Hropt said with a shake of the head, eyeing the layer of spume.

Every charm cast by Hedin was brief and struck true as a fine-made rapier honed to penetrate the rings of any armor. Yet the Castle Mages again betrayed no perplexity, and their squadron advanced once more, much faster now. Indeed, all the vessels would have been driven by a following wind, even had they been heading straight toward each other.

The cerulean blue over Hagen's head had vanished, obscured by myriad steadily beating wings, and only the inert sun still illuminated the field of combat. Rakoth's servants seemed to be panicking, having descended almost to the level of the island's towers and cliffs, their every feature displaying stark fear.

Webbed wings pounded the air ever more powerfully; the broad fins of the sea-bulls dragging those heavy galleys whipped the waves to foam. The first ships were already in range of the fortress's catapults, and Hagen touched without being aware the Disc of Iamerth at his side. *Presently...presently...as soon as any detail comes plain enough.*

A piercing shriek grew overhead as the Castle's winged troops swooped down. Tracing a path from both airborne and seaborne vessels to the island's bastions, long smoky trails extended behind fiery spheres that sparkled in flight, weapons more deadly by far than the pots of liquid fire that had earlier burned almost all the fortifications of Hedinseigh to cinders.

But Hedin had found a means to counter even this threat, since the bright ruddy spheres were made of Magic Fire and therefore susceptible to spells. Just a few dozen yards from the sea-cliffs they exploded, strewing clouds of blinding white sparks, as if they had hit against an invisible barrier. Hagen frowned—his Teacher had had to stop this tool of the Castle by main force, since the Mages had contrived to hide or securely protect the enchantments that guided their flaming spheres.

"But when will this end?" the Father of Hosts sighed in gusty impatience. "I tire of standing here, watching sorcerers trade wizardry!" He drew his Golden Sword partway out of its sheath then thrust it back with a clang.

"I believe we shall soon have occupation aplenty," Hagen said morosely.

There was a roaring directly overhead as Rakoth galloped by on a mount that flew without wings.

"In their place I would have thought long and hard ere I started this tussle," Hropt muttered, staring intently into the distance from beneath his low faceplate. "Even I can feel the power, the great power gathered here at Rakoth's call. And if they do not see that, then woe to them, every one!"

But the aerial regiments of the Castle of All the Ancients at last bade farewell to indecision and made a concerted plunge from the heavens. Brazenly low now, they determined to cover the distance that separated them from the fortress in a single bound.

Had Hagen been in command of Hedinseigh at that time, the winged brutes would have been met by a penetrating whirlwind of long arrows and arbalest bolts, but his Teacher had at hand incomparably more powerful weaponry. The air abruptly darkened, as if great clouds of the finest brown dust had been sprayed across it. Standing in the very heart of that unnatural cloud, the image of a being indescribably fearsome and intimidating to those winged creatures appeared over the island.

The inartful ruse achieved its purpose—the formation of flying things racing toward Hedinseigh broke apart. In disarray and in great haste, they flapped upward with all speed. But the image revealed itself to be no simple mirage. It suddenly extended an immensely wide appendage into which at least several hundred of the winged things disappeared, absorbed by an unknown power, and promptly burned away there to ash.

Even the Father of Hosts' jaw dropped in surprise.

As the surviving Castle servants retreated in disorder, the ships of the Mage Generation's main battle forces crossed some unseen frontier, and Rakoth threw forward his regiments, which had been eagerly awaiting that command.

HEDIN

I MUST OWN THAT MY KINSFOLK'S FIRST ATTACKS HAD BEEN NO SURPRISE TO ME. THEY seemed to be putting me through my paces and had presented me, one by one, with the tried-and-true techniques of magical warfare—only to have them all repelled. The Diviner had promptly deciphered the interwoven Spells of Force and Bidding Spells, leaving me only to conjure a precise Cleavecharm for each. This resembled nothing so much as a childhood game called Find the Thread, in which a player has to find the carefully hidden lacing in a new broom and cut it, whereupon the broom, naturally, falls apart. If he fails, his rump is nicely warmed with the aforementioned broom. The comparison may seem crass, considering the high style normally used in recounting wizardly duels, yet it is, for all that, a wholly fitting description.

When they began fighting with fire, though, I had trouble enough, for one among them had either guessed how I could deduce with such speed and ease the secrets of even their most cunning enchantments, or simply meant to prevent me from finding the thread I needed by casting spells at haphazard. Whatever the reason, the Diviner was unable to discover the fire's Bonding Link, leaving me no choice but to use the information it gave me on the nature of the Constituent Power of those flaming spheres and raise against them as fast as ever I could an invisible wall of enchantments that created a substance absolutely foreign to the fire. Infallible as this uncomplicated expedient normally was, however, it demanded a great deal of my strength, and at its completion I was weak at the knees and struggling with dizziness.

Rakoth's voice, pressing hard into my mind, restored me to myself.

— *They have crossed the line! I am attacking! I am attacking, Hedin!*

That line the Fallen Mage had himself drawn on the bottom of the sea, prompted by certain considerations of his own he had tried to explain to me;

but he was called away before he could finish.

I heard his words, shook off the stupefying dazzle before my eyes and raced to the embrasure. What I saw there was a sight to behold, irrespective of the peril we faced.

The sea was rearing up, flinging flakes of white foam to the sky and sending walls of waves, raised by the composite motion of hundreds and thousands of bodies, crashing fiercely against the cliffs. It had split apart to its depths, revealing a rocky floor coated with slimy patches of seaweed. An unbroken torrent of backs and heads—brown, blue, black—was sweeping skyward. The servants of Rakoth had at last thrown off the languor that had fettered them for ten centuries and more.

The water under the galleys' prows was stained with blood as jaws and horns tore into the underbellies of the beings that towed the vessels. One by one, the monstrous carcasses, in their death throes, were flung high above the water, there to be set upon by Rakoth's many-toothed creatures, which tirelessly gnawed at their flesh.

The Fallen Mage's winged dragons swooped down on the ships, regardless of the hail of arrows and catapult shot loosed against them, and savagely attacked the skyboats' flying dray-teams. Pliant snake-like bodies wound around the giant eagle wings, beaks split dragon-heads, and the huge jaws of Rakoth's vassals bit through the birds' outstretched necks. I saw a massive dragon fold its wings and plummet onto one of the skyboats drawn by eagles, clawing its sides to smithereens and rending the bodies of its crew with fangs and teeth. Immense tentacles suddenly emerged from the waters, twining about the ships and dragging them to the bottom with supreme ease.

At the very heart of the frenzied battle, where the sky seemed about to split from all the roaring, howling, groaning, cracking and crashing, soared Rakoth, a bolt of crimson lightning amid bodies entwined in deadly combat. Above the Fallen Mage's head flickered his staff, its slightest motion directing his servants hither and thither like a conductor's baton.

No shades, no spirits, not even the detachments of humanlike manikins had as yet entered the fray. They remained concealed in the cliffs, waiting their turn.

Rakoth was able to delay the advance of the regiments of the Castle of All the Ancients, but not to halt it. The sunken ships were immediately replaced. The eagle-drawn skyboats fell into the waves but others, their exact facsimiles, rose from the depths. Rakoth had thrown almost all his forces into the battle, and though his servants seemed all but invulnerable, the Castle squadrons were advancing still.

Rakoth's retainers were relying on their bodily weaponry, and had not yet employed fire or any other wizardry. But the Mages of my Generation had clearly erred again, for now that Hedinseigh was sealed under an unbroken dome of grappling beings, their combat magic could not readily find its way to the fortress bastions. They would have to go about, through other worlds, through the Astral Plane; and there I was far and away stronger than them all taken together.

With every instant I expected them to make that maneuver; but time passed, the boiling stratum of battle approached the island, and my kinsfolk were doing as little as I, either because they truly honored the Law of the Ancients or because they had some other plan of action in reserve.

Then I was softly hailed, not by a voice, but by a quiet word spoken in my mind: *Master...*

I turned around sharply, and by Iamerth's emblem stood the one I had named Hervind, his fur ruffled and in places singed. I had seen many look better, but few worse.

As the battle seethed on outside the walls, I summoned Hagen and Hropt and began to show them what my spy had seen. Rakoth assumed full command, I having hastily transferred to him the last keys to my defensive charms—all those sweet surprises I had prepared for our unwelcome guests. Our salvation lay only in the emblem, in the path it had uncovered to us, for since we had as yet received no reliable intelligence about the Unnamable, we could only continue to concentrate on our own petty squabbles.

An astonishing tale began to unfold before our eyes. Neither I nor my kinsmen nor Old Hropt had heard of such sorcery, and the Father of Hosts did not even recognize the world concealed within the emblem, although he it was who in times past had found the trail to the Wisdomwell.

"There was no mountain there," he said, bewildered, "nor any such village."

"Maybe the village came later?" I suggested.

"Then whence the people, strange as they are? Never have I seen such as they. Those that came with the Young Gods were altogether different."

Hervind was already running along the familiar path, circling the strange mountain with swordlike outcroppings, and soon reached the outskirts of the village. Now even I had perforce to give Old Hropt's powers of observation their due, as the village's inhabitants in truth resembled no race of humans known to me. It was as if someone had for sport combined in them the features of utterly different peoples—light northern locks, the swarthy skin of the Southland, the narrow slanted eyes of the Furthermost East and large, prominent Western noses. And their speech, as heard by Hervind, was intelligible to none of us.

My agent observed them attentively and long, and we came to know that they either had no suspicions as to the magical properties of the Wellspring and believed Mimir to be no more than an old crackpot or were themselves uncommonly powerful sorcerers—the latter, at least, being Old Hropt's opinion. He ran on about the "feeling in his bones" that there was astounding magic in those parts, although even he could not explain wherein it lay or if the villagers had any relationship to the emblems or to the Young Gods.

Still, they put me much in mind of someone—someone I had seen in my apprentice's memory...

There! Brann Shrunkenhand! Yet, I chided myself, it could be but a chance resemblance.

Water was drawn from the Wisdomwell by the bucketful, cows and horses drank from the stream that rose from beneath the roots of the ancient oak, and now and again a village urchin would take a running leap into the Wellspring's bubbling bowl.

Hervind stood long, watching the village, and I understood then that time moved differently in that world—faster than it did elsewhere. This must, then, be one of the Branches of the Great River of Time, a manifestation most rare and perilous. And I was even more certain now that there would be no shift here without the aid of the Dragons of Time. Would also that I could understand what this chance discovery might mean to us and how, if at all, it could help us.

Hervind at length quit that puzzling village without uncovering the secret of those who dwelt there. He had made a creditable effort to enter a home; but failure waylaid him there, for the villagers and their four-legged guards took it amiss, and the hunt was on. The dogs' fangs snapped above my envoy's head, and burning faggots were shied at him. He made a hard escape and, choosing not to persevere where perseverance would be futile, moved on to Mimir's Well.

The old Jotunn—if Jotunn he was—still sat by the Seething Fountainhead, aimlessly dipping his staff into it; but it seemed to me the Guardian of the Wellspring's feeble idleness was all for show, and that there was a certain intensity hidden deep in those eyes. Old Hropt was of like mind ("Though Mimir has fair shrunk down since last we parted!").

Hervind crept up to the rim of the bubbling stone bowl and glanced into it. While the emblems were still in place, the dark crystalline globe that belonged to Iamerth was all girt about now with errant sparks of many colors, and we immediately sensed the torrent of magical energies that flowed from it, speeding across the abysses of worlds.

That was when Hervind, to our surprise, clambered over the stone lip and plunged headfirst into the Wellspring.

A cry broke from me unintended, for Sigrlinn's words were firmly planted in my head; and while the children diving into the Fountainhead likely possessed no magic and could not therefore affect its powers, my envoy was a being made of pure wizardry.

Indeed, the emblem's glimmer changed on the instant, agitating the water above it. Mimir's great brown hand plunged into the Wellspring; and even we, installed in my apartments on Hedinseigh, could feel a prompt perturbation of wizardly forces conveyed along endless concatenations. Somewhere in unimaginable depths, a collapse and a crumbling had begun.

But Hervind slipped smartly away from the pursuing hand, descending ever deeper, until the mysterious glitter of Iamerth's emblem was revealed to our sight.

There it was—the grand fabrication of Power, incomparable with the pitiful replica that had fallen into our hands. It was drawn and wrapped in so tight and complex a network of charms that, to our eyes, it seemed a heavy crystalline sphere, although it contained not a jot of inert matter.

Hervind made a careful approach. Although the being my sorcery had created from Light and Darkness had no need of air to breathe, it could not remain long near the emblem. The forces that writhed within that enchantment-swaddled globe were threatening to tear my envoy to pieces.

Yet, even in the brief span of time spent alongside the true emblem, Hervind saw and understood all that was needful. Though I discerned no purpose in unraveling the interminable chain of spells threaded one to another, I was satisfied to see, beyond the abysses concealed within the emblem, the road that led directly to the very heart of the Hallowed Land, and the Bidding Enchantments that guided the myriad currents of magical energy brought together there, and narrowly confined. Some had called them the Creator's Mindworks—the eternal, perdurable, inextinguishable, all-penetrating Thoughts of the Creator—and it was probably so. I knew not. But one day I would, and for certain.

Made to nourish with Power the Creator's most cherished offspring, to bestow upon Iamerth authority over the sun's light and to secure him against any possible rivals whatsoever—such was the emblem of Iamerth, and so it lay before us. Hervind also noted certain other magical offshoots, subtle filaments of charms that reached into the far distance of the Well-Ordered. The Diviner committed them to memory and vowed to trace them to their end in due course.

So, although the proofs I had were neither as thorough nor as precise as I would have wished, it was clear to me the emblems in their sum held sway over All That Is; and that should the ties that bound them to the Hallowed Land to be severed our prime enemies would be left powerless. There it was—the riddle Rakoth had been unable to crack when he had tried—and failed—to vie with the Young Gods on the strength of his regiments alone.

Hervind had, meanwhile, surfaced and was scrambling out of the Fountainhead. Now I understood what Sigrlinn had said—it was most certainly dangerous for a Mage to be not just in the Wellspring's stone bowl but merely close to that focus of power and authority.

Here, my thoughts went their own way. Why were we struggling against the Young Gods? Was it only because we had dared defy their statutes and free Rakoth and were now forced to defend ourselves, if only to avoid being wiped from the face of the Earth? Or was it as I had told myself earlier, that the limits of the Gods' powers could not be known until those powers had been seen in action, and that I would stop at nothing, would even risk my apprentice's life, to discompose the Hallowed Land?

No, I said to myself. *Your dream has been to sit upon the high throne of the Suzerain of the Sun's Light. You have always known that a weak link in the outwardly impregnable chain wound by the Young Gods about the whole world was there for the finding.*

Still, there had been something inchoate, impalpable, elusive—a faint glint in the very depths of my mind, a secret thought that had given me no peace. Only now could I force it to linger.

While forming my plan, how had I envisioned extricating myself from the skirmish that must follow? Whence had come the unshakable certainty I need only do my utmost, need only penetrate realms of knowledge other Mages had long abandoned to find what I sought? Someone might as well have been leading me by the nose to the idea of taking the Young Gods' place, for otherwise how could I have been so blind to all the consequences of that suicidal act? It was as if somebody were using me as a battering ram to destroy the stronghold of the gods.

Just as I was feeling closer than I had ever been to the solution, I saw that my envoy, whose eyes were showing us the World of the Wellspring, had emerged from the Fountainhead and was again on the grass. Now I clearly knew this place was neither more nor less than an unprecedentedly powerful interweaving of the pathways plied by the truly mighty forces of the Universe, of the Well-Ordered, and of Chaos. After time spent in the vicinity of the emblem, Hervind's gaze seemed sharper than ever before, and we could see that the emblems and their powers were but a small part of the immense system of Wizardry—not wizardry, but Wizardry—whose center was Mimir's Well.

By winding paths, my second sight—my Magical Sight—was led far beyond Earthly bounds, beyond the bounds of Chaos, even beyond the dwelling of the Unnamable, which was still a puzzlement to us. I saw there startling scenes that beggared my feeble powers of description. I saw the improbably intricate motions of strange, multicolored forms—their interaction, their development and decline, their birth and their perishing. The sight was as heady as the view from the brink of a sheer scarp.

The spectacle, as I understood it, was a reflection of the primeval essence of All That Is. *The Wellspring is a gathering of the threads that link multitudes upon multitudes of...what? Worlds? Or something even more all-embracing? Or...*My breath caught in my throat....*a multitude of Creators?* The world became boundless, and my thoughts impotent to comprehend it.

All those magnificent powers lay in the hands of one Jotunn, who had been old even in the days when the Father of Hosts and his kin first held sway over the world. But Mimir would rather sit there by the Fountainhead, whiling away his time with the pyrotechny of lightning and firebolts in the sky. Speech had been his great love, and he had invariably held forth in a high-flown, foggily pompous style; but now, it seemed, he had abandoned even that—all so that the Young Gods would pay him no mind.

I finally knew why the Young Gods had, in the past, brought us to the precipice that overlooked the Wellspring of the Worlds. The meaning of that initiation, that consecration, that unification of the Mage with the great swirl of worlds and universes was clearer now in my mind. And no surprise it was that all memories of it had been carefully erased, since anyone coming to Mimir's domains with a sound mind would be able to acquire a truly awe-inspiring degree of might—perhaps even enough to halt the Unnamable Itself...

I would willingly have risked seeking mastery over the Wellspring's powers, being simply unable to resist the greatest temptation of my life; and had I had long decades, perchance even ages, at my disposal and no other matters to concern me, my venture might even have been crowned with success.

But Hervind had shaken himself dry and was about to run off when Mimir noticed him.

"So, there you be!" a low, hollow voice rumbled. A long brown hand reached for my agent, with far more dexterity than I would have expected from a Jotunn old as Chaos.

Hervind made a narrow escape and fled for refuge to the roots of the titanic oak, but from the black pits beneath the thick coils of those wooden snakes dozens of large, round, unwinking eyes stared out at him; and he retreated from there even faster than he had run from Mimir. Bolting between the giant's legs, he sped off toward the mountain with its sword-shaped escarpments.

"Just you wait, accursed wizard—I'll show you what's what!" the Guardian of the Wellspring growled at his back.

Mimir bent, scooped up a handful of water from the Fountainhead and, with a broad swing of the arm, flung a sparkling cloud of spray after him. Each flying droplet became a many-pawed thing much like a rat, but the size of a cat.

Yet the Sentinel of the Well had misjudged, for Hervind fought with the valor of ten, I having had the foresight to give him sharp teeth and make him agile and deft. And, though his foes outmatched him many times over in both numbers and strength, my spy cared not to meet a heroic death in that place. Darting through the concerted onslaught of Mimir's rats, he found safety in the thickets.

The hue and cry soon fell behind, since a being made of Light and Darkness leaves no trace, and Mimir had had no time to weave the needed spell.

Having thrown off his pursuers, Hervind made for the mysterious mountain. Neither overhasty nor unhurried—for Mimir's creations could appear again at any moment—he ran all around it, first to count the number of outcroppings; there were seven. Then he carefully began to climb the smooth cliff face, every foot upward a trial. Twice he was kept from falling only by the grasp of one tiny claw as he crawled across the cutting edge of a stone sword embedded in the mountain.

He was long, very long, on the ascent, but had at least shaken off Mimir's rats for good and all. The unseen sun of those parts set and the daylight dimmed; it was full dark before Hervind reached the spear-sharp needle of white stone that capped the mountain, the meeting place for all seven of the giant blades that clove the mountainsides. And at the foot of that white obelisk Hervind at last found the answer.

All the while, he had been trying to penetrate the layers of gray stone with his second sight but failed each time, never encountering more than a solid, colorless shroud. The mountain's innards had been painstakingly concealed under a powerful spell.

Yet that, I would argue, is not the best way to hide anything. Any charm, to say nothing of a powerful charm, is apt to be discovered, thus proving that something has been hidden there. And sooner or later, those enchantments will be deciphered and removed.

Once at the white stone spear that pierced the dark, starless sky, Hervind tried again, and this time was able to breach the curtain of gloom. The white monolith was discovered to be no less than a knot of numberless spells that encased the mountain like a dense net; and in the faint light that radiated from him, my envoy could discern what lay within those ill-favored gray cliffs.

Seven giant blades were set tent-like, their hilts thrust into the ground and their tips meeting at that white capstone. These were the seven renowned Swords of the Young Gods, which they had brought with them into the world—the seven embodiments of the Creator's own Mindworks imprinted with His Word and His Name—and together a weapon capable of destroying All That Is.

That I recognized on the instant. During our apprenticeship, all we Mages had learned by heart the ballads that told of the Young Gods' battles, which were rife with references to those Swords. Yet for some reason the sagas passed over in silence the fact that the Young Gods' adversaries had not been some fabricated monsters of Darkness but the Ancient Gods, the first masters of our world. I myself had but recently understood that.

Old Hropt let out an exultant cry.

"Thither, Hedin, and with all speed!" he bawled, leaping up and flailing his arms. "We have found them! We have found those upstarts' Swords! Now I shall settle my score with them on behalf of all who once were ours! Conjure away—we must go to that world!"

I saw Hagen stealing up, pale with scrupulously hidden agitation—he understood very well the subject at hand. At another time, I would have been the first to set about forging a path to the old Jotunn. Now, though, my mind was strangely chill, as if a cold rain were pouring down on my face.

There was something awry in the mountain, something troubling in those swords we had so happily chanced upon in the moment of our greatest need.

They had come to us too easily somehow, being hidden in plain sight, as though someone wanted to convince us the swords really were concealed while making sure we would detect them. Hence, the crudeness of the Charms of Invisibility and that soft spot under the white capstone.

No, I shall not fall into the same trap twice.

"'Tis almost certain to be a sham, and a snare to boot," I observed, recalling the Temple of Iamerth in the Sovereign City.

Old Hropt stood dead still, his mouth hanging open, as if he had just run athwart an unseen barrier. Hagen, too, raised his eyebrows in surprise. I briefly divulged my thoughts to them.

"I don't know, I don't know," the Father of Hosts said testily. "Have you not felt the powers concealed in those Swords? My very breath was stopped. It needs only a glance—"

"But even if they are not really the Swords of the Gods, a road to the Wellspring must all the same be found," I went on, "and the sooner the better, before tidings of our spy reach the Hallowed Land."

"And this Rakoth of yours can hold the island?" Old Hropt asked bluntly.

"Save for the unforeseen, most certainly," I said, as confidently as I knew how. "Unless Iamerth himself appears."

"And if he does?"

It was Hagen's first foray into the conversation. I shrugged.

"If we do all in good time, he will come only in passing."

"Then why are we still here?" The Father of Hosts slammed a fist onto the table.

"The way to Mimir is shut up tight," I explained. "The Walls of the World must be reduced to rubble, and I know no means to do that other than by the magic of Those That Dwell by the River of Time."

Hagen and Hropt winced as one.

"I was reserving it...for the Hallowed Land," I said, the words coming hard. "But since matters are at such a pass..."

The Lord of Asgard shook his head. "There cannot but be some other way. 'Tis a path I have trod myself, and more than once."

"And while seeking it, we could lose all," my apprentice objected.

Our peaceable conversation, which had progressed as though no conflict raged outside the walls, was interrupted at that point. First, the floor jolted beneath our feet—once, twice, thrice. Then the battle's noise was many times multiplied, becoming a deafening roar. There was a blinding flash outside the window, and clouds of acrid stonedust flew, finding their way even into my apartments. Something in the bailey was burning and collapsing.

— *A missive from your Mage of Mages,* the Diviner told me. It had taught itself to wax ironical whilst I had been occupied elsewhere.

We leapt up and raced to the embrasures. Merlin's greeting had been exceedingly impressive—flame illuminated the bailey and two towers had fallen. His fiery blade had burst through all my defensive charms, because I had unpardonably allowed myself to become distracted, lulled by the long silence from the Leader of the Council of the Generation. Once again, I silently thanked Fate that all the people were safe below ground.

— *And you did not notice Merlin casting that spell?* I queried the Diviner, rather ungraciously.

— *No,* it retorted. *Had he applied more powers to his magic, of course, he would not have been able to hide it from me.*

We might have expected something of greater substance than fire and explosions from the Archmage—a tear in the fabric of the Real, for instance, into which our island would tumble entire.

And so, Merlin was to be idle no more. Did that not signify he had been making due inquiries regarding the Unnamable, which all others seemed to have utterly forgotten in the heat of battle?

I asked the Diviner to verify the Guardcharms Rakoth and I had dispatched to the far bounds of the Well-Ordered, while I fixed my own attention upon Avalon. It was clear to me now that I could no way quit Hedinseigh, which meant the task of breaking through to the Wellspring must fall to Old Hropt and my apprentice.

Hagen wanted nothing so much as to descend in haste and see to the dousing of the fires, and I had it hard to persuade him to stay. That was for Rakoth's servants to do, and, truly, not a minute had passed before a flock of pot-gutted, six-legged creatures scurried from the shore to the fires and back. They carried water in hugely distended bellies and spewed it onto the flames in long, strong jets—so many as to overmatch even the fire from the Enchanted Isle. It drew off, hissing and flinging charred brands about.

"Shall we tarry much longer, then?" Old Hropt asked me with a heavy look.

Still I hesitated. I was most fearsomely unwilling to bring into play my last resort, the Dragons of Time, having a faint presentiment the moment would come when they alone would be the salvation of myself and all my followers.

Then I determined on a step I had delayed taking all my livelong days.

A wizard may increase his powers by fashioning something that resembles a material embodiment of the axis around which the world rotates when he casts his spells. That, however, renders him more vulnerable than aught else, for should the facsimile axis be destroyed, no memory would be left of that foolhardy Mage. Yet, I could see no other way. Once the magic had been made, I would be able to dismantle what I had wrought, but in no less than a week, which I must spend incessantly weaving the most intricate spells so as not to make away with myself by accident and disappear along with the incarnation of my power.

When the door had closed behind Hropt and Hagen, I drew a deep breath and commenced my wizardry, sequestering myself for the duration from all that was transpiring in my world, seeing and feeling nothing. My last thought before sinking into the trance was *What if I come to myself surrounded by my dearly beloved kinsfolk, with Merlin at their head?*

I shall not describe my magic-making, and shall merely say that it took very little of my strength and time, as is ever so with all those things that may be discarded only with great difficulty at a later date.

When I came around again and saw the floor transfixed by a column composed of interlaced tongues of bright, ruddy fire, a shudder ran down my spine.

"What have you done?" I whispered. "You have built your own scaffold." But it was too late to draw back. Throwing off those craven thoughts, I set to work, but before diving into a dense mesh of Charms of Penetration, I first made contact with Rakoth.

My mind found the Fallen Mage in the very thick of the fray, engirdled by his own powerful enchantments and in control of all. His comprehensive vision of the battle and his ability to respond with lightning speed to the slightest change in it surprised even me.

— *We're holding our own*, he reported, though a trace of anxiety underlay the thought. *Merlin's arrow caused no little woe, but now that the Diviner is alerted, a second such blow I shall not allow. We are being pressed hard, but all is going by the plan. They're already played out.*

There was much bravado in that, for when the battle unfolded in its entirety before my mind's eye, I realized how dire it was with us.

Hundreds and thousands of enemy vessels and skyboats had been scuttled, burned, shattered by dragon-claws, and dragged to the bottom by giant octopuses; and the corpses of Castle warriors had washed up in piles on the shore. Yet still our foes, inch by inch, were nearing the island's bastions.

The dead were immediately replaced by the living, invested by my kinsfolk's enchantments with reckless courage and a false sense of invulnerability. They threw themselves upon the servants of Rakoth, who fought with far greater skill but were at times simply buried under the enemy avalanche. Ever and again, a winged Child of Darkness would plummet strengthlessly down in a bloody, crippled heap, or a kraken in its death agony would lift mutilated stubs of tentacles high above the surface and sink forever beneath the waves.

Rakoth had not yet applied any of my Protective Charms. His adversaries had not approached close enough, certain units of that apparently numberless army had not even engaged, and the Fallen Mage needed to practice patience, for our first answering blow must be the decisive one. We would have neither strength nor time for a second.

I held back, though, for I saw that Rakoth was doing well in separating the enemy forces, and that his servants were herding the humans in one direction and the manikins and monsters in the other. He had created a rift in the very center of their ranks to allow me to work my magic. Still, I was most reluctant to announce to all our enemies that I had at last created a Talisman of my own, a target for them to aim at in hopes of sooner or later dispersing the tatters of my mind to the uttermost corners of All That Is.

Close by, on the other side of the wall, Hagen and Hropt stood on tenterhooks; and a few floors below, in a room securely locked and sealed by enchantments, Sigrlinn waited, too.

My state of confusion was ended by the Diviner. To the far rear of the investing army had come new players in today's Great Game—the Distant Ones.

In the back of my mind, I had all along been expecting them to come calling and was, therefore, not greatly surprised when they did. For long millennia they—ever the incomprehensible, cold, indifferent, disengaged Pillars—had been preparing for this, and as was soon to be seen, they had by no means been spending the time in idleness.

But something else there was, of far greater note.

Approaching the rear ranks of the army of the Castle Mages was a grand fleet of beautiful, steep-sided ships, long and with high carved bows—very like our own dragon-ships, only incomparably more elegant. Adorned with pearls, agate and silver, flying sails of woven mist on single masts, they seemed lovely mirages made real.

There could be no mistake. These were elves, and none less than they did I care to battle. Not, to be sure, because they could be most powerful and fearsome enemies nor because their magic was mighty in repute for, mighty as it may be, it would never be but a small portion of the boundless ocean of Wizardly Energies. I could easily deal with them, especially since Mages had no law forbidding the murder of immortals.

Rather, all my long life I had admired their wisdom, the loveliness created by their hands and minds, and had dreamed every night of their cities, which, seen once, are never forgotten. The Creator's Elder Offspring had since ancient times trod paths known only to them, and their fortresses were hidden behind a curtain impenetrable to mortal and immortal alike. A true Mage, if so inclined, could, of course, make his way there by main force, all obstacles notwithstanding, but elves enjoyed the special protection of the Young Gods, and an attack upon the First-Begotten was tantamount to a declaration of war upon the Hallowed Land itself.

Yet why—why, in the name of all that was holy—had they joined forces with the Distant Ones? Could such great adepts and master craftsmen be in thrall to the cold, cruel sagacity of such as had never known a single living feeling?

I recalled then the request made by the dying elf to Frodi and Gudmund— to go to the monastery of the Distant Ones in the vale of Brunevagar. I had slighted the news, had not sought to learn its significance or determine whence came such an ill-matched union. Now, the elven army was hastening into battle.

There could not have been a more perfect moment; it was as if they had foreknown the boundary at which the Mages' battlecraft would be rebuffed by the power of my wizardry. Could the Distant Ones have offered the First-Begotten a share in their dominion over the world, once they had some way won it?

— *Rakoth!* I cried in my mind. *Do you see?*

He had not seen, of course, for his last push had begun. The regiments of shades and spirits he had been holding in careful reserve were streaming now into combat, and a line of pearly fire visible only to the Rebel and me glittered above the water. I cast off my doubts. It was time to employ all the new opportunities afforded by my fresh-wrought token.

The spectral detachments sliced into the Castle warriors' already wearied ranks. The octopuses and kraken, summoning all their strength, reached long tentacles toward the ships. The sea-beasts' dread tusks punctured the ships' sides and bottoms. A dense net of lightning twined around the skyboats that still held formation; and the dragons belched out their last stocks of fire.

Although elsewhere we had been pushed back almost to the bastions, a breach had formed in the center of the enemy ranks as the horde of monsters labored ever closer to the island while the mortals fell back. Then the hostile forces overstepped that pearly line inscribed across the waves.

I would have liked to stand aside and observe, like a captious artist surveying his own creation, the operation of spells so long in the preparation and now brought to encircle the island; but I had instead to apply myself again to my magic, strengthening old pitfalls with newly acquired power. My memory, therefore, retains only fragmentary scenes—the sky bursting open and a frenzied, icy wind whipping down from it; keen lances crafted of starlight, ferocious and merciless, stabbing into the madding throng; the black funnels of whirlwinds far more powerful than those visited upon me by the Castle Mages; the Moonbeast in the distant Innermoon raising its beetle-browed head and growling as it drove off some tiny, irksome thing that hovered nearby; and a murderous exhalation, speeding down corridors I had opened to the environs of Hedinseigh and gushing over our enemies.

I cannot tell how much time passed in the meanwhile.

When, at length, I glanced outside—with my own eyes rather than my all-encompassing magical sight—I saw that, even though the devastating hurricane had not spared even our fortress and some of its towers were no more, the great press of Castle monsters had been almost annihilated. Thanks to the steadfastness of Rakoth and his army, they had every last one of them been drawn into the battle and had found themselves at the center of a prodigiously powerful magical attack that descended upon them so suddenly and from so many different directions the Sorcerers of my Generation who had sent those frights into battle had been powerless to protect them.

I had not, however, violated the Law of the Ancients. The mortals had survived. Shaken and deathly afraid, they were running for their lives, and no enchantments could turn them back. Emboldened, Rakoth's warriors followed them close, and the Fallen Mage had work enough to recall his overheated servants.

Old Hropt burst into the room.

"A splendid blow, Hedin! I have never seen the like. They're running—running like waterlogged rats from a spring flood."

"Hold, though," I replied wearily. "All my kin are hale and hearty still, and the Distant Ones are on the march. Call Hagen, if you would."

My legs were giving way. An ungovernable weakness rolled over me like a high tide, as is always so after great acts of sorcery. But the time had come to send Hagen and Hropt to the Seething Fountainhead, and I felt that the Distant

Powers, in concert with the First-Begotten, would yet try me sorely. Since I had not predicted their intrusion, Hedinseigh had but one tier of defensive magic left, and that had been intended to meet the gods, were they to come.

My apprentice appeared, seeming somewhat unnerved by all the horror he had seen; but on being told it was time to go, he gathered his strength and after a moment was again the Iron Thane, which had been his name of old in the coastal towns of Eastern Hjorvard.

"We need the real emblem," I explained to them. "Have no truck with Mimir, and make no effort to remove the swords from the mountain, for I am certain that is a trap. I hope I can hold the Gates open for you, although I can't be sure of that. It is, after all, the Wellspring of the Worlds, not some gimcrack Icy Abyss."

"There are matters I can discuss with the old Jotunn, if he it be," the Father of Hosts remarked. "I fancy I can distract him for a few moments."

Hagen, never one to bandy words when all was clear, only gave a silent nod.

We stood in a circle around the fiery pillar, the Diviner droning into my mind the intricate terms of the charms that hid the way to the World of the Wellspring, and my own spells following after. Scarce any other of my Generation, not even Merlin himself, could so quickly find the way to a world the gods had sealed up so tight.

Hardly had I tied up the last cluster of needful wizardry, causing Old Hropt and my apprentice to vanish, when Merlin sent another memento from Avalon, this one more than a match in might to the celebrated Sword that had almost made an end of Rakoth and me in the Netherside—and would have, had not Hagen sundered Merlin's altar of spellcraft with the Disc of Iamerth.

This time, though, the Diviner's warning was timely, and Rakoth did what he knew to do. I, shackled as I was by my Charm of Transference, could not duly counter the Archmage's blow, and it wreaked not a little harm. Cliffs and bastions collapsed, and granite flamed and flowed in rivers of blazing heat. To our good fortune, though, the fire did not extend to the underground caverns where the people were concealed.

My patience snapped, and hatred wound taut spirals of power in me. I had forborne, had postponed my vengeance too long. That latest strike of Merlin's had, I own, broken my self-control. Calling the image of Avalon to my mind, I struck out at it with all the strength I had. A thick, dark cloud formed rapidly over Hedinseigh, taking the form of a long black spear with faint starlight glittering dimly at the tip.

It was a weapon I had never used before, one that combined fragments of the Magic of the Moonbeast and of the Great Harp of Night. Those same tiny stars that had served me so well against Makran and Esteri—who, by the bye, should have been able to extricate themselves by now and be with us again— had assembled into a spear shaft, and the Moonbeast's penetrating sight had taken form and become the tip. I set it into swift motion with sorcery common to all Mages, then aimed it with a disruptive power borrowed from the Magic of the Slow Water, whose drops were capable of seeping even through solid rock, an effect I had only accelerated.

The black shaft disappeared, streaking through worlds to reach the Enchanted Isle. I kept it in sight and watched the first tier of Merlin's defensive magic shatter, the glittering shield of air over Avalon crack and break apart. Merlin's castle, almost completely in ruins now, flew toward me, and all then disappeared into the bottomless gulf of Eternal Night.

The Archmage had—I did not flatter myself—of course, survived, but now would be hard put to regain his Altar of Spellcraft. I had won a little precious time.

But I could not even draw breath, for I had next to speak with Rakoth. The Fallen Mage seemed most satisfied. The Young Gods and the advancing Distant Ones apparently far from his mind, he was reveling in his victory, and his eyes burned with savage triumph—vengeance, albeit only a modicum, had been his.

The Mage armies were fleeing. Though my kin had not been able to stop them they had not themselves quit the field of combat. In the far offing, rocking on billows of air, their great silvery barque still lay, guarded by an entourage of gryphons and flying snakes.

"I shall ginger them yet," Rakoth said heatedly.

"Hold! What are we to do with the Distant Ones?"

"The Distant Ones? I thought that was your bailiwick—pure magic and naught else. You busy yourself with them, and I'll take on the elves."

"No, wait! I don't care to run afoul of the First-Begotten. I've never been at odds with them. We must attempt to reach an understanding with them."

Rakoth made a wry face but did not argue. His defeat and all the torments that followed had left their mark, and he was now willing to take advice.

"First let me try talking with our brethren," I said. "Maybe events will have sobered them a little."

"Is it really worth your time?" Rakoth shrugged. "Hadn't you better be watching after—"

"The less attention we pay to…that, the better," I interjected hurriedly.

"Well it would be if the Masters of the Hallowed Land went calling on Mimir, to restore order there themselves."

"Very well, I'll tend to the Distant Ones," Rakoth promised me. "Only take care that our Generation doesn't play you false."

I placed the Band of Erith on my head, and reached out with my mind to the silvery barque.

They were all gathered—Shendar, Makran, Esteri, and the rest, even Felostei—standing morosely in an opulently decorated hall belowdecks and looking at a small living model of Hedinseigh Castle set in the middle of a low table. 'Twas not a bad model, either, for it showed all, even down to the last tongue of flame.

As one, the Mages turned toward me.

CHAPTER XIV

FIRST THEY WERE FALLING FAST THROUGH THE WINDING CHAMBERS OF A HUGE, transparent shell, down an endless labyrinth with curved crystal walls—or so their senses told them, changing the real appearance of their surroundings in a striving to convey to them matters wholly alien to the human mind. Old Hropt, though, probably saw something of the truth, because even as he flew he was shaking his head, spitting in disgust and cursing unintelligibly.

They were inside the replica of Iamerth's emblem. The charm Hedin had cast, reinforced by the column of fire within which the heart of its creator was now beating, had opened to them a way into a world of startling powers and fanciful beings that scampered along the passageways of that crystal labyrinth. Some of them were indifferent to the uninvited guests, while others, careless of their own safety, came at them, bringing either the Golden Sword or the Disc of Iamerth into play, for Hagen and the Father of Hosts would not waste their time in fisticuffs. There was, however, no killing, and no dark blood stained the transparent walls; the emblem's inhabitants simply disappeared in a scatter of fine gilded sparks.

They must be keeping watch over a tight interweaving of charms, Hagen decided, *and are themselves naught else than animate fragments of the Young Gods' power, posted here to safeguard the great secret.*

He comforted himself with the thought that if Hedin's envoy, the little beast made of Light and Darkness, had already passed this way unscathed then so would they.

Their demented flight ended abruptly when something soft seized Hagen beneath the arms, slowing his fall; and he found himself standing on a dusty road lined with mighty oaks. Up ahead, beneath a sky blazing with firebolts, loomed the Blademount. The air was surprisingly fresh and pure, and Old

Hropt drew a deep and noisy breath, his stern face strangely dreamful.

"The air of Asgard," he explained, noticing Hagen's stare. "Found only here...I think this Mimir will, indeed, be the one with whom I once left my right eye as pledge."

They strode along a crumbling, slab-paved road, alert to the black fissures that snaked here and there beneath their feet. Nimble lizards scuttled from one crack to another, fixing the wayfarers with ruby eyes.

Yet Hagen felt an inexplicable sense of relief in this place—for the first time in many years, he was going into a battle where he had but himself to answer for. Hropt was prattling away, only now causing Hedin's apprentice to ponder how hard his life must have been to render the Ancient God's speech indistinguishable from that of the most rough-hewn and loutish farmhand as ever was in Hjorvard.

That was all idle conjecture, however, and Hagen thought no more of it when a great Eye opened up in the sky. In the very middle of the firmament a huge black pupil—a truly fathomless aperture—slowly appeared, surrounded by an iris of emerald green. The white was crisscrossed by tiny veins, and the Eye, which had neither lid nor lash, turned to stare at the briefly paralyzed travelers.

An instant later, Hagen was lying face down at the foot of an oak, shielded from that terrible Eye by a thick green root and hearing Hropt's heavy nasal breathing nearby.

"D'you know what it is?" he whispered, completely forgetting at that moment he was addressing an Ancient God.

Old Hropt ground his teeth. "I do. It is the Eye of Iambren, Suzerain of the Winds. In olden days he loved such sport as this."

"And what are we going to do?" Hedin's apprentice wanted to know.

The Father of Hosts shrugged. "Our ham-fisted magic, yours and mine, can offer no shelter from the Eye. We needs must issue forth, and what will be will be. We can't stay lying here until the cows come home."

So, they rose, and emerged as calmly as they could. The Eye in the heavens moved a little.

Wondering how far he would be allowed to go, Hagen took ten steps. Nothing happened. They were being watched but not yet obstructed in any way.

"Why wait," he asked between gritted teeth, "if they have noticed us?"

"They never hurry," Old Hropt replied hoarsely. "To my mind, they are but trifling with us, so sure of themselves they are. Why else would they let us go gadding about in here?"

There was nothing for it, so with rapid steps, they set out on the path around the mountain, to the valley where Mimir's Wellspring flowed from under the oak-tree roots. The Eye followed them unswervingly.

The first real hindrance came at a turn in the road under the mountainside, where six Darkling Riders had taken cover, one of them holding a Blazing Chalice. Sigrlinn's apprentices had two of her three greatest enemies in their sights.

The ambush had been set by all the rules of the hunter's art. Nothing betrayed their menacing presence, and the flood of fire cast from the Chalice would surely have cut short Hagen's life journey had it not been for the Lord of Asgard. Old Hropt's ancient, fine-honed sixth sense apprehended the danger, though he made no unneeded movements that might warn those lying in wait on the road ahead. Hagen's mind also offered the hazy shadow of a threat, but time did not allow it to grow into anything more telling, for Old Hropt, in a single stroke, knocked him off his feet and measured his own length alongside. A massy chunk of road stone, hurled by the Ancient God, flew into the bushes.

The road where they had but recently stood flared with a malevolent, insatiable fire, the flame cast from the Chalice seeming capable of devouring even the stone. Hagen rolled sideways and raced up toward the treacherous trembling in the bushes, in motion—in flight, say rather—unsheathing his Blue Sword, since the Disc of Iamerth would be of no use until he saw his enemy's face.

The Hedinseigh thane, ponderous in his armor of gnomish steel, broke through the green curtain of branches, his blade flashing, guided not by mind, not by feelings but by that mysterious martial instinct that sometimes awakens in times of direst danger. Cleft from shoulder to waist, the corpse of a Darkling Rider dropped at Hagen's feet.

Old Hropt was also astir. Time was—long, long ago—when his favored weapon had been a spear, but the ornately carved shaft had been broken in the fearsome battle on Borgild Field when the Young Gods had scattered the legions of the world's old masters. The Father of Hosts had ever since carried a sword, oftentimes proving that in his hands a blade could be every bit as deadly to his enemies as a spear once had been in the hands of Asgard's Lord.

With a wild battle cry, he flung himself after Hagen, his Golden Sword meeting the whirling and glittering of not one but three silvery blades, whose appearance bespoke the mighty magic invested in each weapon not by any spellmonger but by one of the Young Gods.

Hagen was left with only two opponents, but one held an apparently undistinguished chalice, which put him in mind of Gudmund's tale. His first attack was directed against the bearer of that terrible weapon. He knew they had avoided the first spate of fire by pure chance, and that if the Darkling Rider was allowed even a second to raise her Chalice again all would be ended.

So great was his confidence in his armor's soundness, he made no effort to fend off the heavy blow that crashed across his chest, but the blade grated through the first layer of rings of his brigandine and he was thrown back several paces. The second Darkling Rider—the one Gudmund had encountered—raised her Chalice exultantly.

The Father of Hosts had not come lightly by his renown as the best warrior in all of the Well-Ordered. The Golden Sword knocked aside two of three enemy steels, and Old Hropt leapt forward, a cry bursting from his chest that was inhuman in every way. But he was too late to reach the Darkling Rider with his blade. Instead, the erstwhile Lord of Asgard, unexpectedly agile and limber, swung to one side, shielding the Thane of Hedinseigh with his own body.

The stream of fire hit the Ancient God full in the chest. The fiery serpents coiled avidly about him, seizing him by the arms and trying to penetrate the narrow slits of his visor. Shrouded in flame from head to foot, he slowly lifted crossed arms—though a wonder it was he could move at all—while Hagen and the Darkling Riders alike stood stone-still.

The face of the wiccan grasping the Blazing Chalice was a picture of astonishment followed close by horror. She tried to move, and could not; she sought to call the fiery flood away from the grim and motionless figure of the Ancient God, and her weapon disobeyed her. As if draining a goblet of priceless wine, Hropt drank in the power of the Fiery Chalice, giving the wiccan no opportunity to aim the deadly flow at Hagen.

There would be time for only one sword-strike, and Hagen struck so hard his muscles appeared about to burst from the effort of it. He seemed to fly on new-sprouted wings, not touching the ground as he covered the distance that separated him from the Darkling Rider. The Blue Sword rose up and crashed down.

But either Sigrlinn's most beloved apprentice was safeguarded by far more powerful charms than all the rest or she had diverted his attack with magic-making, cunning and lightning-swift, of her own. She remained whole, although the Chalice, cleft in twain, fell at her feet.

Paying no more heed to Hropt or Hagen and saying not a word, the wiccan gathered up the two halves and darted aside, vanishing into the thickets. Hagen was left facing four Darkling Riders alone—alone because Hropt moved no more and resembled more a charred, fire-gnawed old tree-stump than a living being.

Steel forged down the ages by the best of the world's best craftsmen and impregnated with a miscellany of enchantments clashed and rang in a tiny green glade under a mad welter of firebolts. Hagen, surrounded, wove about himself a solid, glittering screen of blade-strokes, the Blue Sword slicing the air in front, to either side and behind with such speed even the most experienced eye could not follow its movements. From whichever quarter and with whatever speed the attack of the wiccans—who had forgotten Old Hropt in the heat of battle, evidently believing him dead—came, every lunge of theirs met the impenetrable wall of his sword's fanlike motions.

Once, twice, and again clanged the swords, flying together and springing apart; and each time Hagen had trouble keeping his balance. He had never encountered such enemies as these, all far more skilful than any swordsman he had ever met.

He had come into this fight with a cool head, his feelings under close control; but since being shielded from certain death by Old Hropt's own breast there had raged within him a conflagration only his enemies' blood could damp, fed by coals of hatred that naught but the pitiful groans of wiccans in torment might extinguish. Yet there was room for none of that in his mind as he battled on—a fearsome, soulless fighting machine. His cold, inhuman certainty was clearly giving the wiccans pause, for all the advantages they had over him. Their caution grew, they glanced doubtfully at each other; but the hail of blows raining down upon Hagen did not weaken, while his own strength was beginning to melt away.

Having failed in this first contest of arms, the wiccans resorted to wizardry; and although Hagen, being Hedin's apprentice, was easily able to parry their endeavors to lull him to sleep—not he himself, that is, but something in the depths of his mind—that could not continue long. He had to seek a source of power to persist in this sorcerous duel, deriving it from the faint echoes of a world-turning evoked by the sorcery of someone other than he. Unwittingly, he allowed his attention to flag, and thrice the wiccans' swords grated through his armor's rings, causing a flare of pain where the blades, although stopped by the chain mail, still left deep scores upon his body.

— *Your end is nigh*, said a delicate female voice in his mind. It could only have been that of the wiccan with the broken Chalice. *However well you* *brandish your sword, you fool, you shall soon be ours, and then you shall answer to us for all that you have done—you along with your fine friend, who is in truth more like to a roast pig now. But no matter, for the hungry—*she said a word that sounded like a name, but Hagen could not make it out—*will be boundlessly content even with such fare.*

All the thane's being—mind and body both—blended then into one, into the faultless military instrument that was his only hope for salvation. Although there should not have been even one unessential thought in his mind, the wiccan's voice still sounded there, measured and clear, pounding the phrases into his head as with a blacksmith's hammer. Will it or no, he heard every word she said; and while his attention was thus divided, another blow fell, bringing a burning, oppressive pain in his shoulder. The sword tip had punctured the skin, and his armor was almost completely perforated.

Hagen was certain his end really was upon him. He could hold out a little longer yet, as his strength ebbed and ebbed; but only until he was at last butchered like a bull in a slaughterhouse. Naught other than magic or the Disc of Iamerth could save him now, but his hand could not even take the second needed to unchain the terrible weapon from his belt.

As in a waking dream, the thane heard the creak of bare bones behind his back. Death, in the form of a skeleton with a scythe, as portrayed by every painter in all of Hjorvard's temples, was very near. Cold breath that hissed through teeth set in a grinning skull burned into the back of Hagen's head through his steel helmet.

Then, through layers of all the worlds, he heard another voice—calm, strong, sure and slightly husky. High above the field of combat, in a thickening, greenish mist, floated two eyes, each with four pupils. Those eyes looked full on the thane; and in them he read, as distinctly as in any book, *Will you really allow them to kill you with so little difficulty—you, who have claimed the attention of the Spirit of Knowing?*

The hatred, the pain of irredeemable loss and the knowledge that Hropt had, by all indications, died in order that he, Hagen, might live now burst from him in a blinding, searing, unearthly flaring that swept away all obstacles, barriers, admonitions and calculations. Come what may, he would not submit humbly to his own destruction!

He cried out, not hearing the sound of his own voice, tearing his throat with the warrior's fearsome roar—hoarse, wild, primeval, and signifying only that he sought death and would in seeking it slay all who stood before him. He was for the first time in his life utterly overtaken by the madness of war; and under the intent gaze of the Great Dragon, he hurled himself into an attack that could only end in disaster for himself or for his foes.

A wiccan sword sliced through the chain mail at his back, and he was pitched forward but did not even know it. Time stood still, as slowly—unaccountably slowly—the Blue Sword came down athwart a rising silvery blade, snapped it like a bunch of dry stalks and, continuing its death-dealing arc, stopped only when it reached the wiccan's heart. An instant later, the blade was drawn from the wound so fast not a drop of blood remained on it. The thane turned and closed fast with the three remaining swords flying toward him, knocking two of them aside while the third penetrated his brigandine and plunged into his body.

Yet Hagen felt no pain. His blue steel streaked through the air, leaving a fiery wake. It sliced the body of the nearest Darkling Rider in twain then dispatched the other two likewise.

The battle was suddenly over.

Hagen did not see the two attentive eyes of Great Orlangur fade away or the mist that enveloped them disappear. Panting, his strength gone, he fell to his knees, racked with cruel pain that bit into his mind like the stinger of a giant scorpion. The heartside of his body was drenched with blood, his left leg would not bear his weight, and his eyes smarted from the sweat dripping into them.

His recovery was long, by his own lights, for every movement brought pain; and he could not adopt the pose required for the casting of a charm to stem the bleeding. Yet no sooner had his head cleared than he limped toward Old Hropt.

The Ancient God's armor, veteran of innumerable battles, had not yet cooled, and the thane burned his hand in drawing off the helmet. He tossed the iron pot aside and shuddered when he saw what the Father of Hosts' face had become. The flame had eaten the flesh down to the bone, burned out both eyes and licked away both hair and flesh.

"Hropt," Hagen managed to say, placing a hand on the other's shoulder with a timidity he had never known before.

— *Hagen...*

The feeble whisper sounded in the thane's mind; the charred remains of the Lord of Asgard's lips did not move.

— *I live, Hagen. I have been on the very brink, but still I live. Lay me down here. And if you can, bring but a handful of water from Mimir's Well, that I may live a while longer. Only a handful. Only a mouthful...*

The voice weakened and finally faltered into silence.

No matter how excruciating his pain and fatigue, Hagen's spirit had not abandoned him. His body seemed no longer his; he forced that mound of meat and bones, brimful of suffering, to rise, and impelled it mercilessly on to the Wellspring. He no longer thought of how to best the incorruptible Sentinel. He but knew there could be no waiting for the right moment and that he must press on regardless of all.

A turn, and another, and yet another. The road rounded the last outcropping, and before him spread the enchanted valley with the majestic oak in its midst that made all the rest look like ten-year saplings. A light silvery steam rose from the Fountainhead, and the thane saw sitting by it a figure of most impressive proportions. Unhesitating, he strode straight toward to Wellspring.

He was tramping across vegetable plots. Someone poked a head from the nearest house and bawled indignantly at him, but Hagen paid no heed. The villager sprang out with pitchfork atilt, accompanied by a pair of most vicious-looking dogs, but still the thane continued on his way. The kitchen gardens seemed endless; the way around was too long; and in a roadside glade, all burned, lay Old Hropt, waiting for him whose life he had saved to bring him but a mouthful of water from the Wellspring of the Worlds.

Hedin's apprentice had likely spoiled more than one gardener's work because three more men, brandishing stakes and axes, were coming to cut him off.

The first to reach him were the dogs; but a few paces short they suddenly cringed away, howled in fear, put their tails between their legs and cowered to the ground, while their master, bolder than they, jabbed at the thane with his pitchfork. Glittering briefly, the Blue Sword split the iron trident, leaving the overzealous defender of the gardens holding a useless stick.

Seeing this, the other villagers made themselves scarce; and Hagen proceeded unhindered through the village, the one with the broken pitchfork following close behind and eyeing him with unconcealed curiosity. He even asked a question, but in a language Hagen did not know, and the enchanter's apprentice did not linger to learn more. The spell that had checked the bleeding needed strengthening or, better, replacing with a simple bandage.

He approached the Wellspring. Hervind had not erred—an aura of Great Powers radiated in waves from this place. He was dizzied, as though he had breathed the fumes of a narcotic potion.

Half a hundred steps away, the villager who had accompanied him stopped but, instead of leaving, dallied where he stood, shifting from one foot to the other. The magic and whatever else might be there seemed to trouble him not in the least.

Delivered of his unwanted companion, Hagen proceeded on to the oak. Mimir—if it was, in truth, he—rose from his bench and silently turned to face him.

He could not be called a thing of beauty, this Sentinel of the Wellspring of the Worlds, as ancient as the sky itself. His hooked nose had clearly been broken in at least three places, the skin of his face had turned bark-brown and hung in creases and folds, scored with the traces of long-healed wounds and sores. He had almost no brows but sported a bony, jutting chin and a straight slash of a mouth under thin gray whiskers.

Yet the Jotunn was no less than twice Hagen's height, his arms were powerfully muscled and, more important than that, the strength of the Wellspring had nourished this giant, had become part of him. It was not impossible the trick with the many-pawed rats was the most harmless of his jests.

"Old Hropt is wounded," the weary Hagen said, looking firmly into the Jotunn's faded eyes, "and requests a handful of water from your Wellspring. He can give no gage, for his eyes are burned away. Help him, I beg of you."

"You have no greeting for me, young wizardling?" Mimir rumbled in reply. "Or is your human kind no longer wont to give greetings?"

"I would wish to hail you for long ages, O Jotunn," Hagen said patiently, "but I did not think you so capricious as to demand observation of all the amenities at such a pass as this."

Mimir was silent a while, scrutinizing the thane closely.

"Then who has sent you, wizardling?" he inquired, still blocking Hagen's way to the Wellspring. "I do not see in you the strength that would bring you here of yourself, and the Divine Pleasure is not upon you. Who has sent you, young wizardling?"

"If I tell you, will you permit me to take one handful of water from your Wellspring?" Hagen asked, in the same patient tone.

"When I ask, an answer must be given, little wizardling—unless you wish something disagreeable to befall you," the giant said with a sententious sneer, and Hagen found himself thinking that this Jotunn—once famed as the wisest of the wise, the last of the giants, stern, incorruptible and just, who had played no part in the war against the Aesir—was greatly aged; and that the change in him had not been for the better.

His wounded side pained him, and he lacked the strength to continue supporting the spell that staunched the bleeding. However, his muscles were still in good trim. Feinting left, he sprang to the right, his mind made up not to waste any more precious time. The Jotunn's long, grasping hands vainly raked the air, but the thane tore off his helmet and scooped up the bubbling water that glittered with every color of the rainbow. He did not allow the sorcery of that place to take him under its spell, although a murky wave of enchantments did come lapping at his mind.

"Halt, madman!" the Jotunn's voice thundered at his back, no longer taunting now but full of fear—and not for himself, either, as the fleeing Hagen understood. "If you give that to Hropt…"

But the rest of the tirade went unheard, for the ground under the thane's feet was suddenly alive. The vegetable gardens through which he ran were thick with odd, dark-skinned creatures, lizard-like except that each was also endowed with two hands made for hard gripping. The heavens awoke with a wrathful thunder like the booming of some improbably mighty—and enraged—voice. The Eye in the sky, which had throughout held Hagen under its keen gaze, was clouded in a crimson mist.

Then the sky shook, in a silence more terrifying than any sound. It was as if gigantic yet noiseless battering rams were pounding at the doors of this world, there being no time to pick their intricate locks.

Hagen evaded lizard after lizard after lizard, trying as best he could not to tip any of the water from his helmet. He was running full tilt, hoping for nothing. Above his head, a silvery fan of droplets spread, each turning in mid-air into the likeness of an air-breathing octopus with a tangle of sticky tentacles; and they fell with one accord to wind about his feet. He could not even fight them off with his sword for fear of spilling the precious moisture he carried.

Out of the corner of his eye, he saw the strange inhabitants of that strange village pouring out of their houses to stand and stare at him, but there was no help to be expected from that quarter.

Mimir's creatures grasped at his legs, clambering up the outside of his clothing. Hagen gagged with loathing and, seeing his way was blocked, settled on desperate measures. Heedless of the paws and tentacles that held him, he unchained the Disc of Iamerth from his belt with one hand, turned to Mimir and shouted, holding the Weapon of Light high above his head, "Call them off, Jotunn, or…!"

Mimir, without a moment's thought, threw up his arm, and his slaves halted on the instant.

"How came you upon that, wizard?" the giant thundered.

"What can it matter? I have it, it is mine and it obeys me."

"Great Powers!" the horrorstruck Mimir said to himself, so low Hedin's apprentice could barely make out the words.

The old Jotunn grasped his head in his hands, slowly turned his back to Hagen and sat hunched over in a pose that spoke only of utter despair. He was, it seemed, not in the slightest concerned with Hagen anymore.

Dragging off the clutching paws, Hagen went on his way. He cared nothing for Mimir's present troubles, cared not to know what people inhabited the village for, down the way, in the wood, Old Hropt awaited him; and the Young Gods themselves could not stay his steps.

In the glade, all—the motionless, sundered bodies of the wiccans and Old Hropt—was as he had left it. The Ancient God was neither moving nor breathing, and seemed to have departed this life; but as Hagen approached, he heard in his mind the familiar—albeit very faint—voice of the Father of Hosts.

— *Hurry, apprentice of Hedin... The world runs mad, and we must make haste...*

"I have brought you water. Drink." Hagen carefully raised Hropt's maimed head, bringing the helmet to his lips.

There was a multitudinous crackling and rustling in the bushes around them; Hagen looked up and saw they were surrounded by the servants of Mimir. But they occupied his thoughts not at all at that time—Hropt was his only care.

The fearful wounds began to close as he watched. New flesh grew through the blackened skin. The eyeballs swelled like sprouting shoots. Amidst the charring, eyelids appeared, pink as those of a newborn babe.

It cannot be said that a few minutes later Old Hropt's face bore no signs of having been burned—weals and wrinkles still liberally scored brow, chin and cheeks—but sight had returned to the eyes, and there is naught more important than that.

The Father of Hosts struggled to his feet with Hagen's help.

"I thank you," was all he said, laying a hand on the thane's shoulder and instilling all that words could not say into one short but strong handshake.

The multitude of unblinking eyes, alert and avid, that watched them were shortly joined by those of people as a good dozen villagers, ignoring Mimir's creatures standing fast all around, came for a closer look at the newcomers.

"Can you walk, Hropt?" Hagen asked, glancing askance at that peculiar circle of spectators.

"I'd say so," the Ancient God replied between gritted teeth. "Time was when that fire would not have harmed me..."

"Away with memories. Better tell me what we are to do with *them*." Hagen nodded toward people and beasts. "Do you know aught about them?"

"Of them I have heard," the Lord of Asgard responded, wincing with pain. "We need to break through to the Wellspring whilst they still stand bewildered."

He picked up the Golden Sword, and they turned back down the path to Mimir's abode, Hagen holding the Disc of Iamerth at the ready.

"Best put that up," Hropt said. "No one knows what will happen if it were to hit the old Jotunn. Mimir, you know, is himself a Power. I have never understood him."

"But the water from the Seething Fountainhead saved you!"

"Me, yes. But you it would not have saved. It remembers me only too well. My pledge lay too long, down the ages, on the bottom of the Wellspring. I am soaked through with that water; it has become part of me and I of it."

Hropt's last words were almost inaudible. His head had fallen to his chest, and his feet scarce shuffled along.

They were forcing their way through a solid wall of undergrowth made more dense by the hands, paws and tentacles of Mimir's servants. The people, too, were slow to disperse, and gazed intently at Hagen and Hropt, neither hindering nor helping them but simply stepping to either side.

"What makes them our tagtails?" Hagen hissed through clenched teeth.

"They're stalking us," Hropt replied in a low, strained voice. "I know not what we'll be able to do at the Wellspring, Hagen. I have no strength left in me, somehow."

Hagen pulled up, and those who accompanied them stopped, too, their rapt gazes unwavering. *Hropt can go no farther,* he thought. *And even should pride goad him on, he'll be of no benefit to me in battle.*

Dull despair, a repulsive snake, crept toward his heart. Many and varied were the predicaments he had faced, but none had seemed to him as hopeless as this. He glared at the Eye up above. Even though branches hid them from it now, still the thane felt that look slinking tenaciously behind them, alien and hostile.

How long must this go on? The fight with the wiccans was easier! And there, at the Wellspring, Mimir awaits us—the Jotunn, afraid as no Jotunn should be. How will he greet us this time?

The Jotunn greeted them in full war regalia, very ancient and made of the bulky hides of beasts that had vanished long, long before, with bone plates sewn to chest, belly and sides. In his hand, he gripped a stone ax.

They stopped in their tracks. The Sentinel of the Well had never thought to hide or to set a trap for them. Again Hagen's insubordinate hand reached for the Disc of Iamerth.

"Approach, then, you defilers of the world! I know all. I know whence you came and why you are here. Approach, and try to take that for which you have come!"

Behind the giant's back stood a figure draped in a light-blue cloak, making intricate magical passes over the Fountainhead. The stranger cast a fleeting glance at Hagen and Hropt then again leaned toward the water.

That figure was elusively familiar to Hagen, and the threat that emanated from it, as perceptible as the sun through closed lids, forced him to forget even Mimir for an instant.

Meanwhile, the Jotunn's creatures came hurrying out of the wood with a whish, a swish and a rustle, running carefully around the feet of the villagers—maybe two dozen of them now—who followed in leisurely pursuit of the Father of Hosts and the Thane of Hedinseigh.

Old Hropt gave a low, menacing war cry. The Golden Sword rose into position, and he moved briskly toward Mimir. *And whence comes such strength?* Hagen wondered.

The giant smiled ominously and came forward, slowly lifting his stone ax.

"Wait, O Jotunn!" Hagen cried. "Mayhap you can tell us what is afoot here, and why you come armed against us, although I did naught but give a mouthful of water from this Wellspring to one who suffered."

The reply was a deep rumble. "When your..." A small laugh. "...your friend went under a name somewhat different, he came to me to ask for water from this Wellspring. I agreed, thinking it would increase his wisdom, but—alas!—I erred. Therefore, I shall not tell you all. You will not understand. But it would benefit you to know, wizard, that the patience of our benefactors, the Young Gods, has finally snapped, and there is something most disagreeable in store for you and your..." Another small laugh. "...Teacher. You have violated the painstakingly established Balance of great and universal forces—"

"The stupid fairytale I heard in my captivity!" Old Hropt roared. "When I alone remained after the battle, I was given long instruction in suchlike folderol. But by the bye, Mimir, the bones of your kin richly adorned the fateful field that day. Almost all the race of the Jotnar perished. Why, then, do you call the Young Gods your benefactors?"

"That is not for you to know," Mimir snarled, not slackening his pace. "My kinsfolk were foolish enough not to understand the need to acknowledge a new power, not to know the Creator had charged that power to rule the world. They paid for their lack of knowing. But you also are at fault. Why did you provoke them to engage in an avowedly hopeless battle? For that, too, you must pay."

The stone ax, terrifying in its aspect and made of a single craggy block, was already hoisted high, ready to deal a single, undeflectable blow. The stranger in the blue cloak continued his wizardry over the Wellspring.

A terrible thought struck Hagen like a scourge—*What if he has come to take the true emblem?*

Before awareness, circumspection or even Old Hropt could stop him, Hagen had dispatched the death-dealing Disc with a short and powerful spell. He guessed, with a presentiment more powerful than any intellect, that this must be one of the Strong—a Mage, a mortal wizard or perhaps even a lesser servant of the Young Gods—but he made no attempt to discover who this sorcerer was or why a chill ran across his skin when he looked upon him. He flung the Disc, entrusting far more than his life to the swift flight of that glittering circle of bewitched metal.

The Disc went right through the strange being's head and, howling its displeasure, returned to the thane's hand.

It was a Spirit Marshal.

Hagen had heard much of them from his Teacher, but had never seen one with his own eyes. They and the Winged Sentinels were among the Young Gods' best warriors. It was said there were but twelve of them, and that the beginning of their path was lost in the mists of the world's infancy. They had served the Young Gods long and faithfully, and had covered themselves with glory on Borgild Field, where none had withstood their might. They had bested all the Aesir in single combat save Old Hropt, then bearing another name. He had been able to defeat his opponent, breaking the thread of the strange life that inhabited a spectral body not susceptible to Earthly armaments.

Hagen now understood why the stranger's form had seemed so familiar to him, from its close resemblance to the astral likeness of Iamerth that had descended into the Chamber of Altars in the temple in the Sovereign City. This, the most powerful of the Spirit Marshals, stood on the highest step of Iamerth's throne. *First Servant of Light* was the grandiose title it bore, and it had even taken on the external features of the great god, which was not difficult, it being itself formless.

Old Hropt set his wounded head at an obstinate tilt. And, though Hagen could not see Hropt's eyes behind the helmet's narrow eye-slit, it seemed to him their reborn gaze burned with a hatred so ancient, profound and unquenchable that even the faceplate glowed. The Father of Hosts was again, after long ages, meeting his enemy of yore.

"So 'tis you has taken Iaal's place," the Lord of Asgard growled. "I lambasted him well enough in my day!"

The Spirit Marshal unhurriedly turned its fleshless head toward him.

"Ah, you live," it said in a wan, dry voice that held no surprise, no mockery, and simply noted the fact to itself. "Wait a little for me to finish, and then I shall occupy myself with you. Our meeting has, by the great mercy of my suzerain, Iamerth the Most Fair, been too long postponed, while your clumsy attempts to exact retribution still amused him. But his patience has run dry, he is no longer entertained, the time has come…"

Lowering his head like a bull, Hropt launched a silent attack. Hagen was jolted by the supple surge of air raised by that first mighty leap. The Father of Hosts sped past Mimir, who stood rooted to the spot, hoisted the Golden Sword as he ran while loosening something from his belt with his free hand. Both the Jotunn and Hedin's apprentice could only follow the Ancient God with eyes full of amazement.

The Spirit Marshal turned to face the unanticipated threat, its raiment swaying and the Fountainhead's stone rim showing through the translucent border. What transpired next—the clash of those two fabled foes—Hagen did not see, because all of Mimir's wrath was unleashed upon him.

The stone ax fell with the speed of lightning, leaving Hedin's apprentice mystified as to how the Sentinel of the Well could have come so close. He ducked away at the last moment, and the great block ploughed the ground at his feet, sending up a fountain of sod.

A few seconds only were needed to aim the Disc of Iamerth at its new target; but Mimir, like as not, was well cognizant of that glittering thing in his opponent's hand, and would not allow Hagen those seconds. Hedin's apprentice could not even make use of his Blue Sword, so fast was the ax wrenched out of the ground, again raised and again brought down. Once more he was saved by only the slightest span.

The thane was left with no alternative to shameful retreat, for in order to employ the Disc there had to be a dozen feet or so between him and the

Sentinel of the Well. But Mimir guessed what his foe was about to do, and again his ax shook the ground, while scores of his diminutive servants—the lizards, the octopuses and the rest—streamed toward Hagen.

Seeing no escape, the thane made a long, desperate leap, and when the great stone mass fell from above, its edge only grazed his shoulder where his armor, already badly damaged in the affray with the Darkling Riders, gave way with a grating sound.

Yet in the short time it took for the jubilant Jotunn to raise his weapon a fourth time, Hagen was able to cast a spell, the deathly danger having increased his strength ten times over, and hurl the Disc.

Mimir had aimed his ax at the prostrate thane's head, and it came down fast; but as it fell, it collided with the weapon of Iamerth. As it had in the encounter with the White Blade in the Temple of the Sun, the Disc saved its master once again. The ax flew upward as if rebounding from an unseen barrier—so powerfully that Mimir, caught by surprise, let it go. In that instant, the Disc hit him in the face.

The old Jotunn, though, was made of far sterner stuff than stone or steel. He made no wizardry to catch the Disc, did not try to stop it as Merlin had, either because the time was lacking or because he did not know the charm. A bloody welt appeared across his broad forehead, as from the blow of a whip, but more than that even the Disc of Iamerth, which Hagen had long deemed inexorable and all-powerful, could not do.

The Weapon of Light returned to the thane's hand, and Mimir did not even trouble to wipe the blood from his face. The Jotunn's helpmeets, in their dozens, seized upon Hagen's arms and legs. In a desperate attempt to beat them off, he brandished the sword, held in his left hand, the blade inscribing a wide arc of dark blood and leaving a swath of cloven bodies behind it. But the stone ax would surely have struck him dead at last, had not a voice resounded behind Mimir's back, halting the Sentinel of the Wellspring of the Worlds in his tracks.

"Throw down your cudgel and look at me!"

That voice, it seemed, would have forced the dead to quit the gray bourns of Niflhel. The ground trembled and groaned at the sound, the Jotunn's servants started back in horror, and Mimir, lowering his weapon carefully, turned, the very picture of utter astonishment, shock—and fear.

It was the second time Hagen and Hropt had frightened the intrepid Jotunn. The first time he had scared himself through his own thoughts, his own visions of horrible catastrophes known only to him. This time it was the voice of Old Hropt that had pulled him up.

Yet Hropt could no longer be called "old." The voice Hagen heard was that of the true Lord of Asgard and Midgard in the flower of his might, when the Jotnar had trembled at the mere sound of his name.

The ax came to rest on the grass. Only then could Hagen see the Fountainhead and the pile of dirty blue rags draped over its rim. It was all that remained of the dread Spirit Marshal.

"Do you know what this is, Mimir?" thundered Hropt. "With it I brought to book that fribbling spirit, which now more resembles a ragged sheet a-blowing in the wind!"

"You have taken leave of your senses, old fool," said the Sentinel of the Well, with the unlooked-for bitterness of despair. "Yes, I know what it is, and I know how it fell into your hands. It is the Staff that wrests out the souls of those whom the Young Gods wish to punish. I see that you have drunk in the strength of the Marshal like strong old wine, and you are overfilled with might. I know you are now able to contend even with me. And I apprehend, too, that the Balance of Powers has now forever foundered, that the Battle of the Gods is inevitable, and my ax will not return to its place until that strife is ended."

"Return to its place?" A hollow chuckle emerged from beneath the iron cap of Hropt's helmet.

The Jotunn gave a wry grin. "Knew you not that my ax is one of the three stones that undergird the Pillar of the Titans, the nail that secures the Worldframe and at whose summit stands the Castle of All the Ancients? I dread to think what will befall if the Pillar does not withstand the coming tempest."

Here the inhabitants of the strange village—keen and close observers still—exchanged sudden glances.

"And you are to blame for it all, you and the Teacher of that hothead." Mimir nodded toward Hagen. "But you it was, all consumed with the thirst for vengeance, who led the young Mage astray from the true path, ignited in him a terrible blaze of ambition and set him, like the mad dog he is, upon the established order of the world. I find that the water from my Wellspring has brought you no benefit...Hropt. You are prepared to transform All That Is into naught—only to gratify yourself."

"Why all these empty words, Mimir?" the Father of Hosts broke in. "You know why we have come. The Spirit Marshal must needs have told you that. So choose now. Either you will let us pass to the Wellspring...or you will have to deal with me."

All was quiet then. Mimir's head was bent low, as in thought, and the hand that lay on his ax quivered faintly. Only then could the thane raise his eyes to the Lord of Asgard.

Outwardly, Hropt had changed not at all, but even a cursory magical glance was enough for Hagen to know the Ancient God had been imbued with new strength—a sure and cruel strength that was no way in keeping with his inner self ere then. It was the strength of another, and was but loosely anchored in him, putting Hagen in mind of water carried in a goatskin by a traveler in the desert, which diminishes with every passing day.

The Father of Hosts was grasping the never-to-be-forgotten Staff of the Winged Sentinel—quite carelessly, in his bare hands. Though its stem still gave off a feeble greenish glow and a light fume of smoke floated over it, the Young Gods' fearsome weapon was dead—Hagen was certain of that. The senses Hedin had nurtured and refined in him told him clearly that its monstrous maw had slammed shut for good and all. The Staff, it transpired, could be used only once; he at last knew why the Winged Sentinel had brought two to the temple.

"Heed me a while longer, Hropt," Mimir said, with a hint of entreaty in his voice. "You know I have never insinuated myself into any war. I hate them, and always have. I did not avenge myself upon you for my slain kinsfolk, because they were not in their right minds. Nor did I avenge myself upon the Young Gods, because under their rule the world has at last known respite."

"And has become peaceful as a graveyard!" Old Hropt interjected.

"Have humans and Mages not had their fill of fighting in the world?" Mimir urged. "True, the Masters of the Hallowed Land have assumed control of All That Is, but think on it—they have the Creator's blessing. Again I appeal to you. You used to love humans—indeed, you loved all mortals and immortals without exception, and defended them against the giants, my own bloodthirsty kin. How, then, can you do this thing? In the war you are fomenting all could perish—even those peoples you formerly defended. Is that not senseless? Trust in me, and I will open the parley.

"And hearken not to Orlangur's flattery! I know him only too well—he has no heart. To him the world entire is naught but a clownish farce. He stages endless charades for his own pleasure—the only difference being that here when the actors die they are really dead."

Hropt shook his head. "I will not argue with you, O Wise One, and shall say only this: you, I, my brothers and my children were the first masters of this world. We did not prevent any shoot from sprouting, and forced none to grow according to our whims. Much has the water from your Wellspring given me,

Mimir. I understood, even before that battle on Borgild Field, that the world has no further need of us gods and demigods, save for you. Something has happened to its inhabitants—the Pillars of the Third Power, Orlangur and Demogorgon, came into the world for good reason.

"Henceforth, mortals and immortals alike shall have no use for our leadership, loath as we may be to own it. I know whereof I speak, for I have lived ages without number in human lands. Furthermore, few mortals ever perished in our armies—no more, in any event, than in their habitual internecine warfare.

"To forbid humans and others to resolve their own quarrels—albeit at times even by force—is to make them our livestock, to do with as we will. It is not merely vengeance I wish, Mimir. I wish for the Young Gods to be forever gone. There are enough other powers in the world."

Mimir shook his head in his turn. "I expected you to speak so. You are in some ways, perhaps, correct, but you have forgotten one thing. Magical Powers exist in the world, whether you will or no, and to prevent them from scattering all the Well-Ordered as dust, gods are needed—"

"Enough of this." Vexed now, Hropt cut short the debate. "Say at last if you will allow us to remove the emblem from the Wellspring."

Another silence fell. Then, after a few minutes, Mimir slowly and morosely inclined his head to signal his agreement.

Hropt drew a relieved breath. "Now, that is grand—an act of true wisdom. Hagen, my son, go and take the emblem from the Fountainhead. I may not be near it, or all the world will fly out of joint."

Hagen rose slowly—he had been down on one knee when Hropt spoke—and walked to the Wellspring as one half-asleep. His head was reeling.

He was about to plunge his hands into the Wellspring's churning, overflowing waters when the silent witnesses of the encounter with Mimir—every resident of that strange village—turned, one and all, and fled back to their homes, shouting as they ran. A chill ran down the fearless thane's spine when among those cries he distinctly heard words spoken in the native tongue of Eastern Hjorvard: "Brann must be warned!"

HEDIN

I STOOD IN THE VERY MIDDLE OF A LAVISHLY APPOINTED SALON, WHERE HEAVY CLOTH-OF-gold draped the walls and long garlands of sapphires a hundred times more lovely than any mined in Southern Hjorvard hung, glowing with an unearthly light, from silver cabinets. My feet sank into soft carpeting woven of charm-strengthened down. My kinsfolk had always been much taken by luxury, a failing that had also been mine in my younger days.

The Band of Erith made me feel that I was no longer in my sanctum of spellcraft but had been magically transported to the barque of the Castle of All the Ancients.

"Why are you here, traitor?" Shendar, still filling Merlin's place as the head of the Council, thundered. "To sue for forgiveness? Too late!"

"Whence came the notion that I propose to surrender?" I asked in genuine surprise. "I'd say it is your armies that are broken and fleeing, not mine. And it is I who would suggest you remove from my fortress while you still may, ere something untoward befalls your own selves."

I caught then the fleeting flow of some strange magical command issued by Shendar but could not grasp its essence, for he was a strong sorcerer and master of many refined techniques of wizardry, and knew how to conceal his magic-making.

"And what else have you to suggest?" he asked with a grin that narrowed his eyes. "Would you have us humbly hand you the keys to our palaces in Jibulistan? Or power over our apprentices, one and all?"

"I have no need for the keys to your palaces," I replied. "But as to your apprentices, of that we may speak. I would like to know why your wrath did not turn against Sigrlinn when she taught the Darkling Riders her magic. How say you—is that not a violation of the Law of the Ancients?"

An alarmed murmur spread throughout the hall. To all appearances, none but Shendar, Makran and Esteri had known of this.

"I rebelled to free my one friend from imprisonment," I continued. "I achieved my purpose and now fight only to compel my foes to peace, for I am not Merlin, and have no desire to kill. You may have marked that I have not broken the Law of the Ancients—my charms were conjured and Rakoth's servants were dispatched chiefly against the creations of your magic and never against the mortals you had besotted. My magic-making has directly caused the death of none of them."

A magical power beyond my understanding was slowly filling the opulent hall. Unable to consult with the Diviner, I could not know the meaning or purpose of that power, and could therefore only be vigilant. I hesitated, wondering again if I should tell the Generation that Felostei was preparing to give life to a new Mage, who would be the beginning of my kinsfolk's end—and my own, too, unless I could contrive a way to prevent it.

In donning the Band of Erith, I had wished most of all to discover if my former comrades of the Generation were prepared to prolong this war, and what they might know about the Unnamable. And once again, as after the failure of their first storming of my fortress, I saw no perplexity in them. Though their look was far from cheery—was even woebegone, in truth—their demeanor was one of exceeding confidence, as if it would be naught to them to raise against me yet more worlds, in their thousands.

In years gone by, Sigrlinn alone, supported by the simple might of the Castle of All the Ancients, had been more than a match for all my Empire of Night; yet now the Generation entire, with Great Merlin added for good measure, could not master me. True, I had created a Talisman, but though that column of flame in my apartments in the Hedinseigh citadel was a source of new strength to me, it also rendered me one hundred times more vulnerable. In point of fact, I could at that time quit the island only in dire extremity. I could not even go to the aid of Hagen and Hropt, had they been in the veriest mortal danger. And while the Mages of the Generation lingered here, nigh to Hedinseigh, I could not fully count on Rakoth.

So, my kin either knew nothing yet of the Unnamable or were startlingly self-possessed. I, too, was calm, but only at great cost to myself, and in the persistent hope that perhaps all would still go smoothly and that an untried spell, especially one as complex as Rakoth had cast, might not work on first trying.

Still, Shendar and his cabal showed no inclination to yield, and Merlin's absence seemed to surprise them not one whit. To look at them, one might think events were transpiring exactly as they should.

I knew the charm cast by Rakoth had perforce delayed the advent of the Young Gods onto the field of battle. What could they care for two rebellious Mages, now that all their domains might be threatened with destruction?

"In sum, you are determined not to leave, and wish to continue this war?" I said. "So be it. Then let us not contend through our armies but directly, with our Mage-strength. But do you not fear that there, too, your hopes will desert you?"

Again I sensed a swift command issuing from Shendar, and the interwoven strengths of my kinsfolk grew taut. The specter created by my Band of Erith had become the target of a bevy of hostile charms. I stood motionless, still not understanding their intent, for the Erithaean Shade had down the ages been deemed unassailable.

A staggering pain, as from a swingeing blow, suddenly exploded in my head. I believe I may have groaned as the crimson deeps closed over me. In my sanctum of spellcraft I was seared as by fire, but there, where my Erithaean Twin stood, was sanctuary. Powerful forces were drawing me there irresistibly, and my mind would gladly have flown like a bird from my tormented body to find peace and healing in that silvery barque. I saw the faces of my kin, all concern and sympathy now. They and only they could save me, and I reached out to them with all the strength left to me.

A sharp cuff hurled me to the floor of my sanctum. My unseeing eyes were filled with a mad whirligig of crackbrained scenes. Then a cold, cruel vice compressed my mind, and the world gave itself one last shake and was still. Someone's hand tore the Band from my head.

I lay on the tiled floor, my back against a wall, blood seeping from my nose and ears, and my head sundered by a strange drawing pain. Leaning over me, looking with alarm into my eyes and holding my hand, was Rakoth. The chamber window was smashed, and the stout rods of its grating had been wrested from the stone frame where they had been solidly set by gnomish artisans.

"Great One be praised, you live!" he sighed in relief, and dropped feebly into a chair. "How could you let them land you like that? I saw their arrow break through both of the defensive barriers over the island and strike the window of your tower, and I fair flew up here, but even so I was barely in time. They had already begun to haul you over to them. You were splitting in two—a gruesome sight, if ever there was one! All I could do was try to cleave the fetters that bound you. And so I did, but I fear that was near as bad as what they did to you."

Still talking, he rose, flung open the door, took from a servant's hands a wide-mouthed goblet of hot wine and carefully raised it to my lips.

"Drink. Drink, and gather yourself—but smartly, now. Our kith and kin have at last condescended to notice the Distant Ones and their allies, the First-Begotten, and I am afraid the surprise of that will drive them to singular shifts. Damn me if the time wasn't too short to deal with them as I ought! And the Distant Ones are already close at hand!"

The glowing warmth of the wine helped restore my strength. Leaning on Rakoth's arm, I struggled to my feet.

He was impatient now. "Decide, Hedin. Decide what we are to do!" His words drilled into my mind like hot augurs. "Or I shall have to go and burn that whole fleet, and your amiable elves along with it."

"W–Wait…" I finally let go of the Rebel's arm and strode unsteadily to the gap where a window had been. The remnants of my Generation's squadron had dispersed without trace, like a mist in a stiff breeze; and all I saw was the irreproachable beauty of elven vessels in tight formation.

They had, without question, had a fine view of everything suffered by the foes that preceded them, yet the high commander of the First-Begotten's forces seemed undismayed, for the even ranks of radiant ships still moved toward my fortress, a magical wind filling their sails. Looking close, I could see rows of silvery helmets glittering above their steep sides.

The Mages' gorgeous barque hung motionless on the waves of the aerial ocean; the leading elven ships had pulled level with it now. And in the further distance, to the north, a huge greenish sphere—a tissue of glowing threads—was approaching. Even a cursory glance disclosed its gigantic might, and while I knew not what was in that monstrous thing, there was no doubting whence it came. The Distant Ones had left their secret abodes at the farthest bounds of the Well-Ordered, and were now closing on us in full strength.

I was slowly recovering from the blow dealt me through the Band of Erith. I had to acknowledge Shendar had performed the complex maneuver masterfully, weaving a spell of great artfulness entirely unbeknownst to me, and had—also unbeknownst to me, if you please—united the strength of all the Mages of the Generation to wrest mind and body apart, enticing my reason into the astral likeness of an Erithaean Shade. Silently, I gave him his due, for I would have been his prisoner by now had Rakoth not come.

But what was to be done with the Distant Ones? They, unlike the Mages, were not about to crouch behind the backs of others. The huge sphere in which the power of the Distant Ones lay compacted had overtaken the orderly ranks of elven vessels and was making straight for the silvery Mage-barque. Its very movement was alive with menace, and here again I had to credit Shendar for his common sense. As if swept up in a mighty tempest, his elegant little craft broke from its moorings and swept away from my island. Its outlines were wreathed in haze, which told me that someone aboard was trying in great haste to open the Gates of the Worlds. Then a bolt of green lightning from the top of the Distant Ones' sphere burst vainly in the empty sky. My kinsfolk were gone.

I rushed to the Diviner, which, well apprised of its duties, was already unfolding before me the intricate runes of the magical formulae employed by the Distant Ones. I gasped for breath, hard put to understand even the tenth part of what I saw, for the power of the Distant Ones was utterly foreign to the world we knew. It rested on a different foundation, and was portrayed in spells that were almost entirely inaccessible to me

Now I knew why the Young Gods were not intervening. They were, without a doubt, fully aware of the Distant Ones' invasion and of its target, and were serenely biding their time. The Unnamable was theirs, and perhaps they were even now extinguishing the remains of the charm Rakoth had cast, leaving it to others to settle scores with the mutinous jackstraw of a sorcerer I was to them. Then, when both sides had worn each other out, it would be the gods' time to appear in the arena, as the dread, all-conquering rulers and chastisers of the world.

"A bad business," Rakoth murmured, looking over my shoulder at the long files of fiery runic symbols. "This is beyond me. The basis seems familiar, but the recasting…damnation, 'tis all topsy-turvy!"

"Yet it works," I retorted. "And for now I don't know what defense to mount against it."

"Excellent. But then what need have they of elven warriors? What benefit are those swords, enchanted though they may be? I'd say it means they do not rely upon themselves in all things."

"Splendid reasoning, but what of it?"

"They won't be able to break through your defenses," Rakoth declared with great assurance.

I made a wry face. The Rebel had, I thought, begun to blather.

The sphere of the Distant Ones was by then no more than a couple of miles from Hedinseigh's bastions. Having drawn level with the elves' front lines, the green monstrosity suddenly slowed to match the speed of the First-Begotten's longships.

A third assault, I thought with weary detachment. *And always the same beginning. Flotilla, ships, squadrons—there's nothing new here. We shall endure. I built this fortress with the foreknowledge we would be thus beleaguered. Perhaps Rakoth is right, and the Distant Ones do, indeed, need something—elven blades, for instance—to supplement their magic.*

Shendar's underhanded strike was still wearing on me somewhat, and I did not have the slightest inkling of what to do next. I eyed the precise alignments of my new adversaries with a strange indifference, although I should long ago have been sending out crews to man the remnant of the catapults and ballistas, or lacing new charms of destructive power, or at least preparing myself to counter a blow from the Great Fire.

Having not received the order to attack, Rakoth's servants were slowly returning to the fortress. The sea-beasts and krakens had hidden themselves deep beneath the waves, the legions of shades had vanished into the crannies of the sea-cliffs, the dragons had perched, like roosting chickens, on the sharp peaks by the shore, their big eyes, violet flecked with gold, fixed upon the oncoming First-Begotten.

The Rebel stood at my side, arms folded across his chest, watching the sphere of the Distant Ones with rapt and silent attention.

"Rakoth, my strength is gone," I confessed to him. "I must go derive more from the Talisman. Take command for now."

The Fallen Mage shook his head.

"This is your island. It is saturated with your magic, and the best I could do would be to send out the last of my servants. But I've never trusted those elves—they have no wish to fight fair. Belike they're awaiting my attack and are prepared for it. Besides, you saw, did you not, how our kith and kin scampered from the Distant Ones? They, who almost had you, mighty as your Talisman may be? The lightning of the Distant Ones is a fearsome thing, and if I were to send my forces beyond your island's defenses, they'd be cut down almost to the last before coming anywhere near that thrice-accursed sphere."

I gave a glum nod. "Well and good. Then let's try to revive our shields, although Merlin's arrows have left us little enough to work with."

The Distant Ones were continuing their approach—calm, confident, unhurried, as if inviting me to test on them all the combat magic I knew. And, though I knew not a little, something held me from that solution, which had offered itself up too readily somehow.

— Diviner, is there a defense around the sphere?

— Their magic passes my understanding, my invaluable aide grated in my mind. *What seems to you a sphere is a skein of sorcery, and such that time itself runs mad there, twisting and tangling. I cannot imagine such a thing and nor, I doubt me, can you. Terrible is the heft of the forces it contains, and if they descend even a little, you will, I think, see that their sphere drinks from the sea. Under the surface of that sphere, new Worldflesh is born. The heft draws...draws from the emptiness new threads for the fabric of the Real.*

Accompanying the Diviner's words, against a portal opened wide into its world, sped the fiery strokes of runes, forming themselves into such elaborate locutions of the Unsurpassable Magic that in a matter of seconds my mind was floundering from the effort of interpreting them.

"What, then—are they looking to make landfall along with the elves?" a mystified Rakoth muttered under his breath, abandoning his vain attempts to understand anything in the sorcery of the Distant Ones and turning to look through the window.

His question went unanswered, for I had at last hit upon some relatively familiar magical constructs. The Distant Ones were defending themselves behind a Great Charm of Reflection, which is otherwise called a Mirrorspell. Any strike against them would circle the sphere and return again to he who sent it, augmented with the Distant Ones' own might. That was achieved, I must say, by ruses quite unusual and hard to understand—tricks played with time, weight and space—but those portions of the charm responsible for "welcoming in," so to say, a stroke of magic from an enemy were entirely ordinary and had manifestly been borrowed from wizardly systems in common use among the Mages of my Generation.

Having seized upon that strand, I began to unravel the skein, searching for even one point of weakness.

The enemy fleet was no more than a mile away.

"What if we asked Sigrlinn?" Rakoth suddenly suggested. "Since she's been a prisoner of the Distant Ones, maybe she knows something we can use."

"More timely you could not be!" I snorted, with less control than I might have had. "I can't speak with her now. But if you have everything ready, be my guest. You know the Unlocking Charm."

"Don't be angry, Hedin," Rakoth said soothingly. "I could set all my regiments afoot this very moment, but even you don't know yet whether to attack your dearest darling elves or send all our forces against the Distant Ones. They are dawdling their way to us. I'll have time aplenty to confer awhile with Sigrlinn. And fear not—I won't let her go."

To lend strength to his argument, he raised a clenched fist. His scarlet cloak flew back, a tongue of fire, and under the Rebel's hand my apartments filled with a flaring flood of impenetrable darkness. Once again there stood before me the grim, merciless, implacable Lord of Gloom.

His steps faded away down the corridor as I continued my all but hopeless quest for a break in the Distant Ones' harmonious, seemingly perfect magical system, summoning to my aid all my knowledge and experience and feverishly combing my memory for all I had ever heard of them. Maybe Rakoth's idea of consulting Sigrlinn was not so unreasonable after all, for if her apprentice of the Fiery Chalice had almost defeated a whole convocation of the Distant Powers' disciples in the vale of Brunevagar, the sorceress must surely know some of our uninvited guests' secrets.

But even if she did, there was no time to wheedle them out of her. I did not need the Diviner to make me vividly aware of the growing strain in the flow of magical forces, of the powerful excitation to which they were being subjected. The Distant Ones were preparing to strike, and I could not wait until that strike came and laid my adversary open, allowing me to launch one swift counterattack—because I knew neither what the blow would be nor how strongly it would be dealt. And it might be the last I ever felt if my Talisman were to perish in the process, even if only under a tumbled pile of stone.

Strike first? But with what? All my reserves were already in play, except those set aside for a battle with the Young Gods. A Black Spear, such as I had recently used to burn Avalon? But that kind of concentrated power was exactly what the Distant Ones expected from a commonplace Mage, exactly what their defenses were designed to counter. Fire? Fire…the Fiery Chalice. No doubt that was Sigrlinn's doing. But what, exactly, is that fire?

As if guessing my unwillingness to destroy the elves, at odds though we now were, the Distant Ones hovered over the First-Begotten's vessels, seeming tethered to them.

"Decide, then, and do something! Anything!" I barked at myself, knowing the power that had accumulated in the sphere of the Distant Ones could at any moment turn all my island to dust. In a fitful search for a solution, I scanned the room unthinkingly.

There was the soul-quaffing Staff from the Temple of the Sun—a fearful weapon to be sure, which was useless to me then but could serve me well in the duel between Mage and God that was almost certain to follow, if only I lived to see it.

Oh, how I longed then for the inventions that Merlin had filched from my apartments in the Castle of All the Ancients! With them in hand, the Distant Ones' lightning would have already been studied from all sides and parceled out into its constituent parts, and I would not have been racking my brains over the formalities of spellcasting. I would have known where and how to smite it, much as I had known how to shift with Merlin's Arrow, which I had easily dissipated before it left the bourns of the Mid-Real.

The survey of my lodgings had been no comfort. I had to hand many and diverse magical devices and instruments—even Iamerth's emblem—but none of them seemed apt to help me now. A treacherous trickle of cold sweat ran down my back. *Very well. If there's nothing else for it, I shall strike with a Firecharm, and then...*

And then we shall see.

That knavish "we shall see" actually turned my stomach—never had I gone into battle armed with such a scintillating plan.

Yet, the time for doubts and hesitations was gone. If I was to attack, then I must attack quickly. Where was Rakoth with his krakens and their kind? Let him engage the First-Begotten, whilst I did what I could against the Distant Ones.

My musings and preparations were cut short when Rakoth burst into the room.

"Quickly, quickly, if you really want to help!" he roared over his shoulder. A dark-brown light glowed faintly about his right hand—he was leading someone on a magical chain.

I was struck dumb when Sigrlinn made her entrance, at once more enraged and more abject than when I had seen her last, her body and throat girdled by the chain whose other end rested in Rakoth's hand.

"Great Darkness, why have you brought her here?" I howled. He could have done nothing more demented than bring one of my bitterest enemies—who had almost made an end of me in the Netherworld—here, into my innermost sanctum of spellcraft, where she could see my model of the world with its schema of the magical traps and defenses that encircled Hedinseigh, and the window into the Diviner's World, and Iamerth's emblem.

I should, I suppose, have been grateful he had at least thought to clap her in chains, but with one look at what I was doing she would be able to disrupt much, if not everything, I had made.

"She says she can halt the Distant Ones—with our help, of course. And should she have nothing serviceable to say, I recall that once I was styled, among my other titles, Inflictor of Excruciating Pain." Rakoth composed his face into an awful grimace.

Sigrlinn was entrancing. Wrath sat upon her like a fine adornment. She was now truly a Goddess of Vengeance, and the fury that burned in those narrowed eyes discomfited me. She may at that moment have hated the Distant Ones even more than she hated Rakoth and me.

"Hedin..." She began to speak in a rapid patter, the words stumbling over each other. "Hed', on' fire can sto' the sphe' of the Dist' Ones! But not a Firech'm..." Then she stopped to draw breath and articulate more clearly. "Fire from the depths, fire from the core of the world that burns in the very bowels of All That Is, the fire that warms the Seething Fountainhead of the Worldspring. I was there. I even made a Chalice to carry its seed. You must break through to that fire by main force. You must pry the Worldframe open here, here and here..."

Her slim fingers slid across my model, showing the places that would need to be punctured. She poured out the instances of the spells she had contrived to subjugate that fire, the Primordial Flame of the Indestructible; and she intimated the ways of turning a fragment of that fearsome power into an undeflectable projectile that would surmount any defense the Distant Ones might care to mount.

The elven fleet could not be more than half a mile away. Meanwhile, though, the krakens had descended to the bottom of the sea, despairing of ever hearing the signal for the general assault.

I was left with no choice, and no time to subject my once-beloved to a detailed test. All I could do was hope that...

"You understand that if the Distant Ones parry that blow, it will turn all on Hedinseigh to ash, leaving not a stone standing?" I asked her point-blank.

"I do," she replied without a second thought. "Almighty Heaven, Hedin, your mistrust will destroy us all! Only the Divine Might or the Fire that was lit by the Creator Himself may avail against the Distant Ones. If there are other remedies, I have not found them. What can you suggest better?"

That I had nothing better to suggest she knew well enough. Although the complex forms of magic—such as, for instance, the Sorcery of the Moonbeast—had succored me more than once in the recent days of veritable insanity, they would now most certainly profit us nothing. The Distant Ones' defenses would simply turn their power back upon us.

Forging a path to those subterranean stores of Almighty Flame required all my strength, multiplied by the magic of my Talisman. I began to braid the spells dictated to me by Sigrlinn—though that is perhaps rather too strongly stated, for she was delineating only their most general, their crudest outlines. Gradually, there formed over Hedinseigh keep a huge spectral pick. Never in my life had I created the like, and I could not fathom what Sigrlinn wanted with this visible embodiment of our intention; but to be on the safer side, I did introduce into the spell some terms designed to protect our island.

At last she was done. Her face shone with the savage prescience of revenge.

"Begin!" she cried, her burning eyes riveted on the sphere of the Distant Ones.

And I set those vast stores of assembled power into action.

It seemed that, for an instant, all life in me was stilled. My ears were rent by such a din as might ensue should all ninety-nine of the Highest Heavens tear loose from their glittering tablets. The gigantic pick slowly descended, but there were no untoward surprises in Sigrlinn's spell, for Hedinseigh remained unscathed.

The pick's tip penetrated deeper and deeper, levering apart the layers of the Real that had been gathered together in elaborate lappets by my ingenious magic-making. Something similar I had wrought when saving my apprentice's life, but that had near ended in a universal doomsday, whereas now my will was sovereign over all.

But we were belated, and that most certainly. As the Diviner screeched in my mind, the sphere of the Distant Ones hurled at us a bolt of green lightning that was a molding of martial wizardry packed so full of power it could not have admitted one more iota.

Rakoth was our salvation. He had intercepted the Diviner's signal of alarm, and with a rapid and unlooked-for movement in the air, a massive whirlpool seemed woven on the instant from the tiniest particles of diffused Darkness. Utterly powerless alone, they surfaced from the torrents of Light and rallied together at their erstwhile Ruler's call to form a huge shield athwart the headlong flight path of that green flame.

The collision was marked by the frantic howling and whistling of air sheared into red-hot slivers. The lightning hit in the very middle of the shield, tore it and scattered it in motes of dust, leaving not a trace of the Rebel's creation behind. The weapon of the Distant Ones continued on its way, greatly weakened. Although not one of us could do anything further to counter it—I being occupied with the high sorcery of the Great Pick, the sweat-drenched Rakoth clutching his temples in an effort to cope with the terrible headache that always besets a Mage when his defensive barriers are destroyed, and

Sigrlinn capable of no wizardry at all—the Flame did no great harm. A few more of the remaining structures—a bastion and two towers—collapsed, but stones were then the least of my concerns, for if my plan were to proceed successfully to its conclusion, we would have no further need of Hedinseigh or its fortress walls.

Assault bridges were being readied on the elven vessels, and at the bows massed tall warriors in glittering, costly armor, their golden locks softly streaming from under star-bright helmets. Yet not one arrow, not one stone flew at them from behind the merlons. My apprentice's warriors were safely hidden away, and Rakoth's servants were slowly withdrawing. From time immemorial they had not been able to abide elven magic, and kept the greatest possible distance from it, absent any orders from their Master to the contrary.

By a sheer effort of will, I drove the fearsome pick ever deeper, cracking and breaking the unseen clamps and braces that held the layers of the Well-Ordered unmoving. Miscreations that had slept for many millennia awoke in their desolate dens and strove upward to the light, sowing death and destruction as they went. In tenantless worlds, mountains fell and rivers burst their banks. I was trembling all over—now with fever, now with chills—and my Talisman shuddered to the spasmodic beating of my overtaxed heart.

At the last, a needle seemed to pierce through all my being, forcing from me a groan of intolerable pain. The pick had shattered the last barrier, allowing my charm to make its way unimpeded to the lair of the True Fire. The pain blinded and deafened me, depriving me of speech, but Rakoth brought me to myself again with the extremely rough but effective expedient of a smart slap across the face.

"Quickly!" Sigrlinn's fists were clenched, and streams of gilded sparks were again running down her hair. Her fury was giving her strength. "Draw up the fire and shape it into a sphere!"

Shape it into a sphere! Easy to say, hard to do. I could not but admire the skill she had shown in creating a Blazing Chalice, since the True Fire cared not to bend to anyone's bidding. It flung itself against the walls of its magical cage; tongues of flame lapped furiously against the unseen thread that was drawing the cage upward, and the charm I had cast could scarce withstand their furious onslaught.

The frontlines of the elven fleet were at the shore now, the bridges were being deployed, and orderly files of warriors under blue banners that fluttered in the wind were attacking, silent and swift.

I molded a sphere of the True Fire, but the layers of the Real were already knitting up the terrible wound dealt them by the pick Sigrlinn had helped me make. I would be given only one chance to dispose of the Distant Ones' sphere, as there would be neither time nor strength to repeat what I had crafted here.

The True Flame incinerated the first charm I cast, and the second, and the third. I exchanged them with a cardsharp's dexterity, at a speed improbable for any Mage, whose every act of sorcery requires five or six seconds at least.

Those charms were Sigrlinn's, and probably only the Diviner could have counted off the variants she discarded before finding those that might serve. In calmer circumstances, she would have had my sincere, albeit unspoken, accolades.

It had taken time, but I at last succeeded in making some facsimile of a fiery sphere fit for flight. I was wrung out, bone-weary—and meanwhile, the elf vanguard was already clambering across Hedinseigh's dilapidated bastions.

Rakoth cracked his knuckles nervously. He was anxious to order his servants into the counterattack, and well enough I understood why, for it would take the First-Begotten only a few minutes now to reach my chamber of spellcraft.

A second bolt of lightning, far stronger than the last, wrenched itself from the surface of the sphere, which had floated very close. In that second, strange changes were felt in time itself. I discerned singular disturbances in its hitherto peaceful currents as the Great River that flowed from future to past chopped and foamed. The Distant Ones were at us in earnest.

But that spear of green flame had not covered a quarter of its path to us before my fiery sphere, born of specks of the True Fire, rushed to meet it, following my aim and urged on with all the Hastening Spells I knew. Let it not be said its flight was a grandiose spectacle, but although outwardly my sphere differed in no wise from a puff of ordinary flame, from it there emanated such power that Sigrlinn and I and even Rakoth recoiled despite ourselves, shielding our eyes with our hands against that searing, stabbing light.

The green lightning collided with my projectile and disappeared into it, only making the True Fire shine even brighter.

Evidently, the Distant Ones realized at the last moment what was astir— the Diviner even detected the initial cadences of diverse defensive charms— but it was too late. Gleaming like a little sun, the sphere of True Fire tore into the very middle of the Distant Ones' sinister vessel. The gleaming green whorls recoiled before it, as if in fear, then again closed up. For a few instants that were among the most awful of my life, nothing more happened. The elves, meeting no resistance and surely suspecting a trap, had paused in their progress. The sight of the flaming meteor making a direct hit on their allies' sphere froze them in their tracks.

Then the green rind of the Distant One's sphere split apart in a conflagration so powerful ordinary mortals standing where we stood would have been instantly blinded. A spate of frenzied flame, spinning into lithe whirlwinds, pelted the shoreline, turning blocks of millennial stone into ash and sending steam billowing up to the sky. Power had clashed with power, and the destruction was mutual.

The rolling roar of that monstrous explosion had not yet died away before Rakoth issued the order to attack. The gray legions of shades deployed amid the clouds of steam; the dragons soared from their sharp summits and swooped down; kraken tentacles again rose above the waves.

But the First-Begotten were showing little enthusiasm for continuing the fight, being clearly not much enamored of standing alone against Hedinseigh in all its might. So, driving off the bravest and boldest of the dragons with heavy white-fletched arrows, they began the most orderly of withdrawals.

Rakoth, for his part, was merciful to his servants, for an elven arrow in the eye is certain death to any dragon, and elves can bring down a fly on the wing in pitch darkness.

I heaved a sigh of relief, and although there was almost no strength left in me for wizardry of any kind, certain details I was compelled to learn. I reached out with my mind to the ornate longboats of the First-Begotten.

Their high commander I found right quickly. A tall elf, richly armored, stood at the prow of the most trim and elegant vessel in the midst of the fleet. It lifted its head in an azure helm with raised visor, and its huge, almond-shaped eyes, blue as the sky, looked directly into my soul. It saw me excellent well across the bridge of thought between us.

— *We shall give you no peace, Hedin the Destroyer,* it said slowly, in a lovely, enchanting, musical tone far more suited to song or protestations of love than to martial commands.

— *But hold, O Most Glorious,* I protested. *You attacked my domains unannounced, with no declaration of war, although I have never been an impediment to you. Unannounced attacks are in no favor among your kin, and would be better suited to humans or goblins. Perhaps if I am told your particular grievances, we can settle this matter without bloodshed.*

— *Do not try, Mage,* the First-Begotten said with a shake of its head. *Do not try to make me divulge to you what you seek to know. I shall say neither how we entered into an alliance with the Distant Ones nor what we reckoned to gain therefrom nor what the Young Gods or Great Orlangur thought of it. Comfort yourself with the knowledge we misprized your might.*

— If you resolve to depart the island, I shall not attack or pursue you, I told it. *While you may have reasons for waging war against me, I have none for warring against you.*

— Soon the whole world shall have weighty reasons to war against you, the elf promised me, lowering its visor. *Enough of this talk—our swords shall now speak for us. But if you wish rather to vie with us in magic-making, so be it— we shall find the wherewithal to astonish you.*

The bridge of thought crumbled. The elves formed into compact groups, back to back and elbow to elbow, bows ready and arrows nocked, under the protection of small triangular shields richly decorated with sapphires and emeralds. All I could do then was toss them into the sea or come to some agreement with them, for I still did not understand what had brought them to this pass.

I should first, of course, have had Sigrlinn removed. I did not need her as an audience for my wizardry. But time, alas, did not permit.

Rakoth turned to me. "Why are we dilly-dallying, Hedin? They'll be knocking at the gates of your citadel in a matter of minutes."

Silvery streams of elven warriors now flowed across the vessels that had hoved near to Hedinseigh's fire-blackened cliffs, their high commander having been quick to take advantage of our confusion. In no time, they would be straddling the shore, and beating them off would be a most bloody affair.

Sigrlinn had, meanwhile, backed up to the wall, to the full length of the magical chain whose other end was in Rakoth's grip. Her lips were twisted into a sarcastic grin. Was she perhaps hoping the swords of the First-Begotten would set her free?

I hurriedly made a mental inventory of all the possibilities remaining to me, since something still held me back from committing mass slaughter. Since I was, as I have oft remarked, saving the magic of the Dragons of Time for the Young Gods, my thoughts turned to a tried and tested weapon—a Firecharm. My Talisman had multiplied my strength to the point at which I could sustain such sorcery longer than before, and I reckoned that a Wall of Flame would force the elves to cut and run.

The most distant ships were empty now, and the warriors they had borne, having passed from deck to deck, were nearing the shore.

Then it was as if some giant had shaken out a crimson curtain that reached from sky to sea as ruddy, twisting pillars of fire, wreathed about with black streaks of smoke, rapidly formed into a solid wall. My proven weapon advanced upon the elves' fleet from the rear, the unbearable heat driving the crews out of the furthermost vessels. The ornate sculling oars cracked in the heat, and the last of the rowers and helmsmen abandoned their doomed ships.

To that moment, all was going according to my design. My intent was to burn a few dozen empty ships then invite the elves to another parley. However, it turned out the elves' high commander had not been whistling in the wind when he said they would find the wherewithal to astonish me. All at once, a huge spectral figure—an exact likeness of the First-Begotten's admiral— strode from the flagship up into the sky. The Diviner grated the details of the spell into my mind, but I had already felt the jolt of frigid power, like a prickly snowball taken in the face.

Before either Rakoth or I could do anything, the commander's Shade brandished a giant battle ax that shone dimly with a dead, pale light. The blade crashed down, splitting my Curtain of Fire from top to bottom. The rebound from my ruined sorcery flung me to the floor, and I could maintain the spell no longer. The strengthless remnants of my flame died in hissing clouds of steam, and in a few minutes, it was all over. The elven crews set smartly to snuffing out the flames.

"My word!" a dumbfounded Rakoth muttered, reaching out his free hand to help me rise. "Now may I attack?"

I stood. There was nothing surprising about any of this. Likely the First-Begotten had carefully studied my magical techniques and favorite combat spells; and it had not, of course, slipped their attention that I had used a Firecharm to defend the island when it was stormed the first time. *Good enough, First-Begotten. I offered you peace. I did not want your blood and your deaths on my hands. I have no quarrel with you, but you have chosen your own fate.*

"Begin, Rakoth," I said calmly, thrusting both my hands into my Talisman's flaming column and feeling a hot wave of fresh strength roll through my weary body.

"Not before time." The erstwhile Lord of Darkness gave a satisfied grin and lifted his hand, the splayed fingers ready to clench into the fist that would give the final signal.

Sigrlinn suddenly strode forward and hit Rakoth's raised hand hard.

"Stop! Stop or not a stone will be left standing here!"

"What is't with you, may the Darkness carry you off?" Rakoth bellowed in fury, pushing the sorceress away.

"Fools!" she hissed scornfully. "I have no desire to perish because you are dullards! If the first to die in this affray is an elf, the fortress of the First-Begotten will loose the Children of Thunder, who will raze the island to its very foundations and will consume all its inhabitants, the Mages among them."

The Children of Thunder. Like the Hungering Stars, hounds of the Castle of All the Ancients, they had long been absent from the Visible World and, like them, were deemed invincible. I had wondered on occasion what would happen if one fine day those two insuperable forces were to meet in open combat.

There had been a time—during the period of my fascination with elves and their magic—when I had been much interested in the Children. In those days, though, the progeny of Thunder had not seemed particularly menacing adversaries.

"The Young Gods are presently prepared to infuse the Children of Thunder with their might," Sigrlinn went on, as if reading my mind. "That is why the First-Begotten are so self-assured. I should know—'twas I crafted the Becharmed Corridor from the Hallowed Land."

My heart leapt, and I stifled with difficulty a joyful cry. I had known. I had always known. I had foreseen there must be a cleft—albeit the most insignificant, the most negligible—in the Hallowed Land's defensive courses, and there it was! The Becharmed Corridor was our chance, and mayhap our only chance, and my ignorance of the way to that place was of little importance. Maybe the false emblem would be of service to us there, too…

"What, then, Hedin?" For the first time in this entire engagement, Rakoth was bewildered.

"Attack, but very carefully," I bade him, rousing a nervous laugh from Sigrlinn and a crooked smile from Rakoth.

"I fear that will not be easily done," he remarked. Then his fist closed at last, and we heard a frenzied war cry even through the citadel's thick walls. For Rakoth's servants, the wait was over.

Sigrlinn shook her head. "You are still the madman, Hedin," she said. "Bold and lucky, but a madman all the same."

I turned to face her. "You think me afraid of the Children of Thunder or the forces of the Hallowed Land? You think I don't know how to manage them?"

Slicing through the howling clamor raised by Rakoth's hideous creatures came the chill whistle of elven arrows, every one a vehicle of death; and I knew that even now dragons were dropping like stones into the waves, while their more fortunate or more nimble brethren, evading the coldly glittering tips on long shafts of yew, tried to hold the First-Begotten ranks within range of their fiery breath. The shades moved behind shields brought from their worlds, which offered at least some cover against those baneful white-fletched arrows, any one of which could impale several of Rakoth's otherworldly troops at once. And as yet not one elf had fallen.

This attack was exactly what the sly commanders of the First-Begotten's forces had expected of us, once they stood beneath the walls of Hedinseigh. The Creator's Elder Offspring knew the contents of the arsenals of Darkness to a nicety. I felt their calm certainty, and signaled Rakoth to halt the assault.

"Are you certain you know what you're about, Hedin?" my friend asked in wonder.

"There may be hope for you yet," Sigrlinn ground out between gritted teeth.

The sounds of battle outside the walls fell suddenly silent, and in the ensuing hush we heard the First-Begotten's triumphant cries. Our flaccid attack had been as a surety to them, and belike they were already tasting a quick and easy victory.

Rakoth's servants hastily retreated before the well-aimed elven arrows. I sensed the elves' high commander sending its magic in a diligent search for my mind. Something it wished to say, but when I plumbed its intentions deeper, I found naught there but mockery, and I would not speak with it.

All my feelings had died. My desire to avoid bloodshed seemed now ludicrous—the elves would give me no quarter, although I had never done them ill. I was now preparing to show them my true strength, the strength of a Mage who had perforce spent many ages honing the secrets of the most fearsome, most death-dealing wizardry.

Already, the bearers of fear and panic, summoned through my Talisman, were whirling in a brainsick dance. Already, menacing inky-black clouds shot through with crimson lightning, the harbingers of a bloody storm, were crawling to Hedinseigh from all sides. The blast of wizardly winds that had come from the furthest bounds of Greater Hjorvard at my call was growing ever stronger when I sensed a sudden cold rivulet trickling through the most secluded and deep-seated corner of my mind, arousing there an all-consuming and oppressive horror.

It was an alarm sounded by the Guardcharms Rakoth and I had sent to the far reaches of Chaos. There began to unfold before my mind's eye fantastic scenes of the roiling, constantly changing outlines of the primordial Fabric upon which the Creator had set all the Well-Ordered. This time, though, the familiar picture was oddly distorted. In the churning vortices, amid those intricately interwoven funnels, were strange constrictions, breaks in the continuous motion—a region, as it were, of utter, dead quiescence, where all was still and nothing happened and where, I sensed, the movement of time itself had stopped. There were stagnant stretches now in the Great River, and the Dragons of Time were restless—never had they been so greatly disturbed in the many serene millennia since their creation.

My sorcery could not live in those regions of quiescence. No Spell of Knowing could break their bounds—the enchantments flickered out vapidly, meeting on their way neither obstacle to halt them nor barrier to reflect them back. Meeting, that is to say, nothing. The road to those places was blocked by powers incomparably more puissant than mine.

Going cold inside, I looked up at Rakoth. The Lord of Darkness was on his feet, and his face, framed in that mighty mane of blue-black hair, seemed to me the fearsome mask of a corpse brought back to life and torn from the grave by horrid spells. The eyes of the Fallen Mage were starting from their sockets, his pupils were wide; and I knew then he was feeling what I had felt. We were both acknowledging that this was the end.

The Charms of Knowing we had dispatched to the very frontiers of the world known to us had brought the dire news Rakoth and I had been expecting at any moment but for some reason had childishly believed we would never hear, although the Lord of Darkness himself had summoned that all-destroying power into our world.

The Guardcharms were warning us that the Unnamable had conquered heretofore insurmountable bulwarks, and had burst into the bourns of the Well-Ordered, devouring the fabric of the Real as it went.

Depleted, dazed, stunned by the awful tidings, I collapsed into a chair.

CHAPTER XV

*D*ID HE SAY "*BRANN MUST BE WARNED?*" A BEMUSED HAGEN THOUGHT AS HE STRODE to the Wellspring of the Worlds, past the motionless Jotunn and the belligerently frowning Hropt. Neither the Sentinel of the Well nor the Father of Hosts had paid any heed to that cry, although who if not the Lord of Asgard, who had sent Hagen to the hermit of the woods, should be troubled to hear that name spoken in such a place and by such a creature? For Hedin's apprentice was in much doubt as to whether these were, indeed, humans or only an artful counterfeit.

What can it mean? If Brann is really an inhabitant of that village, then it is obvious why Iargohor held no sway over him! Of course! Then why, on my return from Gnipahellir, did I and my Teacher and Old Hropt, too, ascribe no importance to it? We could not understand and so simply cast it aside. But what people live in that village? How came it to be in this place? Could they be handpicked servants of the Young Gods, or perhaps, of Orlangur and Demogorgon?

His boot rested now against the narrow ledge of the Seething Fountainhead. His head swam, a strange, stupefying odor wafted around the Wellspring, and he was vividly aware of the fearsome intensity of magic forces massed in this place by a ruthless hand. Overcoming his nausea, he forced himself to lean over the foaming water.

Across the surface ran rainbow bubbles that never burst. He fancied that in those iridescent little orbs he saw himself and Hedinseigh's steep precipices, his Teacher bent over a model of the world in his sanctum of spellcraft, saw flame streaming upward from twisted towers and sundered bastions, and warriors hacked in pieces lying on the bailey's flagstones.

The brief vision flickered and vanished, leaving a heaviness on his soul.

The Wellspring had foretold the future, and who could know the veracity of that foretelling? Little he would gain by asking Mimir!

"Take up the emblem, Hagen!" Old Hropt thundered behind him.

A gauntleted hand slowly touched the bubbling water. There was a burning at first, but the pain disappeared as soon as Hagen mastered himself enough to thrust his hand deeper. He felt a strange lightness spread through his body, as if there had been no hard-fought battle, no maniacal duel with the Darkling Riders, no skirmish with Mimir and his minions. The fatigue lifted, and new strength infused wearied muscles.

Yet he sensed also a disturbance in a deep, primordial protomagic, thrown out of balance by the sudden intrusion of a being who bore within himself the rudiments of forces to which it was akin. Somewhere in otherworldly abysses, there was a shuddering of the indestructible conduits that had long directed turbulent torrents of energy into their assigned channels.

He felt pain once more, this time not in his hand only but in his whole being. That pain pierced every particle of his body, growing stronger by the instant. Someone was set on turning him back. Fear joined itself to the pain, and an alien will tried to take control of his hand; but he resisted and after a struggle brought his body back to obedience.

When his forearm was in the water up to the elbow, a swarm of faerie apparitions burst into his mind. Wondrous strange beings capered before his inward eye; dancers of fay beauty and unearthly agility twirled in a complex and whimsical frolic, while around them beasts such as he had never seen and of which even his Teacher had never spoken—unicorns, gryphons, flying lions, feathered snakes—tripped in an endless roundelay. They were all indescribably beautiful, with lovely eyes of many colors whose every look penetrated to the depths of his mind. Despite himself, he shuddered—such aversion to violence, such propitiation flowed from them and was glimpsed in those eyes that Hagen felt stinging shame for a life dedicated entirely to war and destruction.

That astonishing dance was being performed under a canopy of dark green leaves with fine silvery veins, borne on full-crowned trees that resembled somewhat the palms of Southern Hjorvard but were far more majestic and well-shaped. Bright-scarlet flights of tiny birds fluttered among the elegantly arched branches with their smooth, gleaming bark, and above all that splendor spread the gilded dome of a sky soft and warm even to the view.

The thane fought off the hex that sapped the strength and malevolence so needful in combat. He plunged his hand ever deeper, the water touching his chin now, until his fingers felt the smooth sphere of the true emblem.

There was a slight prickling in the palm of his hand as slowly, very slowly, he lifted the heavy globe. It glimmered bewitchingly, and although at first sight it differed in no way from the false emblem he and Hropt had captured in the Temple of Iamerth, he almost dropped it once he had it out of the water, for it radiated raw Power. It was made to rule, and the energy that gushed from it almost blinded him.

Unable to tear his eyes from this wonder that contained the key to authority over all the Well-Ordered, he rose by degrees to his feet.

He understood then that the visions that had so bemused him scant minutes ago were the truth. It had been vouchsafed to him to look upon the Hallowed Land, to see what no mortal—none but the god-favored heroes of the last battles with Rakoth, whose bravery had been rewarded with an eternal, reposeful life in that place—had seen in ten centuries. It was a stunning, entrancing, becharming world. No Mage could have evoked such artful, such seductive visions, for his mind could never have conceived them.

"Hagen! Hagen, rouse yourself. It is I, Hropt!"

The commanding voice of the Father of Hosts gradually dispersed the golden mist that enveloped the thane's mind, bringing the real world back into view.

The Lord of Asgard had half-turned toward him while still not taking his eyes from Mimir, who stood motionless, his ax lying on the grass nearby. The Ancient God was filled with a strength that shared its origins with the might of the emblem, but having passed through the crucible of his memory, that strength was now doubly deadly to its creators. The Soul-Banishing Staff lay at his side, drained of its power and negligently discarded.

"Are you now satisfied?" Mimir asked in a low, very weary voice. The old Jotunn slowly picked up his ax and, dragging it along the grass, plodded back to the Wellspring. "Can you understand what will befall the world now? I am old, Hropt, very old, even older than you, although you may not think it, and I have always believed I did not fear death. But I was wrong. Come what may, I want to live."

"I, too, fear death," the Father of Hosts answered simply, "if only because no one can tell me if I will then suffer what my kin suffered after their deaths on Borgild Field. I have found no traces of them within the bounds of the Well-Ordered, not even on the Astral Plane—and I doubt they have happened into the Hallowed Land. Yet still I enter this fray, albeit with almost no hope of victory. So, you are left with no choice, Mimir. If we fall, you shall not be spared. The Young Gods will remind you that you gave up the emblem without a fight, although you had been set here to watch over it.

"Ah, Mimir! Where was all your wisdom when you agreed to assume the ignominious role of watchman? For I suppose all was arranged so you could never avail yourself of the emblems—is't not so? And now…" Hropt's expression suddenly changed, and he hastily donned the helmet he had earlier put off. "Now, would you not right that ancient injustice?"

Mimir roared in a voice terrible enough to turn to flight all the armies of the Hallowed Land, and his once-impotent weapon again cleft the air above his head. The stone ax, thrown with enormous strength, hit Old Hropt hard in the chest. The Father of Hosts fell backward; and with one bound, his ax forgotten, Mimir was upon him, clawing at his throat. The Lord of Asgard's neckpiece, although forged by gnomes, bent like parchment under the fingers of the Sentinel of the Wellspring.

With neither consideration nor thought, Hagen did the only thing he could do in the short instants left to him. Hefting Iamerth's emblem like any cobblestone, he flung it with all his strength at the old Jotunn's head.

The heavy globe, a dark crystal in flight, shattered Mimir's helmet; and the Sentinel of the Wellspring dropped like one poleaxed, pinning Hropt under him. Hagen rushed to drag off the heavy body.

Hropt, in a husky, breathless whisper, asked, "The emblem! Where…is the emblem?" before letting his head fall limply back again. Then, rallying a little, but in a voice still constricted from his recent smothering, he took to chiding Hagen for hurrying to his aid instead of retrieving the priceless globe.

Mimir lay insensible, a fearsome wound yawning on his temple. The bones of his skull were smashed, and thick, dark blood flowed slowly onto the grass. The giant's staunchness was no less than startling, for not even all the might of Iamerth's true emblem had been able to dispatch him into Unbeing.

Groaning and rubbing his chest, the Father of Hosts leaned over his defeated foe, tore a fairly clean strip from Mimir's shirt and bound up the wound as best he could.

"All will be well with him, I doubt not," he said, straightening and wiping his hands. "The old Jotunn's head is strong. They do say it was once proof even against Mjolnir, my son's great hammer, although Thor would argue himself blue in the face he never met Mimir in combat. Well, Hagen, 'tis time we were off. We must return to Hedinseigh. Belike your Teacher's patience has run thin waiting for us."

But the thane stopped him, quickly communicating his suspicions about

Brann Shrunkenhand and concluding with "We must tarry here until we know all."

Still wincing from the pain in his chest, Hropt scratched his head in puzzlement, paying no mind whatever to Mimir's servants, which were creeping up on them again.

"Yes, Shrunkenhand is matchless," he acknowledged at length. "But I never suspected him to be one of their number!" He nodded toward the village. "You might call it a Village of the Blessed. The Young Gods, I have heard tell, granted eternal life to all who agreed to become, as it were, keepers of the peace among mortal men. Although if all that is truly so, I must own to you I fail to understand what business Brann has here in the back of beyond or why the temples are manned by so huge an army of priests. I do not know exactly what these Keepers are capable of, what powers they command…"

"Considerable, I'll warrant, if even the Conveyor of the Dead gives them a wide berth," Hagen said bleakly. "Brann promised me war if even one village were set ablaze at my warriors' hands. And one was, damnation take Merlin— for it was he, I daresay, who so distorted our path that while wandering through Avalon we suddenly found ourselves planted square in our own Eastern Hjorvard!"

"What's done cannot be undone," Hropt said, as glum as ever Hagen could be. "Very well, let's go to the village and try to find out what's doing there."

They made for the distant houses, diligently skirting the garden plots and beds, with a rabble of Mimir's servants dogging their heels and the Eye in the sky watching them close.

The village's inhabitants had scattered when the quarrel between the strangers and Jotunn grew into a brandishing of weaponry, and no more than ten or twelve of them came out to meet Hagen and Hropt. Strong, thickset men they were, with stern and weathered faces and drooping gray mustaches. Not one of them carried a weapon.

"What would you with us, uninvited guests?" one of them, evidently their leader, inquired inhospitably. He alone held a thick, polished oaken staff, and the powerful tawny hand and knotty fingers grasping the carved stock seemed but a continuation of the smooth wooden root from which that staff had been carved.

What answer could be made to such a question? Hropt chose the simplest—he told the truth.

"We wish to know what manner of people you are, whence you come, what is your business here, and all the rest," he said calmly, looking the leader in the eye.

An astonished, troubled murmur passed among the villagers, who had expected anything from the strangers except such directness. Even their leader was disconcerted. To hide his discomfiture, he coughed several times laboriously and thrust both hands under the embroidered belt girt about his simple brown smock, which greatly resembled those worn by the townsfolk of Eastern Hjorvard. Then, recovering himself, he returned question for question.

"And what is that to you? We do not give an accounting of ourselves to all and sundry, and especially not to so sundry as you."

"Who forbids you?" Hropt asked in his turn. "To whom do you owe service? If 'tis the Wellspring you serve, then why did you stand aside just now and watch?"

"And still you try to worm out of us what you need, stranger." The leader shook his head, waspishly reproachful. "But all in vain. None here will tell you aught."

"If you have no stake in our quarrel with Mimir, why will you not speak with us?" Hagen asked pointblank. "Why did you come out against us? If we are enemies, attack. If we are friends, help. If it is all one to you, why not talk with us a while?"

"Who are you that we should pay you any heed?" The headman frowned, his temper rising. "Be on your way! No one has need of you here—neither you, old and outcast god, nor you, 'prentice wizard."

"If we do not incommode you, why are you so eager to see us off?" Hropt inquired. "What will you do should we desire to stay? I, for one, like it here." And he made a demonstration of looking around, as if selecting a site for his future home.

"This country is not for you and your ilk," the leader responded loftily, thrusting out a haughty chin. "Begone while you still can, lest we grow angry."

"Have at us, then. I tire of this." With little hesitation, Hropt drew his Golden Sword. "Ask me, Hagen, and I will say these know-nothings are by the very look of them an offense to this lovely place."

And before Hagen could do anything to stop his intemperately mettlesome companion, Hropt swung his blade and the lower half of the leader's staff, sliced in two at one stroke, fell to the ground.

"That was right discourteous of you, Old Hropt," the leader said quietly, after a pause. "But we do not propose to vie with you in the knack of flourishing crude chunks of iron. You have plundered the emblem of the gods from the Wellspring. They will know of it soon, and we shall laugh last—and best."

"And let them!" Old Hropt guffawed disdainfully in the man's face. "They are all-knowing, are they not? Do you doubt their might?"

"This world is, alas, too far from the Hallowed Land, and news is long on the journey," the leader replied, matching Hropt's tone. "But doubt not we will help it along. The roots of the Real here are over-deep and its walls over-thick. They were raised expressly to withstand a crude incursion from without. Therefore, the tidings of you will not reach the Hallowed Land as quickly as might be wished. But no matter—we will help the gods know the truth of what has happened with all possible speed."

"And do you not fear that, being in possession of the true emblem, we will grind to powder all your much-vaunted gods?" Hropt inquired mockingly.

By way of an answer, the headman made a flaccid hand gesture; and the whole swarm of Mimir's servants, which to that moment had been trailing Hagen and the Father of Hosts at a distance and without a sound, launched a concerted, silent attack that was not even discouraged by the glint of the emblem in Hagen's hand.

The villagers hurriedly made way for the lizards, octopuses, spiders and the rest of that nasty brood. The Lord of Asgard's sword cut a first bloody swath through their ranks, but the casualties were instantly replaced. So, with an angry roar, Old Hropt began laying about him. The attackers fell in droves at his feet, but he would have had as much success trying to overmaster drifts of dry leaves carried on the autumn wind.

Behind the Ancient God's broad back, Hagen tore the Disc of Iamerth from his belt. He was well aware it would be senseless to try to mow down the countless hordes of Mimir's servants, and that left only one thing to do.

"Hey, headman!" he cried at the top of his voice, raising the shining Disc above his head for all to see. "Call off those dandiprats, ere they soil my friend's boots, else I swear by the Great Stairway I shall slice your head in two like an over-ripe melon!"

The leader of the villagers must have known what the Disc of Iamerth was, for his face became a picture of indescribable horror. Thunderstruck, he froze in an awkward pose, both hands clasping his head and his neck bent, as if the deadly Weapon of Light would thus pass over him like any arrow. The rest of the villagers, howling, scattered in all directions.

Surmising that a headman in these parts would be at least somewhat skilled in magic, Hagen speedily conjured a Spell of Dispatch to guide the Disc. And he had, it transpired, judged correctly. Assured that this stranger was issuing no empty threats, the leader shook from head to toe and fell to his knees. With recalcitrant lips, faltering and misspeaking, he muttered some rough-and-ready spell. It worked—the beasts halted their attack in an intricate muddle of twitching, rustling paws, tentacles, suckers and armor plating.

Their extreme displeasure was written all over them—and for good reason, since they had been wrested away from their favorite occupation. Death seemed to hold no fear for them, and had they continued to advance, Hagen and Hropt would have been in sad straits, for not one of Mimir's servants resembled any other. The ploy that had saved Hagen on Avalon—Merlin's winged maws being alike as raindrops, which had allowed him to set the Disc to destroying them all at once—could only fail here. The Disc would have to be aimed anew each time.

"Now shall we speak, master?" Hropt exclaimed with a mocking certainty in his voice, lowering his sword. "Now will you give me answer? And, by the bye, I advise you not to move from the spot or it could end badly for you. You understand me, I trust."

But the remaining villagers were about to prove themselves no cowards. Though Hagen had not seen them holding conference, they suddenly fell on him and Hropt from all sides, shielding their headman from the death-dealing Disc with their own bodies. Mere flesh would never, of course, have stopped the Weapon of Light, but Hagen in truth needed their leader alive, not dead, which is why he had not cast the Disc sooner.

The unprotected throat of the first comer the thane slit with the edge of the Disc, wielding it like a dagger, and the Blue Sword was freed from its sheath in time to meet the second.

This, it seemed, was all the headman needed. He gave a frenzied roar; and all of Mimir's servants again threw themselves into the attack while he darted into a nearby ditch, which could not have been better placed for his purposes.

Sadly, the Disc was not a reasoning thing. He who used it could not just point it at a goal with a charm. The enemy's face had to be in view, and the leader seemed well aware of that.

So, Hagen and Hropt had again to take to the sword, the thane cursing himself for all he was worth for the unforgivable error of allowing the leader to live. Had he already met his death, the rest would perhaps have been less eager to attack.

His hands did not require his mind to direct a battle such as this, which left his thoughts free to feverishly seek a way out. Meanwhile, Old Hropt's blade wreaked havoc among Mimir's servants, but the press from behind continued, closing ranks over the dead. The people had retreated after suffering several fatalities, and their canny headman was nowhere to be seen.

"This will be…a capital brawl!" Old Hropt called to him, not turning his head.

The Ancient God, unwearied, was an excellent swordsman; but Mimir's servants came ever on toward the murderous, iron-bright glitter in his hands. He was already knee-deep in gore, his feet wallowing in a bloody mash of hewn bodies.

The two stood back to back, prepared to defend themselves until every last one of Mimir's creatures was brought low or—more likely—they themselves finally succumbed to exhaustion.

"Foolish it is to waste the strength I took from that shade here, on these nullities!" Hropt suddenly cried. "Hagen, is there aught you can contrive?"

"A fine question," Hedin's apprentice grumbled in reply.

He knew several combat spells, among them the Great Firecharm that had brought victory over the priests in Iamerth's temple, but this world was locked up so tight as to be impervious to the faintest echo of the sorcery being made in the bounds of the Well-Ordered. Thus was he left with nowhere to glean the strength he needed for such magic-making, and Iamerth's emblem was most certainly not his to do with as he pleased.

The answer came of a sudden.

"We'll break through to the Swordmount!" *And certes*, he thought, *what else remains to us? 'Tis a strange mountain, to be sure, very strange, with the blades of the gods and all the rest of it. But we can't tarry here, waiting to be eaten!*

"Cover my back!" Old Hropt responded brusquely.

The minutes that followed were enough to convince Hagen the Lord of Asgard had not come idly by the name of Father of Hosts. Thinking no more of defense and depending entirely upon Hagen's support, he swept forward like the Deathwind that will blow over the world on the day of the Last Battle, and none could stand against him. Every servant of Mimir that happened in his way perished ignobly, able neither to protect itself nor to escape. The blade spun madly about him in a whirling, glinting cloud; the dark blood spurted; there was a crunch of cloven bones, the hoarse gasps of dying creatures that knew not they were dying, and a plashing as Old Hropt strode through pools of blood.

Hagen, the Ancient God's rearguard, was being far harder tasked than even during the memorable battle in the temple, for then he had been on the offensive and now he must perforce defend. He had to match his movements to Old Hropt's steps, all the while trying not to accidentally prick him with his blade. His beloved fanning defense was of no use to him, since the very tallest of his adversaries scarcely reached to his waist; and his tried and tested cut-and-thrust, honed in thousands upon thousands of encounters and so excellent an expedient against people, left openings here through which Mimir's brisk, agile, low-slung servants could penetrate.

But still the pair persevered. Leaving piles of riven bodies behind them, they doggedly fought toward the Swordmount, past the vegetable gardens and around the field until they could see, afar off, the thickets where they had been met by the six Darkling Riders.

Yet Mimir's servants were as numerous as ever. Their fervor undimmed, they flung themselves at Hagen, who, shuddering with disgust, hacked and hewed at innumerable octopus tentacles, cleft the scaly bodies of lizards with grasping hands and dodged the sticky silks cast by the spiders. *How strange it is that Mimir did not create servants with keener wits*, he thought fleetingly, during a half-second's respite between the relentless attacks.

But, as became apparent soon enough, some of Mimir's servants were not lacking in wit at all. At some distance from where Hagen and Hropt were fighting through, villagers appeared, carrying dauntingly hefty arbalests. They moved carefully between Mimir's beasts, as if picking their way through a bog, while those horrors paid them not the slightest heed.

When the first bolt broke against his shoulder plate, Hagen thought that here their adventures must surely end. The beastlings about his feet were giving him not a moment's peace, and as long as he was hacking and slashing at their endless onrush he could not employ the Disc of Iamerth.

"Yield now, for you are doomed!" the rustics' leader called to them haughtily, squeezing his arbalest's trigger. A short, thick bolt glanced off Hagen's helm.

"And so, poltroon, you creep from your puddle of filth?" the Father of Hosts roared back at him. "Great is your skill in groveling in ditches!"

But Hagen knew he could not stand long against those arbalests. For all that he was protected by splendid armor crafted by the masters of Hauberk Mount, sooner or later a bolt tip would find its way through a momentary crevice at a joint or would hit square on the breastplate, and even the gnomes' incomparable handiwork would not protect him then. He allowed that the villagers' bolts could not kill the Father of Hosts, but what was he, the mortal apprentice of Mage Hedin, to do?

"Hropt, hold!" he cried to the Lord of Asgard, unchaining the Disc of Iamerth. Spiders and lizards were all very well, but he must make an end of those bolts.

Repulsively warm, damp, viscid tentacles twined about his legs, countless lizard claws clutched at his armor's rings, spiders cast nooses about his shoulders, and a thick gray loop and a pink tentacle with numberless suckers pinned his lowered swordarm to his body. Shameful capture seemed inevitable, and with it, the destruction of all his Teacher's hopes; but the glittering Disc found its target and the leader fell, his skull split in two. The rest, except a few of the braver souls who hurriedly went to ground in ploughed furrows, fled in horror.

With a few blows of his sword, Hropt freed him from the creatures that hung about him. It was but a short way now to the refuge of those gray slopes.

Then, the beasts teeming and dying under their swords were joined by others, never before seen. These were many-headed snakes, their mouths sporting long, needle-sharp fangs dripping with venom that turned the grass it touched to black ash. One bite would certainly bring instant but agonizing death, and at the sight of them, even Old Hropt gave a muffled yell of amazement and alarm.

They reached the rocky spur, though the poisonous fangs scraped against their chain mail often enough on the way. The bowmen in the field treated them to a random shower of bolts through the thicket, six of which struck Hagen on the back as he followed Hropt but happily did not pierce his armor. The two began their upward climb.

That was no simple matter, especially for the thane, whose strength had been taxed to the limit while crossing the field, and the mountain would offer no further escape. It was not so high it could not be easily invested and kept under constant watch, but it was their only choice, and so they continued their ascent.

The snakes and their delightful coterie remained below, baffled by the sheer, smooth bluffs. Even the scrambling lizards were no climbers, and the air-breathing, eight-legged monstrosities could go no farther.

However, the beasts were in no great haste to leave. They arranged themselves in a dense circle around the mountain, gazing avidly with a multitude of empty eyes at the immobile Hagen and Hropt. Joining them from the village, hurrying across the vegetable plots and the field, came an even more awesomely dreadful sight—mormaths, the very substance of nightmares.

Hagen was scarce able to hold back a cry of craven horror when he espied them, for he had not known that, scattered to the four winds after the rout of Rakoth, they had found their way to this once-safe haven. He was surprised, too, that they, excellent fliers though they were, made no attempt to take to the air and pounce upon their victims from above.

"There is mighty magic in this mountain," Hropt said, turning to his young companion. "If the Swords of the Young Gods are really hidden here, any unschooled village wizard within a mile's distance would know it. Could your Teacher have been correct, and it is no less than a great trap to catch the likes of us?"

Hagen finished the thought for him. "And you believe the magic forbids sorcerous creatures from coming near the mountain, much less climbing it?"

"Who can know? But I'd say that so it is, else what prevents those brutes…" Hropt nodded at the mormaths. "…from falling upon us from above? The slopes are steep for the rest, I'll grant you, but those octopuses could easily use their suckers to climb. They are but crawling along solid ground instead of the sea floor, and nothing more."

We're in a bad way now, and no mistake, Hagen thought bitterly as they settled on the narrow outcrop of a smooth gray slope, bereft of the cracks, crevices, mosses and grasses common to any cliff—of all that makes ordinary dead stone come alive and speak. The mountain seemed a huge sarcophagus, or rather, a gravestone lowered onto some deep tomb.

Hagen and Hropt were surrounded, without the slightest chink or the merest bolthole in that solid wall. Human sentries could be fooled or at least bribed to look away, but these creatures were not only unsleeping but seemed not even to blink as they eyed the prey that had for the time evaded them. And ever and again mormaths rose heavily into the air, straining against the headwind, flapped the folds of their grey wrinkled skin, made a circuit or two of the mountain and, evidently satisfied with their inspection, returned to their places.

Hedin's apprentice and the Father of Hosts, who had beaten every foe in open warfare, had been, at the end of all, defeated.

Whyever did I embrangle myself in this? the thane thought suddenly, to his own surprise. *Was my island not enough for me?* And, unable to lie to himself, promptly answered, *No, it was not.* Hedinseigh truly had hemmed him in too close. *Why, like a pitiful ghoul enamored of death, have I submissively carried out all my Teacher's commands, risking my own head and sacrificing my warriors for a purpose unknown? There was he, settling old scores with the*

Young Gods and freeing Rakoth, his friend, while I...

Sigrlinn was right. I am only a tool in the Teacher's hands, albeit a most valuable one. He took care of me, even loved me in his way, against the day when I must bring him that accursed emblem or die in the attempt. And belike I shall not secure the emblem but shall die in any event.

Hagen saw himself forging a path to the lair of Garm the terrible, saw Sigrlinn's nets, his own frantic attack and flight, the storming of Vidrir's Sovereign City, capital of a man who for long years had remained true to his oath to leave the Thane of Hedinseigh unscathed as long as he discharged his obligations as vassal—and for that Hagen had repaid him with betrayal most foul. He remembered the fight in the temple, the bloody sword in his hands, the priests he had cut down, the clash of the White Blade and the Disc of Iamerth, the battle in the Chamber of Altars...and all that followed.

He had fought like a mad thing, like a berserker, sparing neither himself nor his warriors—and for what? So that the one he had for so many years called Teacher, who had been closer to him than any but his wife and son...

But hold! Hedin was no human, who would transgress the laws of his own conscience in sending an apprentice, his ward and follower, to certain death. Hedin was a Mage. And to a Mage, an apprentice was but an instrument to use in knowing the world.

It was short and plain as the life-stopping blow of a battle hammer to the heart. Hagen had been sent here to die. That much was certain.

He grasped the hilt of his sword tightly enough to cause pain. However it be...

He wanted to direct his thoughts, to reaffirm to himself that never, not for anything, would they take him alive, but his mind disobliged him.

Why do I go on? The circle has been closed. Without the emblem Hedin and Rakoth cannot prevail, and they will not get the emblem, because Hropt and I can sit here on this rocky perch until we starve to death. I wonder if Old Hropt can die of hunger? And then the emblem will in any case return to Iamerth. Is it not better, then, to save ourselves? To hand it back without delay? If he is merciful, as the priests say he is, perhaps I can still repent and be forgiven.

Had any of Hagen's men heard those thoughts, they would undoubtedly have concluded that their commander had taken leave of his senses. Never, not even in a sickly delirium, could such ideas have ever come to him ere then. But Old Hropt suspected something was wrong. No one could say what the brave young mortal truly meant to his dour companion, but maybe he reminded the Lord of Asgard of the golden days when he and his own children ruled the world that was Hjorvard, divesting no one of power and sharing it with none. Those fainthearted thoughts had barely begun to penetrate Hagen's mind before the Father of Hosts was troubled.

"I smell some strange sorcery here," he said, giving Hagen a suspicious look and drawing air through flared nostrils like a hound on a fresh scent. "Is all well with you, Hagen?"

"And what if it is not? We—or I, at least—can already be deemed defunct," Hagen retorted with supreme indifference. He let go of his sword hilt, and it was only by some miracle the Blue Sword did not tumble, glittering, down the mountainside.

"Oh, aye, this is a bad business," Hropt said, slow and worried, staring into the thane's dim eyes.

A spell, mighty and ancient—for old Hropt honored no other—rocked the flows of magical energy that surrounded Hagen. The strength of the vanquished Spirit Marshal burned brightly in the Ancient God. The becharmed heart of the World of Magic, Iamerth's emblem, beat slow and mysterious nearby; the cliff beneath him hid the Swords of the Young Gods; and amid that interweaving of enchanted forces he, with a secret sense known only to him, was able to construct a trusty charm. For the first time after long ages of banishment and solitude, his magickry was in full strength.

To Hagen it was like a splash of icy water in the face. An invigorating vortex burst into the darkened mazes of his mind, driving out the treacherous gloom of pitiable pusillanimity. He who was seeking to command Hagen's reason from afar had clearly made no allowance for the powers of Old Hropt.

Once torn from the toils burdening his mind, Hagen did not at first know what had happened to him. He remembered every last thought that had come to him, but fancied he had simply read them in a book that was now, for some reason, nowhere in sight. He knew, though, that they could not have been his. Someone had most adeptly thrust them into his mind, and had Old Hropt not been there to help, Heaven only knows what he might have done with himself.

The poison slithered from his body unwillingly, leaving behind a sense of emptiness and a temple-rending headache. Gritting his teeth, Hagen slumped backward against the cliff, trying to bring his mind into order with all speed.

"Thank you…Hropt," he forced out, surprised to find his tongue disobedient. "What was't with me?"

"Someone was dead set on you casting yourself head-first from this great height, or attacking me," the Father of Hosts said, looking close into the thane's eyes as if seeking in them an answer to his unspoken question. It seemed to Hagen that in Hropt's gaze there lurked distrust of he who sat before him.

Does he fear that I am not who I appear to be? Hagen wondered, feeling the cold, loathsome claws of fear clutching at his soul. Of suchlike he had heard. Mortal wizards could drive mind from body, and doom the soul to long and aimless wanderings until at length it came to the notice of Iargohor and set off on the journey of no return, on the Black Highway that led straight to Hel.

"It wasn't the Young Gods who assailed you," Hropt continued. "And that was a fear to me, I own, for I do not know that I am strong enough to parry a blow from them here. No, I'd say it was Mimir or one of his helpmeets, or perchance the sweet wiccans the pleasure of whose company we but recently enjoyed. Be all as it may, we beat it off. You are yourself, and I see that it is truly you. Your soul is untouched. Yet I'm still at a loss to know what we are to do! To descend from this mountain would be rank madness."

"Perhaps we could try," Hagen suggested. "They are likely not expecting that of us."

"In another place and were the forces differently aligned, that would, mayhap, serve," Old Hropt objected. "In another place, but not here. They are too numerous. I brought off one spell just now, but who shall tell if I can bring off another?"

"Is there aught else to propose?" Hagen asked the Lord of Asgard, not expecting an answer.

But here the Ancient God surprised him.

"I think there is, Hagen. Nothing remains but to climb to the summit and try to possess the Swords of the Gods. Don't argue, listen!" Old Hropt raised a cautioning hand. "I remember your Teacher's words. But tell me what we should do, if not that."

"I believe that's what they are waiting for us to do," the thane remarked glumly, fingering the pits made in his armor by bolts from the villagers' arbalests.

"Is there not a surfeit of false traps that fail to work?" Hropt persisted. "Iamerth's temple emblem was counterfeit, yet here we are, and the true emblem is in our hands. If that first was a trap then, in very truth, those responsible for it would have done well to learn their trade better from any master craftsman of the Crypts!"

"How do you know it failed to work?" Hagen inquired. "We have our hands on the emblem we deem real, but we cannot use it. And here we sit in a world tightly sealed, in a closed circle, and neither you nor I can make magic worthy of the name here, to boot. Besides, what is your intent for those Swords, if we get them? Is their magic known to you? My sword was made by a god, but what good has that done us?"

"Their magic is known to me, sure," the Father of Hosts replied, in a voice so morose and menacing Hagen grew uneasy. There was a wild glister in Hropt's eyes and an inveterate hatred bubbled in his throat. Hagen believed— the Lord of Asgard did know.

"I was on Borgild Field," Hropt went on, staring with sightless eyes. "I saw—I remember—the sweep of those blades. I heard their harmonious song and their greedy murmuring as they bathed in blood. I looked upon the unfurling panoramas of the forces that commanded those blades. I committed to memory the reflections of the might invested in them. My memory held the words of command spoken by the unseen legion that surrounded them. And I hid that knowledge so deep even the Young Gods could not dig far enough to unearth the truth. They—even they!—did not fully understand the danger in me."

Hropt sprang to his feet, his gray beard bristling in his wrath. His hand happened on a stone, and he squeezed it, turning the piece of granite to dust.

"Why did you not tell my Teacher of this?" Hagen asked, startled.

Hropt gave a twisted smile. "My memory is a very strange thing. Time was when it seemed I had even forgotten who I was. Then, gradually, the knowledge began to return, starting, of course, with the most insignificant and unneeded things. I did not remember those spells until now, Hagen, standing on this mountain. With the Swords of the Gods we shall force our way not to the Gates that open on Hedinseigh but to the Hallowed Land itself!"

Hagen was casting about for the words he needed. All his being protested Hropt's plan. His intuition, his sixth sense, told him this should not, could not, must not be done. But what had he to offer in its place?

"I'd as lief try the Disc of Iamerth," he said at last, removing the weapon from its chain. "We are unassailable here, and the target is in plain view. Perhaps they will be put to flight."

Another smile. "They do not know what death is. If you were to exterminate even three-fourths of that rabble, it would not so much as dawn on the rest that their time was at hand and they'd best hie themselves home."

"Yet I shall try," Hagen replied stubbornly, and the Father of Hosts offered no further argument.

They descended a little, and under cover of a ledge, Hagen took aim at a burly old mormath, a veteran of his kind with scarred wings a good fourteen feet across. He conjured a Channeling Charm and a Charm of Dispatch, and was relieved to find he still had strength enough for that.

The Disc flashed briefly, rending both the air and the mormath's repulsive gray flesh. The two writhing, bloodied halves of the prodigious carcass toppled.

"Right nobly done," Old Hropt said approvingly, but with a hint of irony. "And you propose to serve them all the same?"

Hagen said nothing, striking down instead his second victim, then another and another. The thickets at the foot of the mountain were stained with dark blood, the lifeless remains sprawled among the broken bushes; but the rest, with an astounding disdain for death, paid no attention to any of it, showing no inclination to flee, to retreat, or even to take cover. Instead, they began running in circles, flowing around the mountain in a strange, motley river. Round and round they went down below, and when one was cleft by the Disc, another came instantly to take its place. To Hagen it seemed they were rising up out of thin air.

He was beginning to tire. Each deadly, undeflectable blow of the Disc took a little more of his strength, which he could not replenish here, in a world so singularly secluded from the rest of the Well-Ordered. The enemy's numbers were in no way reduced, even though the foot of the crag on which he and Hropt were settled was awash with blood.

Finally, the exhausted thane abandoned his futile efforts. Hropt had been silently watching him all the while, with a wry, glum smile. Panting, Hagen chained the Disc to his belt. It seemed they were left with only one way out— but why, at the mere thought of the Swords of the Gods, was he seized by a shameful fit of shuddering and a desire to run wherever his legs would carry him?

Without a word, Old Hropt led him away. Hagen trudged reluctantly upward behind his guide, balking still.

Their long climb was accompanied by an honor guard of mormaths that closely observed every movement. His patience tried too far, and eager to do anything to stifle the ever-growing sense of doom and destruction, Hagen loosed the Disc on them several times. Split in two, they tumbled down, leaving dark trails of tiny blood drops that hung like crimson clouds in the air. But another sentry rose up below for every one that fell. It was not quite a pursuit and not quite a shadowing, and the thane was mystified by it. Whatever might befall, he and Hropt could not quit the mountain.

Or could they, given their invisible foe seemed to have no desire but to keep them every second in sight?

Whilst he was racking his brains over the inexplicable, they reached the summit, where the outpouring of magical forces was every bit as powerful as at the Wellspring of Worlds. Holding tight to the almost vertical cliff face, they rested a half-hour at the needle-sharp pyramid of blindingly bright white marble that crowned the Swordmount.

Hagen told Hropt of his qualms, but the Father of Hosts brushed them away.

"I don't believe in your traps," he said, out loud and for all to hear.

"And when we come to believe, 'twill be too late," the thane muttered to himself, realizing the Ancient God was like a drunken man, inebriated by the return of his lost powers. "Do you see the Swords? Are they even here?" He greatly hoped to find the Young Gods' cache—be it real or counterfeit—empty.

Old Hropt grew tense, staring intently at the gray surface.

"I see them," he said at length, his voice hoarse with agitation. "They're here, all seven of them." And he touched the nearest of the stone sheaths that held within it a wondrous weapon. "Here Iambren's blade lies hidden. It is blue as the azure sky and is mottled with silver, like scudding clouds in the vaults of summer."

"Do you really want to take them?

"I don't know," Old Hropt replied with unexpected doubt. "I am uneasy somehow. There is a charm here that…but let me puzzle it out."

The puzzling lasted long enough for Hagen to be chilled by the stiffening wind. The mormaths still hovered above them, keeping their distance from the mountain.

Finally, Hropt raised his head; his gray eyes were troubled.

"Something there is that defies my understanding," he confessed. "I feel that I can break the barrier and take the Sword, but that something…" Furious, he slammed his fist into the stone, not even noticing the narrow fissures that snaked out in all directions from the place of impact. "Yet 'tis that or naught. Either we take the Swords or we remain here until the end of time. Hold fast, Hagen! Now we begin."

A well-aimed blow of his fist broke the snow-white needle, and it fell, tinkling like glass as it caromed off the overhangs. The two friends followed it with their eyes as if expecting something terrible to happen when it reached the ground, but it sank into the thickets that girdled the mountain and vanished, without a sound, without a glimmer. Silence fell.

Then, as Hagen watched, the mountain seemed to grow transparent, showing the seven huge blades within—weaponry best wielded by cloud-capped giants. They differed one from the next in color and form, but all had ornate hilts and intricately curved guards, with crests and insignes beyond number embellishing their blades. And in each there was such power that the Disc of Iamerth seemed a plaything alongside them. A primitive, primeval might, maybe the power of the Creator Himself—had bestowed upon those Swords their essence; and who in all the world could withstand them?

Slowly, as if bewitched by the sight, Old Hropt reached toward the hilt of Iambren's sky-blue Sword. Hagen saw his hand, clad in its iron gauntlet, plunge into the stone as into water, touch the sparkling gilded pommel and draw the Sword toward him. The titanic weapon seemed to cling to the fingers of the Ancient God.

Hagen's eyes stung, but he stubbornly refused to blink, afraid to miss the tiniest detail. A serene, iridescent shimmer wreathed the surface of the transparent stone, but in his mind there rang a terrible rasping, grinding sound, as though someone had shouldered open massive fortress gates whose hinges had not been greased since Rakoth's First Incursion. He saw a sky full of stars, their constellations unknown to him, that was quickly mantled in a deep Darkness through which not a glimmer shone. Not the darkness of which Rakoth was lord—it was neither a dark nor a gloom but a universal emptiness, a bottomless opening into true Nothingness. At the sight of it Hagen for the first time in his life felt such fear, such an unreasoning, immutable, primeval horror as was proof even against his mighty will.

He howled like a wolf wounded unto death. His reason did not know it, but his feelings unerringly told him something beyond all understanding had entered the world, something too alien for him to comprehend, too powerful to be conquered by force alone. In his mind there rose to its full, colossal height the diresome shade of the Unnamable.

Then the inky-black skies above their heads seemed to split from within, unleashing a dazzling jet of turbulent, blinding light. Through that ocean of flame raging down from the sky, Hagen saw speeding toward him dozens of dark winged forms encircled by green sparks. The mighty wings beat rhythmically as they approached in serried ranks, as if on parade.

With a muffled groan, Old Hropt quickly drew the Sword from its home in the mountain. Once removed, it seemed of normal size, though heavier than other blades. He plunged his hand in after the next, in great haste now, for the Father of Hosts and his young companion wished if not to live then at least to die quickly, peacefully and without torment.

Closing with them at breathtaking speed were the Young Gods' elite guards—the Winged Sentinels of the Hallowed Land, attended by Spirit Marshals. The masters of the Real had at long last struck back.

HEDIN

A COPIOUS SWEAT BEADED MY FOREHEAD. IMPELLED BY FEAR, THE BLOOD BEAT MADLY IN my temples. That which we so dreaded had come to pass—Rakoth's spell had proved potent, and the Unnamable was approaching, gluttonously devouring all that stood in its way. Every particle of the Real was food to it, and only served to increase its size and its already immense strength.

Rakoth was bent over the table, leaning on his powerful, convulsively clenched fists; his shoulders sagged without strength. He blamed himself for all that had happened, and I would rather have passed untold years restrained by the Young Gods than have lived those moments in his stead.

Sigrlinn was bearing up far better than either of us, even though she had known immediately what was afoot. The details of it she could not know, yet she need only look at us and read but the outer course of our thoughts, for the keeping of secrets was at that time the furthest thing from us.

With all my being, I felt the whole world seized with great shudders of unreasoning horror. Cold waves of dread rose from deep and distant bourns and passing breadthwise through the fabric of the world. The flesh of the Well-Ordered seemed to have a foreboding of the fate in store for it.

"What...What have you let loose?" Sigrlinn's cry was hoarse, and her voice trembled with rage she made no effort to conceal. "What does this mean?"

Belike she had already glanced into our thoughts, but was refusing to believe what was revealed there.

"The Unnamable," I answered brusquely.

She set her teeth and said nothing.

"To see that wretched thing away, Hedin, we must have at our disposal all the might of this world's magic." Rakoth was master of himself again and spoke in a voice almost calm. "We must be done with the Young Gods."

"A sound proposal, but presently beyond us," was my venomous response. "My own proposal is this—we shall make peace with them."

Rakoth was aghast—he appeared more taken aback by those words than by the Unnamable's invasion. Sigrlinn's eyes positively drilled into me, and I felt my mind under open attack as she forced her way in, seeking to understand the hidden meaning of what I had said. She, too, seemed nonplussed.

"Great Powers, Hedin, surely not!" she whispered.

"Surrender is not my intent," I retorted, in a voice as firm as I could make it. "Now all depends on Hagen. If he and Hropt have done as I designed, and the true emblem is in our grasp, we shall have goods worth bartering with the gods."

"*If* it is in our grasp..." Rakoth made a face.

"And how do you mean to be rid of them without it?" I inquired. "We shall never amass even a hundredth part of the powers you commanded in your day. So, let us not quarrel. It's time to bring Hagen out. We must wait no longer."

"Heaven of Truth, and still they hold forth on matters military!" said Sigrlinn with a sneering smile as she dropped into an armchair. "The Unnamable shall devour All That Is, and you will perforce end your squabble in the presence of the Creator!"

Rakoth gave her a heavy stare. "Would you rather we threw ourselves on their mercy?"

Sigrlinn shrugged. "'Tis all naught to me. You are at war with the gods, not I. But this is, I fear, to no purpose. Neither you nor even Merlin can halt the Unnamable. And a great pity it is. This was, in truth, a goodly world."

"And you bury it beforetimes," I protested. "We have wasted enough time. Rakoth—we begin."

Hervind appeared by the false emblem, again with a great deal of work ahead of him. I drew strength from my Talisman's fiery column and had begun to lay the needful charm upon him when Rakoth gave an odd, hoarse cry.

"And the elves? What of them?" He darted to the window, almost upending in the process the marble stand that held the emblem.

We had forgotten them—the Unnamable had driven all other thoughts from us, and the elven assault must have begun while all our forces either remained in hiding, like Hagen's men, or were keeping a respectful distance from the bearers of elven magic, like almost all of Rakoth's servants.

The Rebel thrust almost half his body's length out of the window. And hung there. The shock in his voice was manifest, even through those thick walls.

"Hedin, no one is here. No one! They have gone—I can see the stragglers on the horizon. They are in flight as if the Unnamable Itself were on their tails."

"And who knows, maybe It is," I replied. "But there's no surprise here. They have understood all. They know what has invaded the Well-Ordered—Sigrlinn is, in her way, correct in calling the Creator the last hope, for herself and the others. The elves are not named the First-Begotten for naught. They likely suppose they can still summon the Maker here before it is too late...which is all to the good. I only wonder what the Mages and Merlin will do now."

But they being in no haste to show their hand, we returned to our prior pursuits. Hervind, the being made of gloom and sunbeams, dove again into Iamerth's emblem, following a familiar path into the forbidden World of the Wellspring. Such were the powers bestowed by my Talisman that we could all see through his eyes as he went, without having to wait for his return.

What we saw was the Swordmount, surrounded on all sides by a pack of monstrosities. Their countless multitudes covered all the approaches to the mountain, and mormaths flapped through the air on heavy wings. Any babe-in-arms could tell that my apprentice and Old Hropt had been driven up into that gray fastness.

Then, from near the summit, there was a blinding white glimmer as something flew at one of the airborne mormaths and split it in two. Hagen was putting the Disc of Iamerth to use.

My little agent, stronger now than on his first visit to this world, directed his eyes to the place whence the terrible weapon was being loosed; and we saw Hagen and Old Hropt, weary beyond measure, barely clinging to the sheer scarp.

Then...

Don't touch them! Don't! I wanted to cry when I saw the Father of Hosts taking from the mountain the first of the Seven Swords—the Sword of Iambren, by its color. An instant later, I sensed a compacted blow of horrifying power slamming into the World of the Wellspring, smashing bastions and walls that had once been constructed with care by those who were now demolishing them. The destruction of the Divine Swords' depository had liberated titanic Powers that pounded from within the barriers protecting the World of the Wellspring.

I had not erred in deeming the Swordmount a trap.

We saw detachments of Sentinels, fellows to the one Hropt had defeated in Iamerth's temple, burst through the rift, with Spirit Marshals in the van. Never since the day of Rakoth's last attack on the Hallowed Land had those most faithful servants of the Young Gods, the best of the best and commanders of all the Young Gods' regiments, been sent into battle. There could now be no doubt that Iamerth's true emblem was in my apprentice's hands.

The Young Gods themselves, though, did not appear, and for good reason, having troubles aplenty with the Unnamable. I did not doubt they would survive, whatever the result, but I was also certain their efforts to save the Well-Ordered would continue to the last extremity.

But while those tranquil—oh, so tranquil—thoughts, sober and practical, took birth in my mind, a gaggle of others were laboring to be born there, too: *What shall we do? How can Hagen be saved? What charm will convey to him the powers of my Talisman?*

Time did not permit me to fear as I ought for my apprentice, whose situation now seemed completely hopeless. Yet he would not have broken even at the sight of the gods themselves, I thought, seeing the Disc fleeting toward his assailants.

From the gaping heavens, a bolt of lighting stabbed at the mountain peak, followed by a second, and a third. Hervind watched as, at the summit, cleft now by the blinding Scourges of the Gods, the powerful figure of Old Hropt slowly rose to full height, Iambren's Sword flashing menacingly in his raised right hand. A brief moment later, Hagen stood at his side. The Disc had brought down one of the Winged Sentinels but not timely enough, and now all my apprentice and his companion could do was accept a pitched battle.

I was all afire. Ways of saving Hagen and Hropt, one more absurd than the next, flared up and immediately died away in my mind. Alongside me, Rakoth was driving his nails into his palms and snarling in impotent wrath.

My apprentice raised his hand until it was level with Old Hropt's, holding a blade that shone with an intolerably bright white light. That was not his own Blue Sword. It was the Sword of Iamerth.

Lightning flashed again, the branching strip of fire reaching from a firmament in the throes of agony down to the pinnacle of the Mount, and a fiery net wound about the Father of Hosts. My eyes shut of themselves, but even through closed lids I saw the Lord of Asgard still standing, and the blade he held avidly drinking in the lightning's misspent power as the serpentine currents plunged into it and died harmlessly away there.

Hervind being at a good distance from the combat, Rakoth and I could see only a dark cloud wreathing the summit, so great was the speed of the Sentinels whirling around it. From time to time, though, that cloud was split by bright bolts of lightning, directed not toward the summit but away from it.

"They are holding their ground," Rakoth whispered, his eyes fixed on the unfolding battle.

"Are you ready for a fine fray?" I asked him, rising to my feet. "They cannot stand alone. The walls of the Wellspring's world are down, which has opened the way for us. Sitting here boots—"

I was not allowed to finish. In the very midst of my sanctum of spellcraft, which lay below every course of defensive magic known to me, there suddenly appeared a person tall in stature, costumed all in dark green and with a longsword, wide and thick, hanging from his emerald-encrusted belt.

Our guest had four fathomless pupils in each eye.

"Every second is precious," Great Orlangur said, wasting no time on greetings. "Call to mind the charm you know, Mage Hedin. And ask naught at this time."

I obeyed. The power that emanated from the Spirit of Knowing beggared all belief and was palpable even to my body of flesh, to say nothing of the rest of me.

The three of us stood around the Talisman's glittering column then, to make a charm so strong it wrested a groan from the Diviner and set a-quake all the immense totality of worlds, from their uttermost nethersides to the bourns of the Hallowed Land, including even the spacious realms of Chaos. A few instants later, Rakoth and I were in the gray, spectral domains of the Mid-Real, pursued by the parting words of him who verily was the Golden Dragon.

"If they seize the emblem, all is done. I shall await you here."

I did not put myself to the trouble of wondering fruitlessly why the Spirit of Knowing had not accompanied us. As it was, his interference in the affairs of the Well-Ordered had this time surpassed all conceivable boundaries—only something on the order of the Unnamable's incursion could have moved the Third Power to such open action.

Side by side, Rakoth and I sped through the layers of the Real, abandoning Hedinseigh to the whim of Fate. I could do no more than hope Great Orlangur would be well-enough aware what the destruction of my Talisman or its capture by an enemy would mean to me, and would therefore guard it with due vigilance.

The World of the Wellspring was flung open before us of a sudden, the vast blood-red rent in the world's flesh looming up ahead, its edges seeming still to smoke like the gates of a common castle put to the torch by a besieging army. We were steadily drawn toward that breach.

A few moments passed, and we found ourselves in a sky as alien and black as that of any world where an ordinary sun had never risen. Directly below, the mountain reached toward us, surrounded still by the scurrying servants of the Young Gods, and still we could discern through their close-knit ranks the sheen of two blades that rose and fell. Hagen and Hropt fought on.

Rakoth started up a bloodcurdling howling and hooting in my ear that I knew to be the ancient battle-cry of onrushing Darkness. He carried no weapon but his stave. I, for my part, had silently bared his gift, the never-to-be-forgotten Black Sword.

A new charm washed over us, one of no system of magic known to me. Great Orlangur had sent it after us to invest our weaponry with his own strength, whose compass and might were inscrutable not only to the gods but belike to the Creator Himself.

The Black Sword trembled in my hands.

I became aware I was capable of flying with the best of the Hallowed Land's servants, my obedient thoughts directing the flight and requiring no other effort from me. Thus it was that Rakoth and I, shoulder to shoulder, came from the rear at the unsuspecting Winged Giants and their spectral Marshals.

My sword split the first clean in two before it even had time to turn around. The second did have time for that, but for nothing more. The third tried to brandish its Soul-Banishing Staff, but the fearsome weapon met hard with my blade and broke in twain, and with my first counterblow I sent the Winged Giant back to the place of its making.

They were milling all around us now. Even in such a matter as the purloining of Iamerth's true emblem—more important than aught save throwing back the Unnamable—the Young Gods had begrudged sending in more than half a hundred Winged Sentinels and a handful of Spirit Marshals. Either they were more complacent by far than I had reckoned or all their other forces had already gone out against the Unnamable.

But that is laughable! That ugly brute cannot be stopped by mere swords, human or divine. Surely the Masters of the Hallowed Land understand so simple a truth.

Rakoth and I fought like two war engines, such as are used in the storming of cities by the artful rulers of Southern Hjorvard. My sword did not hamper thought, and my hands acted of themselves, their decisions more rapid and precise even than the movement of mind. Yet it could not be claimed that we passed pridefully through our enemy's ranks, flinging them this way and that, for the Winged Sentinels fought hard and furiously, not retreating so much as a step. A single touch from one of their fearsome Staffs would have dispatched our souls, Rakoth's and mine, forthwith, to be judged by the Young Gods' terrible and iniquitous tribunal.

No, the best we could do was break through to where Hagen and Hropt battled frantically.

"Your hand! Give me your hand!" I cried full in my apprentice's face. He was near raving with joy, and his eyes told me that he and Hropt had already lost all hope. He gripped me in a pincer-like grip with his steel-clad left hand, continuing to work the sword clutched in his right.

Rakoth did the same for Hropt.

Slowly, the mountain spun away below us, while all around a veritable storm raged in clouds of powerful, beating wings shot through with green sparks from the Soul-Banishing Staffs. Somehow, we fended them off with our swords, doing everything in our power not to prick each other. I had the fleeting, albeit belated, thought that we would have done well to have brought with us the rest of the Swords of the Gods that lay hidden in the mountain; but the thought passed when the Staff of one of the Winged Giants slid along the cutting edge of my sword and almost touched my body. I knew then we could only flee, and swiftly, too.

Great Orlangur, I felt, had not limited himself to hastening us into the World of the Wellspring, but had also covered us with an unseen shield that served to weaken our enemy's combat charms and thus thwarted several attempts to send the Spirit Marshals against us. There was no doubt about it— had not the Spirit of Knowing intervened, our venture here would for a certainty have fallen sadly short.

Encircled by our fearsome escort, we rose ever higher, toward that cruel slash in the sky; I was at that instant little concerned about the inhabitants of the Wellspring world or even for Mimir.

We dove into a fog of impenetrable, inky blackness, and when the gloom dispersed, we all four stood in the courtyard of the Hedinseigh fortress.

For a few moments we could only stare at each other with wide eyes, half-mad. My apprentice was quaking, and the trembling edge of his sword ran with viscous drops of greenish blood that dripped slowly onto the paving stones.

I laid a hand on his shoulder. "All is well, Hagen. Come now. You must both rest."

"Take the emblem from the lad, Hedin," Old Hropt said hoarsely. "That whatnot almost cost us our heads, mine not least of all. And in the midst of our battle royal, when I took that first sword...something terrible happened..."

"You are right," I replied, trying to look the Ancient God in the eye. "The Unnamable is here."

Hagen gave an almost imperceptible shiver, but his sweat-slick face was a blank page.

"I want to see if I can strike a bargain with the Young Gods," I went on, "now that we possess the greatest of their emblems. Maybe we can stop the Unnamable together."

But Hagen and Hropt being too worn by that awful battle for debate or decision, I called Ilving, and gave her leave to minister to her husband. Old Hropt, though, refused rest and wanted only a jug of strong ale.

Great Orlangur awaited us in my sanctum of spellcraft; Hropt's eyes started out of his head in stark surprise when he saw the Pillar of the Third Power. Sigrlinn had vanished.

"That which you call the Unnamable is moving with all speed from the Netherside, devouring the fabric of the Real as It goes," Orlangur said coldly. "I cannot stop It alone. There are limits to my powers. This thing you must do yourself, or no one will."

Rakoth ran his tongue over dry lips. "And the Young Gods? Surely, they can stand against It?"

"This from you, who called that calamity into the world? No, they cannot. 'Tis beyond their powers of mind. And I am not warranted to prompt them."

"Not warranted?" I marveled. "Not warranted to save all of the Well-Ordered?"

"Not warranted," the Spirit of Knowing repeated in the same chill voice. "Something there is far higher than I, and 'tis not for me to know it. Mayhap it is the very Balance of Light and Darkness. Mayhap...No, I wot not, but I strive to know. For now, I am vouchsafed simply the awareness that it is so, and the proofs patent we shall seek later. To you I can say only that there is a solution...and also that death would be most painful to me."

Without another word, he left, closing the door carefully behind him.

"Grand, indeed!" Rakoth exploded. "'There is a solution.' And 'tis left to us to seek it. He did not even deign to tell us the time remaining to us. What are we to do now? One..." He poked a finger into my side. "...wants a quiet, peaceful surrender, and the other appears only the Darkness knows from whence, speaks in riddles and vanishes who knows whither."

"But still I think that we and the Young Gods now have a common enemy," I remarked, and Hropt nodded in agreement. "We must try to reach a bargain with them. They likely have already heard that Great Orlangur was here. They must be wondering why the Spirit of Knowing would visit a brace of unruly Mages with whom they have not yet dispensed only because each time their cat's-paws have proven unequal to the task or more urgent matters have arisen. They cannot but be disquieted, for the Third Power is the Third Power, and the Young Gods are no match for it.

"I think we must try sending them a missive. Who knows, maybe the Unnamable can be halted only when all the emblems and all the Swords of the Gods are held in one pair of hands. In any event, the game is worth the candle. We lose nothing, not so? And we may win much."

Rakoth gave a disconsolate shrug. "To my mind, it is a plain waste of time. But...'twas you brought me out of the Netherside. Do as you see fit, and deem me in agreement."

Old Hropt nodded again. "Much as I thirst for revenge," he said slowly, "to defend the world against the Unnamable I am prepared to ally with whomsoever it may be—even with the very Lords of Chaos."

"Be less free with your words," I cautioned him, constantly mindful that in releasing him I had employed forces foreign to this world—the Forces of Chaos—and that one fine day I would be called to account for it.

We were, at any rate, in agreement. I carefully placed the true emblem alongside the false. There was nothing to distinguish them to the sight, but within they differed so greatly it seemed now farcical that I could have begun by taking an artful counterfeit for a true creation, especially since the Young Gods had not troubled to furnish their false emblem with even a dash of magical veracity. Now I was set to find my way to the Hallowed Land, and Sigrlinn must wait for her reckoning.

Obedient to the charm I had conjured, Iamerth's emblem began slowly to unfold before us intricate interweavings of mighty—though tamed for the nonce—sorcerous forces. Ours it was to seek out the one among them that would lead directly to the Abode of the Gods.

Before long it was found, meandering away from us like a narrow silvery path through the abysses of the Mid-Real. Without ever leaving my sanctum of spellcraft on Hedinseigh, the three of us glided along its resplendent, delicate paving through the world's declivities all the way to the forbidden gates of the Hallowed Land. There we stood, awestruck despite ourselves. Rakoth had already seen with his own eyes the chiseled spires of its unimaginably lovely palaces when his dark armies had invested the Abode of the Gods and he had tried on the glittering diadem of Lord of the World for size, but Hropt and I had never been so close, not even in our fondest dreams.

We were looking upon a vast cloud of rosy eddies interwoven with pearly threads. I heard Rakoth's teeth grinding—his regiments had been halted at this very place, fetching up hard against the Young Gods' unexpectedly hardened defenses.

Along the sparkling path we moved, over an astonishing bridge across time and space that rested on the backs of the Beasts of the Mid-Real, and then we were by the gates of the Hallowed Land.

Scarcely discernible in the creeping, oozing billows of pink mist were the outlines of low walls and elegant turrets topped with spires. Under our gaze, the mist wafted unhurriedly apart, revealing diamond doors secured by golden bolts. All of this was, of course, no more than decoration; the entrance into the Hallowed Land was protected by barriers far more powerful than those fine gates, which themselves were guarded by an impressive pair of sentries, a Winged Giant on either side, its Soul-Banishing Staff at the ready.

I strode up to the Gates—the Sentinels of the Hallowed Land grew agitated, unable to see us but doubtless feeling our presence—and knocked.

The guards were promptly calm, as if having received an order inaudible to us from their suzerains. The diamond doors swung slowly open, and we passed within, where we were immediately shrouded in a cloud of impenetrable dusky gray. Beneath our feet a fine, thread-like clew gleamed with a greenish light. A dispassionate voice bade us follow it.

And so we moved through the Hallowed Land, isolated within that opaque curtain from its beauties and wonders, led ever onward by a thin, winding filament of fire. It was impossible to say how much time elapsed in our transit of the Citadel of the Gods, until at length our clew was gone and we stopped, still swathed in that gray curtain.

We heard a woman's voice, tender, sorrowful, and low. "Heretics, why are you here? What do you seek? I am Ialini, she who has wrought harm to no creature living or unliving. Speak and be heard!"

Ialini! She was the last with whom I would have sought an audience. I had surely naught against her, for she had never meddled in the affairs of men and other mortals or even of the immortals. My quarrel was with her brothers, not with her.

But what matter who stands before us? I must have peace, and perhaps

Ialini the Merciful will prove more amenable than the rest.

"O Lady of the Green World," I began, respectful but not fawning, "we come hither bearing not swords but tokens of peace. We come to propose to the mighty gods a truce. The Well-Ordered has need of our alliance."

"But the gods need ally themselves with no one, you nonentity," the goddess's soft voice replied. "You think us afraid of the fiendish thing your unruly and, alas, unrepentant friend has summoned from the abyss? Do not flatter yourself, sorcerer. Do not oblige me to think even less of you than you deserve."

Rakoth muttered something unintelligible that sounded like an oath.

"But what of the emblem?" I prompted her. "'Tis the true emblem, not the counterfeit that was kept in the temple of Vidrir's Sovereign City. Is it not needful to you? May we not speak of it now?"

Ialini gave a faint, derisive chuckle.

"Bethink you, sorcerer. If it had been needful to us, would we have allowed you to seize it with such ease? Would we really have allowed you to possess it, even for a moment, had that run counter to our interests? No, it is not needful to us. Do you have aught else to say? If not, then better it would have been for you to repent with all dispatch and crave forgiveness from my brothers and sisters. I would have spoken on your behalf, and would have elected to moderate your punishment."

Old Hropt unexpectedly pitched forward. I sensed his movement and managed to stop him by grasping his elbow. Who knows how it might have ended—and the incident with my Erithaean Shade had taught me caution. These were, of course, only our shadows there in the Hallowed Land, but still there was a connection, a common ground with our living bodies, which was why Hropt felt my hand on him.

"And what shall you say to me, O Merciful One?" he roared in a voice so terrible it made even me uneasy. The words were laden with the hatred that had accumulated in him over countless ages. "What shall you say to me, O Even-Handed One—you whose brothers slaughtered all my kin on Borgild Field? You who have wrought harm to no creature living or unliving, you who are named the Mild of Heart?"

"What has this to do with the subject of my conversation with the sorcerer hight Hedin?" The goddess's voice rang with unconcealed surprise. "Ancient God, you remained among the living thanks only to my intercession, although you knew naught of it. My brothers are sterner by far than I, and their intentions for you were wholly other. You had, therefore, best repent in concert with Mage Hedin, for I will not, I fear, be able to protect you a second time."

"But why do you tarry, Ialini?" Rakoth said, his voice hoarse. "Go, call your brothers! So mighty are you, what would it be to you to take us captive here and now, and convoke a tribunal to pass judgment, swift and severe, on the sowers of discord? Come, we are they, and in your power entire!"

"Unlike you, Lord of Darkness, I have never dealt a treacherous blow," Ialini replied scornfully. "Nor shall I now. It is dishonorable to seize such as have appeared on their own volition, even if they are enemies. Depart now. Our quarrel shall be resolved elsewhere."

"Very well," I persisted. "You do not wish to make peace with us, and you have no need of the true emblem. The Unnamable holds no fears for you. Then all praise to you, O Mighty Ones! At the moment when the might of the Unnamable humbles Itself to your will, I shall crawl on my knees from Hedinseigh to the Hallowed Land, beating my breast in contrition and begging for the harshest punishment. When you halt that monster we shall all understand that you have rightfully been set here to command and rule the Well-Ordered. Our insurgency will then end of itself."

The reply was slow in coming. We were enveloped in utter silence, deaf to the sounds of the Hallowed Land; we breathed in the gray mist with never an odor in it and could say naught of what was happening without.

Yet still I fancied that I felt uncertainty in the enemy camp. My Guardcharms duly informed me that the monstrous handiwork of Outer Darkness was penetrating ever deeper into the flesh of the Well-Ordered, halted as yet by no one; that the Unnamable was progressing unhampered. Clearly, Ialini's divine brothers had bade her speak thus, but were they really so presumptuous as to assume we would lack the means to test their words? Could they really suppose us apt to believe that the Unnamable's devouring of the fabric of the Real was also part of their plans and intentions?

"The Unnamable has almost completely swallowed up all that was the Netherside," I declared. "Many beings, unreasoning though they may have been, have parted from their lives in torment. And why did you not protect them, did not save them? Yes, we called that monster into the world, but we cannot resist It alone, or we would long ago have set about doing so. Why do you wait? This temporization of yours obliges me to believe you lack the strength, and that your much-vaunted obstinacy prevents you from owning it so!"

We were answered with a silence that to me was more eloquent than any bombast. A lengthy interval passed before we were addressed again, this time by a powerful baritone full of confident strength. That voice could belong only to Iambren or to Iamerth himself, for Iaeth, Lord of the Realm Beneath, spoke in a deep bass, and Ialmog, Master of the Seas, seldom expressed his thoughts in words.

"In the name of universal tranquility and in order to end your preposterous sedition, we agree to grant you peace. Return the emblem to us, and you may leave quietly. None shall touch you or punish you for what you have done. This say I—Iamerth, Lord of the Sun's Light!"

It was much more than I had hoped for. Had I been correct in suspecting that without the true emblem they were powerless?

I feigned great surprise. "But we have only now been told this plaything is not needful to you. I had thought to keep it for myself."

"Indeed, it is nothing to us," the baritone voice confirmed. "But it shall be as a sign of the constancy of your desire to end hostilities forthwith."

"And what shall be the sign on your side?" I asked.

"My word," Iamerth replied. "What other signs would you wish?"

"At least such as would be equal in magical power to your true emblem."

"Oho!" Iamerth, hidden still behind the curtains of gray mist, gave an ominous chuckle. "You wish too much, Sorcerer Hedin! Remember that peace has not yet been made between us. You have still to receive my word."

"Inquire first with the Unnamable, and do not squander your strength threatening me," I said. "We depart now, there being no purpose in taking from you more of your invaluable time. Whilst we spoke, the Unnamable has belike engulfed yet another world."

The Lord of the Sun's Light did not condescend to reply. We were struck rudely in the chest, and an unseen wind, freshening, began pushing us out of the Hallowed Land. It being senseless to resist, we yielded.

Only a few minutes later we were again on Hedinseigh, in my chamber of spellcraft.

"Did I not tell you it was effort for naught?" Rakoth flung at me. "What did we gain from making those social rounds?"

"While we gained nothing, at least we lost nothing," was my rejoinder. "Besides, it's past time we looked on the Unnamable with our own eyes."

Old Hropt gave me a gloomy glance. "You still hope to stop It? I envy you the force of your will. I can think of naught now but a quick end to this. Maybe we should seek the aid of the Lord of Chaos."

"Again you gabble on, and right thoughtlessly, too." I frowned. "'Tis all one to the Unnamable whether It devours the Well-Ordered or Chaos. That aside, did you not hear the words of Great Orlangur?"

"How could I not?" Hropt responded, staring morosely at the floor. "But to my mind, he, too, was wrong."

"You succumb over-early to despair, friend," Rakoth said hoarsely, licking dry lips. "The Spirit of Knowing is, for all that, still the Spirit of Knowing. Don't discount his words out of hand."

The Lord of Asgard made no reply but sat, his head hanging low, drawing complex patterns on the floor with the tip of his sword. Rakoth and I decided to leave him in peace.

"There must be a solution," I said to Rakoth in low tones. "The Golden Dragon cannot be wrong. That solution is only be found."

"Easily said," Rakoth grumbled. "Do you have even an inkling of where to seek it?"

"First, let us see how it looks, this Unnamable that is bolting down the Real," I suggested. My mind was working feverishly, and I was a-tremble with an extraordinary inner tension. A mistake now would be too costly, and impossible to rectify.

With help from Hervind and the Diviner, Rakoth and I looked down, down into one of the farthest Lowerworlds, almost to its netherside. Time was when there had been here a dead kingdom of ancient mountains, a land scarred with ravines and shrouded in dense fog. Now, though, the scene we saw was different in every way. The mighty peaks that had stood changeless for hundreds of millennia were melting before our eyes, fracturing and sinking into an ocean of Nothingness that lapped at their once-indestructible feet. It might have put one in mind of a sandcastle being washed away on the seashore, had the sight not been so fearsome.

I studied closely the black sea that had so readily swallowed up those great piles of solid granite, and saw then my mistake, for the gloom resembled water only slightly. No waves rippled its surface, no glints of light played across it, and it gave off no reflections. All it did was consume—consume all in its path. It was dark yet not dark, gloom yet no ordinary gloom; nothing—no charm nor even magical sight—could penetrate beneath its velvety surface. It stretched for mile after mile in all directions, as far as the eye could see, and everywhere, my understanding told me, the same events were in train.

It was a spectacle of morbid fascination; a terrible dream, it seemed, a nightmare tale of the impossible. Yet it was really happening. My shivering shamed me but was hard to suppress.

The gloom of the Unnamable was not satisfied with mere lifeless stone.

Black threads reached upward to the dismal gray sky of that doomed world as we unwilling witnesses watched.

There opened to my view a prospect I shall remember upon my deathbed, if only it is given me to die in bed. I saw a broad plain beneath a cloudy sky, dotted with the squares of cultivated fields and with outbuildings, houses and huts—some alone, some in clusters. Teams of oxen lumbered along narrow tracks, and an occasional horseman cantered by. Between the houses bustled people—ordinary mortals, were it not for the rack of branchy, almost elk-like antlers each bore on his head. The inhabitants of this world were going about their daily business, with no notion that a magical war was in progress or that the Destroyer was nigh.

I could not at first understand why the Diviner had directed our eyes to these parts.

Then, in numerous places at once—in fields and groves, and on the very streets of the village—black craters appeared, and the ground became something with naught save its color to distinguish it. The craters began to turn, unhurriedly at first, then ever faster as long black threads, much like the tentacles of some unknown sea monster, burst from them, extending in various directions. Everything they touched immediately joined the body of the Unnamable and flowed into Its great emptiness.

Gripped with horror, the people rushed helplessly hither and thither. The more steadfast and stout-hearted among them tried to defend themselves, but no weapon could harm the Unnamable. Others bolted into their houses, as if looking to find salvation there. Soul-riving scenes unfolded before me as mothers already knee-deep in the gloom lifted their children as high as they could above it. I saw a tall man desperately heave a young woman and the little girl who clung to her onto the roof of a barn, and collapse then, swallowed up into that insatiable and bottomless belly. An instant later, even the roof and the two human beings on it, frozen in passionate prayer to the Heavens, had disappeared into the Darkness.

That was when I noticed the gloom had a marked preference for living— nay, sentient—beings, for the people were perishing first. The tentacles of Darkness even pursued them, although I could see no sense in that. Why put out such effort when in a few moments it would all be yours anyway, there being no one to come to the doomed victim's aid?

"Curses upon me, world without end, Hedin." Rakoth's whisper was that of a man half-mad. "Curses upon me for what I have wrought! The accursed gloom cares not what it devours."

"Your curses will not set such a woe aright," I replied dolefully. Those were the blackest minutes of my life. Until then I thought I had lived them when standing before the Tribunal of the Generation. Now, though, I saw how sorely I had erred. Those sights seared my soul with an inextinguishable fire, and I knew peace would not be mine until I stopped the Unnamable, even though I would never find a way to return those victims to life, making all they had suffered seem no more than a frightful dream.

The Diviner, though in a veritable transport of panic and terror, was still valiantly keeping me apprised of shifts in the magical forces that maintained the currents of life in the Well-Ordered, whilst I sought there the solution of which Great Orlangur had spoken. *Maybe in understanding how the Unnamable acts on the energies of wizardry I will find the means to counter Its rampant onslaught.*

But no. The chains of spells that held in submission magical effusions of horrific power were giving way; forces were running mad, augmenting the destruction and shattering whole courses of the Real. Those waves of energy beat against the smooth black face of the oncrawling gloom, yet to no avail.

And still I saw not the slightest sign of action on the Young Gods' part. The Diviner searched for any trace of their spells in the Ether hard by the Hallowed Land, but without success. Either the gods were still most assiduously concealing their wizardry at an elevation inaccessible to us, or they were doing nothing at all.

That, though, I could no way believe, and so asked the Diviner to try again and again.

Like a worm chewing through an apple's soft flesh, the Unnamable moved ever onward, growing yet more bloated and requiring more nourishment with every second that passed. A giant tear had appeared in the fabric of that world, and in that titanic cavity lodged that uncanny Being.

What can stop this fiendish thing? I thought feverishly, watching the spreading black stain. *Magical power? No, the Unnamable has bathed in its tides to no visible detriment. All in a world—any part of that world—is but food to the Destroyer.* Or, rather, served but to make It larger, for, although what the Unnamable was doing to the Well-Ordered seemed very like eating, It was in truth taking everything It touched into Its own body, even though "body" too was as near a misnomer as aught may be.

But the Young Gods—how long would they sit idly by? I could make no sense of it. The Unnamable was coming already upon worlds inhabited by humans and other mortals and immortals, and I waited for the masters of the

Hallowed Land to make answer, but waited in vain.

Rakoth's fist hit the table. "How much longer are we going to lollygag here?"

"Do you have some practicable idea?" I snarled. "If so, do tell. If not, best hold your tongue!"

"Forgive me." Rakoth was abashed. "Forgive me, Hedin. I did not mean to put myself in your way. Sure, none but you can find the solution. The rest simply do not believe that such exists. Hropt, for one."

The Ancient God, immersed still in his dismal musings, said nothing.

I screwed up my eyes. Usually, I required neither silence nor solitude when performing magical tasks of whatever degree of difficulty, and so it had been with me since the days of my apprenticeship. Rather, I needed to be surrounded with the stir and commotion that served as a spur to me and forced me to conduct myself as if I were at war. Even then I was, unbeknownst to myself, preparing for war, although I would not know it until much later.

There has to be a solution. It simply cannot be otherwise. Something in the very depths of my mind was telling me the answer to this riddle did not lie in the sphere of higher magical powers or in some unlikely combination thereof whose elements might take years to select while we had at our disposal only a few days or, at most, a week.

And there was Great Orlangur, with his dark, mysterious words—the proud Spirit of Knowing needed something of us, which was why he was holding us safe, helping us and sustaining us in our almost hopeless battle against the Young Gods. The Third Power never did anything without reason. I was even briefly demented enough to question if the Golden Dragon might not have somehow known the incursion of the Unnamable was imminent, and had begun betimes to prepare to repulse It.

Rakoth rose of a sudden to his feet.

"Sigrllnn has been out of our sight overlong," he announced. "I'll go and look for her."

"Be careful," I responded, thinking of something else and eyeing the trembling at the end of the magical chain that was still wound about the Rebel's hand. Mistrustful of my Guardcharms, he had seen fit to add one of his own.

The door closed behind him, and I plunged again into my burdensome reflections.

So, what power still remained in our world whose might was equal to that of the Young Gods? Orlangur and Demogorgon? Maybe, but the Congregate

Spirit would never enter into any endeavor not also undertaken by his brother. Yet why was I so certain of that? So had said the departed Mages whom we later dubbed the Ancient Ones, but must they assuredly be right?

Orlangur and Demogorgon aside, there was also perhaps the Moonbeast— but no, that was over-reaching. My wish for it was so great that my mind was, despite itself, magnifying the puissance of that greatest of warlocks, the greatest Mage among beasts, which had melded his wolfish reasoning with Darkness only knows what other minds, human and inhuman.

No, do not deceive yourself, I thought. *There is not nor can there ever be anything more mighty than the gods, except possibly the Lords of Chaos or the Creator Himself. And mayhap the Masters of the Hallowed Land are even now employed in trying to convey to Him these tidings. And may the powers divine and sacrosanct strike me down if I know how that may be done.*

Count on no one, I told myself. The solution, if a solution there be, lies elsewhere.

"Soon It will be here," Old Hropt said in a dead voice. "See how quickly It grows. Ere long, It will occupy all of the Well-Ordered, and I wonder who Chaos will choose to feud with then?"

"Get away with you! There will be no Chaos, either," I replied. "The Unnamable will not content itself with the Real and will eat up all of Chaos, too. So, rest easy, Hropt."

"What care I?" the Ancient God retorted dismally, failing to mark the irony in my voice. "'Tis all over with us."

It was beyond bearing to see the fearless Father of Hosts so pitifully downcast. I would willingly have put him to shame, have appealed to his courage; but Rakoth returned then, and following him through the door came a chary Sigrlinn, freed, to my surprise, from Rakoth's trammels.

"She wanted to be with us," he said in reply to my unspoken question. "And I could see no harm in it."

I raised my eyes to her. She seemed calm, even overly calm. Yet I could not believe she had reconciled herself so readily to her fate.

"I cannot urge more strongly that you yield as speedily as you may to the Young Gods," she said quietly. "That is our last chance. The gods may yet quit the Well-Ordered, taking with them all who wish to go. I say again, you must crave their forgiveness. You can do no other."

"But still you dally here?" Rakoth growled. "Be off to your masters, then, and good riddance to you!"

The sorceress gave a wan smile. "That is, by ill hap, a path I cannot tread alone. You forget that the Distant Ones took almost all my strength."

I stepped in then. "Here we are and here we shall stay. For the nonce, that is."

Sigrlinn hung her head.

"Are you thinking of how to stop It?" she asked after a time, her voice, slightly husky now, breaking the dead silence that had come to reign in my sanctum.

"I am," I responded briefly, and not directly to her.

"Poor thing," she murmured to no one in particular, shaking her head and looking off into the distance. I did not at first grasp that she was speaking of the Unnamable. "Poor thing, It must be dreadfully hungry. We would do well to find something to assuage Its hunger before It is upon us."

And then I had it. Of course—find something to assuage Its hunger! What could be simpler, and how had I not come to it sooner? Something to assuage its hunger! *We do not know yet how to destroy the monster, but we can surely stop it.* Never mind that this would require us to bring all the magical forces of the Well-Ordered into our power. Never mind that it would require us to crush the Young Gods and the Mages of my Generation, including Merlin, for that seemed less of a challenge to me, now that the Young Gods had refused to defend the world that had been given them to rule and to tend, and who had yet to do aught to halt the Unnamable.

— *Diviner, can you trace the sorcery being made in the Hallowed Land?*

— *Assuredly,* the grating voice answered. *Behold! Great enchantments are being wrought there now, but I know them. They were made there in the days when your friend was besieging the Citadel of the Young Gods and they were foresightedly preparing for flight.*

I had expected all but this, and was taken aback for a moment. Could it be true? Could the Young Gods have admitted defeat—not by me, to be sure, but by the Unnamable? And were they not able to send word to the Creator?

This last I asked the Diviner.

— *They are,* it grated in reply. *They are, they have, and the spell is well known to me. They created a powerful and swift Astral Messenger and it vanished, as ever is when they are dispatched not to the Well-Ordered and not to Chaos but yet farther, beyond the World of the Unnamable. I cannot understand where its path lay. It disappeared as ever is, leaving no trace.*

So. Word had, if this was no blunder on the Diviner's part, been sent to the Creator. Then why was He silent?

— *And why did you not tell me sooner that the Young Gods can send news direct to the Creator's throne, if such a thing there be?* I was surprised and indignant.

— *You did not ask!* quoth the Diviner, with terse dignity.

— *Very well, but what was His answer? And has He answered them before?*

Inwardly, I was apostrophizing myself in the most unflattering of terms for having been so decidedly dimwitted as to have failed to inquire earlier about a matter of such importance.

— *That I cannot tell you,* the Diviner replied mournfully. *My Spheres of Ether have never shown either answer or action of His.*

Well, then, if the Creator was not intervening either...

But there was more to do than rack my brains over that. I had to act.

I sprang to my feet. The time had come to quit the safe refuge of the Hedinseigh citadel. Hagen must hold it at all costs until our return.

"But destroy first the false emblems from the temple," Sigrlinn said suddenly. I had noticed her studying them intently for several minutes past.

"Why so?" It was Rakoth's turn to be surprised.

"I have no desire to be at the hub of all seven elements in their revelry," Sigrlinn replied. "Surely you know that all the temple emblems are but a trap for anyone foolhardy enough to steal them?"

As if to confirm her words, the wind suddenly began to wail over the keep, and I felt Iambren's Fan stirring in its hiding place. An instant later I stood by their open repository. The emblems quivered, as the wind howled louder and louder.

Rakoth made a sharp gesture with his hand, and a fiery streak flared in the air. The Fallen Mage had opened the Gates of the Worlds—and so deftly I scarcely saw him do it—then thrust into that burning gullet every last one of the false emblems. The maw of flame slammed shut, and we were rid of the deadly playthings between one breath and the next.

Not giving myself even a moment's rest, I concentrated my mind, preparing to cast a charm. Rakoth, Sigrlinn and Old Hropt stared at me, their eyes round, as though what they saw was a great curiosity.

Sigrlinn cocked an eyebrow. "You have an idea?" she asked.

"I have," I said shortly. "Hropt, Rakoth, we must go. The jaws of Fate await us; the Hallowed Land is our goal. Sigrlinn, you are free. Go where you will."

Indeed, she was no longer of concern to me. The riddle of the Distant Ones remained, of course, but it could bide a while. And if we succeeded in stopping the Unnamable, the Distant Ones would be no terror to us.

Rakoth and the Father of Hosts seized on me from either side.

"What are we to do?" they cried in chorus.

"I shall go nowhere!" the disgruntled sorceress sang the counterpoint.

"One at a time!" I appealed, trying to restore order. "Sigrlinn, you have done me harm enough in the past—"

"And her apprentice near made an end to me in the World of the Wellspring," Hropt put in, his eyes glittering.

"But now none of that matters in the least," I continued, affecting not to have heard him. "I say again—you are free. I hope you know it is not in your interests to harm me now. Perhaps you will succeed in explaining that to the rest of our kin."

She gave a crooked smile, her eyes full of unfeigned sorrow.

"And still you understand nothing, Hedin," she said, with a deep sigh. "I have no strength. When will you recognize that? I could not even find my way to Jibulistan, far less the Castle of All the Ancients. And to make me again all I once was is something that only you can do—by destroying the Distant Ones."

I was confounded. "And what makes you think I propose to destroy them?"

"If you do not, they will devour you as readily as will the Unnamable, should you fail to stop It." Infuriated by my lack of understanding, she stamped her foot. "Even if you overcome all your enemies and halt the Devourer, the Distant Ones shall still be at hand. And so, too, lest you forget, shall be the Ancient Powers, who have gone all unregarded in this pother, and who are also apt to demand their share, should your plan succeed." Her voice had risen to a shout. "Yes, of course, you are triumphant now, and you are yearning to bring me to book for the overthrow of your Empire of Night. Then consider it done! But if you send me away, I shall give myself over to the Distant Ones and shall not be silent. They will know all from me!"

"Then stay," I told her. "But—and do not take this amiss—I must leave you in that same...aah...chamber, until I return. I do not care to be unpleasantly surprised."

"What! You would confine me still, under lock and key?" She was aglow with wrath again, and again I saw in her the Sigrlinn I had known.

I hesitated. We were setting out on the most dangerous, the most all-but-hopeless venture, and one more difficult and more dangerous by far than aught that had fallen to my lot in all the long ages of my life. This time, the fate of the whole world depended on us. And here I was, wasting invaluable minutes in empty debate.

Common sense at last prevailed. Let her do what she will!

I gave a short nod. "Very well. You shall remain on the island and may do whatever you wish—within reason, of course. If our undertaking does not carry, we shall not meet again, not even after death. But if the scheme prospers, you may deem all past offenses forgotten and all accounts tallied."

"I never doubted you would conduct yourself so, Hedin," she said, and for the first time in Darkness only knows how many years, she gave me a warm and open smile.

The uneasy silence that followed was broken by Rakoth.

"And now we must be off," he said simply. "Call Hagen."

CHAPTER XVI

THREE THERE WERE WHO LIFTED THEIR LONGSWORDS IN A LAST PARTING SALUTE. THE pale moon shone, black shadows crept across the broad courtyards of the Hedinseigh fortress, and dim, uncertain starlight glinted on the raised blades. Hagen had drawn his Blue Sword from its sheath, having given that taken from the Swordmount to his Teacher, who in turn restored the Black Sword to its creator, Rakoth the Rebellious.

The insane, seemingly endless day was drawing to a close, and Hagen tried to calculate when it had all begun only to go quickly astray. The days and nights had whirled together in a manner beyond belief, and he had forgotten when he last really slept. Since leading his victorious army out of Vidrir's vanquished capital, he had been tossed endlessly from one nightmare scramble to the next.

The insane, seemingly endless day was drawing to a close, and his Teacher, Rakoth and Old Hropt were going to storm the Hallowed Land. He would remain on Hedinseigh, to guard both it and, above all else, his Teacher's Talisman, which had also been entrusted to his care. He knew that should any enemy contrive to come near that fiery column his Teacher's death would be swift and agonizing.

The insane, seemingly endless day was drawing to a close, and the wayfarers departed down a narrow, spectral silvered path. His Teacher was the first to turn and lay foot on it, looking long on Hagen in farewell. Old Hropt followed him, with Rakoth going after. They had found the Becharmed Corridor and were passing along it now, all the way to the Hallowed Land.

They would never have been able to do so with such speed had not Sigrlinn lent her aid. For all their haste, though, Old Hropt had still found time to lay across his chest a piece of skin from the ice-snake he and Hagen had killed during their rescue of Hagen's troops.

Hedin's apprentice felt a light breath of air on his cheek. Sigrlinn, who had stood silently at his side the while, was moving slowly toward the open door that led to the inner apartments of the keep. He gave the figures departing down the silvery path a last look, sighed and, sheathing his sword, followed the sorceress. He did not trust her. To his Teacher, she had been first and foremost a friend with whom, for all their differences, reconciliation was always possible. But to him, Sigrlinn had been all his life long an archenemy, one he had hated and mistrusted since childhood and from whom, moment to moment, no chicanery would come as a surprise. He was afraid to remain with her and afraid to leave her alone, and now he would have to be closeted with her through the wearisome hours to come that would decide their fate.

He knew his Teacher could not have left his Talisman all defenseless, but even so felt profoundly unhappy and utterly desolate, drained to the last drop. His strength, both of body and of soul, had been exhausted in skirmishes without number, his fortress was ruined, and the only good was that his troops had survived. They had rested at least a little, and now glow-worms seemed to swarm across the bastions that had suffered the worst damage as, by torchlight, his men went to plug the worst of the breaches in the walls. They were working fast and furious, but to the thane, the sight of those yawning gaps and the piles of broken stone nearby, of those now-congealed granite rivers memorializing the first attack, was as a needle sliding slowly under a nail.

As Sigrlinn passed through the door, a hand lightly touched the thane's sleeve and Ilving's soft voice whispered, "Hagen, my husband, I am sore afraid! Something terrible prowls…prowls hither. You will protect us? Surely, you know how to contend against it."

The terror exuded by the Unnamable rippled in broad circles throughout the Well-Ordered, and ever more of its inhabitants were coming to feel an oppressive, incomprehensible, unaccountable dread that had, to all appearances, no cause.

"All the women belowstairs are very frightened," Ilving went on in a half-whisper, having been only briefly unmindful of her place as mistress of Hedinseigh, who must think of others first and thus set an example to the rest. "Their thoughts and their hands are enmeshed; they cannot even cry. It is a terrible thing to look on them, but I am trying to calm them. May I tell them you know how to vanquish the Prowler?"

"You may, my own," he said, leaning over her and carefully touching his lips to her forehead with a tenderness that surprised even him.

When Ilving's light step had faded into the distance, Hagen returned to his own thoughts. With all the power of his peerless will, he dispelled the evil premonitions, the prescience that this, their last venture, would end ill. Yet in the very depths of his soul there was born a keen and bitter awareness that his days were surely numbered.

The stars winked peacefully one at another in the sky. The silvery path that had carried the Teacher and his companions away had long disappeared, swallowed up by surges of darkness. In the sea by the Hedinseigh shore deep, muffled, protracted inhalations could be heard. One of the sea-beasts had risen to the surface and was hurriedly turning the respite to good account by breathing all it listed while not threatened by the death-dealing charms of the Mages who had been diligently trying to annihilate the entire brood of Rakoth's creatures these thousand years.

So quiet...and so fearsome, Hagen thought. He knew the Unnamable was moving, inexorably and unchallenged, gnawing ever deeper into the flesh of the Real; that with every instant, Its power grew and the likelihood of overmastering It decreased.

But my Teacher can do it. He will conquer It. Still, the thought could no longer force his fears to withdraw without a backward glance. For the first time, his calm confidence in his mentor was strained to breaking.

The thane had not initially understood why his Teacher had been so driven to return again to the Hallowed Land, but Hedin, with a reproachful shake of the head, had reminded him of the words he had repeated a thousand times over as a child.

"And the first root goes deep into the ground, through Viflheim and the Circles of the Infernal Realm, to Ungoliant. And from below, that root is chawed by a dragon hight Nidhogg. The second root goes into the World and twines about it and goes away into the Abyss of the World, which is now all berimed. And the third root goes into the World and then aloft. It pierces the heavenly firmament and hastens to the primordial light. And three springs feed that tree. Turbid is the water in the first, and black in color. Its name is the Seething Cauldron, and it feeds the first root. The second is styled the Wellspring of Mimir, and all who drink deep of it are filled with wisdom, and it feeds the second root. The root that is in the sky is fed by a well that is esteemed as the most holy of all. Its name is Urd, and the Gods drink its waters. And all who drink deep of it are filled with righteousness..."

Who would have thought that under the old familiar guise of Mimir's Wisdomwell would lie the titanic might of the Wellspring of the Worlds? There, in the heavens—or more precisely, within the precincts of the Hallowed Land—the third Wellspring of Power was concealed. The first had already been secure, long subject to the Fallen Mage.

So now, when the world's strengths were melting rapidly away, engulfed in the Unnamable's insatiable belly, Mage Hedin could do naught else but lock that fiend in a cage whose bars would be worlds constantly created, the fabric of the Real made new time and again, which would feed that eternal hunger. Chaos is endless, or almost so, and could long provide food for the Unnamable, until some better expedient were found.

But to achieve his plan, the Teacher must have power over all three springs. Two were already his; the last remained to be won.

Hagen stood a while longer, looking down on his fortress. The bastions loomed black, the fiery points of countless torches crowded about the gaps in the walls, and the voices of the workers carried up, muted by distance. He could stand there at his ease as long as he cared to—his centurions knew their business. The chiliarch Gerder was a first-rate foreman, and neither Hagen's presence nor his commands were anywhere needed.

The idleness becoming unbearable, he turned sharply away and entered his Teacher's sanctum of spellcraft, where Sigrlinn sat, her wide eyes in a fixed stare. She seemed to be listening. When he appeared in the doorway she gave a slight start and passed a hand over forehead and cheeks, as would one roused from slumber.

"The Unnamable draws near," she said quietly, in a drab and expressionless voice. "In three or four days It will have devoured all the Well-Ordered. The brute grows by the second. I do not know if the barrier your Teacher wishes to raise will stop It aright. Every particle It devours increases Its strength—and Hedin proposes to fatten It for slaughter. I fear one fine day the cage will not hold."

Hagen made no reply. He still mistrusted and feared her, and was all but unarmed, his Teacher having taken the Disc of Iamerth with him. He understood that nowhere was that deadly weapon more needed, but without the Disc he felt most ill at ease. What if all the Mages of the Generation, including Great Merlin himself, were to come calling?

He sat carefully on the edge of his Teacher's favorite chair, hand on sword, and glanced warily at the sorceress. She marked it with a faint smile.

"Calm yourself, war-hungry thane. We shall war no more. The past is gone and will not return, and now I wish victory for your Teacher more than you do yourself, because I know better what will happen if he fails." She shuddered again. "When you came in, I was trying to descry what is transpiring now in the Hallowed Land. But alas, all there is so clouded by a fog of wizardry even I cannot see through it. I understand none of this. Naught of the like has ever manifested itself before in that place."

"You...You have been able to see into the Hallowed Land whene'er you wish?" Hagen asked distrustfully, for he knew how jealously the gods guarded their secrets. The Citadel of the Gods had ever been resistant to his Teacher's magical sight.

Sigrlinn gave another mirthless smile.

"Forget not that I am of Ialini's suite," she reminded him. "That has its privileges. We have been permitted to look all we wish upon the beauties of the Hallowed Land, on the grounds that we would be thus inspired to continue rendering faithful service to the Young Gods. Indeed, we have been promised that we, too, may one day live there."

"For you that would belike have been splendid." He could find naught else to say.

"Perhaps." Sigrlinn slapped her hands on the armrests and rose. "Damnation, I can remain here no longer! I cannot be both idle and ignorant at such a time."

"Then why did you not go with my Teacher?" Hagen muttered. "Did you fear the Young Gods would consider you a traitor, too, if they are destined to vanquish us?"

She flinched as if from a blow, and her eyes darkened with wrath, but after a moment she had herself again in hand.

"Yes, you might well think so," she said, striving to speak with all possible detachment. "I have had my goals, your Teacher has had his. Our ways have crossed, and at times we have stood athwart each other's paths. I sought so long to stop you, even when you had already begun. Do you remember the temple in Erivag? I did all I could then to have your Teacher understand he was under constant watch, while also trying to make him know I was but warning him. It was no easy matter to gull Great Merlin. He was incensed when he learned I had not been able to defend the temple against a willful apprentice."

"Then the zophar..."

"Was sent so your Teacher would know with whom he dealt. Yet Mage Hedin, being so accustomed to traps and tricks, never did comprehend what was afoot. But now none of that is of any importance." The sorceress sighed heavily. "Probably you are in the right. And my reasons for not going with him are very easy to explain. First, he would never have taken me, since his trust in me is no greater than yours. Second, there was no use to be had of me, as I do not command the magic of the Wellsprings. And third…no, the third does not concern you, young busybody."

Hagen deemed it best not to continue the conversation. Collecting his thoughts, he tried to call up the Diviner, but without success, as no mortal could speak with that mysterious being. Then the disappointed thane chanced to look on the empty plinth where the false emblem had been. Alongside stood Hervind, washing itself assiduously with one tiny paw as if it had never had occasion to wander through worlds beyond imagination and had never been chased by Mimir himself. It stared at Hagen with the little black beads of its eyes, and the beastling's thin voice sounded in the thane's mind.

— *I help. We see. Open the road. Look there.*

Hervind's lack of fluency in human speech kept its sentences very short, three words at most. But, being made of sorcery, it had some understanding of magic; and with its help, Hagen began to weave an intricate spell that sorted through the keys for the Gates to the road that had led the Teacher and his companions away. Sigrlinn watched with a signal lack of interest, likely thinking nothing would come of it.

Yet his efforts were crowned with success. He saw a narrow brownish ribbon uncoil before him that passed through the open window, over the bailey, over the sea-cliffs, over the foaming surfline and on, on into the sky, through the walls of the world into the bourns of the Mid-Real, ever onward through the courses of the Well-Ordered to a lonely island amid the gray plains of the Astral, and to the tiny golden pyramid that was the Hallowed Land and Citadel of the Gods, its true appearance cloaked from the unskilled eye.

Hagen and Hervind moved closer to the emblem, their sight separated from their bodies and sweeping away into distances unimaginable to ordinary mortalkind. At the very last moment, Sigrlinn joined them.

"You are, I see, a great wizard, Thane Hagen," she said, her voice tinged with respect. "I should have taken more care when I tried to capture you in the Near Niflhel cavern."

The Thane of Hedinseigh made no reply, taken up as he was by the extraordinary experience of flight. He felt he had sprouted wings that carried him over hundreds of leagues in fractions of a second. The world of Greater Hjorvard was far behind him, the golden pyramid drew closer by the instant, and he saw, to his surprise, that close up the Hallowed Land resembled a scrap of multicolored mist in boundless gray seas that spread heartsickness and despondency all around. The spot of rainbow colors grew, the gates flashed by, ajar and giving off a gentle, silvery sheen, and Hagen was looking into the Hallowed Land.

He saw his Teacher, Rakoth and the Father of Hosts. He heard their voices, and realized he was only a little belated, since he had far outpaced them in crossing the abysses between the world that was Hjorvard and the Abode of the Gods.

They walked abreast, their feet, shod in rude ox-hide boots, tramping irreverently down the wondrous pavements of the Hallowed Land, which were set with gleaming translucent flagstones. Clouds of greenery, fresher and more magnificent than aught in any mortal world, surrounded them on all sides, every flower seeming the handiwork of an artist of great genius, and the colors so bright as to surpass any the human eye might see within the bounds of its customary habitation. Among the bushes, narrow lanes wandered off in various directions. Nowhere was there a living soul in sight.

"Not even a Winged Giant!" Hagen heard the dismayed Lord of Asgard say. "Gates wide open, no guards. This pleases me not, I swear by the Great Stairway. It reeks of an ambuscade."

"All the better for us that there is no one," Rakoth responded. The Fallen Mage moved forward with the careful stride of a hunter, his drawn sword atilt before him. The Black Blade lived now a life of its own, and swift snakes of crimson fire ran along it as it sought a target. "We shall find the Well, do what we are to do and return. I like it not here."

"Stop your chatter!" Hedin hissed at them. "You are not on a promenade."

He had Iamerth's Sword unsheathed and his other hand was on the Disc of Iamerth. The Lord of Asgard set more store by the Soul-Banishing Staff than by his own trophy, the second Divine Sword he had brought from the World of the Wellspring, which he left for now in its sheath.

Hagen could not tell if his Teacher knew the way, but to the bystander they seemed to be wandering at haphazard. He followed the Mage as close as could be, and therefore missed almost all of the Hallowed Land's splendid vistas, catching only glimpses of its fabled beauties out of the corner of his eye. Thus he saw columns set singly, gleaming from within, and near them inert stone sculptures of improbable creatures executed with breathtaking artistry. The statues seemed to have more life in them than those who passed them by, for though they moved not at all, they had a grace inaccessible to the living.

Hagen also saw lovely grottoes from which streamed a soft, caressing light, and crystal pools that held stone maidens, motionless and astonishingly beautiful, with long fish-like tails, and forest giants of spanless girth, with more stone beasts amid their huge roots. The further the three who had come to challenge the gods progressed, the more stone statues they encountered that only a moment before might have been full of life and strength.

Although the path they trod was gradually widening, the sculptures were so thick on it they had to wend their way between them as between the trees in a wood. Hagen could not but notice the statues were placed randomly, with no sense or meaning, and for some reason in the very middle of the road or in the crossroads, where they must surely hamper all travelers. They would have been better arrayed by the roadside, assuming those who lived hereabouts were still inclined to travel by foot, rather than flying or translating instantly from place to place.

Rounding a group of statuary that had completely blocked their way, the two Mages and the Ancient God found themselves before a palace so beautiful Hagen was stabbed to the heart. He had seen perfection, and would be haunted by a burning desire to gaze on it again to the end of his days. A broad stairway of black marble began by the edge of a pool and led upward into a crystallized cloud wherein diaphanous arcs and cupolas interwove. On its steps, in careless poses, stood and sat seven figures, both male and female, clothed in light snow-white mantles and with glittering diadems on their heads. None held a weapon, at least not as far as could be seen.

Hagen froze, unable even to blink. These were the Young Gods, the Seven Most High, the Allfather's first creation, to whom He had granted dominion over myriads of lives in all the innumerable Worlds of the Well-Ordered. Never before had the thane looked on the faces of all those whom he had challenged with such temerity. The image of Iamerth that had appeared to him in the temple was nothing in comparison, being but a weak and unfaithful reflection of the true god.

The seven turned to face the three, and Hagen's gaze crept slowly over the countenances of the Young Gods.

It was, indeed, them—the paramount masters of All That Is: Iamerth, Lord of the Sun's Light, a powerful figure whose glowing eyes—an inextinguishable flame burning inside the skull—had no pupils; his brother Iambren, Lord of Winds and Hurricanes, the tallest of them all, though not as robust and thickset as Iamerth, with white hair and white brows and a nose with a raptor's hook, like the beak of falcon or eagle; the taciturn, scowling Iaeth, Lord of the Dead, his curly mustaches and short beard singed with subterranean fire—as broad in the shoulders as Iamerth but with crudely bulging muscles; Ialmog,

Lord of Waters, as impulsive as the sea itself and with eyes whose color the very waves might yearn to imitate; Iathana, Mother of Beasts, calm, dignified and broad of hip, with hair like a lion's mane; Iavlatha, the light, lively, birdlike Guardianess of the Stars; and slender as a reed, with a gay sheaf of sun-faded hair, cut short, unlike the rest, and with huge emerald eyes, the sweetest and most merciful of them all—Ialini, Mistress of the Green World.

Why have we been at odds with them? What but good could they bring to the world? Hagen was overwhelmed with sudden panic, knowing he would never know their forgiveness.

"What do you wish to say before you are dispatched to Unbeing, you sowers of discord?" Iambren's voice thundered over the heads of Hedin, Hropt and Rakoth, mighty as the roar of a hundred thousand hurricanes, while his brother Iaeth strode silently forward and stretched out his hand, palm downward. From the stiff fingers smoky rivulets of flame streamed down to the steps, and there became fancifully convoluted tresses of stone. A few moments later a clump of granite snakes had formed at the feet of the Silent God, their golden eyes looking coldly on the motionless, boldfaced trio.

"Do you intend to save the Well-Ordered, O Gods?" Hedin spoke first, his voice hoarse.

"That is none of your concern, Mage. You have already been told as much. And are you the ambassador of those who inhabit the Well-Ordered, to pose such questions here? Tremble, then, for your fate has been decided. Our judgment is entered."

"A windy rant, that!" Rakoth growled, raising the Black Sword. "Methinks you have resolved to flee like craven cowards, since the Creator has not deigned to reply to your invocations. Methinks you have resolved to abandon all the Well-Ordered as fodder for the Unnamable. You hope to save yourselves in flight. Very well, then, flee!"

"Only let us pass through to the Well of Urd," said Hedin when Rakoth was done. "It is needful to us. We are not here to wage war."

"Stupendous effrontery!" Iambren raised clenched fists. "Brother Iaeth, carry out the sentence."

"Hold!" Hropt spoke up hurriedly. "If we have been sentenced, is it not the custom of all worlds and peoples to grant the last wish of the condemned? We asked a question. In a few moments we shall be no more. Would you debase yourselves so far as to refuse a reply or to lie to us at a moment such as this?"

"Brother Iaeth, carry out the sentence," was Iambren's only response. Ialini quickly turned away, covering her face with her hands.

"Battle stations, my friends." It was the voice of Hagen's Teacher. "We fight through to the Well! Cover me!"

Iamerth raised a fist that had become a blinding cloud of fire. It was the signal. The glittering, multicolored ribbons of Iaeth's snakes slithered down the steps toward Hedin, Hropt and Rakoth, who stood shoulder to shoulder, their blades drawn. From on high came the beating of countless wings as Winged Giants descended from the skies.

The gods could not bring their power—the magic that was theirs alone— to bear in dispatching the unruly three, could not command them to vanish or consign them to distant worlds where the Unnamable already rampaged. No, naught but brute force could they employ. Thus, in sum, they had resisted Rakoth's storm of their dwelling place—by merely crushing his squadrons with their own.

So, under the unnaturally clear sky of the Hallowed Land, amid lush greenery and wondrous flowers, on the black marble staircase that let to the gods' apartments, battle was joined; and for the first time in the history of the Well-Ordered, weapons were bared in the Citadel of the Gods.

Hagen's heart seemed ready to burst from his chest. He was afraid to blink; his dry eyes burned, but he could not tear them away from the scene unfolding before him. He watched the blades rise to meet the Winged Sentinels' first assault, saw Rakoth's Black Sword parry a Soul-Banishing Staff and answer by running the attacker through. But from his own experience, Hagen knew the great difficulty—maybe even the impossibility—of killing a warrior of the Hallowed Land. The unlucky Winged Giant collapsed onto the staircase, yet almost immediately rose again and returned to the fray.

Not a moment more passed before the cloud of huge wings that beat the air, the enlacement of mighty, half-naked bodies, had hidden the Teacher and his two companions from sight. Iaeth's stone snakes were gliding fast into the very thick of it, and soon only the furious glittering of three blades, seen through the seethe of combat, told of the efforts of the trio that had so disturbed the peace of the Hallowed Land.

They will be broken on the instant. The thought was terrible. *They will be broken on the instant, and that will be the end of all.*

Hagen would have pledged himself to anyone, could that bring him to the Citadel of the Gods and allow him to die alongside his Teacher. He had heard of faithless apprentices who had abandoned their mentors in times of danger, and to him they were the most despicable of all who lived or had ever lived. Now was his time to show that he was cut from other cloth.

The skirmish was proceeding slowly up and across the broad marble staircase as Hedin, Hropt and Rakoth moved step by step to the side of one of the main entrances to the gods' chambers. It was an uneven battle—several Winged Giants had been wounded but quickly recovered and returned, leaving only their viscous, sticky blood to stain the marble a strange, dark green. And the Lord of the Dead's stone snakes were, it seemed, entirely invulnerable—it took all the combat skills of the Teacher and his comrades even to fend them off.

Since the Viewcharm followed those to whom it had been yoked, the Young Gods gradually slipped from Hagen's field of view, but before losing sight of them entirely, he noticed unconcealed astonishment on the face of Iambren, who stood in the fore.

That was encouraging. Something had gone awry in the Young Gods' flawless plan; something had forced events from their allotted path. Hedin and his friends had not yet won, but neither had they lost in the first few moments, as the Young Gods had manifestly reckoned they would.

His Teacher must be leading Hropt and Rakoth to the Well of Urd. Looking on, he saw that the combatants had descended the marble stairway again and passed around the corner of the grand structure at whose entrance the black steps culminated.

Hold fast, Teacher, hold fast! Hagen repeated to himself as one possessed, reaching with all his being across the magical lea that stretched between the sanctum of spellcraft and the distant Hallowed Land.

"Awake, my thane! Rouse yourself!" A voice of authority broke into his mind. The vision faded, and he discovered himself sitting at his Teacher's desk. Sigrlinn was shaking him by the shoulder as hard as ever she could, having evidently already exhausted her magical arsenal. Hagen noticed Knut, Gerder and Frodi standing in the doorway with worried faces.

"Thane, a foreign fleet is nearing the island," Frodi blurted out. "They were first espied by those…those servants of the Rebel Mage—the krakens—and so the news came to the dragons and from them we learned of it. They are already at the entrance to the harbor!"

"Catapults? Ballistas? The ironclads of the first bastion?" The curt questions poured from Hagen, who had been transformed forthwith into a most able commander. It was of little importance who was bent on storming Hedinseigh this time, or with what force—preparations must be made to repulse them.

He was told the catapults had been armed with stone projectiles and the ballistas loaded with sharp-tipped metal-bound beams, that the ironclads of the first bastion, being closest to the harbor, were deploying to the jetties and that the bowmen and arbalesters had taken up their positions in the bastion itself—or, rather, in what remained of it after the first assault, when the walls had suffered sorely from the liquid fire shot from the enemy vessels.

Hagen then issued other essential orders, hastily regrouping his forces in readiness for the worst. He was forcing himself not to think of his Teacher—whoever was approaching his domains would surely take every opportunity to destroy Hedin's Talisman, and then...

He shuddered.

Sigrlinn lifted her pale, strained face to him.

"Can you tell me aught of them, sorceress?" he asked her, donning his armor with the help of two squires who had entered along with his chiliarchs.

"They are not sorcerous beings, nor are they legions from other worlds." Her voice brimmed with alarm. "I feel in them, as they approach, no magic at all. Belike, they are mere humans. Perhaps even yon Vidrir."

"If they are humans, we shall shift with them," he said slowly, turning about and dismissing his attendants with a gesture. "But who would resolve to storm Hedinseigh at this time? Some lackeys of Merlin's? Or someone from the Castle of All the Ancients?"

"Believe me or not, as you will," Sigrlinn replied in muffled tones, twisting a lock of hair between trembling fingers, "but if the hand of Merlin or some other Mage were over them I would already know it. I have my ways. Although...hold...I feel something familiar...Darkness Most Great!" Those last words were a wail of despair. "They are here!"

And she fell into a chair, her right hand covering her eyes and her left dangling down.

"Iamerth scorch my hide! What is it?" Hagen forgot himself so far as to grasp the sorceress's slender shoulder.

"In the train of that army...are my apprentices...you call them the Darkling Riders." Sigrlinn groaned. "They are coming here!"

"And what of it? They're your apprentices!"

"They...They are no longer mine. Something has happened to them. Someone is directing them, tugging on strings like a puppeteer in the marketplace. They are mad. And one of them has a Fire-Bearing Chalice!"

"The one who caused Hropt and me such grief by Mimir's Wellspring? And she is coming here, and you cannot stop her?"

Sigrlinn nodded, her hand still over her eyes.

Hagen took a deep breath. "Very well. If I understand aright, you would rather they not be killed, if at all possible, until you find a way to lift the enchantments from them?"

Again she gave a silent nod.

"I shall do as you ask, sorceress," he told her, strapping on his sword and going toward the door. "Should they be fated to perish today, their death shall come no sooner than mine. If you are willing and able to help us, you are welcome to do so. You will find me at the first bastion."

The preparations to repel the attack were complete. Hagen strode down corridors and passageways already deserted, all the men being in position, but at the doorway leading from the keep to the bailey he was met by a small group of chiliarchs and retainers. Among them were Frodi, Gudmund—well recovered now from the insensibility brought on by that terrible vision on Avalon—and Orc, the fearless goblin chieftain.

Hagen issued his last brief instructions, sending some to the front line, others to the second, and holding yet others in reserve. The faces of his seasoned confederates were calm—Hedinseigh had withstood assaults more fearful than this, and likely none doubted it would again, though Hagen felt a fleeting regret that the Fallen Mage, in departing, had not given him power over the Children of Darkness. Those krakens and sea-beasts would have stood him in such good stead!

Yet the fact they were staying to themselves and not mounting an attack of their own told him there were no servants of the Young Gods among the enemy ranks or that those forces must be so negligible the army of Darkness was simply paying them no mind. *Very well, then, we must wait to see who has come acalling,* he thought as he climbed to the top of the first bastion.

From that vantage point, he had a view of the dark harbor, lit only by a niggardly moon. The lights in the watchtowers by the moles that ran into the sea had been extinguished, and he knew that even then the heavy, creaking capstan was drawing up the thick chain that blocked the harbor entrance. Alongside, by the embrasures, stood his chiliarchs and messengers, awaiting their orders. Down below, the last centuries of ironclads moved to their stations, ready to meet a still-unknown enemy with an impregnable wall of shields.

The minutes passed. The hostile fleet was nowhere to be seen. Weary of waiting, Hagen cast a Charm of Nightsight.

The world underwent strange changes then. It seemed suffused by a steady gray glow, and in that light he saw, afar off, a scattering of vessels of sundry size. At first he was sure his sorcery had betrayed him, and could not believe anyone might venture to storm the forbidding fortress of Hedinseigh with so meager a force.

But in truth, a mere three or four dozen unwieldy, fat-bellied merchant ships were approaching the walls of the citadel, aiming with difficulty at the harbor's narrow neck. His magic helped him see the old patched sails, the oars of diverse lengths rising and falling all at sixes and sevens in a travesty of the well-drilled work of a warship's oarsmen. He could not but remember the regular ranks of the elven fleet, and the concerted and powerful motion of the vessels in that first attack. Set against them, those presently closing in were no more than a piteous handful of malaperts.

"Mayhap they believe no one is left alive here, and they are coming to rob the dead," Knut suggested. "Mayhap they are freebooters."

Gerder would have none of that. "More cocksure freebooters I have never seen."

"Silence!" Hagen raised his hand, and the hum of voices was immediately stilled.

He reached forward with all the magical senses at his command, seeking to determine who was leading the assault. His gaze fixed on the worn planking of a flagship whose place should at best be in a ships' graveyard and at worst at the bottom of the sea. The deck was empty, save for the lone figure of a man at the huge wheel.

Here, the magic art of Hedin's apprentice failed him. Try as he might, he could not discern the face of him who stood on that deck. Something stronger than the spells lent by his Teacher—even those to which he had added the fruits of his own investigations—opposed him here. Like a knife rebounding from steel armor, the charms he cast glanced off the gray curtain that on the instant shrouded the mysterious helmsman.

"Battle stations!" he ordered brusquely, thinking *Magic is as magic does, but the result will still be determined by the sword.* He must hold fast, come what may, until his Teacher gained the advantage in the Hallowed Land and halted the Unnamable.

The enemy vessels drew near, slow and unsure, struggling to catch a following wind in their sails. So few they were that they could not be carrying more than four or five thousand warriors, half the number of Hagen's force. But the thane determined to run no risk, and when the "merchants" crossed the invisible line that put them in range of the fortress' trebuchets he gave the order to fire.

Many of the catapults and ballistas had burned and been disabled during the earlier engagements, but such as remained, he reckoned, would suffice to send this entire miserable fleet to the bottom in a matter of minutes.

The long catapult arms hit the blocking bars, and the first stone projectiles flew into the air—aimed, as during the first assault, at targets set long before. The harbor neck being too narrow for them to come about, the enemy vessels had clustered together willy-nilly, providing a most convenient bull's-eye.

Yet that first volley went for naught. The stones threw up great pillars of water, splintered oars, scraped along sides, but none hit square. Hagen glowered at his catapult captain, who only threw up his hands, nonplussed.

The second volley likewise only churned the water, sending the master sergeant to the catapult platforms at a run.

"Miss no more marks," the thane called after him. He, too, did not understand—Otrag was without peer in the mechanical arts; his machines always shot splendidly and their accuracy was enviable. If he missed, it could hardly be pure chance.

Even so, he waited for the third volley to fall short before taking action of his own. It cost him no particular trouble to uncover the strange system of Protective Spells that safeguarded the enemy fleet. A gray net was deflecting projectiles impeccably aimed, which then fell uselessly away into the water.

Hagen was faced here by one strong in wizardry—or one who would cede nothing to Makran and Esteri, at least, since they had never conceived so simple an expedient when sending their warriors to storm the island. Or maybe they had simply lacked the strength to carry it through.

Then who can it be? The thane was adrift in conjecture. He believed he could read off all the enchanters of mortalkind in Eastern Hjorvard whose strength was even remotely comparable to this. Were the guests, then, from more distant parts? But to what purpose? And how could they have mustered a force and crossed the sea so fast? No, they must be from hereabouts...mayhap Vidrir and his priests? Yet surely, they would never set sail in such sorry tubs.

With a few quick passes, Hagen felt out the strength of his enemy's wizardly defense, finding it to be oddly woven, in violation of all the canons. It was not strengthened by the turning of the world about the spellcaster, and was bereft of all the classical reinforcements, seeming to derive its strength from all that surrounded it, even from the falling stones it was crafted to repulse. The like of this he had never encountered.

But if his catapults and ballistas continued littering the harbor floor with their missiles, there would be fighting at close quarters soon enough. Time to be rid of them, he told himself; and before the thought of what he must do next could form distinctly in his mind, he invested all his strength in a Firecharm.

The Firecharm was faithful as death, and had at no time and in no place betrayed him. It had rescued him in the Niflhel cavern, had brought him victory over the priests in the Temple of Iamerth, had even triumphed over the powerful magic directed against him.

This time it failed, and failed miserably.

For a moment, the bright flame illuminated the gloomy sea-cliffs and was reflected in the black water, bringing the attacking fleet into clear view and showing them to be already upon the underwater chain that blocked the harbor entrance. Hagen's aim was true; his strike fell precisely upon the huddle of enemy ships. The tongues of fire licked avidly at their sides, seized on the oar blades, sped upward along the low-hanging cables...

But before another moment passed, all was quenched, leaving feeble sparks to run along the planking, here, there...and vanish, swallowed up by the uncaring waves. Hagen's spell floated away like smoke.

Merlin? the thane thought, trembling despite himself. *Damnation, the Disc of Iamerth would serve me well now!*

The flagship was against the chain now, and the thick iron links, each as broad as a grown man's hand, held it back—but only for the briefest time.

Still viewing the world through the invisible eyeglasses of his magic, Hagen saw the gray-cloaked figure lean overboard, cup a hand against his mouth, and shout something at the water. A few seconds later, the lead ship was moving serenely forward, as if no obstacle had ever stood in her way.

Hagen was dumbfounded. He had never seen such a thing before.

"Bring the sorceress from the sanctum of spellcraft!" he barked at a messenger, who sprinted away to do as he was bid.

The catapults and ballistas were working still, but always with the same woeful result.

"Arbalesters, stand ready!" Hagen ordered. "Orc, bring up your goblins to the breach on the left, and prepare them for a flanking attack should any disembark. Knut, take five centuries of swordsmen and two of archers to the right-hand breach. I doubt they will try to scale the walls..."

Under the protection of their unseen shields, the absurd vessels were nearing the jetties, their motion so clumsy and so defiantly slow Hagen's warriors were left powerless to do aught but rage.

When the first arrows whistled from the shore, it transpired that the foe's magic was less potent against them than against the stones, in that one of every three or four hit its target. Perceiving this, the archers' and arbalesters' sharp-witted commanders, on their own account and waiting for no orders, brought flaming arrows into play. This seemed at first to bode success, and the flagship even began to smoke; but as with the Firecharm, the strangers' magickry did not permit the fire to take hold.

Meanwhile, Hagen's ironclads had come up to the jetties under cover of the piles of tumbled, part-melted stone.

The task in store for the thane was no simple one. Given that his whole army might yet be useless to him, he had to devise some counter to the enemy's magic. He should, for safety, have at least pulled his handpicked troops deep into the fortress, but the ships were already at the moorages. He was desperate now to know who his opponents were and what kind of magic was being used against him, and all the while he never forgot that Sigrlinn's demented apprentices could also not be far away.

When makeshift assault bridges began reaching from the ships to the moorage walls, he ordered his bowmen, arbalesters and slingers to fire. That was when he first caught sight of the enemy with his own eyes.

Until then, bemused by those ramshackle and unseaworthy craft, the thane could not have hazarded even a guess as to who these visitors were. But he saw what he had never seen, not even in the grip of nightmare, and the very rawest recruit in his ranks would have laughed his thane to scorn had Hagen told him how he had been dreading these perfectly ordinary farmhands of Eastern Hjorvard.

Nonetheless, that is who they were—short and stocky, wearing their great-grandfathers' ridiculous helmets and carelessly patched armor, which for the most part was nothing more than an ordinary leather jerkin with a few metal plates sewn to chest and belly. They carried, almost to a man, carpenter's axes, not battleworthy poleaxes; and the swords could be counted on the fingers of one hand. As for their pikes, they were the simple wooden pitchforks used to hunt bear or elk, which had never been made to pierce real armor, much less that forged by gnomes.

Hagen needed his magical sight, that faithful informant, no more, it being unhandy for use in swordplay. Now he waited for one thing and one thing only—the appearance of the commander of that motley band, he who alone had manned the wheel of the lead merchantman and against whom all the magical skill of the Thane of Hedinseigh had thus far been unavailing.

The wait was soon over. Hardly had the first of the invaders leapt onto the jetties when a figure bundled in a gray cloak appeared on the flagship's bow. The cloak was flung aside, a hand holding a heavy battleax clearly of gnomish manufacture was raised aloft; and over the still black water a low-pitched voice uttered a battle cry such as Hagen had never heard.

"Land and laity!"

At that, the attackers sent up a great roar and, howling fiercely to hearten themselves, began leaping from the vessels to the moorages. There was no thought of loosing a covering barrage of arrows or of erecting a wall of shields, No, the first on shore did not even wait for the rest but rushed disorderly forward, directly toward Hagen's ironclad pikemen, who stood awaiting them.

Their commander, whoe'er he be, should be hung by the heels, Hagen thought. For his part, he need issue no new commands, for his centurions knew their business. The attackers were met by a dense downpour of arrows and bolts.

Whistling death must in a matter of moments have carried off all who had resolved to part so foolishly with their lives, since the men jumping from the ships were in plain view of the bowmen stationed high above them. Their worthless armor would be vulnerable even to a northern savage's short, bone-tipped barb, and far more to the arrows of Hagen's archers, which were weighty, and long as the arm of a full-grown man.

But what came next was strange, indeed. While bowstrings still thrummed against the leather gloves that protected the bowmen's wrists, they peered avidly into the darkness, trying to see in the scant moonlight how well they had made their mark—and saw not one man fallen on the jetties of Hedinseigh.

When Hagen heard the whistle of arrows flying from his bastions, he hastened to aid his bowmen with a Charm of Lesser Light. A small fiery sphere appeared in the sky and hung motionless above the bastion line, shining in the invaders' eyes. The harbor, jetties, ships and fortifications were illuminated by a faint, pale glow, very like moonlight but brighter by far. A chorus of mirth rose from the Hedinseigh battlements as slingers and swordsmen, pikemen and archers burst into helpless laughter at the sight of the preposterous, ludicrous, pitiable gallants who had dared attack the world's best fortress, which had yielded neither to immortal wizards nor to the First-Begotten.

But can all the arrows have possibly missed? The thought was swift but alarming, for not one of the disembarking force had yet died under the shafts that flew unrelentingly from the bastions. The mystery of the commander's person was troubling, too. All Hagen knew was that the unnamed man stood now on a pile of stone that rimmed the moorage, brandishing his ax and ringingly hurrying his men onto solid ground.

But Hagen would not have been who he was—a thane ever successful in the field—had he let slip so splendid an opportunity to resolve this matter with a single shot.

"An arbalest!" was all he said, and he was immediately handed a good strong one, along with a quiverful of short, thick bolts. With all deliberate speed, he drew back the lever to span the bow, aimed, held his breath, pressed the trigger…and in pure astonishment watched the bolt glide over the commander's shoulder.

He could not give way to consternation, though, for below him his ironclads, fully obedient to their orders, were striking hard at the still-disembarking troops. How could erstwhile ploughmen, clutching the first thing that passed for a weapon, contend against an army tempered in numerous campaigns and battles and able to hold its formation, whatever befell, behind an impervious wall of shields? How could those wretched axes endure against long pikes and swords? How could that comical armor protect against death-dealing weaponry that had oft struck through hauberks made by best craftsmen to walk the Earth?

Hagen ordered his bowmen to fire forward at those coming off the ships, to avoid injuring their own. He watched his ironclads close ranks and advance, their pikes at the ready yet retracted a little in anticipation of the first contact.

But then, instead of falling at the feet of Hagen's warriors like mown hay, the impromptu peasant force charged as one at the island's defenders. Though the pikes struck them in chest and belly, the fearsome tips only slid along their strange armor, and the Hjorvard rustics' shabby axes split the pikeshafts of Hagen's ironclads with uncommon ease. In two moments more, the orderly battle had given way to a bloody melee as, instead of pushing those brazenfaces into the sea with one mighty heave, Hagen's men were drawn into the mad carnage of close combat. The jetties were a solid knot of fighting men.

"Give Orc and Knut the order to attack!" Hagen's voice was hollow, as it always was when his battle plans began to miscarry. Yet he still commanded numbers double those of the enemy, and had, he fancied, the means to contest magic-making he had yet to unriddle.

The hail of arrows from the walls thickened, and either the defensive charm—if such a charm there had been—was weakening or the unknown wizard was less successful in parrying them, for they began to make inroads. Hagen's bowmen took first blood on the ships as men fell there, riddled with shafts. Flaming arrows again filled the air, but the ragtag army, now landed on the Hedinseigh moorages, were beating their heavily armed opponents back, step by step.

It seemed impossible, but it was so. The best of Hagen's foot soldiers, who had been trained to advance in tight formations or alone, were in retreat, slapping feebly at the advancing enemy as they went, while the rallying cry "Land and laity!" again shook the bastion walls.

"Gerder, what can this mean?" he asked the chiliarch, an ominous chill in his voice. "Why are they falling back before those bumpkins?"

Though Hagen's tone boded nothing good, Gerder answered stoutly, "There's wizardry being made, my thane. Swords can do naught here. Some charm is entangling our men and helping the seafarers. Freed of that enchantment, we would grind them into dust."

"I sense no wizardry," Hagen said curtly.

"It is hidden, but it is there. Even I feel it, as a ton weight on my back," Gerder replied.

Hagen exploded. "Impossible!" he cried. "What wizardry can there be that acts on all but me?"

"There's no surprise here." Sigrlinn was behind him, her voice cold. "For it is woven so you will notice nothing. It is the magic of those who live in the World of Mimir's Wellspring. I recognize the weft of that charm."

"Can you lift it from my men?" the thane shouted. "Ere long those fine fellows will be throwing us out on our ear."

"Don't shout," the sorceress said, coldly still. "It is not for you to raise your voice to me, mortal. I shall do what I can."

"Then hurry." He gave a twisted smile, glancing down again to where his ironclads had retreated almost to the breaches in the walls. Orc's goblins had at first had some success, but their attack had at length drowned in blood as they lost five for every foe who fell. Unable to hold their position, they, too, had been pushed back to the very bastions. Knut was faring no better.

Although the enemy's losses had been great, they pressed on. Now they crowded into the breaches…now they had broken into the fortress…and still Sigrlinn's hands moved slowly, slowly…

Seeing that sorcery was availing but little, Hagen once again tried to turn the battle with ordinary swords. He hurriedly moved his few fresh centuries up to the breaches, where Knut and Orc continued to retreat, ceding priceless yards of bailey ground. The corpses of Hagen's men, Orc's goblins and the unknown assailants mingled; equal now in death, they lay peacefully side by side, with no further cause for enmity.

More and more of Hagen's warriors joined the fray, all having long forgotten the proper order of battle; and their every wonted strike at the enemy, with only pike-tips protruding from behind an unbroken wall of shields in the style of the mountain gnomes' fearsome *hird*, failed. The adversary had, with unfathomable adroitness, turned the battle into a free-for-all.

The thane's forehead was beaded with large drops of sweat. The instincts of an experienced general were telling him the battle was lost—he could sacrifice all his army, and even so the enemy would prevail. The muscles along his jawline were working, hard as rock. Behind him were Ilving, his son and his Teacher's Talisman. *If I lay down my life now who in this world will come to their aid?*

"Naught comes of this." Sigrlinn's whisper was almost inaudible. "My present strengths will not suffice. A real Mage is needed, and I cannot even appeal to any of our Generation."

"Then I shall go," Hagen said calmly, lowering his visor and signaling his few remaining retainers to follow. "Frodi! Lead out the reserves. We need hold them back no longer."

A short time later, he stood at the head of warriors in close array—his truest and most time-tested, more than ten centuries of hardened veterans and wonder-workers in combat. For many a year they had marched with him from victory to victory, had stormed cities in Eastern, Western and Southern Hjorvard; and they were ever calm and firm in their belief in their thane.

"Onward!" He raised his Blue Sword. Two thousand riveted boots tramped across the bailey stones. A thousand hands rested on sword hilts, grasped pikes, raised strong shields. A thousand bodies clad to the teeth in steel lurched forward, and the formation flowed across the gray expanse toward that seething confusion with Hagen in the van, Frodi to his right and Gudmund to his left.

Hagen's war horns sounded the attack, the familiar sound rousing the warriors of Hedinseigh to wrest themselves from the hopeless, chaotic slaughter and clear the way for their comrades. Judging their movement to signal panic, to foretoken flight, the attackers thronged forward with a wild halloo, and for an instant, Hagen saw their commander.

Through his visor's narrow slit, he stared at the squat figure in uncomely gray armor, at the face half-covered with a forged helm from which only the beard protruded. There seemed to him something strangely familiar in that face, little of it as the steel helmet revealed. Sigrlinn had spoken of magic from the World of the Wellspring. Was there to be another encounter here with his companion on that journey to the fields of Gnipahellir?

By considerable effort, Hagen's men made a place for their commander, and he felt the return of the unshakable serenity that had so often been his salvation in years past. The sensation of the Blue Sword's rough hilt gripped tightly in his hand assured him he would be able to set all to rights.

Ten paces. Nine. Eight. Seven. Hagen saw the surprise on the faces of the enemy. At close quarters they still looked like naught other than simple Hjorvard peasants who had hurriedly taken up arms and determined that merely possessing a piteous facsimile of a pike made them warriors—though to that moment they had, in truth, been routing the excellently drilled fighting force of Hedinseigh. *But no matter—that will change soon enough!*

Hagen felt his cold calm becoming new strength; for all his effort, he still could sense no opposing magic. Never had he been so sure of himself and his handpicked ten centuries. Nor did Frodi or Gudmund betray any weakness or discomfiture.

Six paces. Five. Four. He settled the Blue Sword more comfortably in his grip, preparing a two-handed strike. He had dependable men covering either flank, and had already marked out his first adversary, a hearty, red-headed fellow who had just been so incomprehensibly fortunate as to cut down one of Orc's goblins—well-armored and brandishing a long ataghan—with his short, dented ax.

Three paces. Two. One. The slim blue blade whistled through the air, detecting no resistance as it split the clumsily wielded ax handle, completed a half-circle and clove the body of the misfortunate redhead from shoulder to waist.

First, thought the thane. His hands then dealt the next blow, and the count had risen before the word could even fade from his mind.

For some minutes, he fought on oblivious, surrendering to the bloody eddies of battle and giving vent to a fury that had long been building inside him. His sword met no obstacles, his opponents' absurd armaments proving on closer inspection to be naught more than kitchenware adapted hastily for war. Why, then, had his warriors fallen back, although each of them was capable of exterminating a hundred adversaries such as these?

He found no answer. But the broad breach in the fortress wall was no nearer than it had been, and they were at last pressing the enemy back. *Anon, a little farther now, and they will not hold, will falter, will show their heels. One last effort…*

"Turn, my thane!" Gudmund's furious yell drew Hagen's attention. Not halting for an instant the death-dealing whirl of his sword, he glanced around.

He, Frodi and Gudmund were fighting alone, the rest of his hand-picked chiliarchy having been forced away from them. He saw his warriors fighting like the greatest of maladroits, flailing their weapons as if they had never taken such a thing in hand before. Their blows were slow, their defense weak and easily broken, and they were relying upon feints too simple and artless to trick a child. And they were dying, dying, dying...

Only Frodi and Gudmund, at his side, were fighting as they ever had, each of them leaving a clear-cut path behind them with enemy bodies playing the part of the felled trees. *If there is, indeed, magic being made here, it acts neither on me nor on those close to me*, Hagen thought fleetingly.

"Close ranks with them!" he commanded his two companions.

They pulled back, merging into the main fighting force, which promptly took heart. A center of resistance formed around Hagen; he stood like a rock in the surf, and all attempts to budge him ended as one, with new bodies heaped upon the pile of the dead while not one who stood near him was even wounded.

But he could not replace a whole army. His warriors were still giving ground to right and left, losing two to every one the enemy lost.

Hagen's one last chance to turn the battle was to engage the nameless commander of this unexpectedly formidable force and put an end to him. He was almost certain this death would also end the spell that shrouded his warriors, the secret of which even Sigrlinn had been unable to unlock.

So he began his search. Along with Frodi and Gudmund, he again laid about him, hacking down all to right and left; but oddly, fresh opponents were immediately before him, seeming in no way distressed by the speedy death of their predecessors. None fled from the deadly Blue Sword. Rather, the complement of those wishing to test its keenness for themselves only grew.

The battle was a fracas now. The defenders of Hedinseigh perished one by one, the assailants' numbers dwindled, but still Hagen could find no way through to the mysterious commander. His select chiliarchy of veterans, having suffered grievous losses but still maintaining some semblance of order, was slowly falling back to the entrance to the keep.

Wolflike, Hagen ranged around and around the field of death, which was drenched in human and goblin blood. His sword knew no rest, and he had begun to wonder in all seriousness if the three of them—he, Frodi and Gudmund—could even the odds, since they were proof against the uncharted gramarye, and every cudgel blow dealt by the strapping Frodi, every one of Gudmund's sword thrusts cut short another life. But the commander had vanished into thin air, and Hagen bobbed his head from side to side in vain, placing himself at risk of being struck.

Luck at last smiled not on him but on the sharp-eyed Gudmund, who noticed a flicker of gray armor by the keep that held the Teacher's sanctum of spellcraft and his Talisman.

"Follow me!" the thane ordered his companions brusquely, and they forced their way to the keep.

On the bloodied steps lay six of Hagen's troops and three attackers, all dead. The gray-armored commander had taken up a position on empty ground a few dozen paces distant with a tight handful of his men, and was ready to attack again. Aside from Hagen and his two companions, there was no one to stop him.

Only now that he was removed from the battle for an instant did Hagen realize it was abating, there being so many fewer on both sides to keep up the fight. It had come down to the two or three centuries that remained of the handpicked chiliarchy battling with seven or eight dozen assailants, and victory was going to neither side. The thane gritted his teeth—were it not for his Teacher's Talisman, he would never have left the field.

He did not, though, have long to regret his decision to defend the entrance to the keep, for the gray-clad commander was leading some forty men directly toward the low entrance where Hagen, Frodi and Gudmund stood abreast. One of the attackers loosed an arrow that broke against Hagen's shoulder cop. The next had more success—it pierced Frodi's chain mail and scored his shoulder, but the injury was, fortunately, neither deep nor grave and left the giant with full use of both arms.

When the invaders were some ten paces distant, Gudmund flung his hooked knife at them then tore it from the fallen body with a deft tug on the length of chain.

"Who are you, and what is it you want?" Hagen barked at the commander of the forty. The question's purpose was not to elicit an answer but to show the foe that, despite all, the defenders, even these last few, were no way disheartened.

But the commander kept his silence, a third arrow glanced off Gudmund's helmet, and the thane was at last able to cross swords with him who had acquitted himself so well against an army that had defied the might of Archmage Merlin.

The first clash of those artfully forged blades told Hagen he had joined with an opponent who yielded nothing in strength to a Winged Giant—the Thane of Hedinseigh was hard put to keep a grip on his sword. Meanwhile, on his right and left, Frodi and Gudmund struggled to fend off the blows that rained down on them from all sides

The enemy had stripped some real pikes from Hagen's dead and handled them right ably, outweighing the advantage of height Hagen and his comrades had gained in taking up position on the steps. As the minutes passed, the thane could only impotently curse Rakoth, who had been too pressed to convey to him the Enjoining Charm that would have brought under his command all the might of the Black Brigades that tarried yet on the island and in its coastal waters.

Frodi and Gudmund had moved backward onto the highest step, drawing with them an unwilling Hagen, who continued trading blows with the leader but was still unable to discover the slightest opening for attack. For the first time in many a long year, he had found his match in another human—or at least in one who must deem himself human.

He relinquished yet another step, the next to last, and still he felt in his foe no magic. Yet, when he assayed some magic-making of his own, he found, to his utter astonishment, that his familiar source of magical power was gone. No sorcery was being worked anywhere in Hjorvard! It was as if all the wizards had resigned their business together.

Frodi and Gudmund were backed against the keep door now. It could never be said they were shredding the air with their weapons to no purpose; but the enemy losses numbered only five, and the archer, having found his mark, had contrived to wound both of Hagen's comrades—neither mortally nor even severely, yet under their hauberks the blood flowed, slow but sure.

Hagen defended himself with desperate courage. He began to tire and was calling on all his skill to fend off blows that would be deadly for any less expert swordsman. Again he sought to gain but a little time with words.

"Know you, sirrah, that the Unnamable is devouring our world? Know you that if you kill me, in a few days you, too, will go to wrack, along with all of Hjorvard?"

Silence. The thane had done no more than give of his own strength and spend breath that had better use elsewhere when he shouted those words in his enemy's face.

Behind his back, Frodi gave a stifled cry. A pike had stabbed him below the knee, at the very edge of his chausse.

We cannot hold this position. The thought flickered through Hagen's mind. *We must open the door and retreat farther.*

The door was opened, and evading those hostile swords and pikes with difficulty, the island's last three defenders pulled back into the keep. In all the huge bailey, only they and a few more than three dozen of their enemies fought on, since all the remaining warriors on both sides were already sleeping the eternal sleep.

And so it continued. The invaders hampered each other in the narrow corridor, making the fight easier for Frodi and Gudmund, who brought down five, one after another. Only some thirty were left.

The corridor led into a spacious hall from which a broad stairway spiraled to the upper apartments. Here, though, they did not take a stand, but immediately found themselves in the beginnings of an encirclement that caused them to retire hastily to the stairs.

They faced now eighteen foes.

Hagen and his opponent, who had still uttered not a word no matter what was said to him, kept up their contest of strength that tested both metal and flesh. Neither was prepared to yield, and Hagen was filled with malicious joy to note the enemy commander, too, was showing signs of weariness. Now the thane could carve out a few seconds to help the exhausted Frodi and Gudmund. Ever and again, bodies run through by the Blue Sword rolled down the stairs, their arms flapping clumsily against the stone treads as they fell.

At the head of the stairs, the enemy was down to ten. Only a short corridor stood between them and the Teacher's sanctum of spellcraft now, and there Hagen stood fast. The biting sweat ran into his eyes, the air hissed through his set teeth, his arms seemed vessels for molten lead, but still he fought on. And although his prime adversary was weary, too, all efforts to launch a counterattack still came to naught and his blows were easily warded off.

Leaving the commander alone, then, and only parrying his lunges, Hagen turned on the others. A few minutes later, there were but five.

In the thane's heart was reborn the hope they would yet be able to save his Teacher's Talisman. Although Frodi and Gudmund—both spent, bearing several wounds, their armor bloodsoaked—were scarcely able to ward off their attackers, still he hoped. He cut down another of the enemy cohort—and then a survivor's sword slipped through Gudmund's defense, coming down hard upon his helmet, which was already sorely notched. One of Hagen's best, without even a groan, toppled to the floor.

With a frenzied cry, Frodi flung up his cudgel and with one blow smashed the head of him who had slain his friend; the helmet offered no protection and the skull split like a musty melon. But the wrathful giant had laid himself open, and in that instant a sword wielded by another of the surviving assailants pierced through the stout gnomish hauberk and plunged into his side. Frodi swayed, trying with his left hand to close the wound while the enemy strode forward to deal the deathblow—and met instead the Blue Sword. The head, in its ridiculous helmet, flew aside, and the body crumpled at its commander's feet.

Hagen was alone now, one against three. *Bear up now, Mage's apprentice! This is, belike, your last battle. And Ilving! What will become of you?*

Then Frodi, who had been sitting against the wall holding his spitted side, suddenly rose with a groan. The giant again clasped his cudgel with both hands and, before he could be struck in the chest by two swords at once, crushed both his enemies' heads. The three bodies collapsed upon each other.

And then the commander slowly doffed his helm.

"Brann!" Hagen exclaimed. "Brann Shrunkenhand!"

"Remarked you not that your foe was fighting with right hand only?" was the reply.

They stood facing each other, their feet unsteady on stones damp with blood, their swords bared. Brann's blade dangled from a loop around his wrist, and in his hand he held his helmet.

"Lay on, then," he said calmly. He raised his helmet to put it on again, and in that instant Hagen attacked. A dishonorable attack it was, and he knew full well he would ever after be spurned by the jarls and by his fellow thanes, who prided themselves exceedingly on their observation of all the innumerable rules of single combat between men of…honor. But Hedin's apprentice was now thinking only of saving the island whose fate had been left wholly in his hands.

His blow was beaten off.

"I warned you," Brann said, his voice tranquil. "'Until human villages are set afire, I am no enemy to you.' And set afire they were. Are you ready for death?"

Hagen saw no sense in trying to make all clear to the man who stood before him—if man he was, for one who came from the World of the Wellspring could be anything whatsoever. He had determined to make an end to Hagen and had almost succeeded. Worse, the army of Hedinseigh was no more, and Brann was but a step away from Hedin's Talisman.

But first he had to contend with Hagen.

Hasty steps were heard behind Brann's back—someone was speeding up the spiral stairway. Both he and Hagen stood stock-still. Help was coming to one of them—but to which?

Brann was the first to cast that unwitting caution aside. Either he did not doubt his own men were at his back or he reckoned on making quickly away with Hagen now he was weakened by the lengthy battle. Brann's blade—a most ordinary weapon, with no particular refinement or ornamentation—crashed down slantwise, and the thane's sword came up barely in time to meet it.

As the footfalls drew rapidly closer, it became clear that more than one person was approaching. A few seconds passed, and Hagen caught sight of three figures at the end of the corridor. Short-statured they were and shapely, dark-garbed and with curved swords in their hands. The foremost among them held a simple cup-like chalice.

There could be no mistake. Sigrlinn's apprentices had at last found their way to the fortress that housed their preceptress, and a malicious volition had added something to their desire to free her. What it was Hagen could only guess, but it might well have been an edict to burn everything where it stood. That Fire-Bearing Chalice roused in him only the blackest of memories.

Brann Shrunkenhand showed no surprise at the sight of those unexpected guests. He only glanced at them then turned again to Hagen with a silent invitation to continue. Two of the Darkling Riders in turn paid him no heed but simply walked around him on either side as if he had been a column of stone and bore down on Hagen, raising their curved blades. The third wiccan—the one with the Fiery Chalice—hung back a little, but the thane was only too well aware what that ingenuous maneuver might mean. It was the same Chalice that had once been fragmented by a blow of his sword, but evidently enchantments had rectified the damage.

The miniature sun he had lit still illuminated the island, and by its rays, Hagen could read the look in the eyes of all three wiccans. His death was inscribed there.

Brann still did nothing in response to the appearance of the Darkling Riders. His modest sword atilt, there he stood, all unconcerned, and only grinned at the thane.

"Madwomen, hold!" Sigrlinn's frantic cry rang down the corridor. The sorceress came fleetfoot up the stairs and burst into the short passageway. "Hold! If you kill him and destroy the Talisman of Hedin, we shall perish every one, and swiftly."

But her still-weakened powers must have been no match for the spell that lay upon her apprentices, for the Darkling Riders responded not at all to her impassioned plea—they did not, in fact, even turn their heads. In their eyes, which held Hagen fast, madness glittered.

For an instant, Sigrlinn was motionless, as if listening. Hagen could guess she was seeking to puzzle out the enchantments that entangled her apprentices. Soon, she started back as if in fright, and an astonished, wrathful exclamation tore from her lips.

"Merlin!"

There was naught, then, to which the Archmage would not stoop.

Her cry drew a Darkling Rider's attention to her, and a curved blade soared aloft in readiness to strike. Hagen could give his unwilling confederate no aid, for Brann's sword hissed again through the air, and he had again to fend it off.

But Sigrlinn, with great composure, caught the flying blade between her palms, and a quick movement of her nimble body sent the presumptuous apprentice sprawling on the floor, disarmed.

Before Hagen, who was still holding Shrunkenhand at bay, could rejoice for her sake, the third wiccan—the one with the Fiery Chalice—joined the action. A stream of liquid fire washed over Sigrlinn from head to toe, her garments blazed. A living torch, with a wild cry more terrible than any Hagen had ever heard, thrashed this way and that, slamming into the stone walls, and came to rest at last by the stairway, a hunched, charred faggot with no discernible features.

The prostrate wiccan also showed no signs of life. Hagen, though, was strangely strengthened by the sorceress's dreadful end. He knocked Brann's blade aside, slid under it and found a wiccan throat with the tip of his Blue Sword. Blood spurted, the eyes with their vertical pupils turned glassy but never had time to close, and the thane found himself facing but two adversaries once more.

Brann's sword almost struck the weapon from Hagen's hands. For the first time, a flash of fury could be seen through Shrunkenhand's visor slit, but rage is a poor ally in close combat. Hagen again managed to dart beneath his opponent's blade and come up behind his back, driven to such a desperate shift because the wiccan with the Chalice had turned toward him, leaving him in no doubt as to her intent.

Despite the adroit maneuver, he was still quite soundly singed. Again, mere fractions of an inch had saved him. But when he next struck at the wiccan's head, he held back nothing.

Even her animal address and agility could not preserve the Darkling Rider this time—Hagen's sword cleft her to the chest. He plucked it out and spun around to Shrunkenhand...only to meet a blow he could not parry.

He was thrown back several paces, his hauberk and neckpiece split apart. Crimson sparks whirled in his eyes, but at first he felt no pain, just a great difficulty drawing breath as a sticky warmth flowed down his body.

Still he kept a grip on his sword. A cold voice spoke in clipped phrases for him alone: *You are wounded, and the wound is mortal. To defend yourself further would be senseless.* And he hearkened to that counsel.

Through a bloody mist, he saw only Brann and the unsolved riddles around him—who he was, whence he came, why he had stormed Hedinseigh, what was the secret of his astonishing skills in wizardry, and why Iargohor had no power over him. Then, before Brann could catch his breath after his great accomplishment, the thane sprang forward.

The foretaste of imminent death seemed to give him such strength as no man had ever had. He struck, breaking Brann's sword like a reed and then, with a fearsome charge, also split his enemy's armor. The Blue Sword plunged to the hilt into the broad breast of his erstwhile companion and guide, he who had saved him in the Niflhel cavern.

Brann gave a death-rattle. Blood bubbled from his mouth, and he bent in two, dropping his sword. Hagen, swaying, stood before him, and the certainty of this last victory drove from the mind of Hedin's apprentice even the horror of death. He feared nothing. Come what may, he had triumphed!

The pain announced itself then, and with it came a flare of searing joy. *If there is pain, then I still live! I can wrestle yet with the Reaper...see my Teacher's return...But first I must stem the bleeding...*

But as if hearing Hagen's jubilant thoughts, Brann straightened suddenly, and though his right hand dangled uselessly, in his left Hagen saw the glint of a knife. The shrunken hand sprang into motion, clumsily hurling the weapon as hard as ever it could.

The gift from Old Hropt that Hagen himself had presented to Brann plunged into the thane's unprotected throat. The two foes fell against each other.

When the sobbing Ilving reached them, they were both dead.

HEDIN

I T WAS MADNESS. WE SEEMED TO HAVE BEEN FIGHTING FOR AN ETERNITY, AMID BEAUTIES indescribable by the mortal tongue. Like mechanical manikins, we had repulsed attack after attack by our invulnerable foes. Iaeth's granite snakes were not submitting even to the Swords of the Gods, which threw them back but could do them no other harm.

At a point when we were being pressed most sorely, I failed to ward off a Soul-Banishing Staff that was jabbing toward me; and my body, whether I would or no, jerked aside, leaving the Winged Giant and Hropt face to face. Even the Father of Hosts could not prevent the attack; the greenish Staff hit him hard in the chest. I became as stone, forgetting even the set-to that boiled all around me in expectation of the Lord of Asgard's fearsome demise. But the Staff broke against that preposterous chestplate of ice-snake skin that had given me so much private amusement. The Winged Giant stood aghast, and Old Hropt seized the opportunity to run it through.

For all that, we were, for the nonce, prevailing, since the Young Gods had not been able to stop us; and step by step, we drew closer to the Well of Urd.

For a brief span, a corner of their magnificent palace had shielded us from the Masters of the Hallowed Land, but the pursuit continued. I must own, in all honesty, that I still could not understand them. If they had resolved to flee, as Rakoth assumed, then why that grand performance anent our sentence and so forth? Maybe we had had the foul luck to present ourselves oversoon. A few minutes later, we would perhaps have found the Hallowed Land empty, and would have been able to fulfill our grand scheme unhindered. Or...

Suddenly, my mind cleared. *What if the gods can make their exodus only by way of the Well, and what if, as they left, they were to slam the door behind them—were, in other words, to destroy Urd itself?*

My questions remained without answer, but I did know it was too great a risk for us to run. I could not even imagine the consequences had we broken into a deserted Hallowed Land and found there the Well choked with stones.

While one portion of my mind ruminated in this wise, another was reckoning up the blows and counter-blows of the continuing swordplay.

"Hedin, what are we to do at the Well?" Old Hropt yelled, a little winded.

"I'll know when we are there!" I yelled back, realizing that as answers go that one was not, to word it mildly, worth much. But what was to be done I really did not know, any more than I knew where that all-accursed Well was to be found. Yet I forged on unreflecting, remaining all the while utterly and adamantly certain our course was true. Another's will led us on, or maybe it was only my own sharpened senses.

The Winged Giants and Iaeth's snakes flittered hither and thither. Not one of them did we truly cut down, for, even when stuck through, the Sentinels of the Hallowed Land rested only a minute or two then returned to the fight.

The Well of Urd came to our notice most unexpectedly when Rakoth stumbled against its low stone rim.

"Look you, now—'tis the very spit of Mimir's Wellspring," Hropt said in surprise, driving back a remarkably persistent snake.

All at once it was over. The brutes took themselves off, the Sentinels sweeping aloft and the snakes slithering away. Toward us came the seven gods—or, rather, six of them, for Ialini trailed behind, and seemed to be making no effort to stay in step with her menacing kin.

"Why do you delay?" Rakoth hissed at me. "Here it is. Here's your Well!"

"So, you have recouped your strength, brazen Mage." It was the voice of Iambren, and it set all around atremble. "You have proven too much for our servants, and thus their masters must take up the task."

"Lord Iamerth," I replied, trying hard not to tremble. "Every instant, the Unnamable devours ever more of your subjects' lives. Yet you do not stop It. Why?"

By way of reply, the Master of the Sun's Light reached out his right hand, and, just as granite snakes had appeared from the hand of Iaeth, a short, gleaming, handleless blade woven of sunrays came into being and hung before the outstretched fingers.

The air around us blazed, a fearsome heat enveloped me, and my eyes were filled with a fierce glow. I felt my whole self begin to fall apart as the links between the human and the wizard in it—links that had so long seemed adamantine—snapped. It may well be that I cried out with the pain, but it only grew stronger. I saw and knew nothing.

That would likely have been the end of our war with the gods had not some power urged me forward. It was as though a voice whispered in my ear words I could not decipher. Holding before me the Sword of the Gods, so hard-won by my apprentice in the World of the Wellspring, I blindly ran at Iamerth. I smelled burning, realized it was my own skin starting to char and only by dint of great effort compelled the other part of my mind, the magical part, to assume control of my failing human body. When mere seconds remained to me, I sensed Rakoth sprinting forward to the right of me, and the Father of Hosts to the left.

Insensible of the torrents of fire streaming toward us, we struck as one.

To our utter surprise, Iamerth made not the slightest attempt to defend himself against my blade or Hropt's. The god's mighty hand knocked Rakoth's Black Sword aside, even as our swords—the Swords of the Gods, and the sum of our hopes—plunged unhindered into the body of the Lord of the Sun's Light.

And he laughed, right heartily, as if we had at last done something he had long wished us to do.

There flared then in my mind the doubts and hesitations that had assailed Hropt on the Swordmount, Hagen's persistent feeling that he and the Father of Hosts should not do what they were about to do. Their premonitions, their suspicions had told them something was amiss.

The Swords of the Young Gods could not harm their creators. Worse, the powers that protected those weapons had been revived. I could only surmise that the blades now in Iamerth's breast had flooded him with new strength, though I knew not from whence that strength came or why he could not have availed himself of it sooner. Yet all of my magical being was aware of the deluge, the cataract of wizardly energies that were presently investing the Master of the Hallowed Land with their might.

"And now you shall be ash!"

So thunderous was that voice I even relinquished my hold on the hilt of the Sword that still protruded from the Young God's broad, sun-bronzed chest. But I could thank the blow for this—that Iamerth, occupied in absorbing his new strength, was no longer directing that ravaging torrent of flame toward us.

Hearing then a sharp, mercilessly ear-piercing whistle above us, I raised my eyes—and started back. A blindingly white arrow—twin to the one that had crowned the summit of the Swordmount—had slammed into the greensward directly before me. A few finger-breadths closer and...I could sense the evil magickry that imbued this apparently plain shard of ice.

Like the Disc of Iamerth, the fearsome missile then dragged itself up out of the ground and aimed its tip toward us, leaving no uncertainty as to what would happen next.

With the courage of the desperate, Rakoth slashed at it with his Black Sword, the blade clanging furiously; but the Lord of the Sun's Light bent his will and easily deflected the mighty weapon of Darkness. And it was our doing that he had such strength! 'Twas enough to bring anyone to despair.

That icy needle was the implement of our undoing; we could not stand against it. I began to picture every particular—the giant tip piercing my chest, destroying all the human and magical life principles in me, my naked soul consigned to grisly torments; and also what lay in store for my apprentice, he who had foreseen this danger and had never wanted to take those accursed Swords.

One last possibility there was. Its toll could be the life and death of us all, and with it we might hasten the ruin of all the Well-Ordered, whose other haunch was even then being gnawed away by the Unnamable. But naught else remained.

I was thinking of the Dragons of Time.

While the long, long moments ticked by, I closed off my mind with a shield I had spied human wizards using, and created the most powerful charm of my life. Much was interlaced in it; it gave the denizens of the Great River their freedom and showed them the way, and also the goal to which they should apply strengths that had lain so long in idleness. As in a waking dream, I saw the vast spectral River whose waters bear and lave All That Is, saw its giant yet indescribably lissome denizens. This time, there was no one to restrain their fearful fangs and talons, as there had been on that memorable day many years before, the day of my apprentice's birth.

By the looks of it, I had contrived to surprise even Iamerth himself. The Master of the Sun's Light even stilled the hand that was extracting a Sword from his chest and glanced upward.

It was, to be sure, a sight worth seeing. The blue serenity of the skies over the Hallowed Land had disappeared, as if gusted away by a driving wind. A dark-gray abyss had opened, and against it floated the gentle coils of hundreds upon hundreds of Dragons of Time. Their maws were open, and along talons that hungered for prey ran scarlet glimmers. They hurtled through the magical barriers around the Citadel of the Gods, and there joined battle with Winged Giants sent to the slaughter by the Young Gods in a blighted attack against an enemy whose might exceeded even that of the dark assemblies of the Rebellious Mage at the height of his powers.

Iamerth, Iaeth, Iambren and the rest seemed to have completely forgotten about us. The White Needle slowed to a halt alongside Rakoth; and the Fallen Mage, recovering from his shock, again raised his Black Sword, with the clear intention of stealing up on the God of the Sun's Light. Iaeth was meanwhile trying to bring an end to this protracted tale, but the charm he dispatched fell easy prey to one of the Dragons.

The waters of the River of Time ran even faster now; and the most esoteric charms, compiled in anticipation of their flowing in different courses, lost their meaning. The only charm that might still have effect was the one I would cast next, to halt the incursion of the offspring of Almighty Time, and it had never yet been tested.

The Young Gods, it is true, were working to the same end. Credit must go where it is due—they had very quickly come to an understanding of the circumstances. The sky filled with a glittering of fiery rainbows. The silent Iaeth stood, his arm extended toward the zenith, and the Dragons of Time recoiled in confusion from the iridescence he had willed into being, which was to me a mystery. Rakoth threw himself forward, the Black Sword raised, Hropt and I picked up the White Needle, and we ran, all three, at the tight cluster of Young Gods.

We flung ourselves on Iamerth in unison whilst he was distracted by the affray in the skies. I had done what I could to supplement the magic of the white needle with something from my old reserves, but with no certainty that my erstwhile sorcery would serve me in this place where Time ran mad.

Iathana cried out a warning to the God of Sunshine, but he was, in any event, too quick for us. Rakoth's blade only slightly grazed the shining skin of his left forearm, and although our Needle hit him in the chest and knocked him backward, our future prospects would likely have been dim had it not been for the Dragons of Time. Seeming to sense whose allies they should be on this field, they launched a concerted attack on all the Young Gods but sweet Ialini, who had still taken no part in aught that transpired here.

The sacred Well was witness then to a great rumpus. Rakoth had raised his sword over the prostrate Iamerth when he was himself toppled over backward, one of Iaeth's granite snakes wrapped about his torso; and Hropt and I had no other way to rescue the Rebel but by flinging our wonderful battering ram at its head. Strange to say, that did the job, and Rakoth was able to rise. Only he was still armed with a sword, Hropt and I having lost ours to Iamerth, although he had not yet begun to employ them himself. The other gods were occupied by the battle against the Dragons.

Yet the ascendancy was going to those who had so long reigned over the Hallowed Land. Iamerth rose, and from his hand spurted a freshet of scorching flame. But before those tongues of fire could lash us well, everything disappeared, and I heard a cold, alien voice say leisurely, "Meddle not with them as they fulfill their duty, Iamerth."

I struggled to open my singed lids and saw, standing by me, a man in a dark-green cloak, placid and unarmed. Imperturbably, he folded his arms across his chest, and the Young Gods started back, as if the Unnamable had presented Itself to their view. Even the indomitable Dragons of Time went stock-still.

"Orlangur…" Iamerth breathed in astonishment.

"The same," was the cold reply. "You yourselves entitled me to appear here when you resolved to flee, relinquishing the Hallowed Land as fodder to a monster from other spheres of Creation. I have read your thoughts. Your enchantments are no secret to me. And I know you were prepared to let all the Well-Ordered perish rather than admit defeat. But if a Mage should succeed? So, meddle not with them, Iamerth."

"Best meddle not yourself," hissed the Lord of the Sun's Light. "Can these nonentities of wizards possess such great knowledge, which is hidden even from us? You it was who led them here. Sure, none but you and that brother o' yours knew where Urd is to be found within the bourns of the Hallowed Land."

"Maybe so," Orlangur replied, still calm. "But are we to continue with this aimless conversation or will you take yourself away and let us halt the Unnamable?"

"Brother!" It was Ialini, her voice resonant with unshed tears. "I beg you! I beseech you!"

"Silence!" Iaeth barked at his sister. "Proceed. We shall show them we are still a force to be reckoned with, and that our sentences are carried out, come what may."

"You will, of course, cease to be gods if you fetch up against an unachievable task, if a sentence you have imposed is not executed," said the Spirit of Knowing with a chill smile.

He could enlarge no further on that subject, for Iambren retrieved his sword from Iamerth and six of the Young Gods cast hesitation aside and hurled themselves forward, ready to decide the last dispute between Powers in the history of the Well-Ordered.

Orlangur moved not at all, but only cast upon us a glance brief and penetrating as lightning. I understood then—the Spirit was endowed with knowledge, could aid with his counsel, and would sometimes bestow strength in the heat of battle. Here, we would have to shift for ourselves, for such were the strange and inscrutable limitations laid by unknown hands upon the otherwise boundless might of the Golden Dragon of Knowing.

Exchanging never a word, Hropt and I strode forward, I holding the Disc of Iamerth and the Father of Hosts grasping the Soul-Banishing Staff. Already, Iamerth's gait was less majestic than it had been at the beginning of our contest. We had roundly harassed him, and the other gods had taken a good drubbing from the Dragons of Time. A wave of incinerating fire surged toward us, but we contrived to bear both the pain and the terrible rift it caused between the human and the wizardly within us. There was time enough for me to dispatch the Disc at almost point blank range and for Hropt to run the Staff into Iamerth's outstretched, fire-disgoring hand.

There came a howl so fearsome it fractured the ground beneath our feet, but the shriveling flood ran dry. We sprang backward. The Disc and the Staff had vanished from our hands, but the gods, too, had disappeared, nor did I see, in the level clearing before the Well, Iamerth prostrate, as we would have wished him to be.

Orlangur swung to face us.

"Make haste, Mage Hedin." Never before had I heard alarm in his voice. "A while longer, and we shall lose all. The forces of the Unnamable will have grown so much that nothing will stop It. You have the emblem of the god—use it, Mage Hedin. Or I should say God Hedin, for you and Rakoth and Hropt are now in command of the Well-Ordered!"

At that moment, nothing could have surprised me. I slowly drew from inside my shirt the crystalline sphere of the true emblem, and once again the abysses of space and time were thrown open before me. I saw the stately streams of soulless magical forces that gave life to stars and worlds and made the hearts of myriads of creatures, reasoning and unreasoning, beat. I also beheld the huge black chasm in Nothingness where the Unnamable's great, featureless bulk tossed restlessly, exuding such might I started back despite myself, and very nearly lost my hold on the wizardly energies I was holding on tight rein.

I saw the Distant and the Ancient Ones, I saw the Old Gods, who had been expelled by the Young, saw Merlin and my kinsfolk in the Generation, saw all—except Hedinseigh and the World of Mimir's Wellspring, which were strangely shrouded from me, to which fact at the time I ascribed no importance. Neither could I tell whither the Young Gods had gone.

We—Hropt and Rakoth and I—began to cast a Greatcharm that was Great in very truth, weaving together every power in All That Is, our purpose being to bring Something out of Nothingness.

The Well-Ordered below us was wreathed with smoke. Rivers burst their banks, mountains fell, seas dried up, and whole continents were engulfed. I watched the Pillar of the Titans sway and topple. Mimir had spoken sooth—he had, indeed, removed the Pillar's cornerstone from its foundations. I saw Garm the monstrous hound, awakened by all the tumult, straining to freedom.

But the darkness at the rim of the Unnamable's domains was changing, turning crimson—as if thousands upon thousands of gigantic bonfires had been lit beneath its dense pall. A belt of flame surrounded the Unnamable, and Its fearsome bulk shuddered several times. It shuddered—and stopped.

As the moments passed, we waited, not daring to breathe. Then, that first belt of fire was joined by another, with dozens more following. They merged into one, standing across the Unnamable's path into the heart of the Well-Ordered.

And with this change I felt myself changing, too, and fearsomely; and I knew it to be the precursor to pain such as I had never known.

Were they years or instants that passed before our sight was normal again? Close by seethed the Well of Urd, the loveliest that had ever been within the bourns of the Well-Ordered, a gift from the Creator Himself. Beyond that, words fail me in describing it. At our side was Orlangur, and the first thing I saw was that the alarm was gone from the Golden Dragon's strange, four-pupiled eyes.

"It is done," he said to us. "The Unnamable has been halted, for a time. Now enter your demesne, O New Gods."

"What is't you say?" I asked in a strangled voice.

"Why do you wonder?" was the reply. "The Young Gods are gone away into the world, and now you rule the Well-Ordered. And I feel that new powers shall soon be born in you both—in you, Hedin, and in you, Rakoth."

"Whilst I shall be myself again," the Father of Hosts said quietly, his shoulders squared now and his eyes shining with pride. "And can regain my true name."

The Spirit of Knowing raised his hand. "Very well, the time has come to take my leave. I cannot teach you what to do or how, for that you will know of yourselves. I will only answer the question you surely wish to ask: Why did I do all this?

"Hear you, then, that the Well-Ordered had no further need of such gods as the Young Gods were. My brother, Demogorgon, the Spirit of the Congregate Worldsoul, says thus: 'The mind of any that have trodden the grievous path of Earthly existence and have drunk deep of it becomes such as is capable of helping those that live. Not of holding sway over them but of helping them, calming calamitous passions, and chiefly the hunger for power.' The Well-Ordered needs New Gods, and it has chosen you—not I chose nor Demogorgon, but the Well-Ordered itself. I have been only its blind instrument. And now, farewell."

And he vanished, as if he had never been there at all, leaving us alone in the Hallowed Land with its throng of stone statues. I already knew they had been deprived of life by the Young Gods in their preparation for flight, for I had invoked a Charm of Knowing before I could think of it, and that charm was mightier than any I had ever made or even heard of, which was in itself good cause for surprise.

Hagen! What has happened to Hagen?

A cry burst from me. I saw my apprentice dead, and Ilving sobbing over his body.

The rest I remember ill. With all my new-coined strength, I reached out to my apprentice's mind, to his soul, which had not yet become one with the abyss of Niflhel or with the place that lay under the wardship of Demogorgon.

And I found him—or say, rather, that I saw him, together with Sigrlinn. That must have been when my legs gave way, because when I came to myself I was being supported on either side by Hropt and Rakoth.

There was only one way to return my apprentice's soul to the body it had abandoned. I tore from my neck the cherished amulet that for long years had carried the Grain of Hagen's Fate. It had almost burned out; only deep within it a dim, reddish light still glimmered. I dashed it with all my strength to the floor, where it shattered against the stones and became dust. Then I fell to my knees and began to blow upon that faint smoldering. A moment passed, then another, and tiny tongues of flame leapt up.

Hagen was no longer my apprentice. By breaking the Grain of Fate, I had forfeited the right to teach him henceforth. But through her inconsolable sobs, Ilving heard her husband's heart, once stilled, begin to beat again. Hagen stirred and groaned.

I invested all my newly acquired powers into an effort greater than god had ever made, holding Hagen and Sigrlinn at the very brink of a lugubrious abyss, bottomless and nameless. There they stood, until my enchantments began to draw them back with ever-growing certainty.

That was my proof to Hagen that his faith in his Teacher had not been misplaced.

The Dragons of Time having disappeared along with Great Orlangur, we lingered there, at a loss as to what to do next, while in my mind long scrolls were unfurling, and there I read...

We were the New Gods. We could not domineer, as our imprudent predecessors had before us. We were the guardians of the World Balance. Though much had been given into our power, yet more was subject to unalterable prohibitions we could never circumvent. We could create, but could make only creatures with free will—never brainless slaves or warriors who would unthinkingly kill at our command. We would have no emblems to augment our powers—even Iamerth's crystalline sphere had vanished without trace on the completion of our charm to halt the Unnamable.

I saw the wreckage of the Pillar of the Titans, and my kinsfolk crowding in bewilderment around the gigantic mound of debris. I saw Merlin, utterly pinched and aged, and pitied him. I saw, too, tender Felostei, and knew then that she was with child, the first of a new Generation. She had, after all, fulfilled the promise made to me; and now I must find a way to save my injudicious kin, and to rescue from the horrors of the afterlife every last one of my apprentice's men, who had fought so valorously and laid down their lives for me. There was time still for that, I felt, albeit very little.

Came Mimir, too, with the Old God of the Mountain, he whom I had divested of the Blue Sword to give to my apprentice. The fall of his immemorial enemies, the Masters of the Hallowed Land, had erased the patina of cruelty from his soul, and falling to his knees, he begged forgiveness. We spoke at some length of the Sentinel of the Wellspring, of the God of the Mountain, who had received his punishment and had gone off to serve it, of powers magical and human, of Brann Shrunkenhand, whom I could not trace even behind the Portals of Death, of the new aspect of the world...

But all those deeds and colloquies of ours are a tale for another time.

We also bade farewell to Hropt, who was Hropt no longer.

"I am Odin once more!" His mighty voice rolled beneath the vaults of the Hallowed Land. "I have returned. But, Odin though I am, I shall go back to walk the Earth."

And thus, unable and unwilling to be judge and Guardian, he departed to tread the endless byways of Greater Hjorvard and its neighbor worlds, to fight the evil that still lay hidden—the vampires, ghouls, savage trolls and shatter-brained wizards. There was much for him to do, but that, too, is a lengthy and particular tale.

Then I heard the quiet whistle of a voice at the very verge of hearing, and shivered, knowing I was being addressed by the Black Mages of Brandeigh Isle, who still infested the body of our world. With much gibing, they reminded me I had borrowed strength from Chaos in an extremity and inquired if it was not time to repay the loan.

But I would have no converse with them. Whatever the cost, that festering abscess must be lanced, must be cauterized with red-hot iron before Rakoth and I were brought before our own judges to answer for all that we had done and left undone. And that, too, is another story.

As we stood by the holy Well, I heard Rakoth say quietly, "So, now we are gods, brother Hedin?"

"Yes," I replied after a moment's silence.

"And you know what that means?"

"Yes. You and I shall be prisoners, for untold millennia, until someone stronger or bolder comes to overthrow us."

We exchanged a glance and, having done so, began to speak of pressing matters. We had to step lively, for eternity has a way of passing all too quickly.

END

ABOUT THE AUTHOR

"Nick" is the English short-term for Nikolai (pronounced: nee-koh-LIE). The name "Perumov" comes from a powerful Armenian noble family.

Nikolai Perumov himself was born November 21, 1963; he began creating his first literary works in high school. Having graduated in biophysics from the physico-mechanical department of the Leningrad Polytechnical Institute, he stated working in the field of molecular biology and spent 10 years working in the Leningrad Scientific Research Institute of Particularly Pure Biopreparations, until he switched to literature as his main profession.

After nine years of writing, Nick Perumov has 19 novels with a total circulation of more that a million copies, a record for a fantasy writer in Russia. Four more novels have been published under an assumed name, which the author adamantly refuses to reveal.

Currently Nick resides in Raleigh, North Carolina, where he writes his books and works at a scientific institution in his main profession as a biologist.

ABOUT THE ARTIST

Martine Jardin has been an artist since she was very small. Her mother guarantees she was born holding a pencil, which for a while, as a toddler, she nicknamed "Zessie"

She won several art competitions with her drawings as a child, ventured into charcoal, watercolors and oils later in life and about 12 years ago started creating digital art.

Since then, she's created hundreds of book covers for Zumaya Publications and eXtasy Books, among others. She welcomes visitors to her website: www.martinejardin.com.

LaVergne, TN USA
21 December 2009
167803LV00004B/185/A